The LOST COLONY

Route of rafts
Route of boats
Route of marchers

Miles

0   100

ST. AUGUSTINE

Cape Horse

Abandon boats

RIO DE INDIO

CALUSA

CALUSA

Okeechobee Lake
Gran Laguna de
Mayaimi

RIO SAN JUAN

TIMUCUA

CALUSA

D

CALUSA

CAPITAL
TZIN CACIQUE

CALUSA

OLD TAMPA

F
L
O
R
I

SUWANEE R.

D1064183

Gulf

of

Mexico

map by palacios

BOOKS BY EDISON MARSHALL

Biographical Novels

CORTEZ AND MARINA A novel of Cortez and the Conquest of Mexico
THE CONQUEROR A novel of Alexander the Great
GREAT SMITH A novel of Captain John Smith

Hero Novels

WEST WITH THE VIKINGS A novel of the Viking discovery of America
THE PAGAN KING A novel of King Arthur
EARTH GIANT A novel of Heracles (Hercules in Roman myth)
THE VIKING A novel of Ogier the Dane
CARAVAN TO XANADU A novel of Marco Polo

Historical Novels

THE LOST COLONY A novel about those colonists who settled Roanoke
    Island in 1587—and then disappeared
YANKEE PASHA The adventures of a young American frontiersman from
    Salem to Tartary after the Revolutionary War
BENJAMIN BLAKE A tale of the bastard son of an English squire in
    the South Sea Islands in the period of our Revolutionary War
AMERICAN CAPTAIN The adventures of a young mariner in Maine,
    Malta, North Africa, East Africa, and England at the turn of
    the eighteenth century
THE INFINITE WOMAN A tale inspired by the life of Lola Montez
GYPSY SIXPENCE A novel of a young Lancer on the Afghan frontier in
    India, his character and his story suggested by those of Sir
    Richard Burton
THE UPSTART A novel of strolling players in England about 1730
THE GENTLEMAN The adventures of a Charleston gambler at home, in
    the West Indies, and in South Africa prior to the Civil War

Gothic Romance

CASTLE IN THE SWAMP A novel of the Carolina low country in the
    nineteenth century

Regional Novels

PRINCESS SOPHIA A novel of Alaska in the period 1898–1918
THE INEVITABLE HOUR A novel of Martinique in the period 1890–1902

Personal Memoirs of Big-Game Hunting

THE HEART OF THE HUNTER A looking-backward over hunting trails in
    Canada, Alaska, Africa, Indochina, and India, and where they led
SHIKAR AND SAFARI A factual and objective account of various big-
    game hunts

Books of Short Stories

LOVE STORIES OF INDIA
THE HEART OF LITTLE SHIKARA Stories of animals of forest and jungle
THE ELEPHANT REMEMBERS A jungle book

THE LOST COLONY

THE
LOST COLONY

Edison Marshall

GARDEN CITY, N.Y.

Doubleday & Company, Inc.

1964

Library of Congress Catalog Card Number 64–20577
Copyright © 1964 by Edison Marshall
Printed in the United States of America

*The author has the honor of dedicating this book
to my editor,
LEBARON (LEE) R. BARKER,
as an expression of my happiness
in our eight years of rewarding concert.*

FOREWORD AND ACKNOWLEDGMENTS

No large event in the history of the settling of America is as poorly documented as the founding and then the vanishing into thin air of the second of two colonies founded by Sir Walter Raleigh on Roanoke Island, off the coastal mainland of present-day North Carolina.

We have a list of the names of the colonists but know almost nothing about their occupations, personalities, or previous histories. For instance, we do not know whether Edward Powell and Winifred (Winfris) Powell, both Welsh, were man and wife, father and daughter, or unrelated. Of the westward journey there are two accounts, affording us very little detail, and somewhat contradictory reports of events at Roanoke before John White's departure for England on the same ships that had brought the colonists. After this, there is silence.

The Indian lore in this book is as true in the main as can be researched in the writings of historians, anthropologists, and ethnologists of varying opinions. However, since the source material of these books is not infallible, I ventured to have various tribes range far and wide from their recorded habitats, and have branches of the great Indian nations vary from one another in ways of life. Moreover, I have added customs and ceremonies observed personally in Asiatic tribes of approximately the same level of civilization as that of the North American Indian.

It follows that the solution of the mystery offered in this novel is highly imaginative. Yet I may be on firm ground in my premise that the forces bringing about the evacuation of Roanoke Island were already at work among certain members of the colony before they left England. In the hasty assembling of one hundred and ten colonists, men, women, and children of differing circumstances and histories, largely from three shires, there could have been many curious relationships. My duty as a storyteller was to surmise or invent these, make them as plausible and exciting as was within my literary power, and to furnish as much instruction in anthropology, natural history, mythology, geography, and psychology as is germane to the tale. Thus this is a novel of "what might have been," offering opportunities for dramatic situations which every dedicated novelist loves.

The author is greatly indebted to David B. Quinn, editor of *Roanoke Voyages, 1584–1590,* 2 vols., London, the Hakluyt Society, 1955. This work represents a great deal of difficult research and seems to me the most authoritative on this subject. Particularly useful to me was "Roanoke Colonists and Explorers: An Attempt at Identification" by William S. Powell in the *North Carolina Historical Review,* April 1957. It is frankly conjectural, and Mr. Powell's opinions are highly interesting and persuasive.

The geographical data in my book is substantially correct.

The author's main dependence for Indian lore was on *The Indian Tribes of North America* by John R. Swanton, U. S. Government Printing Office, Smithsonian Institution, 1952; *Indians* by Edwin Tunis, New York, World Publishing Company, 1959; and *Florida on Trial, 1593–1602* by Charles W. Arnade, University of Miami Press, 1959. Also I had access to *The Everglades* (1947), Marjory Stoneman Douglas' enchanting book.

Also researched were *The American Heritage Book of Indians,* 1961; Arrowsmith's *New General Atlas,* 1817; *A Short History of the United States* by John Spencer Basset, Ph.D., 1939; *A Higher History of the United States* by Henry E. Chambers, 1889; Collier's *World Atlas and Gazeteer,* 1940; *Lake Okeechobee* by Alfred J. and Katherine A. Hanna, 1948; *Castillo* by J. Carver Harris and John L. Vollbrecht, 1949; *Indians of the Southern Colonial Frontier* by E. Atkin, edited by Wilbur R. Jacobs, 1954; *Physical Geography* by M. F. Maury, 1880; *Florida's Seminole Indians* by Wilfred T. Neill, 1956; *Rinehart's Indians* by F. A. Rinehart, 1899; *History of America* by William Robertson, D.D., 1844; *The American Indian in North Carolina* by Douglas L. Rights, 1947; and *Red Man's America* by Ruth M. Underhill, 1953.

This is a novel of many inventions, none of which, as far as the author knows, is in conflict with established fact.

Edison Marshall

CAST OF CHARACTERS

The following characters in this novel are fictitious:

THOMAS SUTTON, portrayed as the father of Martyn Sutton.

MAGGIE SUTTON, portrayed as the mother of Martyn Sutton.

ENID POWELL, portrayed as the wife of Edward Powell.

LADY ISOBEL WADE, portrayed as the wife of Thomas Wade.

WEECHEE, portrayed as the quarter-Spanish granddaughter of Dona Antonia, sister of the Spanish Governor Menéndez de Avilés and wife of Carlos, first and great king of the Calusa nation.

ANTONIO, Weechee's father and portrayed as the son of Carlos.

MISTRESS CLARA BARTON, portrayed as the sister of Thomas Wade.

PRISCILLA, portrayed as the daughter of Mr. Thomas and Lady Isobel Wade.

THOMAS WARNER, an English bowyer, long in slavery to the Spanish.

PETE, an old gardener on Thomas Wade's estate.

WILLIAM HOLBROOKE, Thomas Wade's bailiff.

ADAM HARRISON, Thomas Wade's gatekeeper.

REVEREND STEPHEN BURBERRY, an antiquary of Amesbury.

STORYTELLER, a wandering Indian taleteller.

BEAR HUNTER, an English renegade.

CHEEWINK, daughter of a Croatan underchief.

TOMAY, son of an outcaste Indian.

OWEN, infant son of Edward and Enid Powell.

COSSINE SACHEM, father of Cheewink.

The Sheriff of Wiltshire, Deputies, Prison Officials, Housemaids, a Queen's Judge, Indian Chieftains and Chieftainesses, Peasant Friends and Neighbors of Martyn Sutton, various Indians, and a Lawyer.

CAPTAIN SELKIRK of the *Elspeth* and Officers.

The following characters really lived, many with vigor, although most are now but names on time-yellowed paper:

MARTYN SUTTON, a colonist, in this novel the protagonist, his actual personality and history unknown.

EDWARD POWELL, portrayed as a fanatical preacher.

WINIFRED POWELL, portrayed as Edward Powell's daughter.

RICHARD DARIGEM, a colonist who, in this novel, is Richard Wade sailing under an assumed name for a plausible reason.

MANTEO, once sagamore of the Croatan, with Lane's colony and then John White's.

JOHN WHITE, governor under Sir Walter Raleigh.

SIR WALTER RALEIGH

JOHN JONES, colonist, identified by some historians with the Welsh physician of note.

ANANIAS DARE, assistant governor.

ELEANORE DARE, wife of Ananias.

VIRGINIA DARE, the first English infant born in the now United States.

ANTHONY CAGE, a colonist and former sheriff of Huntington.

CHRISTOPHER COOPER, DYONIS HARVEY, and CUTHBERT WHITE, colonists and assistants of John White.

JOHN SPENDLOVE, colonist and gentleman.

DARBY GLAND or GLANE, colonist and deserter.

ELISABETH GLAND, his wife.

WILLIAM BROWN, colonist and goldsmith or jeweler.

THOMAS HEWETT or HEWITT, colonist and Bachelor of Law.

WILLIAM BERDE, colonist and yeoman.

MARK BENNET, colonist and yeoman.

JOHN HYNDE and WILLIAM CLEMENT, thieves whom Sir Walter Raleigh had recruited from Colchester Castle prison.

THOMAS ELLIS, colonist and vestryman of St. Petrock Church, Exeter.

WILLIAM NICHOLES, colonist and clothworker.

THOMAS SMART, colonist and young son of Thomas Smart left with fifteen or so others by Sir Richard Grenville.

TOWAYE, Croatan Indian with Lane, later with White, deserter.

JOHN PRAT, colonist and urchin, son or brother of Roger Prat.

GEORGE HOWE, White's assistant, killed by Indians before the departure of the ships.

RICHARD BERRY, colonist and gentleman.

JOAN WARREN, MARGARET LAWRENCE, ROSE PAYNE, JANE MANNERING, colonists and presumably spinsters.

Other colonists, men, women and children.

CONTENTS

THE LOST COLONY

Chapter I

SERENE BEGINNINGS

1

My name is Martyn Sutton. Quite true, I played a large part in one of the strangest events of my century, a century forever famous because it embraced the first attempts of English people to settle the New World. The first part of the event which I shall chronicle will be given a few paragraphs in every history of the North American continent written in the next ten centuries, but if my writing is never found and published, it may be dealt with as a mystery, perhaps the greatest ever to rise on those and new-found shores.

Others who played large parts in this dramatic event were the great Sir Walter Raleigh, who was not even present at its occurrence, and people of various station and eminence, likewise absent, such as Lady Isobel Wade. She made possible my first great winning, and was the wife of the franklin, Thomas Wade. Others were Mistress Barton, Thomas' sister, and a peasant, Thomas Sutton, who had given me a doctrine to which I was scarcely equal. This statement of mine is palpably a boast because Lady Isobel, Mistress Barton, and Thomas Sutton moved and exerted force in the enterprise only through me. In their varied ways they had shaped me and readied me for the test that was my fortune to stand. The stage of the main action was the vast, loosely bounded region named Virginia by Sir Walter Raleigh in honor of our Virgin Queen, and Florida, discovered and so designated by the Spanish about seventy years before. But the prologue of that part of the drama in which I played the leading part took place on Salisbury Plain in Wiltshire, England. There I was born.

This plain and its mysterious works of ancient man, such as Stonehenge, I will describe briefly, as the scene of various incidents in this chronicle related in proper sequence. But its influence on my life was strong and deep long before what I call my first great win-

ning, the meaningful result of circumstances so trivial that I hesitate
to relate them in the history of a historical episode. I was only sixteen
at the time. Indeed that victory occurred on my sixteenth birthday.

Why not start my tale with this? Only a little filling in of conditions
and happenings prior to this is needful for easy understanding of
the narrative, and from this point it will flow with almost as few
swervings and stillnesses as our river Avon between the towns of
Upavon and Amesbury. My father, Thomas Sutton, was Wiltshire
born and bred, and only a close survey would reveal him as differing
in any marked degree from a typical West Country peasant. Almost
all peasants these days have a first and last name, unlike their ancestors of three centuries before. According to law and the parish
records Thomas Sutton was a freeman; he owed no dues or services
to his landlord other than rent payable in bags of wool; in theory he
could take employment wherever it was offered and he so chose, but
in practice he was as affixed to the land as a Saxon thrall. Mama
was a cotter's daughter from Somersetshire, tall and strong, and no
doubt striking to look at as a young girl; and since she was equal
to the heavy labor of the farm, and because the labor of childbirth
had been lain on her only once—not again and again and again as
is the case with most peasant women—she was still handsome. Neither
could read nor write, although both could do simple sums. On the
other hand, I was as well lettered as the master's son and heir, because Mistress Clara Barton, the master's widowed sister, had taught
me and lent me books. I know not the reason for this great beneficence
unless it was a motherly interest in me—she had no children of her
own—and a wild surmise that I was mentally gifted. Also, she had
time to spare.

The date was October 7, 1584, and the day sunny and pleasant.
I was supposed to be watching a flock of some sixty sheep, cropping
in the rich grass which, as a consequence of its making mutton, had
gained me inches in height, good bone, and strong muscle. Actually
the shepherd's job was taken over by an old ewe we called Lop-ear,
of a strong mind and a strict disciplinarian. I had nothing worse or
less pleasant to do than read *Canterbury Tales* that Mistress Barton
had lent me, admiring their sharp characterizations, moved to revery
by their poetry and to mirth by their bawdry. The antique language
and spelling bothered me not at all. Many of the old-fashioned words
were still employed by our Wiltshire countrymen.

But I laid down the book when I saw Miss Priscilla, the master's
daughter, four years younger than his heir Richard and thus fourteen,
making toward me up the sheep path. In her hands was something
the size of a clay brick wrapped in a napkin and a wicker-covered

flask a little larger than pint-size. She was a pretty girl, neither thin-shanked nor buxom, and the late-afternoon sunlight graced her blond hair. With pleasure, I pounced to my feet and doffed my cap.

As she drew nigh, I saw she was somewhat flushed and a little abashed.

"Good day to you, young mistress," I greeted her.

"Martyn, do you know what day this is?" was her blurted-out reply, a question she had no doubt rehearsed.

"Why, yes, I do, my lady. It is the day that I could lawfully begin to bear arms, if I were gentry instead of common."

"Being common, you can still celebrate it. At least you are liable to military service as a bowman against the dons, if Queen Bess decides to punish Philip's insolence. And being part-common myself —for a franklin stands between the commons and the gentry—even though my mother is of noble birth, I decided it was quite proper to help you."

"To help me—in what way?"

"To provide the materials for your celebration." She spoke rather sharply, annoyed at my intentional dullardism: then her voice warmed. "And how do you suppose I knew this was the day?"

"I can't guess."

"From our bailiff's book. He has listed the birthdays of all our tenants and their families. I just happened to be looking through it. So I asked permission of my lady mother to make you a little cake and take you a bottle of honey mead. She said it was quite all right, since your sire is our best sheep grower, even if o'erstubborn for one of his station. And she said you could be even better, but she doubts if you will stay in England and instead will likely go to one of Sir Walter Raleigh's plantations in Virginia."

"I have given it some thought, I do confess. And the delight and honor that I feel in your birthday gifts are inexpressible."

Well I knew that this last utterance was strange sounding out of the mouth of a peasant. But I knew the language so well, having read so widely, and had harkened with such eager ears to the accents and words of my betters, especially the more learned, that it had become a kind of second nature, requiring only swift, hard thought and a close guard of my tongue. The fact was, I spoke better than Richard, son and heir of the master. It discomfited the gentry, I thought, which tickled me, for many of these employed country accents although with good grammar. Especially it irked the master himself, who was the son of a yeoman but the richest man in the parish, owning his great wool farm of two thousand acres and a haberdashery in Bristol. Yet I did not believe that his son Richard resented the accomplishment and instead was proud of me.

"Well, I'll leave the treat with you," Priscilla told me. "You can take it home and share it with your parents, and return the napkin and the flask at your convenience."

"You know, Miss Priscilla, that tenants are not allowed to enter the park, unless they're sent for." The park was the master's seat, about twenty acres surrounded by a hedge, and embracing the mansion, stables, kennel, and some other outbuildings.

"Then leave them with the gatekeeper."

"I would rather share them with you, if your position permits you to eat and drink with the son of your parent's tenant."

"Why, Martyn Sutton, you know full well that my sire—and even my noble dam—eats and drinks with all our tenants at harvest home! You have a wooden cup with your water bag. I brought along my little silver goblet, given me when I was christened. It won't do any harm for us both to drink to your—your future adventures, for my Aunt Clara Barton says you are a born adventurer."

"Will you eat a piece of the cake?"

"Yes, if it would pleasure you."

"Greatly so, I do aver! Will you unwrap it? My hands are used to rough work and I might muss the napkin."

"Why, yes, and you may unstop the bottle."

When we were both seated comfortably on shady grass I thought of a pleasant thing.

"I know a little ceremony connected with drinking mead, taught me by an old mead maker from Middlesex," I told Priscilla. "It would not apply to us. It could never apply to a young lady and a peasant youth. Still you might like to hear me recite it.

"Yes, I would, if it is not too liberal for a maiden's ears."

"No, it is delicate, although it is a preliminary to a marriage ceremony—or a pledge made at a wedding supper—among the folk. It is called the Bee Bride's Words, and was passed down from the days when beekeepers were a kind of guild, and had customs of their own. First you pour a little honey mead in my cup and your goblet."

She did so, her hand less steady than she wished and her color higher.

"Then the younker sings to his sweetheart—I will only recite:

'Sweet as honey, loving as mead,
You shall be my queen indeed.'"

"Why, it's a lovely custom," Priscilla exclaimed, with shining eyes. "Now what does the maiden sing?"

"She answers this way:

'Flowers unplucked will wither soon.
Eat my honey with a spoon.'"

"Since the young couple are wedded, or about to be, I don't think it's gross. Is that all the ceremony?"

"Since you ask, I'll tell you the rest. The youth and maiden are supposed to kiss, with their lips still wet with mead."

"Well—" She looked at her folding and unfolding hands.

"I don't think there would be any harm in it despite the difference in our stations, since it is part of a ceremony," I ventured.

"Why I do not either, in all conscience. I've given kisses to young gentlemen, whom I did not know half as well as I know you, and you are clean and do not smell bad—"

"Then with your permission—"

I leaned toward her and she toward me. She did not stint the kiss, for she was not unpracticed. Kissing games were commonly played by young people of all stations, in palaces and in cottages, especially at the Christmas season. But my sharp pleasure was cut short as I glanced up quickly to make certain the impropriety had not been seen by anyone.

We had not made sure that our retreat in a stand of elm trees was well-enough sequestered, and that glance was made too late. Fairly running up the path was Priscilla's brother Richard, two years my elder but by no means better grown or more the man. I rose with what dignity I could muster and waited for him with my arms rigid at my side.

Richard and I had had pleasant relations as long as I could remember. Despite the difference in our stations we had managed to obtain a competitive companionship in games and what I had deemed, and still did so, a youth-to-youth friendship. But now his manly, handsome face was fiery red and I did not know what would happen. Still I did not expect . . .

Then I felt the full blow of his fist on the side of my jaw. I reeled from its force, and almost fell. Then in regaining my balance, somehow I collected my wits, for a moment scattered. Richard stood there panting and glowering, but made no further move to attack me.

"Master Richard, you have struck me without cause, and I am a freeman, and you will have to answer for it."

"I saw you kiss my sister—"

"No, we kissed each other!" Priscilla shrieked in his ear.

Richard's whole manner changed. He had noticed the mead bottle and the cake. Before he spoke, his expression told me he repented the violent action.

"Martyn, I clean forgot it was your birthday. Those edibles—Priscilla, you brought those to him no doubt with our mother's permission. It was a birthday kiss, and I made too much of it."

"It was part of a little ceremony—"

"Well, I'm sorry. Can't we shake hands and forget it?"

"Before we do that, I demand satisfaction," I answered. "You can well ask how can a peasant ask satisfaction of the son of his master for a blow in the face. You could order me lashed by the master's bailiff, and no doubt he'd do it, but I don't think you'll give such an order in Queen Bess's England. I am not entitled to wear or wield a sword, but I can handle a quarterstaff, and so can you. Would two good knocks out of three even this up? It would for me."

"It certainly will, and I'll try my best to win, although I deserve to lose. We'll have time between now and dusk."

"Master Richard, I will bring the staffs."

Indeed I was only too happy to quit the scene for a few minutes of self-contemplation. I had taken too heroic a stand for a lowborn swain. The truth was I had dramatized myself in a degree that would have either disgusted or moved to mirth my hard-headed sire. He had cautioned me not once but a hundred times that under no circumstances, or how far I might rise in life, must I ever forget the position to which I was born.

For centuries now, quarterstaffs have been the peasants' fencing foils. Rare was the fair at which neighborhood champions did not compete, usually for a prize donated by some worthy. The gentry knew that a good staffer could easily change into an expert spearman if a big war broke out, or even a swordsman if he were made a petty captain, for there are many quick shifts from yeoman to officer in the carnage of battle. By the same token, a good staffer made a good pikeman, when Spanish or French pirates grappled an English vessel and sought to board her. Not yet masters of the sport, both Richard and I had been schooled by a former champion of the parish, and we were by no means tyros.

Usually the staffs were of light, tough wood, and about nine feet long. With his right hand the player grasped his staff about a quarter from the end, his left hand in front at easy distance. The players fenced until one or the other saw or made an opening, then struck. There was never room for a long swing or time to apply much strength, so the blow, although painful, rarely did serious harm. The same swift gaze and agile muscles admired in fencing were necessary for good play, although lacking flourishes and refinements; and hence a good match with quarterstaffs was never as fine a sight. Yet our rustics relished it, cheered their favorites; and when the contest was decided and the contestants had shaken hands, there was a deal of backslapping from the lads, no few kisses from the wenches, and perhaps unbegrudged praise from some watching worthy.

Obviously such terms as *épée* and *touché* would have meant fully as much to the spectators as the rector's prayers in Latin meant to his hearers.

I shouldered the two staffs kept in our barn well out of sight of the master. He did not favor Richard's enthusiasm for rural sports, and wanted him to fence with his social equals, the contestants employing tabbed rapiers. When I regained the little copse of elm trees overlooking the meadow, I did not see the master but his better half, no less than Lady Isobel. Obviously Priscilla had run to the mansion in my absence, reported the coming match, and returned with her mother and a knowing and well-trusted gardener commonly called Pete. Possibly one reason for their presence was to see that the honorable old game did not turn into a fight. But both should know there was no danger of that. Richard and I were too good friends and respected each other too much to start a real brabble.

While I could not speak for Priscilla, I could swear that Lady Isobel's sporting instincts caused her to welcome the watching of a lively bout. She loved to follow otterhounds which the master's bailiff kept, down brooks and through brush; and only a good bowler could match her on the greens. She was a tall, fine-looking woman, patently of high birth, handsome rather than pretty, with an arched nose and fine, bright eyes; yet there was nothing male about her in her dealing with sick tenants and ailing children.

"Good afternoon, my lady," I greeted her, bowing my bared head. And I did not say "m'laady," as did the household varlets.

"Good afternoon, the devil," she replied. "It's a good match I came to see, hot and heavy, and no piddling patting."

"I think you'll see one, ma'am."

Then we both spied three people crossing a hedge from the lane, a long arrow-cast distant. Patently these too would be spectators, and I could instantly guess by Lady Isobel's invitation. Plainly she, Miss Priscilla, and Pete had come hence by the lane, instead of across the clover fields wet from a recent shower. On that route they would pass the home acre of the second-best house in our parish, that of Edward Powell, gentleman, his wife Enid Powell, and their daughter Winifred Powell. Doubtless Lady Isobel had called to them as she spied them in their garden, told them her destination and what was afoot, and had invited them to follow on.

I was not nearly as surprised by Mr. Powell's and his daughter's presence as by that of Mistress Powell. A shy, modest, beautiful woman of about thirty-five, she was palpably with child although not yet great, and rarely appeared in public.

No family in the parish was of greater interest to me save the master's and my own. They had migrated here from Wales about ten years before, and they were the fair type of Welsh, unmixed with the dark Cornish. At least this was true of Preacher Powell, as the folk called him, and of Miss Winifred, but Mistress Powell may have had mixed blood, for although her complexion was most fair, her hair red-gold, her eyes were brilliantly black in startling contrast. Our countrypeople had it—and they were rarely mistaken in such matters —that she was better born than her husband, her maiden name being Glendower. She was lean in the face, but its bones were beautifully molded, her limbs long and lithe; she seemed to walk on tiptoe, so light was her step. I had even heard the rumor that her lineage was older than Lady Isobel's own, although she had no title of nobility as far as known. Her voice was soft.

Preacher Powell was so handsome that I could well imagine him a seraph sent to earth to implement the works of our Saviour; and no doubt he believed he had a divine mission to save souls. Like our Saviour, he preached in the open fields and commons; and in court-yards wherever folk could gather; but there the likeness ended, as far as my young thoughts could reach. Jesus had employed simple par-ables to convey his truth; this self-appointed evangelist called down thunders and lightnings; and these rumbled and flashed in his words.

Still neither he nor his soft-voiced, shy, beautiful wife mattered a fig to me compared to their exquisite daughter Winifred. I suppose it is not uncommon for a younker of sixteen to have an idol of the opposite sex. Here was mine, well past thirteen and swiftly shaping toward young womanhood, almost too beautiful for my eyes to believe. There was no doubt now that I would strive my utmost against Rich-ard, more than what before had been my utmost, and that if I won I would be generous victor, and if I lost I would make every show of accepting defeat in good part.

But truly, more seemed to hang on the rude game forthcoming, the sport of swains and clodhoppers, than I could rationally explain. It was as if the defeat or victory would set a pattern that would hold throughout my life. From this high ground I could discern, and count if I tried, the still-standing stones of Stonehenge. It was hardly a half mile distant; and always in broad daylight it looked commonplace enough; and only in the moonlight did it cause visions and not quite reachable thoughts to haunt the mind. All who lived near it were changed by it, in inscrutable ways. It was the most mysterious and incredible edifice in all England, moving the imagination far more than the glorious cathedral raised in the city of Salisbury—New Sarum it was sometimes called by the folk—a little more than three centuries ago. Men a great deal like me in all essentials had hewn and hauled from afar and heaved upright the fifty-ton stones perhaps twenty centuries ago—for what purpose and to whom?

2

"Lady Isobel, I heartily approve of young fellows bouting with quarterstaffs for their own sport," Mr. Powell was saying in his rich, resonant voice. "But I feel that today it will be for something more than sport."

"Indeed it is," she answered in her pleasant but firm way. "It is the honorable settling of a wrong done to Martyn by my son Richard —and Martyn is showing himself a true Englishman, regardless of his station, in being satisfied by this test."

"A better way of settlement would have been for Richard to ask pardon, Martyn to grant it, and then the giving of a warm handclasp. This is a pagan, not a Christian, way of settling a wrongdoing, and I hate paganry in all its forms." The ring of his voice and the shine in his eyes were more eloquent than his words.

"Well, sir, the world won't get shed of it as long as you live and for many a century to come. Please don't let me inspire you to a sermon, Mr. Powell. Report has it, they are most inspiring—one of them in-spired a crowd of young people to sally forth from Amesbury and topple down two leaning sarsens of the outer circle of Stonehenge."

The Preacher became deeply thoughtful. "You know, Lady Isobel, you are not the only one who has rebuked me for my remarks about Stonehenge. All I said was, that it was a pagan edifice, and its stones should be torn down and used in the building of a Christian temple. The other objector was, I suppose, a human being, although my old ostler insists and fervently believes that it was goblin of some sort. I confess that my visitor's entrance into the house without being seen poses a puzzle. On my bed I found a brown sheet of paper with a crude but graphic and I must say horrid picture, done with chalk and red paint. It showed the corpse of a man lying on the flat stone that the peasants call—with no good reason—the sacrificial stone, within the circle of Stonehenge. I was identifiable by the chain and cross I wear on my breast. Shall I tell you the rest? It's rather ghastly."

"I'd better hear it. After all, Stonehenge is on our land."

"I had been sacrificed. There was a red gash in my bared abdomen, and my entrails burst out and dangled down the side of the stone, this too portrayed in red paint."

Lady Isobel stood very still and no one spoke. At last she gave a little shudder.

"I happen to believe that the ancient monuments in England should be preserved, whether Christian or pagan," she said quietly. "I am a Protestant, yet I doubt if King Harry should ever be forgiven or forgotten as the destroyer of images. Now it is time for yon two cockerels to take their places."

On later contemplation, I decided I was the victim of an illusion; and the ensuing combat was no more significant than many scores of similar contests ensuing at this moment throughout England. If so, I should omit its description from this chronicle. Still I cannot; not only because of my own deep feelings at the time. In the first place, to my opponent this was no mere game; in our many previous contests with quarterstaffs, or at running, jumping, vaulting, shooting arrows at the mark, and stone-heaving to test strength, he had never been so patently aroused. His mother's presence may have been a factor, especially since she was herself not quite her usual serene ladyship; the flush on her cheeks and the way she stood betrayed an excitement that a mere game in no way justified. Presumably she wanted Richard to win. Yet I could not feel that she was partisan to Richard or to me either; it was as though she passionately wanted to know whether he or I was the better quarterstaffer.

Richard was hardly conscious of his sister's presence: at least he did not give her a glance or a smile as he took his stand. Because she had kissed me, and because young ladies used to kiss their champions before a tournament, I felt her presence keenly, but that feeling had little force compared to those aroused by Winifred's watching. More by intuition than by any sign or gesture made by Richard, I perceived that behind his mind bent on winning she stood foremost. But his contemplation of her was far different than mine.

Young females differ greatly in what can only be called natural attraction to young men. Winifred was some months younger than Priscilla, yet she would waken in almost any healthy young animal of a man far more sensuous yearnings. To these Richard gave rein; because of idealism, far more common in younkers of sixteen than is commonly believed, my mind dwelt on her innocence and purity. I had had my fair share of haycock venery that peasant boys and girls enjoy, but I could not associate them even dimly with the Preacher's daughter, Winifred Powell.

Still the greatest force of all in changing this rude contest into a desperate trial was the doctrine of that strange, terribly intense man, my father Thomas Sutton. He had taught me that with other peasants I could win or lose any kind of game, depending on how much I cared, but in a contest with the son of gentry, I must always win.

I have called quarterstaffing a rude game—thinking that it was generally played by rude peasants. Actually it is a difficult and subtle game when well played; it demands intense sharpness of sight, and lightning-fast muscular reflex. As in fencing—curiously enough like chess in this respect—a capable mind can employ strategy, a present stroke associated with another five or even ten strokes distant. As our play warmed and my joy in the contest began to override anxiety, I had time for a fleeting hope that the time-honored game would never die in the land. It was a wondrous sport for men so poor that they could not buy swords and too lowborn to be allowed to wear them.

Lady Isobel heard the lively clatter of staffs for which she had asked. Richard and I were so well matched that for fully five minutes neither of us had time or room to swing for a strike. When at last with my strong wrists, I was able to knock aside his staff and whip my own backward, he recoiled so quickly that he almost knocked it out of my hand. In that opening he swung, giving me a sharp blow in the side, and the first point was won.

The second round was more violent: although this did not seem possible, the fact remained. Richard took the offensive at first, wild to win the second and deciding point, and my work was cut out for me, as our peasants say, to fend his shrewd blows. But the extreme exertion that he employed winded him somewhat, and I got a precarious upper hand. Then I employed a stratagem; with what seemed a cold ferocity I kept knocking his staff upward, as though to give me an opening to strike at his upper body or at his head. When his guarding it became something akin to habit, I was able to reverse the direction of my staff in the twinkling of an eye, and knock his staff down. With the extension of the same movement I whirled my own and struck him just over the knee. Thus we stood point to point.

While we both stood panting, ere we took our stands for the final round, Lady Isobel raised her strong voice.

"If this were a fencing match between young gentlemen, they would now rest and wet their lips with wine. But there is no wine here, and Priscilla's bottle of mead is drained to the last drop, and since by the code rank descends through the male line, one of you is between gentry and common, and other a full-blooded peasant. And since you are playing a peasant's game, it is for the peasant to say whether you will go on now, winded as you both are, or stop and catch your breaths."

"If left to me, the game will go on now." For although there were few if any visible signs to support my belief, I thought that Richard's breath was shorter than mine.

I reckon that no third or winning point was ever contested more strictly in any match of quarterstaffs. We two contestants parted company with the spectators and almost with ourselves; our staffs', became our selves' projection, moving of themselves it seemed; and seeing it would have hushed and held spellbound an audience at a fair; and haughty noblemen lounging about would have watched perforce, with narrowed eyes and intent faces. I had a dim sense of Richard's manly prowess, and likewise of my own, and the point when it was won would not prove which was the better player, and be only a quirk of chance.

Finally that bawd Fortune, despite her world-wide whoring, could not abjure the scene. My foot slipped on a patch of mashed grass. Richard saw an opening and struck at my lowered head—but over-reached himself by the length of his hand. By a great thrust of my left arm I knocked his staff far to one side, then gave him a hard whack on the shoulder.

As we stood panting, Richard was the first to speak.

"A good match, Martyn, and fairly won."

"Thank 'ee," I answered, speaking as my mother spoke, a peasant expression, with which I thought I was long broken.

"And now for the winner's prize," cried Lady Isobel, and her face betrayed only excitement, not jubilation or disappointment. At once she strode into a low thicket behind the copse of elms and brought forth an object she had hidden there, long, slightly wedge-shaped, and wrapped in rough woolen cloth which peasants called by the ancient word friz. When she came to my fore, she unbared a sword with a plain hilt in a scabbard with belt loops, such as might have been carried by a sergeant in some war forgotten but so desperate that even pressed men, or even capable thralls, were permitted to wear swords.

"Lady Isobel, that is an improper prize for a game between young men," Mr. Powell told her quietly but with great force.

"Because Martyn is a peasant?"

"That has nothing to do with it. Our Lord made no such distinction between Nicodemus and the humblest fishermen—you remember what He said. But remember more terrible words. 'He who kills by the sword must be killed by the sword.' Mark that word 'must.' There is no extenuation, no exception."

"Still I'll give it to him. Martyn, you cannot wear it now, lawfully or at least by granted right. But the time may come that you may wear it and wield it in some great cause."

"I accept it from your hand," I told her, hardly knowing what I said or what it meant.

"And, Mr. Powell, a sword is an especially fitting prize for Martyn to win, on this particular day."

"I do not know why."

"I will venture Richard does."

"No, ma'am, I don't."

"Then, Martyn, you surely do, if your tutor did her duty."

"It is the thirteenth anniversary of the battle of Lepanto, when Don Juan of Austria turned back the Turk. It took place on my third birthday, Mistress Barton told me. Of course I'd remember."

"One of the most momentous battles in all history. The right day to arm all stalwart youths of age to bear arms, whether gentleman or peasant. For the Turks may come again."

"God forbid they ever do, but they will, if God's children disobey His ordinance," cried Preacher Powell.

All tension was suddenly relieved. Lady Isobel fell into conversation with Mistress Powell—no doubt the former perceived the latter's ladyship, for they talked as equals. Mr. Powell began telling Richard and Priscilla about a great fencing match he had seen in Italy, when he had made a pilgrimage there in his youthful days. Pete stood back, mourning his young master's defeat. As I waited alone and apart, Winifred crept up to me, her feet very light, her movements lithe.

"Martyn, if you promise you won't tell anyone, especially Richard, I'll tell you a secret."

"I promise."

"I prayed for you to win. I don't know why, for I like Richard, too."

"It must be that your prayer was answered, because we fought even."

"All of my prayers are answered. That's because I pray to the true God."

Plainly this beautiful young girl, so appealing to a man's most noble and most earthy instincts, had inherited her sire's religious nature. What did that matter to Martyn Sutton, and the same with any other virtue she possessed? Even her bright beauty should not matter; it did so only because I could not be as strong as I desired. Winning a sword did not change my station; I could never win her. But I could win other prizes, and I would, with or without the help of God, who seemed to favor the gentry. These would be great prizes. I felt it in my bones.

3

On my way to our cottage, I stopped by the brook, sat down, and carefully examined my prize. It was a double-edged broadsword, strongly made, and I thought a century old. The look and feel of its metal made me think it was so-called crossbow steel, forged in the Low Countries. Its hilt with stout guards fitted my hand well, and I liked the weapon's balance, and the fact it was a thruster as well as a hacker. No crest was engraved on it, so it was not an emblem of power and position but a plain tool of war. As I studied it, I was listening to the sound of one of my father's tools of peace, stoutly wielded. He was in the wood lot, of free access to all the master's tenants, cutting fuel for our winter fires.

The dusk was heavy, and candles had been lighted in our cottage when I approached the door. In what we pridefully called the front yard, I saw Mama, Maggie Sutton, at work in her flower garden. Oddly enough, almost all the tenant women grew a few flowers; and loving them so deeply, and with strength more than equal to her daily tasks, Mama was markedly successful at it. In the spring, her garden surpassed that of any yeoman's wife living in our parts—and yeomen stood between peasants and franklins, having freehold.

"What is it 'ee be carrying, Martyn, if not a very sword?" she asked in her soft, rather childlike voice.

"Aye, and where do you think I got it?"

"I don't fink Master gave it 'ee. 'En would more like give 'ee the flat o' it, on 'ee side. I fink my Lady Isobel gave it 'ee, for her ha' queer notions about poor folk what stand out. But I can't reckon the 'casion."

"I won a quarterstaff match with young Master Richard."

"Her fink 'ee'll ha' use for it, before 'ee be gaffer. Mayhap 'ee will! Only last night I dreamed of 'ee sailing away in a tall ship, and I was a-cryin' bitter, but my heart was proud."

"It's a fine sword, Mama, and I mean to be a fine swordsman."

"That I'll warrant; but the hatchet Father found in the old copper chest is no earth-good. I was thinning lily bulbs, to plant some in new ground, and I come on a big root in the trough I was a-diggin'. 'En had his ax, choppin' in the wood lot, and I got yon hatchet to cut out 'at root. But the edge blunted at every hack."

Mama referred to a very strange find that my sire had made the year before, while trying to dig out a chicken-killing badger in a stand of oaks near Stonehenge, a remnant of what we thought had been heavy forest. About three feet underground he came on an expertly welded copper chest, and since it was fairly heavy, of course he dreamed wildly of buried treasure. But when he knocked off an old copper bolt and pried out the watertight lid, he found the most strangely assorted objects that a Bedlam could imagine in his maddest fancies. One was the head of a hatchet along with dust that had once been its haft. One was a long-dry human skull, about which were scattered pieces of broken glass. If these were amenable to wildly fanciful association, the presence of some sort of oil, an inch deep in the bottom of the chest, confounded all reason.

But peasant-like, my sire decently buried the skull, fitted a haft on the hatchet head that proved neither iron nor brass, but lead, and sold the box for its worth in copper to a smith in Amesbury.

Mama put away her friz sack of lily bulbs, and went to our storeroom to mix barley bread and make a rich broth for my father, herself, and me. I found my father in a handmade oaken chair, watching the cheerful play of our cooking fire.

Its light fell full on his face and, as always, I wondered at it. It was a peasant face, rugged and strong, with no refinements caused by some lord's bedding a pretty peasant girl, who had then quickly married one of her own sort. Still it was by no means coarse, and it betokened not only high intelligence but intense virility.

"Gossip has it," he began, with barely perceptible contempt in his tone, "that in a great battle ye've won a sword."

"Yes, Father, I have. Would you like to see it?" He had long ago forbidden me to address him as sir.

"Not now. Anyhow, one sword is like another in my sight—the badge of gentry as opposed to peasantry. But I hear ye won it in fair contest with the son o' the master, and that suits me well. And instead of looking at it now, I'll look at ye."

"Here I stand."

"Get in better light, an please ye. You've grown so fast I haven't kept track of ye. I note that ye stand tall."

"One inch under six feet."

"Ye'll make that up, and more besides, ere ye touch one-and-twenty. Ye thrives well on old-ewe mutton, barley bread, honey, truck from the garden, and the master's grouse ye poach with your bow-and-arry, and his trout ye tickle. Ye'll be going some'ere, doing somepin', likely enough amiss, afore ye're much older. Turn your head a little, so I can look well at your face."

I did so, and he looked long.

"A good judge of faces, I be. I find no fault with yourn. Ye are narrow 'twixt the eyes, and folk say that's a sign of foxiness, if not worse, but that I doubt. They be cold gray in color, but with good shine, monstrous quick eyes I reckon. The forehead's broad and high, in that like Sir Walter Raleigh's, but the head with the wisest brain I ever knew was shaped like Jackanapes' at the fair. Your hair's naught to mark, dun-colored I'd call it, and your cheekbones are high like 'em Indian captives which 'at Frenchie showed at New Sarum. Still 'tis a face to note in a crowd, and I don't know why."

"I certainly don't either, if you speak truth."

"And now ye've got a sword. The peasant Wat Tyler had one, when he led that monstrous great throng into Lunnon, and the guards had broke and run, and England was his for the taking. But he didn't draw it when Cap'n Standwick marched up on him. Instead he died like a silly sheep." My father could not keep sorrow out of his voice.

"Father, it happened more than two centuries ago."

"And we've gained a little since, but not much. Still, we might gain a monstrous lot in two centuries more. Maybe the ballot for 'em who can read and write, to vote for the gentleman who 'presents us in House, although he'll still be hand-picked by the gentry. Maybe the jails where debtors go won't stink so bad. Maybe a hungry liddle child won't be hanged by the neck for stealing sixpence. And, Martyn, do you know why I dare hope for wondrous change?"

"No, Father."

"Because o' the New World."

"Tell me exactly what you mean."

"I'll try. 'Tis not all clear in my head. The lords close to the throne will have the mighty grants, some of 'em big as all England. Their friends and kinsmen will have the great manors. But the weight of years, of centuries, won't lie on custom. It can change, Martyn my son, and if it don't make sense, it can be discarded. A monstrous great sea will roll and beat between there and Europe. Life will be hard there, at first, the forest to be felled, land broken, wooden shelters raised instead of marble palaces; painted savages will swoop down at night. The folk'll need wheels for carts. Can the gentry make 'em? When folk are besieged from all sides, to who will they turn to lead 'em? To the highborn at first, for 'tis a habit hard to break, but when the highborn can only fumble, won't they turn to the *natur'l* leader, and care not tuppence who his grandsire was?"

"I believe what you say is true."

"I won't be a fool and say ye're a natur'l leader, for ye ha' done naught to prove it. But Lady Isobel wouldn't have picked an old sword for today's prize in a mere game of quarterstaffs, knowing her son was matched with Maggie's son, both wi' a fair chance to win. A sword is the real symbol of leadership, not a blasted baton; and she's no common sort of noble lady, but a woman o' strong will and mind. Why did ye learn to read and write so well, arter ye'd done a boy's work in the fields? I didn't spare ye the labor. As a peasant ye must win or lose, not as a privileged man." I had not known that my father knew the word "privilege."

"As a peasant I'll win or lose." I made that promise to myself as much as to my sire.

"Now to the meat o' the egg. I want ye to go to the New World, and if ye are not given a chance, make one. 'Tis true that Sir Walter Raleigh is choosing mainly folk of middle station, along with a leaven of gentlemen down at heels, and almost none of our kind. But he will, before he's through. He'll have to, to find enough settlers. 'Tis the nature of folk in middling 'stances not to want to trade a safe living for what might be riches across the sea but what might be starvation or an Indian ambush. Two attempts at settlement of the lands north of Florida have failed—Sir Humphrey Gilbert's and a Frenchie's in Virginia whose name I forget. Sir Walter's readying another, as ye know. But I don't want ye shipping as a boy, wi'out practice in seamanship and war. 'Twill be against ye first to last. And fear not ye'll lose out by not grabbing this first chance. The land's bigger than Fancy's scope. Why, ye can take all England, and hide it for a hundred years in those monstrous forests. Wi' every sea cap'n's log, it proves bigger and bigger. A sailor on a privateer, gale-blown northerly from Florida, counted seven estuaries, every one bigger than the Thames, from the Spanish settlement St. Augustine until they took shelter in a monstrous bay, where there were at least five more. Today is your sixteenth birthday. Not till ye are eighteen will ye be counted a full man. So I ask ye, Martyn Sutton, what will ye do 'twixt now and then, to prepare ye for victory in America?"

I answered without thinking, the words ready on my tongue.

"Why, I'll sign as an apprentice seaman, on a privateer, such as sail with letters of marque on almost every moon to fight the dons and strip 'em of their gold."

4

I did not see Richard again until we were both on the way to church on a bright, cool Sunday morning. Autumn colors in Wiltshire are peculiarly charming. The shire is too far south to have the contrasts of gold and scarlet and evergreen of our northern counties; the tints are timid rather than bold; the herbage is not defiant of the soon onslaught of winter; these are melancholy shades that touch the heart with an unknown sadness. Richard saw me behind him, and had the master's coach driver stop to let him out.

To him I would confide news that to me was important and exciting; and the outward lives of Richard and me, not so our inward, were so close that I thought it would startle him, too. I waited for him to rid his mouth of what he had put there to say.

"You surpassed yourself, Martyn, that afternoon with the staffs."

"I was in good fettle, and so were you," I answered.

"Now the highest type of gentleman, such as is raised in ancient noble families in France and Italy, would not say what you just said. You see, it's a self-compliment, because you beat me; those genuine gentlemen would say I was off my game. English gentlemen are not nearly so well-mannered—how could we be when our mentors, the old and genuine English aristocrats, were practically exterminated just yesterday so to speak in the Wars of the Roses? We have nothing left but upstarts—and my mother and a few more. Yet what you say is perfectly true. I was in excellent fettle that afternoon. I had no doubt whatever, when we began, of my winning. I have had more experience, Martyn; and am a better than passable fencer with foils. With you I played my utmost and my best, and the most I can claim is that your victory was very narrow. You played as you never played before. And when you bore off the prize—well, I had to think hard of our good comradeship, our many games, the good times we have had together, not to take it in bad part."

"I would have been very sorry to lose, although I do not know why, when it would be to such a great sportsman."

"I don't think the latter matters very much. Losing any game is never a pleasure; no second prize ever came close to equaling first. The winner gets not only the spoils but the satisfaction; the comfort coming to the loser is mighty chilly. Still, you may be the exception. You are exceptional in many ways, Martyn; or we would not be talking man to man. Instead I would stand on my dignity as the son of a rich franklin."

"And a noble lady," I reminded him.

"A real noblewoman, truly. I am sorry I didn't get a bigger dose. When is our next game, Martyn? It will be at the butts, will it not? I need a victory over you—and surely I can still beat you there—and yet, curse it, I can't feel absolutely sure—to lift me up after my late fall."

"It must be rather soon," I remarked, as casually as possible.

Richard did not want to ask why. It would be somewhat beneath the son of the master speaking to a tenant. Still he could not resist doing so.

"In the very near future, I'm going to seek a berth before the mast on a privateer."

This should not be a very momentous announcement to a youth

so far above me; and all over England adventurous youths sought berths on ships to fight and rob the dons. Yet it was momentous to him, for some cause I could not divine. I had the wild and senseless impression that my presence in England was somehow necessary to him, perhaps for reasons he himself could not explain or at least justify.

"Now that's a good idea," he said, when the silence grew too long.

"I think so."

"Even men before the mast have a share in the loot. One of Cavendish's sloops of war fetched home, in gold and prizes, fifty thousand pounds, enough for every man jack to buy freehold and turn yeoman. Needless to say, few of 'em did so. The port-harpies got most of it, but since these too are spendthrifts, easy come, easy go, the bulk landed at last in the laps of the Queen and the new class of gentlemen-merchants."

Still I had the impression his thoughts were not on his words. And after I had made commonplace comment, I found out where they had ranged.

"Oddly enough, Martyn, I have recently had a chance for excitement, not on the sea but in the field. To put it bluntly, I've been offered a petty captaincy in the army in the Netherlands."

"That would put you under Buys the Patriot. Still the dons take city after city and no one seems able to stop them."

"They will be stopped at last, and I want a hand in it. My mother would be very proud of me if I join what seems the losing side."

"So would Queen Bess—if it becomes the winning side."

"I might even become one of her favorites! I'm as wellborn as Sir Walter Raleigh—perhaps a shade better, for my mother is the daughter of a lord, and his the daughter of a knight. Everyone knows she has a liking for young men, so it's not lese majesty to say it. She's fifty-one this year, but the older she gets, the younger she likes her flatterers. By the way, I think Sir Walter won't remain much longer as her favorite. Leicester's replacing him, and Lord Essex is coming up fast."

"I reckon Raleigh will last long enough to plant Virginia."

"I hope so. We need colonies there, to prevent the expansion of Spanish colonies, as well as a base for privateers. And that reminds me of something you should consider, if you sail on one. If the Spanish capture you, you'll hang. You'll be on the Queen's business—she'll take her share of the loot if you sail home safe—but she can't own to King Philip that she winks at the traffic, and must disown her own adventurers as pirates."

"I knew that—everyone knows it—still I'll sail."

We tramped in silence until we were almost to the entrance of the Puritan Church, a humble edifice and not yet ten years old, yet in its congregation were some of the richest commoners in our parts, merchants, franklins, and two knights. Also it had one noblewoman, Lady Isobel. The movement had been founded by protesters of the Queen's policy of a middle course between Calvinism and Romanism. Edward Powell preached against all denominations and urged the return to literal practice of the Saviour's precepts.

"You know, Martyn, I'd like to test my blade against some of Philip's gentlemen," Richard told me, at the door of the hushed room. "I think I'll take the petty captaincy."

And fate had it, that he should set sail for the Low Countries before I took ship for the Spanish isles of the New World.

By going to Bristol I had received a captain's promise to sign me on a swift sloop sailing in November. And since Lady Isobel had lent me a nag, to be delivered to a kinsman in case of an earlier sailing, and the distance between Amesbury and the metropolis was only a long day's ride, of course I returned home for the three weeks' wait. There the even tenor of my life was resumed, and I loved it all the more dearly because of the impending change that life at sea would bring. About the twentieth of the month I said farewell to Richard who would ride to Plymouth with a groom in attendance, and a sharp sadness came upon me when we clasped hands. Truly he had dealt most fairly with me, and generously too; and I could not doubt he felt affection for me, which had crossed a bridge between our stations. It was a tribute not only to some worth in me but to breadth of mind in him.

After his departure I began to pack the stout canvas seabag I had bought for sixpence in Bristol. Mama directed, sometimes having to stop and wipe her eyes, and on the whole her sense of my vital requirements was sound, and she did not press upon me unnecessary garments, such as a Sunday coat with breeches. The side of bacon she took from the storehouse, she wept over, then wistfully returned it to its hook. The bag was deep enough to conceal my sword. All vessels ship a Bible, by the Queen's command, so the only book I took was Lady Isobel's gift of *Canterbury Tales,* which no amount of reading could ever make stale. In truth I could not resist dipping into it of an evening, despite a haunting feeling I should spend every waking moment not with the Prioresse or the Parfit Knyght, but with Mama. It was only too possible that when I set sail I would never see her again. Not one or two brave ships bound for the Spanish isles never again raised topsails over English waters.

Middling late in the afternoon of the twenty-fourth of October I started down the land to pay a last visit to Stonehenge, for I proposed to leave for Bristol on the twenty-seventh. Just beyond our gate I encountered Winifred Powell, and with childish joy she told me that her patron saint and namesake, English-born Winfrid, was truly befriending her today, for I was the very person she was looking for; and she had almost missed me! When, greatly flattered, I asked how I could serve her, she told me that her sire who was also her tutor had gone off for the afternoon, leaving a page of sums to do, some of which were beyond her powers, for she did not understand the rule of three. Would I help her? She would be ashamed to have her father return with the work undone. And she had brought pen and inkhorn.

"We could go into the cottage, but the light there is not good in late afternoon."

"Is Mistress Sutton there?" Winifred asked, in dubious tones.

"No, she's taken a bag and gone nutting in the woods."

"Then it would not look right, Martyn."

"Then why not go to Stonehenge, where I was headed?"

"Why, that's perfect. We can sit on one of the big stones that's fallen down, which my sire rejoices to see." And then as we started off: "But I don't feel that way, Martyn. It may be a pagan temple, but some say it was a monument raised to early Christians who died in battle against Hengist the Saxon, the stones moved here by Merlin's magic. Of course I don't believe that last. But whoever moved and set up those stones, and there are none like them for many miles, must have had help from God." Her eyes had become round and her expression solemn.

"The blue stones were brought all the way from Wales, Mistress Barton believes."

"There are many stone circles in Wales, Papa told me, but none as great as Stonehenge. He hates them all. But I agree with Lady Isobel that old ruins should be preserved. She is such a great lady."

True, she was, I thought, and my mother only an illiterate peasant woman.

We gained the circle, and in bravado I suggested that we sit on the slaughter stone. This Winifred would not do, so we perched on a fallen sarsen. I felt none of the spell that the ancient ruins cast at dusk, or in moonlight. The ten or so sums that had baffled Winifred were not difficult for one who knew the rule of three, and because I liked the warmth of her side close against mine as she watched me cipher, I tested the answers she had found to her problems, to discover all of them right.

"How can I reward you, Martyn?" she asked, a little breathlessly I thought, when she had folded and pouched the paper.

"I'd like a kiss."

"Well, that's what Priscilla gave you, which somehow caused the duel with quarterstaffs between you and Richard, or so she told me."

"I am much below you in station."

"My father does not believe in station. Everybody is a sinner until he is saved. That wouldn't stop me if—"

"If what?"

"We're all alone here, and this may be a temple to a pagan god who tempts people to wickedness, as my father believes. You wouldn't try—try to take—take advantage of my maidenhood?"

"I wouldn't dream of it." And truly I believed I would not even dream!

"Then I will."

Her kiss was a little more ardent than I had expected. Immediately she sprang to the ground and started homeward, her lovely face flushed. It came to pass I clean forgot every word we said on my own walk home. The most terrible moment of my yet life was winging nearer.

In the deepening twilight I caught sight of my father in the lane, making, it seemed, for the mansion. But as he looked wildly about, as though in some desperate need, he saw me and came running toward me. When he came close I saw a look of nothing less than horror on his strong face.

"Oh, Martyn!" he gasped out. "We've lost Mama."

My throat constricted and I could not speak and I was in dire pain.

"Tell me what happened—if you can," I pleaded.

"I can and I will." My father rallied his great, inward strength. "I found her at the edge of the woods, her bag of nuts beside her. And Martyn, she did not die from natur'l cause. In her side was a deep, bleeding wound. I think it was made by a knife."

Then he bowed his face in his hands, and wept.

Chapter II

TRIAL BY BATTLE

1

The closest tie in human life is between mother and son, unless it be that of an old couple long-wedded, each having been forced beyond escape to adjust himself to the other's faults, failings, and annoyings, yet to meet and combat the attacks of fate and circumstance side by side. The night following Mama's murder and all the next day I was so shocked and dispotentiated and in such mental anguish that I hardly knew who came and went to our cottage, although I was aware of the brief visit of a minister, a surgeon who was also the coroner, and a constable. I heard the hammering of nails into board by Andrew Fenner, a carpenter whom the master steadily employed; and knew well what he was making, but could not give thought to its soon contents. Peasant women came with needles and thread and worked on a black cloth which my father had bought; and I knew its purpose without grasping its full meaning, and I replied without knowing what I was saying to their heartfelt and simple words intended to give comfort. In late afternoon I put on my best clothes and my father and I repaired to the church, following six men, all of them tenants of the master, who carried a long box. I knew what was in it but could hardly believe the truth.

The parson spoke and prayed, perhaps more eloquently than usual because Lady Isobel sat in the congregation. Then the box, decorated with bouquets of wild and tame flowers brought by neighbors, was lowered with ropes into a hole in the ground in the churchyard, and again the parson gave utterance, and then there was the sound of dirt being shoveled and dropping in the hole, which slowly filled and made a little mound. Then suddenly, where Mama had been, there was nothing.

But I had best come alert, and regain my best wits, for the following morning brought the high sheriff of the shire and two of his bailiffs.

And these began to look in the house and all around it, and at the edge of the woods where Mama had met death. And soon after this they began to ask questions of both my father and me.

These were tolerably civil at first—routine questions the sheriff said. But their faces became more stern, and their eyes more severe, as the information that they gleaned was ever less satisfying. I was watching the official and his first bailiff through a small, curtained window as they were searching a patch of weeds close to our storeroom door. They found nothing, but the sheriff made a significant remark:

"Ned, I don't think we'll need to look far to find our man."

A few minutes later they came grimly in the house and the sheriff informed my father and me that they would question us not separately but together; and since they had a good many questions, we might as well sit. I thought that they hoped that if we became confused and frightened, my father and I might dispute each other, or one of us charge the other with the hideous crime. Still it would have been more sharp, I thought, to question us each alone, to discover if our testimony was identical, and if not, catch one or both of us in a lie.

"Father and son, I take it," His Honor the Sheriff began, when we were seated in the four chairs that the house boasted. "Well, my bailiff, Mr. Ned Willis, will ask most of the questions, and I'll listen sharp. Neither of you is under arrest as yet, but what we've seen so far looks bad for one of you, and I'd advise each of you, my best advice, not to try to protect the other."

"Why, Your Honor, does it look bad?" my father asked, calmly but with strength.

"I'd think that you'd see that for yourself, Thomas Sutton." Yet I felt that the question discomfited both men.

"Well, sir, I don't."

"In the first place your wife was killed by someone she knew well and trusted. That fact's plain. No one sneaked up on her through the brushwood to the hard-packed path. We've found only her own foot-prints, as she gathered nuts. If she'd seen or heard a stranger there she would have run for the house. Instead we saw where she'd walked into the brush a few feet, not ten paces from the place she was found—to gather a few filberts from a bush she had missed. We reckon that when she returned to the path she saw the murderer coming toward her from the house and she came right on. Maybe they stopped and talked a minute. Then with your wife leading the way they filed back toward the house and as they reached the edge of the wood he struck her with his knife deep in the side."

"I ask, sir, if you've found the knife?"

"No, we ain't," the bailiff broke in angrily. "But we will."

And that caused me to recall there was indeed a knife in the house, an ugly dirk that one of Mama's uncles far removed, and who had been a cooper, had brought back from a voyage with Sebastian Cabot. It had somehow come into her possession, but she did not like the look of it, and kept it out of sight.

"I thought myself she was killed by someone she knew well and trusted," my father said. Then, in a voice that he held steady by a feat of will, "I seen no terror in her face, and her clothes were not disarranged to show she'd been running. Ask your questions, sir."

"Was there any money, or any articles in the house, worth stealing?"

"Maggie had put away a little money, most of it white but some red, in an old pepper box in the storeroom."

"Is it still there?"

"Sir, I haven't looked."

"Well, we'll look now. How much was it?"

"The last time she spoke of it, she had ten shillings, three groats, six tuppence, and as I remember, ten pennies and some farthings."

"Get the box, Ned," the sheriff commanded. "Young fellow—your name is Martyn—you go with him, for you know where she kept it."

I did know. The bailiff shook the box, heard it rattle, and carried it to his chief. The latter carefully counted the sum.

"Only one of the shillings is here, and no more white money," the sheriff said in excited triumph. "Where's the rest o' it?" And then turning an ominous glance on me, "I reckon you know."

"Yes, sir, I do know."

"Will you favor us by telling?" the bailiff asked in sneering sarcasm.

"Sir, it's in a little leather pouch packed at the bottom of my seabag. Mama herself put it there."

The officials exchanged exasperated glances. I perceived that while the sheriff had summoned my father and me to the scene of Mama's death and had asked us to show him the lay of the land, a bailiff had carefully searched the bag. But their faces became more grim as they perceived no thief and murderer would have been stupid enough to conceal his loot in his own baggage.

"We have only your word that your mother gave you the money," the sheriff remarked dourly.

"Ye've my word too," my father remarked. "Maggie asked my permission to gi' Martyn the siller ere he went to sea. We had no high need of it, and he would, mayhap."

A silence fell, as the sheriff considered a new tack.

"You say, Thomas Sutton, that you had no high need of the silver. Likely you and your wife had a hidden hoard," he ventured.

"No, we didn't."

"But maybe you had a craving for a new wife, one not so long in the tooth," the lowborn bailiff said with dreadful insolence, which the lowest ruffian in England should not have to endure. But it was my sire's place to speak, not mine. This I felt sharply. And he did speak, with great quietude.

"Mr. Bailiff, I'll ask ye to speak with more respect of my dead wife. And if ye don't, I'll knock your teeth down your lying throat."

"Now, now, Mr. Sutton," the sheriff said hastily. "My bailiff had no call to use that expression, but 'tis his and my duty to find and arrest the murderer, and if you're innocent, you want that, too. No few wife murders have been caused by what he hinted. The pretty daughter of a fellow tenant, who you might have met in the wood lot, when you went there pretending to cut fuel. You were there part of the afternoon of the murder."

"All that afternoon," my father said.

"So you say."

"If ye ask the men making hay just beyond the lot, I think they'll tell ye they heard the ring of my ax from just after noon until sundown."

"We'll look into that. And where were you, Martyn Sutton, that afternoon?"

"I was here, Mama and I packing my bag, until the third hour. Then I went to Stonehenge."

"For what purpose?"

"I often go to Stonehenge just to look at it, and that would be my last good look before I sailed."

"You go often just to look at an old ring of rocks, some of them standing, but the most lying down? 'Tis a mystery, I grant you, but I've looked at it only once in the last ten years."

"Yes, sir."

"Did anybody see you coming or going?"

"I did not pass anyone. This is a lonely region, and the lane's little used."

But this corner was getting close. I did not want to disclose that I had gone there with Winifred Powell. If it were known, I knew several wives of tenants whose tongues would wag, wet and lively with spit, for I was a peasant youth, and Winifred not only gentry but the daughter of a preacher. Of course I could not shield her from this, if I were seriously charged, but truly my urge to do so was greater than I could well explain, except by puerile idolatry.

"Martyn, if after our examination you're the only one who can't clear himself—establish what we call an alibi—that's a Latin word meaning elsewhere at the time and scene of a crime—and everyone

else who might have motive and opportunity has cleared himself—
you'll be investigated very fully, I'll tell you that. You're a queer sort
of stripling, or so I hear. You can read and write better than most
gentlemen, let alone any peasant I know of. Do you know the word
matricide?" And the sheriff was plainly pleased with himself at knowing it.

"Yes, sir, I do."

"'Tis an unnatural crime, yet it's been committed in England
more times than I like to think. Sometimes sons get far above their
mothers, and are ashamed of 'em, and regard them as obstacle to
their own rise. And sometimes they hate 'em for reasons unknown.
Doctors have told me that—'em that know family secrets—and it happens as often among gentry as among common, maybe more often.
I can't swear we're not dealing with such a case right now."

"Say nought, Martyn," my father cautioned me quickly.

"Thomas Sutton, that's bad advice you're giving your son."

"I'll gi' it, still."

"Thomas Sutton, you've looked about the house and grounds since
the murder. You were seen doing it. I ask you, and expect an answer.
Did you miss anything? Has any valuable disappeared?"

"None."

"So theft is not a possible motive. What does that leave but a
murderous desire for the riddance of this woman who was killed, or
the act of a deranged mind? Your son is an odd sort, Thomas. But
those who show the most brilliant at the beginning are the most
likely to fetch up in Bedlam. He admits he frequently goes mooning
off to Stonehenge. Only a few days ago a noblewoman, wife of your
master, gave your son a sword; and 'twas an unsuited gift, as I'd tell
her to her face. Could it have caused Martyn to become grandiose
—to imagine he's not a peasant boy but a nobly born foundling, or
some such moonshine? Suppose his mother told him, in plain words,
to stop his silly talk and posturing, and he became violent. Yes, I
believe we're on the right track now, but what he did would not be
murder. He'd go to the madhouse, not the gallows; and there the
keepers and a good doctor might straighten him out within a year."
And the high sheriff looked pleasantly at my father.

Actually his account of my mother's death was strangely convincing.
Almost every human being questions his own sanity at times; the
curtain between rationality and madness is eerily thin. I thought that
if I were a listener to this account, and I were a learned judge, and
there was even a little factual evidence in its support and no evidence
that any other person had either motive or opportunity to put Mama
to death, I would credit it. The bailiff was slowly nodding his head

with satisfaction. I could see that my father was deeply troubled, if not afraid. I alone of its hearers knew that the story was utterly false, and one other living person would know the same, if she listened to it. The moment had come to present my alibi, "a Latin word meaning one's presence elsewhere." My reluctance until now had been the real touch of madness.

But I was spared the distasteful task as by a miracle. At the least what happened was an almost incredible coincidence—as though Fortune herself loved whimsy, and could not resist smashing flat the sheriff's whole case.

There came a timid knock on the door. The bailiff opened it quickly, hoping, I thought, for some development that would prove my guilt. Then there entered the room a young and, to my eyes, strangely beautiful girl; and her hair glimmered in the shadowed room.

"Yes, miss?" the sheriff inquired, rising to his feet at sight of gentry.

"Sir, I am Winifred Powell, Mister Edward Powell's daughter. I know something that might concern this awful happening, and my father told me it was my bounden duty to tell you."

"Why, we'd like to know it."

"My father said that since no robber or crazy man had been arrested, suspicion would fall on Thomas Sutton or his son Martyn. I do not know where Thomas Sutton was in those late hours of afternoon when the—when it happened, although when I had left Martyn I heard a chopping sound far away in the wood lot. But I know where Martyn was, and that was with me."

There was a long wait. I thought that the sheriff sighed. Winifred stood very still. I recalled her steady voice and mien; among her other gifts was bravery, the real thing. Then the official spoke.

"Are you saying, Miss Powell, that Martyn Sutton was with you every minute from three o'clock in the afternoon of that day, until sundown?"

"That's what I am saying."

"I regret that I must ask how it happened that a daughter of gentry was with a peasant youth all that time, and *where* you both were?"

"We were at Stonehenge. My father had bade me work some sums while he was absent, and I couldn't, and I came to ask Martyn to help me, and since his mother was gathering nuts, I—we—thought it would not look well for me to go into the cottage, so we went and sat on an upset stone. I have the sheet of problems, and some of the answers are in his hand. The sun was down when we separated and each of us started home."

The sheriff was equal to the occasion, although he gagged on it.

"Young lady, I thank you for your evidence."

"Then with your consent, I'll take my leave."

This she did. The sheriff and the deputy looked at each other with what seemed disgust. Then the sheriff remembered his many dignities, cleared his throat, and took comfort that he was not beaten yet, and spoke with authority and force.

"The young lady's story is probably true," he pronounced. "She's gentry and the daughter of a kind of minister. Still our duty will be to investigate it fully. Martyn Sutton, I have no real doubt that you are innocent, but cannot pronounce you so, so it is my official order that you not take sail for the high seas, but remain in this parish, until this case is either cleared up or our investigations are complete. Do you hear me?"

"Yes, sir."

"I must observe that your knowledge of mathematics—and a young lady's sense of duty—but that we can expect from English gentry—have stood you in good stead. I have no more questions at present."

The high sheriff of our shire was not without an acrid sense of humor.

2

That night I wrote a letter to the shipmaster who had promised to sign me, saying that because of the death of my mother I could not sail as soon as I expected, but kindly to remember me if I should again apply for duty under his command.

Then there was nothing to do but unpack my seabag, a forlorn task, and made more mournful by my recurring memories of its packing, whereupon visions rose of Mama's voice and countenance, and of how her eyes had filled with tears, as did now my own eyes.

The sheriff returned to his office in Salisbury—New Sarum in my father's speech. His bailiffs remained, and the fruitless search for Mama's slayer went on, although in a more desultory fashion. Rumors rose and died away—one of a wild-looking fellow, suspected of being a fugitive from Bedlam, being seen on the lane near the fatal spot on a day before her death. Some gypsies who rather suddenly appeared in Amesbury were questioned by the watch and ward. And then I was told by a bailiff that I was no longer under suspicion, and free to come and go. But the stout ship on which I had meant to sail was well at sea by now, perhaps about to make a landfall of the Azores.

And now there was talk unguessed by any official of the crown, and never reaching the ears of the gentry. But I was of the folk, and when I saw Pete trimming the hedge of the park, he called to me that he would walk with me a little way into the field.

"'Ee suffered a bad loss, Martyn," he began, pausing under a solitary elm.

"Aye, I did."

"'Tis like tearing out the root of a man's life, when 'en's dam's turn ha' come."

"Aye, it is."

"I wish 'em wardsmen would catch the renegate, if 'en's flesh-and-blood."

"What do you mean, old man?"

"'Ee know what I mean. All 'em books 'ee read, and 'ee talk like gentry, ha' not parted 'ee from the folk, and I know it never will."

"No, it never will."

"The folk be whispering o'er much."

"What do they say? No one has told me."

"'Ee may guess. How 'em monstrous stones was raised by sorcery, made by 'em Druids long ago. But 'em Roman soldiers under Agycola crushed the Mistletoe Men and put some of 'em to herding hogs, and cut down their sacred groves." Agycola was the peasant version of the long-remembered name, Agricola, the Roman governor under the Emperor Domitian.

"I've heard that, and the last part is true, but there's no proof that the Druids built Stonehenge."

"Well, 'em did," Pete insisted stubbornly. "And when the Druids' power was broken, the temple they built stood empty. And Martyn Sutton"—Pete's voice had dropped to a hoarse whisper—"'ee know, or wish on purpose to forget, for 'ee've read too many books, that no temple ever stays empty long."

"Because the Devil takes it for his own?"

"If not 'en, some of 'en's servants. And plenty of folk have seen 'em servants, slipping through the shadows of 'em big stones, of usual on nights of a waning moon. And one of 'en's servants—his bailiff 'ee might say—has a name 'ee've heard, but which I dread to speak."

"You needn't speak it. Does it rhyme with slow dough?"

"O' truth it do."

"I'll say it for you. Modo. He was one of the Five Fiends, and his department was murder. Mama told me about him, once, and I read about him in an old book called *God's Enemies in Ancient Britain*. The author said there was an extensive cult of Modo after the Romans left Britain and before St. Patrick's teaching became widespread, and it centered on Anglesey Island."

"This 'ere a'ant the first murder nigh to Stonehenge, and the folk say it won't be the last. Only se'en years since, a journeyer on the road was cut open in 'en's chest. 'Twas not in our parish but only half a league beyond the master's lands. The only tracks in the road was cloven like a cow's."

"Did the watch and ward ever catch the killer?"

"That, they didn't. The tracks made toward Stonehenge and then was lost in the grass."

"I remember hearing about it, now, when I was an urchin."

"I hope no man hears nothing like it, any more, and I wish I could believe 'en won't."

Pete walked away. I did not believe that Mama's death was associated with any other, but I wished the whispering would stop. Some day the solution of the mystery, truly a baffling one, would be found, and it would be ugly but commonplace, possibly the desperate deed of a fugitive from jail who knew he had been seen and must shut the eyes of the seer.

Yet a brief conversation I had with my father just before he went to bed caused some darkling thoughts before I too retired, only to toss that night from eerie and troubled dreams.

"I told the sheriff one lie," my father announced suddenly, after a long, thoughtful silence.

"You did?" For my sire was a notably truthful man.

"It was when he asked me if I had missed anything from around the house and shed. Well, I did miss something, but I reckon it's misplaced some'ere, 'cause it couldn't be of use to anyone."

"What was it?"

"That hatchet with the leaden head I found in the copper box."

"It will turn up," I answered, after brief thought.

"I reckon it will, but I don't know where or how."

3

In the morning my father had a sound explanation for the missing hatchet.

"Maggie was digging a trough for her spare lily bulbs when she came on a big root and went for a tool to cut it out. Later she dropped the hatchet, it fell in the trough, and in the dusk she covered it up. Well, I'm not going to dig up the posies she planted there, looking for it." And this made sense enough.

And it came to pass that I had another chance to sail to the Spanish isles, and one far more thrilling to a young man's heart than the one I had missed. A fleet was being organized by Sir Walter Raleigh to harry and sack these islands, and no less a sea eagle than

Frankie Drake was to serve as vice-admiral. As soon as I heard the
news, I began packing my seabag, and on the following day to speak
my farewells to those I thought would miss me. Three of these were
Lady Isobel, Miss Priscilla, and Mistress Barton. Just to entreat their
permission to address the first of these demanded a rallying of my
courage and a firming of my nerves, not only because of the vast
gap between her station and mine, but because she was the wife of
the master, whose mighty import in our lives I had sensed before I
could talk plain. Those who dwell in a later age may find it hard to
understand and believe. By the king's proclamation—the king being
Henry VII—the institution of villeiny had ended in England; but that
was less than a century ago; and as men thinketh, so they are. Even
gentry, let alone nobility, seemed a separate creation of God from us
peasants. My father's and my own mind told him and me that this
was not true. Our ministers told us this was not true; but their actions
belied their words. Mayhap feudalism had received a death wound
in England with the signing of the Great Charter at Runnymede; if
so, it was suffering a lingering death and in all outward aspects was
wondrous healthy still.

"So ye wish to speak to Her Ladyship, Mistress Barton, and young
Miss Priscilla," the gatekeeper, Adam Harrison, remarked.

"Aye, those were my very words." For I did not intend to be lorded
over by this fellow, himself of peasant birth.

"They be bold words, from the son of the master's tenant."

"That they may be, but I spoke 'em."

"I was gi'en the right to turn away visitors, who I didn't reckon 'em
great folk wanted to see, or who I reckoned would waste their time."

"Turn me away, if you feel like it, and I'll report the fact in a letter
delivered to Lady Isobel by Her Majesty's post."

"Why, now, I didn't say I was going to turn ye away, Martyn
Sutton. I have it she takes an interest in ye, as a likely youth, wi'
prospects of high repute in your own station; and 'tis known far and
wide that the master's sister, Mistress Barton, gave freely of her time
to teach ye her letters, and I hope she didn't waste it, but I'd not
wager a penny on't, for ye can't turn a sow's ear into a silk purse.
But I'll send Dora to the manor house wi' your entreaty."

In the first place a franklin's habitation was not, strictly speaking,
a manor house, no matter its richness or the breadth of acres it commanded; because a manor is an outright grant from a king. The master
had bought these two thousand acres from freeholders, with the prof-
its of a foremost haberdashery in Bristol established by his sire. Dora
was the gatekeeper's little daughter, swift of foot.

"But mind ye, Martyn," Adam told me when the messenger was

dispatched, "if they grant your plea, 'tis for this time only. It don't mean ye can enter the park some other day, coming through the hedge, let alone some night; and if I'm not on duty, don't forget that Snarler is unchained at sundown."

Snarler was a mastiff, immense and formidable, and trained as a watchdog. It is said that barking dogs do not bite. A corollary of this might be a biting dog does not bark: certainly this held true with Snarler. I had never heard him bark; he attacked in ominous silence, and snarled only when he had his teeth set in a trespasser's leg, from which there was no release except at his master's command. This had occurred at least twice. Once when he had slipped his chain in daylight he had seized by the calf of the leg an innocent clergyman from a nearby parish, who had come through the hedge to call on Mistress Barton; and once he had bitten and held a peasant from Hampshire who claimed he had lost his way. The minister was given ten pounds to repair his church roof, and the wanderer a month in jail for trespass.

The gatekeeper walked a distance to meet Dora, coming on the run. The glum expression on his face when he heard her tidings cheered me no little: I could not doubt my request had been granted.

"The great folk say they'll receive ye," Adam reported almost with cordiality. "And I see ye are clean—but ye're known for that—and decent-dressed, and I'll open my gate for ye as though ye were gentry."

I walked up an avenue of larch trees, which make a good show when only twenty years old. Then I was confronted with a difficult question, whether to pull the bell cord at the big front door or to use the tradesmen's and servants' entrance at the rear? After brief, hard thought I followed a walk of inset stones to the postern door.

A grumpy maidservant admitted me, not of course to the drawing room but to the curiosity room, where also the master's guns and trout rods were neatly racked. The former included a pair of expensive wheel-lock shotguns, expressly made for wild fowl shooting, as well as three matchlock muskets, shooting a ball. I had little opportunity to examine them, for Mistress Barton burst in with haste.

"My prize pupil!" she cried, taking my hand in both of hers. "And I hear you're off to the wars!"

"Ma'am, I don't believe any war has been declared between Queen Bess and King Philip. I am going freebooting, to put true words to it."

"You've always liked precise terms, Martyn. 'Tis the sign of an orderly mind, 'stead of a cluttered one. Who went searching with a lantern for an honest man—Demosthenes or Diogenes?"

"Demosthenes."

"Martyn, can ye ne'er remember? Demosthenes would not have found an honest man when alone in bed. Nay, 'twas the great cynic, Diogenes. Martyn, will you read books when you're off watch? Not just *Canterbury Tales,* but any book you can lay hand on? The officers will have a few, I reckon; and no lover of books can resist lending them to the young and eager; that very love makes for liberality; 'tis the least jealous in the world. Some of the sailors 'll own that pirated copy of Boccaccio in English." Mistress Barton blushed slightly but went on firmly. "There's a deal of human nature in it, as well as ribaldry. Read Marco Polo, for though scholars aver he's a liar big as Sinbad, the voyagers since Da Gama tend to bear him out. But now come Isobel and Priscilla, and we can talk no more."

Lady Isobel was gracious; and that covered it; yet I felt she was not quite her well-mastered self; and that either the master had protested her receiving me, or she did not want him to know it. In truth I had supposed he was out of the house, for his horse had not been hitched at the usual post, and this was a comfort to me. It would be quite like the master to oppose the condescension, for those gentlemen whose grandsires were peasants are famously the most haughty.

She told me that privateering was not only a necessary but noble pursuit just now, because war with Philip was unavoidable since we had begun to colonize Virginia, and with all her guile Queen Bess could not stave it off much longer. The more Spanish ships we captured or sunk, the fewer there would be to assail England. Then she gave me, in her most domineering tones, some good instruction.

"Now don't be too hotheaded, like your bull of a sire," she told me. "Stay out of quarrels, at least until you know a sword from a—I started to say pitching fork, but I'll change it to quarterstaff. There's a deal of difference, Martyn Sutton. One gives a painful rap, but tother deals death. Maybe you can practice with an old cutlassman aboard the vessel, for everyone likes to teach; 'tis self-flattering. Don't let an insult goad you into a duel; settle it with your fists. Beware of grog. First it gives a pleasant warmth, then an addled head, then over-confidence, and at last the wish you were dead. Beware the French disease—for I'm told it's rife in the Spanish isles, spread by Indian women. But I've preached enough, for you'll pay no mind to it anyhow."

"In that, my lady, you're mistaken." For I was wonder-struck at the great Lady Isobel spending her time and breath in my behalf.

"When the war's done, come back to Mother England. For all her faults, she's the best country in the world, unless her daughter Virginia beats her, when she's settled. Good-bye, Martyn, and that word means 'God be with you.'"

She extended her strong, beautiful hand and took my rough hand.

"Come back safe," Priscilla told me, and I felt sure she would have kissed me, if there were no onlookers.

From the mansion I made for the second-best house in the parish; and at the gate I heard Preacher Powell ranting to himself, no doubt practicing a sermon. And the thought struck me that what I was about to propose was really more bold than a peasant's visit to his master's abode to say farewell to inmates. Mr. Powell heard my knock and himself opened the door to me.

"Well, Martyn?" he queried, his mind still on fire and brimstone.

"Sir, I am taking off tomorrow, meaning to sign on a privateer, and I'd like to walk and talk a little while with Miss Winifred before I go." The expression I had used—walk and talk—was ancient in the West Country and, I thought, native to Wales. The more common expression nowadays was "walk out."

"I'll not deny your right to ask," Mr. Powell answered. "As a servant of our Lord, I cannot hold with worldly rank. Still, it's nigh sunset, and time for supper—"

"Don't make objections, Edward," came a soft voice from an inner room. "There's no harm in what Martyn proposes. Winifred's turned fourteen, and I'd rather her first walking and talking would be with a respectable peasant youth than a lewd young lord."

"Well, so would I. Wait here a moment, Martyn, and I'll ask Winifred if she's agreeable."

Winifred took a good five minutes to make up her mind, or else Preacher Powell gave her extensive instructions. At last she came to the door, her hair glimmering from a very recent brushing, her manner shy, but her eyes bright. For the first time I took note of their coloring. Instead of black like her mother's they were a pale hazel. Brilliance was their outstanding quality. I had a feeling that despite her childish ways and her peculiarly soft voice she lived with more intensity than most maidens of her age; perhaps she had a more lively imagination. This could be her birthright; the Welsh were a highly imaginative people, with a great love of poetry and music. Mistress Barton had told me that the name Welsh meant "stranger," in the ancient British tongue; and the folk's distrust of them had by no means died out.

> Taffy was a Welshman, Taffy was a thief,
> Taffy came to my house and stole a piece of beef.
> I went to Taffy's house, Taffy wasn't home,

Taffy came to my house and stole a marrow-bone.
I went to Taffy's house, Taffy was in bed,
So I took a club o' thorn, and beat him on the head.*

"I would have been sorry if you had sailed without telling me good-bye," Winifred told me, the words perfectly proper on a young lady's lips but her tone taking my breath. It could not have been intentional, I thought. It must have been unconscious, because there was no reason in the world for a wellborn girl to employ it in speaking to a peasant youth unless she was somehow moved by him. It was true Winifred was now fourteen, which old wives said was the most dangerous age for a maiden; and that was why parents wanted their daughters safely married at fifteen. If they were not they were likely to remain unmarried until nineteen or even twenty, in which case many were headed for the shelf instead of the bridal bed. Welsh women were peculiarly passionate, or at least had that reputation. I was going on seventeen, with my innocence long lost.

"I wouldn't miss offering you my good-bye, after what you did for me."

"Oh, you mean what I told the sheriff? I would have told him even if my parents had not bade me."

Without the slightest inattention to her meaning, I was marking for the first time that her choice of words and even her accent was subtly different from that of daughters of Wiltshire great folk, such as Priscilla. Indeed the difference was too subtle to pin down, yet perfectly real. It came to me that English was not her native tongue. In all probability her infant speech was Cymric, a branch of the old Celtic, but she had learned precise English while very young. But this passing thought did not slow down the hurried beat of my heart; and perhaps quickened it still more. Perhaps unconsciously I shared the general feeling toward Welsh immigrants, and thus would dare make bolder addresses to a Welsh maiden far above me in station than to a wellborn British girl. And a remark old Pete had made, at a woolshearing, bore upon the matter with salt and pith.

"They be not much to choose 'twixt a ram and a man in his youth and wigor," he had said, when one of the shearer's spoke of the former's corpulence. "Ary man will go as far as he dare wi' a wench who takes his fancy, and only 'at keep him in bound, not his conscience." And there was a more gross saying that made the same point.

* Taffy is a corruption of Davie, the most common given name in Wales, in honor of Saint David.

"Does this way we are walking suit you?" I asked my flushed and beautiful companion.

"Why not?"

"It's toward Stonehenge."

"There's no better place to be walking toward."

"That's what I think, too."

"You spoke, Martyn, of the little thing I did for you. But you tried to do something for me, too. You were not going to tell, at least until you were forced to do so, that I was with you at that awful hour. How many gentlemen, how many young lords, would have kept silent that long? Why, they'd blat it out the first time the sheriff looked hard at them."

I did not confess that I was at the very point of telling when Winifred had knocked on our door. I did not want to shatter an illusion that was weaving in her mind.

"You thought it would cause talk, considering the difference in our stations. And it did, too, but not the kind you expected. Our scullery maid, Annie, hears everything—so I hear everything. Nobody has mentioned what was at worst an impropriety, as far as Annie knew, but all the people praised me for coming forward, almost making me out a heroine. You know, Martyn—and you can talk plain for no one knows it better than we ourselves—that the Welsh are still under suspicion in Britain. Well, what I did—the natural thing for any girl to do—helped to make it less all through this shire—my father said so."

"That is wonderful!"

"Perhaps I shouldn't mention it, when it concerns such a terrible happening. Instead let me tell you about Wales. Shall we sit on an upset stone as we did before? It would—we would be more proper than if—if—we sat in the grass."

"Still I'd like to sit in the grass."

"Then we will. I won't see you again for years and years maybe, and maybe never."

She quickened her step a little, now that Stonehenge was in plain sight in the falling twilight and in the light of a rising moon only a little thickened from her perfect round. We said no more until we were seated in the dense grass between the outer circle of sarsens and the ring of blue stones. These circles were pitifully broken by stones having fallen, but I could picture them two thousand years ago, when they were perfect, and perhaps the outer circle a series of cromlechs, their tops interjoining. From our low position all the stones looked taller to me than ever before, and their shadows cast by the moon more weird-looking. Would this help or harm what I intended? It was only to woo the beautiful girl beside me and win a few kisses. What was in the dark cellar of my mind, I imprisoned there. It was strangely like shutting and locking a door, and not difficult, since every perception of her beauty in the dimness quickened the chivalry innate in a youth out of a home of love.

But, first, Winifred had something to tell me.

"There is no cause whatever for the British folk to be suspicious of us Welsh," she said earnestly. "And to look down on us is worse, because Wales has the oldest aristocracy on the island."

"I didn't know that."

"How far can your English dukes and earls trace their lineage? The immediate families of most of them were unknown before the Wars of the Roses. Yet my own mother descends directly from King Vortigern and Queen Enid, and Vortigern was a direct descendant of King Lear."

"Then she's the best-born woman on the island."

"None is better born. The Marshalls of Pembrokeshire go back to 1200, and the famous King Rhodri of Wales did not emerge until just before the Danish invasion in the late eight hundreds. Yet my own grandmother refused to be Queen of England."

For a second or two, I thought Winifred might be demented. Young, delicate, and imaginative girls sometimes dwell on such daydreams until they believe them. But my quick glance showed her sitting calmly, her exquisite hands in her lap, with no wild light in her eyes and these lustrous rather than overbright, and her voice was low and sweet.

"How could that be, Winifred?" I asked.

"It happened in 1539—just about then. King Henry VIII—your merry Harry, father of Queen Bess—had just shed 'that great Flemish mare,' Anne of Cleves. A short time before he had granted Wales full union with England, fair representation in Parliament, the same taxation and laws. But there was still unrest in Wales, the people did not want to be English, their loyalty was to the great thanes, landless and impoverished, but mighty men still. The idea struck the king of marrying one of their daughters, in the way of placating the people. None was more eminent that my grandmother, of wondrous beauty too. He complimented her and made his plea; she answered that at least she had pretty hair and a comely countenance, so she did not want her head falling in a basket on the block, as fell poor Ann Boleyn's head. Merry Harry married Catherine Howard, whose head did not stay on her neck for very long. My grandam fell in love with a young poet. Her daughter Enid married a gentleman who called himself a Primitive Christian, a considerable cult in Wales. I am their first child, and a baby will be born in March."

I believed the story, partly because Winifred looked the part, and because of the simple way she spoke. Since her telling it to a young peasant who tomorrow would set out for Plymouth on his way to the high seas was profitless, no doubt she had obeyed an impulse, prompted by our aloneness here, between two Magic Circles of stones looming so far above us, on which the moon gazed once more. These knew each other so long and well, sharing but confiding to no human soul their ancient secrets. It might be that the ruins were once a temple to the Sun, husband to her grace, the Moon. The folk thought so, for the Sun was the highest god in the Druid pantheon.

"You must take me home in a few minutes more," Winifred told me dreamily.

"So soon?"

"Yes. You told my father you would walk and talk with me but briefly. But, Martyn, I had a purpose other than just letting you know, when I told you about my lineage—that I am the noblest born of anyone you have ever addressed. In old time such exalted birth gave rights and privileges mere noblemen's daughters do not now possess. It is told of great Goneril, Lear's daughter, when she was caught conspiring with a lover against her husband's life, that she asked him: 'Who can arraign me? I am the Law, not thee.'† Such Celtic queens and princesses could lie with brawny slaves, if they so desired, and their god Lud—London was once Ludtown—did not punish them. I will not lie with you but I will let you kiss me, for I know it is your desire." She laughed softly. "I knew it when we first began our walk."

"Will you lie with your breast against mine?"

"Yes, but your hands must not wander."

Immediately she was as good as her word, making herself comfortable with the grace and luxury of a cat, but after our mouths had pressed and then clung, and she became palpitant and breathless, she countermanded some of her words.

"I take back what I said about your hands. Let them wander at will."

† The author has no recognized justification for repeating the content of these famous lines, since this chronicle was supposedly written before Shakspere's play. Yet it is by no means certain I am guilty of an anachronism. Throughout *King Lear*, Shakspere evidences close acquaintance with West Country lore, especially in the utterances of Poor Tom (Edgar in disguise) and of the Fool. The legend of Lear and his unnatural daughters is a great deal older than Shakspere's writings.

Truly they were willful, and Welsh blood is fiery. In a few minutes that sped so fast, yet would never be lost in the abyss of time, never forgotten, her body began to stiffen, her thighs pressing together against my hand, her legs straight, her feet arched down, her weight full-thrust against my thighs, although her mouth still clung to mine, and her arms remained clutched, ever more tightly, around my neck. Then a long quiver passed through her whole body, became more intense, then slowly passed away. She relieved her held breath with a long luxuriant sigh.

We rose and walked away from each other until each reached the shadow of one of the towering stones. It was human, I suppose, for me to hope that, along with being some kind of mystic, Preacher Powell was not a mind-reader or did not possess second-sight. When we joined each other, Winifred was her calm and well-poised self, and the only reminder of our transport was the warm clasp of her hand as we began our homeward walk.

Only once she spoke.

"I have told you of things as they were long ago," she said. "I have no longing, openly or covert, to return to those old things. My patron saint and namesake is Winfrid, known as St. Boniface, born in Devonshire. But you are going to sea, perhaps to soon death, at least you will be celebate for many weeks, and I don't think he would blame me for what we did tonight."

"Why, I feel the same!" I told her, in solemn exultation. "And because of that, I want to make you a promise."

"I'd love to have a pledge from you."

"It is only this. If you ever call on me, for any service, anything I can do for you, anything you want that I can give you, you won't call in vain."

I was sixteen years old, no nearer maturity, really, than my beautiful companion, who was barely fourteen.

4

Only my father, Thomas Sutton, and our sheep dog, Hustler, saw me off in the dawnlight of that late-October morning. The former gave me brief advice on matters overlooked until now; the bitch barked excitedly, whined, and sniffed at my new clogs. My sire rented for sixpence a mare owned by a yeoman dwelling down the lane, the charge so low because "'en be going to fight 'em 'Quisition dons what hate Queen Bess" and I could leave the animal with his cousin, who kept a woodyard in Plymouth, and who would return her in due course. I would take the highroad via Salisbury, Ilchester, and Exeter, a journey of four days, or at most five. A penny would buy me a bed at poor-folks inns, and my well-packed seabag was strapped on Stumble's back behind the saddle.

It so chanced that I arrived there none too soon. The Vice-Admiral, Sir Francis Drake, had proposed to Sir Walter Raleigh that he send forth an advanced squadron, under Captain Fernando, to harry the shore of Cuba. Thus we would destroy shipping and gather pelf, and at the same time draw off ships defending Porto Rico, Santo Domingo, and Jamaica, and make them easy prey for his swift galleons. It so chanced too that all berths on the ships allotted Fernando had not been filled, and he and his fellow captains were signing on every able-bodied man who knew south from north, but those who did not know east from west were mercilessly rejected! I applied to the ship's clerk of the *Elspeth,* this name being the Scotch form of Elizabeth, and I had heard some old wharf rats admire as a fine sloop, staunch, "yare," with plenty of weight, which word meant guns. In all truth she was a beauty, built and outfitted in the yards of Glasgow at a Protestant laird's expense, and his son, the Honorable Andrew Selkirk, was her master.

"Age?" the clerk asked after he had written down my name and birthplace.

"Seventeen, sir," I replied, a lie as yet, but truly I was in my seventeenth year on earth, since a newborn babe is in his first year on earth.

"You said eighteen," the clerk remarked thoughtfully, writing the number down, "and a good thing, too, for Sir Walter frowns on signing boys. Cap'n Selkirk is all of twenty-two."

The next question, or comment, was one I answered with pride.

"I don't reckon you can read and write."

"Yes, sir, and with facility."

The word facility jarred the neat little man. He glanced into my face and then at my clothes and I thanked God for Mistress Barton.

"But by no chance you're adept with a cutlass," he remarked.

"I've never had one in my hand, but I'm handy with quarterstaffs."

"Then I'll sign you as a 'prentice pikeman. We've got good long pikes, not those shorty pikes fit only for pinnaces. If you make pikeman first class, your share of the booty will be a third more than an apprentice seaman's. Now sign your own name, not just make a mark after a name I write, and if you talk to any landlubbers before we weigh, remember we're bound for Newfoundland."

This last, I thought with a little thrill, was to confound spies. But common sense told me that half the town knew that our course would be west by south.

The *Elspeth* had a good master—the old salts said so. She was not a starvation ship, a dread name in our fleets, although a few complained at the plenitude of porridge. After certain agonies I found my sea legs; and truly the seas were only middling rough for this time of year. They smoothed as we slanted southward, and soon a sail on the skyline would draw all men not at duty to the rail. We must fear French pirates even now; after a week off the Azores, recently ceded by Portugal to Spain, but still enjoying uneasy peace, we had crossed what was known as the Line Decreed by a Pope. Its existence was stoutly denied by our great voyagers, yet the watch aloft was doubled, for we did not know when we would raise a Spanish ship of war.

What need to tell of the gales we met, which we must ride out with a sea anchor, or those that blew us off our course? This last we kept mainly with an astrolabe and by the sun; but Captain Selkirk owned a Nuremberg compass, on which a needle, one end of what had stroked a loadstone, was said to point straight north by some mysterious power. But it was a foreign device and in it our pilot put little trust.

Perhaps for lack of that trust, the *Elspeth* became separated from her sisters on a day when fog drifted in dense clouds and skiens and slowly wheeling towers before a breeze hardly strong enough to puff our sails. In the first gray of dawn after the worried night all hands lined the rail in the hope of spying a ship light, but soon the heaving up of the sun revealed us adrift on an empty sea. But since he had risen where the needle told he would, we continued our course with confidence.

Our point of rendezvous in case we became scattered was to be southward of Crooked Island in the Bahama archipelago. But we failed that rendezvous because we had been lamed.

Before that laming we had been blooded and baptized in battle. Off islands northward we had encountered numerous Spanish ships, from some of which we must run, and some had run from us, but some we had fought, but only in cannon range, not at close range as yet. Even these indecisive frays had not been contests with quarterstaffs, or even duels between gentlemen over an insult. Often the balls flew wild, but one that we dispatched knocked down the foremast of a merchantman. Yet we could not pursue our advantage, because a ball fired by our foe slanted across our stern, killing two seamen on our poop, and damaging our rudder. In a clash with a heavily armed trader I thought I had seen sea fighting at its utmost heat. Truly we fought to a draw, both ships limping on their ways. This was recorded in our log, but the fight would not be counting worth the ink of its mention in the big black books of the Admiralty, although the seven men we put overside were as stony-dead as those that had fallen at great Lepanto.

But on what seemed a keelless sea east and a little north of Crooked Island we went to a dear school. Only shrieking seafowl and leaping fishes watched at the battle there; and we had not expected any at all, and instead an easy prize, as we gained on a brig not as yare as the *Elspeth,* and, we supposed, not nearly as heavily armed.

As we drew nigh, I waited with aching hope for the brig to strike her colors. But the dons were a haughty people, contemptuous even of death, and more battle-tried than we; and instead of a struck flag we saw the flash of hidden guns, and then heard their thunder, and then a terrifying crashing sound that made the whole ship shudder. Implacably our way brought us alongside, where we grappled, and then the battle raged across both rails and decks; and the din was such that once heard, could never be forgotten, but would re-echo in a man's nightmares all his life long. On a field there is room to maneuver, to attack or retreat, to find shelter in a ditch, to crush a weak segment; but not so on these little floors, slippery with blood, and littered with dead and wounded.

English and Spanish fought with cutlasses, pikes, daggers when in hand's reach, and sometimes a musket was discharged with what seemed a little pop. We did not know what side was winning; each of us had no concern but to avoid death or to deal death. After an eternity the Spaniard struck, and the awesome conflict ended, and we could take our prize—but there was no prize. A wound we had dealt her at her waterline had been stuffed with old cloth, and boards over these were held in place by props, but the whole contraption suddenly gave way, and the vessel's settling no more than a foot opened another hole to the inrush of the sea; and now her hold was filling like a bucket let slowly down into a well.

Her hands made haste to jettison her guns, but this would not save her because of her heavy freight which later I decided must be chests of gold. She had had a company of sixty, and half of these lay on the deck, dead or too direly wounded to seek escape, and half of the remainder fell in their effort to leap aboard our vessel. Not one of the fallen did we save, because of a school of ravenous sharks, drawn here by the smell of blood of wounded and dead men that had toppled overboard.

So the battle ended with our having fifteen prisoners not one of whom could pay ransom, some twenty corpses, Spanish and English over whom to pray ere we rolled them, weighted by the heels, through our broken rail, and about the same number woefully wounded. All the rest of us were hurt, our sails torn, yards had fallen, and the ship leaked.

This had been one little skirmish on a lonely ocean. What mighty strife on land and sea did it herald? A fact plain to the eyes of a few handfuls of adventurers seemed to remain unperceived by Elizabeth on the throne of England, and Philip wearing the crown of Castile and Aragon. The great prize north of Florida and known as North America, perhaps the greatest prize of all human conflict in the remembered history of man, could not be won by wishing.

Chapter III

THE SEA ROVER

1

Commodore Fernando had instructed Captain Selkirk that the place of rendezvous would be the south end of Crooked Island, by way of Crooked Passage, in a vast archipelago known as the Bahamas. This was in case any ships became separated from the squadron, a common happening on voyages as long as this. The *Elspeth* limped her way there, after raising Cat Island, unmistakable for any other because of the extensive westward-pointing cape at its south end. Crooked Island was readily identifiable by the spread of its north end and a nearby islet there, plainly shown on the charts. But when we sailed to its south end, the men in the tops gazed with starved and aching eyes for the sight of even one English ship.

There we lay at anchor a weary three weeks. Plainly the rest of our squadron had had fair winds and no mishaps, lingered at the rendezvous a few, impatient days, and given us up for lost. During our wait, our hands had been busy at such repairs as we could make, and at its end, the sloop was fairly seaworthy; but we durst not make for the south coast of Cuba with almost empty pantries and our water casks nigh-dry. We must needs go foraging, and be not long about it.

Our course was generally southwest. Although we raised a gracious plenty of islands big and small, to our incredulous surprise we saw none with Spanish harbors and towns, and no ships of any nation. Moreover, when we skirted them closely we saw no houses that we could believe were Spanish, no plantations of tobacco, no cattle or sheep, and an astonishingly few Indians, although the land was fertile and the herbage luxuriant and beautiful.

"You know what I think?" a petty officer asked me, after his trick at the helm.

"No, sir."

"'Tis that these countless islands called the Bahamas on our charts have never been settled by the Spanish, and Fernando never got around to tell our Cap'n so. Well, I've heard afore that many islands owned by the dons are for nothing but slave farms, the stock grubbing for themselves until the poor devils are ironed. That would account for the scarcity of natives—the most have been caught and shipped to Hispaniola to work on the sugar plantations, and in the mills and mines. I read Christopher Columbus' account of them people. He said they was docile, loving and gentle; just the sort for slavery, for the Caribs can't be tamed, and the mainland Indians are fierce devils."

This word was soon passed about the ship. I believed it, because Captain Selkirk did a deal of cursing, caring not who heard him, and Fernando was the theme of most of it. But I thought he should save some of it for himself, for if I had been he, I would have gone over the charts with great care with old seafarers, to discover which islands promised booty and which should be passed by. The danger of our ship or any other being separated from the flotilla had been a ready danger throughout our voyage.

We must go ashore anyway to revictual. When we sailed into a cove near an Indian village the people ran away into the woods as though we were fiends incarnate. There was abundant water and plenty of wild plantains; also we caught glimpses of deer; but the food in their huts was strictly Indian, unground maize, vegetables we did not know, a few domesticated fowls different from European chickens that we must run and catch, and in the largest hut, some excellent dried venison. Our whole haul was so short that we dared not sail on through Windward Passage to the southern coast of Cuba, where there were towns and potential prizes, for many of the former had mounted heavy guns and some of the latter were galleons that we dared not engage out of the company of the lost flotilla.

Still our captain—and the Scotch are stubborn folk—could not believe that none of these luxuriant islands, some of them larger than the Isle of Wight, had Spanish capitals. So it came about that we roamed from one to another, barely able to garner food enough to supply our immediate needs. Then Captain Selkirk took it in his head to reverse our course, and seek battle and provision in even larger islands, some of them not far off the south tip of Florida according to our charts. So we cruised along, foraging as we went, and the weeks were logged off one by one, the total rounding out into months, and the hope of our rejoining the Fernando squadron slowly waned, and all talk of it died away.

Still in this almost aimless wandering, Fate had ordained one strange adventure. It began with our hearing, when we were behind a high and rugged cape, the boom of what was surely a Spanish or an English gun. No other reports followed: this was possibly an accidental firing but more likely a warning to a much weaker ship or to a village or populace on the island. With sapience not always manifest, Captain Selkirk ordered the launching of the long boat, manned by twenty musketeers and pikemen, to reconnoiter and discover the situation, whereupon he could decide whether it promised profit or threatened danger. I was in the boat party, by my friend's, the petty officer's, choosing, and we rowed with no danger of discovery to the point of the cape.

Then we beheld a scene that the sharpest men aboard quickly penetrated, but must explain it to the dullards. At anchor in the cove was as disreputable a vessel as I had ever seen, once a flyboat of sorts, lacking paint or any kind of trim, her yards askew, her sails dingy, and her smell, blown straight to us by a seaward breeze, rank and offensive. As far as we could see, she had but one gun. Patently she was not worth the labor and the risk of sailing her home to England.

On the nearby shore were perhaps a hundred Indians, caught by a slaver's gang of perhaps forty Spaniards. A few of the captives wore irons; the rest were confined by ropes. But we had been mistaken in thinking the gun we had heard had fired only a warning shot. Plainly the Indians had attempted hopeless resistance, and the moiling men and women and terrified children had been fired upon. About five, their bodies bathed in blood, lay still upon the ground. The rest were presently being lashed by bull whips, ere they were to be marched to the beach and packed aboard the ship.

"An ugly sight," Captain Selkirk remarked to his first officer. For although there were a few Negro slaves in England—I had never seen any—I doubted if there was even one in Scotland.

"Cap'n, I agree with you," the mate replied.

"I've a notion to make an end to it, in this instance."

"Sir, I wish you would."

"But some of those slavers have muskets, and the rest cutlasses or pikes. And when Spaniards are concerned, they have a pesky way of fighting to the last man. I don't think those slavers are of that ilk, but they may kill a few of us, before they yield, and our gain won't be of the least good to the Queen, for the Good God knows we don't want that stinking hooker, or a parcel of Indian slaves. We'd be doing this for the pleasure o' it, so I'll sound out the men."

"'Tis a good notion."

"Mr. Quartermaster, you've heard what I've been saying to Mr. Ferguson. Would you favor our freeing those new-caught slaves?"

"That, I would, and gi' 'em dons a taste of their own medicine to boot."

"What of the rest of you hearties? Don't fear to speak."

"Turn the *Elspeth's* guns on the stake burners, and kill 'em out to the last man," said a grim-faced Calvinist from Yorkshire. All of us knew that his English mother, married to the Frenchman, had been slaughtered on Bartholomew.

"We can't do that," our captain answered. "King Philip would hear of it, in time, and the complaining he'd do to the Queen! Well, we'll go ahead, first wi' the main job, and decide later how to do the dons. Pull the boat to the ship, and stow her."

This we did featly, and soon the *Elspeth* was making round the cape. We knew the very second the Spaniards left aboard their vessel caught sight of our well-armed sloop of war, flying the Queen's colors.

"Strike your flag!" Captain Selkirk shouted.

Instead the ship watch ran to the rail, staring and waving at their shipmates on shore, for no doubt their captain and other officers were in the shore party.

"Send a shot through their rigging," our captain ordered.

So our bow gun boomed with a fine clap, and some rigging fell on the slaver's deck, and it was wondrous to see how soon her colors dipped. Then we heaved overside every ship's boat on our deck; and into them dropped all hands except the ship watch. Every man had his pike, or musket, or cutlass, and on every face was furious intent, for the English and Scotch of Queen Bess's time did not hold with slave catching, or the sight of strong men bull-whipping helpless folk who had done no wrong, and truly this was a wondrous age.

The dons gathered in a close pack, as though to defend themselves, but quickly they perceived the folly of the attempt, and no brabble ensued.

"Lay down your weapons," was our captain's first command when we had piled out of the boats.

The dons looked to their own captain; he nodded and made a remark we did not hear; and the order was obeyed.

"Now remove the chains and the ropes from your captives, and bid 'em hold their ground, not run into the woods, for we'll not molest 'em."

It must be that one of their number, perhaps an English renegade, could understand the captain's commands and immediately passed the word, for I never saw busier men than these dons, cutting off ropes and removing shackles from the naked, trembling prisoners.

Still I expected some of them to scamper, as other islanders had done at sight of us. But these were human beings, however savage, and the removal of their bonds made no sense to them, if they were to be stowed aboard our vessel, from frying pan to fire. I think the wondrous fact had dawned on them that we were rescuers and friends.

"Half of you men iron or rope the slave catchers, and the other half stand guard with muskets and pikes," Captain Selkirk ordered.

Never was a command obeyed with such zest and dispatch. Our fellows were gleeful and could hardly control their buoyant spirits, and from henceforth they would idolize our captain, with whom lately they had felt somewhat disgruntled, because of our fruitless wanderings and our meager and monotonous rations, without our seizure of one cask of Spanish rum, or an ounce of Spanish gold. If he ordered an attack on a Spanish galleon, he need have no fear that they would quail.

If there was to be a brabble, this was the most likely moment. I had heard that most Spanish soldiers and seamen even of peasant birth will die fighting rather than submit to irons or hempen bonds unless ordered by their own officers or by persons in authority. But it must be that only a low and brutal sort of Spaniard took to slaving, ironing, and making off with people almost helpless to defend themselves, because the circle of leveled muskets and bristling steel had completely cowed them, and not one of these catchers raised his hand except to have it shackled.

Leaving the disconsolate crew standing in the scorching sunlight, Captain looked at the houses and then at the Indians, meanwhile making the motions of eating. The quick perception and the pleasure in the dark faces was a wondrous thing to watch, and instantly all the people, men and women and children, rushed to their huts, their bared brown limbs aglimmer. Out they poured in a minute or two, their arms loaded with edibles. These included maize ground and in kernel, loaves, bunches of plantains, earthen jars of wild honey, the freshly slaughtered quarter of a deer, no little dried venison in sticks, baskets of brown sugar in big lumps, and large pods the seeds of which, so we were told by an old gunner who had sailed with Sir Francis Drake, were used to make a stimulating and delicious beverage called cocoa. Why we had found no such variety of food in the deserted Indian villages we had searched was most readily explainable on the supposition that those Indians had made off with, or hidden, their more prized edibles at first sight of our vessel's approach.

Obeying our captain's gestures, we deposited all this food in our boats. Meanwhile, their minds now free to devote to other matters than strife and righteousness, our men in the prime of manhood were observing the young Indian women and girls. They were naked as they had been born, except for necklaces and bracelets of bright pebbles, which fact did not discomfit them whatever, and truly they were worthy of observation. On the whole they were comely females, with big black eyes and raven hair; their skins looked burnished, and with their forms we could find no fault, most of them being slender and shapely. It was not possible that they remained unaware of the new interest their bearded rescuers were taking in them, for there is a natural communication, a magnetism it might be called, between young people of opposite sex as wonderful and mysterious as that which draws iron to the loadstone. One of the young women asked a question of a tall savage whose cap and amulet worn on a necklace indicated he might be a chief. The latter nodded.

At once the younger and prettier girls and women began to form a group. I took it that some of them were young wives, at least they were of age to be so, although none had swollen bellies, as did a few pretty young women who remained with the older women and the men. If indeed some of the bright-eyed passel were married, whatever they were about to do did not disconcert, let alone enrage, any of the young Indians, who were eying them, giving us an occasional glance, with approval and perhaps pride.

Suddenly one of them, I thought the chief's daughter, cried out something in their unknown tongue. At once they began running not toward the huts but toward the woods, looking back over their shoulders, and laughing rather wildly. My younger shipmates glanced at our captain. Perhaps his strong Calvinist conscience gave him pause for a brief instant, then he remembered the needs of young men, and their nightly achings, and how long they had been at sea.

"Take after 'em!" he directed tersely. "They may show ye some gold mines."

My shipmates shouted, and no pack of beagles unleashed ever darted away with more vim. Only the officers, some old seadogs, and one young pikeman, recently a landlubber, did not join the rush. Of the first two classifications, a dignified ignoring of the invitation could be expected. I doubted if any of our old mariners were impotent, but their anxiety was not such that they welcomed the chase of young women in the woods and its subsequent discomforts. The real mystery that I must search was why the young pikeman, myself, did not seize this opportunity to relieve pent-up strains. Fear of the French disease, against which Lady Isobel had warned me, might have been a factor; but according to sailor talk, it had been brought from the Spanish mainland, and I could hardly believe it had reached this remote island.

I could not doubt that my memories and my dreams of Winifred were a restraining hand. Another, of high credit to me provided I could believe it, was that our slave-catching prisoners needed a stouter guard than our old salts provided. One of them might conceivably wiggle and twist out of his bonds and pass a knife to his fellows; but they stood in the open, and the chance of such a happening was almost inconceivable. There remained another reason for my abstinence, the main reason really, which I might as well face. I had a great deal of winning to do to satisfy my ambitions. By abjuring my fellows' sport, I called the officers' attention to myself.

"Pikeman Sutton—I believe that's right—you're a well-grown and hearty youth," Captain Selkirk remarked. "I am curious why you don't join your mates."

"To tell you the truth, sir, I wished to question one of the prisoners, and I thought I could do it better in my shipmates' absence."

"Now that's curious," Captain commented. "Mate Ferguson remarked to me that you were well spoken in English, could write well, and were a lover and a great borrower of books, but he did not tell me you could speak Spanish."

"Sir, I don't believe the man with a brown beard is a Spaniard. He's tanned and swarthy, but his eyes are hazel and when the men were binding him, he tried to tell them something, but couldn't get out the words. My guess is, that he's a North European, so many years separated from his own kind that he's forgotten the language."

"Why, then, Pikeman Sutton, don't you speak to him and see?"

"Sir, I'll try it."

I went up to the man and his round eyes gazed imploringly into mine. I smiled at him, and then pointing to myself, I said in an easy tone,

"Martyn—Englishman."

His throat corded, a dreadful strain came into his face, and began to make mouths. Plainly he was in fearful struggle and travail. Then his face took the expression of one about to sneeze, his mouth gaped, and he uttered a long and racking sigh.

Then he said, very quietly and slowly:

"My—name—is—Tom—Thomas—War—War—Warner. I—am—Englishman."

Then he broke into sobs, heavy and pitiable, his chest heaving, and I walked away a little distance until he could regain his self-control.

2

When Tom Warner had quieted a little, Captain Selkirk gave the order to two old tars to remove his ropes, and not to frighten him in the doing. When the quick duty was performed, the man walked a short distance from the group of captives and sat down alone on the ground.

"You know, Mr. Ferguson, I don't feel too charitable toward those dirty slave catchers," Captain Selkirk remarked.

"Nor do I. Yet we can't give 'em their own medicine. Treatment of prisoners of war is a part of a very strict code among Christians, and while the Queen is not strictly at war with Philip—"

"Mate, you missed your calling in not becoming a sea lawyer. But the point you made is perfectly true. We can't even keelhaul them, to give them a good salt bath, without rebuke if not worse from the Queen—provided we ever see English shores again. Pikeman Sutton, you seem an observing yokel. I confess I didn't note a whit of difference between your lost sheep—your charge, I should say, for that's what he is, from now on—and yon slave-catching bully boys. And your Tom Warner may be a renegade, as rotten as the rest."

"I don't think so, sir, an' please you. What first drew my attention to him, when the slavers were whipping and clubbing their captives, I suppose for their attempting desperate resistance, he held a whip but only brandished it about and didn't lay on one stroke."

I was aching to say something more, but durst not, without specific permission.

"Well, what's on your mind?" the captain demanded irritably. "You can speak at will, until those roisterers have finished their frolic and are all present and accounted for, and we have re-established some semblance of naval discipline."

"I was thinking, Captain, of a way to pay the slavers in their own coin, without making any trouble for Queen Bess. I doubt if the victims would ever tell anyone."

"Oh, God, he's a diplomat, as well as a lost sheep rescuer and repatriater," Captain Selkirk remarked to Mate Ferguson. Then, to me, "What's your fine scheme?"

"Only to search 'em well for knives and put them aboard their own deck, with their ship watch bound and gagged. Pack the slavers close as they would have stowed the slaves. Stick one of their knives in the bow rail well out of anyone's reach. One or more would finally chew through their wrist ropes, and crawl and get the knife. But

they'd have no key to the irons and 'twould take a deal of chisel-
ing . . ."

"The plan has no brilliance but a certain appeal, and deals a
modicum of poetic justice. 'Twill be a hot and vexatious chore, before
they can free themselves, and they'll feel mighty cramped, and the
roped men will be spitting out hemp strands for the next two hours.
But what's to prevent them returning to the Indian village and
getting revenge?"

"Sir, a solution of that difficulty would be to set all their boats
adrift on the tide."

"Better than that, we'll stow 'em on our ship. What is your rank,
Pikeman Sutton?"

"Apprentice pikeman, Cap'n."

"You are hereby appointed to pikeman first class. Take note of
that, Mr. Quartermaster."

"I will, sir," the petty officer answered. I stood at attention.

"Well, here's the first of our dove hunters coming out of the woods!
He walks somewhat wabbly." Then, with a touch of wistfulness: "I
ween those island lassies are human fireballs!"

Soon our whole shore party had assembled, looking a little sheepish
but otherwise wondrous content. Captain Selkirk and Mate Ferguson
were again correct and aloof as officers of the Queen's Irregular Navy.
The Indian maidens did not appear in our midst and doubtless had
gone from the woods by obscure paths to their huts. My fine plan for
teaching the slave catchers a long-remembered lesson was put into
brisk practice; and truly I had never seen men more aghast with
terror as when, instead of loading them aboard our vessel, we stowed
them on their own. Perhaps they expected us to tow the hooker out
to sea and sink her, or deal them some worse death, perhaps by
fire. They probably had heard and believed more harrowing tales
of us Englishmen than our countryfolk of Spaniards.

When we had taken their boats and prepared to put to sea and
they finally divined our purpose, they were not in the least grateful
for our sparing their scoundrel lives but only wildly infuriated by
their humiliation at our hands. As our sails filled, I never heard such
howling.

At last I had leisure to see to my charge. He must still swallow
painfully and stammer before he could speak any English word; yet
the desperate expression that I had seen as he stood in bonds had
vanished from his deeply lined countenance; and plainly dim remembrance of the language was returning to him swiftly, because he
understood several of my questions.

"How long have you been in captivity? Many years?"

He caught the words "captivity" and "years," I thought; and he would hardly have forgotten that eloquent word "long." At least he nodded sadly.

"Five years?" I asked, holding up one hand with fingers spread.

He touched all these fingers, all those of my other hand, and counted on seven more.

"Seventeen years?"

Again he nodded.

By now I concluded that he was better-born than I, certainly as a yeoman, possibly a franklin, and not impossibly, a gentleman. His manner was courteous, his lineaments refined. Just now he was in mental agony as he tried to remember a word. Finally it burst forth.

"Kent."

I pointed to myself and said "Wiltshire." His face brightened at this mutual orientation.

"Trade?" I asked.

"Arrowsmith," he answered easily and immediately.

"Bowyer also."

"Aye." This word was easy to say, I thought, because it was a simple vowel sound. Then I thought what fools his captors had been, to put him at slaving instead of weaponmaking. Bow and quiver will support a man lost in the woods—even in the great forests of the New World—when all his gunpowder had been spent.

As a craftsman he stood well above a peasant, and if he had owned his own shop he was in the lower ranks of the gentry.

"I, peasant," I told him, so he would suffer no illusions as to my station. He cocked his head a little in surprise, but made no comment. Then, again pointing to myself, I told my name.

"Martyn Sutton," he repeated without difficulty. "You—friend."

"Aye. You my friend."

Tears filled his eyes and he brushed them impatiently away.

"You—s-s-s-*save*—me."

"Good luck," I answered.

"Bad luck"—then he paused and groped pitifully before he could finish the sentence—"gone."

It was a wonderful thing, how quickly thereafter he gained command of his all but lost language. His wrinkled face smoothed out from our good belly timber; instead of a man past fifty, as I had thought, he was hardly forty, in the full strength of his years. I was not surprised to discover that he could read and write; also he could take readings by an astrolabe and make the necessary calculations according to the tables; and I soon discovered he had been second officer on the *Maid of Dover,* a merchantman captured by Spanish pirates off the Azores. By them he had been sold to a slave trader in the Spanish town of Isabela.

His first service aboard the *Elspeth* was that of a common seaman, but soon Mate Ferguson began to use him as a kind of ship's clerk, because our quartermaster's assistant had been killed by a gunblast on the day we had fought the *Santa Lucia,* that lonely fight on a lonely sea, one in which we were the victors, but a Pyrrhic victory truly. But he did not set himself above the common seamen, the pikemen, and the musketeers; and while he showed every respect to our officers, smart and brisk in his obedience to them, I discovered to my great wonder that his real captain, aboard this ship, was a youth hardly half his age and of peasant birth. I am sure he did not try to explain this to himself, and I could find no explanation other than that, by no heroic deed, mere quick observation aided by circumstance, I had redeemed him from slavery and thus restored to him his manhood.

As for other consequences of our visit to what my shipmates aptly called Satisfaction Island, they were trifling. Our store of edibles had been sufficient for Captain Selkirk to order our turning at last toward Windward Passage and the south shore of Cuba. On the long way there, we victualed our ship at various small islands where we spied Indian inhabitants. Again the natives fled like hares at our approach; whereupon we robbed their huts of such edibles as we could find. At one of these islands, Thomas Warner returned from the woods with an armful of carefully chosen straight poles which he had cut. He told me these were lemonwood, possibly the trunks of young lemon or lime trees; but I could not say positively, he having stripped off the bark. Others were looking and listening, and I did not question him further.

These slender poles he put away to "season." Later he confided to me that, since he lacked English yew, they furnished the best wood for bows obtainable on the islands, easily worked, and strong and resilient.

At Great Inagua Island, second only to Andros in the whole Bahamas, and about the size of Wiltshire, we confidently expected to find a Spanish town. Again the green and luxurious expanse was uninhabited by man except for tiny hamlets of sick and languid people, not worth shipping as slaves. It came to me very sharply that of all institutions sanctioned by nations and kings, slavery was the most evil.

Our frolickers remained in excellent health and the only penalty they paid for their lechery, if so it could be called, were numerous insect bites, received in the woods. These were fiery red, dotting their skins, and itched most fiercely, and their bathing in salt water did not assuage their irritation, and only carefully distributed drops of strong rum from the captain's bottle eased them in the least. The punishment lasted only two or three days, and Preacher Powell would have deemed it much too mild, and be put out with God.

3

In the South Cuban waters we caught no glimpse of our lost squadron. They had been here, however, for the town of Manzanillo had been sacked and partially burned. From Trinidad, not the island but the Cuban town, we were resolutely chased by a swift galleon that we durst not engage, and we had to fly nigh to Jamaica ere she lost us in a fortunate fog. We engaged at long range two swift merchantmen, but could not overtake them and take them prize. Along in February 1586, with us fifteen months at sea, and I going on eighteen, the *Elspeth* enjoyed what could be called our first notable triumph.

We came on the town of Júcaro, somewhat famed for a narcotic which could be used in subduing dangerous reptiles, for what benefit no one could explain to me. It had about a thousand inhabitants, an alcalde dwelling in an impressive house, and of course a jail. No ship of any nation lay at anchor, so we sailed boldly to a stone's throw of its wharf, and our captain in our long boat led two other boats, all three packed with pikemen, cutlassmen, and musketeers. The alcalde and some other dignitaries awaited us, the citizens stood back, and the fact was at once plain there would be no brabble.

Because we could not trust our Spanish captives not to gull us, our captain appointed Thomas Warner as our interpreter; and I was proud of him, as he stood beside the master, a fine figure of a man, instantly understanding his instructions and translating them into Spanish. The captain first wanted to know what ransom the town would pay for our Spanish captives.

They were of no value whatever to Júcaro, the alcalde replied; their vessel, the *Santa Lucia,* had been lost at sea and her whole crew had had the benefits of prayers for the dead, with a special prayer for the officers; and their names had been stricken off the list of citizens of Santiago de Cuba, the *Santa Lucia's* home port. Also these fifteen were men 'fore the mast, and Biscayans to boot, while the town was settled almost wholly by Castilians. Still, gratitude would be shown that we had not hanged or abused the prisoners, and the town would make a token payment of fifteen pounds in gold for the batch.

When we heard the word gold repeated on Thomas Warner's lips we were all a little startled, for although it oozed from every tongue when we had first stood to sea, for months now it was scarcely mentioned. Our dreams of sudden wealth had gone down to the graveyard of ships.

The next question was more pertinent. How much ransom, in gold and silver, could be gathered together to save the town from destruction?

There was excited talk, and much gesturing and headshaking between the alcalde and his worthies. It continued so long that Captain bade them speak out, with no more palaver, or he would order immediate looting of every house and office, and men with firebrands would be close behind the looters. His voice was quiet but strong. The voice of Thomas Warner was loud and imperious, and it echoed seventeen years of accumulated hate.

"England is a Christian nation with a Christian queen," the alcalde protested in a tremulous tone. "Surely you would not take from the subjects of a Christian king *all* our gold and silver."

"Also what jewels you may have, such as pearls," Captain Selkirk said remorselessly. "But if you scrape your vaults and treasure chests, you will still have your broad fields of tobacco, your houses with furniture and daughters intact, your orchards, your public buildings, indeed your pretty town, and your slaves. But I warn you, if my searchers find a single hidden hoard, we'll raze the town."

The alcalde flung out his arms in a gesture of despair and called a command to the citizenry, who immediately scattered in all directions.

"We yield to you," he told our captain. "Our vaults and treasure chests will be emptied. But may I speak my thoughts as to the wisdom of your action?"

"That, you may."

"We will be impoverished, but your debt to King Philip will be vastly increased. He is sick of your Queen's dalliance, talking of peace and even marriage, while she shuts her eyes to her pirates' ranging our seas, commandeering our ships, razing our towns, and he will have terrible revenge."

The little, graceful man spoke with dignity. Our fellows laughed when they heard the translation, but the thought came to me that future laughter might be from the wrong side of their mouths.

Within half an hour the citizens began to appear with leathern bags, mainly light but some notably heavy, and our men's eyes began to have a greedy gleam. When the last reluctant victim of our high hand had deposited his treasure on the considerable heap, and the captain had sent forth his searchers, themselves under guard and guarded by pikemen and musketeers, they reported finding not a single hidden hoard. Perhaps no people in Europe had so powerful a concept of personal honor as did the Spaniards. They had pledged their honor in obeying the command of the alcalde.

When the gold and silver had been weighed, and the value of the pearls, jade, and Mexican rubies estimated, the total of our haul came to two thousand and forty English pounds. The Queen's share, and that of the ship owner and contributors to the enterprise, and the officers' portion had been set aside; six hundred pounds were left for the musketeers, pikemen, and common seamen. Again to my satisfaction, Thomas Warner assisted the quartermaster in dividing this sum, one share to each seaman and apprentice pikemen, one and a third share to each pikeman first class, and one and a half share to each musketeer, a perfectly fair division in the seamen's minds, because of the danger of enemy pikes and even greater danger of bursting guns. The outcome was nine pounds for every seaman, twelve for every pikeman first class, and thirteen pounds and ten shillings, for every musketeer. It was not wealth, but a good wage for men of our stations for nigh two years' service at sea.

We would probably glean a little more by raiding small Spanish towns and villages, but not much more. All larger towns had been raped by Vice-Admiral Drake and Commodore Fernando, these long since making for greener pastures, and now great galleons stood guard at Santiago and Havana, so we dared not look there for gleanings. Waiting for summer and hence smoother seas, because our ship needed new rigging that our empty cubbies could not supply, and God knew our bottom should be scraped of barnacles to make our ship cut water as she should, she took to sailing into coves to revictual at plantations, and even to hunt deer in the forest. At a village called Sorena Marina on the north shore of Cuba our seamen received three more pounds, and the pikemen and musketeers shared in the same proportion as before.

About then I received a wonderful present from Thomas Warner. The thrill of joy I felt was second in power only to my receiving the sword from the hand of Lady Isobel. It was a bow of superb workmanship, six feet long and wonderfully resilient and a tug of no less than fifty pounds' weight could bend it to its perfect round. With it was a sheath of forty arrows, of a tough wood very much like ash, these in a leather quiver to wear over the left shoulder, flecked with wild-goose feathers and lacking only iron heads to be formidable weapons, mortal to man and deer when truly aimed and strongly sped. Mr. Warner had made similar bows for Captain Selkirk, Mate Ferguson, and himself, but mine had the finest finish of all.

We set sail for England in May 1586 and without notable adventure, arrived in Plymouth in mid-July. I had a leather pouch containing fifteen gold sovereigns gained by rapine, for I had lost half a pound in a bet with the quartermaster, as to the time of our arrival. It was a good two weeks earlier than I had reckoned, persuading me I was inclined to be distrustful of fortune, expecting not the best or the worst, but somewhere in between. Some of my shillings' change, along with two I had left of my parent's gift, I had spent at the Azores for presents for my near and dear.

There was still uneasy peace in the islands, but it was fading fast as English privateers made nearby waters their rendezvous, and my purchases were made from a Portuguese bumboat: an Antwerp pocket-knife for my sire, a bracelet set with agates for Mistress Barton, island-made coral earrings for Lady Isobel and Priscilla, and a pair of silver buckles, costing a whole shilling each, for Winifred Powell.

Still I had enough shillings to pay for a ride in a wool wagon making through Salisbury, and coppers to buy food en route. The trip took five days, which seemed to lag unduly, while the main of two years at sea had sped arrow fast. Also, I was lonely because Tom Warner had taken off for Kent, there to greet his loved ones if any were left alive. But he had written down and carefully pouched my address in Wiltshire, and neither of us believed our parting would be long. The four pounds that were his share of our last, small piracy would pay his way for several crossings of all England.

Tramping from Salisbury and taking a short cut home that skirted Amesbury, I caught sight of our cottage about suppertime. My heart leaped up, and two anxieties were relieved, one no more than that my supper would be cold leavings and the other that I need travel these lonely lands after nightfall. Road knights were almost a thing of the past in our part of Wiltshire; still there were a few footpads ranging out from Salisbury, and I was sharply conscious of my heavy wallet, containing fourteen gold coins. True, I was in peasant dress, but my seabag over my shoulder would arouse the interest of any robber lurking in the spinneys at the edge of the fields. Most home-bound sailors on shanks' mare had spent their pay at the port, but the more thrifty had white money. Two shillings was a fair haul from a bludgeoning given in the dark, and my small fortune would be worth the while of a practiced gang, with murder the certain end.

But I gained the door, rapped and called, and my sire greeted me with a great hug.

"At least ye haven't starved," he remarked, looking me over, after a few fatherly questions had been asked and answered.

"The fare was good, usually plentiful, but not fancy."

"Did ye get promoted on the voyage?"

"Yes, sir, from apprentice pikeman to pikeman first class."

"I take it, 'twas in gory battle."

"We had some on the voyage, but my promotion was received on a day of good sport, which I'll tell of later."

"You're full six feet and an inch more, and weigh twelve stone?"

"Five pounds more by the wool scale at Plymouth. Now tell me how matters stand at Court, for we've had no dispatches. And have Sir Walter Raleigh and Sir Francis Drake hove into port?"

"Raleigh long since. Frankie Drake the like, and took himself a new wife, and long gone again. 'Twas a wonder you didn't run into him in the Spanish isles."

"No great wonder. There are countless islands, and to use your own word, a monstrous lot of sea."

"Well, there's a report that he's back in Plymouth. If it's true, it's in good time, for he's the best admiral the Queen has got, even though Lord Howard outranks him and would be in the high command if war breaks with Spain. Let me speak of that first, Martyn; although the rumor about Drake, provided it be true, would count more with ye just now."

"Is the war with Spain any nearer?" I asked with tension in my throat. My sire's judgment of great affairs had always been wonderfully keen.

"Philip has conquered Portugal and got all their ships; and now he's persuaded that he can't master the Dutch and sweep the seas of English privateers without conquering England, won't he send those ships to our shores? Rumor has it he has established great yards to build more. Still, I don't think he'll strike until he has a fleet outnumbering ours ten to one. It might mean the end of England, and again it might not, for England has stood a long time, and got strong legs. I hear that the Spanish Ambassador Mendoza is about to be sent home; and maybe he's gone already. He had conspired with Mary Stuart's party, which may mean the loss of her pretty head, for Queen Bess does not stay her hand when there's threat to her throne. As for ye, I hope ye'll be in the New World when the storm breaks."

"What chance is there of that?"

"Well, Sir Walter's begun to talk of another plantation, farther up the coast. The master's thinking of putting money in it, his bailiff told me. Again he's recruiting gentlemen down at heels, mainly from Hampshire and Devonshire, tradesmen and yeomen, and promising five hundred acres to every man or head of a family. The folk say he's inviting no peasants, but he's going to have to, if the rumor about Drake is true." My sire's gray eyes were shining with excitement.

"What is that rumor?" I asked him straight.

"That he's brought back every mother's son of the other settlement, those still alive, that is, and all with empty pockets."

"I can't believe it. Lane would not give up this soon."

"According to the story, the settlers were so bent on leaving that they threw all their goods into the sea, to crowd in small boats and get aboard Drake's ships. A gale was about to break. They threw away a mighty lot of pearls they'd got from the natives. Maybe it was panic. But as I told ye once before, settling Virginia a'ant no picnic."

4

In the next few days rumors were as numerous in our neighborhood as plover in the grassy hollows of Master's lands; and appeared to fly as fast. Detail differed, but the main fact remained indisputable: that Sir Walter Raleigh's 1585 planting of an island called Roanoke off the Virginia shore had proved a dismal failure. Attacks by hostile Indians had not been the cause; rather it was shortage of food, wasted labor, and perhaps solitude most of all. Report had it that one hundred Negro slaves had been drowned or somehow lost in the exodus or on the homeward journey. The story persisted obstinately; but what were our settlers doing with Negro slaves? Had these been captives on the ships of Sir Francis Drake? The most ugly theory of their deaths, whispered in the main but plainly spoken by some bold hangers-on at taprooms, was that they had been jettisoned to lighten the ships in tempest. Also quite a number of Indians had been lost, although two chiefs of the Roanokes or the Croatans had been fetched home. Their names were Manteo and Towaye.

Truth was slowly established. The first news had been brought to Plymouth by a pinnace that had spoke Drake's squadron below the Azores. Most of the returning colonists had landed finally at Portsmouth. Before visiting Roanoke, Drake had made some highly profitable raids on the Spanish island capital of Hispaniola and other West Indian towns, and one story had it that he had taken at least a tribute from St. Augustine. This last was stoutly denied by the big-wigs, for no reason that I could guess other than such a raid might have political consequences. Fighting between English and Spanish was an old story in the islands, but this later attack, if it occurred, had been our first on the North American mainland. It would surely throw Philip into a fury, and if the English attacked Spanish settlements in Florida, the Spanish might play tit for tat in Virginia.

The failure had evidently not even dented, let alone broken, Sir Walter Raleigh's spirit for Virginia colonization. His explanation for the defeat was that the arrival there of Sir Richard Grenville, his ships loaded with supplies, had been delayed by heavy weather; if the colonists had delayed even a few days, their desperate position would have been relieved, and no exodus would have occurred. Also, Sir Walter published a list of Virginian sources of wealth, to make water the mouths of money-loving English, which included our whole nobility, almost all our gentry, and our rising class of merchants. As for our peasants, they never got hand on yellow money, rarely on white, and their meager handful of red money ebbed and flowed with the harvesting and planting times*; and this had been true so long that thoughts of wealth very rarely crossed their minds, except as a possession of those God had made for its possession, the nobility, the gentry, and, in a few cases, where God's plans went mysteriously awry, the yeomanry.

I, a peasant, studied Sir Walter's list with avidity. The veins of gold were barely scratched by the Indians, yet some of the tribes wore golden chains and ornaments as island Indians wore pebbles; and gold the weight of ten pounds had been traded for a tin cup. Twenty buffalo skins was the price of a copper kettle, each of which would bring a sovereign in England. There was a prodigious wealth in furs—otter, bear, mink, beaver, a kind of ferret called marten almost identical with Russian sable, and a kind of polecat called skunk. There was frankincense and myrrh, the names having a biblical sound and associated in the mind with the fabulous riches of India. There was tobacco, which some thought a cure-all, even though its use was turning into a common vice. There were medicinal plants of which Europe had never heard, effecting wondrous cures, and dyes that sold at their weight in gold in London apothecaries. As for the staples, it was impossible for an energetic man to starve in Virginia. Besides the abundance of game, maize grew wild, peas and beans yielded mighty crops in the rich virgin ground, the boughs of certain fruit trees bent down with exotic and delicious fruits. A kind of common tuber would of itself support human life; and walnuts, butternuts, chestnuts, hazelnuts, and a New World species, chiccora nuts, oily and delicious, were so abundant that a ship could be loaded with them, in trade for a hundredweight of tin ware. The finest

---

* Folk use of the terms red, white, and yellow money, meaning copper, silver, and gold coins, is ancient in the extreme.

lumber was to be had for the cutting. Certain kinds of fish known but expensive in England swam in schools of millions in the shoal waters just off the shores. To reassure the more insular English, with no taste for exotic foods, Sir Walter recited the abundance of our familiar herring, whitefish, grunter, cod, sole, haddock, and sea bass. In his description of shellfish, Sir Walter wrote lyrically. The abundance of these along all the coasts and especially in the great bay, as large as the Straits of Dover and called Chesapeake, could not be believed unless seen. Lobsters were not the length of a man's forearm but his whole arm. A dozen of the giant shrimps made a man his meal; twelve of the huge oysters made a big stew; Indians hardly bothered to scoop up scallops. Common crabs grew as large as a dinner plate.

But in discussing oysters Sir Walter arrived at his breath-taking word, pearls. True, pearl-bearing oysters were more common in waters from twenty to thirty feet deep, but the settlers did not dive for them, and instead traded trifles and toys to the Indians for a total worth of five thousand pounds. These had been tossed overside, along with charts and priceless records, in the frantic and demented rush for Drake's boats.

Why were the colonists in such haste to leave a land flowing with such milk and honey? Why did they need supplies from England? Raleigh answered both questions in the conclusion of his statement. They wanted to get rich too fast and too easily, and hence had neglected their first duty, making themselves a living and piling up stores, and instead depended on the Indians for these necessities.

If I had been their leader Lane, I thought, I would have ordered a whipping for every gentleman and commoner who did not spend five hours out of every day working with his hands to preserve the colony.

"Martyn, I wish to ask ye a question," my father broke into my thoughts. "Ye need not gi' me an answer now, 'less 'tis already fixed in your heart. But I'll demand an answer from ye within the week."

"Ask your question, my father."

"There be a war coming, a great and noble war, to save England from Spanish rule. And there be a passel of people going to Virginia, to plant a colony, taking wives and children, and this time they'll stay, unless the first batch have mistreated the Indian so bad they'll be killed out."

"Why, there's no chance of that. Sir Walter says they're docile."

"There's no such thing as a docile human being, if he's bad enough abused. And there's a tale being whispered, that along with the hunnerd Negro slaves that was killed or died, there was two hunnerd Indians."

"How could it happen?"

"A gale struck Sir Francis' ships all on a sudden. They had to cut their lines and make for the open sea. There could have been two hunnerd Indians aboard 'em, gawking, and fingering things, and trading; and English officers and seamen, and passengers too, don't stop to read their Bibles when their ships are nigh to floundering, and the cargo must be jettisoned. Black cargo. Brown cargo. Yes, we are a civilized nation, along with France and Flanders and the Netherlands and Germany and Spain. But I trust civilization when the weather's fair. When it's foul enough, men turn foul."

"Now I can answer your question. I'd rather go to the New World than fight against the dons."

"Some would call that treason—or at best, desertion."

"I suppose so. I do not feel it is either one."

"Can you tell me why? Feelings that men can't put in plain words may be deceitful. They gull the man who has 'em."

"I'll try. If the Spaniards fail—and their galleons are immense, towering, awkward ships, hard to maneuver, unfitted to our narrow seas—Queen Bess will rule all the seas, and that's fine for Queen Bess, but I don't think it would greatly change the lives of us peasants. Philip is a Christian king, not an infidel Moor, and if he'd win, he would not dare rule England harshly. His rule would not last long, and anyway, what real difference does it make to the folk whether our Kings and Queens are of English blood, or Castilian? It will be another war between royalties, with the folk doing the main of the fighting. They might make English folk attend Mass and adore images, but I don't know that that would hurt them any. Yet I'd join in the fight, and if I were rich, I would contribute gold for building ships. As it is, there is something greater to do than fight Philip, and the greatness that I mean I heard out of your own mouth."

"I don't remember."

"And I don't forget. You spoke of building a new nation across the monstrous sea, where a man's merit will count more than his pedigree, and where the folk can find new hope."

"I did say as much."

"My risk of being killed will be great or greater than if I were a pikeman aboard a Queen's ship, so I couldn't be charged with cowardice."

"And on a Queen's ship you'd stay a pikeman, wouldn't you, Martyn, and you'd never gain the poop?" He was watching me closely, and I flushed.

"No, I'd never gain the poop, but maybe make petty officer."

"But in the New World you just might become leader, and that's the yearning of your heart and soul."

"Is that a base ambition?"

"No ambition is base, when it's to lift a man up, and lift others with him. And we're all a long way from angels. I won't ask ye what counts the most wi' ye, a new nation for the folk or leadership and power for ye yourself. I be a rude peasant, but not rude enough to ask that kind of question of any man. Working for the good of the folk is a noble thing, but the full exercise of a man's own powers, those he believes in, is a mighty useful thing for the whole race. The race moves forward by following its leaders as much as its dreamers. The matter's not *why* men perform great deeds, of benefit to all, but whether those deeds get done. Martyn, I'm perfect satisfied to have ye go to Virginia, although I'll have less hope of seein' ye again than if ye went to the wars with Spain. I'd like to shake your hand as I lie on my deathbed, and know ye've fulfilled what I dreamed for ye; still I'd rather ye essay it and be killed, than turn away from it and live."

My father fell silent, wiped his eyes, and packed his clay pipe with tobacco smuggled to him from his cousin on the Isle of Wight, who had obtained it from Spanish smugglers. When it was lighted from a coal and he had taken a deep puff, he spoke quietly.

"Now I know your intent, I'll give ye a bit o' news."

"I thought I'd heard it all."

"No, one thing happened that the folk don't like to mention. I don't like to either, for it don't concern thrones and great folk, and the mighty world; it concerns us that live in this section of Wiltshire. It may be—what you call it—coincident. But there was another murder while you were away at sea."

I had heard of blood being curdled by scenes or tales of horror. Nothing like that happened to my blood, but I did distinctly feel a chill from the top of my backbone along its natural curve to its very base.

"Well?" I asked.

"Martyn, it wasn't well. It was wicked as hell. The victim was a poor woodcutter, a peasant like us. He wasn't connected with anybody great or rich, no more than was Maggie. He'd never harmed a human soul that I know of; he was not quick in his mind either. You've seen him a few times—Davie Stewer. You know that stand of very big oak trees south of the master's land, above Pike Creek, and owned by Mr. Fortworth, in Amesbury? He'd hired Davie to fell 'em, trim 'em, and lay out the trunks to be moved with timber sledges. Straight-grained oak timber brings a high price now, because the shipbuilders want it for decking; Mr. Fortworth thought 'twas a good time to sell. Then, when his brother Jan went to bring 'en his lunch, and called out his name, he didn't answer. Jan looked everwhere for him for about ten minutes before he found him. He was lying behind some cut boughs with a knife hole in his chest. That's all there was to it."

After a long time I spoke. "There weren't any tracks in that deep moldy ground? I've been to that very clump, for partridge fly in there when Master and his guests hold shoots, and I've poached a few with bow and arrow."

"There was nothing like a track, except Davie's own. True, some young herbage looked mashed down some'at, as though weight had been on it, but there was nothing like heel and toe. Of course the whispering among the folk became mighty worse, and then suddenly stopped, for no reason but they was *afraid* to whisper."

"It was a despicable deed by a heartless human being and I'd like to be hangman." For so well I remembered Davie Stewer, his slow wits and speech, his somewhat vacant stare.

"I don't reckon you'll be called on, nor a Queen's hangman either. There was no clues, nought but a dead man stabbed through the chest, and the high sheriff could do nought but bustle about a while, and go back to his office in New Sarum."

Chapter IV

THE DARK ROOM

1

The thought came to me to seek out Sir Walter Raleigh at once and apply to join the proposed colony. But my second and better thought was to wait a while, until he ran short of gentlemen and yeomen, when he would be more amenable to accepting a peasant. Also it seemed to me almost certain that he would meet with Captain Selkirk well before he sailed, to ascertain what our captain had observed in the way of islands that would supply water and victuals and reasonable safety from Spanish ships. His route would certainly be by way of the West Indies, if only because astrolabes were inadequate, and compasses too unreliable, for charting a fairly safe course directly from England to Virginia. In the course of that conversation, Sir Walter might ask if our captain knew any likely fellows fit for settling in the New World.

About my fifth day at home, I set forth to deliver my presents that I had brought Lady Isobel, Priscilla, Mistress Barton, and Winifred Powell. None of these could be as pleased as was my sire with his small, deadly sharp clasp knife of Flemish steel; for none was as useful, and taking the will for the deed is a sorry substitute; still I thought the other gifts were well chosen, and not improper for a peasant youth to present to benefactors. I had assumed I must contend with a gruff or perhaps sarcastic gatekeeper of the park, but instead Mr. Harrison greeted me warmly and shook my hand. Why, I was now a far-traveler and a proven adventurer, and he had hearn tell that we had sunk a Spanish galleon, which was good service to the Queen, deserving of the written thanks of one of her ministers, and he cared nought who heard him say it!

"'Twas not a galleon, but a well-armed trader."

"'Twas a hard fight right on, and 'tis one less ship for King Philip to send agin Queen Bess. Why, I've half a notion to let ye through without asking her ladyship's leave, but I'll not, for the time might be unoperatune. So I'll send Dora, and I'd wager a groat agin a penny, ye'll have favorable reply."

Dora scampered off, but not without one meaningful cast of her eyes on mine, for she was thirteen now, with a high swell in front and a low one in the back, and she had begun to walk out with neighbor lads.

"I hear that Miss Priscilla is wedded," I remarked in Dora's absence.

"And high time too. Why, she was going on sixteen when Squire Hudson's son, heir to Widow Lacey's two hunnerd acre o' hops, and a fine house too, brought her to lawful bed. The old lady's nigh to ninety, and in feeble health, so the two be waiting about like, and the master himself wouldn't hear of 'em not staying in the mansion, until they had a home o' their own."

Mr. Harrison would have won his bet; Dora was almost overcome by the cordiality of Lady Isobel's invitation. Her ladyship and Priscilla entered the curiosity room together, and the former seemed not merely astonished but even shaken by my appearance, changed more than I knew or she had expected since I had seen her last. What did she expect of an English lad, peasant or no, of sound heritage and well fed all his days, after nigh two years at sea?

"Well, did you, or did you not, make good use of the sword?" she demanded, in a more imperious tone than usual, which for some reason I thought forced.

"My lady, I didn't wear it, but I looked at it often, kept it in good edge and shine, and 'twas an inspiration to me always. In battle, I used a pike. I was made pikeman first class."

"I heard there was a sea fight, and a bloody one, but I thought the story exaggerated."

"You wouldn't have thought so, my lady, if you'd been in it."

"You're not only a sight taller than you were, with more meat and muscle, but a deal bolder, and of stronger voice."

"It has to be let out, if you want to be heard, when a half gale's blowing. And in a full-reef gale, you must shout in your shipmate's ear."

"Storms. Battles. Fantastic islands. Strange folk. Gigantic whales. St. Elmo's fire. You've seen all these. And I—what have I seen and done in this year and a half? I wish I'd been born with—something I'll not say, for it would shock Priscilla, although Queen Bess has said it straight out, according to court rumor."

"Mama!" Priscilla reproved her.

"Richard has been made a full captain of fusiliers; but a lot of good it's done him, with that dullard Lord Leicester in command.

Why did the Queen appoint him? Because he was adept at flattery? Battles lost, cities taken, fortresses overthrown, the patriots' cause at the lowest ebb since the rebellion. My hope lies in Maurice, son of the great William. He's only nineteen but he's showing genius in command. Now if he'd only cooed with Bess in her private bower and kissed her painted lips—"

"*Mama!*" Priscilla cried, shocked to the marrow of her bones.

"Forgive me, my sweet daughter. Elizabeth has been a great Queen by and large—or else the times have been great—and it bred brave men like Richard—and like Martyn. And I'm a bitter old hag!"

A long silence fell which at last I ventured to break.

"My lady, I hope a trifling gift I brought you from the Indies will give you brief pleasure." This was not strictly true, since I had bought the gifts from the Portuguese in the Azores, but I reckoned they had come originally from the southern islands, so the truth had not been abused.

"Martyn, you brought me a *present?*" Lady Isobel asked in genuine astonishment, if not something deeper than that.

"Yes, ma'am, such as it is." And I fished out of my jerkin pocket a scallop shell, from which a Portuguese craftsman, earning as much as a groat a day, had detached one side, then fitted this back with a little hinge and hook. On damp moss, each with its tiny silver ring, lay two pendants of coral, translucent and the color of a pale red rose.

"God's blood!" she burst out. And then, as if almost in a rage, "Martyn, you had no business buying me such a costly gift! A rag doll would have satisfied me . . . I lost a rag doll when I was a little girl; it was pretty and I loved it . . . Those Levantine jewelers in Soho would have charged five shillings each for those rings."

"I paid nothing like that sum. They're a token of gratitude and respect. In fact I got a pair for Mistress Priscilla, too."

"For Priscilla?"

"Yes, my lady."

"I gave you a sword—at least I put it up for a prize to the winner of a contest. What did Priscilla ever give you?"

I gaped, at loss for words.

"You needn't tell me. A birthday kiss. Wench, did you ever tell your lawful wedded husband, Benjamin Lacey, that you kissed a peasant youth?"

"No, ma'am, and I'll thank you if you don't tell him either," Priscilla replied.

"Have no fear; I won't. 'Twas a heinous sin, and the Bishop o' Canterbury would have rebuked you sternly, and belike preached a sermon on the maintenance of due distinction between high folk and low, as ordained by God. Ordained not by the wayward Son but by the Old Man himself. Well, Martyn's got a like pair of earrings for you. Bring 'em out, Martyn, and put 'em in her pretty hand, and see what she'll say. 'Twill be pretty, I assure you."

I had always thought that Priscilla was somehow jealous of her mother. No doubt this explained the shine in her eyes when she saw the baubles, fully as rare and roseate as her dam's.

"I'll say nought," she said, looking at her mother, and speaking very slowly. "But Martyn risked his life, fighting the dons, and these represent a little of his loot, and if Martyn pleases, and you can keep your big mouth shut—"

"Good for you, Priscilla! You're a true daughter o' mine, not a foundling put in my bed! Martyn?"

"I do please, if she'd condescend—" I said quickly.

"Condescend my foot!" Lady Isobel broke in.

Priscilla came up to me, put her arms around my neck, and gave me a plenteous kiss. She had learned a good deal about kissing since her marriage.

"Thank 'ee, Mistress Lacey," I said, proof that I knew who she was and what I was.

"And now you can't wait to see Mistress Barton, and no wonder. You know she's been sickly lately, and this is one of her bad days, still when Dora brought word you wanted to come, she said to send you to her room, and that we'll do." Lady Isobel pulled a bell cord, and the same parlormaid that had admitted me made quick appearance.

"Harkins, take Martyn Sutton to Mistress Barton's room, at her own request."

"That I will, m'laady."

That lady's last four words had told on Harkins' natural distaste for waiting on some one equal, if not below, her own station. The sulky look I had seen before was not in evidence as she guided me civilly enough through the great parlor. I had entered it, after all, and now caught a glimpse of its glories, such as gilded chairs, high-backed couches cushioned in velvet, and tapestries and paintings on the wall. I had never before walked on carpeting. This was almost as soft and deep as wood moss. Then she led me up the first flight of a broad stairway with a railing of a lustrous dark-red wood from Santo Domingo. But she stopped at the first landing, making sure that no other servant was watching or listening.

"Old 'ooman can wait a minute," she said spitefully. "Martyn Sutton, 'ee be getting up in the world, a'ant 'ee?"

"Not that I know of, Harkins."

"'Ee and 'ee fine talk. 'Ee can call me Lucy, what 'ee know is my Christian name. 'Ee're not gentry yet a while."

"I'll never be."

"In 'at you speak Jesus' truth, 'though I didn't 'spect it o' 'ee. 'Ee can't make—"

"A silk purse out of a sow's ear. I've heard it before. Now if you'll take me to Mistress Barton—"

"I just want to tell 'ee that if you'd ask to walk out wi' me, I'd not do it. Maybe 'ee don't put on airs on purpose, but 'ee 'pear to, and I'd not be seen wi' 'ee. 'Ee wi' 'ee fine talk, and making calls on gentry!"

With this Parthian shot—for Mistress Barton had told me that "parting shot" was a corruption of a classical phrase—Harkins led me to Mistress Barton's room, knocked, heard a faint "come in," and opened the door. At once I forgot all about Harkins. I rushed to the bed and took my mentor's pale, frail hand and kissed it, my eyes brimming with tears. She had been sick lately, Lady Isobel had said. She should have said she was in last sickness, a fact apparent in her wasted face.

"There, there, Martyn," she said in a husky whisper. "Don't cry."

I could only cover my face with my hands.

"Ye know, don't ye," she went on. "Ye've seen wounded men, for ye've been in battle besides traveled the world. But it doesn't hurt, Martyn, my dear one. Ye took the place of a son I never had. But I couldn't have done aught for ye, save for your mother wit."

"It was a wondrous lot!"

"Now what can you do for the folk, to make me proud? My soul would be proud in heaven."

"All that I can."

"Not for queens, for some words writ on vellum, not for great folk, who might ask ye to outdoor suppers, or even to their boards with your seat well down below the salt. Do what you can for them that need it most, the desperate, and the hopeless. That opportunity will come. 'Tis a vision sent to me by God before whose judgment seat I soon will stand. What can I tell Him of my service unto Him in my days on earth, save that I taught, deep as I could, a boy of lowly station? That opportunity will come, Martyn Sutton. The whole world's in turmoil, and if you're ready to answer, ye'll be called. To tell you so, and to bid ye make full answer with all your might, is my farewell to you. My deepmost prayer."

"I brought you a bracelet from the Azores," I said with a twisted throat and streaming eyes.

"Put it on my wrist. I'll be buried with it, and 'twill still hang on the bone when the bone's dry. And come no more to visit me, 'cause I'm wasting fast away, and I'd not have you see me."

I brought forth the trinket, and its agates had a pretty shine in the dim room, but it could not hold a candle to the shine that came and slowly died away in Mistress Barton's eyes.

"I love you, my lady."

"Then kiss me, and go your way, and a long way, and a hard way, and unless you die too soon, a victorious way."

So I kissed her wasted cheek, and some of my tears fell upon it, but she did not let me wipe them away. At the door I stopped and raised my hand. She lifted hers and moved it so that in the slanted light its cheap stones shone and glittered like precious diamonds.

2

On leaving the great house by the postern door I caught sight of Pete, working in a trellis. I had not met with him since my return, so I made haste to him and clasped his rough hand.

"Ye look tall and fine," he said, "but just now your eyes be red, and ye've had a hard blow, and I reckon ye've looked on Mistress Barton."

"Yes, I did."

"She'll be tooken in a few days now. Only yesterday she had me coom to her room, and she gi' me half a crown, and some words I'll treasure more than if 'twere five crown she gi' me."

"That I know."

"But 'twas ye o' who she was most proud. Well, she's lived to middlin' age, fifty I reckon, her very window overlookin' 'em goblin stones, yet she'll die natur'l."

"Is that still on your mind, Mr. Pete?"

"Didn't I tell ye there'd be another murder? And them that it strikes has no connection I can see, 'cept they lived nigh, or they passed by, 'em stones. Mayhap I'd best not speak o' 'em, or I might be found wi' my chest split open."

"If they're slain by the Powers of Darkness, defy them, Mr. Pete! Speak me your mind."

"I've little to say, for you know well that stand of oaks where Davie Stewer was found. I used to see you sneaking there, with your bow and arries, to get the grouse that settled there when the master held his shoots. Just a stand o' oak, where Davie was at honest work. One time Master sent me there, to drive home some hogs that had gone there to eat mast. Well, I did, and where one of 'em had dug a deep hole I found somepin' I'd never seen, and still don't know the use of. It was a hook made of some black metal. It was thicker at one end, and had a hole in the bottom."

"Had it a sharp edge?"

"Not a bit."

"You said you didn't know it's use. Could you make a guess at it?"

"None 'at you'd believe. But I noted it was the size to fit around a man or a woman's neck. It was big enough that its ends would come under his jaw bones. If a pole was set in 'at hole I spoke of, and somepin' had hold of the end of the pole, it could drag along the person who's neck the hook was fixed on."

"And drag him down to hell and fire?" Without knowing quite why, I had lowered my voice to a murmur.

"Aye, or to 'at tower that the old people call the Dark Tower. Ye know the rhyme 'most as old as Stonehenge. 'Childe Roland to the dark tower came.'"

"What did you do with the iron—it might have been bronze—hook? Have you still got it?"

"No, I reckoned I'd better get shed o' it. So I gave it 'at minister of the Queen's church in Amesbury, the Rev'rant Stephen Burberry. Ye know he like odd sorts of things, curiosities and the like, and he keeps 'em in glass cases. I reckon he got it yet."

"Did the reverend know what it was for?"

"That, he didn't."

"Well, if it was buried in a ground till one of the master's hogs dug it up, it could have had nothing to do with that murder in the oak grove."

"My common sense tell me the same, supposin' the knifeman was flesh and blood."

"It's a good, sound supposing. Stick to it, old Pete." I walked away, leaving him mopping his brow with a pocket rag.

My presentation of the gift I had brought Winifred was a wholly different experience than the others. Timorousness was not quite the word for what I felt: rather it was strain, a strange thing, considered our intimate experience at Stonehenge when I had bade her good-bye. Perhaps she repented that amorous episode and wanted to forget it; she was going on sixteen and contemplating a good marriage; perhaps she and some son of a knight or even a nobleman had already plighted troth. She would be more beautiful than ever and more enticing.

It so chanced that both her parents and their baby boy were in Salisbury on business of the Crown, meaning generally the paying of taxes. The only other occupants of the house were a parlormaid and a scullery maid; I was shown into what was called the sitting room, pleasant enough, as it overlooked the garden, and not nearly as formal as the parlor. Winifred entered at once; and her strange beauty shortened my already flurried breath. I call it strange without knowing where its strangeness lay. Thinking of her when far at sea, I had found myself doubting that her ancestry was as old or as exalted as she had told me—descent from King Lear through King Vortigern and the Gwynedd kings, and especially that her grandam had declined marriage to our much-married Harry. In my repeating the story to a knowing old Welshman aboard the *Elspeth*, without mentioning Winifred's name, he too was inclined to scout it until I had remarked that her mother's maiden name was Glendower. The old fellow had been instantly arrested.

"Why, if she descends from Owen Glendower, like enough the rest is true as Gospel!" he exclaimed. "Owen came out of the kings of Gwynedd, and he 'roused the folk against Henry IV, and beat him back, and was the last real king of Wales. Also he scattered bastards thick as hares from the mouth of the river Dee to Cardiff on the Taff."

I had been mistaken in thinking Winifred's welcome might be cold. It was most cordial, and if she were a whit embarrassed over what had passed between us at Stonehenge she gave no sign of it. She had prayed to the true God that I might safely return from my perilous journey, so she told me, and she had herself written to Richard, in care of Maurice, Prince of Orange, of my home-coming. She wished to hear of all my adventures when the time was propitious.

At my bringing-forth the silver slipper buckles, I thought that her genuine pleasure in them was clouded with consternation. This could mean a sense of impropriety in accepting a personal gift from a lowborn swain, amounting to embarrassment if she were betrothed to a highborn swain. It proved to be neither one.

"Why, they're fine enough to wear at Queen Bess's court," she told me, meanwhile her thoughts flying some in another direction.

"I doubt not, you'll wear them there in due course."

"What should you have as your reward for your remembrance of me, and your generosity? Why, twice as many kisses as I gave you at Stonehenge, but here I cannot give you even one."

"I do not know why not."

"Martyn, if it was undutiful of me to disobey my father's most strict injunction beside a temple to a pagan god, how much greater my offense in his own house, where he ever prays and wars with sin?" And her eyes grew big and wistful, and—so I deemed in my youthful fancy—unworldly beautiful.

"I would be a rude swain indeed, if I did not perceive such a delicacy of feeling."

"Martyn, my sire is almost free of sin—he has struggled all his life against it—but I am not. The temptations of flesh, itchings and sometimes burnings, afflict me as they did Saint—I cannot recall the name. Often I have lain awake at night, even as my father prayed with fervence in the next chamber—thinking of that scene, the moon and the tall stones—but I should not speak of it. Let me give thought to these gifts, costlier than you should have bought for me. But you can count on it, that you are relieved of the promise you made me, that day."

"If you ever called on me for any service, I would not fail you?"

"That is what you swore."

"My giving you those little buckles has nothing to do with that."

"Martyn, you don't mean it!"

"I never meant anything more. I was only a stripling when I made the promise, and now I'm a whole man, but I feel more bound than ever."

"What if the favor I ask brings you into danger. It is slight, I think, but I must warn you, it's perfectly real."

"I've been in danger before." And I could not resist saying so, although I fear that my tone was a little too grand for a peasant, and my father, if he heard me, would break into his raucous laughter.

"Still I won't tell you now, what my need is, and how close it is to my heart; and fortune may have it that I'll not need to call on you at all."

"You do not mean, do you Miss Winifred, that you will call on some other young man to do the service for you? That would cut me to the quick."

"Of course I don't mean that. What other young man would be equal to it, even if I did not want and choose you, Martyn Sutton, for my champion? And Martyn, when the time comes, if you succeed in the mission, I will want you to meet me at Stonehenge, deep in the night, to put in my hands the—I came nigh to saying the Holy Grail, for it is akin to that in my mind—but I will say a token most dear to my heart. More than a token, a talisman, such as our knights wore in the Crusades." She was speaking in a low, soft voice, wondrously sweet in my ears, and her expression was childlike, and I was carried out of myself, by happiness and wonder.

"I will meet you at Stonehenge."

"That is what I believe. And anything we should do there, will not be held against us by my patron saint's intervention in our behalf. And if there are evil spirits, which I cannot wholly deny since Stonehenge is without doubt the ruins of a pagan temple, they cannot seize us in their toils."

Winifred was truly the daughter of Preacher Powell, I was thinking, as I took my exultant departure, but she was somewhat more tolerant of human needs and pleasures.

3

What thought I gave to the call upon me that Winifred might soon make—provided it was her fixed intent or a passing whim—was most pleasurable. She had said it would put me into danger, but this last, I felt sure, would be almost altogether a figment of her imagination. She was a great dreamer, really. I had once had a close look at a gentleman named Edmund Spenser, as he lay at the inn at Amesbury. He had since become a renowned pastoral poet, his having written *The Shepheardes Calendar* becoming an open secret. He had had a flowing mustache and a romantic beard, and even Winifred's eyes reminded me of his, brilliant when he spoke, dreamy when he stood in thought; whereby I wondered if she might develop into a great poetess, for England had never had any such, to my knowledge. I hoped more fervently than my common sense could tolerate that she would not abandon the enterprise, and could not abide the thought of her assigning the adventure and the risk to some other youth far above my station.

But my mind was in bleak twilight when it confronted the almost incredible fact of the "Wiltshire murders," as circuit judges and visitors at our inns had come to speak of them. They wasted no wind on the homicides committed well-nigh weekly in the vast metropolis of London, with its two hundred thousand folk. Almost always these were done by nameless footpads, or by broilers in taprooms, or by married folk in squalid hovels, each at most a nine-day wonder, and then forgotten. Wiltshire was rustic England. Most of our people led serene and innocent lives; even our great folk rarely visited court. The first of three had occurred ten years agone, and its detail had become disputed and vague. But the other two appeared to me monstrous in the extreme—the victim of one of them a sweet and guileless peasant woman, gathering nuts in the woods, and the other a dim-witted but harmless woodcutter. There was no credible motive for either.

But I refused to believe goblin-ridden old Pete that there would be another.

On the winter solstice of 1586, Preacher Powell took himself off for Salisbury, his purpose easy to guess. He had always raged at the frivolity and the passing of brimming cups in great houses and small with which Christmas was celebrated; and he had declared the burning of the yule log a pagan rite. He meant to thunder against these blasphemies in a holy season, and as was his common practice—he adored his daughter—he took Winifred with him. Mistress Enid Powell remained at home because—so neighborly gossip had it—their little toddler, named Owen, no doubt in honor of his ancestor Owen Glendower, and now a year and nine months old, had an inflamed throat. She had also given leave to the kitchenmaid to spend Christmas at home, six days' vacation in all, and the parlormaid could go to Winchester for New Year's Day and Twelfth Night.

On the night of January fourth a northeast wind chilled the whole countryside. At midnight when it died down, the cold drizzling rain changed to a somewhat heavy fall of snow, not rare but somewhat uncommon in our parts. In the first light of dawn, Harry Blake, old Pete's nephew, came to our door, warmly dressed, and with his fine yew bow in his hand.

"Martyn, the snow's just right for tracking hares," he told me jubilantly.

"I'll be with you as soon as I get my lemonwood bow," I answered, with the lift of my heart that was always given by the promise of a day's sport.

No field work needed doing; the master permitted the hunting of hares on his broad lands, provided the hunters carried only time-honored longbows, not newfangled firearms. It went without saying that they must not enter the park, regardless of the enticing tracks leading straight to and through the hedge. Harry was a capable archer, often winning the prize at arrow-shoots at fairs, and since we would take turns at shooting, my own prowess would be taxed to beat or equal him.

While encircling the park to the Great Meadow beloved by hares, he told me the latest news, for his parent, Hugh Blake, was the master's coachman, who made many stops at inns. The three items would appear to any other listener in a descending scale of importance.

The first was that King Philip of Spain had been flung into such a fury by the Queen's ordering home his ambassador, Mendoza, that he had fallen in a fit. The second was that Lady Isobel had had a letter from young Master Richard, now a captain if not more under Prince Maurice, that he had suffered an attack of swamp fever, and was coming home to regain his wasted strength. This report gripped my attention more than the first; it seemed to bear out a kind of inkling that I would see Richard again before I again set sail, whether to dire battle with Spanish galleons or, if luck was with me, with colonists bound for the New World.

The third item was trifling of itself—that according to a neighbor, who had it from another neighbor, Preacher Powell and his daughter Winifred had returned from Salisbury. It was somewhat astonishing that the fiery reformer should leave the city before Twelfth Night, notorious for its revelry, always high on that night, often unseemly, and sometimes downright pagan. Still it did not cross my mind to doubt the report, and indeed I rejoiced at it, for I was eagerly waiting for the chance to pay a call on Winifred. The occasion would be the loan of a new publication by Edmund Spenser. She had a great love of poetry; and Lady Isobel, who had lent me the book, had given me permission to lend it in turn to "Mr. Powell and his family."

Our rabbit hunt was moderately successful, each of us bagging three, and promising our families at least three delicious dinners. At three o'clock we were hungry and tired, and the sun hung low, behind cold, gray clouds. We parted at our door; I went in, washed, put on my best coat, picked up the book, and began the short walk to the Powell house.

Its chimney was giving forth no smoke on this raw, chill evening. This puzzled me, for if the report of the return of Preacher Powell and his daughter had been false, still Mistress Powell would crave a cozy fire. Still I mounted the porch and rapped on the door.

No one answered. Plainly the mistress and the parlormaid were both absent. I do not know by what impulse I softly turned the knob; perhaps it was waked by a kind of creepy silence, perhaps imagined, that overhung the premises. To my profound astonishment and a strangely dark foreboding, the door was unlocked.

I opened the door. The light was exceeding dim, yet my eyes rapidly adjusted themselves to this condition, and I walked a short distance into the front room. And now I was severely shaken, the back of my neck prickling, and unpleasant quivers chasing each other up and down my spine.

"Is anyone here?" I called, my voice hoarse and strange.

There came a reply that dealt me a wracking shock, because of its very commonplaceness. It was the wail of a little child from an adjoining room. I had clean forgot about little Owen, the Powell baby not quite two years old. Plainly my call had wakened him from deep sleep. But at once he began lisping and crooning to himself, and the thought flashed through my mind that he would take no harm—I had seen the latticed pen in which he played and took his naps when he was not toddling about the rooms or in the yard on sunny days. And instantly I forgot him again, for all was not well with his castle; and I must find out what was so terribly wrong.

I did not like the look of the open door of the dining room. I could almost, not quite, see into it; yet I felt there was something there that must be seen. As the baby babbled in the nursery I walked to the opening. Something *was* in there, a shape which at first made no sense in the gloom; and then suddenly it made horrid sense.

It was a human shape, but its feet dangled a full foot above the floor. Then making a great effort to obtain sharper vision, I saw that it was the body of Mistress Powell, hanging by the neck on a rope fastened to one of the beams bracing the domed ceiling. With a desperate surge of my will I crept forward and touched the hand of her dangling arm. It was cold as a stone.

4

The thought came to me that I should search the house. I did manage to glance into the nursery; and because its window faced westward, enough wisps of dusk remained to show me the child's shape, laying on his back in the little pen, trying with his chubby hands to find his toes in the stockinged feet of what was no doubt a warm and fleecy undergarment. He would take no harm in this accursed house; the room was chill but not bitter cold. But the homey scene finished my unnervement; it was in such contrast with the grisly scene in the adjoining room. I had no will power left to look into other rooms, and chilled to my soul's depth with horror, I fled the house. Into the open and early night I fled, into the day's last dusk indeed, from whence I could see the distant glimmer of windows behind which people talked and moved about.

Now I must seek companionship and help. I had carefully closed the door and now I shut the gate. Instinctively I started homeward, seeking my father. It would not be likely that I would meet or pass anyone on this lonely country lane at suppertime.

But luck was with me in this respect. I heard the footfall of a horse on the sunbaked earth of the road, and then dimly glimpsed a rider. I ran to meet him and at his first word—"Martyn?"—I recognized him as Mr. Billy, William Holbrooke being his real name, who was the master's bailiff. I stood gasping, my throat corded; and he peered down at me, and then sprang off his horse.

"Compose yourself, Martyn, and tell me what's happened."

"I went to the Preacher's house, to take a book to Miss Winifred. The house was so still, no smoke from the chimney, that I went up on the porch and tried the door. It was unlocked, and that didn't seem natural to me. I saw no candles burning and all, so I opened the door and went in. I called who's there, but got no answer but a wail from the baby, Owen, in his nursery. He was all right."

"Go on, Martyn," he drove me, when I paused to catch my breath.

"The rest is just awful. I had a feeling there was something—something wrong—in the dining room. I went on tiptoe to the door and looked in. It was awful dark, but I made out what looked like a woman standing very tall, and then I looked hard and saw that her feet didn't touch the floor."

"Jesus Lord! 'Twan't Mistress Powell?"

"Yes, sir. She was hanging from a beam. I touched her hand and it was stone-cold."

"Another one! Your mother, and then poor old Davie Stewer, and now the second lady of the parish. What ha' we done, to bring this curse on us!" He had been speaking his horror; but now he stopped, and looked me straight in the face.

"Did you say, Martyn, that her hand was cold?"

"Stone-cold, I tell you."

"I hate to speak of this, but I must. 'Member you were under suspicion when your mama was foully murdered. You're finding the body will put you there again, unless you can 'count for how you spent the day . . ."

"From dawn until just now I was with Harry Blake, tracking hares."

"Thank God for that. Thank God for the snow that set your mind on't. Could she have been killed last night? No, for I seen her myself this morn, soon after sunrise, when she was a-looking if her early spring posies had been frostbit. Now I'll tell you what to do. Hurry back to the gate, and if anyone comes by, tell 'em I sent you there, and to wait and watch with you, until I come with Parson Burberry, and one of the watch and ward, if I can find any. Have you the nerve to go in again?"

"I'll find it."

"See if there's a blanket at the foot of the baby's pen and put it over him. Have you got flint and steel and a little tinder?"

"Yes, sir."

"Then light a candle, and leave it burning in the stick in the little boy's room. Then go back to the gate and look and listen sharp."

These orders I obeyed; my skin crawling on my body, then took my post at the gate. The first wayfarers were a young man and his sweetheart walking out, both of whom I knew, and I bade them stop and stand watch with me. When I told them what was in the house, a mother hanged and a baby boy playing or asleep, the girl declared that she "was fair took," and asked her lover to hold her up, or she would fall in a faint. I suppose I seized upon the wholly human incident to rid my mind, for a brief moment, of the awesome fact. Presently came a sober-citizen, walking his collie dog, whom I recognized as a magistrate from Rochester, visiting his kinswoman, Mistress Lacey. He was carrying a lantern, for he was aged and unsteady of foot, and in its glimmer he saw the pallor of our faces.

"Something dreadful has happened," he remarked. "What is it?"

I told him in a rush of words.

"And you found the poor lady!" said Justice Willard. "No doubt she took her own life in a fit of despondency."

"If so, your honor, I didn't notice any stool or box she could've stood on, while she fixed the noose, and then kicked away."

"Do not tell me it is foul and heinous murder! Yet it is not rare, in these rustic scenes. And the babe is in its crib, unguarded. The bailiff that gave you your orders seems not to know the maxim that a murderer almost always returns to the scene of his crime."

"I'll go and stand guard of him now, if you will take my place here."

"Do so, and here's my cane of stout thorn and a weighted top. I'll keep the collie. She'll bark if her keen nose detects a skulker."

"Don't go alone, Martyn," the young wench wailed. "'Tis the Devil himself who might come in 'orrid form—"

"This young Englishman will be a match for him, no fear," the magistrate told her in reassuring tones, firmly authoritative and at the same time gently paternal; for the lantern light had revealed the peasant girl as noticeably comely of face and form. It struck me as strange that the dignified magistrate would notice such things in such an hour. It seemed that the Devil himself could not knock the humanness out of human nature.

It so happened that I need not enter that minatory house alone. A long shadow swiftly shortened as a young man came running—I knew this youth by the ease of his stride—and he soon proved to be my companion of the day, Harry Blake, his longbow still in his hand. Plainly he had heard the news, thought I might be under suspicion, and had come to my rescue. Together we went in, and with the first candle I had lighted we set blazing a three-pronged stick in the front room. The only sound was the whimpering cry of the baby boy, not of the least fear, more likely of lonesomeness or hunger. This last was relieved much sooner than we thought. The news had sped with wings; and a pleasant-faced motherly yeoman's wife, whose cottage was two furlongs down the lane, brought a bowl of gruel, a spoon, and a bib no doubt used by some little child of her own.

The child ate greedily and gurgled happily. This was such a homely

scene, human and warm, and I could not keep my thoughts from
wandering to an inhuman scene in the next room, beyond the pale,
mercifully concealed by the pall of darkness. How much longer must
it endure, unmitigated and stark? Until a duly authorized officer of
the shire or of the Queen could be notified and formally arrive on
the scene of the crime. But before long, our little charge was well
fed and yawning. Might his dreams be sweet!

"I wish one of 'ee would light a little fire in the hearth in the front
room," the woman said wistfully. "There be kindling and fuel in the
box. 'Twould bring no cheer to her who's gone to heaven, nor to the
babe that's left, but I don't like to think—"

"I'll do it, ma'am."

Soon the small flames were leaping, and relieved the bleak chill
of that room, and a little of the warmth crept and found its way
into the nursery. None could enter, I thought, the once cozy dining
room; a dread spirit stood on guard at the threshold. But now a
sudden bustle in the gathering crowd outside, and the ring of authoritative voices told Harry Blake and me that our present vigil
would quickly end.

It turned out that a constable had been found in a taproom in
Amesbury, and had ridden hard on his own horse, and sent a messenger on another horse to the high sheriff in Salisbury. The officer
was not one of those who had questioned my father and me; his
station in society was a good deal higher; no peasant woman had
been done to death but the wife of a gentlemen, herself of a noble
line. He entered with the magistrate, both of them carrying lanterns.

"I'll speak to you young men later," the officer called to Harry and
me, "and see you don't leave the premises." Then with a quick, firm
step he entered the dining room, the big-eyed justice close behind
him.

In about five minutes he reappeared and called in Mr. Blake, Harry's
father; also he asked that someone fetch a strong box or chest that
would not break under a man's weight. The latter errand took about
ten minutes to complete; we heard the murmur of the three men
talking in low tones. A suitable box was brought; the coroner and
his assistant had now arrived and these joined the conferees. I knew
that a litter and bearers were not far behind.

They came, entered the room, and very quickly reappeared bearing a sheet-covered figure of human shape, which was at once carried
up the stairs and doubtless into a bedroom. And now the coroner
made an announcement from the front door.

"Hear ye! Murder has been committed on the person of Mistress
Edward Powell, and any of ye who have information or suspicion

that may be of use to the Queen's officials, remain in call. The rest of ye may disperse."

The constable, Mr. Hardy, now appeared in the door of the nursery.

"A horseman has been sent to Salisbury to notify Mr. Edward Powell and his daughter," he told us civilly enough. "There is nought more that we can do until daylight, so while this good woman remains with the little boy, you, Harry Blake, wait with her, the door closed, until I summon you. Martyn Sutton, since you found the body a-hanging, I'll save time by questioning you now."

He had me seat myself beside the fire, and relate in detail how I had come to make the grisly discovery. This I did, and when he asked me to show him the book of poems that I had intended to lend to Winifred, I had to look for it a full and rather flurried minute before I found it on a stand, not far from the dining-room door. I could not remember at what point in my harrowing experience I had laid it there. The officer thumbed some of its pages.

"Martyn, the high sheriff told me you could read and write—surely a credit to a young man of your station—but I didn't know you read Master Spenser's poems."

"I do, when I can get hold of any."

"The front sheet has the name of Lady Isobel Wade written on it."

"She lent it to me, sir, and gave me leave to lend it to the Powells."

"The gentry around here are right neighborly to a young man of your station."

"They have been most generous with me, sir."

"I heard too, after your mother had been killed, that you frequently visit the stone circles on your master's land, and stay there several hours, mooning."

"I am deeply curious about them, sir."

"An odd thing, that you would be involved in—I should say, have a close connection with—two murders in this neighborhood."

"In one of them, the victim was my mother, Maggie Sutton, and the other was our near neighbor. I will answer any question you ask me, sir; may I ask you a question?"

"I'll not stop you."

"The coroner undoubtedly examined the body of Mistress Powell. Did he form any opinion as to when her death occurred?"

"He said that *rigor mortis*—that means stiffness—had begun to set in. Of course the room was chilly—that would hasten the process—still he believed that she was killed not much earlier—or hardly any later—than noon."

"Will you ask me, sir, where I was at noon, and in fact since sunrise, until just before sunset?"

"No, because I know what you'll answer. A reliable witness told me that you and Harry Blake were hunting hares the most of the day."

"Then—excuse me, sir—I do not see much point in your other questions."

"I wouldn't ask 'em if I didn't see any point in 'em. Two youths a-hunting hares don't stay close together the whole time. They wander off from each other, that's natural enough."

"Sir, Harry and I were shooting against each other. The snow hasn't melted—if you'll send someone to look at the Big Meadow he'll find two pairs of footprints, never more than ten or fifteen feet from each other. He'll find blood on the snow where we killed six hares. He'll find where we sat on a log and ate the wheat cakes and dried mutton that he'd brought in his pouch. During the day we saw John Higgins mending a fence, we met Jan Pierce taking a short cut across the meadow from the park to his cot, and just about noon we noticed Simon Tuttle likewise tracking hares, on the Lacey lands south of the meadow."

He waited a long while in silence, then sighed.

"You've got sharp eyes, Martyn, and an excellent memory," he remarked. "Well, we'll look for those tracks at first light, and I'll question Harry Blake, but I must say in all fairness that you appear absolutely in the clear. As for your familiarity with gentry, I guess it's their business, not mine, but I don't know what England's coming to. I reckon you can go home, while I talk to Harry. The coroner will call an inquest—that's the law when gentry are killed by persons unknown—and you'll have to testify, but until then I have no reason or right to hold you. And I'll say too, that I'm glad I haven't."

Instead of going home, I hung with the little crowd of neighbors, mainly waiting for news. A few might have information to report to the sheriff, although I would wager a crown against tuppence that it would be wasted breath. Some of it might arise from spite, but very little; poor folk had to work too hard—and must sleep soundly when they may, not lie brooding—to have time and energy for hating neighbors. Most of it would be instances of second sight, in dreams or awake; but very few would report ghosts and goblins, for great folk, deaf and blind, made light of such specters.

I intended to linger here until Harry had been questioned, but when he came forth, we both stayed on, awaiting the coming of dignitaries including the high sheriff. This gentleman with two bailiffs arrived on winded horses not long after midnight, and the sheriff's mouth was grimly set but his eyes were wild-looking. Hearing the horses, both the magistrate and the coroner came into the yard to greet him, and we heard a brief exchange.

"Bad business, Mr. Sheriff," the magistrate commented.

"This is one case, your honor, *that must be solved.*"

The inference was plain. Queen Bess herself would ask her ministers if the miscreant committing the Wiltshire murders had been caught, tortured, and hanged, and if not, why not? And that set me to wondering if she had ever heard of her father Harry proposing marriage to Enid Glendower's mother, a tale I did not doubt. Had she accepted, and borne him a son, Bess herself would be merely a lady in waiting at the court, not Queen of England and the isles. Nor would Anne of Cleves be famed throughout Europe as "that great Flemish mare" and Catherine Howard's head might have set securely on her neck until old age. Consequences of even small events are like the ever widening ripples of a pond, when a stone has been cast.

Harry and I stood about till dawn, a watch not in the least harmful to sturdy youths of our years, but which furnished us little, if any, excitement. For some three hours he and I followed a deputy sent to verify his and my account of never separating during our long day's hunt, and the fellow was most blasphemous because of wet feet and the tiring, futile tramp when his search was done. The sheriff, who had come into the case like a lion, went out of it a fortnight later like a lamb; a better comparison was like a whipped dog. On the whole my fellow peasants were rather gratified that he had not fastened the crime on flesh and blood, since this fact sustained their own convictions. But witch-masters did a lively business in selling charms and amulets, many bolts were fixed on cottage doors and windows, and hardheaded workmen did not like to work out of sight of fellow hands.

Two weeks later the sheriff resigned his office, and another worthy was duly appointed by the Queen. He too set about the solving of the mystery, and with great vim; he sought the source of the rope and the blunt instrument that had struck the victim lightly on the back of the head, by no means cracking the skull, indeed so light a stroke that it could have done no more than stun the lady a few minutes. From this fact the officer deduced that she had regained consciousness before the rope tightened, to find herself probably standing on a dining-room chair, which only needed setting aside for the completion of a gloating killer's fiendish purpose. Indeed he showed that the noose itself had loose and broken strands, indicative of clawing hands.

"And that there meant," the big-eared innkeeper late from London told all who cared to listen, "that this 'ere was a crime o' passion. 'E hated 'er, with 'ellish hate 'e did, and wanted 'er to suffer. Or else 'e was a 'ooman fiend who loved the sight of folk in ter'ble anguish, for there be such men, floggers at prisons, and 'ficial torturers to get confessions, and 'Quisitors in Spain."

But in any case—and this was the sheriff's main contention—the method of murder separated this from the two preceding, and he would wager his warrant that they were committed by different people.

And this was as far as the inquiry went. And then I remembered a scene on the dark road, when I had told of my finding to a horseman, William Holbrooke, the master's bailiff, and of the awful question he had asked.

"What ha' we done, to bring this curse on us?"

Chapter V

ERRANT KNIGHT OR ERRANT FOOL?

1

Another week passed by, one gray day amazingly like its predecessors, before I met Winifred face to face. She was coming out of the churchyard, her lovely eyes red from weeping, and she quickened her step, and slipped both of her hands into mine.

"Martyn, we're in the same boat now," she told me in quiet sorrow. "Your mother—and now my mother."

"That is true."

I thought upon this, and wished I could wring the neck of a little, coiling serpent of a thought that Winifred's words were not quite true. What remained of her mother and mine lay under the same kind of dirt, the mounds were indistinguishable, and although hers would have a somewhat finer stone, its writing chiseled by a mason, the other that my father had erected was good enough, bearing my mother's name, the year of her birth and of her death, and the epitaph *R.I.P.* But they were in different ends of the churchyard. One corpse laid in proximity to those of men and women of my mother's own station; and the other in the company of its own station. Well, God Himself, His eternal, merciful, omnipotent self, had ordained these stations—all proper clergymen said so.

Winifred and I strolled down the lane side by side—only the merest violation of God's ordinance. I was not worried about that, but a question had risen in my mind, and it was of such urgency that I would not wait long to put it in words.

"You know, of course, that Sir Walter Raleigh is swiftly enlisting settlers for his new plantations in Virginia," I began. "He is meeting with difficulty, so I hear—folk are reluctant to go to sea and make homes on a distant coast that Philip's ships might raid—still, nearly a hundred bold wights, some with wives and even children, have set down their names. In a few days I will be setting out for Plymouth

to entreat him to include me. I will have a letter from the master—
he will write against his will, with Lady Isobel at his elbow—and
one from our parson, and if I am lucky, one from Cap'n Selkirk. Well,
that leaves something undone, but I take it, the matter is no longer
of great importance to you, now you have suffered this loss."

"Martyn, it is of greater importance than ever before."

"I can hardly believe it."

"It should be obvious, I think. Of course you do not know exactly
what it is. Martyn, I feel so alone. I love my father dearly, and he
loves me as much as he can love anyone, when all his heart and
mind are so occupied by what he believes is his divine mission. He
thinks of himself as a latter-day prophet of very God. But I can't
live up to him—to his expectations of me—he wants me to be a heroine
in his cause. I am not the stuff of heroines. He does not need any
support—any emblems—any tokens—to hold in his hand when he prays.
He need not pray for strength to do right; he has not the least doubt
of himself; but I am torn with a thousand doubts. I told you that
something I had lost, and wanted you to help me regain, was an
amulet. My father would think that my longing to get it back was
almost heathen. I will tell you what it is. You would call it a locket,
I suppose, although it has no key—it is a round disk of silver or some
other white metal, with a hinged back. It is about a thousand years
old; it was passed down through my mother's ancestors and her
mother gave it to me when I was six years old. It contains a lock
of white hair."

"Cut from the head of a great Christian martyr?"

"He was a saint, but not a martyr, except in coming among the
barbarous Saxons to preach the Faith. I was named after him; he is
my patron saint. He was born in Devonshire and he was canonized
as St. Boniface. But the Welsh and the English too knew him as
Wynfrith, or Winfrid."

Winifred's treasuring of the talisman—or sacred memento if the
former word smacked of superstition and paganism—was no girlish
whim. It was heartfelt as any emotion of her being. Her voice told
me, and the expression on her face. She did not belong to this
iconoclastic age, ushered in by Henry VIII, the image breaker, the
despoiler of the ancient treasures of Canterbury Cathedral. I knew
then that my boyish idolization of her had lingered on, and by proc-
esses of mind and heart I did not wholly understand, I felt that it
was justified.

"You say you lost this relic?"

"I'll tell you how it happened. I unhooked its ring from a clasp on
a silver wire to show Mistress Barton at the mansion—one of the few

times in my life I opened it. We were in her room, and Richard called us from outside to look at a fine red deer stag that must have wandered all the way from Savernake Forest. We went to a window in a room called the chess room; Mr. Wade kept his boards and men there—and there were two tables where he and his friends diced or played whist—and some worthless mementos he had won at sporting events—I remember noticing a red ribbon with a metal clasp and with writing on it, won at a horse show I supposed—three or four canes in a basket—some staghorns on the wall—and some bronze medals fixed on a cushion. Mr. Wade keeps the key to this room— his chessmen are ivory and jade and very fine and valuable. Either Mistress Barton or I laid down my relic in this room. With the excitement of rushing downstairs and outside while Richard was getting a musket to shoot the stag, I didn't miss it until I was almost home; then I thought that on fastening it back on the wire I had not securely closed the clasp and it had fallen off in the path. I searched the path carefully, but did not find it. And by now Mistress Barton had gone with the others to Mrs. Lacey's; and I had to wait till morning before I could tell her of my loss."

Winifred paused, and drew her hand impatiently across her eyes.

"Well, Mistress Barton and I searched both rooms. We couldn't find the relic anywhere. Later I bribed one of the housemaids—she was about to get married and needed money—to make a further search. She found it without difficulty—in a metal dish on a desk in the chess room, along with three silver shillings owned by King Harry or some earlier king, horn buttons, a tarnished silver medal, and some brass thimbles. What I think happened was that another housemaid picked it up from where one of us had laid it down, and had kept it overnight, thinking the silver in it was worth stealing. But when Mistress Barton and I looked for it, she became frightened and put it in the metal dish. I promised the maid a halfcrown if she'd get it for me but she was afraid to—a maid in Dorsetshire had just been sent to jail for stealing sixpence. I thought I'd have a chance to recover it, but the inside door is almost always locked, and I never did."

"Why didn't you ask Priscilla to get it for you?"

"Simply because if she knew I valued it, she'd keep it from me. She's been jealous of me as long as we've known each other. I think she hates me."

"How could I get it for you?"

"There's a tree just outside a window that won't close. I've looked at it from the outside at least twenty times, and sometimes it's open for two feet, and always for at least six inches. And that's the whole situation."

My thoughts raced, and I spoke, wondering if I were in my right mind.

"Winifred, I doubt if you are very well acquainted with English law. Your life is such that you wouldn't hear much talk about it. My entering the park would be trespass—the penalty these days is usually a month in common jail, but if it was a flagrant case the trespasser can be ironed and imprisoned for six months. Breaking and entering is always a felony, punishable by five to twenty years in prison. If loot above a certain value is taken, the penalty can be the gallows."

"Don't say any more. Just refuse me. It's the sensible thing to do. I release you from your promise."

"These penalties I speak of are paid—only if I'm caught."

"I tell you, don't think of it again."

"The chance of my being caught is unlikely. The dog would be loosed but he can't smell what is downwind—it would have to be done on a windy night—an east wind, in fact. If I were fool enough to try it, and by bad luck was caught, you would feel it your bounden duty to come to court and say you had asked me to do it, and you would be an accessory before the fact. I would have to be sure that you wouldn't come to court, or tell anyone, or I will withdraw here and now."

"That's what I want. A little disk of silver with some white hairs in it, cut from the head of a dead saint by a loving priest. It's the wildest folly."

"So were the Crusades. The knights were not looking for a short route to India—not for treasure of any kind—they could not bear for a Holy City to be in infidel hands. I wonder if any knights ever did go in search of the Holy Grail? It was a beautiful idea. Well, I fought the Spaniards, the risk a hundred times greater than this. I wonder why I fought them—I had nothing against them but the Inquisition, and its victims were usually Spanish too. If I refused your request, I feel I would always be wise, never be a fool, and that would mean I would never do anything of mark, never prove something that I want very much to prove. So if you'll give me that promise not to tell why I did it, I'll go and get your trinket."

"Well, I make the promise and I can say no more."

Thus it came to pass that I had talked myself into committing the most wanton folly.

The wind from the east in wintertime is bleak, biting, and dispiriting. Yet before noon it had marked the day, on the night of which I must undertake my demented knight-errantry. I had waited a week for this east wind; there had been a north wind and a gentle southwest wind, and it seemed a wind from every point of the compass except due east. The pertinent fact was that Snarler's kennel lay directly east of the mansion; by approaching it from the west my smell would be blown behind me and thus not into his alert and incredibly sensitive nostrils. There was still another advantage to a wind out of the east; it was heartily disliked in England, perhaps beyond its deservings, and folk were not prone to go abroad when it was blowing, and instead kept close to well-tended fire or snug in blankets.

I thought it was the wind that "cold through the hawthorn" blew in a very ancient song. This song was still sung in Devon but it was not in the Devonshire dialect; I reckoned it had been Anglicized, as the saying went, in the thousand years it had been passed down from mother to son, and from son to daughter. To get my mind off of tonight's undertaking, I sang it to myself to the wistful tune that Mama had learned and which my sire had loved:

> Still through the hawthorn blows the cold wind,
> And the lowering clouds are gray.
> I will search the lorn moor, but who will I find
> To take my forlornness away?
> Wild are the winds that blow through a life,
> Until heart, hope, and happiness chill;
> But the wind through the hawthorn cuts like a knife,
> And gone are white blossoms and little bird's fife,
> And in death and decay lies all that was blithe,
> And the deep frost violets kill.
> Once the hawthorn and I, our hearts could meet,
> White was my blossom, my perfume sweet,
> He gave me his shadow, I slept at his feet,
> And I would that I slept there still.
>
> Still through the hawthorn blows the cold wind,
> Now I pass him unknown, he is deaf, he is blind.
> Bed, I will come to thee, sleep I shall find.
> Blow rain, blow snow, blow soft, blow shrill,
> While I drift with the mist where I will.

I did not know exactly what the words meant, but I thought it had to do with a maiden's hopeless love. My heart must hold a hopeless love for Winifred, who ever reminded me of Elaine of the Lake, the lily maid of Astolat, who appears in Malory's book as fatally in love with Sir Lancelot. But the song was sung long before Malory was born, before the Roman legions tramped away, before the first knight rode in tournament, so said antiquaries whom Mistress Barton had questioned.

I would have liked to compare myself with a knight-errant, about

to set forth on noble and chivalric quest, but my common sense refused to let me. I had not the least notion why I should risk jail, even
a hanging, to restore to a beautiful girl, obsessed by dreams, what
was at most a holy relic and at least no more than a good-luck charm.
Yet I knew I must run the risk; and there was no getting out of it
on any excuse I could invent.

I prepared for the adventure; so I termed it in my thoughts, although almost with a sneer. I put on a pair of leathern boots I had
never worn, that no one knew I had bought cheap from a strolling
cobbler—he had made them on an order for a gamekeeper who had
since left the country—and I knew a place to hide them on my return
where no minion of the law could likely find them. I dressed warmly
in dark clothes and, for the first time in earnest, belted on my sword.
If my plans went awry and I had close dealings with Snarler, I
would have use for it. With my left hand pressing down on the hilt
and the scabbard projecting behind me it would not interfere with
swift flight, if this were in the dice of fortune that would fall tonight.

A scarf over my face would be no advantage. If anyone at the
mansion caught close sight of me, he would know me anyway, by my
height and shape, and any sort of mask would imply criminal intent.
In my wallet I carried one gold sovereign and three shillings. I brought
these in case, by evil fortune, I encountered another trespasser, conceivably a burglar, more likely some field hand who had located the
winter nest of a hedgehog, the strong flesh of which certain poor
folk were meat-hungry enough to stew. The gold piece, or even a
shilling, would buy a deal of silence from such a hard-up fellow.

At midnight I sallied forth without waking my father, out of our
back door into grass that would not hold a human footprint in this
high wind, circled through Preacher Powell's yard, and leaped across
the footpath into one of the two well-worn ruts of the lane. Today
was market day in Amesbury—one little stroke of luck—and several
cartwheels would be following these ruts before sunrise, effacing any
boot tracks.

Where the ruts skirted closely a patch of high grass across the lane,
I leaped into this, over which I could pass with safety to the hedge
surrounding the park. This I crossed directly west of the mansion and
made for the tree that stood beside the window of the master's chess
room.

A gibbous moon, in a few nights to die, then to be buried in daylight for a week ere she was reborn, had newly risen. Now and then
the wind-harried clouds gave me glimpses of her, and at such times
the blackness of night paled a little, and I could make out flower beds
and stone benches at fifty or sixty feet. But not a sound, not even the

eerie screech of a mousing owl, ruptured the heavy silence. I supposed these fowls huddled in thick treetops on such nights as this, preferably yew trees in graveyards, for in naked trees or in flight the wind would blow their body warmth from under their feathered coats. At the foot of the tree, and by swift and grateful thought, I removed my boots that might scar the bark of limbs or damage twigs, leaving sign of a climber. The lower boughs were in my easy reach, and in stocking feet I swung myself up. Once more the harlot Fortune gave me a smile. On a night that the window should be closed as far as the sills would descend, it was open for a good two feet. I supposed the upstairs maid had been in haste to seek her warm bed, and her conscience had been eased by the thought that the tree would fend off the gusts of the east wind. Anyway the room was locked from the inside, and no gamesters had use for it tonight.

With one squirm of my body I made entrance headfirst, and braced myself with my arms until I could draw through my legs and stand on them. In my pocket was flint and steel, and a little well-dried tinder. The first spark ignited the latter, and I lighted a tiny taper that I had also brought.

In a matter of seconds I had located the metal dish atop a desk. I experienced a moment's panic lest the relic had been removed from the depository—proof that however I had cursed myself for this under-taking, my mind and soul were devoutly bent on its success. But the pale gleam of the taper revealed in my first glance the silver disk; and I could not mistake it because of the small ring on its top and a worn engraving on the corner in the shape of a convention-alized tree. I slipped it into the upper pocket of my coat, wedged it with a rag, and headfirst, still in absolute silence, made out the window into the tree.

In seconds I was on the ground, pulling on my boots, then making for the hedge. And I had gained a third of the way, running lightly, only occasionally glancing over my shoulder, although cursing the moon for emerging into a big patch of open sky, which the blowing clouds had left clear. Once more I glanced over my shoulder. What I saw sped an icy chill through every vein and nerve in my body. At his swiftest gait, and straight toward me, charged the great watch-dog Snarler, as large as any wolf still said to prowl in the Forest of Dartmoor.

Perhaps then, but more likely a good deal later, the thought struck me of how he had come to scent me upwind. Well-trained watchdogs often leave their kennels at night, sometimes making a wide circle about the houses in their charge. On such a reconnaissance he had caught a whiff of me in a cross draft, and in scenting it out had caught sight of me in the ghostly moonlight.

It would be the wildest folly to take to my heels. I did what I must do, without thought, which was draw my sword. No doubt Snarler saw its faint gleam, which had no meaning in his brute mind; for he charged on in deadly silence. His shape grew large. I drew my right hand back to my chest, the sword blade pointing slightly downward. At what my brain told me was precisely the right fraction of a second, I thrust it full length. The point entered just below the base of his thick neck, and so keen the well-filed edges that it plunged fully half a foot into his breast. He uttered one sharp yelp, his death cry, his legs already wilting under him.

I wiped both sides of the sword on the grass, swiftly indeed, and then resheathed it. But the awesome fright the brute had given me was on me yet, and I sped not in the direction I had started, the route I had entered the park, but toward the nearest point of the hedge. I thought that thus I would cross a good hundred paces from the gatekeeper's cottage, but I had misjudged the distance, so difficult to estimate in treacherous moonlight, wherein the eyes play tricks, when small structures at one hundred feet look like large structures twice as far. Actually I crossed the hedge within forty paces of the gatekeeper's window.

Still I refused to believe that the single outcry of the dying dog had wakened the fellow from heavy sleep, and if it did, he would lie a few seconds wondering over its source and cause before he would rise and go to his window; and the darkness would have swallowed me by then.

Again I walked in the ruts until opposite the Powell house. I had told Winifred I would essay the adventure about midnight, so I was not surprised to see the glimmer of a lighted candle in a downstairs window. At this I rejoiced, not that I might have a few words with her, but that I could pass her treasure into her hand at once, and be shed of it.

She was standing, a dim figure strangely spiritual-looking, saintly perhaps, in the open doorway differentiated from the darkness by a few feeble gleams of an invisible, burning candle. Without a word I handed her the relic.

"Oh, thank the True God!" she murmured in ecstasy and worship. "Oh, I know it by its feel. And you, Martyn—"

At once she threw her arms about my neck and gave me a long and ardent kiss.

"But I smell something and I think it's blood," she went on.

"I killed Snarler with my sword."

"You killed the Dragon! Of course you would! But won't that—?"
Her words died away.

"I don't think it will cause any trouble. No one will know who did
it. As far as I can tell, I wasn't seen."

"Then that's all right. We can't go to Stonehenge, as I promised,
but we can sit a few minutes on the steps of the portico. Papa won't
wake—he sleeps like a baby. You've earned my favor. I was going to
give myself to you—my whole self—but that might be my ruin, and I
dare not. But I know a young man's needs—my father is forever warning me against them. Don't touch me, but I'll touch you. Wouldn't
that make you happy, and ease your worked-up nerves, so you could
go home and sleep well?"

A moment ago I had been in almost frantic haste to deliver the
trophy and hasten home. Now I was engulfed in a warm flood of
craving, nature's inevitable response to her suggestion, and I could
not think of danger in the delay, or else I dismissed it as unreal. Such
is the way of lusty youth, and all the angels in heaven, and all the
dictates of conscience, cannot change it.

I loosened my clothes to admit her hand. It did not falter in the
least, it was a purposeful, almost a greedy hand, and in hardly half
a minute she uttered a gasp, spread her knees and with her free
hand fairly jerked upward to her waist the loose garment she was
wearing. The invitation would have been irresistible if I had tried
to resist it, which act was unthinkable. After brief convulsion we both
uttered long, happy sighs.

"Go home now, Martyn. Have no fear—you're in the care of St.
Winfrid. We haven't sinned. He was the most understanding of saints.
Be happy as I am."

In a moment I was on my way, the same way I had come. The
minutes sped, and I was in our cottage, with the door locked, my
sword soon carefully washed, the pink water thrown out, and my boots
behind a loose board in the back of a cubby. I undressed without
haste and got into bed. I lay awake not more than twenty minutes,
fear at odds with exultation, and then suddenly I fell asleep without
knowing I had fallen there.

Just after dawn—I saw its grayness on the window—I was wakened
by a strong rap at the door. Then I could be glad I had been rewarded
for my quest, for in the door stood Joe Brook, the constable at Amesbury.

"What do you want, sir?" I asked, my heart fainting but my voice
strong.

"Martyn Sutton, I want ye. Here and now I put ye under arrest, for trespass and for breaking and entering, and I warn ye anything you say can be used against ye."

2

Surmising the main of what had happened did not take me very long. In all truth, my head remained wonderfully cool, and a rush of what were probably right guesses came into my mind apparently simultaneously. I had been mistaken in thinking that Snarler's dying yelp had not waked the gatekeeper, and instead of tardily, he had sprung straight to the window. A cowshed, painted white, had stood about fifty yards from the cottage, and about twenty yards farther back from the hedge. I was running west, the gibbous moon had hung behind me in the east; and for a brief second my shape would loom against the shed's palely glimmering side. Mr. Harrison had recognized me by my shape and height, and undoubtedly he had seen the lower part of the sword—scabbard thrusting backward from my side.

"Do you intend to take me now?" I asked the constable.

"I'll not march ye to jail in your nightshirt, but I'll stay close to ye while ye dress."

I went to my father's bedchamber to dress. He would be out of bed already and pulling on his breeches. Instead of in my own closet of a room, I chose to carry my clothes into his room; he might have something important to tell me while I was dressing. This I did slowly, at which the constable made no protest. He was enjoying this show of his authority before a peasant highly regarded by the folk and by Lady Isobel Wade. Also my sire was known as stubborn, refusing to suffer any illegal humiliation at the hands of his betters.

"Wi' what have ye charged Martyn?" my father asked.

"With willful trespass of Mr. Wade's park, and breaking and entering his house."

"When did this occur, an please ye?"

"About half an hour after midnight."

"The charge strikes me as cur'ous. Why do ye put in 'willful trespass?' Breaking and entering alone covers and includes willful trespass."

The constable did not like this question, and could not immediately lay tongue on an answer.

"Well, he had a sword with him, and he killed Mr. Wade's fine, trained watchdog, worth all of five pounds."

Still he had not answered the question of my sire, who had not asked it from curiosity as to the niceties of the law. I at once perceived his real reason for the two charges; on the first my guilt could be readily proven in court, but of the second there was little or no certain evidence.

"Do you reckon if Martyn broke and entered, his purpose was burglary?"

"'Twould be a charitable charge, considerin' he was wearing a great sword, and he'd been a suspect of one murder—you'll excuse me for mentioning it, Mr. Sutton, it coming so close home—but ye asked me a question and in respect to ye I answer it man to man. Also he was the finder of the remains in another murder."

"In both cases my son was absolutely cleared, as ye well know. So I don't find your charge charitable. Were articles of value stolen from the house?"

"Mr. Wade hasn't told us o' any yet. But it's got hunnerds of pounds of articles o' value; ye wouldn't expect him to miss any of 'em, yet, would ye now? But he'll or her ladyship will find out what's missing before he comes to trial, and ye can put that in your pipe and smoke it, Tam Sutton."

"My Christian name is Thomas. And if Martyn broke and entered, what did he break and how did he enter?"

"'Tis a term o' law, as ye know. I don't know that Martyn broke anything. But there's a tree just outside what Mr. Wade calls his chess room, and the windy won't quite close. But 'tis the upstairs maid's custom to close it well as it will on cold, windy nights, yet she found it two feet open. Martyn had climbed the tree, opened the windy more, and crawled in."

"Are you going to take Martyn to jail without first searching for the loot he supposedly stole?" my father asked. "If you are, I want to tell you he has twelve or thirteen gold sovereigns and some white money brought home from his sea voyage fighting the dons."

"That's common knowledge. Now, Martyn, ye'll walk beside my horse to Amesbury. I'll not put ye in irons, for ye know better than to try to leg it, for then you'd be a man wanted, with a price on your head, and be chased with musketeers and dogs."

"No, I'll not try to leg it."

I was dressed by now, and had put my best coat, breeches, and shoes in a friz bag, light on my shoulder, to wear when I appeared before a magistrate, or, as was perfectly possible, in a solemn court of law. Ere we departed from the house, my father managed to whisper brief instructions. The constable and I started for Amesbury, with my walking meekly beside his horse. He seemed somewhat grumpy. At last his rather slow wits collected themselves, cunning glimmered in his eyes, and he spoke.

"Martyn, the judge has a lot o' leeway in passing sentence on breaking and entering."

"Yes, sir."

"He can order the gallows, or as little as five years in jail. He has the right to suspend sentence, if he thinks 'tis justified. Suppose you confessed to me you were tempted, you wanted money for this or that, but when you had broke into the house, you took thought of the 'normity of your offense, and didn't take nothing. Then while you was running, you killed the dog to save your own life."

By these remarks he had told me what I had wildly hoped but of which I dared not try to verify without self-exposure. Very plainly the searchers had not missed the silver locket.

This my wonderfully astute father, of long experience at listening to tones of voice and watching facial expressions, had surmised. Thus his parting advice:

"*Admit nothing but trespass of the grounds.*"

"I didn't break into the house, Constable Brook."

"If ye do what I tell ye, I think Judge Willoughby would suspend sentence. He's not one of these hanging judges, nor a long-term judge, and if a young fellow shows he's not a criminal at heart, he'll go out o' his way to grant mercy."

"I'll not confess what I didn't do."

"When ye tried the inner door, leading to the other rooms, ye found it locked."

"I didn't try it, because I wasn't there. But I knew it was kept locked."

"How could ye know that?" the constable asked triumphantly. "Ye're not one that Mr. Wade invites to game with, and play chess."

"Mistress Barton told me, one day when she was telling me about the master's wonderful set of chessmen, brought from India."

"Mistress Barton's long in her grave, and can't bear witness in court. And it was them chessmen you came to steal. He paid a hunnerd pounds for that set, hand-carved in ivory and jade, and brought from Cathay by way of India. Then you got to thinking you couldn't sell 'em without getting caught, and you leaved them be."

"I wasn't there."

"Ye didn't look into a metal dish on a desk. If ye had, ye'd found some old silver coins." He was watching me sharply.

"I wasn't there."

"They was silver crowns of Edward VI, and Queen Mary's shillings with the picture of her husband Philip. Knowing young man like ye would know that curiosity shop in Lunnon would give gold sovereigns for them old silver crowns and pay double or treble for Queen Mary's shillings."

"Were any of them missing?"

"Didn't I tell ye, ye didn't find that metal dish?"

"Yes, sir, you did. How could I find it when I wasn't there?"

"Ye were seen in the park. Ye can't poach hares at night, or tickle trout on windy nights. What was ye doing there? Come to pay a social call on the master?" The constable was getting angry, as much with himself as with me.

At Amesbury, I was not confined in the little keep, used mainly for disturbers of the peace on festive nights, and instead my wrists were bound with a hempen rope while another piece secured both ankles against my taking more than a two-foot stride. Something rather extraordinary had occurred. An empty lumber wain was leaving at noon for Savernake, only twenty miles from Devizes, where Assizes had begun the day following Twelfth Night. The rhyming of the town's name with that of solemn court amused me briefly, for I could think of little else in the least pleasant. The driver would carry me that far free, provided the constable rode with him on the seat, his pistol ready for roadknights who were thick just now at the edges of Savernake Forest, where much woodcutting was being done for the Queen's ships.

"The shire's responsible for your transport, and provision en route," Constable Joe Brook told me. "'Tis a provision agin you proving innocent, in which case you could levy agin the shire if ye must pay your own way. In this case the driver's charging nought, 'cause he knows me for one handy with a pistol, but I warn ye, the fare bought by the shire is bread and water, and if ye want to eat well, in the courtyard of inns, ye'll pay it out o' your own pocket." But I could wager that the officer would collect from the shire treasury just the same.

We traversed the forty or so miles in an even two days. At Savernake I hired a horse at my own expense, rather than walk, reaching Devizes in about seven hours. Here I was put in quite an elaborate jail, at the moment fairly crowded with men and women under arrest and waiting trial, besides those serving terms for offenses less than felonies. It was a gloomy hole withal, rat-ridden, dirty, and often pestilent; but the town was festive. Trade was never half so good when court was not in session, for it brought here not only learned, free-spending judges, but lawyers, clerks, bailiffs, constables, and the loving families of prisoners to be tried.

"Do ye want a lawyer?" Constable Joe Brook asked me. "'Tis my duty to tell ye, ye need not go to the expense unless ye so request, for his honor the judge will let ye tell your story before the bar. One who's worth his salt will charge ye a whole pound."

"Still I want a lawyer."

"If you're convicted, his charge will be the same."

"That I know."

"Well, I'll get ye Mr. George Peabody, who's Wiltshire born." I reckoned that Mr. Peabody would clear about sixteen shillings out of twenty.

The young man came to see me, and I was pleased with the constable's selection. If Mr. Peabody cared not a fig for my future, he was zealous to maintain his reputation as an adroit and, on the whole, successful barrister. He questioned me with the greatest care. I told him not a very likely lie to excuse my trespass of the park, still by far the best that I could invent, all others insulting the intelligence. Mistress Barton had been my benefactor; because of her I could read and write and employ the good speech on which the lawyer had commented with some amazement. I had been allowed to visit her on her deathbed and there she had told me she had left a gift for me, concealed behind the loose footboard of a bench in a wicker structure in the rose garden. This stratagem had been needful to conceal the giving from her brother, Master Wade, who did not approve of "spoiling" the peasantry. I had brought my sword for protection because of the series of murders lately perpetrated in our part of Wiltshire. But I had not gained my destination; the wicker house was southerly of the mansion and I was afraid a crosscurrent of air would permit Snarler to scent me.

I told him that the window fronting the oak tree would not close within six inches of the sill, and could be raised somewhat only with a loud, scraping sound: this I had had from a housemaid with whom I had walked out ere my voyage on the *Elspeth,* and who had since moved to Scotland, leaving no address. At this he questioned me about my adventures at sea. Had the *Elspeth* sunk or seized any Spanish ships? How many men had we lost in the fight?

I told him of my knowledge of the precious chessmen kept in the master's gaming room, and of it being kept locked from the inside— again naming Mistress Barton as the source of my information. I thought of her, as I lied so fluently, but knew well that she would not contradict me even if she were able to raise her voice from her deep grave.

Still the point that impressed the barrister most was that no charge had been made against me for theft. "But I wish you hadn't killed the dog," he remarked.

"I didn't want his fangs in my leg," I answered patiently.

"Well, I can only hope that his honor isn't a dog lover. The French-men say we English care for nothing but horses, dogs, and bottles—leaving out their own preference above all things of earth."

He left presently, advising me to plead guilty of trespass, but in-nocent, with all the earnestness I could muster, of breaking and enter-ing. In that case my sentence would not likely be more than thirty days in a common jail. The lie would come easy on my lips. In all truth I had not "broken" into the mansion; I had crawled in through an open window.

The case was called two days later. I wore my best clothes, minded my best manners, but did not bow and scrape to anyone. When I glanced about the court room my awed heart was given a great and solemn lift. My grave father, sitting there with his head up, was its main thrust. Of course the gatekeeper, Harrison, was pres-ent, for he was the mainstay of the Crown's case, but present also were Preacher Powell and his daughter Winifred, and which counted vastly more in impressing the court, Lady Isobel Wade. Since sum-mons to appear could not possibly have reached them in time, beyond all question they had come as volunteer witnesses. The master was also present, looking somewhat glum. I thought that his main purpose was to try to restrain his nobly born wife from speaking too em-phatically in my behalf, thereby signifying that she was too partisan in the peasantry's favor, too lenient toward their failings, and in fact a traitor to her class, which his marriage to her had brought him nigh. Why, he was often addressed as Squire and sometimes sat in almost noble company!

Somewhat to my surprise a considerable number of yeomen and peasants, plainly countrymen, sat on the back benches. Knowing very little about the case, still they were biased in my favor. The only plausible reason was the current belief that despite the Great Charter and the Queen's liberality, a peasant stood a poor chance in court against the nobility and gentry.

Despite his impressive robe and big wig, the judge did not look formidable, only serious; and his countenance was handsome and dis-tinguished. After the Queen's prosecutor and my advocate made their opening statements, the Crown called its first witness. Mr. Harrison told of his wakening and his clear view of me through the window, making swiftly toward the hedge. His voice and his manner carried such conviction that Lawyer Peabody did not ask him a single ques-tion.

The Crown's second witness was Annie, one of the mistress' up-stairs maids. Her testimony was brief, that the night of the crime was cold, with "an east wind that fair bit her to the bone," and she had closed the window, as far as it would close, in the master's chess room. And when, next morning, she had seen it open a good two feet, it gave her a start, it did, and she was all a-tremble. No, there was no bad feeling between her and the defendant. "I leave him be, and he leaves me be." Had she ever any reason to believe that the defendant was a thief? She couldn't say she had, but she didn't hold with young men of his station reading and writing, and using big words, as though they was gentry.

"I think that last is irrelevant to the case," the prosecutor remarked dryly, at which my fellow peasants laughed, and the judge reproved them.

Mr. Peabody questioned Annie with great courtesy, but with great care.

"Annie, is the window in question ever opened as far as it will open, to air out the room?"

"I grant ye, that it is, 'specially when the master and his friends have been gaming, and smoking pipes."

"Had they been doing so on the night before the alleged crime?"

"That, they hadn't."

"Had it been opened the day before the alleged crime?"

"Yes, sir, by Katie Small, the other upstairs maid. But it didn't need it. 'Twas the very thought that struck me, when I shut it."

"When going about your nightly duties, just before you go to bed, have you always remembered to close it?"

"'Tis my duty, and a habit wi' me beside."

"But on the night in question, you had an engagement to walk out with a young man." And this was a shot in the dark.

"What if I did? 'Twas a young man of my own station, not one wi' big and high-sounding talk. The master and the mistress too—they don't mind our walking out a little while."

"What time did you meet this young man?"

"'Twas no more than half an hour after I heared the big clock of St. Mary's Church in Amesbury strike nine. The sound carries wondrous far on still nights, and comes clear as you ever heared when there be an east wind."

"You were to meet your young man at nine, so you were already late when you left the mansion."

"That was 'cause Katie and I had to take down and set up some beds."

"How did that happen?"

"Some bugs got in 'em."

This caused a gale of laughter from the back benches. The judge rapped the bench with his gavel.

"'Twas no fault of the mistress," Annie protested indignantly. "I think they was brought there by a couple of nephies of the master who had visited him in the fall, but he himself said they was roisterers and scapegraces."

"The subject of bugs will be dropped," the judge said sternly.

But I could not resist a glance into the faces of the master and Lady Isobel. The latter seemed to be trying to control her amusement; but the former was plainly furious with Annie. This was too sharp a reminder of his own sire's humble origin.

"I propose, Annie, that on this particular night, when you were already late in keeping your engagement with your young man, you forgot to lower the window."

"He's not my young man. He's just an old friend, and what harm be there in—"

"Annie, you have not answered my remark about the window."

"Well, if I forgot to lower it, and I'm almost sure I didn't 'twould be a wonder."

"You said 'almost sure.'"

"Who can remember every little thing? I believe I shut it, and that's Jesus' truth."

"I have no more questions."

The lawyer threw me a half smile, although wholly triumphant. His ruse had succeeded, and the whole trial was going exceeding well. Then a Dark Spirit whom I had known always, who had his lair in the deepmost of my mind, confided in swift intimation that it was going almost too well. I was missing something, failing to catch a sign of dire import.

The Crown now called to the stand Amos Little, the master's gamekeeper.

"I suppose there's a certain amount of poaching of your master's fish and game," the prosecutor asked.

"Yes, sir, more than I like, I'll tell you that, but it's a hard thing to stop."

"Has the defendant ever poached?"

"I've never caught him at it, or he'd heard from me, still I don't doubt he's done it. Shot grouse with his bow and arry, and tickled trout."

"Has any trusted man ever told you so?"

"No, the tenants won't peach each other."

"I have no more questions."

My lawyer had only one question, which he asked with a slight smile.

"It's a rather old custom in England, isn't it, Mr. Little?"

"I reckon 'tis older than Domesday Book."

Now the Crown called his last witness to the stand—the victim of trespass and the alleged housebreaking, and swearer to the warrant for my arrest.

"Mr. Wade, have you had any trouble with, or suspicion against, the defendant until now?"

"I was satisfied he poached my grouse and tickled my trout, but I never proved it on him."

"Did you keep any valuables in what you called the chess room?"

"Yes, sir, I kept my chessboard there, and the finest chessmen in West England. They were ivory and jade, and a curiosity shop in London, or even one of those scoundrels folk call a 'fence' would have given twenty pounds for 'em. I take it, that's what Martyn came in to steal, then got to thinking they could be traced—"

"Your honor, I object to the question, and the accuser's answer," my lawyer cried sonorously. "The question should have been, had the accuser missed anything of value. I ask that his attempt to predicate defendant's thoughts be stricken from the record."

"Your objection is sustained. The clerk will strike Mr. Wade's final remark from the record."

"He's your witness," the prosecutor said sourly to my advocate.

"I will detain you only briefly," the latter remarked with great civility to the master. "Did you, or did you not, miss anything from the room, of value or of no value?"

"No, sir, I did not."

"Did you find any evidence that an intruder had been in the room, such as mud from boots, drawers open, and the like?"

"No, sir, I did not."

"Then your allegation was based wholly on the maid Annie's statement that she had partially closed a window that in the morning was found open?"

"I reckon it was, but what was he doing around my house, and he killed my dog?"

"Your first question will be answered when I call the defendant to the stand."

The Crown had no choice but to rest its case. My advocate asked permission to call character witnesses, which the judge granted. These were Edward Powell and Lady Isobel; both were told they could legally decline, since they had not been served with summons, but both accepted. Their testimony was substantially the same; that I had never been arrested on any charge until now, engaged in no broils of which they had ever heard, and was of good moral character as far as they knew. Lady Isobel remarked that I had served the Queen against the dons and had received promotion.

When my time came, Mr. Peabody questioned me closely as to my relations with Mistress Barton. When the prosecutor charged that this matter was irrelevant, my advocate told the judge he would presently show its relevancy. He pictured a childless widow who had taken such an interest in a peasant boy with a quick mind that she had taken much time and many pains to teach him reading and writing and the love of books. With these facts established, he asked me my purpose in trespassing in the park, in fact drawing near the mansion, on the night of the alleged breaking and entering. I told the specious lie of looking for a remembrance from Mistress Barton in the so-called summer house in the rose garden, and most members of the audience nodded with satisfaction.

In "summing up the case," my advocate devoted all his breath to my service on the *Elspeth*. I was not an officer—I was an English peasant, born in a humble cottage—and I had been signed on as an apprentice pikeman. Before the cruise was over, I had been promoted to pikeman first class, the kind of promotion that really counted, not brought about by preferment, but by behavior in battle. I had taken a cutlass cut, and the judge could tell by my appearance, walk and posture, that I was an English fighting man.

The prosecutor made no concluding address of any kind. I took it that he was fearful of trying the judge's patience. Then his honor sounded the bench with his gavel, and began to give his decision.

"The Crown's charge against the defendant of breaking and entering is based wholly on a housemaid's testimony that she 'believed' she lowered a window, despite her haste to walk out with a young man. There is not a vestige of other evidence, and I hearby find the defendant innocent of that charge."

Applause began in the back benches which the judge quickly arrested by sharp raps of his gavel.

"The defendant has admitted committing trespass on Mr. Wade's park," the learned judge went on. "All that remains is to declare the penalty he must pay. The trespass occurred on the home acres of his kind and generous master, and he went there armed with a sword. Therefore, it is my decree that he serve the maximum sentence for trespass, which is six months in prison and in irons."

Six months! Great God, did he say six months? I saw the color drain from my father's face, and from many peasant faces; and I could not doubt if it drained from mine. Instead of winning a victory I had suffered dire defeat.

"In the act of trespass, the defendant killed a valuable dog belonging to Mr. Wade," the judge went on. "In lieu of a fine, I order that he pay the former owner the dog's worth. Mr. Wade, what do you declare a fair valuation?"

"Why, I'd say ten pounds."

But Lady Isobel had leaped to her feet. She could not do much for me, but she might do something, and I knew she intended to make a mighty effort. She stood tall and imperious with a spot of color in each of her pale cheeks.

"Your honor, have I your leave to speak?" she asked in her strong voice.

"It is somewhat irregular, your ladyship, but you have my leave."

"Snarler was not my husband's dog. He was my dog. He was given to me as a puppy by Lord Woodward, of Cheshire, when a traveler was waylaid and killed near by husband's estate. Long I have perceived he is too savage a dog to be turned loose in the park where he might attack innocent visitors, as indeed he once did. So is it not my place, rather than my husband's, to declare his value?"

"What do you say to that, Mr. Wade?"

"I believe that by law a wife may possess personal property, even though her real property becomes that of her husband. I will be satisfied by Lady Isobel's estimate."

"Then, Lady Isobel, you may state the sum."

"I will say five shillings. But in all truth I would have freely given five pounds to be rid of him."

Not one hair of the judge's wig was turned. He spoke with great dignity.

"Martyn Sutton, you will serve six months in the prison of Devizes and pay Lady Isobel Wade the sum of five shillings for killing her dog while committing a crime in the dead of night. I declare the case closed."

At that he rapped three times with his gavel, rose from his chair, and started to depart for his chambers. Many of the spectators, especially my fellow peasants, were tardy in stumbling to their feet, and then they stood with bent heads and downcast eyes, sorrow and what seemed shame on their weathered faces.

In my face was all strength of spirit that I possessed. I had been acquitted of housebreaking, I was not a felon, but all the signs lately had foretold this: these cards had been in my hand, Fortune had befriended me. But she remained the errant whore that all thoughtful men had long deemed her, kissing and embracing him she seemed to favor, her hand meanwhile reaching for his purse, or aiming her keen knife between his ribs where his heart beat. By my spending half a year in a loathsome prison, Raleigh's ships would no doubt sail without me. I would suffer whippings for trifling or accidental breach of the rules, or for a jailer's spite; I would eat slop, my clothes and body would be befouled; it was easy to catch jail fever and be buried in haste in the prison yard.

All this was my reward for the obtaining for a dreamy, fanciful young girl a silver disk containing some white hairs, quite possibly a chapman's cheat to start with. Still I was not such a self-liar to lay any blame on Winifred; she had offered to release me from my romantic promise. There was only one fool whom I must watch and guard and discipline all my life long, and that was my fool self.

Chapter VI

CROSS WINDS

1

Now that it is long done, still I wish that I could lift out of my life, and somehow obliterate the fact of the term I spent in prison. If its purpose was to teach me a lesson, I had learned it the first day, if not the first hour; but I do not think this was its purpose. Rather it was to show that no matter how poor or humble or troubled a man's life might be outside the walls, how much worse it would become, how wretched and shameful and hated by its possessor, by his life inside. Indeed it did not have the worth of a healthy rat's—if he should be caught breaking a law ordained by the mighty and the great.

My lot was no worse than a hundred others'. My offense—not that for which I was convicted but that for which I was acquitted—was in many instances of less affront to my betters than was theirs. Most of my fellows in the foul dungeon had stolen a little red money with which to buy drink or food. There were no great criminals here, famous road knights or coiners, for these when caught were invariably hanged, and that ended it.

The prison itself was no worse than a score of others: experienced jailbirds said so. The food was bad but not worse; our wretched coverlets were as louse-ridden; the rats were as numerous and as hard to catch to half bake over the meager blazers and eat. As for the stench, a man got used to it, it was such a verity of prison life, that a prisoner could hardly compare it with that of some other jail; there was not a farthing's worth of difference really. There was the same bribery and vice; the same scurvy tricks were played on prisoners if they had no money to grease the hands of the guards. Wisely I had turned over to my sire every gold piece in my pouch; he would change one of them from time to time into pennies or, at most, to groats and bring me coins when he was permitted—again by bribery—to visit me. These coins were not stolen from me by my fellow prisoners: partly because I was a light sleeper and partly because I had not yet been weakened by vermin bites and semi-starvation and hence could defend myself.

The weight of my irons was less than most—this concession had been made because I was not a felon—but chafed as badly and caused the same kind of sores. But there were sores within my soul which were more irking, caused by its degradation. The guards were not allowed to lash us without the warden's consent, but they could cuff us about and kick us on the shins or even in the groin, and their most common insult was to spit in our bowls of mush. But I ate my portion just the same. I did not have an especially strong stomach, but I had a strong enough will to do everything possible to maintain my bodily strength.

I made no friends with fellow prisoners and I did not even learn to speak their language. This caused no abuse from them or concerted attacks; they were restrained by fear. That fear was the consequence of one fact: that my term was half a year while theirs was mainly from five to twenty years. When I walked free, they did not know exactly of what I would be capable in the way of revenge. Also it was soon evident to their wits, some of these dulled by despair and some whetted rat-sharp by a powerful instinct to survive, that I had powerful friends.

Except for my sire, only one of these ever visited the prison, but he was the delegate of other friends. The visitor was a brown-bearded man, who had been a slave for seventeen years in the Spanish isles. The news of my imprisonment had been slow to reach Kent; but when two months had passed without my answering his letter I had received just before my arrest, he had set out for Wiltshire. There he had talked to my father, to Preacher Powell, and been given a few fruitful moments alone with Lady Isobel. He had obtained permission to visit me, as an old shipmate, by presenting to the warden a beautifully made yew bow along with a quiver of arrows—the finest that this official, who liked the butts, and had more than once held a stand at a lordling's stag hunt, had ever seen.

I did not weep at sight of him, perhaps because in gaining some mastery over the effects of humiliations, I had obtained the same over those of jubilations; but my eyelids smarted and burned. He was plainly dressed; he did not wish to attract attention from the keepers. His first words were, that he had no news of assured goodness, the reason being that Thomas Wade had made up his stubborn mind that I must serve my sentence, which he fancied would reduce poaching on his lands, this last offense the only one that his tenants knew I had regularly committed. Also he had lost some face with the gentry for having charged me with a felony of which a stern judge had found me innocent. His wealth gave him power; and even his nobly born wife could not move too openly in my behalf. Yet she was moving cautiously and, my friend thought, with some hope of success.

Tom Warner would not tell me the direction she had taken—she had asked him not to, lest it raise my hopes in vain—but he himself believed she might succeed in her enterprise.

My father had supplied him half a pound, which he delivered to me in groats. The quiet and complete earnestness of his resolve to help me lessened greatly the pall upon my spirit, making all physical abuse easier to bear. He told me too that Richard Wade, almost fully recovered from swamp fever, had moved to help me, but had picked the wrong man to whom to appeal. It was his friend, the son of a rich wool buyer in Bristol, who in turn knew the Earl of Lockstone, on a friendly footing with Lord Essex. But if Essex ever mentioned to the Queen an obscure peasant in a North Wiltshire prison, which intelligence denied, her reply was hoity-toity! In the midst of her mourning for her beloved cousin Mary Stuart (so I fancied Queen Bess scolding) to call her attention to such trifles!

I have boasted of my self-control. One morning, the second monthly observance of my ironing, I lost it completely, and could thereby have lost my life by the slow torture of attrition. A guard we barely knew, called Lambeth Joe, had been assigned to our hall of the prison, and since it was in the way of a demotion, his mood and manner were vile. I had read aloud to a fellow prisoner a new set of rules posted on what my fellows called the Bad Luck Sheet, the contents of which were always quickly circulated because of a half dozen of our number being able to spell out its words. But I read it rapidly, with precise pronunciation, and unhappily had not noticed the guard in hearing.

"Why, you're the best reader we've got in this crib, and that 'cludes a thieving lawyer's clerk.

"Thank you, sir. I had hard schooling."

"I 'member your case. You was 'quitted of breaking and entering—some toff managed that for you—and they only got you for willful trespass. Yet you was son of a tenant who couldn't read and write."

"Yes, sir."

"You couldn't of took that schooling without a sharp mind. Now where did you get it, you reckon?"

"Some illiterate people have sharp minds, and my father is one."

"I reckon he did have. Didn't I say a toff fixed it with the judge?"

"Sir, I don't see the connection."

"There was a connection, all right. I reckon that eighteen or twenty years ago your ma was right pretty. The toff don't come no more, but he ain't forgot them good times, or what he left one time where he shouldn't have left it."

"Sir, my mother is dead, and I respectfully request—"

"Cut out 'em big words. I'm talking plain talk. I don't reckon that toff had to come on the sly. Your pa always had work to do, away in the fields, on them days. I reckon he welcomed the shilling, or maybe two, that the toff gave him. And besides he gave you that 'bility to learn reading and writing. Siller and a bright boy, too. That whore did herself well."

"Sir, isn't it the rule of this prison that the guards cannot personally insult a prisoner?"

"You don't like what I said? Maybe you'll like this better."

With that he gave me a vicious slap on the side of my face. Both of my arms lashed out, the iron wristcuffs and the heavy chain between impeding them not at all, and one fist caught him full on the jaw. He reeled back, stumbled and fell. Because this had attracted the attention of many prisoners, he dared not strike me with his cudgel. He rose, livid with fury, stepped to my fore, and spoke in low tones.

"I was reprimanding you for leaving your bowl unrinsed—"

"Sir, too many using the well—"

"And I seen you gather your chain in your hands to strike me with it. I slapped you for that and you strook me. 'Tis not 'xactly so, but even Mistress Strictland won't know that, and you wite and see what happens."

I had never heard of Mistress Strictland and did not see the connection; but very shortly I saw what happened.

In about the center of the big, chill chamber an iron pipe fifteen feet long and about two inches in diameter was clamped to the stone floor at each end. One of the clamps could be unfastened by a big iron key, and that end raised high enough to slip through an ankle ring of my leg irons. Then the clamp was relocked, and I was a prisoner in the bilboes, a name hated worse than the lash in the prison because, although the bilboes was not as brutal as the lash, in the long run it was more cruel. The mind was tormented and the soul was wounded and what was left of manhood was abused.

"This will be your 'appy 'ome," the jailer informed me with mock courtesy, "for the next two weeks."

The inmate became the shame of all his fellow prisoners, for unless one of them was merciful enough to put his slop pail in reach of the bilboed man, the latter must attend to his natural needs on the floor in sight of all, and offending all unless the bucket was likewise emptied and washed by some other Samaritan. One such must bring within his chain's reach the inmate's canvas mat and lousy quilts, or he must try to sleep on the cold, damp stone with no cover but his clothes, and two weeks of such exposure usually brought inflammation to the lungs and swift, merciful death.

My fellow prisoners drew away from me as though I had the plague. Great misfortune, at the hands of Fate or men, such as a twisted body or a terrible mangled countenance or the depths of poverty are indeed like a catching sickness in repelling people; not always because of pitilessness of heart, and perhaps as often because of sensitivity of soul, whereby the person cannot come near another of extreme affliction without sharing that affliction. Also most of the prisoners had detected reptilian malice toward me in Lambeth Joe's actions and his voice; they could not be blamed for desiring to escape his notice; it would take real heroism to do anything to ease in the least my torment and shame. They knew I had finished eating my breakfast much less than half an hour ago; that nature's call would soon, if not already, become irresistible.

A grizzled old villain had just washed his slop pail in the flowing well. Its outlet was an open sewer but its inlet was through clay, and thus the well was not so foul as to demand abolishment by inspectors, one of them a doctor, who visited the prison four times a year. He stopped a moment, gazing thoughtfully at me, meanwhile trying to catch a louse biting him under his befouled shirt. His name was Cockstreet Jim. Thus he and the guard were both Londoners and quite likely had known each other in the gutters of the capital. Jim had been sentenced for life for homicide of a fellow ruffian.

He made up his mind, went to the corner where I slept, got my slop pail, and set it in my reach. Then he brought what must be called my bed, and the friz bag assigned to me by the warden to hold such personal belongings as were permitted in the prison, soap, a comb, a washrag, a prayer book, if I wished it, a few old clothes, a box of ointment for jail sores, and even a little hard bread or dried meat that might be brought me by kinsmen. Of course no metal objects, capable of use as weapons or tools, were permitted.

"I'll come and git your bucket and wash it out for ye, when ye've used it," the old man told me, "but don't thank me. I'm not doing it for ye; I don't know ye from Adam's off-ox, anyhow ye're not our kind. I'm doing it to spite Lambeth Joe, and he dassn't punish me. He did, one time, and was caught at it, and was fined two shillings by the warden."

I did not know whether to believe this last. Jim would not want me to think he was so mushy as to do a good deed for its own sake.

But while the minutes passed at such snail-pace, Event was moving unknown to me on the Wings of Morning!

I had passed but one whole day and the fourth part of a second day in the bilboes when the flight of Event became known to me by a sudden flurry of excitement near the entrance of the hall. It was not a flurry, really; no one ran about, but all the prisoners near enough to gaze into the entrance sprang erect if they were sitting, squatting, or lying down, and all those standing stared in that direction, their arms hanging, and leaning a little forward from their hips.

Presently I perceived that someone very great was entering this chamber of the prison. Neither his ruff and plumed hat and sword, nor the lordly cut of his beard and mustache, were certain evidence of his eminence; for these might mean no more than that he was a rich lord or knight; and his being escorted by Mr. Morton, the warden, and followed by four armed pages fully certified no more than limited prominence and fame. What cinched it in my mind was his long, graceful stride, supremely confident of his bent and of obtainance of his object. He held his nose a few seconds against the room's stench, then cut down the warden, of such stature in our sight, to pygmy size by one withering, contemptuous, sideways glance. And now a notion I scarcely dared believe was bursting starlike in my brain—that this was Sir Walter Raleigh in the flesh.

I had seen his picture crudely painted on cardboard, selling for a groat in shops at Plymouth; and the trade had been lively. I thought I saw resemblance between the portraiture and the man; but my own imagination was still my main persuader of his great identity. If he was Sir Walter Raleigh, why had he visited Devizes Prison? Report had been brought by a prisoner moved from the general jail at Colchester Castle, near London, that Sir Walter Raleigh had chosen two fellow prisoners to be members of his forthcoming expedition to Virginia. Doubtful of the story, I had questioned the man and had become convinced that it was more than jailhouse rumor. The two felons were named William Clement and John Hynde, both convicted of theft.

If Sir Walter took prisoners from Colchester Castle, it was conceivable that, in passing, he had stopped to look over the prisoners here, and might choose one or two to fill empty berths on his ships.

There were two hundred of us in this immense cell; the chance of even the most upright, or the most skilled in trades useful in the colony, was pitifully small. There was absolutely and literally no chance for a rough, refractory fellow confined in bilboes unless . . .

I would not have been human, I would have been a man of iron, not sentient flesh, if I could have utterly repressed one warm wave of delicious hope that somehow Lady Isobel had reached his ear and he had stopped to question that very fellow so refractory that he had knocked down a malignant guard and was now in bilboes!

Frequently the heart of a little child bleeds with yearning. Its object may be only a brightly painted toy, costing tuppence or at most a groat, yet his desire is more intense and all-pervading than a strong man's yearning for a wench. The child cannot reckon the enormous odds against fulfillment of his passion: he knows only the craving of his heart and believes that somehow, somewhere there must be a Power that would know it and gratify it. For perhaps the duration of a second or at most two ticked off by a solemn clock, I returned to childhood, and credited that the great Sir Walter Raleigh's express business here was with me, me, Martyn Sutton. Then I cursed myself for a silly fool.

The visitor had stopped, Mr. Morton close beside him. The former asked a question; the latter began to look among the prisoners, his gaze moving rapidly as possible and yet not to overlook whom he had been told to find, and I knew he was under intense strain. Then he turned to the great knight and offered some sort of excuse or explanation. No doubt he was taking care to employ a reassuring voice and words . . .

They began to move deeper into the chamber. Their direction was generally forward, certainly not toward me. They stopped about twenty yards from me. Sir Walter spoke again; although I did not catch the words I distinctly heard their tone, cold and gray as ice. I thought that he might have asked, "You cannot identify your own prisoners by name?"

Just then the guard we knew as Jones emerged from the room where he and his fellows ate and slept when off duty. His widening eyes took in the famous knight, the warden, the armed attendants, and now a small, neatly and plainly dressed man, with a portfolio under his arm and an inkhorn hanging from a strap at his side, his position behind the armed attendants until he should be called. At once Mr. Morton imperiously beckoned to Jones. No doubt he hoped to lay on him the disfavor he himself was under from Sir Walter. The man obeyed the summons on the run.

Then the single most thrilling instant my life had ever known moved out of the curtained future into *now*. In later contemplation I wondered if the babe's first consciousness of life in the world outside the womb was its equal in intensity. In that dark warm chamber perhaps it knew it was alive, but in the thrusting and battering it had received in its descent likely it lost what little consciousness it had had until then; at least it was storm-tossed, but suddenly it perceived light, its chest hurt, it sucked in air which it gave forth in a lusty bawl; yet at this same climactic instant its soul knew of some great change, charged with hope and strength. What happened was, the terrified guard had pointed a shaking finger at me!

At once Sir Walter Raleigh came toward me in long, swift, powerful strides, Mr. Morton almost trotting to keep pace, and gazing fearfully into the handsome, lordly face. The great knight stopped a few feet from the bilboes, drove one searching glance into my face, then turned to Mr. Morton.

"Is this man Martyn Sutton?"

"Yes, your honor. He's new here, and I didn't know him well by sight, among so many, but Guard Jones will tell you—"

"You tell me, Mr. Morton, why he's in the bilboes."

"Why, I'd not rightly know. You see—"

"Men can be put in bilboes in your prison with you not knowing it?" And the speaker was not now the rollicking cupmate and prince of good fellows that his intimates recognized; he was Sir Walter Raleigh, bold adventurer into far and keelless seas. He was the grappler of Philip's ships, Lord of Virginia, and a favorite of the Queen. His tone was biting as the east wind.

"Your honor, 'tis the custom here for guards to put prisoners in bilboes, if the jailors say—"

Sir Walter turned his head, his body motionless, and faced Jones. "Did you put him in the bilboes? If so, why?"

"That, I didn't, your reverence!" Jones stammered in haste. "'Twas the guard we call Lambeth Joe—"

"Mr. Morton, please be so kind to summon the guard known as Lambeth Joe."

It was just possible that Mr. Morton misinterpreted the courteous form of the great explorer's command. His face wet with sweat in this cold room, still he did not at once obey.

"Need you waste your time on that detail, your honor? I know 'tis precious, and I'll tend to Joe, and have no fear I won't. If he put Sutton in bilboes without just cause—"

"I bade you summon him, and I mean immediately."

"Yes, your honor. Run for him, Jones, and no loitering, or you'll both lose your posts."

Sir Walter waited in grim and dangerous silence, and the wait was brief indeed. I had last seen Joe's face flushed and exultant with activated malice. Now it was gray and his eyes held no longer a snaky glitter and in roundness and emptiness were curiously like those of a dying codfish. Did I feel the least pang of pity for him? I felt only a cruel jubilation.

"Are you Lambeth Joe?" Sir Walter asked quietly.

"That's what I'm called here, your 'onor, but my rightful name—" Like most gutter-Londoners he spoke fluently, despite his terror.

"Did you put Martyn Sutton in the bilboes?"

"Aye, your reverence, I did so, but when I tell you what 'e did—"

"Make it short."

"When I rebuked 'im for not washing his breakfast bowl—"

"What time was this?"

"'Twas just six, yestaday morning—"

"Prisoners are commonly fed at five, I believe. He hadn't washed his bowl. What then?"

"As I was a-saying, I rebuked him, and when 'e cursed me, I gave him a slap, and 'e caught me off guard and knocked me down—"

"Martyn Sutton, is Joe speaking truth?"

"No, sir, he is not." I too had tried to speak quietly and calmly, but my voice trembled.

"Tell your side, and take great pains that every word is true."

"Sir, he spoke to me about reading aloud a bill on our board for a prisoner who can't read. Then he said that my mother, who is now dead, had entertained our master, and I was the master's son, not Thomas Sutton's son. He called her a name I'd like not to repeat. When I reminded him that a jailer had not right to insult a prisoner, he slapped me, and I knocked him down."

"He didn't mention the unwashed bowl?"

"No, sir, he did not until after he got up; when he boasted of what he would tell the jailer, virtually what you heard."

"Well, sink me, I've got to choose which of you to believe, but I've had that choice before now, and sometimes it was harder. Lambeth Joe, or whatever your name is, unlock the bilboes and liberate the fellow."

Not only Sir Walter's manner of speech but his voice and posture and his very mood had changed.

"Are you the Martyn Sutton who shipped under Cap'n Selkirk?" the great knight asked.

"Yes, sir."

"Your father is John Sutton, tenant under Thomas Wade?"

"His given name is Thomas, too, sir, not John."

"Why blow me down, I must be getting senile! You others wait. My business with you isn't finished. Martyn Sutton, would you like to sail on the *Lion*, one of the ships for my new venture in Virginia?

If you agree, will you remain there, one of my new colony and serve your best to make it thrive?"

"Yes, sir, I will."

"Mr. Clark, fetch me one of those forms, and a pass too, while you're about it."

The neat little man who looked so clerklike was indeed a clerk, and it was fate's little whimsy that he should also bear the name. He handed Sir Walter an impressive-looking parchment with a gold seal, and also a card.

"Now in the blank spaces, write the name Martyn Sutton. Martyn with a y, and S-u-t-t-o-n."

The clerk obeyed handily.

"Would you like to see this?" Sir Walter asked Mr. Morton, his eyes twinkling. "'Tis a full pardon for Martyn's offense, and an order for his immediate liberation, signed by the Lord Chief Justice of Elizabeth, Queen of England."

"'Tis my duty to see it, your reverence, not that I doubt—"

"Spy it out, Mr. Warden, spy it out! Hand it to him, Mr. Clark."

"I see 'tis all in order, Your Excellency," Mr. Morton decided after one swift glance at the handsome vellum, and was trying to force a note of joviality in his voice.

"I'll not report your recent laxity of discipline of your guards, but I would recommend, most earnestly I do assure ye, the immediate discharge of this liar and bully, called Lambeth Joe."

"Don't say that, your reverence," Joe pleaded. "I 'fess I did wrong to Sutton, and told a lie on 'im, but I don't hold with men of 'is station and mine reading and writing."

I had been in prison long enough to understand Joe's abject terror. He had been a prison guard a good many years, a good many former prisoners who had suffered from his abuse were now free and ranging the grogshops and the alleys of the big cities and towns, and Joe's chances for living much longer were not good. But for the second time in my life I knew hate; the first that my heart had harbored was for a wanton murderer in the quiet scenes of Wiltshire. As for Lambeth Joe, the knife or the leaded bludgeon or the garrote could not be put in use quick enough to suit me.

"Lambeth Joe—Joseph Wilson—you're discharged this instant!" Mr. Morton pronounced in his most stern voice.

"Pikeman Sutton, the *Lion* will sail from Cowes in April," Sir Walter announced in an easy tone. "No, that cuts your time too short—go aboard at Plymouth on the first day of May."

"Yes, sir, I will."

"Well, that ends our traffic here, and I might as well weigh unless—"

His voice died away and he looked curiously, with boyish eagerness, I thought, into my eyes. "Unless you, Pikeman Sutton, have private affairs to settle, which I've time to watch."

"Sir, I have private affairs with Lambeth Joe, which could be quickly settled in the courtyard before the entrance."

"Why, I'd admire to see it, when a wretch has employed foul language about my pikeman's dam. But don't waste my time with any sparring; 'twill be a full, old-fashioned trounce, known as the Devonshire Wight's Delight, or I'll ha' none of it."

"Sir, I'll not waste your time."

Sir Walter started striding toward the entrance. Before Mr. Morton fell in behind him, he looked at Joe and pointed a stern thumb in the same direction. Joe wobbled and quaked as Guard Jones marched implacably beside him, for his own skin had been barely saved, and he saw Joe as his scapegoat. In all justice to Lambeth Joe, he steadied when we gained the open ground, and for a full minute or more he fought cunningly and doggedly, dealing many a painful and at least two all but winning blows.

But his gutter agility was no real match for my peasant strength. In the end it was his own dogged courage that brought him to the awesome beating that he received. It was deeply taught in Wiltshire youth not to hit "a man when he was down," and I would not; but Lambeth would not stay down when I smote him in his eyes and nose and on his cheekbones and on his gums to break out his teeth; and I would not help him by smashing him low on the jaw, which impact carries to the brain, and makes further resistance impossible. In all truth I was in love with my own fists and the long, iron-hard muscles that drove them, and I loved the sound of the blows, the blood that spurted, and the feel of firm flesh softening into pulp. I was not avenging a woman's honor; I was the victim of no such absurd illusion; I had forgotten his dirty charge; I remembered only his locking the clasp of the bilboes. When he struggled to his knees and then by frantic will power tried to resume his feet, I gave him full time, only to blast him down again.

At long last he lay prone, the most terribly beaten man by fisticuff I had ever seen. I waited patiently and hopefully for him to rise once more—my fist against my side, the muscle quivering a little like the tail of a cat watching a mousehole. His hands went limp. His bleeding eyes closed. He breathed stentoriously through his grotesquely swollen and scarlet mouth.

"Pikeman Sutton, you hate hard, and that's not a good thing," rose a quiet voice beside me. "Or else you take your full pound of flesh as in the old tale—Italian, I think; I read it on the *Falcon,* in 1578—and that's wickeder. But you gave me what I asked, and I'll say no more."

At once Sir Walter Raleigh and his armed attendants mounted their horses. But they had to wait more than a minute for Mr. Clark to finish retching.

2

For a moment I stood in blissful revelry, hardly able to believe how much had happened in so short a time. Of course I knew that the best was my pardon and my acceptance as a colonist in Virginia; but the most rapturous was the cruel and savage beating I had given Lambeth Joe. My eyes felt small and hard and deadly; I wished he would reel to his feet and I could smash him between the eyes, not caring if I blinded him; my mouth was partly open, my lips drawn back. What this meant about myself, what it betrayed, I did not think now, or care; rather I gloried in it. Yet I had a faint awareness of having to confront it later.

I had forgotten Guard Jones, standing round-eyed and pale behind me. Suddenly I felt the need of speaking to him.

"Wasn't Sir Walter splendid?"

"*That,* he was," Jones agreed.

"I wish I could serve directly under him."

"I did *so,* on the very voyage of the *Falcon* he spoke of. I 'membered him, all right; he didn't remember me, 'o that I took care; I was in the brig when we docked at London. He was splendid, as ye say, and all who saw and heard him would agree, but do ye know the one to who he be most splendid?"

"I don't read your riddle."

"'Tain't no riddle. Every man who was ever under him knows full well. To Sir Walter Raleigh hisself."

"Don't imply to me that he was showing off."

"He never does anything else, 'cept in bloody battle. Even then, he's always in the forefront, where he can be seen and admired. Now if ye want to mangle me forever as ye mangled Lambeth Joe, I guess ye'll do it; still I've spoke truth."

"Those great eyes! Still, I'll not harm you."

"Then I'll tell ye something. You're a lucky man, Martyn Sutton."

"By and large, yes. You wouldn't call six months in prison for trespass very lucky, would you?"

"Ye had the harshest judge in all the circuits, Martyn. The jailers and us guards take note of the trials at Assizes here, talk 'em over like, and wonder who'll get what. Not one of us would've took a bet you wouldn't get five years for breaking and entering."

"There wasn't any evidence! The judge said so!"

"He was speaking of evidence 'cited in court. Could there be some that didn't get to court? A housemaid that would testify, but didn't get no chance? But I'll say no more. Like enough 'twas only guard-room rumor. It don't pay no guard to know too much, and leastwise to talk too much." He turned to go.

"Guard Jones, won't you at least tell me from whom I can hear the straight of it? Lambeth Joe spoke of a Mistress—Mistress Strickland—who wouldn't hear the straight of something he meant to do."

"She follows the circuits. She's a trimmer of ladies' gowns, touching 'em up to the latest fashion. Ye see, there be always dinners and receptions 'mongst the gentry when the big judges come, and she's one of 'em that likes to hear all the gossip, and she do hear it. She don't tell it, but she hints. But if I was you, I'd let well enough alone. You got the longest sentence his 'onor could give ye for trespass and now ye're pardoned. What need to know what strings were pulled, and such as that, to save ye five years for breaking and entering?"

"There was a noble lady who spoke for me. But she wouldn't try to influence a Queen's judge. She wouldn't suppress evidence—I'd pledge my soul on that—she's a true noblewoman."

"Could there have been anyone else?" With this grinning and tantalizing question, he left me.

Of course I thought of Richard. He had ample means and he might feel a far deeper friendship for me than I had ever hoped. My own father had no means, and would have no inclination for saving me the dread consequences of committing a felony: he was a Roman father. It seemed impossible that I could sail for Virginia, perhaps never to return, without knowing if Jones's hints had any basis, and without my making some expression to an unknown benefactor.

It was easy to learn that Mistress Strictland had rented a small, pleasant house at the outskirts of Devizes for the sixty-day term of court. I thought it would not be hard to gain admittance to the lady's presence: after I had thoroughly scrubbed myself and put on my Sunday clothes, I prepared a big paper parcel of appropriate shape. Seeing this, the lady could easily mistake me for the peasant errand-runner of a well-off household. When I confessed the cheat, she might well order me out of the house, but great gossips love gossip for its own sake; it is an uncommon but not really rare idiosyncrasy, most of its possessors being women but by no means all. I resolved to make the attempt before setting off for home.

I went to the side door of the house and a maidservant admitted me at first sight of the parcel. I was told to wait in the hall; after a muttered conversation in the next room, a lady of middle age, sharp-featured, with peculiarly innocent-looking eyes, came into the room.

"I am Mistress Strickland," she announced, "but I'm so overwhelmed with orders—"

"Madam, I do not wish to place an order," I told her when she paused for a closer look at me, "and in all truth I am an impostor."

"At least you are engagingly frank, still I have no time—"

"Let me say only this, I will sail in May for Sir Walter Raleigh's plantations in Virginia; and I was once a pikeman first class on one of his sea raiders. I owe a great debt to someone—or so it was hinted. My name is Martyn Sutton. I think if anyone can tell me to whom I owe that debt—my being saved from a long term of prison—you, madam, are that one."

She mused a while, and then asked,

"You say your name is Martyn Sutton?"

"Yes, mistress."

"Then the thought strikes me that you are indeed what you said you were, at first. Martyn Sutton—yes, that was the name of the young man—was peasant-born in Wiltshire. Your accents and grammar and diction are better than that of most rustic gentry."

"I had a wonderful teacher, now gone to heaven."

The lady moved to a chair. "You may sit down, Martyn," she told me. "It is true I heard rumors about your case, but I cannot vouch for their truth. You are leaving England—you wish to make acknowledgments—I know of no reason for withholding some of them from you. Why not question me?"

"Is it true that evidence that I was guilty of breaking and entering as well as trespass was withheld from the trial?"

"'Withheld' is a strong word. I will report that some such evidence, not of a conclusive nature, did not reach the courtroom. A summons might have been lost—something of the kind."

"Ma'am, do you know the witness' name?"

"Not her full name. She was a maid at the home of the warrant swearer, Thomas Wade—I believe her given name was Lucy. She had been secretive about her evidence, it seems, reporting it to a bailiff in Salisbury. It was that something was indeed missing from the master's chess room. A small silver disk she had seen in a metal dish."

"Do you think that evidence, had it reached court, would have brought about my conviction?"

"Not if I had been judge. It was of trifling value—otherwise it would have been locked up—and it could have been misplaced or previously stolen by a servant. But I was not the judge—His Honor Judge Willoughby was."

"Is it common for summons to be lost, or for a witness not be called?"

"Far from common. Someone in a position of authority must have provided for it."

"Ma'am, I know no one in position of authority as concerns this trial. I had never seen Judge Willoughby or any other circuit judge. None would have a motive."

"I believe that the weird evangelist, Edward Powell, was at Devizes just before the trial opened. But Judge Willoughby is a fervent member of the Established Church. It seems highly improbable to say the least—"

My brain made a powerful surge, and my scalp crept and my skin prickled.

"Did he come here alone?"

"No, I believe his young daughter—I did not hear her name—came with him."

"Well, they couldn't have done anything for me, even if they had tried. They're well-off but not rich. Preacher Powell wouldn't want to—he believes in evildoers being sternly punished."

"Please do not get the idea, Martyn Sutton, that any amount of gold could seduce Judge Willoughby from what he thought was his duty. He's a rich man by inheritance. But I'll say one thing more, after which I expect you to go without comment."

"Yes, ma'am, and thank you—"

"There was a report, whether true I have no idea, of a young girl, her identity unknown, very lovely of appearance, going to Judge Willoughby's lodgings the night before your trial, and remaining there a little more than an hour."

Abruptly she rose. I was already on my feet, my head reeling. Out of the door I went without looking back with my present eyes; but the eyes of my mind were gazing back at Judge Willoughby, as he sat with dignity and austerity at his bench. He was a big florid man, not more than fifty, and in full strength and vigor. And I remembered too well a saying I had heard more than once in Wiltshire, one of those rising from the experience and observation of the folk. It was that St. Ursula herself, to whom virgins pray, would not on her way homeward from very Rome be safe from a gentleman of fifty.

3

Only a few brief weeks intervened before I must set out for Plymouth, there to go aboard the *Lion* on the adventure of my dreams. In the first of those weeks my father recovered completely from his depression, amounting to illness, caused by my confinement in the prison. I had no doubt, now, that he would live to hale old age, working early and late with his flocks, cooking his own meals, adjusting himself to two mighty lacks, one of them the company of Mama and the other of me.

When Richard and I met for the first time after our long parting, he gave me a long, slow, quiet grin, because as well as I had known him, I would have failed to recognize him in a crowd. In the custom of soldiers, he had grown a handsome pale-brown mustache and beard; his hair had a different cut and dress; his countenance had weathered from the frosts and fogs of the Low Countries, being out-of-doors by day and night; it was more manly than before and even more impressive. His posture and his manner were those of a captain of men.

"I have some news for you," he told me. "I hope you will feel about it as I do, which is good. We are not going to be separated when you sail on the *Lion*."

"Master Richard, it is the best news I've heard since—" But I could not bring myself to mention that brought by Sir Walter Raleigh. "Still it strikes me with wonder, for riches are yours by inheritance, you have won promotion in Flanders, a brilliant future is assured you."

"As a soldier, yes. But I have no great fondness for military life. I want to fight the raw powers of nature instead of my fellow men. Anyway, it was my father's wish that I go, even if I return after a few months on one of the many ships that will be plying between Virginia and England. You see, he has invested a large sum of money—two hundred pounds—in Sir Walter's enterprise. He has asked me to sail not as Richard Wade but under the assumed name of Richard Darigem—Darigem being his granddam's maiden name. It is under that name that John White, in command of the colony, has enlisted me. The truth is, my good sire does not trust White. He doesn't think he's a strong enough man to lead a hundred and twenty or more people in settling a completely virgin land, dealing with the Indians, and fighting Spanish raiders for all we know. Almost no Wiltshire folk will be on the *Lion*—they're mostly Cheshire and Devonshire. None that I have known personally will be aboard—a little group from around Plymouth will ship on the flyboat or the pinnace. At least I'll remain incognito until I have a chance to observe White and the *Lion's* officers."

I recalled an errant thought I had once had, that for reasons inscrutable Richard seemed to like to have me in his company, or to remain in mine. It was a seeming only; it must be, because it made no sense. The fact remained, we were likely to be together a long while.

"War is at once dirty and magnificent," Richard was saying. "Cruel —killing men from ambush—a blood-crazed colonel crying 'Havoc!'— yet soldiers bravely dying for duty to—what? They don't themselves know. The Spanish die just as bravely as the patriots—perhaps with even more hauteur. Well, some Indians will die to hold their lands. Some Englishmen will die to seize 'em."

"Instead of Englishmen and Indians killing each other, why not unite with each other?"

Richard's eyes rounded very slightly; he knew the reason no more than I.

"How can you say that? We're a civilized people. Indians are painted savages."

"What difference does that make? They're human beings. Raleigh and other explorers think North America is a vast continent—the size of its rivers well-nigh prove it—perhaps bigger than all Europe including the Russias. Yet judging by the scarcity of villages, they think that the total number of Indians may not exceed the total number of Englishmen—three or four million. They'd absorb us at first, but in time we would absorb them. What do you think of that idea for settling the New World?"

"I think it's crazy!"

"Well, it may be. But it seems like common sense to me. We'll discuss it further under a giant tulip tree in Virginia."

In exactly three days there was something other to discuss—much closer to home. In one way it was rememorant to my mind of a fire that was started by lightning in the master's forty-acre field of ripe wheat in a peculiarly dry summer when I was about twelve years old. All hands rallied to fight the fire, with friz sacks soaked in water buckets, and some of the sharper men tried to burn off, extinguishing the flames as they advanced, a narrow strip of wheat to check the wind-blown fire, and from time to time it appeared the main of the field would be saved. However, the blaze seemed Devil-guided as well as wind-harried, and ever it worked around the lines, or some we had thought extinguished flared up again, and in the end the whole crop was lost, and up in smoke went a cattle barn along with the lives of several oxen.

The affair in early April 1587 began with a series of minor incidents no more spectacular and not nearly as unusual as the sight of a little flame and a stream of smoke not far from the windward rim of the big field. Mr. Edward Powell had come home, spoken to Winifred and little Owen, and withdrawn to his library. Owen had tagged his father into the room and thus escaped the care of the housemaid. What Winifred did not know was that Preacher Powell almost immediately left on an errand to the Lacey home, and so she felt free to go to the edge of the wood lot to gather a bouquet of spring flowers. She had started home when the housemaid, Emily, came running toward her and crying that Owen was not in the house or in the yard, and had the master—Mr. Powell—taken the child with him?

Winifred had tried to reassure the maid, saying that her frightened guess was probably right. But both girls remembered all too well that there was a deathtrap for toddlers just at the back of the Powell garden, which was a slow-flowing brook, almost a stream, and for a reach of about forty yards the water was four feet deep at this season of the year. True, the little boy had been strictly warned not to go near the bank, and at least until now had straitly obeyed the warning.

A passing urchin was sent on the run to the Lacey house to fetch Mr. Powell. Both girls began a frantic search of the house—the lawn and garden were all too empty of his chubby shape—looking in closets and under beds where he might be hiding. Then both ran to the brook, but it gave them no good news or bad news either, because thick grass that would not retain a footprint grew clear to the brink.

The urchin had cried the news at every cottage that he had passed, so several neighbors gathered, pale and round of eye because too clearly they recalled tragedy striking this very house only the past winter. One yeoman was astride his horse, and immediately raced off toward Amesbury to recruit a large search party, for it was possible that Owen had gone to look for Winifred in the wood lot and had fallen in a steep-walled ditch. The search was rather noisy at first, as men and women shouted back and forth, but gradually the shouts died away, and more and more people came to the bank of the brook, and stood gazing with parted lips and glazed, rounded eyes into its still waters.

First one man waded in, and then three more, and then at least a dozen in all. Some had broken branches from the garden trees, stripped them of twigs and leaves, and were using them to probe the bottom. The most frantic searcher was Mr. Powell himself. The scene was now almost deathly still, except for the little splashings made by the waders and the drawing along the brook bottom of their poles.

The silence was broken by a cry from old Pete, the gardener.

"I've found something!" he cried out. And instantly he immersed his whole upper body into the brook, and almost instantly it raised, and a long moan went up from the onlookers when they saw something, covered with mud and streaming water, in his arms.

I was among the waders, but I stood still, and so did all the others except Mr. Powell. He splashed his way to Pete's side, and I could never forget, the remembrance returning often to my waking mind and occasionally in evil dreams, the expression on his face.

"It's him, Mr. Powell," Pete said in low tones. "It's little Owen."

Mr. Powell's lips opened and he too spoke, in quiet anguish, and I was one of those near enough to catch his words:

"*Eli, Eli, why hast thou forsaken me!*"

Then Preacher Powell took the body in his hands, rinsed the mud from its garments and its face and hands, and in a reeling run made for the house. The neighbors and other searchers began to disperse, speaking in low tones or not at all. One kindly woman put her arms about the heaving shoulders of Winifred, who was crying as if heartbroken, but the girl rejected the condolent proffer and she too ran for the house. On Pete's face and in his whole posture there was incredulous horror.

Then Preacher Burberry spoke to me in low tones.

"Come with me, Martyn. You have younger eyes than I have."

We walked a little way up the bank, indeed to the boundary of the Powell home acre, and as he was plainly searching for human tracks, large or little, I did also. We found none; we could scarcely hope to do so on this grassy ground; then we retraced our steps and followed the bank downstream, passing the scene of the body's finding, again to the Powell boundary and through the hedge to the home acres of a prosperous yeoman. The brook's pace quickened slowly at this point and a narrow strip of clay between the grass and the water would have revealed tracks; but we saw not one, except the old tracks of an urchin angler. But a fallen tree limb slanted athwart a shallow about fifty paces down, and I noticed an odd-shaped object, unidentifiable at this distance, although it vaguely suggested a large rectangular basket, caught in the foliage.

I ran to get it, and still did not know what it was, knowing only it had been fashioned by human hands. It was no kind of basket. It was a curved, although far short of semicircular, piece of worked wood about four feet long, and three feet from rim to rim. I would have thought it was beech except it had nothing like the weight of beech; the thought struck me that it could be beech, bone-dry from ancient age. Certainly it had been carefully and cleverly carved from the exterior of a very large log. What was most remarkable were three strong metal bands, whether bronze or iron I did not know, shaped by a forge to fit the curve of the interior, one near the bottom, another near the top, the third in the middle. I marveled that it had remained afloat with its weight of metal until I observed that the carving had been inbent a little at the top and the bottom, whereby its whole shape suggesed a small, shallow boat.

I carried it to the Reverend Burberry, and he stared at it as might a witless man.

"You do not know what it is?" he asked.

"No, sir."

"I do not either, but I think it is very ancient, washed out of a gravel bank by a freshet somewhere upstream."

"Could it be a primitive wooden shield?"

"If so, its makers had metals and knew how to work them. Heed me, please, Martyn. I will hide this object in the high weeds yonder, and take it home after dark. It could not possibly have any connection with the child's drowning: such a thought would be madness. But our superstitious folk would think that it did; their whisperings would begin again—"

"If you please, sir, I don't think they have ever stopped."

"No good would come of their brisk resurgence. The folk would connect it with the bronze hook old Pete had found in the wood where Davie Stewer was murdered, and which is now in my collection of antiques. Both would be associated with Stonehenge, probably not a pagan temple but some kind of sepulchral monument to some early king or queen, possibly Boudicca.* The coroner will sensibly pronounce that little Owen met his death through misadventure. He tried to wade in the brook, or fell in."

I rallied my courage and remarked, "Sir, I would like to suggest an alternative to that explanation."

"I can't imagine what it might be," he answered, palpably irritated.

"I confess that the suggestion is wild in the extreme. I would not make it if I did not know something about the late Mistress Powell that Miss Winifred told me. She did not tell me in deep confidence; still I'd not want you to repeat it, please, sir, unless you think some good would come of it. Mistress Powell was the direct descendant of Owen Glendower, the last real king of Wales."

* As far as known, this theory was not advanced in writing until 1624.

"That is true. I had it from other sources."

"Also, Henry VIII proposed marriage to her mother, after divorcing Anne of Cleves, in order to placate the nationalism of the Welsh people, soon after he had admitted Wales to England in equal status with the rest of the kingdom. But the lady declined."

"If that's true, which I doubt, she knew what she was about in doing so."

"Suppose rebellion against England is being fermented in Wales—and a return of rule of their ancient royal family. Now would be a good time. England is about to fight for her life against Spain; she may win, but she would have no surplus strength to suppress an uprising in Wales. And suppose too some great English duke in Wales wished to nip that rebellion in the bud. Mistress Powell and her baby boy might have been the only living descendants of Owen Glendower."

"'Tis ingenuous," the minister remarked after a thoughtful pause, "but it won't hold water."

"I confess it will not account for two other murders, Davie Stewer's and—and—"

"Martyn," he broke in, not knowing yet what he was going to say, his only impulse to save me having to speak of Mama's murder. A sensitive man was the Reverend Burberry, a considerate man, and a gentleman; I doubted if the great gentlemen of France and Spain, with whom Richard had unfavorably compared English gentlemen, were his superior. "Martyn, most if not all those killings had to do with—but I'll not say it; it makes no sense; why should I say in the Queen's English what superstitious peasants say in dialect? I have not forgotten, Martyn, that you too are a peasant. But you are a peculiar peasant."

"I may have some rare accomplishments, your reverence, but am a peasant right on."

When we parted, I had the feeling that of all intelligent and educated men observing but not connected with the Wiltshire murders, Reverend Burberry had the deepest knowledge of them and by the same token was the most mystified by them.

4

The coroner's inquest into the death of Owen Glendower Powell was a simple and positive affair. The maid at work in a bedroom, the windows of which were open, had heard not one wail of pain or alarm, despite her quick ears, in the half hour in which the child had drowned. She had heard no splash of water caused by his falling in the brook, but there would have been very little, as the bank was only a few inches above the flood, and his weight was slight. His body had shown no bruise. Inevitably the coroner's verdict was "death by misadventure."

The time of leave-taking drew nigh. At first it was with neighbors that I knew, with the gatekeeper Harrison against whom I bore no grudge, with Mr. Holbrooke, the master's bailiff, and with Mistress Priscilla Lacey, with whom I had once shared a birthday feast. The master himself, riding down the lane, stopped his horse to speak to me.

"You would have made a good woolgrower, Martyn, if my sister Clara, Mistress Barton, had not stuffed your head with reading and writing and the bless'd God knows what else. You've heard the saying, 'educated fools.' I don't say or hint you are one, although you played the part when you trespassed my park that night, and I'll say 'trespassed' and no more, for the court found you innocent of all else. Sir Walter Raleigh has got too big for his boots, or he wouldn't go around with blank pardons, no doubt authorized by Queen Bess and signed by her Lord Chief Justice, for such prisoners as take his fancy to work his plantations across the seas. He has three jailbirds in his company that I know of. Still I've put good money in the venture, and I trust you to do your utmost to make it prosper; for you may soon long for home, where only owls and not screeching naturals break your sleep, and I'll have a place for you, a pasture and some stock, and you can live respectable, if you'll put aside this fancy stuff and buckle down like your good sire, and not ape the gentry but be respected by 'em, as the Good God intended. So I'll advise you not to look above yourself, and pay heed to what Richard tells you, for he'll not advise you wrong. And with that, I'll wish you a safe journey and good fortune."

The thought struck me that Thomas Wade had rehearsed this speech while laying awake at night. He would never quite get over the sting of making a charge against me that the court had thrown out.

I went to Pete's cottage, after work hours, to bid him farewell, and he and I talked alone, seated on his doorstep.

"Ye be lucky to be going across 'em great seas," he remarked, wiping out and putting in his pocket his tobacco pipe."

"I think so, for 'tis a wonderful opportunity for a man to get ahead, but why do you think so?"

"'Cause you're going so far away from 'em great stones."

"Pete, I don't reckon they had anything to do with what happened here."

"I told ye once, ye' be read too many books, and I told ye true. Them stones is accursed, a mighty black curse, a curse out o' Hell, and when we'll be shed of it, only the good Jesus know, for only Him can bring it about. I can't figure what your mama done to anger 'em evil spirits, likely nought on purpose, but she did somepin, and that ye can know for sartin. A good woman, she war. Once she took a barry, and filled it with broken rocks she picked up from that dark and evil ground and wheeled 'em home, and made a border for her walk to the door. On Allhallow's Eve she drawed a cross on her back door and on her front door. Still, I reckon she did somepin else, what enraged 'em hot, or she'd be alive today. Davie Stewer! A-choppin' down a tree, and hisself chopped down. It don't make no sense. But he was not right in his head, and maybe he did somefin 'at threw the Devil hisself into a fury."

Dusk was falling, and a nightingale tuned her pipe for song. It was a liquid sound, indescribably lovely.

"Pete, I don't believe a word of it," I told him. "There's evil in the world but men make it, not demons. I dare all the goblins in Hell—"

"Be still! Or if ye must speak so wild, go from my doorstep."

"Forgive me, Pete. I'm truly ashamed."

"'Tis no offense, from one so young as ye. When ye're old as me— if ye stayed in these parts, and wa'n't gone somewheres across the sea—ye'd know God hain't beat down the Devil yet, and his ministers flit about the earth, and this very corner o' it is their assembly place. Take thought o' Preacher Powell. He fought 'em the hardest, he cared nought what he said, he defied 'em in the Name that they hated most, and look what they done!"

"Pete, Mistress Powell was hanged by human hands. We don't know what was back of it and may never know. And the little boy, toddling about the yard, fell into the brook."

"I don't 'spute the crowner. Who am I, to make so bold, but I ha' my own ideas. But I wish to very God that Preacher Powell would stop his ranting against 'em stones, or else move off some place. It looked like God didn't look arter him very good, don't it?"

"I heard him say the same, only in different words." I rose and took Pete's worn old hand in both of mine. "Old Pete, we may never meet again."

"That be full true, Martyn Sutton."

"Thank you for all you've done for me."

"I've done nought, that I know of, 'cept wish you well."

"You've been my friend. I have very few friends—Mistress Barton first of all, Richard so far above me, Harry who went hare-hunting with me that snowy day. Lady Isobel herself did me a mighty good turn that day in court, but that was not from friendship but what she owed the son of a good tenant."

"She be a great lady, true as God. And as for ye—ye'll ne'er ha' many friends, Martyn Sutton, not in this world."

"I think you're right, but I don't know why."

"Nor do I. I jes' feel it in my bones. Ye strive too hard for what ye want to win. Folk can't keep up wi' ye. Ye'll tire 'em out. That's part of the reason, but not all."

"Good night and good-bye, old Pete."

"God be wi' ye, Martyn Sutton, for I reckon ye'll need Him mighty bad."

We parted; and it turned out that I need not seek a last meeting with Lady Isobel. The report was soon out that she would journey to Plymouth to bid Richard farewell. And it was my firm intention to say good-bye to Winifred in the presence of her sire; because of their late loss the ceremony could be brief and somewhat formal. Truly I had been utterly disoriented in regard to Winifred since my talk with Mistress Strictland at Devizes. My mind refused to treat with the suggestion the lady had implanted in it; for all of the strangeness I had always sensed in Winifred, and despite her romantic imagination, her paying a debt of honor owed to a peasant with her maiden treasure was beyond my credence, and I wished it to remain there. I had made a fool of myself by accepting the criminal mission; I did not want her to make a martyr of herself to redeem me from its worst consequences. Perhaps it was true that the maid Lucy's testimony had mysteriously disappeared; it was quite likely true that Judge Willoughby had entertained a pretty young girl in his lodgings at Devizes; but Madam Strictland was a congenital gossip and sensation-lover. What I wanted, was to forget what she had said. I would soon be on a ship with swollen sails; every puff of wind would carry me farther from Winifred; every moment of my voyage would thrust all my dealings with her deeper into the past. I had idolized Winifred, at the same time experiencing her common humanity; but for her to do what Mrs. Strictland had hinted was—unnatural. The French had a saying that Richard had brought back from the Lowland wars —*noblesse oblige*. It was a wonderful saying to apply to Lady Isobel's saving me a payment of twenty pounds for killing a savage dog; but, as Mistress Barton had once told me, a saying of one of Seven Wise Men of Ancient Greece, "moderation in all things."

Still, in my best raiment, and with a complaining but ruthlessly driven will, I did call at the Powell house. Emily admitted me; to my great relief Winifred was out "visiting." Would Mr. Powell care to see me a brief moment? I knew that he was grief-stricken, and if he was not receiving visitors, I could leave a message . . .

"I think he'll see ye," the girl told me. "The master is not one to shrink from any duty; and he counts it his duty to see anyone, high or low, who seeks him out."

As it happened, Mr. Powell had observed my entrance into the yard and immediately appeared in the hall.

"Martyn!" he exclaimed. "I was hoping you would call, because I have news for you."

As he spoke, I could hardly force my gaze from his face. It had changed greatly since I had seen it last. It was thin and worn and pale; still it suggested that of a seraph but one who had just witnessed the murder of a holy martyr by a Nero. Still, he gave me a wan smile.

"I came to tell you good-bye and to thank you—"

"Come into the parlor and sit down. I myself have come to a great decision that would affect what you had to say. Martyn, I have somehow taken the wrong road. I did not come to this conclusion because God did not defend my wife and little boy from a cruel death. Death comes to all; in his omniscience God wills the time of that coming. What I realized, really, was that I could do very little here in Wiltshire. In most of the people pagan beliefs are mingled with Christian beliefs; all my preaching could not weed them out. But what if I started, as the people say, from scratch? That is the way St. Winfrid, one of my favorite saints, began; he preached to a completely pagan people, and, Martyn, they caught fire! That was true of many of the early evangelists. The Christian story was not an old story to their listeners; it was fire-new. I recall a story of a Frankish pagan—I forget his name—let me call him Cedric. When he heard the story of the Crucifixion, he was heard to ask himself, 'Where wert thou, Cedric, when these things were taking place?'

"And that is the kind of innocence I could work with. I can obtain tangible results—not a brief revival of old faith, but a new, all-pervading faith." And his sick eyes had begun to gleam.

"I don't know what you mean, unless—"

"Martyn, I have talked with Sir Walter Raleigh at Cowes, on the Isle of Wight. He is a Christian knight, despite his piracies and his lecheries. He accepted my petition to be a member of his new colony in Virginia—the only man of the cloth. I will be sailing about the day you sail, not on the *Lion*, but on the flyboat—you know she's big and comfortable. And, of course, Winifred will be with me."

My spinning head remained capable of one inquiry. Although there would be other women in the colony, married and unmarried, as well as several children, how could Mr. Powell bring himself to expose his daughter and his delight, the last of those he could call his own, to the rigors and the genuine perils of the long journey and of life in a settlement at the rim of the primeval forests of the New World? The only answer I could hit upon, was that he dared not leave her in England.

5

My last evening ere the dawn on which I intended to start for Plymouth, I spent with my father, Thomas Sutton. Gazing at him in his old chair of gnarled wood, I saw that he too was gnarled, not a fault with his growth, but the consequence of hard labor and stress, over all of which he had been victorious. It had left its mark in his countenance, his corded neck, and especially in his hands and wrists. These last were mighty. And no one could gaze into his face and mistake him for a nobody. Here was a true man, honorable, steadfast, dogged, loyal to his own, intelligent by natural endowment, then self-taught.

"I wish I had some advice to gi' ye," he told me, "but I've not."

"You've given me a good deal ere now, and I feel I've profited by it."

"Ye've profited more than I can rightly explain, even counting a good woman, your mother, who loved ye a mighty heap, and the mighty good fortune of having Mistress Clara Barton love ye, and school ye in the patient way she did, never scanting the time she spent with ye, or begrudging the labor. In your name, I'll put wild flowers on her grave on every anniversary of her death as long as I live, and tie on a piece of paper which Mr. Holbrooke will gi' me, and write on it, 'From Martyn,' which I can copy if you write it for me on the flyleaf of our Bible."

"If her spirit has gone to heaven—and it will, if there is any heaven —she'll know of it, and her blessing will come down to both of us."

"Martyn, I do not believe the spirit dies, at least as long as folk remember it. I cannot dream where it lives on, I cannot picture such a place, because my eyes be of earth earthly, and it need not be made of matter; and it may be the mind of God, which is infinite, as seems the vault of heaven on a clear night. There be a bond, I believe, between the souls of living men and the souls of the dead, and I think it might be love, which is a mighty mystery too, when ye try to take stock o' it."

"She'll never be forgotten as long as my mind lives, in this world, or in any existence that might come after I leave this world. In my dying breath she'll be with me, and so will you, Papa, and so will Mama, and all else whom I have loved."

"Ye owe her a mighty debt, that much I know. And that causes me to think of them who in their youthful vanity and folly, some of 'em sons o' lords, who was given a chance to obtain learning, but who spurned it, devoting themselves to lesser things, and passing pleasures. I, an illiterate man, grieve for 'em, for I know what it is to stumble through life like a blind man, never to behold the common wonders about us, or having even an inch-deep understanding of 'em. Missing the concourse of one knowledgeable man with another, for I've marked that they seek one another out, and won't waste their time on the ig'orant. Ye be wondrously well-read, Martyn, for a man of your years. How will it help ye, in a wild, rough colony across the mighty sea? I've took thought o' that, and found the answer, if ye'd like to hear it."

"Yes, sir, I would."

"Ye can't read wi'out using your mind; if ye don't use it, then you're not reading, which means listening to a great student, or a deep thinker, or a man of mighty vision, such as a real poetry writer, or a storyteller of bounding imagination. I speak of such who set down the tales of Roland that ye read, and of Lancelot, and of Hercules. Them writers captured your mind. You'd begin readin' right after supper, and ye wouldn't believe when I called to ye that 'twas midnight. Never believe that they didn't make your own 'magination bound, and growth comes through use. Ye talk better, and ye think better, and more ideas come to ye, than an unread man can dream. Ye want to be a leader in the colony. Ye wouldn't dream it if ye didn't think ye were equal to it, and if hard times come there, as is almost certain, ye'll have ten times the chance than a lord's son whose head is thick and slow. Get riches if ye can. Riches mean added power, and who denies it is a fool. But use 'em for the good o' all. It comes to me, Martyn, that the success or failure of the colony will lie in the hands of a mighty few men, and ye can be one of 'em. And if it thrives, or bare survives, or if the colonists live, not die, and that is what ye've worked for, your main thought and purpose, then you've done which God meant for ye to do, when He gave ye human life. Ye know the word that great men use when they lay the corner stone for some noble church or building? I can't put my tongue on it, but ye can."

"I think you mean dedicate."

"Aye. I ask ye to dedicate the main of your gifts, the best of your abilities, to what's best for the colony. I'll be mighty proud of ye if ye do. Now I'm done. I've got a jug of good ale put by, and let's drink a mug apiece, enough to sleep good on, and then go to bed, for ye've hard travel before ye, down to Plymouth, and ye'll want to make a good start tomorrow."

So he brought the jug and poured the brown ale; and then, standing face to face, each of us touched his mug to the other, and we both drank.

The hours sped, and I dreamed strangely and wildly and betimes fearfully, and rose at the first paling of the stars. My sire was already up, and had prepared a hot, rich broth with wheat cakes for our breakfast. I lashed my crammed seabag behind the saddle of my borrowed horse, and I petted our sheep dog, who did not frisk about me as of yore, for she knew that all was not well with our household. Then I took my father's rough hand in mine.

"Martyn, I don't reckon we'll ever see 'tother no more."

I started to deny this, but my heart knew its likelihood, and I could not be false to that true man, my father.

"I reckon not, either."

"Ye've been a good son to me, and God bless ye."

"You've been a good father, and may He bless you, too."

Not to my amazement but to my quiet and profound wonder, tears filled my father's eyes, and then my tears filled mine.

I did not attempt to speak but I kissed my father's wrinkled cheek. Then I swung into the saddle and rode away, now and then glancing back. He was still standing at the gate, his back straight and his head high, when I came to a bend in the road. I raised my arm and he raised his, and so parted his presence with my presence and as on I rode into a new life, I must bow my head and weep.

Chapter VII

VOYAGE AFAR

1

Report had it that our fleet would count six ships, and at least one hundred and fifty colonists besides the crews. But the return of Raleigh's colonists under Lane had put a damper on the new venture; and so had the worsening threat of war with Spain. An impalpable but real obstruction was Sir Walter Raleigh's slow loss of favor with the Queen, her trust and affections bending more to Lord Leicester and youthful Lord Essex. I had the temerity to think that she should have stood by Walt. Leicester had proven a bungler in the Lowland wars. Essex had held the line at the Battle of Zutphen, but since then had done nought but dance attendance upon Elizabeth, for which skippery he had been made Master of Horse.

In any case, the plain fact was that we had three ships instead of six, and one of these a pinnace. The *Lion* was our flagship, a stout vessel of one hundred and twenty tons, under command of Captain Irish, but above him stood Fernando, a kind of commodore of the flotilla. The flyboat—meaning a coaster—was almost as large, and under Edward Spicer. Captain Edward Stafford, whom the sharp petty officers said was the best mariner of the four, commanded the pinnace. Instead of increasing as the tide on which we were to sail drew nigh, the number of colonists steadily decreased. Those same petty officers could count but one hundred and thirteen head. About eighty of these were unmarried men, or else they had left their wives at home; the number of husbands and wives were said to be ten, two of these couples having a child each and two more appeared to be expecting a child each; one woman had a babe in arms. There were four "boys"—youths of sixteen or so—and six young, unmarried women. I did not reckon these would stay unmarried very long.

Under White, dispersed on the three ships, were at least five assistants, George Howe, Ananias Dare, Christopher Cooper, Thomas

Stevens, and Dyonis Harvey, the latter the son of a knight. Cuthbert White did not have visible authority, but was on intimate terms with John White, and evidently his kinsman. A truly impressive number of my shipmates were gentry. For instance, Anthony Cage had been Sheriff of Huntingdonshire only two years before. John Spendlove was plainly rich, had his own horse and servant aboard the vessel, and held a master's degree from Cambridge.

Richard Berry had been a muster captain, according to swift-flying deck rumor. Edmund English had attended Eton College twenty-five years ago. John Jones was a somewhat famed Welsh doctor, who had written and published books concerning his art. Thomas Hewett was a lawyer, trained at an Oxford college. William Brown was a goldsmith, his presence greatly prized by the main of the colonists. No doubt he knew where to look for gold, how to mine or wash it to remove impurities, and to evaluate it. Doubtless he would shorten their road to riches.

There were three jailbirds, all on our ship—William Clement, John Hynde, and a young peasant named Martyn Sutton. As far as I knew there were only two out-and-out farmers in the fleet, Mark Bennett and a powerful-looking yeoman named John Baird. Our ironmonger— at least he was the nephew of one who had been knighted—did not look as if he had ever shaped a plowshare on an anvil. There were no cartwrights or wheelwrights that I heard of, none who had given his trade as cooper, mason, brewer, boatwright, millwright, carpenter, candlewright, glassmaker, swordsmith, or gunsmith. For that matter Richard Wade, signed on as Richard Darigem, and Martyn Sutton had no trade but fusilier and pikeman respectively. Common sense seemed to say that no poorer candidates for colonizing wilderness could hardly be assembled. I reckoned Sir Walter Raleigh had been too worried about his faltering favor with Queen Elizabeth to give much care to his choice.

The ship was well victualed, had several cannons, and a Bristol gunsmith had sold our governor forty matchlocks, cheaply but strongly made, at a pound each. These were an old-fashioned type, the match, or fuse, being a slow-burning cord stowed in a hole in the stock and running up through the hammer to ignite the powder in the pan when the trigger was pulled. Our kegs of powder seemed of scanty number, no doubt because gunpowder was being hoarded in the Queen's arsenals. If Captain Fernando gave way to his old passion for taking Spanish prizes on the journey to Virginia, we would soon have none. In this case, I could conceive no comfort more consoling than the presence in our midst of Thomas Warner, an expert bowyer and arrow maker.

Yes, there were two other consolations for the more thoughtful. These were two Indians, whom Lane had brought to England from Roanoke and who were now homeward bound. One, an impressive chieftain, was named Manteo. The other, a sullen fellow who kept to himself, was Towaye.

I decided to attempt to make immediate acquaintance with Manteo, since the fact seemed both plain and frightening that even bare and brief existence in the New World, let alone our survival and conquest, might so largely depend on him. It was a good time, for our officials and more important colonists spent most of their days in the town, or else receiving visitors and kinfolk. Mistress Priscilla Lacey had given me a little box of sweetmeats as a farewell gift. These I immediately shared with the chieftain, when I found him sitting alone and dis-consolate in the stem of our vessel, now riding at anchor in Plymouth Harbor.

It came to me with a kind of thrill that there was no clear separation in his mind between a peasant and a lord. The clothes of either one were equally strange to him; our speech about the same, our customs as curious. After making my gift, and he had munched a while, I riveted his attention by pointing to our dingey boat that lay alongside.

"English—dingey boat," I said, pointing at it.

"*Um,*" he answered.

"Indian—what?" And I pointed to his own tongue.

He shook his head, failing to understand.

"Croatan—what?"

"Canoe," he answered promptly, his dark face lighting somewhat, so happy he was to speak an Indian word.

A young spinster, Rose Payne, crossed the deck to the companion-way. I pointed at her and said,

"Woman?"

"Algonquin—squaw. Croatan—crenepa."

I had seen the word Algonquin in a paper published by Sir Walter Raleigh. He thought it referred to a great Indian confederacy, occupy-ing the coasts from Roanoke Island and the mainland halfway to New-foundland. The colony founded by the Huguenot Ribaut, now taken by the forest, was in Algonquin domain. The Croatans, with whom the colonists of the expedition of 1585 had made friends, were likely a branch tribe or kinsmen of the Algonquins.

A fisherman's wife came aboard from a bumboat with a basketful of shellfish. As she offered them to the cook, identifiable by his leathern cap and apron, she held up a wiggling lobster.

"Lobster?" I asked.

"Ah-sha-ham." Manteo pronounced this with great care.

I pointed to a loon winging its way from one freshwater pond to another. Before I could speak, Manteo pronounced,

"A san-am-aw-queo."

Then I learned Manteo's tribal word for a bucket, rope, porpoise, sea gull, water, tobacco pipe, knife, ax, leather, north, south, east, west, cloud, and the verbs to eat and drink—twenty words in all. Because my ear was keen, my tongue nimble, and my memory precise, I was able to recite all but one of these. The chieftain appeared enormously pleased with me, stamping his feet and clapping his hands. This caused me to remember what Mistress Barton had told me, of the pleasure almost everyone took in instructing a quick pupil.

Two months would surely pass, and more likely three, before our ship dropped her hook in Virginia waters. As a colonist I would not be expected to help sail the ship; in fact all passengers would be ordered to go below in heavy weather; and only in case of a sea fight would I exercise my only trade as yet, which was that of a pikeman. Manteo too would have a great deal of time on his hands. It was my firm resolve than when I disembarked somewhere in Virginia I would speak and understand the Croatan language not merely as well but better than did John White.

2

Because of the niggardly count of powder casks in our magazine, fully half of which our captain would hold for the defense of his ship on his homeward voyage, I fell to wondering how many of our fifty or more male colonists on our ship had brought long bows. We had stowed twenty of the forty rude muskets Sir Walter Raleigh had supplied, but I reckoned that we would be lucky to keep more than ten. Our gentlemen, of whom we were said to have twenty in the companies of the three vessels, would hardly condescend to the time-tried yeoman weapon, although most of these would presumably have swords and a few wheel-lock pistols. I had noticed only three bows in the baggage brought aboard, belonging to farmers Mark Bennett and John Baird, and to the yeoman, William Berde. Richard Wade, who had not yet embarked, would have his fine yew bow, and of course I had brought my own lemonwood bow, the gift of my fast-friend Tom Warner. Besides his own, and at no word from me, but by John White's consent, Tom had brought aboard forty yew staffs six feet long and four hundred ash sticks, three feet long and about an inch square. Governor White had assured him he would be paid five shillings each for every bow he fashioned during the voyage, along with ten arrow shafts. Iron heads for these Dyonis Harvey, the son or nephew of the rich ironmonger, Sir James Harvey, agreed to provide for a groat each. In fact White had ordered one thousand extras, at a total sum of more than sixteen pounds.

With the help of a "boy," Tom could fashion a bow and about ten arrow shafts in a long day's work. But attaching the head and fletching the shafts was a delicate task, and learning to hit even a large mark at forty yards demanded long and faithful practice. The fact was already plain that only a stern captain could force that task and practice on a body of men whose main intent was to get rich on Indian gold and pearls, then hasten back to Merrie England . . . But a vague vision of some fate far different passed before my eyes.

There were not more than five yeomen in our company as yet, these identifiable by their dress, and in some degree by a slight refinement of peasant accents and by their independent carriage and manner. I had heard it said that the strength of England lay in her yeomanry, industrious tenders of their small holdings, good archers, sturdy well-grown men and women, unbeholden to any landlord. To my dismay, petty tradesmen were numerous, men who had kept small shops where they had handled enough money, not only red but white and sometimes yellow, to acquire a great greediness for more, and who had rented or sold their little shops to trade tin pans worth sixpence each for buffalo skins each worth a pound.

Two men were carters. Where would they find cartwrights and wheelwrights, horses to pull carts, and roads on which to travel? A perfumer had been enlisted, since frankincense and myrrh were believed found in Virginia, and we had high need of Doctor John Jones, the Welsh physician, but I feared he was taking the voyage for a brief glimpse of Virginia and would return to England with the ship. If we needed a judge in any dispute that might arise, Thomas Hewett, a Bachelor of Civil Law from Oxford, might serve well.

Only a few colonists had brought more clothes than they were wearing. Our store of woolen cloth was small, although we had many bolts of bright-colored linen cloth, and cotton imported via Portugal from India or smuggled from the Spanish islands. This was for trading with the Indians for corn, if need be, but preferably for gold, pearls, furs, and buffalo and deer skins. I wondered if William Nicholes, the clothworker, had ever handled rawhide. I doubted it; and I would trade three of him for one tanner, leatherworker, or cobbler.

Our churchgoing might be scanted in the New World, not so much for lack of Sunday clothes as for ministers. Thomas Ellis, formerly a vestryman in Exeter, could no doubt handle temporal problems of a church, but not matters of faith and spirit; and the avowed purpose of Edward Powell, shipping on the flyboat, was to preach to and convert Indians. The truth was, Sir Walter Raleigh seemed to have had as little care for our immortal souls as for his own; for he was famed as much for impieties and blasphemies as for lecheries. But if we could do without sermons, we certainly needed a curate, or even a deacon to solemnize christenings and funerals. In fact two women, one of them John White's daughter and the wife of Ananias Dare, "had swallowed a pumpkin seed" as our West Country rustics say. If a new colonist did not join the company late in the voyage, it would happen not long after our landing.

The largest of our three ships, the *Lion*, would transport most of the women colonists, married or unmarried. Four young unmarried women had already found one another, roamed about together, and were berthed together in a small cabin vacated by the ship's clerk. Their names were Margaret Lawrence, Joan Warren, Jane Mannering, and Rose Payne. In the bachelors' eyes they already looked pretty, and they would turn to beauties in those eyes before the voyage ended. I ventured to the yeoman William Berde that they would soon choose husbands.

"Ye say that, Martyn Sutton, 'cause you're yet too green to ken the nature o' womankind," the knowing fellow replied. "By and large, wenches marry when a good catch comes in reach, playing safe one might say, but it can't come up in 'citement to being wooed by a swarm of swains. These 'ere are shopkeepers' daughters, so I reckon by their look and dress, but they'll all have their heads turned, before we touch the Spanish isles, let alone Virginny."

I fell to wondering if Winifred Powell would have her head turned by the lecherous bachelors on the flyboat. Truly not one of our bevy could compare with her in beauty, grace, and all the gifts of good breeding. I was well aware of her sensuality; she might no longer be a virgin if the gossip of Mistress Strickland was all that it implied, which I refused to believe. I would continue to perceive her as wistful, dreamy, devout, highborn maiden, both spiritual and passionate, almost fey in the modern English meaning of that word. It stood to my hard-gripped reason that when she married, it would be to someone like Richard Wade. The fact remained we would likely have crossed a mighty sea ere that, and become colonists on a remote shore fronting the primeval forest in which Danger prowled, and old ways of thought and feeling might change with now incredible rapidity. My common sense forgave some dreamy glowings . . .

What it found hard to forgive—and the same, I thought, with the common sense of all hard-headed colonists—was the amount of space in the hold occupied by trade goods. Almost none belonged to John White, so rumor had it; the main was the property of Captain Irish,

Simon Fernando, Ananias Dare, John Spendlove, and perhaps Sir Walter himself. Certainly the great knight had given the others permission to barter with the Indians for gold, skins, and pearls during their stay on the Virginia coast, and perhaps to cruise along the coasts for the same purpose after the colonists had disembarked. There were many boxes of copper kettles, cheap metal dishes and utensils, carefully packed mirrors, crates of assorted bells, toys, and other knick-knacks, as well as bolts of cloth. To my dismay, there were almost an many casks of cheap spirit as of powder in our magazines. It was common knowledge that for this the Indians would trade their dearest belongings, including their wives and daughters, after they had downed half a cupful. Sober Indians were easily aroused to violence; half-drunken Indians would present a danger awesome to contemplate.

The time drew nigh when we were to stand to sea. Indeed Captain Irish was waiting for the full-moon tide and a favorable wind. I had assumed that Richard was already aboard either the flyboat or the pinnace—instead he had been the guest of a rich knight in Plymouth; and he had either chosen or been ordered to sail on the *Lion*. When he came aboard, as Captain Richard Darigem, he caused a great stir among the passengers, especially the chattering quartet of young spinsters. Truly he was a splendid figure of a man, with his blond mustachios and pointed beard, in fine attire, and wearing his sword. My heart warmed, not wholly because he would not be thrown with Winifred on a long voyage. Our ancient bond, so real however strange between a landlord's son and a tenant's son, was a dear possession.

Nor was he alone. Obviously a great lady had come with him to bid him good-bye. As far as I could tell not one of my shipmates, none of whom were Wiltshire, recognized her, and she appeared to know only one of our company, a lowly born pikeman. This fact caused a considerable rise in my repute among both passengers and crew.

When they approached me I doffed my cap. While Richard stood silent with a guarded smile, Lady Isobel Wade wished me a safe journey and advancement and prosperity in Virginia. She did not offer me her hand but something much more prized, just now an expression of feeling on her face that was more than kind, and I could not doubt that her good wishes were heartfelt, and that she harbored a considerable affection for me. I thought that it had been deepened by the very favor she had given me, by saving me a ruinous fine at the trial in Devizes and by recommendation that had reached Sir Walter Raleigh. It has been said that deeper feelings are wakened by serving than by being served. It could easily be true, so unplumbed and mysterious is the human heart.

"You and Richard won't play at quarterstaffs any more," she told me in low tones. "Your contests will be far more demanding on your powers, and I know that they will benefit the whole enterprise, and help to win a new province for the Queen."

She turned away to meet Captain Irish, who had come down from his poop deck to greet her. Yet as far as I could discover from his address, he did not know her, but was merely paying tribute to a great lady who had honored his ship. At once Richard spoke to me with a quiet smile.

"What my dam told you is true. We will continue to try to out-match each other, in the same spirit as of old. There will be wonderful contests."

Then he went to the rail where presently his mother joined him. There they talked quietly a few minutes, embraced, after which Lady Isobel wiped away her tears and went overside into the boat that had brought her here.

3

We expected to sail at sundown but at noon were notified we would lift anchors at dawn the following day. Colonists and crew were not allowed to go to shore, but the captain permitted some men off watch, and three or four avid passengers to take one of the boats and go fishing. If we made a good catch, we would not only please the company by a meal of fresh fish, but would postpone encroachment on the ship's pantries. Manteo and I were of the number, and we rowed to likely waters of Stonehouse Pool.

Our purse seine, cast by an expert, soon boated more herring than the whole company could possibly devour before spoilage, and Heaven knew the pantries were overstocked with salt herring. Then for the sport of it we rigged hand lines, and made a respectable catch of sheepshead, croakers, a very few striped bass, and such trash as salt-water catfish, lampreys, sting rays, and a small turtle. Obviously all these varieties of sea creatures were common in shoal water off the Virginia coasts, because Manteo called the Croatan Indian names of the first of each kind brought aboard. This was for my express benefit. The other anglers were not interested in Indian names. A zealous student, I repeated these names in an undertone and locked them in my memory. As long as the knowledge would be useful to me, I would know that catfish was *keetrank*—possibly the Croatan had the same name for edible catfish—the lamprey was *kokohoch*, croakers were *manchauemec*, striped bass were *mesikek*, and a small turtle had the euphonious name of *saccuenickot*. Manteo remarked to me *quin-ziuck*, when a fish duck flew nigh. Far more valuable to me than the primary grounding in the Croatan language was the fact that Manteo and I were surely making friends.

The day was early in May; the dawn broke early and swiftly, and I was on deck to see its first pale glimmer in the oriental sky, while all the rest of the cobalt vault was still studded with stars. As might any sailor—my close to two years on the *Elspeth* had caused irremediable changes in me, including the fall into little habits I would never break—I sniffed the wind. It was in the northeast, the most favorable wind to smack us along our course, and fresh. We were lying off the east shore of the great estuary Hamoaze, and our captain must sail close to the wind to round the cape.

These were historic waters. Ten years ago Sir Francis Drake had from hence stood to sea on his journey around the world; four years ago the great Sir Humphrey Gilbert had set sail here on his second attempt to colonize Newfoundland, never to return. Bound back to England when a gale had struck his two ships off the Azores, he had refused to leave the ten-ton *Squirrel* and board the forty-ton *Golden Hind*, crying, "We are as near to heaven by sea as by land." At midnight his ship lights were suddenly lost sight of in the dark; his brave little vessel had been swallowed by the ever avid seas.

Suddenly Tom Warner stood beside me. I told him the brief tale as rose and yellow bands decorated the low sky above the eastward bay. Because he had been in slavery to the dons at the time of its occurrence, he had never heard it. It moved him to sober utterance.

"Did aught come of the colony?"

"Not yet that I know of. His drowning blasted the venture. But Devon fishermen run to its banks, 'tis a short sail compared to ours, forty-five degrees of longitude compared to our seventy-five, and besides we're going the long way round."

"Ain't it queer, how often death of one man will wreck a venture, or lose a war?"

"Or how the strength of one man will save a venture or win a war."

Our talk ceased, because all hands were on deck, and the captain was shouting orders. There was no doubt now of our present departure. Soon we heard the creak and grind and the "Yo, heave ho," of the capstan weighing our bow anchor. Presently such sails as the hands had spread began to fill, and the ship moved with a little start, as if surprised by her sudden freedom from her chains.

I was going with her, and I made a close search of my mind to find out if I were a fool. What was the searchlight I did not know, perhaps only a swift summing up of what I would lose thereby, and what I might gain. My sire had not been jesting when he had told me that in his opinion my chances of survival in a fire-new colony amid the wilderness of North America seemed no better, and perhaps less, than if I fought for the Queen against Spain. But this was not the main issue, or so it seemed in this moment of insight; perhaps it was irrelevant. In Wiltshire, like the ship at anchor, I too had been chained. In Virginia it was possible to loose those chains, if I were enough of a man and Chance was at all fair in her dealing. My separation with my sire would be almost as wide as if he or I had died. I would be parted for years and perhaps forever with much else I loved. It might be I would never again lay eyes on the wondrous Circle of Stones.

I realized what seemed a sudden jerk to a stop of my meditations. My last conjecture was quite true; but was I saddened or relieved? Certainly I had not put a jot of credence in Pete's superstitious mutterings. I remembered well a question of a hardheaded man, the master's bailiff, William Holbrooke. "What ha' we done, to bring this curse on us?" But my common sense had denied any relationship between five peculiarly horrid crimes, the murder of a late traveler ambushed on the road, of a sweet and innocent peasant woman who was my mother, of a slow-witted woodcutter, of a highborn lady from Wales, and finally, for deep in my soul I did not believe it was an accident, of a trusting toddler at his play.

By departing Wiltshire, these atrocities I could now forget, or else they would draw so far distant in space, and drop so deeply into the dim vault of time, that they would no longer haunt my dreams. If it were possible, which I denied, that ancient evil could somehow linger about and emanate from those mysterious fallen or upright stones of a heathen temple, certainly it could not cross the wind-swept Ocean Sea.

Then I faced the truth. No amount of self-mockery or derision of fairy tales, could make me regret my departure from Stonehenge.

By now the railing was lined by colonists gazing at the slowly shifting shore. In the wan light, the lines of their faces were accented; the men looked determined, as if fighting something; many of the women were in tears. Suddenly I felt brotherhood with them all. It was a strong wave of feeling; inextricably bound with it was a dim, glowing sense of my own strength. They represented not a cross-section of England; the number of gentlemen was far too large for that; the number of craftsmen and yeomen far too small; only two that I knew of had partaken in the previous attempt at colonization that had ended in frantic flight from the wilderness and the loneliness. One was John White; the other name I had heard mentioned was Humphrey or George Newton, but the latter had stayed only a few

months. Were we a poorly chosen, ill-assorted band for the venture
toward? In any case, we were irrevocably committed to it, now that
the ship was underway.

4

Three more prospective colonists had embarked the night before
we sailed. They were Darby Gland, Elisabeth Gland presumably
Darby's wife, and Dennis Carroll, evidently a close friend of the
couple. Elisabeth was the comeliest young woman I had yet seen
among the passengers, and the best dressed and spoken. Both men
had been seafarers, as was evident from speech, gait, and sunburn,
and I could not doubt that Darby had called commands from the
poop. He had the manner of an officer if not of someone more lordly;
I suspected he was the younger or the bastard son of at least a knight
and possibly a nobleman. The wild notion struck me that he was
one of Sir Walter Raleigh's bastards, if the tale of the admiral's many
lecheries was true. I suppose it had occurred to me because of some
obscure physical resemblance between Darby and Sir Walter, but the
only feature I could pin down was the two men's eyes, alike in color,
in setting, and particularly in boldness.

It would not be unthinkable or hardly unlikely that Sir Walter
had sent a scapegrace son, whom he admired but for one of many
possible reasons had not acknowledged, to ship as a colonist, and to
take command of the colony in case John White proved an inadequate
leader. It was hard to imagine two more different personalities than
those of Sir Walter and Governor White. What might be one cause
of sympathy between the two men amused me. Jovial Sir Walter's
family might include bastard sons; staid John White's family certainly did number a bastard grandson. He belonged to Ananias Dare,
the governor's son-in-law, and his name was John Dare, and he was
old enough to have been left in England. Plainly John White had
forgiven this little slip, for Ananias Dare had been appointed assistant
governor.

My amusement did not in the least reduce my concern over the
newcomer, Darby Gland. Any blood relationship with Sir Walter
Raleigh was in all probability a figment of my fancy; but the strength,
vigor, and boldness of the man were only too real. Greedy for power
in the colony-to-be, I would compete not only against Richard. Among
the strong contenders almost certainly would stand Darby Gland.

Our southeastward journey began; a diminishing number watched
the coast of England recede; an ever greater number were appraising
or getting acquainted with their fellows. Our quartet of maidens,

fiercely competitive with one another, united in their suspicion of Elisabeth Gland, despite her having what appeared to be a lawful husband. At least they watched her covertly with a sheen of envy and resentment on their eyes. They had learned long since that flighty young wives could be formidable rivals. They marked, as I did, that Darby paid little attention to her and indeed roamed the ship with his friend and understudy, Dennis Carroll. When she moved aft along the rail presumably for a last glimpse of the spires of Plymouth, being hidden one by one behind the westward-jutting cape below the fishing village, I deemed they did not fail to note that the shift brought her within one landgazer of handsome Richard. Very naturally, since he was not bashful and she was attractive and of a station not far below his own, he made some comment to which she replied. And when the intervening colonist went elsewhere the two fell into casual conversation.

I could imagine the virgins' comments to one another. "And her a wife!" would be the most mild. And another more denunciatory could well be, "She's an errant Jezebel, and ye can set your mind on't."

But as the journey progressed, one long-drawn day after another, Richard remained unattached, for he was not now a wellborn rustic; indeed his manner and mind had always seemed urbane compared to most young gentlemen I had ever watched. He was more attracted to Elisabeth than to any of our bevy; nor did Darby Gland pay any attention to their deck-walking and cozy talks; but a crowded ship offers few opportunities for serious love-making. Meanwhile the spinsters had their fill of flattering attentions. Almost every bachelor under forty paid them court from time to time, hanging on their words, laughing heartily at their jests, and waiting on them at every chance. Indeed in this respect an observer could not distinguish bachelors from lusty fellows who had left their wives on shore.

I paid little attention to this, having been wisened by the yeoman William Berde, but my curiosity in regard to Darby Gland steadily deepened. He and his shadow Dennis Carroll were unaccountably busy making friends with about twenty of our male colonists. To the remainder he was merely civil; and I sought for a common denominator in those of his choice. It was hard to find; the only obvious fact was that none was of rank above a yeoman, and this was a strange fact, considering my deepening conviction that he himself was wellborn, whether or not on the wrong side of the blanket. His closest associates apart from Dennis Carroll were John Hynde and William Clement; and I never for a moment forgot that they, as was myself, were jailbirds. This fact was well known to all of our company, but it was not held against them, naturally enough since they

were unobtrusive, modest-seeming men; and all of us were in a sense
beginning a new life. The run-of-the-mill Englishman is woefully conscious of caste in those above him; he becomes self-conscious in their
presence; but he has quick sympathy for the underdog. His sense of
fair play is one of his most admirable and outstanding traits; and
Hynde and Clement had paid the lawful price of their thievery and
that ended it.

I observed too that Gland's new friends were the most eager
talkers about trading trifles for Indian treasures; and the prospects
of gathering gold and jewels. The grandeur of the idea of a new
English colony fronting a continental wilderness did not reach them,
much less move them. But these twenty had no mirrors, pots, or
kettles to trade for stacks of buffalo skins each worth a pound, or
for even more precious pearls.

There was more and more talk beside the rails of the sudden and
frantic flight of Lane's colony. Why had they been in such wild haste
to sail from Roanoke if it were indeed an El Dorado? Half-veiled
expressions of doubt of John White's leadership became more common.

When Tom Warner and I discussed the matter—happily he brought
up the subject, which assured me I was not prey to idle fancy—I
found his concern fully as deep as mine.

"You spoke once, Mr. Martyn," so he always addressed me, "of the
Elspeth being a happy ship."

"She was a happy ship."

"Sailors know what that means, 'though they can't quite put it into
words. This here was a happy ship too, the people united-like, while
Cap'n was loading and making ready, but 'tis not a happy ship no
more."

"What do you reckon happened?"

"Two men have been putting out poison—one man, I should say,
for the other's just his echo—as though to kill rats. But themselves are
the rats."

"They're a busy pair—but why?"

"Rats will gnaw away on a timber until it's weakened. There seems
no point but pure deviltry. But there's something more than deviltry,
more point I mean, in Darby Gland starting all this talk."

"He's somebody's mouthpiece, you think?"

"I think he's his own mouthpiece. He doesn't strike me as being
anybody's agent but his own. There's a bold man, Mr. Martyn. A
mighty ambitious man. I'll go further and say a strong man. Look at
those eyes, sharp, hard, and bold."

"Why hasn't Captain Irish heard the talk, traced it down, and
stopped it?"

"There's a mighty drop from the poop to the deck. It's like that from the gentry to the commons, back home. I was an officer once—I didn't tell ye, because being a slave for seventeen years set it at nought—and although I was usually the first officer to know what was in the men's minds, it wasn't till after the very cabin boys knew it bottom to top. But I'm not an officer now, but maybe I could find out enough that you and I could set our own course."

"I was hoping you'd suggest that. How would you go about it?"

"I'd make just one remark, offhand like, in Darby Gland's hearing or, better yet, in Dennis Carroll's hearing. It's known already that I was in slavery to the dons, and can speak Spanish, and that I'm your man. I'd well-nigh bet that Darby Gland will stop and have a little chat with me 'fore tomorrow's sunset."

5

The plot we hatched was simple in the extreme. On my previous sail I had acquired a taste for Spanish cheroots—*cigarros* was their native name—and had bought a string of them, patently smuggled, on a dock at Plymouth. Dennis Carroll also smoked cheroots and had an abundant supply. I furnished Tom with one of mine, and he was to wait until one of those rare times when Darby Gland was with his wife, whereupon Tom would ask a light off Carroll's cheroot. The brief conversation that would follow would be of the most commonplace kind, after such an incident. A remark about the weather, so good until now, but this was pure trickery, for a gale lay in wait for us sure as God, not a hurricane, for it was too early in the year for these, but a real boiler just the same. Then, after Carroll had agreed, Tom would remark, "Well, I hope Cap'n Irish will have sense enough to heave to, but I'd not bet on it."

But Tom agreed with me that from henceforth he should listen, not speak. Such civil utterances as were called for must be rigidly guarded; Carroll must not be emboldened to say too much. I felt that if we knew too much, and yet did not become party to the plot whatever it might be, we would go into grave danger.

The meeting occurred as we planned it; that it had been rehearsed almost certainly had not crossed Carroll's mind. Still we were little the wiser.

"He would not have been my choice to be master of the ship, or John White to be governor," Carroll had replied to Tom's remark about Captain Irish. "'Fact, I know several men in our company better fitted."

Tom had not asked who those men might be. He had made the

safe response that time would tell, and he reckoned that if these officers proved imcompetent, Commodore Fernando would replace them with others. Meanwhile Carroll had made a swift, furtive, but perhaps shrewd, examination of Tom's physique, countenance, and hands, noting his prematurely gray hair. Tom thought the examiner had dismissed him as too old and "set in his way," to be of worth to the project, whatever it might be.

Yet our timid stratagem bore a little fruit the following morning. Darby Gland was pacing the deck alone, ostensibly for exercise, and I posted myself alone, out of hearing of any other watchers, by the rail. Actually these were few. The ever restless sea had evidenced no apparent or dramatic change in several days; the wind had shifted between northeast and northwest, never more than a point or two off our stern; it had remained brisk and I thought the heavily laden ship was clipping off between five and six sea miles an hour, a good gait indeed for a fat-bellied trader. Abruptly, as on sudden impulse, Gland skipped a step, then came quickly to my side.

"You're Sutton, aren't you?" he asked civilly enough.

"Yes, sir. Martyn Sutton." Meanwhile my impressions of his voice were sinking in and clarifying. It was a very pleasant voice, resonant, forceful, one that implied directness and great self-confidence.

"You shipped under Cap'n Selkirk on the *Elspeth*."

"Yes, sir, I did; but I didn't know it was generally known."

"I've been in rather close touch with the Admiralty. Our Queen did not know what ships came and went—she made it her business not to know—or their intents. But Selkirk's report to Sir Walter Raleigh gave you favorable mention, despite your low rank. It was concerned with an incident in the Bahamas—I forget what."

"It was not worth remembering, sir."

"Still it caused him to look you up and get you out of Devizes prison. I dare say there were other recommendations, too. And when you were free, you beat the stuffing out of some guard."

"I was not a felon—I was jailed for trespass, a sentence of six months —and he had put me in the bilboes without the least cause."

"I saw you reading a book on the foredeck."

"Yes, sir. I can read and write. I had a benefactor."

"The voyage is going well, isn't it? Almost too well, to last. There's bound to be rough weather before or soon after we raise the islands, and if not sent by Jupiter—I reckon you know—"

"Yes, I've picked up a little mythology," I said when Gland paused.

"Good. Some of White's assistants wouldn't know, I'd bet on that. If the storm god doesn't make us trouble, it will strike the same. Not likely from a Spanish sloop of war. Philip is keeping most of those in port, putting on all the weight they can carry. The trouble will rise, mark my words, because White and Fernando are at logger-heads. White's whole thought is for the colony. Fernando's mind is on prizes, and for looting the islands while their guard is down."

"Fernando is above White, but White has Sir Walter's trust," I ventured.

"Still, it's a pity we have women aboard. This might be the chance of a lifetime. If we could take enough prizes and enough Spanish gold, we'd cripple Philip, and maybe he wouldn't be so bellicose."

"Spanish gold may not be as plentiful as it once was."

"That's the common view. There are some islands in the Lesser Antilles that haven't been scratched—in fear of the Carib Indians. I think they're a bogey—they can't stand to cannon and musket fire any better than the Cubans did—but of course that's no business of ours. Our business is laying out farms and herding sheep in Virginia."

"Those are Sir Walter's orders and the Queen's wishes. White learned a great deal from Lane's failure, and I hazard he'll be success-ful. And the hunting and fishing will be better than on a duke's preserves."

I remarked this last with boyish enthusiasm, because Gland had talked as much as I dared let him. I did not want him to give me the least hint that he would regret. I had no real doubt now of the general aim of the conspiracy, let alone of its existence. I wanted to be dismissed from the thoughts of Darby Gland. For him to trust me or to fear me would be equally dangerous.

But hard thinking told me that he would take no action in the near future. He would certainly wait until the morale of the colonists had fallen much lower than now, a fall that would almost certainly occur if our good luck turned to bad. This last was almost a certainty also, if not because of circumstances, by the clash of temperament and intent between Fernando and White. Darby Gland was a bold man, and he would take calculated risk for what he wanted, but he was far from a fool. In prison I had heard of the captain of a privateer, who had called himself Gary Dane, and who had mys-teriously disappeared when the Admiralty had begun an investigation of his log and accounts.

A brief southeaster, a capful o' wind but far from a gale, slowed the *Lion's* steady pace west of the Bahamas, and we gained not more than fifty miles in the whole of two days; then it did a turn about, and at noon of the third day thereafter the lookout shouted "Land!" What tremendous meaning in one four-letter word! Old sailors off watch left their meat to hasten to the rail; the colonists watched with eyes shining in flushed faces. The officers pored over their charts.

Soon we heard their verdict that we had sighted the eastern tip of Santo Domingo, probably Cape Engaño. We did not draw near enough to verify this guess, for the capital island of Spanish West Indies would be too well guarded by Spanish galleons for an enemy merchantman to venture there, but we sped boldly through Mona Passage and then turned eastward to gain the Lesser Antilles, which at last report were not guarded at all. On one of these islands we must certainly land, to refill our water casks and obtain such edibles as we could seize or obtain in trade from the Indians. In two days of wandering, we sighted a beautiful island lying well westward of the main group, called Santa Cruz by Spanish sailors, although this was not its name on the chart. No Spanish sail was in sight.

The colonists went to shore, happy as children, and gawked at the luxuriant foliage, admired the laden fruit trees, and listened to the incessant chatter and shrieking of great flocks of parrots. No Darby Gland would attempt a daring *coup-de-main* in this hopeful climate.

Precious little water and almost no food had we obtained when the topsails of a far-distant sloop, whether Spanish or English or French we did not know, caused us to re-embark in haste and set sail. At the next island that we touched, we met with a curious although not serious accident. Our fruit-hungry colonists ate what looked like green apples, only to suffer from a painful burning in their mouths. The ship's baby barely tasted a tempting slice, and its tongue and delicate membranes caused it distress all that day and the next night. Yet the incident was memorable because of a remark of an old frigateman, known as Gunner Hopkins.

"If the apples in the garden o' Eden had tasted like them, there wouldn't of been no human race."

A more serious mistake was made at a nearby islet, bereft of water except for one pond the water of which had a brassy taste. All who drank from it fell almost immediately sick, choking and retching, and those who had merely washed suffered from swollen faces. These mishaps obviously disheartened the colonists. The islands were so verdant and beautiful to the eyes; the flocks of parrots and parakeets were so animated and colorful, as well as noisy; no doubt the sight called up their visions of heaven and everlasting bliss. But they had already shown their treachery to the innocent visitor.

Our next side trip was to a neighboring island in search of tame sheep. Governor White himself spoke from the poop to the assembled passengers, explaining the importance, indeed the urgency, of the journey. This island had been stocked with sheep, they had been allowed to multiply, and they were to be had for the taking. They would prove of incalculable value to the colonists, for the Virginia

shores provided abundant pasture. The winters were so mild that
the animals would require almost no care, except perhaps at lambing
time, and because they were purebred marino sheep they would provide abundant wool, for spinning and weaving, and delicious mutton
from surplus rams and antiquated ewes. True, the ship was already
crowded, but room could be found on the decks for a hundred head.

Feed for the animals on the journey presented a problem, the governor conceded, but not a difficult one. Stops would be made at
verdant islands and shores along the route, and all hands would "unite
their labor" in cutting and gathering grass.

It appeared that Fernando had acquiesced to the proposal, and
no one remarked, although all were aware of the fact, he would
rather spend the time seeking and capturing Spanish traders in the
poorly guarded harbors of the larger islands. Nor would the majority
of our male colonists have the least objection to the latter pursuit,
and probably would prefer it to chasing and roping sheep. Gold and
Christian edibles and trade goods were more appealing just now than
a flock of blatters on the deck, the gain from which lay in the hazy
distance. Piracy was not nearly as objectionable a word as it had
once seemed; anyway, England and Spain were virtually at war,
despite the protestations of love, or at least of friendship, between
their sovereigns. In fact, Fernando might be the more far-sighted of
the two men; he was the realist, White the dreamer. After all, war
is war; and any crippling of Philip's seapower would benefit England
and hence her colonies, more than the acquisition of a passel of sheep.

In all truth, I thought, the deterioration of the morale of my shipmates was accompanied by a weakening and muting of their consciences.

It chanced that White had chosen a day of peculiarly miserable
weather for the passage to "Isle de Mutton," as our jokers had it. A
chill wind, bringing rain squalls, blew across our beam, our vision
was restricted, our progress slow, and the way much longer than Governor White had indicated in his reference to a "nearby island." We
sailed part of half an afternoon, the whole of an uncomfortable night,
and well into the morning of the next day before we made landfall.
And then the watchman on the masthead climbed glumly down to
report that he saw wide meadow, winding brooks, pools, and what
appeared to be old folds, indeed all appurtenances for sheep raising,
but no slowly moving patches of white.

And this was sorry outcome of White's venture. No hide or hair
of a sheep was seen on the island. A number of our young and more
restless males exchanged triumphant looks with Darby Gland.

"I been on wild-goose chases afore now," remarked bold Gunner

Hopkins, caring nought who heard him, "but this is my first tame-sheep chase."

The colonists' spirits rose somewhat at Coltea, on the south coast of Porto Rico, to find our pinnace riding at anchor. But they fell again when Captain Stafford was rowed alongside in his long boat—this so large in comparison with his ship that it reminded a jokester of a ninety-pound woman carrying a nine-pound bouncer—to announce that the flyboat had failed to keep the rendezvous. Indeed he had seen no hull or rigging of her the whole voyage. True, she had met no foul weather that he knew of. But she was an old tub that Raleigh should have never trusted, and likely her seams had parted in a little squall, and she was on the bottom. And could we let him have some salt, because some of his dried herring were spoiling in the heat?

Still I did not for a moment believe the flyboat lay on the bottom, Winifred's white body a pale blur in the sea gloom. Preacher Powell's thunderous prayers would have kept her afloat.

We furnished Captain Stafford with salt, and without waiting for any sort of celebration of the uniting of the two ships, we hastened on to Musketas Bay to refill our water casks—these inclined to spring leaks in this weather. On the south side of the island was a famous spring; but it must be that the region had suffered drouth, for the pool had shrunk, its shallows were muddy; and the haul, on which we had spent three days coming and going and dipping, was so scant that Richard Wade, put in command of the shore party, remarked that more ship's beer had been consumed in the venture than water brought aboard.

The very thought of rationing drinking water—not ordered yet, but expected any hour—cast our colonists into gloom. As we cruised the south coast of Porto Rico, their spirits became dangerously low. Talk against Governor White became openly bitter. Sir Walter Raleigh had organized the colony as a gesture to the greatness of England and to flatter the Queen; for the colonists' fate he cared not a fig. Even Captain Irish did not know his business; it was well known he was using charts more than twenty years old; and he had not kept abreast of conditions in the islands, or he would not have sanctioned the sheep-catching venture or ordered the water-fetching fiasco at a mudhole.

'Twas a pity that colonists and crew were not permitted to elect governors and ship's officers when those appointed proved to be bunglers. That was the English spirit—Englishmen had shown it when they had forced King John to sign the Great Charter of Runnymede; Wat Tyler had asked for no more when he had first led the peasants to rebellion; but he had let the mob rule and his enterprise had died with his death. Now there were gathered together a hundred or more people intending to make their home in the New World, where they could be truly free, and a start should be made right here on this ship!

If ever the time was ripe for a successful mutiny, led by a long headed and masterful leader, it was now.

6

This very night! Suddenly I knew, as though I had been told, that Darby Gland had so decided in a flash of inspiration. I thought that he had notified his followers, probably with an innocent-looking movement of his hand. But Darby Gland did not intend to lead the colonists to freedom in a New World; he had sung a siren song of sudden riches. Once in command of the ship, its former officers chained or dead, he would be more likely to sell the colonists to the Spaniards as hostages or slaves, or hold them for ransom. I had hurried and secret talk with Tom Warner, to discover he had arrived at the same conclusion.

"His men will have to be well-armed, or he won't attempt it," I told him, as his eyes burned into mine.

"There are plenty of muskets and powder in the magazine."

"He wouldn't try to force that great door. It would make too much noise. He either has the key or had it long enough to make a replica. It would be no more than one night's job by a craftsman skilled with a file."

"One or the other. And if I were he, I'd chose the change of watch at midnight for the attack." And I observed that Tom did not employ his usual careless speech that he had picked up since the recovery of his memory of the language. He spoke the precise English of his raising.

"Then the sensible thing would seem to be to warn Captain Irish."

"You said 'seem.' What do you think we should do, Mr. Martyn Sutton?"

"If it's at all possible, I'd like to block it by ourselves—then say nothing. Twenty or more of our fellow colonists are involved. They're good enough men—they've been debauched by the glitter of promised gold—they've pinched pennies all their lives, still most of 'em will make good colonists once they are persuaded that they must do so, in order to survive. Also, Irish is a stern captain—he has that name. He might order the lot of them hanged, once their leaders have been put in irons. I wouldn't like to have that responsibility on my soul."

"How can we fetch it alone? I know how, if we could get into the magazine just before they rush the door. Wait! They'll be pressed for time. Won't the magazine be unlocked a little while beforehand?"

"I believe Gland would arrange that, and load the twenty muskets, and put powder in the pans, and have candles burning to light the matches."

"He'll do all that an hour or so before the watch changes."

"We have to know the moment he's made ready. Well, have you observed Thomas Smart?" This was one of the "boys," about sixteen years old. His father, Thomas Smart, the elder and about fifteen more had been left at Roanoke by Sir Richard Grenville, and had not sailed with Lane's colony. I was under the impression, disputed by some of my shipmates, that they had been put ashore after, not before, Lane's flight. The younger Thomas Smart's main motive in obtaining enlistment under White had been to find his father.

"I've marked him well," Tom told me.

"He's reliable and loyal. We can hide in that cubby just aft of the magazine door. I take it that one man, or at least no more than two, will unlock the door and load the muskets. It's a post of danger for a younker, but he'll face it, if his getting to Virginia is at stake."

Thomas Warner meditated briefly. Then he answered, "Yes, I think he will."

"He'll report to us, the moment the man or the men emerge. If they lock the door, we'll have no choice but to alert the captain that someone was seen tampering with the lock. But if the loaders haven't a duplicate key and only a few minutes' access to the gunner's key, they'll leave the door unlocked. It would be almost a sure shot that no one else would try the door until tomorrow's inspection."

"That's all good headwork. And if the loaded muskets are found spiked, there would be no time to unspike them, or even to reload them. Those powder casks are of heavy oak, and only a crowbar could break out the tops, and that's a noisy job."

"Gland had his own canisters of powder."

"Mr. Martyn, you're risking everything on the supposition that Darby Gland hasn't armed the men with wheel-lock pistols that have been smuggled aboard."

"Wheel-lock pistols are rare in England. Also they're unreliable contraptions that such a man as Darby Gland wouldn't trust. Twenty of them would need a heavy box. I saw his baggage when he came aboard, and no heavy freight was loaded then or since. Still, it's a risk. If no one comes to meddle with the rifles before eleven, we'll have to alert the captain."

"Well, the sun's setting. You're the captain in this venture, and it's your place to talk to young Thomas. I'll do what you tell me."

Sounding out Thomas Smart was one of the most gratifying experiences of my life so far. His depths were great, and their treasure was a brave and loyal heart. Only two years ago he had heard the news of his father's failure to return with Lane's colonists, and the time was less since he learned for certain that he was not with Sir Richard Grenville. He had told me that his elder brother had a wife and little children to care for, and I reckoned that Thomas had to grow up fast. But an aging uncle had agreed to help his mother till their little farm; and he was the only man available to inquire into his father's fate.

He listened quietly, his mind intent on every word I uttered, as I told him of the likelihood of mutiny and Tom's and my plan to nip it in the bud. When he heard of the part I wanted him to play, his eyes lighted wonderfully. Great God, what stalwart sons old England bred!

The dusk deepened and the stars glimmered palely, then grew bright. These were the great tropic stars, attendants of the magnificent Southern Cross. Deck strollers disappeared; a flirtation in the shadow of our stern was ended for the evening when first Jane Mannering hastened to the companionway and, a few minutes later, Richard Wade took the same route. For a moment I wished I had recruited Richard in our enterprise. I could not find any satisfactory reason for not doing so. As a matter of fact, only two men were needed for the light duty Tom and I had assigned ourselves, if event followed my expectations. Still Richard would have loved a share in the excitement, far more than kittling in the dark.

From an obscure station Tom and I watched Thomas Smart making his stealthy retreat to his hiding place, making reasonably certain that this was not observed by others. Then we two set ourselves for a long wait.

It was not as long as we expected. We observed a stealthy movement near the forward hatch no later than ten o'clock; but a nearby ship's lantern hung on the foremast did not reveal the countenance of the skulker there, and only the dimmest profile of his form. Evidently Darby Gland was an impatient man, or else he put his trust, reasonably enough, in none of the nightwatch trying the door of the magazine before midnight. After midnight he intended to relieve that watch with his own followers!

For another hour Tom and I waited, now under deep and harrowing suspense. We did not *know* what was happening, if anything; but I was born with an active and somewhat pessimistic imagination, and

Tom was as far from a clod as any of my shipmates. Then again we perceived the barest outline of a man's shape in the distant glimmer of the lantern near the forward hatch, and if there had been an intruder in the magazine, he had finished his task.

There was as yet no relief from Tom's and my watch. We breathed slowly and deeply, almost calmly it appeared, but our hearts were thudding and our eyes under intense strain. Then suddenly, only a few yards distant, we saw the shape of Thomas Smart. The thought occurred to me that he would make a good stalker in the forests of Virginia, whether of deer or of an Indian spy; but this thought was a protective trick of my mind, to dull the awful strain of the main surge of my thoughts, which were so fixed on the news Thomas Smart might bring. As he had been told, he came obscurely to our hiding place.

"I saw Dennis Carroll come to the door of the magazine," young Thomas told us in a low tone. "In one hand he had an unlit lantern and in the other a key on a chain."

"Well?"

"He let himself in, stayed nearly an hour, and came out."

"It would take about an hour to load twenty muskets and put powder in the pans; and fast work at that," Tom said in a hoarse whisper.

"Did Carroll lock the door behind him?" I asked, in deepmost anxiety. So much might depend on that.

"No, sir, he left the door unlocked."

"Thank God. Thomas Smart, that was fine work," I told the stalwart youth, who appeared not at all triumphant, but rather anxious lest he had left something undone. "If you like you can go to your bunk, but if you want to help us a little longer, you can. It is only to wait at the hatch and if you see a number of men assembling, rush to the powder magazine and warn us. But I warn you if they rush us, you may be knifed or shot by a wheel-lock pistol."

"If that happens, you both would be killed too, wouldn't you?"

"That's right."

"No, I'll stay with you till you're through."

Tom Warner and I left him to his post and made our stealthy way to the hatch. I had an unlighted lantern; Tom about twenty sticks of ash each about three feet long, square-cut to whittle into arrow shafts. We found our way into the magazine, closed the door, and there with flint and steel and a little tinder I lighted the lantern. Then in desperate haste Tom began thrusting the sticks into the barrels of the muskets, having to push them hard to plug the barrels, while I drew back triggers a short distance so I could blow and wipe powder out of the pans. The task seemed to take forever; actually we had finished it in less than a third of an hour. Then we blew out the lantern and went out, closing the door behind us.

In a moment more we were on the deck, largely open except for sleepers. Thomas and I slept there also, on hot, clear nights; and presently we had spread our pieces of heavy canvas that served as our mattresses and placed the rolled coats that were our pillows. I pressed the hand of Thomas Smart between both of mine and warned him to silence ere he took off for his own cot.

We had hardly lain down when Darby Gland—I knew him by his lithe form and bold stride—was seen making his way from the after hatch to the forward. About a minute later Dennis Carroll appeared, then one man after another at about the same interval. By an effort of will I did not try to identify these and only about ten minutes had passed before there was a flurry at the forward hatch, and three or four men hastily emerged. They spoke quietly to the others coming to join them, and waved them back.

Darby Gland was not only a bold leader but a trusty one. He waited by the rail until all his followers who had yet appeared had vanished from the deck, and he was making in that direction when I, obeying an impulse I could not resist, sprang to my feet.

"Mr. Gland?" I called, just loudly enough for him to hear.

"Who is it?"

"Martyn Sutton. Sir, you're up late."

"So I am, but what business is it of yours?"

"The whole ship's business, sir. I suppose you're making ready to keep the appointment you and Dennis Carroll have on shore." By now I was close to him, watching his hands. But they hung at his side.

"Mr. Sutton, I was not aware I had an appointment on shore." But he spoke in hushed tones.

"Either there, or with the yardarm."

"God damn you! Still, you must have warned John White; and he's the sort to give me this chance, weak reed that he is. I'll make no threats. They'd sound too silly now. You can tell him Dennis and I will keep our appointment on shore."

He turned his back on me and strode off with a fine swing. I did not doubt that Darby Gland, Dennis Carroll and our dingey boat would all be missing at daybreak, and a good riddance for the whole ship and especially for me. If his ambition had been a little less, if he had waited to seize command of the colony in Virginia instead of our ship while still at sea, I would have had a competitor fully as formidable as Richard Wade, and a great deal more dangerous to my person.

7

The absence of the dingey boat was observed by the boatswain on his morning rounds. This petty officer was mightily upset, not so much from its loss, as by his failure to remember whether or not he had ordered it shipped or had left it moored alongside the preceding night, which lapse would ordinarily excite Captain Irish to utterance violent and profane. As it happened, a previous report had so bewildered the rather unimaginative master that he refused to listen to such trifles as a lost dingey boat. The report was that the watchman, at his sunrise rounds, had found the door of the powder magazine unlocked, the barrels of twenty muskets spiked with wooden sticks, and signs of powder having been put in the pans and then blown or brushed away.

A second report, from a muster officer, that two colonists, Darby Gland and Dennis Carroll, had vanished during the night explained the disappearance of the dingey boat, but threw no light on mystery of the magazine. If bewilderment could cause apoplexy, Captain Irish would have no doubt suffered a stroke. He was gasping at his desk when one of his officers appeared with the message that a colonist, by name Martyn Sutton, wished to speak to him on an important matter.

"Who is Martyn Sutton?" the captain demanded. "Be damned his important matters! Anyway, his business is with Governor White, not me."

"Sir, he says his business concerns the powder magazine."

"For God's sake, send him in." And when I appeared, "Sutton, if you know anything about that crazy business, let me hear it, and be mighty certain that every word is Jesus' truth."

I had rehearsed the report with some care. Standing at attention— for I was a pikeman first class—I spoke first of my talk with Darby Gland. He had been sounding me out, I thought, as to whether I would be of a mind to participate in mutiny, the purpose of which would be to seize command of the ship and turn her into a gold seeker and pirate, forgoing altogether the planting of a colony in Virginia.

"Why did you not report this to me at once?" Captain Irish demanded. "By God—"

"Because, sir, I had nothing definite to report. His words were open to an innocent interpretation. But there was discontent among the colonists, the disappointing search for sheep and for fresh water—"

"I had advised Governor White against undertaking either. He believed his own charts instead of mine. He was appointed by Sir Walter Raleigh, our admiral. But go on with your report."

"It occurred to me and my friend, Thomas Warner, that the plans for mutiny were well advanced, and in fact we surmised it would be attempted at midnight, last night. Still we had no certain evidence to lay before the high command. But we reasoned the attack would be hopeless unless he first seized the muskets stacked in the magazine, and as we were deliberating whether to disturb you, we tried the door of the magazine, only to find it unlocked. Fearing the mutineers might act at any moment, we went in, found the muskets loaded and primed, which had not been the case when the colonists were allowed to inspect the magazine to reassure them as to the ship's stout defenses. So we decided to spike the muskets with Warner's unworked arrow shafts, and remove the priming. Sir, we would have reported the matter to an officer if we had time, and if we had been certain he was not himself in the plot. But we had both been at sea before. Our first instruction was that in an emergency, when there was no time to seek official permission, to do what needed doing according to our best judgment."

"Yes, Sutton, I agree that's the first law of the sea. I'd not have a man in my crew, down to the lowest cabin boy, who would dawdle if he had a chance to stop or plug a leak that might swiftly grow worse. I take it, your man Warner ran for his arrow shafts while you removed the priming, and when the job was done, you beat a swift retreat, which was only common sense. Still you should have reported your action at once, so I could summon all hands to catch the scoundrels and iron 'em until we could rig a noose for every man jack of 'em."

"Sir, there was very little time. We were making for your cabin when we saw Gland and Carroll go down. We hid the best we could, for other men were following them and we feared we'd be seen, captured, and silenced. But we would have run the risk if we had not seen the two leaders of the mutiny immediately appear and wave back their followers. These scattered like sheep, and we knew they had abandoned the enterprise. Still I ventured to speak to Gland, who was completely crushed, and tell him his jig was up. I suppose he inferred that you and the other officers were already cognizant of the plot, and in panic he and Carroll climbed overboard into the dingey boat and made off. I did not cry an alarm, because I feared that multiple hangings would cause the spirits of the colonists to fall still more."

"Sutton, you should have left that for your captain to decide! But I hope you identified some of Gland's and Carroll's followers."

"No, sir, not one. The moon was behind clouds and the light dim."

"'Tis most irregular and disorderly. Still"—and the captain wiped his brow—"I cannot, in good conscience, order punishment for you and Warner for what you did on the spur of the moment to prevent mutiny." Captain Irish sighed heavily. "To try to catch those deserters would take time, and we've none to spare. And like as not Governor White wouldn't consent to their hanging—divided authority is always a vexation." He brooded darkly, then came to a heartening decision. "Perhaps 'twould be wiser—aye, I'm sure it is—to let the matter rest. I'll enter the two desertions in my log—the less said about the rest, the better. You understand that, Mr. Sutton. Most of those colonists are landlubbers." And he looked at me wisely.

"Yes, sir, and if I may say so, I agree with you."

"You can go now." Then, as I turned, he added quickly, "And don't think I'm insensible to your own and and Warner's quick thinking—and quick acting. That's what I like. Not to dillydally in a crisis, *get busy*. I hear that one of White's assistants has decided to resign his post and sail home with us. If so, I'll request Governor White to consider you for the place."

"I'd thank you kindly."

I stood at attention, gave a smart seaman's salute, and returned to the deck.

Chapter VIII

THE WAIF

1

It so happened that Captain Irish had a good excuse for not pursuing the two deserters, Darby Gland and Dennis Carroll. I had hardly finished reporting to him when the man on the masthead called down "A saill" Close watch soon revealed a very large, tall ship, obviously a Spanish galleon since she was high-decked, round-stemmed, with castles fore and aft. Obviously the *Lion* was no match for her, but she could outrun the mighty vessel, a full fleet of her like being King Philip's hope of crushing the English navy. A light fog, tenuous to those in its midst, permitting easy vision for a hundred yards, but impervious to the sight at a league's distance, permitted our easy escape.

Yet the incident gave Fernando an excuse to forbid Governor White to drop the hooks of the two ships at unguarded Mayagüez Bay, where he wished to gather young fruit trees to plant in Virginia soil. The colonists were disappointed and depressed—all their hopes of a happy or profitable day on shore had been blasted lately—so he gave permission for a brief call on Saona Island, at the southeastern tip of Santo Domingo. Dons dwelling in the Spanish towns had cattle rancheros in its valleys, but its only permanent dwellers were peaceful Indians. The animal and birdlife there was said to be rich.

So it came about that Richard Wade, Tom Warner, and I planned a day's hunting with bows and arrows. As soon as we were ashore we discovered a hunter's paradise, and since we could carry to the ship only a limited amount of game, we made some rules that the highborn chasseurs of France would have applauded. We agreed that only one arrow would be launched at any one target, unless the beast was wounded. In fact we would take turns at shooting or otherwise obtaining any quarry that we saw, and he who had the turn could keep it until he failed to kill or capture the bird or animal on his first try; thereupon another of our trio would take his place. None of us would take the risk of losing or blunting an arrow at a cat-sized marsupial which the crew relished, and which could be run down and clubbed, or at a henlike bird, which at this time of year was well grown but could not fly. Each shooter had the privilege of trying to obtain any bird or animal we might encounter, or of passing it by.

I had suggested these rules, for no other reason than to make the hunt as pleasurable as possible, and the test of our skills as difficult. I suppose I wanted to compete with Richard more than obtain a heavy bag. The thought did not cross my mind that they would bring about the winning of a strange prize for me.

Thomas Warner won the toss of English pennies. He was a deadly marksman, and he killed cleanly in succession what was called a tree duck, a rabbit, and a large and very handsome squirrel, also chased and wrung the neck of the henlike fowl, its wings unfledged, when we had flushed a flock of the mature birds feeding on mast. Then he missed another tree duck and retrieved the arrow, and now the turn passed to Richard.

He was fully as skillful as Tom, and I would have to hold my best, and loose most true, if I were to equal him. To beat him seemed beyond my powers. He made a brilliant shot at a rabbit, moving slowly and dimly through the brushwood, then shot down a very large tree duck perching at great height, and transfixed the neck of a fer-de-lance, a horribly poisonous snake that I did not know was found in Santo Domingo, although it was all too common in the Lesser Antilles. Then, in a stand of immense vine-draped trees we came upon a scene of such sylvan beauty that a truly civilized man would refrain from molesting it with his musket blast or even with his humming fang-on-a-stick which he could launch with deadly accuracy and dispatch. But avid hunters forget their civilization, their eyes are dimmed to the beauty and vivid and harmless lives of their quarry. When in dire need of meat their blood lust is natural and without sin; but we three were hunting for sport and to outdo one another.

A noble stag with a burnished coat was the central figure of a small herd of deer, numbering a young roe, four hinds, and five fawns. The wind that they trusted to bring them scent of danger had betrayed them today, blowing from them to us, and the soft turf had muffled the sound of our tread. They remained utterly unwarned as Richard nocked his best arrow with its whetted fang and raised his bow.

His movements were slow and steady, not to take the quarry's eyes. The draw was flawless; and an impressive figure of a man he stood, tall, graceful, his right shoulder drawing back with great power. The resilient yew formed a deep and perfect crescent. Then he loosed in superb archer form.

The arrow sped on its arching flight. From the top of its arc it darted with incredible swiftness, as though it had life of its own. But as its point seemed to dip to the stag's shoulder, its course was slightly higher than it seemed. It appeared to slide across the top of the shoulder ere it plunged into the ground some thirty yards beyond.

To my astonishment the stag raised his head in a startled way but did not bound off, his herd behind him. No doubt he had heard the whistle of arrow flight, but since probably no shaft from a powerful bow had ever been launched at him before, he did not recognize it as a seeker of his splendid, vital life. Again he lowered his head. I looked at Richard, and there was not only ignominy, and almost self-hatred in his face; there was desperation.

"I am going to shoot again," he murmured, reaching toward his quiver.

"It's against the rules," I reminded him in the softest undertone.

"For birds and such, those rules were all right. But that is a big stag, and the pantries need fresh meat."

"It's still against the rules."

"What do you say, Tom Warner?"

"Mr. Richard, I agree with Mr. Martyn."

"I suppose you're right. I forgot I am almost, but plainly not quite, a gentleman." And then he raised a great shout, at which the entire herd sprang into flight. In a few seconds they had disappeared in the thickets. His face pale, Richard picked up what I thought was a brown seed, hardly larger than a field pea. This he put in his pouch.

"I'm going to pouch this until I've made up for that miss," he told us gravely. "I'll take it out and look at it, every time I hit, and remember this moment, and cast out the pride that goes before a fall. But I'll be punished for it, just the same. I don't know how or with what, but it will surely come."

"To err is human," I reminded him, unslinging my bow from my shoulder.

Not to punish Richard, but in a sense to honor him, paying the respect that his manhood deserved, I resolved to shoot my utter best. I killed cleanly a large grouse perched on a stump at fully a hundred paces, tumbled a giant pigeon from his treetop, and was about to shoot what I thought was a wild boar, as so were called domestic pigs that escaped from plantations and grown tall, lean, and swift in the woods. Then I perceived that he had no long tusks, that he was rotund, and his tail was coiled. It was plainly a farmyard hog, and I could not doubt we had drawn nigh to the plantation of a Spaniard. He might be in residence and own a musket. The hog would certainly utter his far-carrying squeal if he was wounded mortally or slightly. The hunter taking his turn to shoot had right to lead the way. Immediately I beat a retreat on a quartering course.

We had not gone a hundred paces when I heard a faint rustle in a thick clump of brush. In a swift glance I saw movement there, which in the first flash of thought I supposed was another hog. But the glimpse I had had of a living thing revealed it pale brown and too tall for any kind of swine; and not nearly broad enough of body.

The wildest surmise I had ever made struck my brain.

"There's my quarry, and I'll run it down," I cried to my companions. Instantly I took off into the brush.

The living creature there heard me and after a brief flight pitifully tried to hide. And I knew now what it was.

"*Amigo! Amigo!*" I cried in a reassuring voice, one of the few Spanish words I had learned.

Then speaking quietly in English, trusting to my tone to convey my meaning, I came up on the crouching figure of a young girl, possibly eleven but more likely going on thirteen, small because of scanty rations. Her pale-brown skin was crusted here and there with dirt and well-nigh covered from scratches from thorns and brambles. But I noticed something else that sped a flood of pity to my heart and rage into my brain. Across her shoulders was a welt that had been made by a white man's whip.

Obviously the whimpering child was an Indian slave in desperate flight from her master.

2

I took her small, hard little hand and pressed it. At once her whimpering ceased; she knew this was a sign I was her friend and meant her no harm; I think that newborn babes can thus interpret this sign, but by what mysterious process such an instinct could obtain I had no time now to think. The young girl walked beside and very close to me to the edge of the thicket, but shrank back at sight of Richard and Tom. "*Amigos, amigos,*" I assured her, thanking God that I knew the word and that she did also. Then to them, "Please come up slowly and smile big smiles." Again a wonder, a newborn babe seems to understand the meaning of curled lips as opposed to lips straight and prim.

"Ask her her name," I bade Tom. He did so, in Spanish.

The girl answered what sounded like *Weecheepas*.

"That's odd," Tom commented. "It's very close to the Cuban word for swallow, the bird, not the act. Yet I'd swear she's not native to Cuba. Her skin is too pale; there's a different conformity of facial features."

"*Amigos,*" I reminded the child, pointing to my two companions, for their strange talk, obviously concerning her, had dismayed her somewhat.

"*Sí,*" the young maiden answered happily.

I pointed to myself and said slowly, "*Me—Martyn Papa.*"

"*Sí,*" she agreed, nodding vigorously and with the first trace of a smile.

"*Tú—Weechee?*"

"*Sí.*" This with emphasis amounting to enthusiasm.

And then, thinking fast, I took it that Weechee was in imitation of a swallow's shrill, pleasing shriek and would be a natural name for the bird in many Indian nations. The affix *pas* might well mean bird in her own nation as well as in Cuba. Long ago, when my curious mind had caused me to ask Mistress Barton of the origin of words, she, wondrously well-read, had told me that many words were "onomatopoeic," and had then explained the meaning of the jawbreaker.

"Ask her if she has been a slave?" I prompted Tom Warner. Again her answer was "*sí*" but in a faltering tone, as though the very word slave was not only sorrowful but shameful.

"Ask who was her master?"

The child's answer was "*el señor.*" Then her face paled and her hand trembled in mine.

"Ask her if she has run away?" Her reply was a feeble "*sí,*" but this had been a thoughtless question, for renewed terror came into her eyes and she turned them into mine in mute and pitiful petition.

But a greater fright was in store for her, for at the next instant we heard the ominous bay of a hound. Still holding one of my hands, she clutched my leg with her free arm. Again I smiled at her upraised pleading face, and nodded.

"Tell her not to be afraid," I said hastily; and when Tom had done so I bade both men unsling their bows and nock arrows on the cords.

"What do you mean to do, Martyn?" Thomas asked anxiously. "There may be a big party."

"I think not, chasing one little runaway." After listening a moment, I was sure there was not. Dimly across the silences I could hear voices, for walkers following a hound are forever shouting back and forth, and in this case I could distinguish but three. One was loud, angry, and commanding—obviously it belonged to the foreman or more likely the master himself—the other two were those of Spanish-speak-

ing Indians, somewhat shrill as Indian voices become when the shout-
ers are excited, and in this case servile and placative.

"What are they saying?" I asked Tom.

Tom answered with the grin.

"The boss is saying he'll flay them alive—burn them at the stake—
lash them to quivering corpses—unless they catch the runaway. They
have fanned out from the master and his hound and are replying that
the brush keeps getting in their way, and they're coming as fast as
they can, and they'll surely catch the little ingrate, never fear . . . Just
now the *señor* is cursing the dog for leaving the girl's tracks to flush
a rabbit."

"We'll step into the thicket to take a look at them."

Reassuring the child, patting her back, pressing her hand, and once
bending down to kiss her dirty, thorn-scratched cheek, I drew her back
from the open glade, Richard and Tom beside me. The girl had
flinched from the touch of my lips, as though she feared I would bite
her; and I recalled from reading that kissing was unknown to many
primitive peoples, the more fools they, for there is no sweeter or more
gratifying caress on earth, or one more mutely meaningful, always
accompanying high civilization. But at once she divined its meaning
and her terror diminished in a marked degree.

Soon we came in sight of the hound, avidly sniffing the trail, and
then the three hunters. The dog was a hound of sorts, no doubt a
mixed breed; the two naked Indians were indistinguishable from most
Hispaniola natives, not to be compared to the stalwart, warlike Caribs
of the Lesser Antilles. While coaching Tom, I let the hunting party
draw within a hundred paces. I had already observed that the *señor*
was too dark to be purebred Spanish; presently I decided he was
mestizo and had a brutal countenance. In his right hand he carried a
whip with a long lash, as handy for dogs as for slaves. Over his left
shoulder was a rusty musket.

When they were within forty yards of us, Warner stepped into their
plain sight.

"We've found the little girl," he called.

"*Bueno! Bueno!*" the man called in great satisfaction. Then in sudden anxiety, he asked a question.

"We are Englishmen," Tom replied. "Our warship lies at anchor in
the bay. Please stop where you are."

As Thomas told me in English what he had said, the hound began
to bark, at which the *señor* swore at him and struck him lightly with
his whip. At this Richard and I emerged from the thickets and stood
at Tom's side, Weechee close beside me; but her hand was no longer
in mine for I had partially raised my half-bent bow with a nocked

arrow. Richard and Tom had done the like, which the three slave catchers had not failed to mark.

"I am the Señor Pedro Mondego. You are hunting on my land. But I will not report it to our alcalde if you deliver to me my runaway slave, and in fact you may then hunt to your heart's desire. What are quarrels between kings and queens to good fellows such as we?"

Of this Tom gave me a brief translation. "Tell him to lay down his musket and be sure it does not fire."

When Tom had translated the command, Pedro dropped his whip and swung the weapon into position to raise to his shoulder. But we three companions drew our bows somewhat more deeply.

"Why this foolish quarrel?" the man asked plaintively. "I want only my lawful property, a captive girl of some Carib Indians blown on my shore by a gale three years gone, and I paid for her with foodstuffs worth a golden peso. Since then I have cared for her well, and her gratitude for that care was to steal away in the dead of night. Deliver her, and I will tell you where you may find many deer, fat stags and sleek hinds, and if you call at my 'cienda I will give you a flagon of wine for your trouble."

When Tom started to condense this long speech I bade him take his time—we were in no hurry—and to translate it in detail.

"Tell him we will count to five, and if by then he has not laid down his musket, we will give him not the maiden but three arrows, one for each of his Indians and one for himself. They will not be warming as wine in his and his men's bellies, but will have more tang, until they induce a heavy chill." And I knew that my lips had drawn back as when I had fought the prison guard, and taut muscles there and around my eyes felt good.

When Tom had translated this, I told him to begin his count aloud, not rapidly but distinctly. When he reached "tres" Don Pedro laid down his musket.

"I have no choice," he cried plaintively. "Two of my men are unarmed but as a caballero—"

I had caught the last word and interrupted Tom's translation.

"Caballero? Son of a bitch!" This last was in English, but I did not doubt that the slave catcher grasped its meaning. There is no group of words in any language so quickly picked up by people of other tongues as profanities and obscenities.

At my direction, Tom ordered the man to draw back twenty steps and kneel down. Thoroughly cowed now, he obeyed. Shouldering my bow but with a barbed arrow in my left hand, I picked up the whip Pedro had dropped as he had started to raise his musket. I need glance but once more at the red welt across the top of Weechee's back and shoulders to know what I craved to do.

Rolling up my prisoner's shirt and stuffing the tail of it around his neck, I struck his bared back with all my strength. It was a strong whip and my arm had been phenomenally strong, and Pedro screamed with pain. At once drops of blood seeped up through the mangled flesh from one shoulder blade to the other, and the vicious lash curled up over his opposite shoulder, to leave no doubt a red welt.

This was all the punishment I had intended to administer, but the matter was taken out of my hands. Snatching the whip, Weechee began to lay it on, her eyes blazing with fury, and her little naked arm was far stronger than it looked. He howled at every fall of the lash, although a strong man would have only grunted. I let her lash him to her heart's content, which I thought would never be gained, but at last her arm tired and she began to weep. His two Indian slaves watched their avenger with starbright eyes.

We gathered up our belongings, with the new addition of Weechee, and her late owner's musket and his whip, and started toward the *Lion's* anchorage, Weechee firmly clasping my hand. Before long we emerged from the woods to the stream that we had ascended a distance from the beach where our ship's boats lay. Soon thereafter we heard the wind-blown shouts and laughter of our fellow colonists bathing and enjoying their holiday from many days at sea. They were in no danger of captivity by Indian or don; Captain Irish had ordered their coverings by his demicannon. Nor was there any danger of pursuit by a stronger party assembled by Weechee's late master.

It happened that I had planned to take a sea bath after the hunt, and had had the forethought to bring along a cake of soap in my small kit. I fell to thinking of a better use for it, for I did not want to present my acquisition in her present state of grime. Also her long black hair was matted and intertangled with burrs, pieces of thorny vine, and leaves. I had no comb because I wore my hair short, in peasant-fashion, but Richard always carried one, in respect to his fair hair worn long and his fine mustachios and pointed beard. We had now come to an almost still pool, perhaps three feet deep, in a hollow in the creek bed, and in easy hearing of the beach. So I asked him if he would lend it for a good purpose.

At once he put it in my hand.

"You intend to tidy her up a bit, and a good thing, too," Richard remarked. "But what about a fig leaf of some sort for your pale-brown Eve? On your previous voyage you became accustomed to seeing naked savages of both sexes and all ages, and they're to be seen every day on the Spanish wharves, but our colonists are mainly insular, and the Puritans inclined to be prudish."

"I've a piece of linen around my spare arrows in my quiver," Thomas Warner broke in. "It was to protect them from breakage if the quiver got a hard rap in heavy brush. I think it's long enough to ease outraged Puritan consciences."

He produced the cloth, then he and Richard prepared to sit down to watch the ablutions. I considered this, felt like a fool, then acted as my instincts bade me.

"It occurs to me this should be a somewhat private affair," I said. "I don't exactly know why, unless it's in the way of starting Weechee out in so-called civilized procedures. At present I'm her finder, her guardian, and as far as I know, her owner. She's used to going naked but she might object to onlookers to her being bathed. I was long enough in the islands to know that Indians observe what Raleigh, and before him, Magellan's men, reported regarding the islanders of the great southern sea. Certain actions, supposed to bring bad luck, are called *tabu*."

"If you know what I think," Richard said with only an undertone of humor, "you are going to enjoy the little rite, but don't want to share it with anyone but Weechee."

"Yes, it will be enjoyable," I said with complete honesty. "But it won't be underhand."

"I didn't mean that, old friend. No such thought could cross my mind. I think you're on the right track, even if it doesn't make palpable sense. Tom and I will wait for you around the next bend of the stream. If you see Spaniards coming, give us a shout."

The two men trudged cheerfully away. I removed all my clothes in as matter of fact a way as possible; her quick mind had already leaped to the supposition I was going swimming in the pool. As for naked men, she had seen them all her days; I was merely a *white* naked man. She became interested only when I stood waist deep and soaped my wetted chest and arms. Presently I called her name, and beckoned for her to join me. She did so with perfect trust and what seemed to me joy.

She caught the idea of the soap when I scrubbed her dirty face, hands, arms and chest. She saw the dirty soapsuds and said, *"bueno!"* The bathing of most of the remainder of her body was no problem whatever; still I did not know what would be her response to my bathing her vulva, the first step in an examination I felt I must make, to discover if she had been raped and that was reason for her desperate flight into the forest. I thought her color rose as I did so, but she made no objection when, as she lay in shallow water, I parted its lips. There were no bruises in that region, no outcry of pain when I applied a little pressure, and I concluded that the act I feared had not occurred. Still the cruel lash across her back must have been dealt in fury, so it seemed likely, but not certain, that it had been given her for refusing a degenerate lecher's proposal.

As for me, I was so intent on my inquiry that no sensuality enveloped my mind. Perhaps it was partly a feat of will. I could not deny that to her the examination was pleasurable, simply a physical response, for her color heightened and her eyes had an unmistakable shine; but as soon as it was over, she evinced the same curiosity in regard to the soap.

She stood in the shallows, admiring her own body. Truly it was lovely, her legs slim and long and shapely, her waist narrow with what looked like elastic skin; her breasts barely beginning to swell. I could not make up my mind about her countenance, although I never doubted it was attractive. The cheekbones were of course high, the forehead slanting, her nose was no longer a childish lump, but was straight and narrow, her mouth was sweet-looking and her teeth even and snowy white. Her eyes had an extraordinary bright sheen, and a sparkle when she smiled, as she was smiling now.

I was not done with her toilet yet. I began the pleasant task of combing her hair, a difficult task too because it was matted. I had washed out most of its dirt, but the burrs had to be combed out. She closed her lips tight when the pull hurt, made no sound, and brushed away the tears that frequently filled her eyes.

But my reward was plenteous. Drying her hair on my own shirt, I saw its raven luster. It was not at all coarse, as is most Indian hair, but as fine as an Englishwoman's, and that was my first inkling that she might not be West Indian, but had been brought as a captive from some distant land inhabited by people of the same basic stock but of definitely different appearance because of a different environment. The Carib Indians, from whom the mestizo said he had bought her, were known to range far on their piratical journeys, and one of Cortes' captains had written that they had occasionally visited the mainland.

In any case, I felt an unbounded pride in her, and could hardly wait to show her to my countrymen.

Finally I took Tom's linen cloth and found it of ample size to go around her waist and conceal her loins. Fastening it was a problem until suddenly she made a little outcry and ran to a nearby clump of thickets. I felt an absurd fear that she had run away—as Morgan le Fay had faded away from Roland's sight when he had failed to grasp her by the forelock—but was reassured by her slow movements in the brush. Meanwhile I dressed, wondering what new surprise she would give me. In a moment more she appeared, pridefully showing me a dozen thorns about two inches long, as sharp and almost as slender as needles. She herself inserted them at the folded joining of the strip of linen, weaving them in and out, and leaving their points on the outside where they would not prick her skin.

Then, her hand in mine, I made my triumphant advance around the bend in the stream to a grassy bank where Richard and Tom awaited us. They both stared, then rose to their feet as might men newly wakened from a dream.

"Oh, *Santo Dios!*" Tom exclaimed, showing that his seventeen years of learning and speaking Spanish had underminded the reflexes of thinking and speaking English; and that in moments of great astonishment the adopted language sprang to his tongue.

"Bless'd God!" Richard broke forth, oddly enough expressing exactly the same thought.

Then they stared for long seconds in silence. Finally Tom gave me the big grin of which I was so fond.

"This is the second slave you've saved from the Spanish chain, such a coincidence that I would think it was ordained by Fate, but I stayed an ordinary man, while this child—"

"Your waif is a second Cinderella," Richard broke in, with far more intensity in his tone than he had wanted to reveal.

"Comely, I confess," I remarked with all the nonchalance I could manage.

"And if I hadn't missed that deer . . . I told you I'd be punished. But I didn't think it would be this severe."

"Richard, she's only a pretty young Indian wench."

"I suppose so. But finding her so dirty, and her hair so matted, and then seeing her now . . . Good heavens, that raven in her hair. And the gloss of her skin. What are you going to do with her, Martyn?"

"Keep her, of course. I mean until she grows up. Then maybe I'll marry her off to Thomas Smart, who's a likely lad."

"The people are moving back to the boats," Tom broke in. "We'd better go too. They'll stare at what we've got, Mr. Martyn, but they won't be astonished as we three, and in fact they might not even stare or feel any wonder. A few will—the more imaginative. But your English shopkeeper is hard to startle. An Indian wench is an Indian wench. They haven't seen her as we saw her first."

Richard and Tom started off together. But they had gone hardly twenty steps when Richard fell back to walk with Weechee and me, the child still tightly clinging to my hand.

"See here, Martyn," Richard said rapidly, in an undertone. "You've seen me be a fool before, but never such as big a fool as you'll see me now."

"What is on your mind, Richard, old friend?"

"You're poor and I'm rich. You're of peasant birth and I'm the son of a lord's daughter. Naturally I can sway power that you can't, and I don't think the authorities will let you keep that child—particularly John White. Yet I'll give you ten pounds for her, the deal made right now, and pay you when we get to the ship."

"Richard, I'm not a slave dealer."

"You fool, don't you know that your only hope of getting something out of her, or of keeping her either, is that you've seized her from an enemy Spaniard and slavery is a legal institution not only in Spain but in England? Our privateers catch and sell slaves. And who else would pay you ten pounds for a child of that age?"

"Still, Richard, I won't sell her. If I sold her to anyone it would be to you, but I'm not permitted to sell her. I simply could not bring myself to do it—to count her as a slave when Fate let me find her. It would mean betraying her and myself too."

"Within a week she'll trust me as she now trusts you."

This might be true. But I had not failed to see the extreme anxiety in her eyes as Richard and I talked. Well she knew that she was the subject of that talk. Her hand pressed mine with great strength and she looked imploringly into my face.

"What if I made it twenty pounds? That's insane, I know, but I can afford it, and you can't afford to refuse me."

"I do refuse, Richard. It would be like selling myself for twenty pounds."

"I don't see the connection, but I plainly see it's no deal. All right. You were always stubborn and your father the like. I'm not angry. Maybe I think more of you than ever for being a fool—anyway I'm a fool too. Shake hands with me."

"Proudly and gladly."

We shook hands and he quickened his step until he caught up with Tom.

3

Thomas Warner had been quite right in his surmise as to the colonists' attitude toward the newcomer. All day they had beheld wonders, beautiful flowers for the plucking, luscious fruits for the picking, fairyland scenery for the looking; and had exhausted all their exclamations of wonder and surprise. They could hardly fail to note Weechee's exquisite symmetry of form but her face was alien-looking and thus unattractive to their conventionalized tastes, and they would have evinced more admiration for any ordinarily pretty and winsome white girl of this age. They quite failed to note the dignity of her behavior in the presence of numerous strangers. She had released my hand and walked behind me, but with her head proudly raised and her face serene. For three years she had been a slave; but I made the sudden guess, the truth of which I had no real doubt, that before then she had been the daughter of a great chieftain, possibly the king of a powerful Indian nation.

However, my obtaining official permission to keep her and not have her put in the care of "some good woman" might not be smooth sailing. Thomas Ellis, the former vestryman, looked shocked at her presence in the company of two lusty youths, although white-haired Thomas Warner lent some respectability to the association. When the quarter-master caught sight of her and was told she was a runaway slave, he suggested that she have a mat in the hold with Manteo and Towaye, since she would no doubt be more content with people of her own race. I demurred at this, saying that Weechee was obviously of a different tribe with a different language from the two Croatans; and I would be responsible for her until some better arrangement could be made. The petty officer replied that he "wa'n't sure that would look just right, meanin' no aspersion agin ye," and in any case Cap'n Irish must be notified of the young squaw's presence on the ship.

Captain Irish, not occupied with ship's business at the time, was immediately notified, and took a long, guarded look at the girl from his poop deck. Since we were not to sail until tomorrow, he had time to meditate the matter, and as a consequence he summoned to his cabin John White, Vestryman Thomas Ellis, Doctor John Jones of Wales, the lawyer Thomas Hewett, and, in all fairness, my lowly self to assist him in making a decision as to her disposition. After asking the master's permission, I brought with me the girl to speak for herself and Thomas Warner to interpret her Spanish.

We met as might any committee, around the chart table, and all the gentlemen were courteous in the extreme. Doctor Jones alone seemed mystified by her appearance and could hardly keep his eyes off the child. She did not sit in the ring, but on a stool to one side, and although her eyes were sharply alert and on guard, on the whole her manner was serene.

Captain Irish first suggested that Governor White speak to her, and hear her story, told in her own tongue. This attempt had completely negative results: Weechee did not understand one word of White's Croatan—I had already discovered her complete ignorance of the word when she, Tom, and I had had supper together. Governor White confessed himself at a loss when she spoke in her own tongue. I sensed a resemblance between the two languages but since his knowledge of Croatan was straitly limited, he did not seem to do so and gladly concurred in my suggestion that Thomas Warner act as interpreter, both he and Weechee employing Spanish.

Her story was brief in the extreme. She had been captured by marauding Carib Indians three years before, her brother had been killed, and she had been carried off and sold to *el señor*. *El señor* was a *hombre malo*. He had struck her with his whip when she would not consent to a shameful thing; all could see the welt across her back. So she had run away and was hiding in a thicket when Martyn *hombre* had found her, cared for her kindly, and then hit *el señor* on his bare back with his own whip. She desired to stay with Martyn *hombre*. Please let her stay with him.

The first comment on the story was by the vestryman, Thomas Ellis.

"I sympathize with the child's feelings," he began pompously, "but what she asks is impossible on a Christian ship or in a Christian colony."

"Your reverence, I see nothing wrong with it, if it is her desire," Doctor John Jones replied. "She may be close to thirteen, but more likely hardly twelve, and is already attached to Mr. Sutton, he having treated her kindly. Before leaving Plymouth, my fellow Welshman, the Reverend Edward Powell, told me he is a man of good character. In fact, a friendship has developed between Martyn and Edward Powell's daughter Winifred."

"That is indeed surprising, considering the difference in their social stations."

"I believe, sir, that English social stations will matter very little in the colony that is to be established in Virginia. Character and courage will be far more important."

"But, Doctor, I am thinking of the future as well as of the present. In one or two years Peewee—I meant to say Weechee—will be of marriageable age. She of course should marry a young Croatan brave. If this attachment between her and a young Englishman is permitted, it could easily start with our governor and other leaders—including myself—most wish to avoid, which is sexual communion between our unattached colonists and native girls."

"In all respect to you, sir, it would be a mighty wonder if you could prevent it," Captain Irish remarked with a faint smile. "It happened in Lane's colony—open living together—and he could do nothing about it, whatever his feelings. In the Spanish colonies their

Church has provided for it, only insisting that the girls be baptized before being taken as concubines."

"The Church of Rome—I never use that vulgar term, the Whore of Babylon—is not *my* Church," said Thomas Ellis.

"It happens to be my Church," Doctor Jones remarked quietly.

"Pardon me, sir. I greatly admire the great establishment, truly the cornerstone of Christianity in Europe, but I regard it as too lenient in many of its dealings."

"And I regard it as too strict in as many more. In any case what you call its leniency is intelligent recognition of what you might call human frailty and what I call human nature."

"The doctor's profession has made him tolerant," Captain Irish broke in. "I must say that mine has also—I have dealt with sailors all my mature life, and sailors are somewhat famed for their human frailty. But Governor White, you have not spoken as yet. Pray give us your opinion."

Our governor pondered. I waited in deep suspense. Weechee also knew that a crisis in our discussion had arisen, and her brilliant black eyes were fixed on his.

"I am somewhat at a loss. My instincts would be against a young Indian maiden cohabitating, even as a foundling, the relationship akin to that of a foster father and an adopted daughter, with a young man, whatever his good reputation. On the other hand, I feel for Weechee. She has been a slave for three years to a bad and lascivious master. She is now in charge of someone whom she trusts. I do not think Martyn would betray that trust in any way. After what she had been through, to be parted from her finder and protector would be a cruel blow to her. I would say for their relationship to continue, she his charge, at least until she is a year or two older."

"I feel the same, your honor," Doctor Jones offered.

"And I also," remarked Captain Irish in his robust voice. "Also, I can inform you gentleman on a matter that you do not know. Martyn Sutton, pikeman first class, and recommended to me by Sir Walter Raleigh, displayed not only courage but high character and intelligence in a matter arising out of the defection and later of the desertion of two colonists, and quite possibly prevented a bloody disaster. This is confidential intelligence."

"Mr. Hewett, what are the legal aspects of this affair?" the vestryman asked. "Have you given them any thought?"

"Yes, sir, I have. Slavery is legal in England and her possessions. The Queen has not sanctioned privateering against the Spanish islands, but not forbidden it either, and as a result Englishmen raid those islands, and carrying off among other things Negro and Indian slaves and selling them, some of the former in England itself. I see no essential difference between that and what Martyn Sutton did, except it was on a larger scale. Pikeman Sutton took a young female Indian slave from a Spanish slaveholder. By the precedent set by our privateers she now belongs to him. It is for him to say with whom she lodges and has her meals; her labor and services are his also; the law requires only that he give her no cruel and unusual punishments and provide for her decently. I would suggest, for propriety's sake, that he get her some more suitable clothes. The steward may, by the captain's consent, make a reasonable charge against Martyn Sutton for the food she consumes on the journey, the same as charged John Spendlove for bringing a personal servant. What I said is perfectly self-evident. As for her marrying, I am not well informed as to the rights of slaves, except that they are meager in the extreme, but offhand I would say that Martyn Sutton may select her husband if he cares to do so, or forbid her marriage all together. All this, of course, is true on an English ship and in England. That, gentlemen, concludes the statement of my opinion."

A long silence fell, during which the vestryman breathed heavily. It was broken at last by Captain Irish.

"Since Weechee may prove of value to the colony as an interpreter, no charge will be made for her rations."

"I accept your statement, Mr. Hewett," Governor White finally pronounced. "However, in this case, for the good of the colony, I think I may ask a favor of Mr. Sutton. However legal slavery may be, I trust it will never gain a foothold in the colony soon to be established on the American shore. It is my hope that much that was ill with England will obtain cure in the New World. Therefore I respectfully request Mr. Sutton in the presence of these gentlemen to give us his solemn word that he will treat his slave kindly, take no advantage of her youth and innocence, and make her no amatory addresses until she is at least fourteen, and for a full year after the onset of puberty. Indian girls can be considered mature by then—earlier than that by Indian thinking—and many English girls marry at fourteen. If he does so, I will be fully satisfied to entrust her care to him."

"Your honor, I give my solemn promise to do all you ask," I replied, looking into his face.

"In that case, gentlemen," Captain Irish intoned, "our conference is over, and I am grateful for your participation. As for me, I must chart the safest and best route to Virginia."

In the way of arraying Weechee, I asked John Chapman if I could buy two shifts from his wife Alice, a tiny vivacious woman who was long a favorite in our company. I had told him my use for them;

and John not only named a reasonable price but promised that his wife would make over the garments to mid-thigh length and fit the child fairly well, still allowing for her rapid growth. I had not the least intention of providing her with a wardrobe fit for an English girl of lowly or middle station, for in wearing such clothes, her Indian countenance would make her appear an anomaly. However, "shift" was a peculiarly significant word in England. Women and girls wore shifts or were shiftless, which spelled the difference between wantonness, or at least disreputability, and respectability.

It turned out that John Gibbs, before he had obtained employment with a saddler, had been a leatherworker. Among the stores in care of our steward, salable to colonists, was an oversupply of pliable calfskin which the chandler had thought would be useful as aprons for metalworkers and perhaps as long boots for the gathering of a New World species of tree, growing in swamps and famed for its durability, and hence a possible product of colonial export. From him I ordered two jackets of the right size for Weechee, both of which could be enlarged, one with collar and sleeves and the other sleeveless and with an open neck. Also I had him make two knee-length skirts and two pairs of sandals. This would complete her summer attire, and I meant to provide her with Indian-sewed deerskins before the onset of the chill but not severe Virginia winter.

When, in privacy, I presented her with the garments, she turned shiny-eyed, for she had begun to feel conspicuous when wearing her loincloth in the presence of the other passengers. She instantly stripped it off, feeling not the slightest shame in her nudity in the eyes of *Señor Marteen*, the name and title with which she addressed me. After trying on both costumes, she sensibly adopted the cooler of the two for present weather, and there could be no doubt of it becoming her. Indeed, with her flowing hair, she suggested the romantic portrayals of the American "naturals," now popular in England, some of them painted by John White. In thanks she timidly gave me what must be an Indian caress, which was gently to sniff my cheek. In acknowledgment I kissed her cheek, as I had done once before, and then I could not resist kissing her happy mouth, which was a poor way to go about keeping the pledge I had made to Governor White.

"*Bueno*," she breathed, then drew back in slight shame of her obvious pleasure in the caress.

"*Dos?*" I asked, for I had learned to count up to ten—*diez*—in Spanish.

"*Sí*," she whispered, with a little flush on her cheekbones.

Her lips lingered on mine a little longer than she or I had intended.

I did not appear to notice this fact, and at once, pointing to her costume, and in a casual tone, employed another of my stingy stock of Spanish words, one known to every sailor who had ever set foot on an inhabited West Indian island.

"*Bonito?*"

"*Me—feliz—ahora.*"

Feliz was near enough felicity that I understood the word, and I put *ahora* in my memory to refer it to Tom.

A literal interpretation of her expression would be, Tom told me, "I am happy this hour." Well, I would continue to make her happy, I vowed, in ways suitable to a child, or young girl, and not in underhand ways. I could kiss her at times, I thought, in the way of affection, but the subtle serpent that nests in the cellar of every young man's brain must be rigorously chained. Otherwise I would dishonor myself and bring her unhappiness in the long run. I have once spoken of "haycock venery." It was by no means an uncommon practice between peasant children younger than she—the impulses that prompted it were natural enough—and in some eastern lands I had heard that it was condoned or even encouraged, but Weechee was a child and I a grown man. Besides, I had pledged my solemn word.

I wished that Winifred was aboard. I idolized her, but that would not keep me from wooing her, well knowing that, while sensual, and not banning amatory bliss, she would accept it from me only in the degree that was acceptable to her conscience. It was true that she leaned backward considerable from her father's puritanism, or rather puritanicality if such a word existed. Still I had the feeling that Winifred would never be swept off her feet into committing any act she would regret.

To the contrary, Weechee was a young girl and helpless in my hands.

4

The winds made up Captain Irish's mind as to our course. Southerly wind bore us swiftly through Mona Passage and most conveniently shifted into the southwest. When we were well out of wrecking-range of Navidad Bank, we sailed generally northeast of the main Bahamas archipelago, but we made a landfall, just where our charts would indicate we should, in a dim glimpse of San Salvador* which cosmographers had identified with Guanahani. There at ten o'clock on the night of October 11, 1492, the frantic probing of Columbus'

* Watling Island.

eyes discovered what seemed a light. At two o'clock the following morning its reality became indubitable, indubitably too it had been lit by human hands, and the Great Admiral had discovered the New World.

According to our reckoning with the sun in accordance with such timepieces as we had aboard we were about on the seventy fifth degree of longitude. If so, assuming Lane's reckonings had been reasonably correct, we were directly south of Roanoke. How far south?

Since the corrections of the tables in the last years of the fifteenth century, the astrolabe had become a trusty instrument of navigation provided its user knew elementary astronomy, and Captain Irish made bold to answer about ten degrees. One degree was reckoned at sixty miles. In six days of fair sailing, or even five if the still favorable wind remained brisk, we would be entering Croatan Sound. The colonists could hardly wait. All their dismal forebodings had come to nought and their spirits had ascended to what I feared were dangerous heights, not only because of the proverbial slip between cup and lip, but from distrust of weather and reef.

As for my own reckonings and accountings, I judged my progress since we had set sail not equal to my first and rosier dreams, but greater than I had had any right to expect according to Fate's usual dispensation of fortunes and misfortunes. I did indeed speak the Croatan language better than did Governor White, who had not a good ear, but not as well as did Weechee, who by frequent association with Manteo was picking it up as—our Wiltshire peasant's expression—a hen picks up corn. This would have been impossible, I thought, if Croatan language and her native language had not been at least distantly related, perhaps in as great a degree as French and Italian. Needless to say that when I wanted easy converse with her I had her speak Spanish, which Tom readily interpreted.

I had become a marked man on the ship, although I had no such following as had Richard Wade. The hint that his family name was not Darigem was common gossip throughout the ship and rumor had it that he was the son of some nobleman close to the throne, or a kinsman of a favorite such as Lord Leicester or Lord Essex. His very denial of such exalted place seemed to heighten its likelihood with romantic-minded shipmates. My helping to foil a mutiny, my only accomplishment that had the lightest smack of heroism, remained unknown to all except a few close-mouthed crew members and the gentlemen to whom Captain Irish had hinted some such service. These respected the secret as they had been told. My modest fame arose from three things—that a noblewoman had spoken to me when Richard had embarked, that I was obviously the master of the capable

bowyer and arrow maker, Thomas Warner, and that I had captured
an Indian slave girl whom the passengers had begun to regard as an
addition to the company and even pretty. To condone for the latter
heresy—the only word fitting for regarding any young pagan female
as personable, utterly against their insularity and religious concepts—
over and over they told one another that she would serve the colony
well as an interpreter, her interpretations to be checked against those
of Manteo and Towaye, both of whom had close-set eyes and were
thus not wholly to be trusted.

Truly my shipmates did not know how pagan, or at least uncon-
ventional, my charming captive was, although the right word could
well be innocent. It had happened that when, on account of Weechee's
fears, and I confess my own inclinations, I had asked the quartermaster that she and I share a cubby of some sort, he had protested
that the ship was already crowded as a keg of smoked herring. Then
he had remembered an adjunct to our arsenal, where was kept spare
wheels for our guns, ramrods, matches, swabs, extra fire buckets, and
the like. There was room for two mats; there being no key to the
door was "right and proper" under these circumstances. But when
Weechee had stripped her shapely little body, in complete compla-
cence, it was plainly her intention that we use only one of the mats.

In all honesty I would have enjoyed cuddling with her on cool
nights; but not because of ship talk as much as of mistrust of my
own self-control, I had to deny her her wish. This she did not in the
least understand, and in fact it hurt her feelings. She said, "*Tú no
amar me*," which was bad Spanish, but as good as I could comprehend, which fact she seemed to realize. Her eyes were brilliant with
tears in the glint of our guttering candle.

When I still refused, she told me "*Me detestar tú.*" But I persuaded
her to sit on my lap, where I gave her more kisses than my conscience
could justify. One was longer than I intended, for the inner stirrings
it caused she was not prepared, and with a startled expression she
hastily left my knees and quietly and docilely repaired to her own
mat.

What I was not prepared for was her saying in mixed Spanish
and English one day, "*Me verdadero hungree!*" There was no longer
any doubt that she had a gift for languages, which I had previously
heard was not at all rare among Indians. I reckoned that she would
master English before I could speak tolerable Croatan.

She never evinced the slightest desire to imitate white women in
dress. Indeed, when we celebrated our first landfall—obviously Cape
Hatoraske—with the best we could do in the way of a gala dinner,
she had prepared a "surprise" mainly for my benefit. First she had

asked me for a piece of silver, her wants perfectly apparent when she patted my pouch and said, "Jingle, jingle." I had given her a shilling, and she had persuaded Tom to buy for her, from our store-keeper, one of the brass headrings, among our trading goods, and this she had polished until it shone like gold. After combing her hair straight back, she had fitted the ring over her scalp barely above her forehead and then dressed her hair in two glossy braids, fastening the ends with bits of red ribbon. One of these she wore in front of each shoulder, and in contrast with her brown vestments and pale brown skin, their effect was attractive and rather startling. The island Indians had the repute of being mentally sluggish. Very patently Weechee had a lively mind. She sat with great dignity between Tom and me, and any scoffing of the report that she was a princess of some sort was silenced.

The wind turned foul after midnight, and Captain Irish was hard put to it in the drizzly, windy dawn to find the passage through the barrier reefs into Croatan Sound. More than once we felt sand under our keel, and only the strong puffs of the western wind into a hastily spread sheet kept us from being grounded.

All our colonists were up, close behind the sun. All were aware of the confusion on the bridge; and presently they were lining the rails, anxiety on every face. I stood between Weechee and the youth, Thomas Smart, who had given such staunch help to Tom and me on a night of the attempted mutiny. I was truly alarmed by this danger-ous sailing, as Weechee well knew. But my own apprehension, and hence hers also, were forgotten in sudden sympathy for the youth, who had just made a wistful remark.

"I wouldn't wonder but my father is standing somewhere on the shore, watching us and praying for us."

I had forgotten for the moment that Thomas' father had been one of a group of men, numbering from fifteen to eighteen, who had chosen or been ordered to remain on Roanoke Island by Sir Richard Gren-ville. At the time Thomas had been little more than an urchin in an English shire; now he was almost a man, and expected to do the part of one in the upbuilding of the new colony. But I did not like to contemplate what might be the fate and fortunes of such a small num-ber of white men at the edge of the forest sparsely inhabited by primitive natives. The mistake of one might mean the death of all. Most heartily I hoped that the vision Thomas had just revealed to us was a true vision.

"Thomas, is your mother alive? I believe you told me that she is."

"Yes, and I have an uncle to help work the farm, so I could make this trip. My mother has never for a moment let herself doubt that she and Papa would be united. She gave him a ring her grandfather had given her, of solid gold it is, and it has a seal with a unicorn engraved on it, and it's been in the family since the battle of Crécy, or so the tale goes. Mr. Sutton, doesn't it stand to your reason that those fifteen or more men are all right? It's a rich land, Sir Richard left them seed to make a crop, they had falconets in the blockhouse, besides muskets to kill deer."

My thoughts were flying and not very steady, perhaps not very sensible. One of them was of English lords and Scotch lairds and French monseigneurs shooting deer for sport. They had powder and balls to waste, and the latest wheel-lock muskets. A feast or a famine did not depend on whether one of them missed his aim; it would be only a subject of raillity.

"Thomas, we'll have to wait and see," I answered. For I would not insult this earnest young man, his eyes pouring their plea into mine, with an easy, wish-thinking answer.

"If he is all right, I'll want him to go home on Cap'n Irish's ship, and I'll take his place in the colony. I'm well grown for my years, and can do a man's work."

There was another contingency which had not occurred to the youth, as far as I could tell. Thomas the elder might have taken an Indian woman. It was a common thing indeed in the Spanish colonies, when a colonial made any extended stay on the island, and it had made for easy living. Often when their legal wives had come out to join these husbands, they had not been welcome, and trouble, sometimes bad enough to cause bloodshed, had come to pass. The colonists' standing in society had not been a considerable factor. The Spanish hero, Hernán Cortés, governor of the Spanish mainland, had been a conspicuous example. When his wife Catalina had joined him at Vera Cruz he was mated with an Aztec princess, Marina; and legend had it that Cortés and Catalina were never again man and wife, and she had died a mysterious death. Two years is too long a parting for a husband and wife to be sure of everything; time and event have continued their irreversible and irresistible flight. Thomas Smart senior might not want to go home. He might not be able to do so. Also he might be lost without trace.

At that moment the pinnace, of much less draft than the *Lion,* and sailing two hundred fathoms on our port stern, flashed a signal light in the rain squall and her crew raised a great shout. Her captain, Edward Stafford, had found the break in the reefs that Captain Irish had missed. Some of our crew nodded to one another, as they set about shifting sail. They had said from the first that Stafford was the best officer in the fleet.

So the giant humbly followed the midget through the pass, and in his well-deserved humiliation Captain Irish let the pinnace lead the way northward toward the old settlement at the northern end of Roanoke Island. The weather was clearing now, and in about four hours' sail in a cross wind modified by the lee of the land, the man at the masthead cried down he had raised the island's outline. Less than an hour later all of us could see it plain.

In two hours more we spied "Fort Raleigh." The cleared land had grown to low thickets. If there were any standing houses, they had been covered and obscured by vines, and the entire scene was one of desertion and desolation.

Chapter IX

THE GREAT CHIEFTAIN

1

Governor White's original plan was that the site of Lane's old colony be abandoned and the new colony be established on the shores of Chesapeake Bay. This plan he had been forced to discard for a number of reasons. The main one, no doubt, was the objection of the financiers who had invested substantial sums in the present venture, and all of whom had kinsmen or friends to whom they had entrusted their interests and conveyed their instructions. Lane's colony had cleared away forest and built houses. There would be positively no sense in wasting this labor, since the shores of Chesapeake had no richer soil than those of Roanoke and the nearby mainland. The Lane colonists had won the friendship of the Croatan Indians, whose eager purchase of trade goods would help sustain the economy of the colony. Final pressure against going farther north had now been put on by the captains and crews of both ships now nearing port. The ships needed supplies unobtainable except in England, as well as shoring up for repairs and bottom-scraping. The voyage hence had been much longer than anticipated; they were barely seaworthy for their return, and certainly not for sailing farther north and back again. If White's extravagant notions were permitted to prevail the danger of mutiny by the sailors would become acute.

White had no choice but yield, although as a sop to his discontent, the ships would lie in anchor here for at least two weeks, the colonists living aboard them, until the ruins of Lane's colony could be made more habitable and other shelters erected. In the meantime fishweirs could be set out, the catch to be salted or dried in the now verdant sun, and supplies of Indian corn and dried venison could be obtained by the Indians with such trade goods as various colonists owned, these to be "dispensed"—the plain word "sold" was carefully avoided —to less affluent colonists. The Lane colonists had amassed some gold and a considerable count of precious pearls. It stood to reason that most of these had been hopelessly lost, but a few might be recovered, in which case the finders could exchange them for goods more useful in a colony so far from the courts of Europe.

But I saw Captain Irish and his ship's clerk exchange knowing glances. Plainly they scoffed the notion that even one pearl could be recovered from the ever shifting sands and gravel of the shallows and beaches. To my mind there had been something specious about all of their declarations. Certainly the arrangement for the colonists to live aboard for a fortnight was to give our plutocrats an opportunity to skim the cream of the trade with the Croatans—cheap and gaudy wares in exchange for two years' accumulation of pearls, gold, furs, and buffalo skins. On the excuse of spying out the country, short jaunts up and down the coast could be made in ship boats. When the colonists had been discharged, I doubted if the vessels would make straight for England. A search must be made for the missing flyboat, which would fetch them to Spanish islands undefended now, some of which had working gold mines and pearl beds barely sampled.

Sir Walter Raleigh would probably be far at sea on one of his knightly ventures when the ships hove in home; at least he would be out of favor with the Queen. As for the financial backers of the new colony, they did not know the ropes of smuggling, or any of the wiles by which masters and trusted officers could dispose of ill-gotten treasure.

To the captain's amusement, the colonists refused to share in his pessimism in regard to finding lost pearls. They had builded on it throughout the journey; now half of the men waiting for their turn to land in the ship boats had draw buckets, slop buckets, or something that would serve as a washing pan. The present intent of every seeker was to beat his shipmates to the most likely grounds. A number who had heard me talking Croatan with Manteo had asked me to find out for them the exact point of departure of Drake's overloaded ship boats. This I had done, but the chief could answer only that the frantic people had embarked from the beach or in shallow waters off a small inlet on the northern end of the island. It was suspected that John White had more detailed information, but as far as anyone knew he had not revealed it except possibly to a few favorites. No one, as far as I knew, had the effrontery to question our very Governor.

No one in my hearing had mentioned the fifteen or more men left on the island, except one misanthrope who proposed that they had in the meantime probably recovered the pearls and were hoarding them. No one demanded an immediate search for the men themselves. No speculation was offered as to their subsequent fates, and no one remarked

on the mystery of the appearance of not one of them waiting on the
shore. But back from the crowd stood a disconsolate couple, hardly
speaking to each other—there was nothing to say—but drawn together
by a common fading hope and advancing despair. One of these two
was Agnes Wood who was somehow connected with John Wood, who
had come to Roanoke in 1584 and had never returned to England. The
other was young Thomas Smart.

By and large our colonists were admitted to the ship boats in order
of rank. Governor White was in the first boat, as was of course his
daughter and son-in-law, Master and Mistress Ananias Dare, his main
assistants, Vestryman Thomas Ellis, Captain Richard Berry, John
Spendlove, and my friend Richard, along with some other gentry. Our
run-and-ruck were so used to the precedence of "great folk," that they
took no thought of this, and did not resent it, no matter how long they
had stood at the rail, because they considered it the natural order of
nature. Manteo was admitted as interpreter in case the newcomers
would encounter Indians, but actually his English vocabulary did not
exceed one hundred words. But Manteo was my fast friend; Indians
put a higher value on friendship than did most white people; and I
thought I would find him at my elbow soon after the landing. Of our
maidens only Jane Mannering was admitted, mainly, I thought, because
it did not make conspicuous the inclusion of Elisabeth Gland, Darby
Gland's deserted wife, on whom the ship's officer in command of our
boat was presently sweet.

My repute had indeed risen during the voyage, or I would not have
been ordered into the second ship's boat that was launched from the
Lion's deck. There I found myself in worthy company, the choicest in
my mind outside of Thomas Warner, Weechee, and Richard. This
included the physician and scholar John Jones and the lawyer Thomas
Hewett. Learned men of course could not hope to rank with people
of title, to which fact they were so long accustomed that they did not
give it second thought. Cuthbert White, John's kinsman, was in our
boat, as was Dyonis Harvey, a younger son or nephew of the rich
ironmonger, Sir James Harvey. So was Anthony Cage, once High
Sheriff of Huntington. So were Richard Brook, John Bright, and Roger
Prat, lesser assistants to the governor; the gentleman, Edmund English; and two other of our maidens.

Presently I set my foot on New World soil. Beside me, Weechee
took a long and happy sniff. There was indeed a taint of rotting wood,
I supposed from the houses enmeshed in vines, but the dominant smell
was of healthy and vigorous growth, fresh and hopeful. An exciting
aroma of conifers was borne to us from the mainland on the brisk west
wind, this smell unnoticeable on shipboard because of the reek of tar,

fresh paint, and perhaps crowded humanity. The whole scene was cheerful except for one detail—a half dozen or more men already washing gravel. They dipped and scraped and tipped and shook the utensils with much vehemence.

The pinnace had already landed her small component of passengers a short distance down the beach. And then for a long-drawn instant I could not believe the trusty witness of my eyes. Among them was a tall, lean man in clerical dress who looked like Edward Powell—and then he *was* Edward Powell! He saw me and gave me a big wave along with a big smile. Obviously he had transferred from the big, slow pelican-like flyboat to the skimmer-bird pinnace, for one of any number of possible reasons, when the ships were anchored off some island, or even in mid-ocean on a calm day. Nor had the company soured on one another in the long sail, for their company stood in a close, genial group. Then my eyes searched, a brief search indeed, before they fell on Winifred Powell. She stood a few feet behind the group, partially hidden by it, until I changed my own position. Then I saw she was talking gayly with Richard. This was a perfectly natural happening, I assured myself, since they had been neighbors in England, and were both bursting with talk.

Winifred had stood the journey well. This was my conscious thought, intentionally moderated to temper my feelings, which were highly intemperate. In all truth she was more beautiful to look upon than when I had seen her last, for my visions of her in dreams had been gray and somehow remote.

She too threw me a smile, small and secretive. Well, we had shared secrets, some of which stirred my pulse. Then I remembered my enchanting little ward. She too was gazing at Winifred, her ever-strange countenance utterly impassive.

"*Tú—desear—señorita,*" she said slowly.

"*No—señorita amiga.*" But *amiga* could mean either a friend or a sweetheart.

"*Tú dormir verisimlente esposo.*"

Perhaps I divined more than interpreted her Spanish corrupted for my better understanding. *Dormir* certainly meant "sleep." *Verisimlente* was a long word for an Indian waif to pick up but its resemblance to "very similar" was unmistakable, as was *esposo* to "spouse."

"No, never," I answered.

"*Pronto.*"

"No *pronto.*"

She gave thought to this, and her thoughts reduced her childish passion of jealousy. It was as though she were contemplating what actions she might take to make "no pronto" mean "never." My thoughts

were, that the little savage's emotions were perfectly natural under
the circumstances of her rescue, and they would change greatly in
changing circumstances as she grew older. She had been nearing thirteen when I had found her. She had told me so by counting on her
fingers.

Suddenly I had something much more serious to contemplate, a
matter not a little sorrowful as was Weechee's childish jealousy, but
one that might be deeply tragic. Young Thomas Smart had landed
from a boat immediately behind ours, the precedence probably obtained by the boat-officer's knowing the part he had played in foiling
the plotted mutiny. Now he was standing apart, for Agnes Wood had
not come with him; and at the edge of the excited and growing throng,
he was the image of sad solitude.

I joined him, but dared not say a word of cheer. The most I could
offer was, "Let's set about looking for signs of those men Sir Richard
left on the island. They're not here, or they would have heard the
ship bells and the gun we fired, but they may have gone to the mainland, and we might find out something. Thomas Warner will help us.
Richard will also, if I tell him the situation. I'll ask Governor White if
he'll appoint a small detail. At least we can search out the region of
the village."

"Thank you, thank you."

I went first to John White, at that moment talking to Richard. I
asked and obtained leave to speak.

"The youth Thomas Smart wants to look immediately for his father,
Thomas Smart the elder, one of those left by Sir Richard Grenville.
I would like to help him, and perhaps a few of our colony would
volunteer."

"I will, sir," Richard told the governor.

"I hope others will, for a first survey," the latter answered. "Please
keep your eyes open for any sign, Indian cooking fires, old and new
cultivation, anything of mark. I suggest you ask Doctor Jones to join
your party, and Manteo might be helpful. You should—but on second
thought, it's better not to take muskets, although Mr. Warner and yourself might carry your bows and arrows, as though you were hunting
deer. Take a glance into the stockade. Stay close to the beach, where
sign is most likely. I advise against entering the denser thickets."

In a moment I had spoken to Doctor Jones and Richard had his
longbow, for he had brought it to shore with him in hope of a soon
shot at a deer. The doctor was a robust man, no more than forty, equal
to any exercise. He agreed immediately and Governor White called
in one of his chief aides, Christopher Cooper. Humphrey Newton, who
had dwelt a year in Lane's colony and knew the lay of the land, soon

heard of our scouting trip, asked to join it, and was welcomed.

We fanned out through the low underbrush that had grown up in Lane's abandoned cornfield. Here and there we found young stalks, where fallen corns had taken root, reproduced themselves once and then again, but these were so few that I concluded the Croatan squaws had come across the channel in their canoes and harvested the main of both crops. We converged on the stockade, a ditch and an earthen wall in great need of repair, and then looked at the blockhouse in one corner, covered with creepers but otherwise stout, it being built with achicory wood. Our main find within was a falconet Lane had abandoned, rusty from the damp, but in condition to be fired, if powder and balls were handy. Of these we saw no sign, although we did see a rock that someone had chiseled with the idea of firing it in the falconet. However, the chiseler had not finished his task, for it was too large as well as jagged to fit the barrel.

There were prints of moccasined feet in the dust on the wooden floor but no sign of boot tracks.

But we made other finds on which none of us commented. One was a soapstone bowl, usable for cooking and eating, and a very large leather-covered account book or log, from which the first fifty or more sheets had been torn out. There remained about five hundred sheets of what Doctor Jones identified as John Tate paper, of good but not fine quality, and perfectly blank.

"Do you suppose Lane kept a log and tore out as much as was written on when he pulled out?" Christopher Cooper asked.

"Possibly he did," Doctor Jones replied. "On the other hand, Indians might have ripped out the sheets and made medicine over them, and finally burned or buried them. The writing would seem magical to them—perhaps black magic. But let us go on with the search."

Since there were about ten of us, only a moment or two was lost as someone glanced into all the twenty or more houses, in various stages of decay, and dismally vacant and enmeshed in vines. But a little farther on, in a small clump of brush at the foot of an immense elm tree, Tom Warner raised his voice enough to be heard by all.

"All of you come here, please."

He spoke with enough urgency that all of us made haste. What we saw was the skeleton of a tall man, intact except for the fallen jawbone, and separation at the joints on the left leg and the right arm. The left wrist and hand lay half-hidden under the pelvic bone; the legs were sharply bent at the knees, and I could not escape the grisly impression that he was in hiding, or trying to hide, when he had died. Then Doctor Jones pointed out four adjacent ribs broken on the left side.

"A big stone did that, or the ferocious blow of a war club," he said quietly. "And there's the stone lying where it fell, fully twenty pounds and hurled with terrific force. I don't doubt the crushed-in ribs killed him instantly."

Then we stood silent, until at last Doctor Jones spoke again, asking a quiet question.

"Thomas Smart, could these be the remains of your father?"

"Yes, sir, they could be. My father was a tall man, and broad-shouldered."

"Had you ever heard of him breaking an arm, a leg, or even a finger or toe? If so, I think I could detect nature's mending."

"No, sir, he never had a bone broken that I heard of. But, please sir, I'd like to look at his left hand. The fingers are out of sight under—"

Bold Richard kneeled down and, seizing the wrist bone, drew the skeletal left hand into view. On the bone of the third finger, close to the knuckle, was a dark-colored metal ring.

"I want to take off that ring and look at it," Thomas Smart said in a firm voice, his face stark white.

"You may," Doctor Jones replied. "I think it will slip over the joint in front. If not, separate the whole finger from the wrist bone."

The ring slipped easily over middle joint of the finger, and Thomas Smart began to polish its oval-shaped seal against his breeches leg, glancing at it now and then. Since the ring was gold, it had not corroded, and was only discolored by dust caked into mud by rain. At once the seal began to gleam bright. Thomas Smart gave it a long, searching glance with narrowed eyes.

"It's him, all right," he said quietly, looking into our faces. "It's Papa."

"I doubt not that more than one of the lost party wore seal rings," Christopher replied at last, his voice infirm.

"This seal shows a unicorn, plain as day. I hope that he died fighting."

"I don't doubt he fought until he was hopelessly outnumbered, then maybe he tried to hide to fight again," spoke Tom Warner who had been a slave for ten and seven years.

Thomas Smart was manly in mind and spirit if barely so in years, so Doctor Jones did not hesitate to put forward a matter puzzling to him, whatever its effects might be upon the youth.

"I wonder why the ring was not taken by his killers. Indians know gold, and it is a handsome ring besides."

"I speak!" Manteo, who had stood silent until now declared with a chieftain's dignity.

For a few seconds he groped for English words meaning what he wished to say. Then with a look of relief he turned to me and spoke in the Croatan tongue. This I immediately translated for the curious listeners.

"He said when the Indians examined the ring they saw the engraving of the unicorn. Manteo called it the 'horned horse.' They said his tribesmen feared it—it resembled a demon beast in their mythology —and they did not want to anger it. So they replaced the ring on the dead man's finger."

"I'll keep it as a memento of my father and his forefather," Thomas Smart told us in a voice shaking but very little. "As for Papa, I was going to ask him to go home with Cap'n, while I took his place. Now he can't go home, but I can take his place just the same. If you please, sirs, I'll ask you gentlemen to count on me."

Then he covered his eyes with his hand.

2

Christopher Cooper made our brief report to his chief, Governor White. The latter looked shaken, and then directed that none of the finders make known that Thomas Smart senior had been killed by Indians. Among our colonists were several hotheads. They could well demand that immediate vengeance be taken—to teach the redskins a lesson. White personally did not believe the friendly Croatans were guilty of this murder or any others that might be revealed. The Renopoaks, their hunting grounds generally north of that of the Croatans, frequently crossed to the island, especially to kill bears that fed on the oak mast here. The Wingineos were far the likeliest assassins, since Lane had had trouble with them and had been forced to kill several of them, because of their repeated raids on the fields and storehouses. Friendship between the English and the Croatans was our colony's best protection against the Secotas and the Pomiock tribe, not enemies as yet, but potentially so.

The fact had begun to dawn on me that Raleigh's last two ventures had both been rash, perhaps to a degree that some sober men would call foolhardy. The mainland tribes were by no means the docile agrarian people Columbus had found on Hispaniola and other West Indian islands, easy to enslave. Those Indians had weak bows and arrows; their spears had no flint heads but only fire-hardened points; they appeared to lack tribal organization. On the other hand our neighbors, the mainland Indians, lived mainly by hunting. Their bows were far inferior to the English bow, but Lane had seen some with "weight"—meaning the force necessary to draw them fully—of thirty pounds. Their arrows and the spears both had well-worked flint heads and could penetrate to the vitals of deer, although probably spears were thrown to dispatch buffaloes. I wondered how many of our colony would meet fates not unlike that of the elder Thomas Smart before it was strong enough in armament and fortifications to defend itself.

One high card in our hand was that Manteo's mother was chieftainess of the Croatans. Apparently matriarchal societies were not uncommon in the New World. But the Croatans were not strictly so; Manteo's father had been chief until his death.

When I asked Manteo how the pearl seekers had fared he uttered a short bay of laughter. Not a single pearl had been found.

"Why not?" I asked in the Croatan tongue. "Pearls valued at five thousand pounds were said to have been cast away in those waters."

"The white men are not looking in the right place, but if they will keep on looking, they will find many pearls."

He made this heart-stopping remark in his usual low, calm mutter.

"Manteo, do you know the right place?"

"I think so."

"Can you tell me?"

"I tell you what comes into Manteo's head." Then he began to speak rapidly, and now and then I had to ask him the meaning of a word.

"Pearls are not heavy as the broken rock of the bottom. They will wash with the waves in shallow water. There are no heavy waves when the wind blows from the west, the water is very calm, and when it blows from east, the waves break, first against headland but some drive shallow waters against a peninsula shaped like hook at tip of island. North wind, south wind, do not roughen the little cove formed by hook, long way, arrow-cast from where men looked today. But maybe they look there tomorrow."

"I think they will. Manteo, I need those pearls—as many as we can find—to buy trade goods in the ship's hold. With plenty trade goods we can get corn, meat, skins, logs, anything we need that Indians have."

Manteo took a long survey of the sky.

"Clouds almost all gone. Moon one day from full, rise before sundown. If you, Tom, and Manteo want look for pearls tonight, we do so. We can tell pearls from round gravel by feel, moonlight will show shine. But we better take lanterns, tell people we go to spear sea bass that chase little fishes into shallows. Sagamore White"—the first word appeared to mean Great Chieftain—"have fish spears, six the sailors put on shore. Also sagamore send for shovels to dig grave tomorrow morning for bones we found."

I lost no time in reporting all this to Thomas Warner, who thought the chance was at least worth trying. When in the late afternoon the

colonists prepared to return to the ship for their evening meal and
night's sleep, Tom announced that tomorrow they might dine on fresh
sea bass, as Manteo was going to show Mr. Sutton and himself how to
spear them in the shallow water. I was afraid that Richard would ask
to participate in the sport, a request I would not know how to refuse,
but his only remark was that he himself would promise to eat our
whole catch. Since he had always taken a lively and optimistic interest in any sport, I surmised that he had other plans he did not
wish to confide in me. I hoped that they were no more important
than a rendezvous with Elisabeth Gland, but they might be a visit to
the pinnace, to spend the evening in cozy talk with Edward Powell
and his beautiful daughter Winifred.

The dark thought struck me that however I might beat my friendly
rival Richard at quarterstaffs, at spiking guns, at capturing a winsome
slave girl, or even, by great fortune, at garnering pearls, I could never
run close to him in any contest the prize of which was Winifred.

The sun had barely set, although the snow-white moon, only a trace
askew from her perfect round, was well up over Homer's wine-dark
sea, when Tom, Manteo, and I feigned going fishing. Actually, when
we saw the parting of the shallow waters, forming a swiftly moving
miniature swell, as sea bass pursued their prey, we fished in earnest
until the light failed. The trick was not to pursue the bass, but to stand
perfectly still until one lazied along in reach, then thrust quickly.
Manteo made four thrusts and caught three fish, weighing from six to
eight pounds each. Tom stabbed downward thrice and speared two.
I had three chances and won once. These fish we left in the small,
moored boat our boatswain had put to our use.

Ere the light failed I had marked that the deposit of gravel which
we were to search was only about thirty paces long, and by no means
heavy. I could explain the latter fact only by the bottom being covered with broken rock, none of the pieces larger than hen eggs, yet
too heavy to wash in such small waves as swept through the less than
knee-deep water of the shallow cove. When the deepening dusk obscured all sight of us from chance watchers on the ship decks, we
each took a shovel and a bucket and began washing the fine gravel
of the deposit.

I had held no high hopes of finding even one pearl. Manteo's rea-
soning seemed sound enough, but pearls were small, and the waters
into which the colonists had cast their pearls so relatively wide. Yet
Tom found one, its smoothness, shape, and glimmer asserting its reality, in the second bucket of gravel that he washed. It was fully three-
eighths of an inch in diameter and we did not doubt that in London
it would bring ten gold sovereigns.

My incipient fever immediately rose to unseemly heights, and I could not wield the shovel and wash the gravel fast enough. If there were seed-pearls in the deposit, we did not recover them or try to do so; anyway Lane's colonists would not have traded for these when medium-sized and large pearls were obtainable in abundance; and I doubted if the Indians would have collected any. In hardly a moment Manteo's grunt told me he had found a pearl; and in fact he had found three in one washing. All three were large enough to decorate a ring, a broach, or to match shimmering fellows in a necklace. Only seconds later, I found one, larger than any but not as shapely.

Just now we were digging in what seemed a trove of pearls. We recovered more than forty in an hour's digging, then we came on a reach of gravel, perfectly resembling that which we had just worked, that contained not one. Later I had wonder at what whimsical behavior of wind and wave had worked this wonder, but now I could only dig and wash with dogged industry and not-yet-flagging hope. Then we again reached a stretch of rich gravel.

Gleaning pearl after pearl, we spoke hardly a word, only pouched our find and dug again. I found it hard to believe that three men could get rich so fast—it was my intention that the whole haul be divided—but the patent fact was useless to deny, when the evidence was so unmistakable. There was such a thing as fool's gold, its real name being mica. I wondered if there were fool's pearls, white, light pebbles smooth as silk to the touch and with such beautiful shimmer in the moonlight. Still my head remained hard and I knew that Manteo's observations had led us three to a prodigious find.

Again we came upon a reach of gravel barren of pearls. We worked through it, to find the richest trove of all in the very crook of the hook-shaped spit of beach. Here Manteo made the greatest find of the night's treasure hunt, which was a matched string of pearls on the finest of golden wire. I could not believe that the primitive civilization of the Croatans could have produced such a marvel of jewel-smithery, and it caused me to recall what I had read of Aztec jewelry, the wonder of all Western Europe when Cortés had returned from Mexico with his trove. Could this marvel have passed from hand to hand, given in tribute from a conquered Indian king to his conqueror, or won in battle, or even traded for trifles, all the way from the highlands of the incredible Aztecs to the shores of Virginia?

Soon after this we had searched the entire bed and the hour was late. We had no heart, and heaven knew no need, to search nearby banks, so we shouldered our shovels and made for the main beach. Here we put our three lights together, brought out our deep pouches, and slowly poured their glimmering contents into Manteo's English-bought hat. My quick eyes could count five at a glance, and I counted by fives, of course with a few mistakes, but the total figure that I gave my two wide-eyed friends was a hundred and twelve pearls besides the necklace. Certainly they would bring an average of nine pounds each from London jewelers—who could sell them in Antwerp for eleven or more each, or fetch seven pounds each from our store-keeper. Multiplying one hundred and twelve by seven fetched a sum of seven hundred and eighty-four pounds, the total fortune of many an English squire. After division among the three of us, our new-found fortune would be just over two hundred and sixty-one pounds apiece. How many sacks of wool such a sum would buy!

"You take charge of my share," Manteo told me quietly, speaking Croatan slowly and distinctly so I would understand.

"I do not know that I want the responsibility," I answered in the same tongue.

"I wish my friend to relieve me of the burden," Manteo remarked after deep thought. "I would give the lot to the first trader who would get me drunk enough, long enough. If you lose my share, I will not mourn or hardly care. You will buy trade goods with a good part of them. Some of these I will take, to buy a young wife, or beads, or apparel splendid in my sight. Your dream has become my dream, Sachem Martyn—that your people and my people may keep peace, and the settlement of the white man may thrive. We Indians— we have more land than we know how to use. Why should we make war because our skins are a different color, and your ways are different and better than our ways? We have much to learn and per-haps a little to teach. Let us bury deep the war ax, as do the Algonquins. Let us be as brothers."

"That we will. I think it is foreordained. And if this colony thrives, there will be other colonies, more and more, a place of refuge, new hope, and a new life, for countless of my kin in Europe. That is a noble thing. But maybe at last it will bring great trouble between your people and mine."

There fell a long pause. Sorrow came into the strong face of the great chieftain.

Then Tom Warner, of sensitive and delicate mind, had an impulse to speak.

"Manteo and I are in the same boat, as to the pearls. I would not know what to do with my share if it remained in my charge. I have few kinsmen living in Kent, most of them died while I was in slavery. For seventeen years I was a slave, and sometimes in my nightly dreams I am a slave again, and I wake up weeping. Then I remem-ber I am a freeman. Señor—sir—you use my share as you use yours, that the colony may thrive under your leadership. What would I do, or where would I go, without you?"

"Then we will regard these pearls not as our own but in our trust," I answered after a moment of profound revery. "What we want for ourselves we will buy, but Manteo has told us what we want most." And this I translated as well as I could for Manteo's understanding. He nodded gravely.

At that he raised his hand and uttered a great "Hough!" I had never before heard the word but I divined some of its meaning. Then we stood up and clasped our right hands.

3

I put the three pouches in one of the buckets, and in a few minutes we had dug enough clams to conceal them well. When we had strung our fish in the silver moonlight we launched our little boat on a silver sea, and the moment that Tom and I dipped our oars was somehow magical. The air was strangely fresh in my nostrils, and it seemed that if I wished to gaze with my whole soul into the future, it would be revealed to me, but this I dared not do. I could not bear for my present exultation to be cast down by so many sorrows that the years would surely bring, whether or not the end we sought should at last be gained.

To gain the room occupied by Weechee, I had to remove the barricade that I had told her to place there, running from shelf to shelf. Knowing exactly how it had been laid I was able to insert my hand in a crack in the door and lift down one end, so noiselessly that I did not believe my little companion would waken. However, it could not have been forced by a drunken sailor or passenger without a good deal of noise. On entering I barely glanced at her mat, to make sure she was on it and had not vanished hardly more mysteriously than she had come into my life. Then into the barrel of the falconet I thrust the three pouches, first removing and then replacing a woolen swab. The chance of it being fired tonight and my trove discovered, was too remote to consider.

Weechee had seemed in sound slumber, but now that I had leisure for a long gaze at her, I decided she was feigning sleep. True, her position was so easy and as graceful as that of a sleeping kitten, but suddenly I was by no means certain that this was not studied. The room was rather warm from the day's outpouring of summer sun upon the deck above, and the rainy squall at sundown had not cooled it noticeably. She had drawn only a corner of the blanket across her loins, and lay naked above the waist, and halfway down her thighs.

The lantern picked up the gloss of her skin and the heavy silence of the sleeping ship let me hear her breathing, not as slow and deep as a childhood sleeper.

Presently she feigned waking, rubbing seeming-sleepy eyes that were actually as alive and alert as a young vixen's. Then she sat up.

"*Wah*, you have been gone a long time," she remarked. *Wah* was an exclamation I had not heard any other Indian use, and I reckoned it a single rendering of an exclamation learned on some shore which I scarcely dared dream I would ever see or she behold again.

"We caught some fish," I said.

"I do not believe it was your main purpose, when you left me all alone. It was to go to the little ship and visit the beautiful *señorita*." Weechee told me this in an amazing mixture of Croatan, Spanish, and English.

"I did not go near the little ship. I have not laid eyes on the *señorita* or any maiden. If you promise to tell no one, I'll tell you a secret. Señor Tom and the chieftain Manteo and I went seeking pearls."

"Well, I dreamed you found some and hid them in the barrel of the big gun."

"Tell no one about your dream, for it was a true dream. *Tú promesa?*"

"*Sí.*" And with that she crossed her heart, and where she had picked up that ancient sign meaning to keep faith I did not know, unless she had been spying on lovers.

"Now I will tell you good night, for I have a busy day tomorrow." And I stooped to kiss her on both cheeks, then her soft throat I could hardly ever resist, and then her young, soft mouth.

"You know what I saw?" she asked suddenly.

"No, tell me."

"The woman who came with the man who has run away, and the handsome man you call Richard standing in a dark place on the deck. He said something to her, and she drew her finger longways and crossways across her chest as I did. And then he held her very close and kissed her a long time."

"Well?" For Weechee's eyes had a gleam I had seen before.

"Isn't kissing a long time supposed to come after some maiden crosses her heart, but you didn't do it to me, because you think of me as a child, not a young maiden."

"I've never heard of it coming after that sign. I suppose it does, frequently, after a maiden has given a promise. I'd love to kiss you a long time, Weechee, if I were your age, but as it is, it would be against the rules. Do you know how old you are?"

"*Sí*. On the big moon before the sun's shadow grew short, then started to grow long, I was—*dies* and *tres*."

It was quite wonderful, I was thinking, how well we were able to communicate, mainly in Croatan, her fluency being a recalling, with changes in word endings and other substitutions, of the speech of her own tribe. Nothing ever learned is ever quite lost—folk who have gone into a trance can remember events of their earliest childhood. Weechee had reached thirteen on the first full moon to follow the summer solstice. Since she had been in slavery for three years, she had been nearly ten when she was captured, and master of her native tongue. Yet her adaptability to a different dialect was truly remarkable.

I suppose I was dwelling on this fact to keep my mind off her sensuous suggestion. I need not be told that a maiden of thirteen and indeed younger can feel sensuality, kissing games being common in children younger than that, but that I, a man grown, and her protector forsworn, need exert his will to resist ignoble temptation startled me. This was a dangerous moment in my life. The hour was late, the night was balmy, the grace and beauty of this naked maiden was exciting my imagination.

"Kiss me just twice where it itches, or I will think you do not like me as well as the pale-haired girl, and I will not be your little girl any more, but stay with Richard, who is fine-looking and who wants me."

"Where does it itch?" I asked as calmly as I could.

"Here, and here," and she pointed to the small pink buds of the swelling mounds of her breast. "When I scratch, it does no good."

I could not possibly refuse. Her needs were as real as if she were ten years older. My refusal would mean to her that there was something wicked, dishonorable, even unnatural about her request and she would suffer guilt. My two kisses were tender but not prolonged; then she gave a long, happy sigh, yawned, turned on her side, and almost instantly fell asleep. I covered her a little more against the cool dawn and went to my own cot.

There I lay, recalling all I could of my own childhood, and of experiences I had had with girls of my own age. Our peasants made no great to-do about prepubic sexuality; they lived close enough to mother earth to perceive that sexual life and perception was not a sudden onset when a "proper" age was reached; that it was a slow and natural growth in boys and girls; and its signs were not shameful and were not to be associated with guilt. Sweet, wise mothers taught modesty and the preservation of a maiden's treasure until marriage; they did not fly into fits of denunciation about "sin"—perhaps they remembered their own childhood better than did shopkeepers' wives whose god had become "propriety." No doubt the idea was hatched by the widely taught and thunderously preached doctrine of original sin. Would preachers have preferred a world inhabited by only two human beings, handmade by God, and stuffing vegetables in a verdant Garden?

Weechee had not been so taught. Neither were the beautiful children of the south sea islands that Magellan's men, and later, other explorers had seen. It might be that she was somewhat precocious, perhaps from having been born and living all her days in a torrid climate. I had already learned she had never seen snow and frost, that her native tongue had no words for these things, and that Manteo had to explain to her the Croatan words, to her big-eyed wonder. Just before Preacher Powell had boarded the pinnace, after I had told him my intentions of going fishing, he had informed me that he wished to have a "quiet talk" with Weechee, since he had assiduously studied Spanish, Captain Spicer being his first teacher, and an officer of the pinnace his second. I wondered if the subject of the talk would be Christian morals with accent on salaciousness. I wished he would leave my little heathen alone. I had begun to believe that Weechee's bright mind could be, indeed, of great value to the colony; but if so she must be able to think and feel like an Indian, not like a Puritan.

Dwelling a while on the future fortunes of the colony, potentially so happy or so disastrous, my mind soon switched to my own good fortunes, lately. Actually I had achieved, or Fate had provided for me, three major coups since my fortuitous escape from the bilboes in Devizes prison, the latter brought about by Lady Wade and a recommendation from Captain Selkirk. Previously to this I had somehow won the loyalty of Thomas Warner, mainly through the accident of my identifying him as an Englishman, but the boon was indeed great. The three ensuing on this journey were divining, with Tom's help, a plotted mutiny and our rash but successful effort to prevent it. We had moved impulsively but escaped punishment therefor. The wildest piece of pure luck, and the only credit I could claim was taking advantage of it, was the finding of a thorn-scratched dirty runaway slave girl in the bushes. Our finding of the castaway pearls was the direct result of my making friends with Manteo, through the process of my learning the Croatan language, which demanded no great wisdom on my part, but merely common sense. The fact remained that the main of my shipmates did not employ their common sense in this direction.

4

Disposal of the pearls, to the advantage of the colony and hence to us finders, required a deal of forethought. Happily Captain Irish had openly declared "finders, keepers"; the same applied to all abandoned property by English common law, except where it conflicted with sea law, or at least the customs of the sea, in regard to abandoned vessels; in this case there might be a question of salvage, the procedures of which I did not know. It stood to my common sense that if colonists, their lives in no immediate danger, threw pearls into the ocean to expedite their own abandonment of their enterprise, those pearls could not be reclaimed from the finders.

I thought of other questions that could be raised as to the course I meant to pursue, and re-examined the cards in my hand. Then I went to sleep in peace.

With my jacket pocket half-full of pearls, in the morning I went down into the hold and told our storekeeper that I wished to look at trade goods which were on sale for colonists with the means to buy them. Other colonists were in the hold, buying little, but wistfully gazing at the stores, so I spoke clearly for all to hear.

"Sir, Governor White declared publicly that all these stores, whether supplied by Raleigh or privately owned by various officers and passengers, were for sale to colonists at their purchase price plus a twenty-five per cent charge including their storage and transport."

"That, Mr. Sutton, is correct."

"Also he made the statement that any pearls recovered from the sea or otherwise found could be traded in for stores at this same price, the pearls to be valued at seventy-five per cent of the price English jewel buyers would pay for them, according to the estimate of the goldsmith William Brown."

"Yes, and if you find any pearls, you'll also find that Mr. Brown's estimate is eminently fair. He himself is a colonist and he is not going to cheat a fellow colonist for anyone's benefit; he is a gentleman born and ethical in all his dealings. In fact, the owners of much of these goods had to insist that he accept a fee of two shillings for every pearl that he examines."

"I've already found some."

The storekeeper's eyes rounded perceptibly, and his vocal response was slightly delayed by his effort to control his voice.

"Where?"

"In the gravel beds."

"Why, that's what I call good news."

If I guessed aright this was not good news to the storekeeper but highly disconcerting news. I suspected he was hand-in-hand with the owners of the stores, and they wished to buy pearls not from the colonists at seventy-five per cent of their value in England but to obtain them from Indians at five per cent of their value.

I fished a pearl from my pocket: it happened to be one of our largest and finest. The storekeeper's jaw distinctly dropped.

"I will gladly pay Mr. Brown's fee," I said, "if he would estimate the value of this pearl."

"I don't know if he can come down just now. I reckon he'll want to wait until he can estimate several at the same time, if that many are found by the searchers."

"Do you think he would come down to estimate twenty pearls? His fee would thus be sixty shillings, or three sovereigns."

By now there was no sound in the whole hold but our voices. The other persons present were standing mute and motionless.

"Are you sure that pearl is a real pearl?" the storekeeper asked, in considerable disorder of mind.

"By no means sure. But Mr. Brown will know at first glance."

"And you have *nineteen* more?"

"Yes, for immediate purchase of trade goods on the terms agreed."

"I'll go for Mr. Brown myself." And the man hastened up the ladder.

No one spoke for some long-drawn seconds. Then Arnold Archard, who had a wife and son aboard, and limited means, came shyly up to me.

"I guess you're not telling where you found them pearls."

"When we go to shore, I'll show you. Manteo and Thomas Warner and I found them together—I'm in charge of the haul. We worked the gravel bed thoroughly last night, but we may have missed a few."

"Will you show me, too?" Ambrose Viccars asked. He too had a wife and son in the colony.

"I'll show anyone who's interested."

"When will you be going ashore?"

"As soon as I've finished my business with the storekeeper. But if you'd like to go now, I can tell you and the others where we found the pearls. Off to the west of where the men searched yesterday there's a hook-shaped peninsula forming a little cove. Search the gravel at the water's edge. If all of you want to go, and you ask the boatswain, I think he'll provide a boat."

"Please, sir, don't tell anyone else until we've washed the bed," John Prat asked.

"I can't promise that, sir, if I'm asked where we found the pearls. But if you hurry, you can get a head start."

I was happy to give that to both the Archards and the Viccars, as among the most needy and worthy of the colonists; and all the other people who rushed away with them were among our poor, and not one had been among the twenty who had such friendly intercourse with Darby Gland. I thought it entirely likely that almost everyone would find at least one pearl.

I waited alone at least five minutes for the storekeeper to reappear. When he did so it was at the end of a file of personages, the greatest being Governor John White. Behind him came Captain Irish, the jeweler William Brown, Mr. Hewett, Vestryman Thomas Ellis, and John Spendlove. The last two were believed to be owners of a large amount of trading goods.

"Well, Mr. Sutton, we meet officially again," Mr. Hewett remarked dryly. His eyes twinkled and I thought him a man given to secret amusements.

"To my pleasure, sir," I answered.

"In fact, Mr. Sutton, you have become a conspicuous figure about the ship," Captain Irish said with a touch of sarcasm.

"I recall that I played not a conspicuous, but perhaps important, part in the affair of Darby Gland," I replied to the master. He did not welcome that reply in the hearing of Governor White. If the latter's curiosity was sufficiently aroused, it might lead to an investigation of Captain Irish's competence by the Admiralty. In any case my ready answer to the insinuation would do me no harm. The captain had befriended me in the matter of Weechee; but today he was opposed to me.

There was no chart table over which to confer; the only chair in the room was taken, in the dignity of his office, by Governor White. The rest of us sat on nail and even powder kegs and varied boxes. Seated on a small box, the goldsmith put pen, inkhorn, a sheet of paper, and apothecary scales on a large box. Then he affixed his spectacles.

"With your permission, Your Excellency, I will examine the stone in question," Mr. Brown remarked to the governor.

"Pray do so."

I produced the pearl and laid it in the goldsmith's palm. He examined it for not more than ten seconds, then balanced it against fine leaden pellets.

"This is a superb pearl, of perfect skin," he announced, "and weighing just under two carats."

"What would a Flemish or English jeweler pay for it?" White asked.

"For that pearl, either would pay fifteen sovereigns, and get a bargain."

"Mr. Sutton, the storekeeper said that you had nineteen others?"

"I have a good many others, sir. They are the joint property of Mr. Thomas Warner, the chieftain Manteo, and myself. You have just looked at one of our finest. I would like to request that you judge a dozen more."

Every eye fixed on my hand as I dipped into my jacket pocket and brought out what I guessed were a dozen. Not one was as large as the one just weighed, but none was under a carat, only one was blemished, and only two were the least misshapen. Mr. Brown took note of the skin, shape, and weight of each and, after laying it in the row he was making in a shallow crack between two boards of the box, he wrote down a figure. Finally he announced the result of his examination.

"There are eleven pearls here, counting the first; one of which is worthless. Two would bring five pounds each; the remaining eight will bring from six to twelve pounds each. As for the batch of eleven I can confidently predict London buyers would pay ninety English pounds."

This announcement created no sensation. No one here except possibly Mr. Hewett was unacquainted with pearls.

"And we do not know," John Spendlove remarked thoughtfully, "how many more those three gentlemen have."

"And there is no reason for Mr. Sutton to confide in us, unless he wishes to do so," the governor said pointedly. "The matter does not seem to me relevant to the two questions asked. Captain Irish, will you please repeat the question you put to me?"

"Yes, Your Excellency. These pearls, how many we do not know, are in the possession of Mr. Sutton, who tells us he is acting for Manteo and Mr. Warner, which I have no reason to doubt. What I asked was, sir, who are the owners of these pearls?"

"And Mr. Spendlove, will you repeat your question?"

"My question was, Your Excellency, if the pearls are declared the property of the three men presently possessing them, whether owners of trade goods are bound to trade at twenty-five per cent over their cost in England, and accept the pearls at seventy-five per cent of what Mr. Brown reckons they will bring in England."

"If they do not belong to the finders, to whom, Captain Irish, do you propose they might belong?"

"They were once the property of some of Lane's colonists. They were cast away in a moment of utmost danger—"

"Pardon me, Captain," Mr. Hewett said gravely. "It has never been put forward by these colonists or Sir Francis Drake's officers, that the colonists were in any immediate danger whatsoever."

"They thought that they were—"

"I do not believe, Captain Irish, that this committee can predicate or pay the least attention to the thoughts of a hundred or more people in a big hurry to leave their colony."

Governor White cleared his throat. "I am of the opinion the matter of the ownership of the pearls be dropped here and now. They are very plainly the property of their present possessors. In fact Captain Irish announced to the whole company that if pearls were found, they would become the property of the finders."

"Perhaps I did not have the right to say that," Captain Irish protested, feebly indeed.

"Why not, when it was a self-evident fact? Since the trip began, one of the avowed purposes of the colonists was to seek the pearls abandoned by Lane's colonists."

"Mr. Sutton told me he was going fishing—"

"I will ask you, sir, not to bring up irrelevant matters. As a matter of fact, Mr. Sutton and his friends *did* catch some fish." Mr. White smiled wanly. "As for Mr. Spendlove's question, it is hardly deserving of an answer. Sir Walter Raleigh himself made the arrangement as to the colonists' rights to exchange pearls for trade goods, and at what valuations of trade goods and pearls. Mr. Hewett, can you, as a lawyer, see how any honorable answer can be made other than that arrangement is in force?"

"No, sir, I cannot."

"Then I wish to withdraw the trade goods belonging to me from the entire transaction," John Spendlove said with an ugly pout.

"Sir, you have already committed them to the arrangement, and you will not be permitted to withdraw them." Governor White spoke rather sternly, and plainly all who had doubted his strength of character, at least where the human and lawful rights of the colonists were concerned, had not a leg to stand on.

"I do not think that those of you who were permitted to buy and ship trade goods should bemoan this outcome," the governor went on. "You will be selling these goods at twenty-five per cent above their cost, the cost of shipping being only five per cent, and you will be buying pearls at seventy-five per cent of what they will bring in England. That is, of course, if Mr. Sutton and his partners wish to exchange pearls for said goods. I ask you, Mr. Sutton, if that is your intention."

"Yes, sir, perhaps to the amount of about five hundred pounds."

What one could only call a stunned silence followed this announcement. Five hundred pounds did not represent a week's expenditure of the Queen's court, or not more than a fifth of Thomas Wade's entire fortune, but it would build and perhaps arm also a pinnace, or buy the home acre of many a well-to-do gentleman in England. King Philip was said to be spending five thousand golden pesos to build and mightily weigh every one of his great galleons, for Spain had become fabulously rich with New World gold. But our venture was a minor one in cost and prominence, whatever its great aims. The main of our colonists were poor folk; not one was rich as the word was applied to noblemen. The total trade goods aboard the *Lion* had been bought for fifteen hundred pounds or less.

"Did you say five hundred pounds?" White asked quietly at last.

"Yes, your honor, I did."

"I take it you have found most of the pearls cast away by Lane's colonists."

"I do not think so. By far the greater part is probably lost forever. Manteo knew where to look for them, from knowing about where they were cast overboard and would then wash to shore."

"It sounds very simple, as you explain it. But they were sure to be found by someone, and I must express my hope that the finder will make such use of them that the whole colony will benefit."

"Your Excellency, our intention is to buy goods useful to the colonists and for which we can trade for useful things. I was a poor boy, Thomas Warner was a Spanish slave for seventeen years, and Manteo is a great chieftain, wanting the colony to thrive and thus help his people to thrive. Also he is a wise man and thinks the colony will not even survive unless it is made greatly stronger than was Lane's, and able to stand a siege by hostile Indians. With the trade goods we can buy from friendly Indians corn, deerskins, and all the logs we need for houses and fortifications. We can buy their labor to help till our own cornfields and with woodcutting."

I felt I had already said too much. I must remember that I was a peasant, talking to our governor, and our sudden riches were almost wholly Manteo's winnings and not mine. But remembering that last, I must say something more.

"You have taken this venture to heart, Martyn?" our governor said with a quiet smile.

"Yes, sir, I suppose I have. It was my father's wish I do so."

"I hope a great many of our people have. But you were about to say something more."

"Yes, sir, I was going to speak about a request that Manteo made. For you to believe it, I have to say again he is a great chief, and I say now he is a great man. He asked me to buy all the spirit that was to be used for trade and give it to the steward on the condition that it not be used for trade with Indians, or else dump it in the sea. He knows by experience that spirit is poison to his people. With your permission, I will do what he asks."

"You have my full permission," the governor answered in a strong voice.

Then up spoke John Spendlove, who was pale with fury.

"Your Excellency, in all due respect I ask that you reconsider, at least briefly, the giving of that consent. We have not come here to shelter Indians from their own vices. Many are friends one minute, and murder you the next. Some of us have invested capital in spirit. From that we hoped for the most gain. It was perfectly lawful for us to do so. I regard Sutton's suggestion as fantastic."

"I will not reconsider my decision, and you will get your money back, and a fair profit."

"Your Excellency, I yield to your high office."

"Thank you. Gentlemen, we will now go our various ways and attend our various duties."

But I went to the deck with a frightened heart. I could not help but divine that this was the greatest victory I had ever won, and it had come to pass because of Manteo's friendship; but I had made a powerful and deadly enemy.

Chapter X

ANCHORS TO WINDWARD

1

Our storekeeper looked quite ill when I had exchanged about seventy pearls, reckoned at seventy-five per cent of what they would bring from European buyers, for trade goods at twenty-five per cent above their purchase price in Europe. Governor White had promised that the colony should have twenty of the forty muskets racked in the magazine, and for these I bought all of the gunpowder offered for sale, along with fusees, ramrods, and spare parts. Even so, there were frighteningly few kegs. I determined that as little as possible of the powder would be used in hunting deer and other game, and this only at first, before the colonists could become tolerable shots with their longbows.

Also I bought all the tools available for colonists' purchase, such as axheads, saws, crowbars, anvils, sledge hammers and smaller hammers, awls and augers, wedges for splitting logs, pliers and wrenches, planes, a large assortment of files, screws and screw drivers, shovels, forceps, a hundred clasp knives to be used or traded, butcher knives, and every purchasable keg of nails. I could buy only twenty cast-iron buckets, to my regret, because the making of oaken buckets was a delicate job of carpentry, and the time would be long before colonists could learn the craft. I obtained several big spools of wire, and large skeins of fish net. I did not forget to buy scythes, rakes, and hoes, reaping hooks, heavy twine, graters, and three bellows and leather for which tanned deerskins would not substitute. I bought some of the gaudy cloth, because of its worth in trading with Indians, but a great deal of canvas, and all the bolts of good woolen cloth in the store. Remembering the concern with their children of parents of every skin, I bought a big bale of cheap, brightly painted toys. Not forgetting the squaws, I took two crates of well-packed mirrors and a crate of big scissors.

Seed corn the proprietors had provided, but had been derelict in providing the tools for its planting and harvesting, and since these had been expensive, as were many other supplies, the four hundred and ninety pounds in credit that I had received for seventy pearls were now expended. The barrels of spirit, mainly the property of John Spendlove, would have cost one hundred pounds in addition, but the steward agreed to take all but two ten-gallon casks, to dispose of it, not through a smuggler, at the Azores on his homeward sail. These remaining casks I bought and put among our stores for the use of the colonists, as Doctor Jones advised, as medicine for chills and fever, applications for infected wounds, and for a cup of cheer for all on the Queen's birthday and on Twelfth Night. I thought that the three pearls that they cost were well spent.

Much remained to buy, so I now asked Mr. Brown to appraise our pearl necklace, and because the jewels were of such good size and quality, and so perfectly matched, he estimated that European jewelers would pay three hundred pounds for the treasure, we to receive two hundred and twenty-five pounds in credit at the store.

"'Twill end up about the Queen's throat, and mark my words," Mr. Brown had burst out after patient examination of every pearl in the necklace. "'Tis a pity she's not a younger woman, with a younger and less string—I mean plumper—neck."

He still had it in his hands when no less than Winifred, accompanied by Jane Mannering, the best-born of our other spinsters, appeared in the lantern-lighted storeroom. They had come, I supposed, to buy some little article that one of them needed; but all thought of it passed from their minds at sight of the shimmering string. A covetous shine came into Jane's eyes, but only a strange wistfulness appeared in the lovely countenance of Winifred.

"Martyn, is that to be sold?" she asked.

"It is to be traded for things the colony needs more," I answered.

"What could it need more than that beautiful thing, reclaimed from the sea? Don't you perceive, Martyn, it is a sign sent to us by the True God? It couldn't have been fashioned by Croatans. It is a wonder of artistry; I cannot believe it was fashioned by any human hand."

"The Aztecs could have made it, and somehow—trading, raiding, I don't know what—it fetched up in Virginia and was obtained by one of Lane's colonists, and then thrown into the sea."

"I do not believe it. That is the way with people—always they deny miracles. I warn you, Martyn, that if you part with this sacred symbol, some awful calamity may be visited upon the colony."

Meanwhile she had taken the necklace into her slim white hand,

and I could not help but observe how her delicate skin enhanced the pale shimmer of the jewels. She was examining it very closely.

"Martyn, let me keep this in my charge," she proposed, not as a request but as a matter of due. When I hesitated, she went on in deep sincerity, "it would be best for the colony that I do so."

"I think that what it will buy will be of more importance to the colony."

She handed me the necklace with a serene expression. I examined it again, and noticed a detail I had not marked before, although I could not attach the least importance to it. The expertly made clasp of gold bore a miniature engraving which had no meaning for me other than it suggested a conventionalized tree. It seemed to me I had seen its like before but I could not remember where or when. I supposed it was a rather common conventional decoration in many parts of the world.

"If Richard will furnish the same amount of credit as you will get for this necklace—two hundred and twenty-five pounds—will you leave it in my charge?"

"Certainly."

"I'll speak to him. Wait just a few minutes."

She ascended to the deck, and in a few minutes she returned not with Richard but with John Spendlove.

"Richard did not have enough notes or coin to buy the necklace," she told me, in a soft, confiding tone. "But Mr. Spendlove has a packet of notes of La Casa di San Giorgio of Genoa of a hundred gold ducats each. That comes out thirty-seven pounds and six shillings per note."

Since Winifred had once needed help in doing sums, I took it that Mr. Spendlove had reckoned their value beforehand.

"He said that six of these notes would come to two hundred and twenty-three pounds and sixteen shillings," Winifred went on, "and that he would make up the difference with two gold sovereigns."

"That would be perfectly agreeable if the storekeeper will accept the notes."

But the storekeeper demurred. He would have to ask the paymaster of the ship. The latter made prompt and emphatic refusal.

"Our vessel has no intention of going near Genoa. It was a French possession fifty years ago—it may be a Spanish one by now. You can ask the cap'n if you please, but 'twon't be the least use. We're more than three thousand miles from home, and we're not money-changers, and only the good old pound, shilling, and pence is legal currency on this ship."

John Spendlove turned courteously to me.

"I think, Mr. Sutton, that yours and your partners' find in pearls is by no means exhausted. Will you accept six of these notes in lieu of two hundred and twenty-two pounds in pearls, as chosen by Mr. Brown?"

"No, sir, I cannot."

"I remind you, sir, that La Casa di San Giorgio is the soundest financial institution in Europe. It was the mainstay of Genoa throughout the long French occupancy. Pearls, on the other hand, fluctuate in value as various troves are found. When you return to England they may not be worth a pound apiece."

"They are worth seven pounds apiece to me now, the average run, and I have much more to buy."

"The English Jew and the English peasant are alike in their thinking. It's either jewels or coin with them."

"Sir, I think you pay undue credit to English peasants and withhold credit from English Jews. Our peasants know nothing about jewels—they could not tell a ruby from a garnet. On the other hand, English Jews are the most cosmopolitan people of our nation, in regard to finance and currencies."

I felt a soft hand on mine and heard a sad, soft voice.

"Martyn, won't you do it for me?"

"I would give you the necklace, Winifred, if the colony could afford it."

"I am not angry. I am only disappointed in you. And I fear you are making a tragic mistake in trading this Gift of the True God for mundane things such as corn and gunpowder."

I steadied and strengthened my will and answered in the only way I could.

"I take it on my head."

2

With five pounds of our new riches I was able to buy a forge, old but perfectly serviceable, that Captain Irish had in his ship's stores. Twenty pounds bought a boat that he could spare, for no provision whatever had been made for our crossing back and forth to the mainland. This was an excellent boat, with four pairs of sweeps, and could carry safely up to twenty people. Also from the stores I bought lanterns and one barrel of whale oil, this to last until we could obtain oil rendered from venison fat and from blubber obtained from small whales we could capture with our boat. The thought of whaling caused me to seek long lines, which proved impossible to obtain without Governor White's intervention in our behalf, and even so there was not one whaler's spear aboard either vessel. Well, we could improvise a few, by removing broadsword blades from their hilts and inserting them in strong, light poles. Nor need I beg these from our armorer; about a dozen were among the trade goods for purchase by Indian chiefs.

With part of the proceeds from the sale of the necklace I bought cans of paint and turpentine, and goods for trade with Indians. I took one crate of clasp knives with plain handles and good blades, and also eight burning glasses, useful to the colonists, and workers of miracles in the eyes of savages. The main of my purchase was metal pans and kettles. The latter would be scorned by the braves, but coveted by the squaws, and if Indians were at all like Europeans, which Governor White averred in respect to their fundamental natures and customs arising therefrom, the Indian women exercised far more power than they or their husbands pretended.

My question now was where to store my large and bulky purchases. I brought it to Ananias Dare, second in command, and he at once suggested the most strongly built and best preserved building in Lane's village, which was the stockade. He himself would discuss the matter with Governor White; which discussion resulted in the latter's full approval. Any trouble with Indians was unlikely as long as the ships were in port, with thundering guns and power to deal death afar. However we must build a new storehouse as soon as possible.

I would also need a storekeeper, on duty at least one hour every day, for the lending out and receiving back of tools and other transactions. I immediately thought of Thomas Smart, perfectly capable of filling such a post.

At the very last I thought of a hand mill. We would have need of such very soon because if the Indians had corn stowed from their last harvest, it would be maize, hard to reduce to meal with Indian bowls and pestles. Fortunately I found one in the hold, old but perfectly adequate, with good stones and a cast-iron frame, which could do the work of fifty pestles pounded at once. Its ownership was hard to establish; at last it was shown to be the property of a steward not now with the ship; and I sent him by the present steward one pearl worth in England about eight pounds. If the steward pocketed one, as his commission, the millowner would still be well paid.

Despite all this buying, Manteo, Thomas Warner, and I felt what Mistress Barton would have called *embarras de richesses,* for we retained numerous pearls and as yet had found nothing on the ship for which to trade them. It occurred to me that by emptying our pouches we could have let Winifred take charge of the necklace, whereby I would have won her deep gratitude and deep esteem and conceivably more than that; and it would have been a tribute to her social position, much higher than our other women. Still I did not feel that this last should be emphasized in a new, raw colony. Also the act could have caused jealousies and possibly a rift in our solidarity that could become a crevice. We now had all the goods we could store. Our armorer went so far as to give us twelve leaden cannon balls and a half cask of gunpowder for our falconet, but told me for love nor money he could spare no more without a rebuke and perhaps graver punishment from Fernando. He refused to let us have even one more musket and a further supply of shot. In all truth the pearls that we had left, although not tradable to Indians for any respectable percentage of their value, could buy labor or the fruits thereof from colonists, whose yearning was to return rich to England, and on the first ship that would remove them there.

It so happened that I did manage to buy two more boats, one with four oarlocks and the other hardly larger than a dingey, with locks for one set of oars. For this last I gave a small pearl reckoned at five pounds; and it was not worth nearly that much on an English wharf; still one workman could repair it in one day with planking and tar. In all truth I was so obsessed by boats that I frequently dreamed about them. To explain the aberration I could only recall the emphasis, recorded in every history of a great soldier or conqueror that I had read, put on the military necessity of keeping open a line of retreat.

Our colony was being established on an island. This gave us a certain safety from wandering bands of marauding Indians; in a manner of speaking it was a castle surrounded by a moat of great width. But in case of a war with united tribes of Indians, all of which had crafts or boats, it would turn into a pen unless we too had water transport. The three boats I had bought would be good for fishing and for scouting; but were a drop in the bucket in the way of means of escape to the mainland. At times I had visioned a large fleet of canoes, but in the first place their making required much time and great skill, and in the second place Lane had discovered that the warriors would not ordinarily sell their crafts; these being their dearest inanimate possession. At least this was true of the coast tribes.

It came to me that some way must be found for a fairly safe and quick exit from the island, before our colony could be reasonably secure from sudden and dire destruction.

I had asked my partners if they would consent to sending one hundred pounds in pearls—amounting to about thirteen—to my father, Thomas Sutton. They of course could send pearls to any one to whom they owed debts at home. Manteo at once replied that he could get what pearls he needed, enough for a coronet fit for king of Roanoke, from oysters taken from the sea. Thomas Warner said that he had no kinfolk other than nieces and nephews whom he barely knew, and who were in no need of such frumpery, and the gift could well interrupt their steady progress in the pursuit of learning or following honest trades. I explained that my father might spend the proceeds on buying land, thus rising in status from a peasant to a well-off yeoman; but if war broke out with Spain he would more likely contribute them to one of the various funds that must be raised. I thought with pleasure of a peasant giving more for England's survival than would many gentry or the sheriff's deputy who had behaved so inexecrably on investigating my mother's death, and others who had not realized my father's worth.

In the end I ventured to ask Captain Irish if he would provide for the delivery of the thirteen pearls to my sire. He told me that if he could not do it personally, he knew an honorable wool buyer in Salisbury who would gladly accept the mission. I wrote down my father's name and address which the captain put in his chest and I put the jewels in his care. As Governor White was in hearing, I had no misgivings whatever. When I turned to go, our leader spoke to me.

"Mr. Sutton, I wholly approve of the use you have made of the trove you and your partners have uncovered. Actually, it filled a need that had given me much concern. I was only too aware that the supplies our proprietors had provided for the colonists were wholly inadequate, but the threat of war closed their purses and I could not obtain greater contributions in time to arrive here this summer; and if we did not sail then we might never sail at all. I was even contemplating the confiscation of much of the trade goods for our use, which would have alienated the owners and turned many powerful men against us, in England itself. You have a level head, a deal of foresight, and good instincts. I am glad you are with the colony. It may be I will make many calls on you hereafter."

"I will answer them, sir, the best I can." And my voice was not as steady as I would have liked, for I had thought of my stout father, now lost to me, and how he would have relished this commendation, and of my dead mother.

On the following day all able-bodied men whose position in society permitted them to do physical labor without offense to their position and hence, by a long chain of circumstances, to the Queen, went ashore to make more livable the vine-grown houses of Lane's village. I was put in charge of a detail to begin cleaning up and strengthening the blockhouse. Some of our gentlemen went hunting for deer, to provide venison for all. Most had their own firearms; still I deplored every blast of a musket, expending powder and balls, when a well-aimed arrow would have done as well. Manteo took charge of the building of fishweirs in the shallow bay—better weirs than the Indians' own because the willows would be strengthened by wires. The arrival of about twenty unarmed Indian braves caused a ripple of excitement throughout the ship; but Doctor Jones stared as though he could not believe his eyes.

"Why," he remarked in a tone of wonder, "they've come in canoes!"

"What is wonderful about that?" I asked.

"Nothing—really," he told me after a moment's thought. "After all, this region is the divide between Indians of the Algonquin stock and the Muskhogeans, a tribe of many branches commonly called Creeks, whose lands stretch far, very far, southward on the mainland. Jean Ribaut's men who survived reported that the Muskhogeans did not employ canoes, but flat-bottomed boats made of North American cypress. De Soto, who ventured well north of Port Royal, observed the same. Manteo used the word tomahawk—an Algonquin word meaning war hatchet. The Muskhogeans have rude axes but not war hatchets."

Doctor Jones was plainly a greater scholar than I had realized. Of course this was the main cause of his coming to the New World, whether to remain with the colony or to sail home to England on the ships I did not yet know.

The Indians had brought deerskins and a few buffalo skins, and one had a handful of pearls which he found not a drug on the market but good only for buying toys and colored cloth because the more prized goods had been sold. They had come at dawn, before we workers had disembarked, and I had my first good look at Croatan Indians not far from their habitat.

They were stalwart fellows, taller, I thought, than the island Indians we had seen, with more bony and stronger faces. Perhaps from remembering visits to Lane's ships and villages none was quite naked; the women wearing leather cloaks, and persons of both sexes wore belts with flaps. Also the women wore headbands of small shells or white coral. Many of the braves wore copper pendants on their ears. They had turned sullen on learning they could not trade for spirit, on the other hand they seemed stupefied at sight of Weechee. When we workers re-embarked, the Indians had gone, and the Indian we called Towaye, of whose mind and intentions and loyalties we knew nought, had gone with them.

My detail had cut away the thickets that enmeshed the stockade, and strengthened its roof against the rain. Richard had killed two deer, both with arrows, for he had declined to use one of the ship's muskets; nor had he the least thought of borrowing one that I had bought, knowing our shortage of powder and balls. Doctor Jones had worked with his hands, along with other men, at cleaning out and repairing the Lane colonists' main well, and they had even rigged a log frame from which could hang a pulley with rope and bucket, because in case fire broke out in one of the houses, swept along by a brisk wind, a swift filling of fire buckets might prevent a mighty loss.

Other details had worked on the houses, some in a sorry state of preservation, and although they had made progress, some days must pass before even one was made livable, and several had to be virtually rebuilt. Richard Berry, the former muster captain, had charge of the large crew dispatched to labor on the dirt wall and ditch, both of which needed extensive repairs. Our spinsters and most of the wives aboard had spent most of the day weaving wicker baskets out of reeds which some sailors had cut and gathered from the shores of a fresh-water pond not far beyond Lane's village. Oddly enough their teacher was Elisabeth Gland, plain proof that she had made a previous visit to the Spanish islands where such baskets were in wide use. Weechee had needed no teaching; her little pale-brown hands had plied the reeds with marked rapidity; but whether she had acquired the skill before going into slavery or since then I did not immediately discover.

Thomas Hewett had gone with the sailors to cut reeds and returned with them, and while they had labored he had visited an Indian burial ground. What he had learned there he had confided to Doctor Jones, but to no one else.

This day set a pattern for several more. One discouraging fact emerged in this period; that the Croatan corn bins were perilously low. The harvest had not been good the preceding fall because of a summer drouth, and we could not hope to buy much corn until the following fall. This year's crop was small-eared and scant, and such seed as we could plant this late in the year, in relatively dry soil, had little chance of growing swiftly and maturing before frost, which could be expected in late October and which might strike before then.

Governor White took half our work force to clear land and plant corn as well as peas and beans, of which we had abundant seed. Still he was heard to tell Captain Irish that "he hoped Sir Walter Raleigh would not dally in sending that second supply ship," which was due to arrive "well before July first." It would not arrive "well before" that date; because the latter was at hand, and we had not yet raised her topsails. This fact disturbed our colonists about as much as the continued absence, day after day, of the flyboat. The common opinion held that the latter had turned back to England, a discouraging premise, and causing such comments as "maybe we ought to of done the same." The most gloomy ventured that she was on the ocean bottom; the more cheerful reckoned she lay at some safe port, undergoing repairs of damage done by some sudden and violent squall.

3

In this interval of waiting, Captain Stafford employed the pinnace to pay a visit to Manteo's tribe on the mainland west and slightly southward. He did not ask me to be one of the party, for no reason that I knew of, other than that my popularity among the colonists had waned in the last fortnight. There was no patent reason, other than a rumor that some one of Lane's colonists had confided to me where to look for the lost pearls, and that I had bought all available supplies useful to us in order to become "the Great Mogul"—this last term coming into the language since Vasca da Gama had established communication with India. However, no less than Manteo had wanted my help as interpreter, and also requested the presence of young Weechee, to see if the far-travelers among his people could identify her tribe.

The town lay between two inlets, accessible to both, yet to reach the house of the chieftainess I experienced my first entrance into the primeval forest. The northern part of Roanoke Island did not have such forests, nor did the tropical islands of the Spanish; or at least the latter had a different aspect. It was a moving experience.

The village was relatively new, I thought, since only a few trees in its immediate precincts had been cut down. In the necks of the inlets, low lands, yet well above normal tides, there grew a tree I had never seen, the peculiarity of which was a large stem swiftly receding in diameter so that from any view the trunk appeared concave. The tree appeared to have no name other than an Indian expression which translated meant "no rot in water." Manteo explained that its wood was used in the frames of fishweirs. It had no side branches but a lushly green top. This was the American cypress Ribaut and De Soto had described, Doctor Jones had no doubt.

Among other trees I recognized oaks, ash, elms, beech, and cedars. Even so, their identity has seemed to change in the New World climate, for they reached such magnificent height and breadth of bole. There were several varieties of oaks, one especially verdant, and which Manteo told me always grew close to water, and did not shed its leaves in the winter season. The village stood on relatively high ground, and on the hillside we flushed a flock of very large fowl, bronze in color, which were eating last year's mast. They closely resembled, and were no doubt a species of a barnyard fowl we knew as turkeys, the supposition being that their native home was Turkey. I made the likely guess that it was the fowl that one of the early travelers in Mexico had described.

The deep and thrilling silence of this forest began to worry me, because we were surely nearing the Indian village and could discern a faint, blue haze of smoke from cooking fires. No children shouted at their play, no human voice resounded, and no hatchet chopped firewood. But Manteo showed no concern.

Presently we came in sight of the houses, which appeared not much more than corner posts, to which slabs of bark and broken limbs were attached to form fragile walls. The roofs were thatch of some sort, with no visible apertures for the escape of smoke; and I reckoned that most of their cooking was done outside the houses, and in winter they depended on animal skins to defend them from the cold. Then we saw the entire population of the village squatting in rows, the men in the front ranks, naked except for their headdresses, pendants, necklaces, and belts with leather flaps, the women wearing leather cloaks, and their naked children. At their very fore squatted a fine-looking squaw of about fifty, tall and muscular, and her cloak was large enough to conceal most of her body. Also she wore a long necklace of pearls, large but mainly misshapen. And now I perceived that every Indian warrior was armed either with bow and quiver or with a spear. Moreover, there was no smile on any face. I would not say the sixty or more warriors were in an ugly mood but they were by no means in a friendly one.

"Wait; keep guns on shoulder," Manteo directed in his scanty English. Then to me, "I speak to Weoanza." The latter word might be his mother's name, I thought, but because of his solemn intonation I was more inclined to believe that it was a title, probably translatable as chieftainess.

The noble-looking squaw rose to greet her son, and they talked a moment in low tones. Then he beckoned first to Captain Stafford and then to me to come forward. Both of us did so, whereupon Manteo presented us in this turn.

"Cap'n—sagamore," he said, indicating the officer. And then, "Martyn—sachem." It was the second time he had applied the latter word to me, and I assumed it meant underchief. In this case *sagamore* might mean head chief. In acknowledgment she bowed her head slightly, and whether this was a native courtesy or one she had seen Lane's colonists practice I could not know. However, head-bowing appears a token of respect among all peoples of whom I had ever heard, and was perhaps as universal as a nod of the head to mean yes and its shake to mean no.

Then Manteo spoke rapidly to me in the Croatan language, with the admixture of a few English words.

"My mother, the Weoanza, wishes to know if the white men come in peace or in war. She says that the warriors have not forgotten how Lane Sagamore killed one of our kinsmen with his thunder gun and wounded one who is still lame. Also they killed one woman with a baby on her back, both dying from the same clap. Lane Sagamore said he mistook them for Wingineo warriors, very bad Indians, but this did not bring the dead ones back to life. They lay with blooded breasts, and they did not answer when their brothers called their names. When the dead ones were put in the ground they did not rise up, and their faces were seen no more, and their voices heard no more. We are not Wingineo, we are Croatan. If you kill one of us, we will kill all of you—so speaks Weoanza. And if your numbers are too great, we will build signal fires and call in our kinsmen the Secotas and the Pomiock, who will come in their canoes from the north, and their numbers are like the red-headed ducks that light in the bays when the leaves fall."

"Tell them we come in peace, my brother Manteo, and in sign of this we will give a gift to every warrior, every woman, and every child."

Having heard from our sailors of Lane's tragic mistake, I had made the easy guess that we might find the Croatan somewhat truculent. Oddly enough, if any of our commanders had considered this, they had not spoken of it; I think that as a whole, most of our ship's company, whether sailors or colonists, who had visited the New World before, found it difficult to regard Indians as completely human beings, with entirely human feelings; and thought that the death of three of their number three years before meant as little now to them as to themselves. It was commonly said Indians "lived from day to day," and almost with the same breath in saying that "Indians bore grudges."

In putting aboard my peace offering, which I meant to make to the Croatans regardless of their mood if I were permitted to do so, I had been addressed by Captain Stafford.

"Evidently you hope to do some profitable trading," he had remarked with a grin. "A good Jew was lost in you, Sutton."

This last was a rather typical remark concerning Jews, not at all ill-willed toward them but rather an expression of a concept so widely held that few people had ever given thought to its truth or its untruth. It was certainly true that Jews were good merchants. But also they were among the most idealistic of all peoples, perhaps to the point of mysticism—my wise father had told me this. Also he had told me that their preoccupation with jewels and coin had been brought about by persecution by the Christians, whereby they were forever being evicted from some city or kingdom, and must have their riches in as portable form as possible.

"Sir, I may find use for some of these goods," I had answered with discretion.

When I spoke to Manteo, asking that he take four stout warriors aboard the pinnace and bring to the village the three crates I had designated, Captain Stafford had caught the word "pinnace," and his interest in our babble had immediately quickened.

"What did you tell Manteo, Martyn?" he asked. "I'm in at least nominal command of this party and am supposed to know what goes on."

"Sir, I asked him to choose four men and bring three boxes of trade goods."

"I suppose you have the right to do that, but I have the right and in fact the duty to question whether this is an appropriate time to start bargaining. These fellows hardly look in the mood for that. I feel something like hostility. What did the chieftainess say? I heard her mention Lane's name."

"She had asked whether we came in peace or in war. She recalled that Lane had killed one man, wounded another, and killed a woman and the baby on her back, mistaking them for Wingineos."

"Well, I had heard that."

"I thought to placate them with a clasp knife for every man, a mirror for every woman, and a toy for every child."

"It might be a good idea—and again it might not. Placation means only one thing to an Indian—or so I've heard—and that's fear. We must not give these savages any notion that we're afraid of them."

"And in that, if I may say so, Captain, I couldn't agree with you more," said John Spendlove.

"I did not know, sir, that you had had any experience with Indians," I ventured.

"As much as yourself, *Mr.* Sutton." The emphasis on the title was palpable sarcasm, to remind all in hearing that I was not a gentleman but was presuming to act as one.

"That is true, sir, but I have the benefit of an Indian's advice."

"I am not a member of the colony—and this is a colonial affair," Captain Stafford remarked after brief thought. "You are on your own, now, so to speak. Still it is my duty to see that this visit here, which Governor White has sanctioned, does not lead to trouble." He turned quickly to Richard. "What do you say, sir?"

"Why, if Manteo approves of them, I say for Mr. Sutton to go ahead with his plans," Richard replied in a bold voice. "Our governor puts every trust in Manteo."

"I wish I could share that trust," John Spendlove muttered.

"Then, Sutton, you can go ahead," Captain Stafford directed. "But be sure and have Manteo explain that the gifts are tokens of friendship, not in any way of homage."

"I doubt if the savage mind would discern the rather fine point of difference," John Spendlove remarked.

I spoke again to Manteo, giving him added instruction. He nodded, his fine eyes gleaming. Actually I thought of a little show easy to put on, before presenting the gift that would increase our prestige with the Indians and hence their own valuation of the trifling gifts.

When he and four lithe young warriors had made off, Richard and Spendlove fell into easy conversation. Stafford turned thoughtfully to me.

"Sutton, you are a very long-headed man, or an ambitious one, or a very lucky one—perhaps all three. You began this journey as an obscure Wiltshire peasant, plucked bodily out of jail by Sir Walter Raleigh."

"You fail to mention, sir, that I was a pikeman first class under Captain Selkirk of the *Elspeth*," I said when the officer paused.

"Yes, I did. On that raid you displayed initiative and good conduct. Such was the information Captain Irish received. Well, you've certainly initiated a mighty lot since then. I am mentioning only what I know by observation. I know nothing of the events preceding the desertion of those two fellows—it is officially off the record—but there was more to it than meets the eye. What are you now? The richest man in the colony in the way of negotiable goods. Riches give power to a man, but not necessarily good judgment. Yet you trust your own judgment mighty far."

"Sir, I trust Manteo's judgment in matters such as tonight's."

"He's behind you, all right. I've heard that Indians make staunch friends—and I'm beginning to believe it—but others say they are treacherous. Well, we'll soon be taking off—we can't wait much longer for the flyboat. It would be interesting to see where you'll stand six months from now. Here comes your stuff."

Every Indian present watched the bringing of the crates, one of them large and light and two small and heavy. But I did not open them yet. I wondered if it would be good policy to have Manteo open them; certainly I meant for him to distribute the gifts. But I took from his hand the shimmering disk, rimmed with metal, that in afterthought I had asked him to fetch. This was strictly white man's business, the seeming miracle-working which all conquerors and dealers with Indians had employed, from Columbus through Cortés to Sir Walter Raleigh. The object was a burning glass, of which I had bought the whole store of eight, at the cost of four pounds. And the sun, two hours after the zenith, was blazing hot and bright.

I laid the glass on the edges of two stones, square-cut by Indian tools for some purpose I could not guess. They were about the height I wanted, and the glass gathered up the brilliant light, causing a brilliant ring, no larger than a groat, to be focused on the ground. Then I took from the metal box in which I carried flint and steel a pinch of very fine, dry moss.

Well the intently watching Indians knew what this was. They had seen the pale-faced men build fires with flint and steel—and with wondrous facility compared to their own method, which was the spinning of a drill with a cord worked back and forth, the point in a hole containing tinder. But they had never before seen fire made with neither flint nor steel, only a glass through which the sun shone in a small ring upon the tinder. When the latter began to smoke, all the watchers drew a deep breath of wonder.

When the dry moss broke into flame I added leaves and little sticks. Some young men in the audience sprang from the crouching position and began to collect sticks and to break dry branches. There was none of the usual Indian taciturnity in their faces; these were animated, and their black eyes sparkled. Plainly they proposed no little fire, fit for cooking, but a big fire, proper to a celebration.

When it was leaping high and crackling, I asked Manteo to distribute the gifts and he in turn invited several old warriors to assist him, with brief instruction in rapid Croatan, which they grasped instantly. The clasp knives, with cheap handles holding a single blade of well-smelted steel were quickly passed to the men; the receivers immediately opened these, tested the blades with their forefingers, and grunted with satisfaction. Obviously they perceived the usefulness of such knives especially for shaping arrow shafts and scores of other tasks for which their heavy, although sharp flint knives were not well fitted. I wondered how the myth had grown that Indians were a thick-headed, even a dim-witted people. True, their civilization was primitive, perhaps they were not markedly inventive; possibly they were conservative in the extreme, wedded to old ways.

The response of the women to the small, square, brass-mounted mirrors was much more amusing and dramatic. Apparently very few of them had ever gazed into a looking glass, perhaps because Lane's colonists and earlier traders had not brought goods of especial appeal to women, being under the impression that they were virtually slaves of the men, who would trade their gold, pearls, and skins for objects of more practical value. To some of the women, the mirrors may have seemed magic. They kept peeping at the reflection of their own faces, then covering the glass with their hands. A rather large number broke into laughter. A few shouted in mirthful surprise. One young woman tried to show her own image to a woman crouching beside her, only to be astounded when the image changed. Another, a slender, pretty girl in the front rank of the women immediately found use for her gift. A strand of her black hair had escaped from under a headband of white coral and small opalescent shells; with her finger she poked it back into place.

The children were the most apt in apprehending their gifts, little girls first admiring and then cuddling their cheap dolls, roughly carved manikins mostly, painted a pale brown but without any representation of clothes. Some of the boys had jack-in-the-boxes, the operation of which they learned instantly, whooping with delight; others had brightly painted whistles or small, brass horns, the right use for which they immediately discovered, and the age-old quiet of the forest was hilariously broken. Boys who had been given hoops were slower to learn their use than the receivers of other gifts. They handled them with puzzled expressions; then one bright urchin began to roll his hoop, at which one boy after another imitated the feat, found it easy, and evinced their pleasure with shouts and laughter. I was given cause to recall a most strange and indeed mysterious fact—that American Indians south and north had never discovered the wheel. Early Spanish conquerors had recorded that even the subtle Aztecs of high civilization, marvelous masons, clothmakers, and jewelers, had never seen a cart, and indeed their only beasts of burden had been human slaves.

The impression came upon me that the gifts to the children had been the best diplomacy we had employed. Other ships had brought toys and knickknacks, but possibly they had made the mistake of giving them to grown men, who had been amused by them until these were broken and the owners tired of them, and then the Indians had regretted parting with their skins and other treasures in exchange for baubles, and the end-product was resentment rather than good feeling. I began to sense what seemed to be exultation, or at least excitement, in the faces, gestures, and tones of voice of the warriors.

4

"If you want to ask about Weechee you had better do it now," Manteo told me in low tones. "I think my people are about to spread a feast."

So I asked Manteo to summon the most widely traveled of all his tribesmen. This was a man, well past middle age, of almost regal dignity, and a countenance betokening intelligence. His name was Eracano, which stood for nothing of which I knew. I shook his hand, which act he seemed to recognize as a gesture of friendship, and then I called Weechee who was now playing and shrieking with girls of her own age.

I had asked Manteo to question Eracano as to Weechee's origins, while I merely listened, for I could understand both the questions and the answers well enough.

"She was a slave of *hombres* in the southern island," Manteo explained. "She ran away and the sachem found her, and she is now his slave. But she is too pale-colored to be a native of the islands."

"I have never crossed the salt sea, and I would not know," Eracano answered, without apparent interest.

"You have traveled far, Werowance. Have you seen any people like her?"

While Eracano looked long at Weechee, studying her countenance, I gave thought to the word with which Manteo had addressed him. Since the old Indian's name had already been given me, *werowance* might be a title of some sort, perhaps a high title; on the other hand it could mean something like grandsire, or wise one, although the word had no resemblance to the common Croatan words meaning either of these. Then I observed that his hair was dressed differently from most Croatan warriors', knotted at the crown of his head and then hanging in three braids. Also on his forehead was the faint remainder of a mark made by tattoo, which seemed to be a small equilateral triangle, within a circle, its points touching the rim.

I had seen such a sign printed in an open book Doctor Jones had on his lap when I had stopped by his bench to make some comment.

"Aye, I have traveled far, Manteo Sagamore," Eracano replied in a dreamy voice. Then he began to speak rapidly, with distinct animation. "Long ago, I and three more were fishing for *chigwusso* (channel bass) off Hatoraske. The north wind rose, the sea rose also, and we could not make to shore, we were blown very fast, and we must paddle hard to keep the canoe lengthwise with the wind and wave, for if we keeled about, we would flounder. For two days and two nights the wind held. When it slacked a little, we cut up and ate one of the big fish, and there was enough water in the raw meat that we did not drink of the salt sea and go crazy and die. But at last the wind died away, the sea grew calm, and we made to the shore. And there we found a people who called themselves Montoak. The name meant the sons of Manitou, the Great Spirit."

At the pronunciation of the name of Manitou both Manteo and Eracano extended their forearms, palm upward.

"My companions and I stayed among them for nearly four moons. Because their speech was much like ours, I learned quickly to understand. Being a young man then, also I took a woman, who taught me much. Among the Montoak was a stranger—indeed they called him the Stranger instead of his true name—although he had been among them for four years. He had been a captive in battle of a tribe far to the southward of the Montoak, and his capturers had traded him to the Montoak for twenty buffalo skins, the price so cheap because his capturers believed he was attended by evil spirits, who brought the tribe drouth, sickness, and other misfortune. In all truth, he knew many things that the tribe did not know and I have no doubt they had feared him. So he dwelt with the Montoak for ten suns and more.

"Now you ask me if I know the tribe of Weechee. I do not know for certain but it is my guess it is the same tribe as the Stranger's. His color was deeper than hers, more like to copper. But the bones of his face were of the same setting as hers, and his nose was thin like hers, and his forehead had the same slant. Also his eyes appeared to be lifted at the outer corners, as do hers. This is my remembrance only; I cannot give my word the two are of the same tribe. But sometimes the Stranger spoke to me of his tribe and country. The men were tall, the women very strong and sat at council with the braves; the shadows there were shorter in the height of summer than were the shadows of the land of the Montoak, a sign that the sun was higher. The Stranger knew nothing of snow, and the only frost he had seen was in the land of the Montoak. All his people were great canoeists, the Stranger told me; so much of their land was underwater. They had bows made of the limbs of the tree that gives forth gum, and their arrows dealt death even when the skin was barely broken, because they daubed their arrow points with a paste made with chalk mixed with a viscid fluid that they pressed from the fangs of large mottled snakes with rattles in their tails—although the quickest and deadliest fluid came from a small snake of many bands of color. Their food was mainly venison—there were countless deer—and the flesh of waterfowl, such as the *woanagusso** with the sunlight gleaming through his fluffed wings alike to pearl. For this they use a light arrow with a head sharp as a needle point, and sometimes they swim underwater, so bold are they, and grasp *woanagusso* by her big black feet, and pull her under and drown

* Whistling swan.

her, and when they meet the dragon *aligador,* they do not fly from him—but of this I will speak later.

"Give me ear, white sagamore! Harken to what else do these people of the Land of the Short Shadows. There come in enormous flocks what we call *taraohow,*† and these perch in myriad numbers on the sand hammocks that lie amid the waters. These have beaks as long as a skinning knife, and sharp as a serpent's fang, and the hen will fight to protect her young. Yet these people shoot them with the same light arrows, and sometimes run down the young, which are brown and fuzzy and very fat, and fight off their mothers who sweep to their defense.

"Nor would I have you think the Strangers hunt only creatures of feather and shrink from those of fur!" Eracano went on, his voice very deep, his head erect, his manner eloquent of hauteur. "In their country, dwell black bears that fatten and grow huge from a heavy diet of fish and of mast from the water oaks. They be savage and proud, and when struck short of the death by arrow or spear they not only bawl mightily, a rising and falling noise like thunder, but rush upon the bowman or the spearman in frightful passion of revenge. Yet those archers or spear throwers stand firm, to deal the death stroke, although sometimes their thrust does not end the life of the fury-maddened beast, and the hunter is torn down, and the white fangs sink deep into scarlet flesh, and his limbs are torn from his body, and so he dies.

"And think not that the Strangers turn from *cuguara*‡ in his awesome fury! Some of these great cats are raven-black, and some brown as an old stag, and some tawny, but they are alike in their hearts, which are of fire. In our land the *cuguara* fly from the hunter, but not so in the land of the Strangers; and often they will attack unseen and without warning from their lairs. And they too will not tamely die, but only after battle most dire, and they seem to have not one life, but seven, all to be extinguished, like to a grass fire in the high heat and drouth of summer, to sink down only again to blaze up, ere he will lie still in kingly death. And the kings among the Strangers wear necklaces of the talons and the teeth of both the mighty bear and forever savage *cuguara,* and unless a king's son, or a young chieftain of high birth, has made such a necklace by his own killing, and bears wounds showing that his kill were not old and feeble, he may not become king.

"And in the waters of the land of the Strangers there dwells a

† Sand-hill cranes.
‡ The cougar or puma.

dragon that I have spoken of ere now, the skins of which white
men from distant islands had long ago come in tall ships to buy,
and which they called *aligadors*. Now this same dragon was often
seen in the rivers and swamps and on the sandbars in the land of
the Montoak, but rarely were their bodies longer than three strides.
In the land of the Strangers the same monsters often grew to a
length of four strides, or even five, and they had long and fearsome
jaws, studded with many score of teeth. And no youth among the
Strangers could sit in the magic house until, armed only with a short
spear, with a long sharp head with whetted edges, he had swum
naked in the waters where these dragons lived, and killed one of them
in battle to the death, his spear against the myriad teeth and the
awesome lashing tail of his foe. This trophy he must drag upon the
shore, and pull forth the teeth, and string some of them on a thong,
and this thong about his neck was the sign, provided he was tall
and strong and hairy in certain parts, that after magical ceremonies
he could become a warrior, and sit in the magic house with the rest.

"Now my spirit whispers that this maiden, Weechee, was snatched
from this very land, doubtless by the people of the Carib who were
wont to travel vast distances in long dug-out boats, and that they
caught the child on a riverbank or on the shores of some lonely inlet,
unprotected by the warriors, for even the Carib could not stand in
battle against the Strangers. And she wears a headband of yellow
metal, gold or perhaps copper, which taken alone would be a sign
that she is a daughter of the Strangers, but if there is still not
another sign, then she is not of that nation but some other."

"My brother Eracano, I know not your meaning, so I bid you speak
not with veiled meaning, but plainly."

"Know, then, it is not the custom of most daughters of this tribe
to wear headbands of bright metal, although these may wear headbands of white coral, or of many-colored shells, as do some of the
daughters of the Croatan. In the land of the Strangers only the daughters of the king, or of great sagamores and sachems of the blood of
the king, may wear headbands of bright metal. Also, if she is the
daughter of the king, called by the Spanish name Antonio, her color
so much lighter than the Stranger's could be readily explained. The
Stranger told me that thirty suns ago the sister of the governor of
the Spanish, Dona Antonia, married the king of the Calusa, known as
Carlos. He died young, leaving two sons, the elder called Felipe. But
Felipe was not a strong king, so the younger son of Carlos, known as
Antonio, became king, although he did not call himself by that title,
instead using an Aztec Indian title, the Calusa being distant kinsmen
of the Aztecs. It may be that Weechee is the daughter of Antonio,

but if so she would wear golden plugs in the lobes of her ears, in the custom of wives and daughters of Calusa kings. Still she might have done so once, and they were removed by her master when she was a slave. So by your leave I will look at the lobes of the ears of Weechee, to see if they have been pierced not by a fine needle, as is used when an earring is to be worn, but by a coarse needle for the admission of the bar of earplugs. Even if the aperture has closed, it would still leave sign."

I turned to Weechee, whose gaze was locked on my face.

"Did you, as a little child, wear earplugs of gold?"

"*Sí. El señor* cut them off with a small file."

"Her word is not enough to give proof," Eracano said quietly. "It was long ago. She might have seen one once, and craved it, and the dream has come to seem like truth."

"Weechee, let me look at your ears for the sign."

She turned her head, and I gazed at the cleanly molded lobes. In each there was a healed slit, perfectly perceptible in the brilliant sunlight.

"This much is proven. If she is a daughter of the Strangers, she is a daughter of the very king or of a great sagamore, his kinsman. But the daughters of other, more distant tribes, or some deep within the land, may wear earplugs and headbands of bright metal—I do not know."

"Weechee, in the land where you were a little child, and from which you were taken, was there much water, and many *aligadors* and bears, and *cuguaras?*"

"Much, much water, and my father wore a necklace of the teeth of those great beasts, just as the sachem told you." She spoke very slowly, almost as if in a dream.

"Eracano, where is the land of the Strangers? Is it close to the sea, and nigh to any island?"

"It was not on the seashore, for the Stranger never spoke of the salt sea, or of catching crabs, lobsters, and such like. Yet it must have been fairly close to the sea, for the Caribs do not raid far inland. Mark you, I have never been there, so how can I tell you where it is. I have been only to the land of the Montoak. From thence I and my brothers made our way home in our boat. We were given dried venison and parched corn, and vessels of water, and bait for our fishlines, and day after day we journeyed northward—for how many days I have forgotten.

"And now we may speak no more, for my brothers have prepared a feast. See, they have built the fire high, and they bring food from their cabins, and soon the drums will beat, and the people dance."

5

While I had talked to Eracano, several of our party had made ineffectual attempts to fraternize with the Croatan warriors. The barrier of different languages was too great, although a good many hands were shaken which the Indians perceived was the white man's sign of friendship. Richard Wade made far greater progress with the slim, pretty girl I had noticed before, who had made immediate use of the mirror given her in poking a strand of her raven hair under her headband. Now I took closer notice of the latter decoration, and perceived it was far superior to the headbands of white coral and pebbles worn by most of the women. Opalescent shells were cunningly alternated with coral beads and polished white pebbles.

Richard had played an old game, almost always successful between man and maid who did not know each other's language. He would point to some object of her dress or surroundings, after which he would speak the English name, then inquire as to the Croatan name. The latter he would try to imitate, and because his pronunciation was always faulty, she would giggle and sometimes laugh heartily. When she took the part of the questioner as to his apparel, his sword, and the seal ring he wore, it was tit for tat, for her pronunciation always sounded strange, at which he laughed, then patiently tried to instruct her in the right pronunciation, to the amusement of them both.

"Who is the pretty maiden, or is she a wife, in speech with Richard Sachem?"

"Cheewink, the daughter of Cossine Sachem, not yet wedded."

I could not fail to observe the syllable *chee* was also in the name of my young charge. Both were imitative, I thought, of the cry of a bird; in Weechee's case the swallow, while Cheewink had probably been named for a shore bird, such as the curlew or sandpiper.

The other Indian women had now brought food on wooden platters, which were decorously passed first to Captain Stafford and then to myself. Not by chance but by design I had moved very close to him, and by this action, we both appeared to be served the same time. I was not seeking an honor, but avoiding one—that of being served first, which I had thought highly probable had I stood apart, since I had directed the distribution of gifts. This might not have offended the officer under the circumstances; still it would have caused talk in our party and to permit it would have been poor diplomacy on my part. As it was, Richard was also close to Captain Stafford, and the three of us partaking of the dried venison, dried fish, and of maize cakes at the same time attracted no attention and caused no comment.

We took only a very little. The platters held only a meager amount, and were a ritualistic offering—merely a breaking bread together by white men and Indians, as a prelude to tribal celebration in our honor. Of far more import was the carrying out by two young warriors of a cask of liquor of some sort, along with half a dozen or more wooden cups. The barrel would have been of interesting construction, had I the opportunity to examine it carefully. It seemed to be a wooden frame, barrel-shaped, covered with expertly seamed birchbark. It had no cover.

We three were handed cups which we immediately dipped in a brown fluid. Its taste was not good but by no means bad, and I guessed that every fermentable fruit and vegetable obtainable at this season had been utilized. Wild plums, crab apples, and wild cherries were its main ingredients, I thought, the fruit crushed to emit its juices but not strained out. Probably wild strawberries, grapes, and currants had been used, and possibly yams, melons, and grain. I estimated that the cask held no more than twenty gallons, and if only the warriors partook, of whom there were at least sixty, the danger of a drunken orgy was not great. The drink was of higher alcoholic content than ale, but not as high as of well-made wine.

The cups were not passed to the women and I surmised that they would not take part in the dance which I expected to follow the imbibation. Presently drums were brought from what I thought was the magic house, *machucomuck* being its native name. There were four of these, all hollowed out stumps with skin covers; the drumsticks were of crudely carved wood. Young men squatted behind the drums, and as soon as every warrior had emptied a cup of the brew, they began drumming.

The rhythm was simple but exciting, one hard resounding *boom* followed by two lighter beats. The first of the warriors to arise and begin dancing were very old men, no doubt by the courtesy of the young warriors, and these lank and scarred veterans of many a battle with enemy tribes and wild beasts and adversity were at first stiff and lame, but it was quite wonderful to see how they gained agility as the hypnotic beat continued and the brew they had drunk warmed their spirits. Younger men began to join them. They danced in the open space between the fire and their squatting places, and roughly in a ring; but there was no pattern of steps or motions that each followed; rather they moved or cried out according to individual impulse. Some of them stamped, some jumped up and down, some tossed their arms wildly, some did a kind of hornpipe; one after another clapped his hand to his mouth, meanwhile shouting, whereby the effect was that of a high-pitched la-la-la-la-la. Despite their bodies' violence there was very little contortion of faces. I could not even say that the elders lost dignity by their prancing.

Yet the franzy of the dance gradually heightened. The women did not arise from their positions but they uttered shouts and wild cries, and some old squaws howled like wolves. Perhaps the rate of the beats increased somewhat, but so gradually I could not be certain of this. But it seemed to intensify, as though the utter silence of the forest about it was like a wall that threw back and re-echoed the sound.

During what seemed a spasmodic climax the beat abruptly ceased. Without crowding, with calm faces and with measured tread, the dancers refilled their cups and drank. During this interval I took from Manteo's hand the burning glass I had used and approaching Weo-anza, I put it in her hand.

"As this glass makes fire, may the honor you have paid us make warmth in the hearts of your people and my people, whereby we will forever remain friends," I told her, in careful Croatan.

"May the sun ripen in its season the corn your people plant, and that my people plant, and there be peace between us," she answered without an instant's hesitation.

When I returned to my group, my glance into Captain Stafford's face asked a question. He nodded, as I had hoped, and spoke to the others.

"I think we should go now."

We departed without ceremony except that every one of us raised our right hands. Amid the silence of the forest we heard the drums commence their rhythmic *boom,* boom-boom, *boom,* boom-boom, of such strange and wild persuasion, which the Indians could not resist, and presently their shouts and hand clapping were resumed. Manteo was greatly elated by the visit and its apparent consequences, which fact I could detect more by his stride and posture than any other expression of his countenance. He had not joined in the tribal dance, a tacit but obvious declaration that he had joined our camp.

But I was troubled by a dim haze of feelings that I could not at once isolate and examine. When I could do so, it proved to be my realization of the great gap between Indian and white. They were no less "human" than ourselves; which was to say no more beastly. Our naked bodies were identical except for less or more pigment in skin, eyes, hair; their limbs might be slightly longer in proportion to their bodies than were ours; the cheekbones were higher and more prominent than ours; their eyes appeared longer; perhaps their lips were not as fully rounded; their cheeks were more severely planed. They responded to friendship as eagerly as did we. I gravely doubted the charge that they were more treacherous; I was by no means certain that they might keep faith longer and better than did we, because of a keener sense of that abstraction we call honor.

Their culture was far more primitive. In all truth it was of the New Stone Age, as Doctor Jones referred to flints found in Devon, or of the Old Stone Age, as he termed a period of much older, more crude flints. If civilization taught anything it was not to act on impulse and sudden emotion; to take a longer view and consider the future. It is the degree of civilization, not its antiquity, that gave or withheld these advantages. Certainly the Greek and Persians and the Egyptians and the Jews of today, who had been civilized for millennia before we Germanic peoples, had no more self-restraint and perhaps less than we. In its broadest meaning, a sense of personal honor should make men more forgiving of an offense received, but in a narrow meaning it might make them more vindictive.

All that I knew for certain was that we colonists must walk with care. We must take thought of all our dealings with our neighbors, more primitive in their feelings and behavior, and consider with utmost precision of thought all our dealings with them. The Indians we had just visited and kindred tribes were in a position to wipe us out in one surge of fury. A single mistake by one of our hotheads or our fools could destroy the colony and all of its bright hope.

Pulsing through the silence of the forest I could still hear the *boom,* boom-boom, *boom,* boom-boom of the tribal drums, and a rising and falling murmur of wild shouting. It would certainly persist until the cask was empty and perhaps until the tranquil stars came out, and the savages went to their mats and sought, as did the Grecian hosts on the Trojan shore, the boon of sleep.

6

A brisk wind out of the southeast had risen at midafternoon, causing Captain Stafford to tack across the strait to the deep channel that set in close to the shore of Roanoke Island. Here in the lee of the land he could make the best of the northern thrust into his sails. Almost at once a small herd of deer on the shore reminded one of our party that his larder lacked venison, and by happenstance this proved the condition of the larder of several other colonists. Richard at once suggested that one of the pinnace's boats put Tom, himself, Manteo, and me ashore, we whites acknowledged as the best archers in the English colony. Manteo knew the midland of the island well, its ponds where deer foregathered, and its game trails through the thickets. Captain

Stafford at once agreed, and inevitably Weechee expressed her intention of going with us.

There was no reason she should not, since she was a hardy traveler, and as hunters we would not walk fast. Not only I would relish her cheerful company; the same was true of Richard, Thomas Warner, and our grave guide Manteo. We hunters thought it possible that we could get two or even three deer: more than this number we could not butcher and carry to the settlement before dark.

Except for one grisly find and one thrilling forest scene the tramp was void of exciting event, although a rich experience in the observation of flora and fauna. There was very little sign of man in this part of the island. Although it had been named for the Roanoke Indians, these had moved to the mainland since its first discovery, and the Croatans had occupied their former hunting grounds somewhat southward. The middle and northern parts of the island had evidently been forsaken perhaps since the coming of Lane's colony and certainly since their departure, except for one raid, by what tribe we did not know, and which we could only postulate, resulting in the murder or at least the killing of some of the fifteen men who had remained after that departure. This lack of occupancy and even of hunting had resulted in an influx of wild animals.

Our expectations of seeing deer proved well founded. Manteo had not brought his bow and quiver on today's visit to his tribe, for reasons of his own finding, and of which I did not speak; but Richard, Tom, and I decided to play the game founded by lordly archers stalking deer in the English and Scottish forests, exemplified by the ancient rhyme:

> First to espy,
> First to let fly.

Unarmed Manteo was the first to spy a stag in easy arrow range and pointed to it. Since Richard was in the best position to shoot, Tom and I watched him make a flawless shot, at which the animal gave one startled bound and fell dead. At once we chopped off its head with Tom's hatchet, I gutted the carcass, and while Manteo cut and trimmed a long pole, I tied the front feet together with stout vines and did the same to the hind feet. Then we slid the pole between the front and rear legs, and Richard and Manteo raised it to their shoulders. Each was carrying a full seventy-five pounds, but we meant to double the load, adding one more bearer; and if the chance came to take three stags, all four of us men would tote.§

§ This ancient colloquialism is of West African origin.

Weechee was an Indian child and it was bred in her bones—or taught her as soon as she had learned to talk—to help as well as she could with any tribal labor; and neither her sex nor her social position bore upon this. So I cut out the stag's heart, excellent meat by any counting, and put the bloody organ, as large as a man's fist, into her eager hands. In return she gave me an inkling into primitive thinking; and in fact, on due consideration, perfectly natural thinking based on a natural and intelligent concept, however mistaken it might be.

"I would like to eat all of this," she told me, "and then I could run very fast."

As soon as I caught the idea, I pursued it.

"What if you ate the heart of a bear, Weechee?" I asked.

"I would become very cross." And drawing her pretty mouth, she gave utterance to a quite ominous-sounding snarl. I took it that she had heard a wounded bear make such a sound in the years before she was enslaved. Bears were extremely rare or non-existent in the West Indian islands, and since she had blessed me with her companionship, she and I had never encountered any.

"What if you ate the heart of a fox?" I asked as we walked along.

"Fox meat smells bad, and I would eat the heart of one only so I could become very sly, and tell lies to you that you would never find out."

Then, to test her, I carried the idea to its ultimate, grim conclusion.

"What if you ate the heart of a very great and brave chieftain?"

She appeared awed, rather than shocked, and her eyes rounded. "There is a tribe toward the sunset called the—the—I cannot remember—"

"Try, Weechee."

"It is no use. It is something told me long and long ago. They do what you said. I don't want to think about it."

I did not doubt her in the least degree. Ritualistic cannibalism was practiced here and there long ago or still, all over the world; I had read of it and Doctor Jones had spoken of it only recently. Cortés had recorded it, as well as a worse sort.

To my own and Weechee's delight, we saw many other kinds of animals, and these gave us nought but pleasure, because they were not dangerous, and we were not compelled to kill them to obtain meat. We saw a fat opossum, who had no business being out of his treetop before sundown, a raccoon bitch with four pups, rabbits and squirrels, and Weechee's sharp eyes spied a porcupine in an achicory tree. We also saw a large black snake with yellow stripes, that Weechee told me solemnly was a good snake, because he ate snakes that killed people, but he was not *tesicquio,* the snake that was himself good to eat.

We saw various varieties of woodpeckers, thrushes, and blackbirds, some of the latter having scarlet splashes on their wings that made their flight a beautiful thing to see. I saw a red-breasted bird, resembling our English robin, although somewhat larger; and a long-tailed bird that Manteo told me was wonderfully gifted of voice, its night-song falling only a little short of a nightingale's. A bird whose cheerful cry was chu-chee was kin to her, Weechee told me soberly, and would bring food to her if she was lost in the woods. She was not able to explain the relationship other than by the "chee" in the name of both. Given names have far more significance among what we call savages than among whom we deem civilized folk.

I learned more of New World flora in this tramp with Weechee, Richard, Tom, and Manteo, although it did not interest my little companion as much as did the fauna. This was natural enough, I thought, since she herself was so brimful of animation. I identified the tulip tree, described by Sir Walter Raleigh; and truly it was equal to his description, cone-shaped with dense olive-green foliage touching the ground and at this season adorned with immense blossoms, white as a swan's wing, and of lovely, delicate smell. Manteo showed me a gum tree, growing in swampy ground; its wood was resilient, he said, and made excellent bows; the achicory tree yielded an edible nut, the name abbreviated to hickory nuts. I was already acquainted with the beautiful walnut tree, its oily nuts so prized by Indians, each encased in a green husk that stained the hands; the tree itself related, but not closely, to the English walnut tree.

He also showed me *winauk,* the source of a tealike beverage of pleasant taste and supposed medicinal value. Also he pointed out *uppowoc,* the tobacco plant, the leaves of which were rolled into cigarros, or pounded to smoke in the peace pipes, or ground to use as snuff. This was indeeed a New World. My head swam when I tried to conjecture how its discovery, colonization, and riches of all sorts would change human life in the Old World.

As Tom, Manteo, Weechee, and I were gazing everywhere, beholding new sights that Manteo identified, Richard continued his purposeful search for deer. Presently he caught sight of another stag in a stand of oaks, and as "first to espy, first to let fly," again he took the shot, and again with remorseless aim. While I was gutting the carcass, sleek and fat, he took from his wallet the nut or berry that he had put there after he had missed the stag on Saona Island, that narrow miss that had cost him the capture of a runaway slave girl. He had said he would do this whenever he became too pleased with his marksmanship, and the sight of it would cast down his dangerous pride.

Fortunate was I that he was my friend. This man could be most dangerous and, as far as I knew, a ruthless enemy.

Yet a few minutes later he and all of us missed our chance at the greatest wild-animal trophy any of our party had encountered in the New World. He had burst suddenly upon our view; our stare of amazement was too prolonged; then as Richard, Tom, and I snatched for an arrow, the beast darted away.

"That was an elk," Richard said in hushed awe.

Oddly enough, I did not think so. I had never seen a live elk, but I had studied a picture of one, as they were known in the German and Scandinavian forests. The picture showed a coal-black beast, with wide-spread palmated horns, and a horselike head. This animal was as large as the elk, or nearly so, but was reddish brown in color and it had a pointed nose like that of a red deer. Its horns were in the velvet, as hunters say, but well grown for mid-July, and these were tall and branched, not flat and palmated.

"What is his name in Croatan?" I asked Manteo.

"We call him by his Algonquin name, which is *wapiti.*"

"I am sure it was an elk," Richard said.

Still I thought it was a giant species of red deer, or else a distinct species similar, except in size, to the English red deer. Perhaps we were fortunate not to have shot. We could have hardly missed, but we would have needed not deer arrows but the heaviest war arrows, with long, knife-sharp heads, to have put an end to the leaping life in that magnificent, vital stag. We might have merely wounded him, of which wounds he might die, and then he would not be here to furnish the colony five or six hundred weight of meat in the hungry days of winter.

7

We were not to gain the settlement without making a grisly find. I was astonished it had not been made before now, since it was almost in arrow-flight of the wall; and the only obvious explanation was that the grass here grew high, the ground being exceptionally rich, and this the settlers were reluctant to enter, fearing the sting of an unseen serpent.

Tom made the find, which was of three human skeletons, so close together that they must have met death together. I had started to ask Manteo whether he thought they were Indians' or white men's bones, when I saw him pick up something from the ground, which he immediately held up for me to see. It was a horn button, with holes for thread, and indubitably of English make. Soon we perceived other evidence, including the wooden heel of a boot or shoe, and a rotted piece of wool that had once been part of a white man's cloak.

A few feet distant Richard found in the heavy grass a rusted match-lock musket, its stock chewed by an animal and almost rotted away, and a hole in the iron barrel eaten through by rust. The hammer was down as though it had been fired, and its distance from the skeletons caused a picture to leap to my mind, that of an Indian, one of the murderers, picking up the gun of the newly dead, and starting to carry it away, only to perceive it would be of no use to him, and might be harmful, because the spirit of its owner might come looking for it, and take unearthly revenge.

"How old are these bones, Manteo?" I asked.

"Not more than three suns. Human bones rot away in our rain and sea mist in four suns. More likely two suns. But since the joints are gone, more than one sun."

"Then they are the bones of three of the fifteen or more men who stayed on the island."

"That is what I believe."

"If they had powder and balls, the brutes made off with them," Richard said, fury in his voice and countenance. "Maybe they had only one charge left. Yet I hope they didn't waste it. I'm going to look and see."

He began searching the grass not far from the bones, then took thought of a clump of thickets about thirty yards distant. He went there in his purposeful stride, glanced once, then shouted aloud and clapped his hands together hard in certain proof of exultation.

"By God, he got one of the devils!" Richard cried.

Tom and Manteo and I went there, as big-eyed Weechee clung tight to my hand. In the brush clump was another skeleton, the skull detached, and in the cheekbone was a hole as large as a silver groat. Manteo turned over the skull. Low in the back was an even larger hole, the place of egress of the heavy musket ball. My own heart made a joyous leap that my three countrymen had not died without a small pre-payment of revenge.

"I tell you what happened," Richard broke out, excitement roughening his voice. "The Indians had their ambush in this thicket. The three Englishmen caught sight of them, but too late to save themselves—the man who carried the gun had just enough time to take a quick aim and fire. Thank God, it was good aim! Then I suppose all three were sewed in and out with arrows. But note the gang was in a big hurry to get away—they didn't take their tribesman's body for their hocus-pocus burial. They didn't like those two big holes in his head, and that means there were still Englishmen on the island when these three were killed."

"It might mean that," I said.

"Notice, Martyn, that they took his bow and quiver and beads and his leather belt and everything else that might give a clue to what tribe they belonged."

This last I translated for Manteo's understanding, and explained Richard's explanation of the facts.

"Perhaps the white chief speaks truth, but perhaps not," Manteo replied. "Often Indians leave their dead where they have fallen in battle; it has something to do with their spirits. And often they take their clothes and weapons and ornaments, and bury these in the floor of the *machucomuck*."

"What did he say?" Richard demanded harshly.

"He spoke to me, Richard." But my only reason for answering so was the rough tone my friend had used.

"I suppose you have the right to keep it to yourself. You and he are good friends, and that's a good thing for the colony. That was shown at the feast today. But if he said anything that made you believe the murderers were Croatans, it's your duty to tell Governor White."

"He said nothing of the kind, Richard, I assure you. So I would suggest that we report the finding of these bones only to Governor White. Then it will be left to him what to tell the colonists and. how soon. Just now they are hardly in a mood to stand up under it well. They are depressed by the delay in arrival of the flyboat—that delay is drawing awfully long, and it may not be a case of delay but something much worse—and well the colonists know it."

"'Fore God, I wish she would show up before the *Lion* and the pinnace must stand to sea. That will be a bad time. Martyn, I'm so glad you've learned Croatan—my Aunt Clara always declared you had the quickest mind she had ever worked with, including mine—"

"She never worked with yours. You went to a proper school."

"She made it pretty plain that she included mine. Anyway, I started to say your knowing the language will stand the colony in good stead, and very especially if Governor White has to return with the ships to hire and dispatch another supply ship."

"Is there any likelihood of that?" Tom Warner asked quickly.

"A good deal, or so I believe. We're well fixed for trade goods, thanks to Martyn and you, but I don't like the look of those corn bins and our powder magazines." Then, turning to me, "Already you can communicate with the natives better than White does—I think he'll appoint you official interpreter—whether he does or not, you'll be chief interpreter and the true interpreter. I do not mistrust your aboriginal friend now in our midst. Still, there's the old saying that blood is thicker than water. You may have to amend and omit and perhaps invent in the parleys between the two tribes; at the last two you would serve better than His Excellency, who is inclined to be almost too honest and forthright."

So we went to the settlement, and since Tom had made the gruesome find, he and Richard, our best-born, made our report to Governor White. If the latter did not know by now that Richard was the son of Thomas Wade, one of the financial backers of the enterprise, which I suspected, I believe that Richard told him at this meeting. The governor received the tidings of the find with his usual fortitude, but we could see deep trouble in his eyes.

The colonists' spirits were raised; a fact not at all strange under the circumstances, by a commonplace and natural event occurring to one of their own number. Actually it was of immense importance to whom had been two of our number and were now three. Mistress Eleanore Dare was brought to bed, and Doctor Jones was summoned, and the consequence was the birth of a baby girl, the first white child born in Virginia and probably the whole New World north of the Spanish possessions, St. Augustine in Florida, and the vague borders of the vast land called Mexico. Almost every colonist prayed for a safe delivery, and the prayer was granted. No soul was so self-centered that it took fright at thought of a helpless baby in our troubled midst, needing protection and care. A great shout arose from the gathered colonists when, deep in the night, Doctor Jones came to the door of the Dare house and announced the babe's emergence, and that she would be duly christened Virginia Dare, and both she and her mother were doing well.

And her appearance among us seemed to us a sign that our luck had turned, for on the very next day a watcher shouted, "A sail! A sail!" Only the vessel's topsails were visible at first, and the Good God knew she might be a Spanish sloop that could outgun our vessels, and all of us might be captured and sold into slavery or sent to the Inquisition; but the Reverend Edward Powell led us in fervent prayer that she be either the flyboat or the supply ship Raleigh had promised to dispatch. If a few, a very few, were so belly-minded and so fearful of the future, that they hoped she would prove the latter rather than the former, I wondered if they could be blamed at the Last Counting. Happily for the majority, she was soon identified by a colonist gaining the crest of a low hill; and he returned on the run, shouting the good news.

"She's the flyboat. I would know her by her wallow from here to Trinidad. And Captain Spicer has hoisted the Queen's flag."

So our colony was strengthened from eighty souls to one hundred and eleven, counting Virginia Dare, Weechee, and Manteo, and minus our two deserters. Also to our great joy, our arsenal was increased by a flagonet with a full score of balls, five muskets with a hundred leaden bullets, and five casks of gunpowder. The paltriness of the latter number was a sharp blow to me, because rumor had it we would receive at least fifteen casks. Actually Captain Spicer's total allotment had been fifteen casks, five of which he must keep to protect his vessel from pirates, and he had expended five casks in a two days' running fight with a Spanish sloop of war, who had yearned to make the flyboat his prize. Happily the sloop was no better gunned than her would-be captive, but much more strongly manned, and Spicer's tactics had been to keep her at a distance by frequent cannon fire.

My disappointment was greatly mitigated by the flyboat's plenteous bins of wheat and barley, several casks of smoke-dried herring, a ton or more of pliable, well-tanned leather, several hundredweight of half-inch hempen rope, ideal for trotlines and countless other uses, a hundred pairs of French-made boots well-oiled with a single waterproof seam, and, no doubt obtained from a French smuggler, a hundred knee-length military cloaks of oiled cloth, circular, with a hole in the center through which the wearer thrust his head, and giving well-nigh complete protection against rain or snow. Supposed to be sailing two days after the *Lion* departure, she had been held up three weeks for the lading of these stores. I could not help but conjecture that Sir Walter Raleigh had arrested his attention from other great affairs and even his attendance upon the Queen to take thought upon the three ships he had appointed to a reckless enterprise, and somehow found the money for greatly increased stores.

But in this same guessing, my mind stumbled upon an unwelcome possibility if not probability; and indeed it seemed to fall from the stumble, and carry down a deal of hope. It occurred to me that because of the threat of war, Sir Walter may have found it not within his means to send a supply ship, and had done what he could to remedy our loss, and from now on our sky-rim gazers would keep their watch in vain.

Chapter XI

AUGURIES OF STORM

1

In all truth our colony was reasonably well supplied for almost every likely contingency except attack by a Spanish galleon or by combined tribes of Indians. With such game as we could shoot, we could subsist until next year's corn crop, cut abundant fuel for our little houses, and keep warm and fairly dry when we worked in the fields or hunted or gathered nuts and edible plants in the forest. The great equation was a purely human one—would our intentions to maintain friendship with the Indians be sufficiently well kept that no reckless or wicked deed would lose us that friendship and force us into dire and well-nigh hopeless war?

It was impossible to forget we were in a pen the walls of which were deep water over which we had no means of crossing quickly at threat of death.

Tom and I discussed this matter, taking no one at this point into our confidence. Whereupon we hatched another stratagem, which we could not execute without Manteo's help. So we consulted with him, on a night of waning moon, the date being between the twentieth and the twenty-fifth of July of the year 1587. I marveled over how easy it was to lose track of five days for lack of a calendar, a well-kept log, or even of notches cut in a stick. The first question we put to him was one over which he must scratch his head.

It concerned the blood ties and other strength of the bonds between the Croatans and other tribes loosely or strongly bound with what we called the Algonquin Confederacy in the region about and southward of Chesapeake Bay. Doctor Jones had already given us his opinion that this confederacy had ancient treaties with the Powhatans and the even greater confederacy of the Iroquois and that all these tribes spoke dialects of the same basic language. However, the distances were so great between Roanoke and the upper waters of the Chesa-

peake, and communication so scant, I did not think that we need
consider either the central and northern Algonquin Confederacy or
its northward and westward allies.

"I tell you what I think," Manteo broke out suddenly. "My tribe, the
Croatan, will not dance the dance of war, their faces and bodies
painted red, their spears or bows in hand, unless your people do unto
us great evil. You may kill the deer in our hunting grounds, as many
as you need to eat, and although we would rejoice if you use the
silent and deadly bow and its humming arrows when you hunt deer,
still we will not protest your using thunder guns, although their great
noise frightens from our grounds twenty deer for every one that is shot
and eaten. Even if you kill the Little Fisherman with the ringed tail,
whose soul is kindred to our souls, my people will not make war upon
your people, because Weoanza will tell them you meant no harm, and
perhaps wanted the skins of the Little Fishermen to make a warm
cloak against the north wind. But if you kill one of us who had not
drawn his bow against one of you, that killer the Croatan will kill in
our own way, and if you do not deliver him up to us, thus to die according to our laws, then my people will send messages far and near
to summon the warriors of closely kindred tribes, and no man, woman,
or child, or babe in arms will escape their fleet arrows, their deadly
spears, their hatchets, or their avenging fire."

He spoke very calmly, as though of a deed done long ago, irretrieva-
ble, almost forgotten. And I rejoiced that John Spendlove and certain
others who did not recognize fellow manhood in an Indian brave, and
find in him the image of their own fierce pride, and discover in him
the same dark passion of revenge, and could not conceive of Honor
wearing aught but a white skin, did not hear the quiet statement, for
they might have been inflamed to slay Manteo then and there, as they
might kill a snarling dog, and then take satisfaction in the act, and
preen themselves, and even believe they have done God's will.

"What tribes would answer that call, and what are their numbers?"

"The Wingineos would not answer that call, despite their quarrel
with Lane Sagamore, because they are a stranger tribe and small.
The Secota, Agriascagoc, and the Pomiock are mighty peoples north
of us, of Algonquin blood and speech, and their sons have taken our
daughters for their women, and often we send gifts of meat to them
when we have made a great kill, or corn when Manitou has blessed
our fields, and our harvests are heavy. The mother of Eracano is a Secota, very old, but like unto—um, um, medicine woman in the tribe.
All these will surely answer the call of the Croatan, if we send up
smokes."

"How many warriors in those three tribes all told? Are there twenty twenties?" For twenty was the largest number by which the Croatan counted, the numbers of his fingers and thumbs added to that of his toes.

"Martyn Sachem, the numbers of their warriors twenty-twenties."

This number of warriors, four hundred, I repeated to Thomas Warner. His eyes rounded a little. "Cut it by half—" he began.

"No, we cannot cut it by half. The chieftain does not exaggerate."

"I can hardly believe that amid this mighty forest—"

"I think Lane believed it. In any case he sent gifts and other peace offerings to the Secota, Agriascagoc, and Pomiock tribes."

"They have very great and rich hunting grounds. The spring run of herring into the estuaries of the Chowan, the Roanoke, and the Aligador rivers is prodigious, all that the women can smoke, dry, or pickle in brine, and many left to plant with the corn seed to enrich the ground. Their fields are mainly patches of a few acres in the forest, where they ring the trees to kill them so that they cast very little shade; even the next year they can plant seed, and the trees ultimately die and fall, and Indians burn trunks and limbs. The soil is very deep and rich, and yields heavy crop year after year. And the forest itself has many achicory, chestnut, and walnut trees, hazelnut bushes, and edible plants, including the sweet tuber called *inhame*."*

This conversation occurred on a Sunday afternoon. The day being fine, most of our colonists listened to Edward Powell preach in what was once the cornfield, his topic being Our Lord's stay in the wilderness with John the Baptist. In the morning, with Thomas Ellis as lay reader, an Anglican service was held in and about what was once the meeting house of Lane's colony. Most colonists attended both services, although Edward Powell, his daughter Winifred, and Richard were conspicuously absent from the morning service.

I gave thought to these events of the Sabbath, wondering if the three latter persons had remained in one another's company, or if Richard and Winifred had strolled off into the woods. I regarded this as an important matter, as indeed it was in respect to some of my inward longings. But preoccupation with it was sharply arrested the following morning, and its importance took an abrupt fall.

George Howe, one of Governor White's lesser assistants, had risen at dawn to catch a mess of crabs, the white meat of which he was particularly fond. He chose the hour in order to fish at the low turn of the tide, when crabs were reckoned to feed greedily, and the water in the bay was no more than thigh-deep. The night before he had rigged a line, and he had some chunks of meat weighing an ounce or

* Yam.

two in a bucket; and from a six-foot pole hung a net he had made from some old mesh.

At about the same hour Thomas Smart, an early riser, had walked out on a peninsula extending a short distance into what we called Croatan Strait, carrying a shovel and a bucket, and his inclination although not a settled purpose was to dig clams. From its extremity, he could see George Howe about three hundred paces distant, out about thirty yards from some low brushwood on the muddy bank, assiduously tossing his line, and rather frequently netting, or failing to do so, a crab. Then he had an occasion to turn his back on Mr. Howe, in order to watch a game of some kind played by a school of porpoises.

These had shortly disappeared from sight, and he glanced idly again to the scene of Mr. Howe's crab fishing. To his enormous amazement he could make out the bucket floating on the water, the pole and the net, but not the least sign of the fisherman. His gaze searched wildly, and then he dashed to the settlement. The first person he met, walking about in meditation, was Governor White, and to him he swiftly imparted his tidings. Thomas Smart immediately set off running for the scene of the crab fisherman's disappearance but Edward Powell, passing Ananias Dare's house, called him loudly. I heard the call as I was dressing, and perceiving its note of alarm, I seized my bow and arrow, spoke briefly to Weechee half-awake on her cot, and rushed out to join Mr. Powell and Mr. Dare. Other colonists joined us; and quite aware that something serious had happened, hurried to get what weapons they could lay hands on. Two of the men brought muskets, Richard and Tom Warner each seized their bows and quivers, and John Spendlove had buckled on his sword.

With ill-forebodings we followed Thomas Smart. When we had a view of the muddy beach, we saw him knee-deep, towing to shore what was very obviously the body of George Howe. There might be life in him yet, we thought, and our hope quickened somewhat by Thomas' care to keep the motionless man's head and shoulders out of water. But of course that same care would have been taken if his charge were only the remains of George Howe.

In a moment more we perceived the awesome truth. With a thrill of horror we saw the body stretched on its back a few feet from the margin, and thrusting upward from its trunk were three staffs, indubitable Indian arrows. The light was so clear just before sunrise that we could distinguish the gay feathers that fletched them.

We made a grim ring around the corpse. We could now perceive the shorter butts of two more arrows that must have transfixed his body, the outthrusting tips undoubtedly broken off. Also blood was seeping from a thigh wound and smears of blood on his jerkin indicated wounds made by arrows not piercing deep enough to stick in the flesh or which George had plucked out.

John Spendlove was the first to find his voice.

"This is wanton murder," he said in low, strong voice. "We'll hunt down the devils—they couldn't have gone far. Anyhow that big a party will leave tracks that we can follow."

"Sir, I do not believe we should take any action without the governor's consent!"

"To hell with the governor's consent! We're white men, aren't we, and one of our number has been ambushed and killed. And if we delay a minute, the murderers will escape. Richard, don't you agree with me?"

Richard drew a long breath. I would never know what reply he was about to make, because I had cause to interrupt him.

"Here comes Manteo! Whatever we do, we need his help. And there's the governor not far behind."

Balked for the moment, John Spendlove shot me a look of disdain; but his posture changed, no longer that of a hound on leash when he catches sight of the quarry. Manteo came, bent over the body, looked at the fletching of one of the arrows and then with a twisting motion jerked it forth. Closely he examined the bloody shaft and head.

"Manteo, are those Croatan arrows?" I asked him in that language.

"No!" This word he spoke in English, for all to understand. Then, looking into my eyes, he went on, "They are Wingineo arrows."

"Are you sure?"

"As sure as the rising sun! I was sure when I saw the fletching; but the shaping is by the hand of a Wingineo arrow maker, and the flint head with its jagged instead of sharp edges is unknown to any people but the Wingineo."

Governor White came up, and the men waited with a strange patience while he surveyed with unflinching gaze what remained of his friend and assistant, stalked in deadly silence and murdered when, pursuing his innocent occupation, he had not the shadow of a hope of self-defense. His first question was addressed to Manteo.

"Croatan?"

Manteo shook his head. "Wingineo."

"Lane killed their chief. This is their revenge, for which they have waited long. And now we must take revenge, and then 'twill be their turn, and so killing will breed killing until the hope of Roanoke is dead. Such is human life."

"I ask you, sir, what else can we do but take revenge?" John Spendlove asked. "What other choice do we have? If we do not act, they will believe us cowards—they will call us women—that name we will have, not only with the Wingineos, but up and down the coasts, and they will take our goods and our women, and of those of us they do not kill, they will make slaves."

"Yes, we must act. Martyn Sutton, you speak the language better than I. Ask Manteo what way we are to turn. Where will the assassins go? What will be their retreat? How large is their tribe? What allies will they have? What will be their next move?"

These questions I put to Manteo, his eyes on mine. His answer was so long delayed that I feared my fellow Englishmen would fly into a fury, but they did not, indeed showed no sign of impatience, because they knew from his countenance that he was in deep thought. At last he replied at considerable length, pausing between statements so I could transmit them to my fellows.

"I think these killers were a war party, young braves who intended to kill and run . . . They are traveling fast . . . They can travel more fast than we, because they know the paths through the forest and the high grass . . . Their canoes are probably hidden on the west shore of the island . . . But the Wingineos have no friends; they are troublemakers between tribe and tribe . . . They are latecomers from the west and belong to no great nation . . . I say to make for their village with twenty men, including every good archer in the colony, and the rest with muskets . . . That white men can launch arrows farther and straighter and faster than themselves will darken their spirits, far more so than a few of them killed with muskets which take so long to load, and which they knew from Lane's fights with their tribesmen . . . If the Wingineo have fled their houses, burn them, and lay fire to their cornfields . . . Let that word fly with wings up and down the coasts."

"Still that won't be an eye for an eye, and a tooth for a tooth," John Spendlove said in a bitter voice when I had finished translating Manteo's address. "We might have killed two or three if we had given chase soon enough. Burning their villages and fields won't satisfy my hate."

"Nevertheless," Governor White answered with great dignity, "the course this chieftain proposes is the one that we will follow."

2

Governor White was not now the meditative dreamer of great dreams, a gazer into the far future, but the man of immediate action, terse, and decisive. Before the other colonists gathering here could give proper care to George Howe's body, he had ordered Captain Stafford to make ready the pinnace to sail within the hour. He appointed Thomas Warner to command the archers, these being Richard,

Mark Bennett, John Baird, the yeoman William Berde, four other yeomen who had arrived on the flyboat, and myself. John Spendlove would command the musketeers, ten in all. Every man would carry his own rucksack, containing ship biscuit and dried meat, and such spare equipment as might be needed for his weapons. The musketeers would have powder and balls for twenty rounds each. We archers must have twenty war arrows in our quivers. No one need carry water canteens for the terrain occupied by the Wingineos had numerous brooks. Manteo was to be our guide, and I was to serve as interpreter between him and our party.

Croatan Sound, between our settlement and the mainland immediately west, was less than ten miles wide. But our sail to Duckhead Peninsula, jutting into the mouth of Albemarle Sound, was about twelve miles. Since all pinnaces are fleet, and ours a flyer, and the wind was in the southeast, we anchored off Duckhead Peninsula in seventy minutes after weighing anchor. With her shallow draft, she was able to launch her longboat, containing our force of twenty and extra rowers within arrow-cast of the shore. Twenty minutes later we had gained the beach and, led by Manteo, begun our march to the Wingineo village.

Throughout the journey we had hoped to overtake the raiders' canoes. If so it was our purpose to run down and smash every one, and shoot all swimmers, whereby their taking of George Howe's life would cost them at least ten lives, a price that I reckoned blood-hungry John Spendlove would consider fair. This hope failed—the canoeists had at least an hour's head start and when stroking with might and main before a brisk wind they could cover water almost as fast as the light and shapely pinnace with wind-pregnant sails. When we came in sight of their village we heard no sound, or saw no human shape.

There were no more than thirty flimsy huts, for these were their summer abode, where their weirs harvested great quantities of herring during the spring run into Albemarle Sound and up into the two great rivers emptying there. Thousands of these lay on racks, brine-dipped and drying in the sun; and nearby lay their best cornfields, the ears formed but yet green and their tops ripe. Curling smoke from dying cooking fires was whisked away by the wind, and the pots contained sweet corn and boiled meat, and yams baked in the ashes.

We entered the houses with readied weapons, but all save one were empty of human kind. We found the reed mats of the fugitives, but not their deerskin blankets; strewn about were bowls and pestles for pounding corn into meal, but no flint tools or weapons; we saw tin pans and one copper kettle which they had no doubt obtained from Lane's colonists; but such essentials as fire-making apparatus and amulets for good fortune had been taken away. In the corner of a hovel was found a piece of pure copper, roughly egg-shaped, weighing about five pounds, but whether it was the virgin metal or whether it had been smelted from an ore bed by some far more advanced tribe in some undreamed realm of the continent, we did not know.

It happened that I was with Manteo when we entered the largest of the huts, in the building of which a few rough planks had been used. It was as silent as the others I had entered, the sense of forsakenness was as deep, and the only light came through the gap in the bark slabs that served as a door. Manteo uttered a little grunt, and then I saw what he saw. Against the wall, on a tattered buffalo skin, lay a human form. My first thought was that the person was dead and the tribe had left in such haste as to deprive the corpse of burial.

Then the occupant of the lowly bed turned her head to look at us. She was a very old woman, and her legs were twisted and wasted from some crippling disease. And then I noticed that about her scrawny neck was a string of pearls. They were chosen more for size than for perfection of skin and perfect roundness; and most would have no value to traders; yet the few that were marketable might be worth thirty pounds.

"Weoanza?" Manteo asked. For the first time I was positive that this Croatan word meant chieftainess, and was not a female given name.

"*Ehh.*" This was almost identical with the aspirant that the Croatans employed to mean yes.

"Your sons and grandsons have left you defenseless?"

The old woman began to speak in what I supposed the Wingineo tongue. If so, it was wondrously like Croatan; on the other hand she might be employing Croatan, her use of which the happenstance of the two tribes being neighbors; and the slight differences of accent were explainable by it not being her native tongue. In any case I understood what she was saying with entire ease.

"No, I bade them leave me. I would have been a burden upon them, slowing their flight. From a treetop on the hill one of my grandsons saw the tall ship, and we knew you were coming to take vengeance for the death of the white crab-fisherman. I told them it mattered not what you did to me. I am very old; I have baked the corn cakes for four times twenty winters. In these last years, I have endured such pain that I laugh at any pain you could give me, whether to break my crooked bones one at a time, or cut me into eel bait with your wondrous knives, or bake me over a slow fire. Aye, I would laugh into your faces, even as the flame licked my heart. For I die proud. I will die triumphant."

I was deeply moved without quite knowing why. She spoke in a feeble voice; she did not move her hands or her head; no posture betokened either pride or triumph; still I knew she was speaking some heartfelt truth according to her seeing; she was expressing a glory within her soul. My perception of this might be no more than seeing a gleam deep in the watery pale eyes of the very old.

"Weoanza, do you wish to tell us of the glory?" Manteo asked. "None of my palefaced brothers will lay hand on you, whether you speak or whether you keep silent, but if you will speak, they will not forget, and you will come to honor in their sight, and they will tell the tale to their sons and their grandsons, and it will be known in this land and in lands afar, and in this age and in ages yet to come, when the Great Swamp of the White Herons is dry cornland, and the Signal Rock at Buffalo Leap has been worn away by rain."

"Great Chieftain, my husband, Wingineo, was felled by the thunder gun in the hand of Lane Sagamore." And I had marked before now how frequently the chieftain of a tribe was called by the tribal rather than by any given name. As a matter of fact the same custom had existed in Europe during the Middle Ages and before then. For instance, several of the Carolingian line were publicly addressed as France, and Burgundy was a common cognomen of the dukes of that great province.

"The son of his loins, out of my womb, had become Wingineo, but our son was aged, three times twenty years, and he could not lead a great feud of blood. But his son out of Weoanza, chieftainess of the Chowan, went into the *machucomuck* where the kewas dwell, and unto Manitou he swore to slay Lane Sagamore, or one of his brothers, and his revenge would be more sweet if his slain were the sagamore's brother than he himself, for to die by the darting arrow gives only a moment's pain, but to lose a brother brings pain and sorrow a whole life long. But when Wanchese was ready to strike, and had painted his face, and donned his headdress, Lane Sagamore and his brothers also fled in great ships into the boundless sea.

"Then it was that my grandson Wanchese grieved greatly, for it seemed his vow made unto Manitou was forever broken," the aged woman went on in her calm, low voice. "But two suns brought first two ships, and then one more, and my warriors spied upon the newcomers, and lo, they were also the brothers of Lane Sagamore, palefaced, bearing thunder guns, speaking like to him, eating like food, ever seeking pearls with a like hunger. So again Wanchese painted his face and body, and donned his headdress, and from two times twenty warriors he chose ten, to go forth and slay Lane Sagamore's brother. And so these went in their swift canoes, and in the dawn they spied this brother netting clams, and they stole upon him, and Wanchese drew an arrow from his quiver and nocked it in the string. And with his strong arm he bent the bow to its perfect round, and as he took his aim joy flooded his heart, for he would not miss, and he could not miss, for he knew that if he did, I, Weoanza of the Wingineo, would slay him with my own hand; and it is a great shame when a mother must slay a son or a son of a son. And the arrow darted away on its sure flight, and it hummed with joy, and down it bent a little, and it struck the brother of Lane Sagamore in the region of his navel, passing clean through his body, but still he did not fall, but reeled about in the hip-deep water. And then the brothers of Wanchese rejoiced, for by our law of the blood feud they now could launch their own arrows, to leave their mark upon the blood enemy of their brother Wanchese. And this they did, and not one missed his aim, although not all their arrows plunged deep, because of the leather coat that the paleface wore. But his body was no longer pale under its garments. Nay, it was as brightly painted as the bodies and faces of the warriors. And he finished his death dance, a reeling about and staggering, and fell dead in the salt sea. So now what can you do to me to harm me? My husband Wingineo dances the Dance of Fulfillment in the Hereafter. What can you do to Wanchese to harm him, now that he has kept his vow. Fools!"

Weoanza turned on her side in infinite disdain. Manteo took three lithe strides and put her across his arms and swiftly carried her to a nearby structure, by far the largest and best in the village, and I followed him, knowing not else to do. Inside there were four rudely carved human figures in stone, called kewas, one much larger than the others, and wearing a headdress of bright feathers, and necklaces of white coral and shells, and long ear-pendants of polished copper, and copper bracelets. Before this image, Manteo lay the chieftainess Weoanza, the lame bitch-wolf of the Wingineo, and then we both tiptoed out the door.

3

When we emerged from the *machucomuck*—Manteo could not tell me the derivation for this Croatan word for temple—my companions were already setting fire to the houses. I hastened to Governor White and told him that an aged, crippled woman lay beside one of the images. It was an unnecessary errand—he had already ordered the fire setters to spare what served the Indians as a church. Then I filled a stone bowl with water from the brook and gathered a dozen or more dried herring from the rack, and with these I re-entered the temple and put the food and drink in the old woman's reach. Mindful of her needs, I took thought once again, and found a shallow stone pan, of what use I knew not, and also gathered a big armful of so-called Spanish moss that grew and draped the limbs of the water-oaks, and these too I put in reach of the crippled crone, so that she need not defile the temple and be shamed.

Carrying burning brands, the arsonists made for the nearest corn-field. The leaves had begun to turn sear, although the ears were not yet mature; still the fire would not have swept the field except for the brisk wind.

Then Edward Powell, armed with the musket, and who had just made a complaint to Ananias Dare, hastened to my side and seized my arm. His face was pale with what I thought was fury, his eyes flashed, and his usually pleasant voice was rough.

"I saw you speaking to White. Did he tell you why he spared that heathen temple from the flames?"

"No, sir, he did not."

"It should have been the first edifice fired. Thatch from the roof should have been piled up inside, so its flames would leap into the sky, and be seen for miles! I would have spared all the houses to see that abomination reduced to ashes! Did not the Hebrews at God's command destroy the temples and the groves of Moloch?"

"What I told the governor was that an old crippled woman lay before one of the images." And I did not tell Mr. Powell that Manteo, without protest from me, had lain her there. In all truth, Mr. Powell's violent hatred of heathenry frightened me a little.

"She could have been carried out before we brought the torch. 'Forgive them, Father, for they know not what they do!' But it was the Son who spoke thus, not the God of Vengeance, the God of Wrath. My own spirit is so weak that I would have condoned—nay, I would have urged—the sparing of the old creature. But well I know that many a man, woman, and child will have to die before the souls of their tribesmen can be saved. Did the Sons of Abraham spare the Canaanites, the Philistines, the Amanites? Did not the Lord Himself smite the Assyrian host, not one of them spared that night of His revenge for their worship of false gods? Did He spare the oldest son in every house of the Egyptians, when Pharaoh would not let His people go? If that temple had been burned, I would have thought the life of George Howe would have been well lost; I would have seen the hand of God behind what seemed wanton murder. Who is Governor White that he dared interfere? I must lead this colony, Martyn; and you must tell Manteo so, and you both must help me become leader. You will be rewarded, never fear. I think you could attain your greatest heart's desire."

Except for the violence of the scene itself, the jubilation of the fire setters, their wild running with torches to set new fields on fire, and their exultant cries, I would have feared that Mr. Powell was not in his perfect mind. When he had told me his dreams and visions of converting the heathen he had been sane and humane. The thought came to me that our living on this little strip of earth peopled by our own kind, between the vast, ominous, and mysterious forest, and the mysterious, ominous, and vast ocean might implement the worst impulses in our natures, or put into practice the best.

Before long we had burned all that was worth burning. John Spendlove proposed we only pretend to depart, but instead lie in ambush at the brushy brink of the village, with arrows ready to nock and our matches alight and our pans primed, for he argued with strength and conviction that when the flames died down and the smoke clouds ceased to billow, the Wingineo warriors would come creeping back, for surely they had not fled far, and we would catch sight of some of them, for the debt of their killing one of our number was not half paid, and thus we could pay it doubly or more, and with good fortune ten times the score, with well-aimed shafts and a hail of musket balls. But Ananias Dare did not favor this, nor did Richard, or Preacher Powell, or Thomas Warner. When John Spendlove became enraged at what he called milk-livered retreat, and with flushed countenance and angry eyes demanded that Governor White take this action he had proposed, our leader stiffened with indignation and replied full-voiced and with unmistakable emphasis.

"Mr. Spendlove, you are of highest birth of any man among us, and you are the richest in possessions beyond the seas. But I have been appointed to this post by Sir Walter Raleigh who spoke for Her Majesty the Queen, and my will under God's will be obeyed; and my instructions, not yours, will prevail; and if you approach me again in such insolent manner, you will receive severe and unremitted punishment. Gentlemen, we will take ship at once."

I reckoned this was John Spendlove's first wide wakening to the fact that the shores of Virginia were not England, and new ways had given way to old, amid these scenes so greatly changed, and he had best curb his lordly manners. He thought upon his horse, which he had brought aboard, of no use to anyone as yet, and indeed a nuisance as one of our men must stop his work in the field to see to changing its pickets and leading him to water twice a day. Also he thought upon his ancient escutcheon, and the peasants in his ancestral fields who turned pale and quaked when he rode nigh. But still he knew not what to say, so he said nought.

Yet the fury of his defeat and what he thought was an affront to his rank was still hot in John Spendlove's brain. This fact was perfectly evident in his appearance and manner, and as soon as we weighed anchor, in his actions. It happened that the wind had shifted into the southeast, so Captain Stafford tacked across the strait into the deep channel that set in close to the southwest end of the island. Here the lee of the land prevented a westward drift, and he could make good progress northward. John Spendlove posted himself in the starboard bow, and although he stood seemingly at ease, often smoking a *cigarro,* I perceived he was keeping a close watch of the shore. I could think of no reason other than that the raiders had been more numerous than Manteo thought, and some of them had not yet returned to the village and were in fact still bent on murder. I supposed he hoped to glimpse ill-hidden canoes and perhaps some of the raiders. If his supposition was sound, the latter could readily occur, since in this deep channel Captain Stafford sailed within a stone's throw of the coast.

After half an hour's sail he suddenly left his position and approached Ananias Dare. There was such grim purpose in his face that I hastened to hear what he had to report.

"I've sighted canoes in the reeds two cables' length ahead. Also I saw movement in the brush close to the reed bed. I have no doubt they are Wingineos and I think they intend to launch war arrows at us as we pass, at less than a hundred yards, kill as many as they can, and drift away into the forest before we can drop our hook and give chase in boats."

"Then summon your musketeers and I'll speak to White," replied Ananias Dare.

Two cables' length is only twelve hundred feet. Since the pinnace was sailing seven sea miles an hour, we were advancing on the scene at about twelve feet per second. This meant we would reach it short of two minutes, so there was a great bustle among the musketeers in priming their pans and getting into position beside the rail. The canoes were becoming rapidly visible to all, and I was astonished that any war party would not have concealed them in taller reeds, a bed of which lay not far distant. John Spendlove, duly appointed leader of the musketeers, resumed his position at the bow, ready to give orders unless ordered otherwise by Governor White, now hurrying up the deck.

"I saw some of them. They've ducked down into the thickets, and they're Wingineos as sure as God. Get ready."

Governor White, excited by the sudden alarm, and himself a man of thought more than of action, did not question Spendlove's report, and indeed cocked the hammer of his musket. I was far from as sure as God; it only stood to my reason that the skulking savages were

Wingineo, so far from any other village, still I yearned mightily for Manteo's trained vision. He had descended to the hold on some errand, and although Captain Stafford had sent his cabin boy to summon him, I feared he would not arrive in time.

The time sped. Suddenly one of the hiding Indians stood up, his bow in his hand, although I did not see he had nocked an arrow.

"Shoot, Mr. Governor!" John Spendlove cried in extreme excitement. "He's about to—"

Spendlove did not have time to finish the warning. Governor White threw his musket to his shoulder, pulled the trigger, and the blast cut short the other's shout. This was not the only consequence. This wild shot, taken almost without aim, sped only too true, and the Indian tumbled into the thickets. But it was not answered by a hail of humming arrows. The other Indians in the party huddled close to the ground.

I glanced at Governor White to find a look of horror on his face. It was perfectly obvious that a sickening doubt had engulfed his mind. The slight doubt that I had had before rose swiftly to the horrid conviction that all of us had lost our heads, in greater or less degree, and an innocent Indian had lost his life.

4

With a gaping mouth, White shouted a command to the other musketeers.

"Do not fire! Hear me? Lower your guns."

Then Manteo arrived on the run, touched my right arm, and glanced once into my eyes. All the other men but one stood stunned, as the same likelihood seized upon their thought; only John Spendlove still looked defiant and belligerent. From his bridge Captain Stafford shouted the command, to drop anchors fore and aft, and the crew leaped to obey him. The ship fetched up against the cables with a jerk. Then again spoke Governor White.

"Captain Stafford, will you ship your longboat? I'm going to shore."

I thought that several men started to protest, only to close their pale lips.

"I wish to go with you, sir," said Ananias Dare.

"You may, if you wish, but I am taking no weapons, nor will any man who follows me. Martyn Sutton, you are our best interpreter. Will you go unarmed?"

"Yes, sir," I answered without thought.

"Then ask Manteo if he will go. If what I fear is true, he may be the first to be slain."

I spoke quietly to my friend. He nodded his head.

"How many more wish to come, leaving their arms here?"

I knew that Richard and Thomas Warner would step forward, but I did not expect every colonist in hearing to do so. John Spendlove had hesitated, then joined the rest.

"I will come, Your Excellency, but I feel it my duty to say we are taking a needless risk."

Governor White did not answer him, but turned again to me.

"Martyn Sutton, ask Manteo if those Indians are Wingineos?"

The answer was made easy by first one and then another Indian rising to his feet, and presently a woman stood up also. Not one held a weapon. Manteo spoke to me and in the deliberate pauses between his sentences, I interpreted them.

"Manteo says they are certainly not Wingineos, or any kind of war party . . . He believes—he is almost sure—they are Croatans . . . He does not believe they have weapons, only hoes for digging wild yams; they may have gathered pumpkins from an old field nearby . . . My brother told me the fallen man had a bow . . . One or more always carry bows when they go into the forest, in fear of bears."

Another silence fell as the longboat was being shipped and the rowers took seats on the thwarts. And then it was as though an evil spirit possessed John Spendlove's tongue, for he said an unseemly thing.

"That redskin raised his bow. You saw him do it. I didn't see the arrow, but it doesn't pay to look too long when you deal with Indians. Our coming without weapons will mean only one thing to them, that we're asking forgiveness."

"That is what I mean to ask, if they're Croatans," John White answered.

"It seems to me, sir, you're making too much of one dead Indian."

"I haven't asked your opinion, and I don't want it. Mr. Sutton, ask Manteo what we may do to atone for my horrible mistake?"

My mind had been marching with Governor White's, naturally enough for our position was critical.

"Manteo, should we bring the hit man to the ship, tend his wounds if he yet lives, and do him honors if he's dead?"

"Yes, that would go far in placating my people, provided I can persuade them that the killing was an accident."

So without further speech with Manteo I put forward the idea that had come to me, letting my hearers believe it was his advice.

"Governor White, will you ask Captain Stafford to have his men prepare a coffin with rope handles? He has enough planks, and they couldn't be put to better use. Also ask that it be whitewashed, for it will dry in an hour in the sun, and white, not black, is the Croatan sign of mourning. And appoint six men to bear it in state to the long-boat, then to the ship, then to the Croatan village."

"You heard Manteo's advice, Captain Stafford," the governor responded immediately. "I expect to follow it. Please put your carpenters to work at once. We all remember the word of Weoanza. God knows we must seize every chance or hope of keeping peace with the Croatan. Now we will go ashore."

The Indians on shore did not fail to notice that man after man dropped into the longboat with his hands empty of arms. Those still in hiding at once rose into view, and we saw that nearly half of them were women, some with baskets made with reeds. When we touched the beach, White took the lead, Ananias Dare behind him, and the rest of us, without regard to rank, in the rear. We made our way with grave steps, and there flashed to my mind that we should make an even more solemn procession when we brought the slain man's body into the village. Captain Stafford had a piper, or at least a sailor who could play his piccolo well enough to pipe Governor White aboard or for the crew, when feeling festive, to dance the hornpipe.

We came to the scene of the death. An elderly man lay with his naked chest bathed in blood; he had been struck on the right side by an ounce ball. Manteo said one word, "Pemecum." I could not doubt this was the victim's name. Edward Powell knelt beside the corpse, and laying his hand on its forehead, he spoke a fervid prayer. Its matter was that may God forgive him for his idolatry, because he had known no better, and be merciful to his soul. The other Indians did not comprehend the words, but they perceived the entreaty was made to the Great Spirit, whom they knew as Manitou. Their eyes rounded somewhat but otherwise their brown faces remained impassive.

Manteo then addressed them, explaining that the Wingineo had murdered from ambush one of our colonists, and the great Sagamore White had mistaken their band for the killers. One or two of the men nodded, but with no great conviction, and the rest made no response. Truly the accident became ever less excusable, as more closely we surveyed the scene. No attempt had been made to hide the canoes. They had been paddled into a thick reed bed to prevent their drifting off in the light wind and to save the labor of hauling them up a rather steep bank. There were several reed baskets in plain sight, if we had looked closely enough, these containing roots called *habascan* and *coshushaw;* their plants unknown in English woods but used as edibles by Indians. What was worse, none of the men wore warpaint or feathered headdress, which alone was plain proof that they did not compose a war party. No doubt they had crouched in the brush because of Indian fear of large vessels, which to them still seemed miraculous, capable of emitting thunderclaps and great spurts of flame.

All of our men but one looked pale and sick, and our governor, although he remained steady, could hardly conceal his despair. The exception was John Spendlove, almost as much to blame for the accident as White himself, for his explosive shout, "*Shoot!*" had caused the otherwise cautious governor to trip his trigger. Spendlove stood a little apart, and the expression on his face could almost be called a sneer. He had listened with contempt to Edward Powell's prayer, and he did not conceal his feelings that the rest of us were fools for being touched with remorse and pity for the killing of a friendly Indian. Evidently he had not taken seriously the quiet threat Weoanza, Manteo's mother, had voiced; and Manteo, perceiving this, had trouble maintaining his self-control.

"Pemecum was a good friend of the white men, from first to last," Manteo informed me. "Always he urged peace between my people and yours. I thank Manitou that he has no son, for if he did, that son would go into the *machucomuck*, and make his vows before the kewas to undertake a blood feud with the colonists, and lurk in the thickets, and strike at any hour of day or night, to kill as many of us as he could before he himself was killed."

This I repeated to my companions, despite it would rowell Governor White's feelings even more deeply, but thinking it would be beneficial to the other men, and might even lessen the cruel arrogance in John Spendlove's face and posture. In this respect, it failed completely. All it did was inspire him to an outrageous suggestion.

"Governor White, I have an idea. I do not believe in trying to placate savages, and if we succeed it is only a matter of time until united tribes will attack our fort. Then it would be better for us if we attack now, because the cannon on our two ships could tear their howling mobs into scraps. We would have no more trouble with them, that's certain."

"It is far from certain, Mr. Spendlove. Our ships will sail within the next month; more distant tribes would fill the gaps in their ranks. Even now, with our ships to help us, a determined attack would wipe most of us out. Remember, sir, we are not dealing with a cowardly people."

Richard and most of the other men nodded, which Spendlove observed. But his brain, unstable or at least weak to start with, wise only in its own conceit, hit upon another idea, hardly less base.

"Then tell them a harmless lie that will satisfy the Croatans, and the same time show them we mean business. It is in my code, that of the nobility, not to tell lies to my own kind or to gentry, but these painted devils are animals, not human beings. Say that this dead Indian—and the only good Indian is a dead Indian†—had nocked his arrow and was ready to loose when you shot him. The people with him were watching us, not him; they can't swear it isn't true."

"Manteo could swear it isn't true," White answered. "He had just gained the deck when I fired."

"Manteo can be bribed to support your story. If he can't, we have no more real need of him, since Martyn Sutton can serve as interpreter."

"Governor, may I speak?" I broke in.

"Yes, Mr. Sutton, you may."

"Is Mr. Spendlove suggesting that we get rid of Manteo, in the most certain way? If he is, I'm going to fix his mouth so he can't speak at all for the rest of the week."

"I don't fisticuff with peasants," Spendlove answered. "If you're ever of a rank to wear a sword—and o'ermany upstarts have done so, lately —then I'll be pleased to meet you. Governor White, I was not suggesting that Manteo be made away with, although it would be a good riddance, for he's certain to betray us to his own people before he's through, but he can be put in chains aboard one of the ships and landed on one of the Spanish isles."

"Mr. Spendlove, I find your suggestions odious in the extreme, shameful to the lowest beggar, let alone to one of your high birth. You will please refrain from making any others; and I will ask Captain Irish to take you back to England when he sails as an undesirable colonist in Virginia."

"I do not think you will go that far, Mr. White, considering who I am and what friends I have in England."

"Sir, you are fated to receive an unpleasant surprise."

The Indians had paid little attention to our discussion, only occasionally glancing up when the tones of our voices changed. They were listening to the sounds of hammer and saw aboard the pinnace, which carried clearly to our ears across the short reach of water. Thereafter we stood about in silence, until we heard Captain Stafford's shout.

"The coffin is ready," he called. "The whitewash isn't dry, but it will dry in the sun before we make the Croatan village. Send the longboat for it, because it's too big for my gig."

Governor White gave his orders. At once the longboat crew took their seats and made for the ship, while we colonists kept our watch over the dead. In about ten minutes the coffin was put aboard the

† This ancient cynical saying, attributed to Pizarro, is probably of colonial American origin.

boat, rather precariously balanced between thwart and thwart, and the rowers must cluster fore and aft. Still the crossing was made fairly quickly. Indeed the whole procedure had been brisk, and I reckoned that a crew of five or six handymen had worked on the box.

Still it was stoutly made, with a plank cover and leather hinges. The sailors carried it to our waiting place, and there were at least ten volunteers, including Governor White himself and Richard, to lift the corpse gently, holding it straight, and laying it in place. Again the sailors served as pallbearers, and Governor White, Manteo, who had been Pemecum's friend, and I, Manteo's friend, would accompany the body. The other colonists were asked to wait for a second trip to bear them to the ship, as the boat would be top-heavy with its present burden. Actually I should have remained for the boat's return, for as it was a group of colonists were left with a group of Indians, whose inward feelings we did not know, without an interpreter. Still, I could not suggest this when I had caught the plea in Manteo's eyes.

No untoward incident occurred in our absence. Our burden was placed on the sunlit deck, where the late-afternoon sun could finish drying the whitewash. Presently all our colonists were aboard and with their baskets of edibles the Indians had entered their canoes. Captain Stafford had set out for the Croatan village, with just enough sail that the canoes could keep pace with our ship.

I made bold to speak to Governor White.

"Sir, I think the Indians would understand and appreciate it if we flew our flag at half-mast," I told him. "I suspect they have seen Lane's ships do so when they buried some of their crews or colonists."

"'Tis well thought of," our leader answered, "but I had better consult Doctor Jones, who has made a study of Indian customs."

The wise doctor concurred and the pennants were duly lowered. White announced that he would lead the procession from the beach to the village, Manteo behind him, while Ananias Dare, Christopher Cooper, Richard Wade, Dyonis Harvey, Cuthbert White, and I served as pallbearers. All of these but myself held the rank of gentlemen. John Spendlove declared he would remain on the ship. I was the only commoner, God knew the only full-blooded peasant. The other appointments did not mean that Governor White was especially rank-conscious. However, he was steeped in English tradition; he was being true to English social customs. I was somewhat surprised that I had been appointed instead of Roger Prat, no peasant, but, as the son of franklin, better born than I. But White was perfectly aware of my good service today and this was his public recognition of the fact. I could not say that any of the gentlemen serving with me in the rite appeared to resent my presence.

Just before the procession started, Manteo bade Governor White order that Pemecum's bow and quiver be laid on the coffin. The relationship between this ritualistic act and the carrying of the empty boots of a general killed in battle on the saddle of his war horse was immediately obvious. It caused me to reflect that no matter how the tribes of men varied in appearance, customs, tribal organizations, and in hundreds of other respects, their natures were strangely alike and every man jack of us was the son of Adam. All were touched by the borning of a babe, despite the commonality of the act, and all were awed by death.

Another custom had existed in Weechee's tribe. She was the first to touch land from our boat, and immediately she sped to a nearby stand of sunflowers, immense, golden, and gaudy, whether growing wild or planted for their seed used as edibles I did not know, and plucked a big armful. Unmindful of their rough stalks against her naked arms, she brought them to the coffin and laid them on its cover. Governor White gave brief thought to whether this would please the Croatans and glanced at Manteo. Manteo was astonished by the act—it was certainly a new thing to him—but presently nodded, then gave Weechee one of his rare smiles. The piper put the piccolo to his lips and began a wailing tune I had never heard, and which was certainly not of English origin, although it might have been imported from eastern Europe, possibly Transylvania occupied by the Magyars and ruled by Prince Sigismund of the incredibly ancient house of Báthori. If so, it was quite possibly of gypsy origin and it was so strongly punctuated that it could have served as a dance of death. In any case we marchers fell easily into its rhythm.

We found the entire population of the village assembled in a close group, Weoanza in their fore, and all with grave if not impassive faces. I could not doubt that they had already surmised that the body of Pemecum was in the coffin, since they missed him from the food-gathering party, and no doubt recognized his bow and quiver on the cover. They knew too, I thought, that the blame for him being there was ours, and we were paying him these honors to express our penitence. We set down the coffin in Weoanza's fore, and after reverently laying aside the decorations, Governor White opened the casket and stood back.

After a long glance at the dead warrior, Weoanza turned her gaze to Manteo. It was his turn to speak, and he knew it, and on how well he spoke, and how persuasively, only the Good God knew how much depended. Every Englishman knew this was a moment of utter crisis in the very existence of the colony and in all our lives.

Manteo told what had happened in a solemn but ringing voice, audible to all. I perceived at once that he put his faith in absolute truth, trusting his own people to weigh it justly, and his only attempt to excuse the wild shot was that we had been enraged by George Howe's murder, in an excited state from our fruitless search for the murderer and the burning of the Wingineo houses and the fields, and that we were such newcomers to the land that we had failed to observe the lack of warpaint and feathered headdress which would have instantly shown that Pemecum was on a peaceful mission when he was slain.

White Sagamore was a man of peace, Manteo declared. His great aim was that his people and Croatans live as peaceful neighbors, helpful to each other. He reminded Weoanza that her own husband, now dwelling in the Hereafter, had once slain one of his close kinsmen, mistaking him for a deer. The sagamore wished to atone for his disastrous blunder in every way possible. He and his followers would give generously of their stores to make up the material loss to the tribe resulting from the death of a great hunter, but were helpless to fill his place at the tribal councils and in the rings about the winter fires, or to dry the tears of those who mourned him. And our priest had implored Manitou, who was our God also under a different name,‡ to bring happiness to Pemecum in the Hereafter.

Manteo ceased speaking. A long silence ensued. The sun was now low, and the shadows were long and to me seemed sinister. As inconspicuously as possible I glanced into the faces of the Croatan warriors, and some of these were sullen, but no fury was manifest as yet. There would be no doubt that the honors we had paid to Pemecum's corpse had gone far to stay their wrath, and perhaps what amazed them the most was our coming here unarmed. This was a stronger argument of our contrition than any Manteo had presented. Yet I was almost certain that we stood in deadly danger, and whether it struck or passed us by would depend upon Weoanza's answer.

I knew the very instant that she came to her decision by her long sigh and a slight and unidentifiable change in her position. Then she began to speak. She addressed her words to Governor White, pausing at intervals to permit me to translate them for his understanding.

"You and your people have white skins . . . I and my people have brown skins . . . You know many things which we know not and you do works that are wonders to our eyes . . . But we also have knowledge that you lack, where to seek deer in what seasons and even in what phases of the moon, what plants in the forest are good

‡ The name Manitou was translated by early settlers as the Great Spirit. The Indians they encountered did not grasp the idea of godhead. To them Manitou was the great magician.

food and which are poison; on what tides the fish will run; how swiftly
to erect shelters against the chilling rain when our marches take us
far from our houses; how to track the bear on sun-baked ground, how
to trap hares, fowls, and even the glutton and the fox without iron
traps; and how to choose ground in which the corn grows tall with
heavy ears . . . But in one thing the white man and the Indian are
alike . . . Neither can forgo the making of mistakes, wisdom overcome
by folly . . . No werowance was ever so wise that he did not in some
unhappy hour make mistakes you would not expect from a prattling
child; even the priests misunderstand, sometimes, the messages of the
Great Spirit Manitou, who made the sun and moon . . . It comes to
me that you feel brotherhood with us, although many of the acts of
the followers of Lane Sagamore seem to deny it; and it comes to me
that this day you have put trust in a brotherhood that you feel within
your souls but which your lying tongues dispute, and the proof of that
is that you came to us without weapons . . . Our hearts are warmed
by the honors you have paid Pemecum, still we could not be sure they
were not a cunning cheat, if you had brought your thunder guns that
deal death, and if the men on your ship stood with burning brands
beside the mighty guns . . . Because you put your trust in us, we will
trust you once more . . . We will take no vengeance or accept a blood
price for what you did in folly and we will put *uppochappa* in the
peace pipes, light them with red coals from our supper fires, and pass
those pipes from white hand to brown hand and back again; and that
is the sign we and our kindred will not make war against you until—
until in folly or in wickedness you strike at our hearts once more."

5

So we smoked the pipes of peace and thereby knew that we had
escaped punishment for our awesome folly. A great happiness surged
through me, and I thought the Indians had been made happy by their
own forbearance, and there was only one wisp of cloud in the evening
sky, soon to be studded with great stars. This was only a glance exchanged between Richard and the daughter of Cossine Sachem, a
slim girl with shapely features, no more than fifteen, whose name sug-
gestive of Weechee was Cheewink. I remembered her well from our
previous visit here because of her beautiful headband. I recalled too
that one morning had seen where our dingey boat had been landed
in a slightly different place than I had marked it the preceding evening. I had the frightening suspicion that the two had met elsewhere
than at the village.

We had been warned against folly that might lead to bloodshed. So soon after our arrival, a clandestine love affair between one of our leaders and an Indian maid could be monstrous folly. But perhaps I had read too much in what could be merely a flirtatious glance between a lusty swain and a pretty girl.

Peace having been secured between the Croatans and ourselves, the captains of the three vessels were in haste to sail to England. They were generous with their predictions that Raleigh would soon dispatch a supply ship—'twas more than likely she was already far out at sea and could be expected any day—but stingy with guns, cannons, balls, powder muskets, and shot. The ships had greater need of these than had been at first expected, the gentlemen explained; the flyboat passengers had reported seeing many Spanish sails in the more easterly Spanish islands and one of the number, who spoke Spanish, had heard a rumor of Sir Francis Drake having attacked the Spanish settlement of St. Augustine. Their very ships might have to run a gantlet of Spanish galleons and sloops of war ere they could drop their irons in an English harbor.

Our colonists could hardly bring themselves to face the fact of the imminent departure of the ships. Partly this was their realization, which could not be dispelled by boasting or easy talk, of our lack of preparation for serious war, whether with raiding Spaniards or hostile Indians. By the same token, they must lay the most of the blame for this condition on themselves. More than two months had passed since we had first set foot on Roanoke, yet the wall and the ditch surrounding the settlement was little stronger than on the day of our arrival. The stockade had been repaired, but the water in the well was low; there were no fortified bins in which we could store corn for a siege; there was no keep for the trade goods I had accumulated wherewith to buy Indian corn; yet it would have to be cast forth to give even sleeping space for our hundred and ten colonists in case of determined attack by either Indians or Spanish.

I had almost persuaded myself that with the supplies brought by the flyboat we were in no great need of a supply ship sent by Sir Walter Raleigh. It was true that if we were able to abstain from war we could maintain life in our bodies a long time, if not indefinitely, with corn we ourselves raised, forest products, and meat procured by bows and arrows. But as I tallied our strengths against our weaknesses, my heart fell. Captain Spicer announced that he could let us have very little powder, despite his generous words which under examination proved to be generalities; and he durst part with none of his cannons. The tools he had promised he would leave with us, also the skeins of rope and netting; the canvas and raincloaks and boots had already been put on shore; but he must hoard the muskets he had intended to furnish us; his own danger of being grappled by a Spaniard was too great. We could help ourselves to a generous portion of his corn, but where would we store it?

Any colonist big enough to lift a musket could point and fire it, and could hardly miss the target at close range. On the other hand we had only ten passable or better bowmen.

Tom Warner and his helper had fashioned about forty bows, each with a full quiver of arrows, and these had been furnished to our younger colonists who lacked firearms, and they had expressed their thanks. But they practiced archery almost none at all. When they had gone hunting in the woods, they had begged or borrowed muskets. But a worse fault was their obsession with finding pearls, and even better, what the Indians called *tapisco,* which is gold.

Governor White had not ordered this practice, only urged it, and himself had set no example for the men to follow. Indeed he had spent no few of his idle days making journeys either in the *Lion's* longboat or the pinnace, to various points on the shore, as far south as Hatoraske, as far west as Ohenoak on the great river Chowan and as far north as the land of the Chespians where he had exchanged tokens of friendship with the great Sagamore Okisco, virtually a king. A good deal of gold had been obtained by trading, and it was quite possible that White's distinguished presence and dignified ways and professions of friendship would prevent their tribes and chiefs from taking part in any war that neighbor tribes might wage against us. But some of the El Dorados he meant to visit had proved legendary, and now that the time was getting short ere the ships' departure and the soon onset of winter, and especially since those hours of peril of our last dealings with the Croatan, I thought that he regretted his search for treasure to show the Queen, and wished he had devoted his energies and leadership in strengthening the colony against attack.

About the twentieth of August he called a council aboard the *Lion* to discuss matters of utmost moment. Of course Ananias Dare and other chief aides were invited, so were the masters of all three vessels, Doctor Jones, former Sheriff Anthony Cage, Muster Captain Richard Berry, Edward Powell, Thomas Ellis, Thomas Hewett, and Richard Wade. Because Tom Warner alone could organize the providing of bows and arrows to help substitute for musket balls and powder in frightening lack, he was directed to come to the parley, and for various reasons, the main one my ability as Manteo's interpreter, I the like.

We met on the open deck on a sunny afternoon. Governor White began the meeting with an optimistic address about our good provisioning for the winter, the impossibility of our starving when the woods thronged with game and the shallows of the sea with shellfish, and with our cloaks and good footgear and abundant fuel, we would not suffer from cold provided immediate attention was given to some of the houses. It was true that more men must become expert archers. In the advancement of this good intention, his assistants and he himself had been remiss. Moreover, he had no real doubt that peace with the Indians could be maintained certainly through the winter, in which season warriors rarely took the warpath, and probably until the next corn harvest, and possibly for many years, since both peoples would perceive the advantages of peace. Still it was our duty, as leaders, to prepare for the most remote contingency that we could conceive. He could not deny the possibility of a great war over some trivial matter, breaking out next spring.

For that reason the arrival of a supply boat would not be only a good thing, but a necessity. It would have come by now if Sir Walter Raleigh had perceived the situation, not only the danger of Spanish attack should their galleons prevail over the Queen's ships, but of attack by united tribes of Indians, a people steadfast in the promises, but excitable, prey to imaginings, and prone to take offense when none was meant. The situation came down to this: Someone close to Sir Walter Raleigh and having great influence with him must sail on one of the soon-departing ships with no other bent than to induce Sir Walter and the investors in the Roanoke enterprise to load a vessel and dispatch it without delay. It would be stowed not with the necessities of life but with implements for dealing death—falconets and demi-cannons not only for the blockhouse but for every corner in the wall and at all vulnerable places along the ditch. With these we needed many casks of powder, hundreds, not scores, of balls, and muskets for close-range fighting. If the situation were well described to Sir Walter Raleigh, he would perceive the peril threatening his second venture, and lose no time in removing it.

Well, who should be sent on this crucial mission? He had given thought to Ananias Dare, Doctor Jones, and Thomas Hewett, all of whom were held in high opinion by Sir Walter Raleigh. Richard Berry had served with Sir Walter in Ireland. Anthony Cage had been received by the Queen. Still the governor did not wish to appoint any one of these until all nominations were duly weighed by the leaders of the colony.

He paused, and there ensued a long moment of silence. Then Richard Wade rose respectfully to his feet, glanced about to see if any of the other consultants had risen, then asked a question.

"Your Excellency, I am among the youngest of the gentlemen here, and do not wish to appear presumptious. Have I your leave to speak?"

"Sir, I consider you one of the most able of the men under me. You may speak freely."

"There is one of our number who is eminently fitted for this mission, not only by intimate friendship with Sir Walter and by mental grasp of our situation, and that is yourself."

At once every man whom Governor White had named and several others showed their approval of Richard's proposal by voice or by a brief clapping of hands.

"But gentlemen, how may I leave my post here?" Governor White protested. "I am recognized as your leader by the Indians with whom we have dealt; would they not be disoriented and confused, and thus be less constant, if my post were filled with some other? I am well aware of the administrative ability of Ananias Dare as well as of other gentlemen I have mentioned, still the change might upset our Indian allies."

"Your Excellency, I propose that you question Manteo on that score," said Doctor Jones.

"That is a good notion. Mr. Sutton, will you repeat to Manteo the proposal made by my young friend Richard, and my protest at it?"

The others made no sound as I addressed Manteo in the Croatan language. He listened with his head on one side, sharply alert, and when I had finished, he sat with his head bowed in deep thought. Finally he spoke his answer directly to Governor White, although pausing between sentences for me to interpret.

"Great Sagamore, your council and commands are deeply needed here, especially when the great ships have gone, and the people here feel forsaken . . . But it is true as the star's burning, each at his wheeling post, that the need of strengthening our fort is a great need . . . Our defenses are more flimsy than we ourselves perceive . . . This, I believe, the Croatans know, and what is known will be told, without any meaning to do us harm, and the Indians will carry that word afar . . . I believe as you believe we can keep peace until the corn harvest a year from now—provided only our colonists or only one colonist does not commit some great folly or wickedness against the Croatan . . . If by then the relief ship has arrived, with abundant guns and powder and balls, and the settlement is fortified, the possibility of war with united Indian tribes will be greatly reduced . . . My people are not fools. They know the thundering might of cannon; they know of the sudden death that the dread mouth of a musket deals . . . It comes to me that not one of our fiery young warriors will urge war with the white men unless the tribe has suffered great cruelty and abuse at your hands . . . Great Sagamore, we will greatly miss your presence in our lead, but we have other chiefs who can advise the people well, so they may thrive, but we cannot, so I believe, hope for their thriving or perhaps survival unless, before some trouble comes, the settlement is made invincible to Indian attack . . . I know not who among you stands the most high with the mighty Sagamore Raleigh . . . But whoever stands the highest, he should be your choice to go."

"There's no doubt who stands highest, by far," remarked Ananias Dare when Manteo fell silent.

"Your Excellency, it seems to me you have no choice but to go," said Doctor Jones.

Governor White heaved a long sigh.

"I cannot make light of what has been said," the governor declared sorrowfully. "Still, I cannot consent unless my going is the written wish of the great majority here. Captain Irish, will you ask your cabin boy to prepare ballots—a blank back sheet of your log can be folded and torn or cut into small slips—and bring pen and inkhorn?"

"Yes, sir, I will."

The order was given and promptly obeyed. On the top of a chest Captain Irish set the pen and inkhorn, and there he laid his cap to receive the slips as soon as the voters had marked them. The men hung back, unwilling to take precedence, until the governor wrote a name on a ballot and placed it in the cap. As the most learned man here, Doctor Jones was thrust forward, and he too voted. The masters of the three vessels voted next, followed by Edward Powell, some sort of a minister, Thomas Ellis, Richard Berry, and Thomas Hewett. Three of the governor's aides voted after Anthony Cage, and Richard, Tom Warner, and I brought up the rear.

"Reverend Powell and Thomas Ellis, will you tabulate the ballots?"

Both men accepted, and Edward Powell passed each ballot in turn to Thomas Ellis. No tabulation was made; both trusted to their memories. In a few seconds their task was done.

"What are your findings, Reverend Powell?" Governor White asked quietly.

"Sir, there is one vote for Ananias Dare, in handwriting that I recognize as not his own, and all the rest are for Governor John White."

"Gentlemen, I accept the mission," the governor said quietly. "I will sail with Captain Irish, and do my utmost to fulfill its purpose. I appoint Ananias Dare to fill my duties here. This party may now disperse."

Chapter XII

FLIGHT OF THE FURIES

1

The news of the ships' early departure was received bleakly enough by our colonists; and its beglooming effect was multiplied by Governor White's accompanying them, his purpose to hasten the sailing of a relief ship. I think that more than a few of our number would have been happy to sail also, returning to England menaced by probable war with Spain, yet a safer land in their sight than this narrow strip of English territory between the forest and the sea. Still not one petitioned the governor for permission to depart. I think that the main persuader of their loyalty was the stigma, which was very real upon those guilty of quitting under fire.

The departure could not be otherwise than a dismal occasion. As long as the ships had ridden an anchor, their boats in touch with our shore, we had not felt wholly cut off from home. In sad silence the colonists thronged about Governor White. The women old and young were in tears; several men knelt and kissed his hand. Then the expressions on my fellows' faces as he boarded a ship boat revealed not their emotions but their responses to these, in which their basic strength of character became patent in some degree. Some were grim expositions of determination. Others revealed what might be close to panic. But one fact was undeniable—that despite his mistakes, major and minor, Governor John White had been trusted by his followers. They had not been left leaderless but perceived a great loss.

No one deplored the departing of John Spendlove. Highest born of any of us, the richest in possessions across the sea, still English common sense had convicted him of having bad judgment and a base spirit. No one knew exactly what his connections were with an unnamed English duke but all felt that instead of an upholder of his order he had betrayed it somehow; in his person he cast doubt on a belief cherished, which by the nature of things the English folk must cherish for their own hope and content, that their aristocrats were great not only in power and riches, but in dignity and personal worth. I had not been taught to swallow whole favorite English concepts, and I feared that among our betters were a frightening number of John Spendloves and even his inferiors.

With our departing governor waving at the rail, the crews weighed their anchors. The sails filled; the three bridges between us and home began to fall. Acting Governor Ananias Dare waited until the hulls had begun to lower under the skyline and the crew and his passengers looked like little sticks, then to our assembled colony he made a brief address.

After due praise to his chief, he minced no words in making plain what the colony must do, in order to survive. The quest for gold and pearls must from henceforth come second to the obtainance of abundant supplies for the not distant winter, and to every sort of labor that would strengthen our defenses against attack by disease, famine, or hostile tribes of Indians. Meat and fish not immediately consumed must be salted or dried. Every deerskin must be tanned and then sewed into some garment or article of use. The three ship boats we had obtained—one of these a longboat, with a hoistable sail; one with the two sets of oars; and one a two-oared dingey—could no longer be taken at will for excursions up and down the coast; they were for official or trading visits to the Croatan village, and for appointed fishing and hunting parties. For those that had bows and arrows but were not yet archers, Thomas Warner would act as tutor, every day except Sunday, between the hours of five and six in the afternoon, the summons being three clangs of an old ship's bell which Captain Irish had given the colony. As soon as more men became passably good archers, the shooting of deer with muskets would be reduced to a minimum, to save powder.

His address ended on a note of hope—that he himself did not question that Governor White would succeed in dispatching to us a supply ship by which we could strengthen our defenses, that by careful behavior we could keep peace with the Croatans, that war would be avoided, and the new dominion of Roanoke would become a pride to us, to our kinsmen across the sea, and to our Queen.

After the address I sought out Manteo, who was not at all surprised by my wish to consult with him, and we walked together into the woods. At my first remark he knew that I wanted to discuss a stratagem we had before mentioned, the details of which we had had no time to settle.

"Supposing, Manteo, we would have to clear out of the island and gain the mainland in a single night," I began.

"Our departure and our landing unseen?" he asked. It was a very astute question. Certainly we would not embark upon any such drastic action unless the extremity was extreme, and the failure of the enterprise was death.

"Yes."

"Martyn Sachem, it could not be done with three boats. Our best luck would be an almost windless night, or a light northeast wind. That would help us on a west by south course to Man's Bay* above Firewood Point,† but the paddlers would have to buck it on the return trip. We could make the round trip in four hours, two or even three trips on a long dark winter night, no more than two on a short summer night. If such a need comes, it will not be in winter, when Indians do not make war. Two trips, twenty-five colonists each trip besides the boatman, half of our number."

"There is no marsh close to Man's Bay," Maneto went on. "The people landed there could enter the forest at once, and Croatans do not hunt that forest; it is disputed ground from there back to the inhabitable marshes. So you told me when we spoke of this before. The party might be safe while encircling the marshes of Callaghan River, and gain Marsh End."‡

"If all went well. And from there we would deal with Indians of no kinship with the Croatan. But what of the half of our people left at Roanoke?"

"They must not be left there, and that is why we must play our trick. Nothing will be lost if the crisis never comes; just some sweat that our brothers can spare. And the rafts might be useful in other ways."

Our stratagem was simple in the extreme. As usual a good number of our bachelors lounged about the cooking fires after the evening meal; and Manteo's showing of an otter he had shot on the afternoon following our talk brought most of them to our fire. He had seen a good many deer, he said. The stags were rubbing velvet from their horns against tree limbs and trunks, still he had looked in vain for any buffalo that might have swum the strait.

"They are good swimmers, that I know," Manteo said for me to translate to about three score listeners. "They readily swim from headland to headland at the gulf where Croatan Sound meets Northwest Sound."

* Manns Harbor.
† Fleetwood Point.
‡ Roanoke Marshes. These represent the southern end of a great coastal marsh including Callaghan Creek. The latter name sounds more Irish than Indian and my use of it is probably an anachronism.

"Once a Croatan chief gave twenty skins for one of Lane's copper kettles," a *Lion* passenger told a late arrival on the flyboat.

This ancient scrap of gossip had never grown stale among our colonists. The skins had brought a golden sovereign each in London. Actually the beast himself was of enormous interest to all, for only one of our mainland hunting parties had ever seen one, the bull merely glimpsed in a rift in heavy brush before he had galloped away. Truly he warranted out fascination, for not only was it the largest beast by far inhabiting our part of the New World, but the most magnificent. Doctor Jones had examined the skull of one fastened on a tree at the Croatan village. Its teeth showed plainly it was not a browsing animal, as was the *wapiti*. First of all it was a grazer; and the fact related by Manteo that he did not drop his horns in winter, these growing heavier and more deeply curved every year, indicated it was not closely related to the true deer but was *bos*, which meant bovine. The mainland Spaniards had called him *búfalo*, and probably mistook him for the plow beast with back-flaring horns seen in India; but Doctor Jones surmised he was nearer kin to the European bison, known to the Teutans as aurochs.

Manteo spoke to me in a low tone. Because it was pitched only for my ear, the colonists were immediately curious.

"Manteo says he knows where buffaloes assemble, probably to get salt, and where forty hunters could kill a hundred with muskets or war arrows; but the assemblage occurs only once a year."

This statement aroused so much excitement that I, as if to oblige them, questioned him further; and presently I reported to the colonists an invention we had devised many weeks before.

"Manteo says they congregate on the lower end of Man's Bay, where it meets the marsh, a little short of a mile northwest of Firewood Point. They lap the rocks there, and the hollows in the beach, but they are there only about a week before and after the full moon following the spring equinox."

"The hides would be of great value to us as beds and the like," remarked Christopher Cooper, one of White's assistants, "and at that time of year, usually early April, there's enough sun to dry and smoke the meat."

"I'd be in favor of a big killing," Thomas Stevens, another assistant, hastened to say.

"Sir, what could we do with a big killing in three boats?" I replied. "The hunters would take up all the room." And this I translated for Manteo's ears.

He replied in four words. I looked thoughtful and somewhat dubious, still the men wanted to know what the chieftain had said.

But my reply was a lie. What Manteo had really said was, "You have them hooked."

"Manteo said 'All hands make rafts,' but that's easier said than done."

"Still, it's possible—we could appoint teams—and Lane's men declared that buffalo meat is as good and filling as English beef," said Christopher Cooper.

"The rafts would have to be built of close-set logs with slats nailed between them so sea water wouldn't wash up and wet the hides and meat. In any case we'd have to have an almost calm sea. We could probably make only one trip, and that would require eight or ten rafts to carry a big kill. Well, we've got plenty of saws and God knows plenty of trees and we could reclaim the nails. For each raft there should be at least eight paddles. The rafts would be good for fishing in cool weather. Mr. Cooper, if the men approve, you might appoint eight or so foremen."

"Will you serve as one, Mr. Sutton?"

"Yes, sir."

"Will you, my good friend Richard?"

"With pleasure. Martyn, I'll bet you six first-class arrows that my team finishes its raft before yours."

"I'll take you."

"Manteo will be foreman over us all," announced Mr. Cooper. "Ask Manteo how large to make the rafts."

This I did, and after the chieftain had mumbled, I reported that his answer was ten feet by twelve feet.

The body approved, and Mr. Cooper appointed six other vigorous and handy young men to be foremen, and their various stations in England did not influence his choice. He announced further that all rafts were to be completed and moored in the cove below Hook Jut before Christmas, or the teams could not partake in the hunt. That cove was well protected from any wind but a very strong northeaster, and its extreme backwaters adjoined a swamp where stood half-grown poplar trees, the logs of which were light, resilient, and easily worked.

Some truth as to our condition became apparent by the easy success, so far, of Manteo's and my ruse. The departure of the ships had aroused the self-reliance instinct in Englishmen and their zest for competitive sport. The appointment of men of all classes, including one yeoman and one jailbird, myself, for the positions of foremen indicated a slow but sure falling away of the accent put on hereditary position, almost all-powerful in our mother country.

Manteo and I had a right to give each other a furtive slap on the back, my giving a natural action, Manteo's somewhat foreign to his aloof and dignified conduct. It would be a vast relief to both of us

when the rafts were completed and moored in such easy reach of
the settlement. Eight rafts of such size could carry twelve colonists
each, each with such baggage as he himself could carry on his back;
the three boats could easily transport the rest with extra baggage. If
sudden exodus was forced upon us, if we must steal away in the night
at the threat of sudden death, some of the passengers from the boats
could be landed with those from the rafts, leaving only necessary
crews and otherwise untransportable baggage. In my most dismal visions I could image such an exodus, the boats keeping pace with the
marchers.

To where would we march? One answer might be to hunting
grounds of Indians that had no feud with palefaces, and no treaties
with them and little blood bond with the Croatans and allied tribes.
For two days march southward through contested ground we would
be relatively safe, unless the Croatans and their somewhat distant
allies could organize pursuit much more rapidly than I could believe.

Certainly, when we had the rafts, the pen in which the Roanoke
colonists were at present confined, would be no longer so difficult of
egress.

During the putting to the test of the ruse that Manteo and I had
hatched, I had scarcely been aware of Weechee squatting decorously
behind me. In fact I was now so accustomed to her presence that
I was scarcely conscious of it, but I would have been sharply conscious of her absence. She had been with me more than half a year
and was well past thirteen. In that period she had learned hundreds
of English words, merely by hearing them, and if she wished she
and I could have carried on an intelligible conversation on a not too
complex matter; however, she preferred to talk in her oddly accented
Croatan, which I thought similar at least in form and in the root
stems of words to her native tongue. Most of the time I was only
vaguely conscious of her physical development in this period; although
occasionally I became sharply conscious of this, and must force my
mind in some other direction. She had gained about four inches in
height, and now stood at least two inches over five feet in her leather
sandals. It was a significant fact that I could not well estimate the
dimensions of her bosom, because lately she had not bared it to my
sight in her innocent way as of yore. Months had passed since I had
glimpsed her naked body; partly, perhaps, in imitation of white
women, she wore one of my old shirts, belted at the waist, when she
went swimming. She no longer invited herself to my lap and I had
to urge her to sit there from time to time, and in accepting my kisses,
which I made as brotherly as possible, she had developed a decided

shyness. I thought that the great event in the life of any girl of about her age was drawing nigh.

My fellow colonists were equally accustomed to her tagging me about or walking at my side or darting ahead of me to gratify some curiosity, that they not only did not speak of it and in fact were actually almost unaware of it. We shared a small hut, with Manteo sleeping in a kind of lean-to at the rear. She had already found in the thickets a stone pan which in winter was used to contain red coals from the fire, really the Croatan concept of a blazer. She prepared Manteo's and my meals and her own and kept the hut and the lean-to brushed and reasonably clean.

When we returned from the parley by the fire—it was not a powwow, the Algonquin word for a noisy dispute—I perceived that she knew something which, if not a joke on me, of which she could make game. I guessed it by her sober manner completely belied by the shine in her jet-black eyes.

"I noticed that you did not understand the Croatan language very well tonight," she remarked, combing her gleaming jet-black hair.

"I do not know what you mean, Weechee," I answered, feigning indifference.

"When Manteo spoke to you, and you were supposed to translate what he said to your brothers, you did not get it right. It seemed to me you made up a good deal that you told them. Is that being truthful?"

"I suppose not, but we had planned something together, and we were both trying to make it succeed."

"I know what it was. For them to build rafts. I do not believe the story about the buffalo coming to the beach for salt. They have their own salt licks all through the forest—my father the sagamore used to shoot many deer and once in a long time a buffalo, by lying hidden beside a salt lick and not making a sound."

"Weechee, do you remember your father's full name and title?" The latter might easily be the name of his tribe, according to the custom in many tribes. I wanted to test what she could recall against what Eracano had told us about the Stranger in the land of the Montoak.

"No, Marteen Sachem, I try to remember but I cannot."

After a long pause, she added, "I am no longer a little girl. Much that I knew is lost—now that I am a young maiden—perhaps forever."

"Yes, in two years, or perhaps even one, you may take a husband."

"A Croatan boy! Pew!"

I did not know she knew this exclamation of contempt; plainly she had picked it up from some Englishwoman.

"What have you against the Croatans? They have been very good to us. They are very good Indians."

"They cannot compare with the Indians of the Wide Dark Waters." She pronounced the last three words as though they were the translation of a place name. "They are not as tall. They are not as proud. Almost all their arrow points are flint, instead of shark teeth. Their houses are not so good. The girls are not as pretty—except Cheewink."

"Weechee, how do you know all these things?"

"I—I do not know. They come into my head when I am half asleep, or when I have nothing to do but sit and hold a fishline."

"Try to remember them all, and tell me."

"I will try but I do not think I can succeed. As for Cheewink, she is pretty as a—a—no, I cannot think of the name. But I think you may take her for your woman, before long."

"I do not think so."

"You would rather have Winifred, I know, but I think she will take Richard as her husband. I see how they look at each other, and he is very handsome, and she most beautiful. Still you might get her, if great trouble comes to the colony, and you take the place of Sagamore Dare. She admires you now, and would admire you more if you are the sagamore, not a sachem. That is no fault in her; that is only wisdom, when she herself stands so high. But it may be that Richard Sachem will take Cheewink."

It came to me I must take thought before I spoke. I had surmised that my friend was deeply attracted to the pretty Powhatan girl and perhaps they had met secretly in the forest. Still I could not possibly imagine how. Weechee had arrived at the same idea.

"Richard is more often with the Mannering maiden."

"She will not get him. She is not a sagamore's daughter. He is not in England now; he feels himself what you call a prince, and he will want a princess."

"Maybe he wants you, Weechee. So you told me, once."

"If he does, would you let him have me?"

"He is my good friend. Still I would not let him have you unless you want him with all your heart, and are tired of me."

This touched her, perhaps more deeply than I could realize. She tried to conceal the fact but failed; I did not know how the truth was conveyed to me, whether by an expression in her eyes or my briefly touching her lips.

"If you asked me to sit on your lap a little while, I would do it," she told me, not very far from tears.

"I do ask you."

"Is it bad for me to do it? Would you be breaking your word to someone? If you want to kiss me, it needn't be on my mouth where I most like your kisses."

"I will make no amatory addresses," I said for my own hearing. "What does that mean?"

"In all truth, I do not exactly know where they begin but I do know where they end, and I will keep my promise."

I held out my arms to her, and very slowly she climbed on my lap. I kissed her young, warm, and silken mouth, but somehow I repressed passion and let it veer into tenderness. The nearest I came to breaking my vow was when she raised one arm and then the other, for me to kiss the silky hollows. Then she gave me one long hard kiss on the mouth, and with great sedateness went back to her place.

In only a few minutes I was listening to her quiet breathing, as she slept.

2

The building of rafts went forward swiftly and admirably. There was a good deal of competition between the teams; much shouting back and forth, and ribald jests. The men employed half-grown poplar trees, their wood very light, soft, and easy to work with ax or saw. In a sense because it was an open secret, I do not believe that occasional Croatans visiting our settlement knew or hardly cared what wonder or what folly the white men were doing now. They could easily hear the ring of the ax or the scraping of saws a mile or more away when spying out the island, and they listened briefly with idle curiosity in their faces; and when we told some of them we were building a "swamp house" they nodded and dropped the matter from their minds. By and large, the Croatan mind was not instinct with curiosity. Perhaps this was a factor that had prevented a higher civilization among the seaboard nations known to English adventurers. The idea struck me that no people can become what we call civilized except under compulsion by their environment. Corn growing, hunting, fishing, shellfish gathering, and the pursuit of edible plants satisfied the peoples' immediate and basic wants. The winters here were not so severe that extensive preparations must be made for their endurance. Chipping flints was a long and laborious process; but the Indian does not count hours, these would pass no matter what he does. The fire drill was a positive device, demanding only patience on the part of the user; the flint-and-steel outfits traders had offered were a drug on the market. On the other hand if sudden bitter onslaughts of fatal cold could be expected the Indians would have found some quicker means of making fire. For excitement they depended on magical ceremonies, dances, and not infrequent tribal war. Infant mortality was high but the bereaved mother soon dried her tears; it was easy to get babies. Doctor Jones thought that the rate of populace increase was very small if not almost zero: the reason might be occasional onsets of plagues, of which we had heard, but which he could not identify or explain. To the Indian these were the work of wicked werowances or of very Oke, who seemed to be an approximation of the Christian Devil.

I found myself harboring a sneaking admiration for the murderous Wingineos. They had an intense tribal consciousness and what I gathered was national pride if not hauteur. Certainly they disdained all neighbor tribes and had never come to truce with white men. And all this fruitless thinking made me wonder about Weechee's tribe. She was as eaten up with curiosity as a jackdaw. Also the molding of her bones and the texture of her skin and hair and her quickness to learn all caused me to believe that the little castaway belonged to a superior tribe.

The summer gave way to Indian summer, a term of which everyone knew the meaning but no one the origin. These were delightful days, and saw the first influx of migratory fowls from the north, those that were the least tolerant of frost, or had fonder memories of the warm lands where they had wintered. Among these were teals, species of curlews I had not seen before, New World robins, a bird we called blue jay, a species of gallinules, and a great many blackbirds, some with scarlet splashes on their wings. These first comers were the vanguard of a mighty host. I doubted if the stilt-walking folk of what we called the Wash and its surrounding marshes in East England had even seen the sky so darkened by ducks, geese, and swans. Many of the species I did not know. One was a duck resembling the pochard in his manner of flight, but this American duck, with his forehead and bill making one continuous line, flew so fast that I doubted if a Greenland falcon could keep pace. English mallards, all with radiant blue on their wings and the drakes having heads green as young wheat, arrived in numbers beyond estimation; there were ducks that had pale blue bills whose flight was peculiarly and charmingly decorous, moving in line and formation like well-trained cavalry; there were ducks closely resembling and perhaps identical with English widgeon. The ducks that fed on waterweeds lighted in enormous numbers in the bays. Sitting close together their flocks would often measure a mile in width.

But these ducks, having bred in little pools and ponds throughout that vast terra incognita, the American North, or in unimaginably vast beds of reeds, did not enthrall my spirit as did the countless wailing flocks of geese, often flying in V-shaped formation. Even these did not lift and exalt my spirit as did the wild swans. I thought if I were an Indian werowance I would found a cult of the swan. She would be our totem, and a captive white girl with fair hair would be our priestess, and I could well understand and almost believe the swan cults of my ancient Germanic ancestors, and how the swans chose dead heroes from the battlefields and bore them to Valhalla. Aye, these were also Norns, which meant the mistresses of Fate itself. But sometimes they changed into radiant maidens and made love with shepherd lads. And I did not forget that it was in the guise of a swan that Zeus had wooed Leda, whereof she laid two eggs, from whence hatched Castor, Pollux, incomparable Helen, and Clytemnestra, murderess of Agamemnon and Cassandra.

And with the countless flocks of the beautiful and magnificent fowls came one whom I could almost imagine was their shepherd. And he came peculiarly to us, out of the unknown north, a presentation so it seemed by unknown gods. He was an Indian of a tribe unknown, and at our first sight of him he was approaching our island in a canoe of a type we had never seen, and his rhythmic strokes had a kind of dignity no words could express, and one could only think of a great king returning to his people after a long pilgrimage, or of someone greater than a king. A north wind had roughened the strait, and he rose and fell with the waves it rolled, still he advanced without seeming effort.

He came straight to our landing and I looked into his face and I knew I had never seen a nobler countenance, and no king upon a European throne could boast its equal. Manteo was with me, and at sight of that face, he dropped on both knees, and so remained until, without a glance at me, the newcomer gave him his hand to raise him to his feet.

"Is this Manitou?" I asked Manteo, well knowing the Great Spirit never took human form; still my question was a natural and proper one.

"No, my friend," Manteo answered, "but he is sent by Manitou, one of a small number that journey from tribe to tribe, and who are greater than any chieftain, and whom we call the Blessed Man, for lack of a fitter name."

"The sagamore exalts me beyond my worth," the stranger told me in fluent, if oddly accented, Croatan. "I am only a Storyteller. But because I tell ancient tales of gods and spirits and heroes and their deeds and of their loves, I am made welcome at any fireside from the seashores of the sun westward to the Father of Waters, and from the vast fresh-water seas in the northwest nigh which the Father of Waters was born to the southmost tip of the Land of Immortal Summer, which white men like you have named for its plentitude of flowers."

"Sir, do you mean Florida?"

"Aye, that is its name. How then, you ask, may so far a traveler speak the Croatan? Because knowing languages is one of the tricks of my trade. A man who loves his trade, and would serve his brothers, can learn all he needs to ply it—and I have learned perhaps twenty basic languages, never to confuse or forget them, and Croatan is basically the same language as is spoken in the eastern nations of the Iroquois, the Algonquins, and the Powhatans; and I mastered the little changes when I spent two moons with the Croatan, one hundred moons gone."

"This is a wonderful thing," I said out of my awed heart.

"No, it is only the practice of my trade. The sagamore—and I think I remember him as a child—will tell you that all peoples are my people, I belong to all peoples, and even if two tribes are at war, I may pass freely through their lines of warriors, and no hand is ever raised against me, and their maidens vie to serve me their best meat. Why have I come here? No Indians—so you call my brown-skinned race—occupy this island now. But I had heard of the tall ships bringing white men here, to replace those that fled from here in their tall ships, and I am curious to behold how they differ from their brethren, and from brethren of another speech who have built a stockade on the shores of Florida, and who have many stockades in what was once the land of the Aztecs, amid the mountains. Seeing and listening and watching is also part of my trade, to behold how one tribe differs from another, and sometimes I hear a tale of some great hero of whom I had never heard, and that tale I put with those I already know. So I ask your leave to remain here at least a moon. I am no longer young, and I caught the cold in my left arm, and it gives me pain, and I wish it to mend before I make for Hatoraske, and it may be there is a wizard among you who will hasten that mending. And who is this daughter of generations of sagamores who clutches your hand?"

In my wonder at the newcomer I had been all but unaware of Weechee, clutching my right hand and gazing wide-eyed into the visitor's wondrous face.

"I wish you could tell me, Blessed Man. Her name is Weechee, but for three years she was a slave on the Spanish islands, and she has forgotten the language of her tribe and even its name."

"I think that I know the tribe but not its language, and I will not speak until I am certain, for such is unfit for a Storyteller when he deals with facts, instead of with legends, and the wild creations of his mind."

A number of my colonists had gathered, gaping at the newcomer. These I presented in order of their rank, and there was not one who did not realize that an Indian greater than any they had even seen had honored our island by coming hence. Ananias Dare bade me to inquire where he wished to lodge. The huts were already crammed, but all hands would join in building him one, of such comfort as we could provide.

"If you have enough skins, I will build myself what the Algonquin call a *tepee*," the Storyteller told us.

"We have something better than skins, and that is canvas, the same fabric that hangs from the tall trees of our ships, and catches the wind," Ananias Dare had me answer.

"That I have seen, and this warm clear night I will sleep in my own buffalo skin, and tomorrow build my *tepee*."

So came to us Blessed Man, the Storyteller, and I wished with my heart he could be persuaded to stay with us all the remainder of his days. But in any case I had a vision that the fate of the colony might in a large measure lie in his square, powerful, long-fingered, and beautiful hands. Unknown to himself, unknown to almost all of my fellow colonists, he was our hostage against a sudden and treacherous attack in the deep of night or from out of the forest shadows.

3

The winter advanced apace. It could not be called severe; our bedding and our garments, turning more and more to skins and furs, were adequate against its lowest temperatures. Fresh-water ponds were frequently frozen over for one or more nights; there was never a particle of ice on the salt-water bays. The worst days were when high wind blew spates of rain and snow. On these the colonists did not like to leave their huts, except to gather fuel for their blazers, and do necessary tasks for the sustenance of the settlement.

In late November, when shallow fresh-water ponds froze solid not to melt wholly until spring, and their fishes lay half insensible under submerged logs and refused all bait, and small amphibians and catfish buried themselves in the mud of the bottom, our fresh-water ducks began to take flight, first in small bands, and then in enormous droves. Ducks feeding mostly on salt-water plants, especially what we called wild celery, these fowls being the blue-billed ducks, the large red-headed ducks, and the even larger ducks with sloping heads and bills, all of them with rather short, exceeding swift wings and deep divers,

stayed a little longer; but they did not like the increased chill of
the waters, and in December these too made off. The wild geese had
long gone. No longer we heard their wailing cries when they flew in
the lonely skies, or their gabble when they fed. The beautiful and
holy swans were seen no more, catching the sunlight on their pinions.
Deer were still plentiful, but moved about very little on windy days,
taking refuge in heavy thickets.

Fish bit on certain tides in certain phases of the moon, these mainly
what we called sea trout, not very large but tasty; these would take
live shrimp which we netted in shallow bays. On some of these fishing trips we used the boats, and now and then a team would try out
its raft, highly pleased with its performance, for although almost un-
handable in strong wind, on still days they could lay a bed of gravel
in the middle and build a warming fire with perfect safety. Since I
asked Ananias Dare that only one raft be launched in the strait at
any one time, on the excuse that in case of a sudden gale we would
have trouble rescuing more than one, I did not believe the Indians
watching from the distant shore or from fishing boats knew that we
had more than one. This, no doubt, was the "marsh house" we had
told them we were building. The name made as much sense to them
as most English words.

No man, woman, or child begrudged the hospitality we furnished
our guest, Blessed Man, and the wives vied with one another to
furnish him his meals. On every night mild enough that we could
gather around a big fire, he told us stories that I quickly translated.
Mainly they were of great heroes of long ago, such as Hi-a-watha
and his granddam Nokomis, who had belonged to one of the Iroquois
tribes on the shores of an enormous inland sea or lake, which a
French explorer had discovered. The tale dealt mostly with a great
famine, and the hero's journey to a land of lakes amid vast prairies,
where he obtained corn for his people, and a maiden for himself. Of
all his tales, this was the favorite of Weechee. She like the idea of a
great warrior wedding a beautiful maiden from a far-distant tribe.

When his store of tales was nearing exhaustion, I told him some of
ours as we set out trout-lines, or tracked deer in the snowy forest.
He was as excited by them as would be a little boy. I told him of
Hercules and Jason and Perseus and Theseus, of great-hearted
Aeneas, and the heartbreaking stories of Niobe and of Oedipus, and
hero tales of Achilles and Ulysses, Siegfried, Ragnan, and Ogier the
Dane, King Arthur and Roland, and of the water witch, Morgan le
Fay. I knew enough of the legend of the Cid to recount in a fashion,
with many inventions; and oddly enough he knew the story of Marina,
the Indian maiden who was sweetheart and mouthpiece and adviser

to a half-god, half-hero out of the sunrise whom he called Cort. And he had heard, God knew how, of a blue-eyed, red-haired man who came out to the west in the first tall ship the island Indians had ever seen, whom he called by the correct name of Colon.

Staying longer than usual at any one village, he became fond of us, delighted with Weechee (who could help it?) and established brotherly relations with Manteo. Very plainly he regarded me as the sagamore, and I had a hard time concealing this fact from Ananias Dare. I was certain now he would not make off until well into the spring; and I thought if trouble developed with an Indian tribe, its signs would be apparent in early spring. It was in the winter that wandering tribes planned and made ready for their raids, and Indians in their councils nursed grudges.

The Virginia winter was chill, with frequent frosts, some of them severe. The worst weather brought blowing rain, and sometimes sleet and snow. But it was not arduous, and none hungered or slept cold. Governor White had had time to reach England, load a supply ship, and sail with her into our view, but no watcher had yet spied her topsails on the skyline. There were many pleasant, sunny days between periods of foul weather, and on these the colonists, reconciled to hard work and less expectant of immediate riches, improved their houses, cut wood for fuel, and hunted in the forest or fished in the bays. With practice our number of fair to middling archers slowly increased, until we had about forty. But those who could not get the hang of bow and arrow still must hunt deer for their tables, and the powder in our casks slowly but steadily dwindled.

There was now another indication, plain as day—that Winifred had almost, if not quite, made up her mind to marry Richard. On nights of good weather, when the colonists were wont to sit an hour or so around a big central fire, often toasting strips of venison over the coals, Winifred and Richard lingered there awhile after the others had retired to our huts. How long they lingered I did not seek to learn. A castle in Spain that I had built was falling down; a boyhood dream was becoming tenuous and losing its semblance to reality. Between Sunday morning service in the rebuilt church and a kind of vesper service that Edward Powell held in the late afternoon, the pair walked often into the woods, returning with a basket of walnuts or some such offering as a weak but at least an indisputable excuse for their long absence.

Sternly I reminded myself I had no cause for heaviness of heart, or Heaven knew for the least complaint to Fate. By English thinking, by no means dispelled from English minds by our distance from England and our new ways of life, the two were well matched. Wini-

fred was no doubt the highest born but by the book Richard had the
highest rank: her mother being the great granddaughter of a Welsh
king did not put her on a par with Richard's grandfather having been
an English lord. Besides, he was one of the very foremost in the colony.
He had evinced good if not excellent leadership; he was not particularly inventive but an efficient lieutenant, and all our people admired and respected him. He had not accomplished nearly as many
daring coups as had a Wiltshire peasant, but one of these, the foiling
of the mutiny, remained unknown; another, the finding of the pearls,
was the result of an accidental friendship with Manteo; and the building of the rafts and the practice in archery were not sensational ideas
and so far had proven of no dramatic value to the colony. Indeed
except for my mastery of the Croatan language, whereby I served as
interpreter at our infrequent meetings, I would not be counted among
the leaders.

In mid-March, when signs of the coming spring were increasingly
manifest, the glance of a clam digger revealed ten Indians in a very
large dugout making northward up the strait, hugging the mainland.
Plainly they had no intention of stopping at our island, and it was
useless to try to guess their mission, yet Blessed Man chose to intercept
them in his small, fleet canoe and hold speech with them. This he
did, the parley was brief, and the report he made to Manteo and,
through him, to other colonists, was likewise brief and lacking in
significance. The Indians called themselves Hatoraskes, and they belonged to the Chowanoc branch of the Algonquin Confederacy who
had voluntarily gone into exile some thirty years before. Now they
were making for Chowaneok for a great intertribal powwow. I thought
that the Storyteller had used this last word in its English meaning,
a conference, not a noisy dispute.

But as soon as the opportunity presented itself, the Storyteller told
me some news for my ears alone. It was that Sir Francis Drake, whom
the Indians called Sagamore Montoak, the last word meaning a super-
natural being, had attacked the Spanish town of St. Augustine more
than a year before, burned its houses, killed no few of its inmates, and
caused the rest to flee into the forest. I could not see how this action
could affect the fortunes of our colony, except as it might cause reprisal by the Spanish. But the thought drifted into my mind that if
St. Augustine, the nearest white settlement, had been abandoned, our
aloneness on the unthinkable reaches of the North American shores
north of Mexico was now complete.

The spring equinox fell on a night of waxing moon. The colonists
had not long to wait for their great buffalo hunt on and about the full
moon. Manteo and I did not know what lies we must tell to explain

its failure, but fate had it we need not give these a second thought. She was rising some hours before sunset, setting well before dawn, when there occurred what seemed a strange but minor incident. Richard, who in the earlier hours of the previous night before had sat with me, Christopher Cooper, Manteo, and Weechee on a log that served as a bench in front of the shed that housed our forge, watching William Berde shaping a plowshare out of an iron breastplate one of Lane's men had lost or thrown away, came to me before I had eaten breakfast to look about for his horn-handled hunting knife. He had noticed its absence from its sheath when he was dressing, and he thought he might have left it on the bench, for sometimes he drew it with no better purpose than to whittle a stick, not a rare habit of men in idle moments since time out of mind. We looked for it, but saw no sign of it. At once I called Weechee to find out if her bright eyes had noticed it anywhere, only to learn that Richard was wearing it when we parted company, for she, bored with our English talk, had looked at it in its sheath, wondering if the handle was part of the horn of a common stag or a great *wapiti*.

"It will turn up," I assured him.

"I wish I were sure of that. The blade is of the best Flemish steel. I brought it from home—the handle is red-deer horn. To save my life I cannot remember removing it from its sheath since skinning a cony with it late yesterday afternoon. I looked there first—and saw where I had wiped it on a dry grass, but saw no sign of the knife. It could hardly have been stolen when I was asleep or awake. No one could use it—its hilt could be recognized instantly. We have two colonists who went to jail for thieving—John Hynde and William Clement—but I haven't been near them and I'd feel a fool and a knave even to question them."

"You forget the third jailbird in our company," I told him, grinning. "But I have a good knife."

"It's no laughing matter, Martyn, old friend. I'm not in a habit of leaving it about. Its disappearance is quite a mystery, truly. Richard Berry and I sleep with our door unlocked—but everyone does. Well, I'll pursue my search, but it is murderously sharp, and I won't feel at ease till I find it." And I thought that I read heavy worry, if not deep trouble, in his eyes.

There seemed no connection, only a strangeness, when we saw six Croatan men, one of them the chieftain Cossine, paddling along our coast in two-man canoes. They seemed to be looking for something along our shore. It turned out that their search was not long. Plainly they landed not far from our harbor, for in a few minutes two of them appeared at the opening of our wall, and beckoned to Manteo. He joined them at once and the three disappeared.

Manteo was gone not more than ten minutes and perhaps less. The time had passed slowly for me, for I had begun to feel a deep but indefinable fright. Manteo beckoned to me, and then called Richard, who was searching the grass in front of his hut. Both of us joined him at once.

"What has happened, Manteo?" I asked in the Croatan language.

"You will see. It is very bad trouble. I think that Oke came out of his black cave to our island."

He led the way a short distance up the path into the forest, then turned off sharply toward the beach. As we came nigh I saw a small Croatan canoe moored in high reeds, some of these tough strands intertwined with and fastened to a leather thong which was in turn fastened to a copper ring in its stem. But the other Croatans were not looking in that direction or on the beach, but about a hundred feet back in the woods. All were gazing at something on the ground, and they did not raise their eyes as we came nigh.

Then Richard, walking ahead of me, joined them and gazed down, and I saw a ghastly pallor come into his face. A second or two later I knew why, and what my countenance revealed I never knew, but I knew of a great fainting and sickening of heart.

The body of an Indian girl lay there, on her side, her neck turned so I saw her face. Although her identity had been largely wiped away by the fell hand of sudden death, I knew her as Cheewink by her beautiful headband of white coral set with many-colored shells. From her side protruded three inches of steel and the horn hilt of a hunting knife. There could be no flickering hope that the knife was other than Richard's.

Chapter XIII

BITTER CHOICE

1

It seemed to my sick imagination that we were sharing this moment of silence and immobility with the dead girl. She could not enter our element of the living breath and all that was given with it, sensory experience, awareness of time and dimension, of the irredeemable past and the minatory future, but it seemed we had entered her element, that of lying so still with open eyes that saw nought, of a soul forlornly lingering nigh, for it had loved its housing ere it was cast forth.

But I cast forth these eerie fancies to confront the fact. Only in its most superficial aspect did the scene consist of seven Indians, Richard, and I standing roughly in a ring about the body of a comely Indian girl in the hushed forest close to the strand where she had been murdered. The faces of six Croatan braves seemed carved of pale-brown wood without grain, immovable and impenetrable. I saw Manteo searching them, a weakness he had suffered from dwelling with white folk, since as a great chief he too should stand remote and alone, neither cringing before Fate nor defiant of Fate, and wait. Presently I knew for what five of the Croatan warriors waited. It was for Cossine Sachem, father of the murdered Cheewink, to act or to speak.

Presently he moved. Bending down, he seized the horn handle of the knife, and slowly, but with great power, drew it forth. A white father could not help but have looked at the bloodied blade; Cossine looked only at the handle. Then he spoke in gutteral tones to Manteo.

"Manteo Sagamore, do you know whose knife this is?"

"Aye, I know, Cossine Sachem."

"What did the warrior say to Manteo?" Richard asked me quickly.

"He asked Manteo if he knew whose knife it is, and Manteo said he did know."

"Then tell Manteo to tell the warrior it is my knife."

When I had done so, Manteo spoke again to Cossine.

"The paleface Richard says that it is his knife."

"Did the paleface Richard stab Cheewink in fury or in the evil of Oke, or did some other use his knife?"

This too I translated, and Richard's reply as well.

"The paleface said that he missed his knife at dawn and has searched for it since, and although he lay with Cheewink last night ere the moon set, he did not harm her, but parted with her in the deep of midnight, amid the great stand of water oaks by the little pond one hundred paces up this dim path, their usual place of meeting." The merest movement of my hand indicated an old deer trail.

Cossine spoke quietly to his companions.

"We knew already whose knife this is, because all of us had seen it on the paleface's belt on both visits of his tribe to our village. We knew already that Cheewink met him by the little pond amid the ancient trees, although she left her canoe last night in a different bed of rushes, or we would have found it sooner. But since he declares he had lost his knife, I will return it to him."

Cossine lay the blade on his open hand in Richard's reach. The latter took it, and either by true instinct or unerring judgment, he knelt and wiped away its blood stains on the dew-wet grass. My heart stood still, in this case not a saying but a fact. Meanwhile I was watching Cossine out of the side of my eyes, and not only did he remain motionless except for dropping his arm to his side: his countenance remained utterly impassive. Then again he spoke, in a slightly different tone than before, one in which a sensitive ear detected command.

"Wait here with Cheewink." And Manteo need not tell Richard and me that we too must wait.

Cossine vanished in the brown brushwood. The effect was curiously like that of a shadow's disappearance when in late afternoon the sun is swiftly lost behind dense cloud. We waited, I believe, ten minutes. The Indians stood in relaxed positions, completely motionless. This ability might not be wholly native to the race; it might be developed by their long waits in ambush beside game trails, but the wonder of it remained. Neither Richard nor I looked up the deer path; the Indians may or may not have taken note of this. Both of us as well as Manteo knew Cossine's errand: it was to search the grass carefully for Richard's and Cheewink's couch, and then for footprints leading off. My great heart-chilling fear was that the dense grass would not hold footprints from moonset until now: it was luxuriant, young, and green because of warm days and abundant rain; stems bent down would soon spring erect; moccasins such as both Richard and Cheewink wore would break off almost no stems; finally against our fates, a hard warm wind had risen as the tide fell; brushing every glade that was not wholly sheltered by the dense foliage of trees.

No more than had Richard and I, the Croatans had not glanced up the deer path. Yet they were aware of Cossine's approach fully ten long-drawn seconds before I was; as was shown by their calm exchange of a brief glance. My own senses could detect no sight or sound or smell of him, until he materialized in the thickets.

He did not speak, or glance at Richard and me. Instead, he gathered his daughter's body into his arms and carried it to her own canoe at the edge of the bed of rushes, then laid it full-length. This procedure I had watched between the trees; I had feared that Cossine's self-control might be nearing the breaking point, and that the chilled flesh against his own and the scarlet ooze from the wound staining his breast might drive him to a frenzy of revenge. Apparently that fear did not cross Manteo's mind. He knew his tribesmen; he too calmly waited the event.

"I will take Cheewink home in her canoe," Cossine announced to the Croatans. "Manteo, if you choose to do so, you may take my place in my canoe, along with Ensenor. I go to speak to Weoanza. Then you can carry her word to your foster brothers, the palefaces."

2

When Richard and I returned to the settlement, we found the colonists in profound but well-controlled apprehension and dismay. They did not know the worst; but the word had passed during our parley with the Croatans that great trouble yet unknown had smote the colony; and from their lookouts various colonists had seen the lading of the body of a young Indian girl into one of the canoes and then Manteo paddling away in the company of the body bearers, obviously on their way to the Croatan village. All our people swiftly gathered about us, silently and staunchly waiting to hear the news we brought.

"I'll tell them," Richard murmured. "They've got to face it, and I won't throw the best light on what you believe to be my innocence, as you might do. How do you know I'm innocent? Every man has a black cavern in what we can call his soul; only he can know the demons that dwell there, in rusty chains; especially they break those chains when his lusts are frustrated. I seem a pretty good sort. You don't know me; I only half know myself; what remains unknown appalls me. Next to Cheewink's death what I hate worst is Winifred finding out I've been untrue. Her angel beauty given to me, as a queen bestows a gift; only two nights ago we became betrothed. But there was something about that beautiful heathen I was not man enough to resist. I'll say I'm innocent, but I would anyway, wouldn't I? But we've known each other a long time and I'll ask you to take my word for it that I am."

"Richard, I know you are." And I did know it, short of us both having gone suddenly mad. I knew it like my own breath.

As we had talked in low tones the colonists gathered in a circle, their faces drawn, their voices low, their stand strong.

"What happened, Richard?" Ananias Dare asked in quiet authority.

"Last night I lost my knife. A Croatan girl, Cheewink, daughter of the Chief Cossine, did not return to the village after a midnight assignation she had with me. He and some other warriors came to look for her at first light. They found her canoe in the reeds and then they found—her. My knife was found thrust deep in Cheewink's side. She had been murdered."

"God have mercy upon us," cried the wife of Ananias Dare. Naturally she would be the first to think of the deadly perils inherent in the situation. She had a late-born baby at her breast.

"I don't understand, Richard," Edward Powell said in his resonant voice. "Less than a week ago you asked my permission to woo my daughter Winifred. I gave it and two nights ago she told me you two were betrothed. With that promise and that hope, you couldn't have made ignoble and treacherous intrigue with a heathen girl."

I observed the adjective heathen. To one of Edward Powell's mind, it was the most damning he could use.

"I had made it weeks before. I couldn't stop."

"Perhaps—in order to make her let you stop—No, I reject that, but will the Indians? I am deeply shocked and wounded; still not for your sake but for all our sakes, we must stand together now."

"Reverend Powell, every man is innocent until he is proved guilty," broke in the lawyer Thomas Hewett. "The evidence against Richard is too pat. Any jury would see that. He could as well signed his name to this crime as to leave that knife that all of us knew, and the savages also, so well. Manteo will plead your cause. God help us if he fails but God help us in any event, because we'll still be held to answer. That old chieftainess will not forgive this blood debt. She warned us fairly."

No one else spoke; no one had anything to say. Winifred had turned her back on the others to hide her convulsed face and streaming eyes.

"What can the old Storyteller do?" Vestryman Thomas Ellis asked. "If you spoke truth, Martyn Sutton, he has more power than a king."

"Not temporal power."

"Shouldn't he take his own canoe and go to Manteo's help?"

"They might confine him," Doctor Jones answered quietly, "to keep him from being killed in a battle ending in massacre."

"I will go apart and pray to God," Edward Powell said, a wild brilliance in his eyes. "I will confess how more than one of us has sinned—how well I know it—how well He knows it—but to have mercy on the sinners, and hence upon us. Richard, even if you are acquitted —even if the colony is spared—I publicly withdraw my permission that you marry Winifred."

"I think the whole force of our thought should be given now to how we may prevent being wiped out," Ananias Dare reproved him in courteous tones.

"And you think too that with that prospect, a father should forgive the betrayal of his daughter?"

Winifred whirled on him, her face stark white but her head erect.

"My father, he did not betray me in the degree you think. I pursued Richard. I craved his embraces and tempted him and gave them freely. I loved him too much. I don't think any man can stand that."

"My God, I must pray for you, also. Are we the Children of Israel, lost in the wilderness? For they too forgot God and worshiped a golden calf! Every event circles back upon itself. Mr. Dare, only God or a Servant of God can save us now. I request—I demand—that you turn over to me, now, at once, full command of the colony. Then with one trusted follower I will take the two-oar boat, and go swiftly to the enemy village. Doubt not that they will heed my words. They will be of fire. Aye, I will ask Martyn Sutton to go with me, to interpret some of them the best he can, but meanwhile they will behold the Gift of Tongues descend upon me. Do you not see, do not all of you see, that there lies the only hope of our survival and the doing of God's work?"

"No, sir, I cannot turn over to you command of the colony," replied Ananias Dare.

"Sir, when you are refusing me, you are refusing God. Or, I will say, disobeying God's will."

"I take it on my head."

"And on your head will fall the retribution most dire! The prophet will point his finger and you will cringe when he tells you in the voice of doom, 'Thou art the man!' I alone, with the help of God, may save the colony in this dread hour. Thus I must go, whether by your consent or no; it is the command of God. Martyn Sutton! I will need an interpreter before the Gift of Tongues is given me. This is your great hour, your moment of opportunity. Will you row me to the Croatan village and stand at my side to assist me in saving the settlement?"

"No, your reverence, I cannot," I heard myself answer.

"*You cannot!* What do you mean? You can, and you must."

"Sir, I believe the settlement will be served best by our present ambassador, Manteo. He will report to us soon. Then we can decide in open council what to do."

"You refuse me? You, a peasant whom I let keep company with my daughter, the granddaughter of true and near descent from the Gwynedd kings!"

"Sir, I must speak to our appointed leader . . . Mr. Dare, will you post lookouts with good view of the Croatan landing? If one or two or three canoes put out, we need take no action. But if twenty or more put out, and the paddlers wear paint and headdress, the archers and musketeers should be assembled. Will you also bid the people watch for signal smokes, north and south and also west of the village, and count the smokes from each site, and bring word to me, so I may ask their meaning of Storyteller?"

"That, I will, and I appoint the yeoman William Berde to select the watchers and appoint them their posts." And this was a good choice, I thought, for William Berde had made it his mission to learn the topography of the island, exercising the same kind of care he had had for his handful of acres in England.

"As for me," broke in a ringing voice, "I turn my back on this company, and go to seek God alone and apart. I will pray for you, and you had best pray for yourselves, because except for direct intervention from Heaven not one of you will live to see another sun. O, generation of vipers! You have brought it on yourselves. The bachelors in our company, and men with wedded wives in England, have committed fornication with our unattached women and I fear with heathen women. My own daughter has lain in sin with her betrothed, without the sacrament of marriage. Richard! Richard! You whom I trusted! Even this unholy surrender did not satisfy your lusts; in the same week—the same night, perhaps—you have copulated with a daughter of the idolatrous Philistines against Jehovah's ordinance. And you, Martyn Sutton, were among the ringleaders in preventing the burning of the Temple of Baal, when we harried the evil Wingineos! I spit upon the ground in disgust!"

Edward Powell strode away. Every man watched him out of sight with his brows drawn; no man knew that his fellow did so, so deep was his own trouble; and I returned to sanity and hope when I felt a small, warm trembling hand steal into mine.

You will not perish this night, Weechee, or any night while you are in my charge. So declares my soul unto Fate standing beside us here in her threatening dark veil! So I declare unto you, the words un*ounded but burning in my heart. For you, so strangely sent to me, I will rally my yet untested and unmeasured powers, those I dimly divined and greater powers that by some great reaching I can attain and wield. Be of blithe spirit yet. Let it soar high as does your namesake in the summer afternoon!

3

The watchers reported no signal smokes, no canoes putting forth manned with warriors in warpaint and gaudy headdress. Only one canoe was visible, a barely visible dot on the quiet waters of the strait, bearing one paddler. He was making straight for our settlement, and that he was Manteo we could not doubt. But what tidings he was bringing we could not dream.

Nearly an hour passed from the moment that William Berde first spied Manteo until we could plainly see his face, in a stone's throw of our landing. In all his desperate errand had occupied five hours; and the sun had passed its zenith. I had long since observed he was not paddling at a desperate speed but with a rhythmic, steady stroke. This could mean the news he brought was not as evil as we feared, but knowing Manteo well, I also knew that it might mean he was conserving his strength for an impending crisis not yet known to us.

Immediately Ananias Dare ordered a continuous ringing of our old ship's bell, this ordering the assembly of all our colonists. Most of these were already in the open space back from the blockhouse, every musketeer with his weapon primed, with rested hammer, but his match not yet lighted; every archer had his bow and quiver. I looked in vain for Storyteller. But the thought of his desertion did not cross my mind; I took thought of how he never attended our colonial parleys unless especially invited. I went in search of him and found him squatting in his tepee, for he had demurred at our building him any better shelter. I had already told him all I knew of what had happened. His strangely lighted eyes had turned dark, yet they had kindled a little when he took thought of other crises he had watched in his long wanderings, these rising only to fall away. Some of these, perhaps, had become embodied in the tales he told.

He came with me, and remained at my side until Manteo squatted beside Ananias Dare. A place in the ring had been left beside Manteo for both Storyteller and me. A deep hush, somehow very strange in this warm and sunlit hour, silenced all whispers in the assembly. I studied Manteo's face and although I knew its every lineament, I could not forecast his tidings. Presently he gave voice to a deep-toned "Hough!" Once before I had heard him utter this sound, that occasion being one of high pride. I did not know, and I doubted if Manteo himself did, exactly what the utterance meant. It was an Indian formality, I guessed, before or after some momentous experience or declaration. Before it had been spoken in a moment of success and pride. But it could as well signal great defiance.

"Martyn Sutton, ask Manteo what news he brings us."

When I had translated, Manteo leaned forward and spoke, with his hands cupped over his knees.

"I bring the word of Weoanza, Chieftainess of the Croatan. Her word is, 'Bring to us the slayer of Cheewink, daughter of Cossine, to be slain according to our time and pleasure.'"

What else could we expect? Why had we yielded to the least, dim, flickering hope? Every paleface became more pale at the announcement, yet the silence held except for long, hushed sighs. Most of the men's eyes were fixed on the ground. The women gazed prayerfully at Ananias Dare, Manteo, Storyteller, and one or two at Richard.

"Ask Manteo if he told the Croatans we do not know the identity of the murderer?"

"Aye, I told them this," Manteo replied when I had interpreted the question. "'That,' said Weoanza, 'is not our affair.' We are given until sundown tomorrow afternoon to find him and deliver him into the hands of the Croatan. Four unarmed men are to bring him, his hands bound, and a halter about his ankles so he may not break and run. If we do not so tomorrow when the Sun gives his last red wink ere he dips beneath the western hills the Croatan will send up smokes on the great rock called Buffalo Leap and on Reed Point and the headlands of the southern shore of Northwest Strait. As darkness falls, the fires will be fed by driftwood heavy with salt, that burn with red and blue and green flames, itself the call to war, and these flames will be fed all the night long. At every place of burning the smokes or the fires will be five. This is to call in the other four nations of the Confederacy of Five, armed, painted, and adorned for battle—Weapemeocs, Secotas, Agriascagocs, and Pomiocks, the Croatans being the least of these by far. It is the word of Weoanza, made before the kewas, that surrender of the slayer or any plea for peace made after sunset tomorrow will be useless, for runners have gone to all four tribes, bidding them make ready, and when they see the smokes they will begin their march. And once they have set foot on the warpath, there is no recall, their warpaint will not be mocked, their arrow points and sharp spears will not be denied their warm bath in blood, and every paleface man, woman, and child, and babe in arms in the settlement will be slain, and every runaway hunted down, and not one will be given burial, and all will lie upon this hated island until their flesh dissolves or is eaten by the birds of death who will gather here, and by wolves and bears. And in that slaughter, I, Manteo will die with the palefaces, because I have joined their camp, and of all dwellers here only the Blessed Man will be spared. And these are the words of Weoanza, Chieftainess of the Croatans, spoken before the kewas, and I, Manteo, born unto Weoanza, have not changed one word of her words, or twisted the meaning of one. Now I am silent."

Also silent were all of his hearers. Most of them had expected heavy threat but not a downright ultimatum of acceptance of Croatan demands or annihilation. A few had been so misled by optimism and loose talk of Indians being weak-willed, their bark worse than their bite, that they had predicted not much more than a demonstration of Indian rage, fizzling out like a musket match in a rainstorm.

"Those redskins wouldn't *dare* press their grievance against white men," was a remark attributed to one of Lane's colonists, and eagerly quoted. Comfort was taken in the story that a single blast of cannon reduced the painted warriors to scuttling curs. Those with harder heads expected at least arbitration with the savages, and the payment of a mighty blood price. Now they could hardly believe their ears, and worse yet, their eyes, which locked on Manteo's face and searched wildly and in vain for the least sign of doubt of his own declaration. His countenance remained perfectly still. There were no self-conscious movements of his hands or shifting glances.

Finally Ananias Dare spoke to the hushed assembly.

"You have heard Mr. Sutton's translation of Weoanza's message," he said, controlling his voice. "Now I will address Doctor John Jones, a newcomer like almost all of us to the New World, but who has made a study of Indian people, as they were described by English, French, and Spanish explorers and adventurers. Sir, what do you make of the threat of the Croatan chieftainess?"

"What is there to be made of it, sir, except that she means what she says?" the wise physician answered.

"She meant it when she spoke it, but has she the will, the determination, to keep it? Has she that much power over tribes other than the Croatan, or even the Croatans themselves?"

"Sir, I do not think she is a braggard. At her husband's death she obtained the chieftainship by the warriors' will and consent. Women chieftains are not at all rare along this coast; there is a small tribe on the Chowan River that is completely matriarchal. Indians in this part of the world are not at all like the mild, defenseless Indians Columbus found on most West Indian islands; they are probably kin to the Caribs. And they are a proud people. Never forget that fact. Now the Croatans' chieftainess has spoken, they will fight to the death to make her words good. There will be no more parleys. There will be only battle. And at the end of that battle—but I can say no more."

Then up spoke Richard, a flush on his cheeks and a glitter in his eyes.

"Sir, may I speak?"

"Yes, you may."

"I did not kill Cheewink, or harm her in any way, but—"

"What do you mean, sir, that you did not harm her in any way?" broke in an angry voice. It had a ring that used to hold spellbound, even more than the prophet-like words it uttered, throngs of rustics in the open fields of Wiltshire. "Base fellow, you harmed her only short of killing her. You lay with her in sin, by which she might have a babe, a mixture of brown and white—*pah*—who will be rejected both by his mother's people and his sire's."

"Sir, I hope you will pardon me for saying so," broke in Doctor Jones, "but I consider your statement that Richard's copulating with Cheewink was a sin second only to killing her as so much claptrap."

"Sir, did you say *claptrap*—to *me?*"

"Yes, sir, I did."

"You forget how wanton boys made mock of Elisha the Prophet, and the Lord Jehovah caused bears to come out of the woods and devour them. Beware, Doctor Jones, of a like retribution for your contemning of one who speaks God's ordinance."

"We have heard enough of that," pronounced Ananias Dare. "Richard, you may continue."

"Sir, I had just said I did not kill Cheewink," Richard went on, with soldierly voice and bearing. "I have no notion who did. But it was my knife by which she died. If I had not met her in the way I did, for the purpose that I did, I might not have lost my knife. Some one of us has to pay for her death. I do not want anyone to suggest that we cast lots. I will wait until early tomorrow afternoon on the wild hope that some miracle may come to pass, or that the murderer confesses his crime. Then if neither of these things happen—which is my expectation—I shall surrender myself to the Croatan. It is a high price to pay for carelessness with my knife, but I'll pay it."

Richard resumed his seat, his face fiery red. I had never been so proud of him, never before realized his courage and his troth with what he conceived was duty, or was so touched by the fact that he was my friend.

"By God, I'll see them in Hell first," cried John Hynde, my fellow jailbird. "We have twenty musketeers and twice as many archers, and one cannon and two falconets. I say for all to gather in the stockade when we see their war canoes, and fight to the last man."

"Before the last man fell, he would have to kill our women, children, and three babes in arms," I said, for the moment to make my long-planned proposal was almost at hand. "I wouldn't like to be he."

"If you had kept God's ordinance, we would not be in this desperate plight," Edward Powell shouted. But I thought this was his last out-burst, which he could not resist. I could tell by his countenance that his fanaticism was burning out in this bleak wind of hard and present fact.

"What choice do we have?" Mr. Dare asked in a bitter voice, reflect-ing all too clearly his growing despair. "To cast lots for a human sacrifice—I would not hear of accepting Richard's manly and brave proposal—or to fight against hopeless odds? Martyn, ask Storyteller if he believes the Croatan will carry out their threat."

When I had done so, and all the staring spectators had seen the slow, sad nod of his grizzled head, I rose to my feet.

"Mr. Governor, I think we have still a third choice, one fraught with peril, but still preferable to human sacrifice or to hopeless war. Have I your permission to present it?"

"Do so, for the love of God!"

4

"Mark you, the strait is almost calm this afternoon," I began, my voice more quiet and steady than I hoped. "There is not a cloud in the sky that might augur hard winds tonight. The breeze is from the northeast, which would be the very best we could ask for. In the harbor below Hook Jut, at the edge of the marsh, we have eight rafts of light, strong poplar wood, well made, with slats nailed between the logs to keep little waves from bursting up, wetting what stores we bring. These would carry eleven, even twelve people each—eleven comes to eighty-eight—the remaining twenty-two can use our boats. The teams that built these rafts know how to handle them in light wind with their paddles. Most of the teams have fished in Man's Bay —the beach is gravel and sand, not swamp—and it would not be hard to find in the dim moonlight or even in the dark, for that beach will show gray while the two headlands north and south are swampy, and will look dark. Every one of us could take only such baggage as he can transport on his back in a canvas carrier, this baggage including his weapons. There would be some room left in the boats, and what heavy baggage we would stow there would be for the leader to de-cide.

"On the beach we would pour the rest of our whale oil on the rafts and set fire to them," I went on, having no trouble with words.

"The Indians might see the flames, even at that distance, they would think it was a peat fire that often starts in the swamp from rotted vegetation. The rafts would be of no further use to us, and any Croatan, scouting in his canoe, must not see them and in that way guess our whereabouts. From the beach we raft passengers would move straight west into the forest. The rowers in the boats must row with all their might, to round Firewood Point before dawn. Then they would continue southward, hugging the shore, to a point on the mainland directly west of the southernmost islands at the southern tip of Roanoke Island. That would fetch them to what Lane's men called Marsh End; this would be their rendezvous with the marchers. From thence on we would make our way by land and by sea to St. Augustine. It is a Spanish settlement, but we are fellow Christians, fellow white folk, and I do not believe they will turn us away. I say again that the journey would be dangerous, still it is our best chance if not our only chance."

"Do you mean, sir," Ananias Dare demanded when I paused, "that you would have most of us march God knows how many hundred miles, our boats staying abreast, through utter wilderness inhabited by hostile Indians?"

"Sir, we do not know that they would be hostile. At least they would have no cause to hate us, as have the Croatans. And it so chances that the land westward of Man's Bay, around the upper waters of first Spanker Creek and then Callaghan Creek, and southward to Marsh End is dry ground and contested ground between the tribes of the Algonquin Confederacy and the Muskhogean Confederacy, these last of no kin to the Croatans. I do not believe the marchers would encounter any Indians until after they reach Marsh End, a two days' march. Thereafter we would have to contend with situations as they arise."

After many seconds of keeping silent, of deepmost shock felt in every bosom, Ananias Dare broke forth in a voice rough with anger, and in the same breath, charged with awe.

"God in Heaven, will someone tell this fool that his scheme is utter madness! Will you, Doctor Jones? Why should we be tormented by a false hope against all hope?"

"No, sir, I cannot. I cannot feel that Mr. Sutton's plan for the saving of our lives arouses hope against hope in our hearts. I know now why he questioned me so closely as to adjacent mainland terrain, as described to me by Lane. As to the rafts being ready—the only adequate transport available in our great need—I think that he and his friend Thomas Warner employed deceit, or I will say ingenious invention, clearly perceiving that if he left the matter to our foresight instead of taking advantage of our men's love of adventure and hunting, our sloth would have held sway, and no rafts would have been available. I grant you, sir, the enterprise is perilous in the extreme, but even a frail chance is better than none at all. I plead that we give it the utmost consideration."

"But to forsake the colony—letting it be taken by the wilderness —all our labors thrown away—" As Ananias spoke, his voice became hoarse, and then he could not go on.

"I remind you, Governor Dare, that we will be leaving our cannon also," rose the accusative voice of Richard Berry, muster captain, who had overseen in his haughty way the strengthening of our ditch and wall.

"Oh, I can't stand it!" a woman broke forth, wildly sobbing.

Winifred Powell sprang to her feet. She took every eye as her own eyes fairly shone, partly with anger but partly with fire of purpose. The slowly dipping Sun graced the pale gold of her hair, but mainly he showed her off to us, under his early spring effulgent beam. "There she stands, behold her," the Sun declared in his high and haughty pride. "You could not see her except for me. In the light of my daughter the Moon she is lovely, I confess; still a mockery of what now you see; at once spirit and earth, melody in human form; visual poetry; the remembrance of a lost dream."

"We need not go," Winifred declared. "Manteo or the Storyteller will take me to the Croatan village and leave me there. You can wait in your own houses, around your own fires; the bowmen need not nock their arrows or the musketeers load their guns. Your hearts may be assured and content. I will make peace with the warriors; how can I fail when my hand is held by the hand of the True God! Still, sometimes he lets his children die cruel deaths. It may be so with me. Why should it not be me, instead of one of you? If it will comfort you, you may think of me as the murderer of beautiful Cheewink, now driven to this act by remorse . . . Why, I am the best suspect anyway. Cheewink had lain with my lover, so I stabbed her to death with his own knife. Now let this gathering break up, all of us go to our own place, and Storyteller and I will set forth at sunrise. Master Dare, tell the people it is settled; the danger has passed; all will be well; they can be comforted." And then after a brief pause, "Why are you waiting?"

"Mistress Winifred, I do not doubt—"

"Give them their instructions; do not hem and haw. The women are weeping."

"And still they must weep," answered Ananias Dare in a strong voice. "Mistress Winifred, your heroism is beyond question, your nobility awes us all, and you may be one of those few mortals who have been sent to us, whence we know not, whose footsteps in our mean paths lend glory to them, one of those whose presence among us endows us all with a measure of grace; and I cannot deny that you might perform the miracle which you feel called upon to perform. Still we are merely mortal; we must do what our manhood bids us, we have not the faith to put our trust in miracles; we must act on what we call reason and on what seems likelihood. By the power vested in me by Governor White, I refuse your petition. I command you not to attempt what you propose, openly or in stealth. I order you to do the same as the other colonists, to fight or to flee, which will be presently decided. Please resume your seat."

Winifred bowed her beautiful head. "The True God knows I can do no more. Tall, ancient, and noble trees, bear witness!" Then with her lovely face twisted by grief she dropped on her knees, then resumed her seat beside her sire.

"We have heard all we need to hear," said Doctor Jones, a look of amazement on his face. "Pray you, Mr. Dare, let the people vote. Is it not enough to show hands?"

"It is enough to show hands. May God let us choose the better—the less bad—of the two courses open to us. I will vote only in case of a tie. The earlier proposal was that we refuse the Croatan ultimatum, and if the warriors attempt to carry it out by force, we will first try to frighten them off by musket and cannon fire, and if this fails, to fight—and I must speak plainly—to the death. All in favor of this course, raise their hands."

Muster Captain Richard Berry lifted his arm straight over his head. Former Sheriff Anthony Cage did likewise; so did William Nicholes raise his hand, so did the goldsmith William Brown, so did John Hynde and William Clement, once inmates of a general jail on the charge of stealing. Thomas Ellis started to raise his hand, glanced at the lawyer Thomas Hewett, but when the latter shook his head, the vestryman lowered his hand. Edward Powell sat motionless with bowed head. There were only a few more hands raised, these of young men mostly, Cuthbert White, kinsman of George White, and some of his gallant friends, race-proud, bold wooers of our unattached women, first to volunteer for any hazardous enterprise. I could expect Richard to be one of them, and I watched him in deep suspense. He saw my questioning eyes and spoke in a low tone.

"I'm going to stick with you, Martyn, for all that I hate turning tail and I believe we're both making a mistake."

"Vote as you see fit, Richard."

"No, I've made up my mind."

"Only fourteen in all," Mr. Dare reported, after a swift count. "But we'll go through the formalities. All of you who favor Mr. Martyn Sutton's proposal, to flee to the mainland on rafts or in boats, please raise your hands."

All who had not already voted except Edward and Winifred Powell raised their hands, and the number included two sons of colonists, both urchins, who voted with their parents. Manteo raised his hand. With instinctive propriety, Storyteller did not vote, but his fine eyes lighted at the dimensions of our victory.

Mr. Dare must wipe his own eyes, then he spoke firmly.

"Now I will give my last commands. Mr. Sutton, all of us will hold you responsible for the success or failure of the enterprise you proposed. But it is not fair to impose responsibility without bestowing power. Sir, I appoint you leader of the colony, myself resigning that position, and my request to this assembly—indeed it would be my command if the power were still mine—is that you obey his orders as you have obeyed mine. Mr. Sutton, take my seat, and give your instructions."

My head reeled, but my legs bore me firmly and briskly to the big log that had served our former leader as a throne.

5

Manteo was already beside me; and at once I invited Storyteller, who had squatted behind Ananias Dare, to draw nearer. And it so chanced that my first business was with him, which I explained to my fellow colonists.

"We must make our exit as soon as night falls. This must not be suspected by the Croatan, and by the same token they must not discover our absence if we can possibly prevent them doing so until after sundown tomorrow, the time of the expiration of their ultimatum. The noise of our getting ready will not carry to their village; if one chance canoeist hears it, he will think we are strengthening our fortifications. But it would be most helpful if they could see smoke as from cooking fires rising from the settlement at meal times tomorrow. So I will ask Storyteller to carry out this stratagem, then set out at sundown tomorrow to overtake our boats which he can easily do in his light canoe. By then, if all goes well, the boats will be out of sight around Firewood Point and our marchers will have gained the contested ground, at least a long head start and possibly safe from pursuit. I say for your comfort, his post is not as dangerous as you might think. The storytellers, called the Blessed Men, live by their own laws. No hand will be raised against him, despite Indian fury. He is sacrosanct. Every tribe confederated with the Croatans would break bond with them, causing them to become an outcast tribe, if they abused, much less killed, a storyteller."

Then I turned to him and explained what I wanted him to do. He folded his arms on his breast and nodded, which amounted to his vowed assent.

"The first task of the young men will be to cut enough fuel for about twenty fires, to be fed once at suppertime tonight, and three times tomorrow. This will take you only a few minutes. The next task in which all will engage is to make bundles. In the storehouse you will find abundant canvas, in rolls five feet in width, and a box containing forty pairs of scissors. Cut the cloth in six-foot lengths. Every man and woman and well-grown child is to have such a piece as a covering for a blanket, and the roll you make of these will contain those possessions most essential for your survival in the forest. Every roll carrier must consider that some accident may separate him briefly or for an extended period from the main group, so take great care in your selection. At such times fishhooks and a long thong might save your life; a tinderbox with flint and steel would give you fire. Wonders can be done if you have an ax or even a sharp hatchet when otherwise you would be helpless."

"How much should the rolls weigh?" someone asked. "We can carry only so much. And how do we fasten them?"

"The ends will be tied with the lines you find there, and the bundles worn across the top of your backs, the ends over your shoulders, and fastened in front. Sixty pounds should be the maximum for a man of ordinary strength, forty pounds for a woman of good strength, twenty for a well-grown urchin. Each of you will need a utensil that will serve as a cooking pot or a water carrier. The marchers should each have a pound or two of food and his water utensil filled from swamp creek near the rafts just before we push off for use tonight and all day tomorrow if our landing is somehow delayed until then. But each of the three boats must have a water cask, because these will continue to make southward after the marchers forsake their rafts, and they will be in danger of sudden squalls driving them farther to sea. As said before, the teams that built the rafts will use them, each with an additional three people. The boats will carry the others, with such heavy freight as is most needed. I appoint Cuthbert White to command the longboat and to select good boatmen to command the other two, also to decide in what boat the extra people —our number is a hundred and twelve with the piper and the Indians —will travel. In brief, Mr. White, you will command under me our sea division, both when you journey with the rafts and after the rafts are put ashore, burned, and the passengers begin their march, both divisions remaining abreast as far as possible. Is that clear?"

"Yes, sir, it is."

"I appoint as my assistant Thomas Warner, who is responsible for forty of you having excellent bows and arrows and being able to use them; also he can speak Spanish and hence negotiate with Spaniards when that time comes. His first duty will be to choose what heavy equipment is the most important to us, deliver as much of this to the boats as Mr. White feels it safe to accept, and try to find space for more on the rafts. This will include a crate of pocket knives and one of mirrors, which we have discovered are most prized by the Indians, and which will be used as gifts and peace offerings. The archers will procure from our stores spare arrowheads and bow cords; the musketeers' canisters of powder and spare flints and matches. For your bundles spare clothes will be needed, but no gold or coin. Divide among them enough oiled cloth to make a total of eleven pavilions, under each of which ten people can huddle. The women may wear what jewelry they have, for the sake of prestige. One Bible will be taken by one of the stronger men, and if he wishes, Mr. Powell may bring his own. You will change your moccasins for French waterproof boots, although bring your moccasins for dry-land travel. Mementoes you have brought from England are not forbidden, but remember that our march will be difficult by any count, and every ounce of tare lessens our chances. You may disperse to make your preparations for the journey."

My own first intention was to carry out an agreement our company had made with our three ship captains who had sailed us here from England, by prearrangement with Governor White. The latter had not been blind to the possibility, perhaps in his darker thoughts a probability, of conflict with the Croatan; also he perceived that the tribe might be our refuge in great trouble. The agreement was, that if we deserted Roanoke Island for any reason that concerned the Croatan, we were to carve the tribal name on the trunk of a big elm tree standing about a hundred paces from the stockade. If we were at peace with them, only that name would be carved there, but if we were forced to go with them or to flee the island on account of them, a cross was to be carved below.

Before I set about this minor task, and realizing it could as well be the last performed before we boarded the rafts and boats, I checked through my mind to see if any more vital provision had not yet been made. Almost instantly I thought of three, immeasurably important to the safety of tonight's journey. In all truth I had put too much trust in weather-sign—the cloudless sky, the balmy afternoon, and the gentle wind that in its present quarter would bear us south-west. I had forgotten how quickly and completely weather could change on this coast, exposed to the great reaches of Northwest Sound and of Pamlico Sound* on the south and to great oceanic winds that did not pause to catch their breath as they swept over the barrier reefs and the island itself out of the east.

Christopher Cooper, one of John White's assistants, had been to sea previous to this journey, serving as midshipman. He had told me that his vessel had touched Amsterdam, Le Havre, and Genoa; certainly he knew the fundamentals of seamanship. We had abundant cord, some pierced lead sinkers for weights on fishnets, and an abundance of hempen cable, half an inch in diameter. I bade him press a com-panion, and the twain prepare ten sounds, with twelve foot-cords with weights and as many anchors—crowbars in this case—each with hundred-foot cables, this length chosen since Captain Irish had told me no water in Croatan Sound exceeded fifteen fathoms in depth. These were to be put aboard the rafts as soon as ready.

Also I had Cuthbert White and his assistants take from the stores or the houses eleven lanterns filled with oil and supplied with tinder, one for each raft and boat. I was well aware at what great distance a burning lantern could be seen on a dark night, but in the first place I did not expect any need of them tonight, and if the need arose, we need not burn them long. Finally I asked Manteo to make me two Croatan torches, which were tightly bound reeds, soaked with whale oil. If need be, one of these I would use as a guiding light for the fleet of rafts, so we would not become separated, and the other the master of our largest boat could employ to prevent strag-gling by the other two boats.

The torches would blaze with a bright flare, visible as a point of light over many sea miles of water. Still I did not think any Croatan would associate them with us, three leagues down the strait; marsh-lights, which our rustics called will-o'-the-wisp, were frequently seen over our own marshes and occasionally on the mainland; some lights we had seen might have been St. Elmo's fire. In any case the risk was small; while the disasters that can ensue in the blind dark may be great indeed.

These preparations well underway, I began the prearranged signals on the tree trunk. I had spelled out the word Croatan and was ready to affix the cross, that would indicate our exodus had been forced by the Croatan. Then a thought struck me that made me hold my hand. My countrymen, the English, were by no means a people temperate

* The author could find no evidence that Pamlico Sound bore this name on the sea charts of 1588.

in their conduct when aroused to fury. For some centuries we had had no great massacres of Englishmen by Englishmen, such as the massacre on St. Bartholomew's of Frenchmen by Frenchmen because of religious differences; but several hangings and head-choppings had occurred in the reign of Queen Bess, and worse than these in the reign of Bloody Mary.

In due course, if England was victorious in a naval war with Spain, English battleships would visit these shores. Their crews might find a double-incentive to deal dire punishment for Indian abuse of Englishmen, in case these same Indians had pearls, gold, and precious furs. In all truth the Croatans had treated us as brothers throughout the stay of Lane's colony and our own, tolerant of our misdeeds; and even now, when their princess had been cruelly murdered on our island, they had only demanded the surrender of the murderer on the threat of wiping out our colony. I did not want these Indians wiped out by English cannon, or the chiefs hanged, or even their houses burned.

I was the appointed leader, now, and I could employ the power put in my hands. I did not carve under the tribal name the sign that throughout Christendom signifies brotherhood and mercy.

Now the sun was low and had begun to pitch toward the western skyline, jagged with treetops. It was as though he was in haste to extinguish his radiance in the dark and endless forest. A number of our colonists, each with his bundle, began to appear on Hook Jut, close to the marsh where the rafts were concealed. They arrived in parties roughly representative of the teams that had built the rafts, and I ordered that each team float its raft and its members and accompanying passengers get aboard. In almost every case the foreman of the team acted as captain. To my great pleasure, Doctor Jones chose the raft that my team had built somewhat longer than the others. Also I made room for Weechee and Manteo.

All the raft captains were instructed to follow me throughout the crossing, and after moonset or even before if needed, my reed torch would be their beacon.

Edward Powell had declined travel on Richard's raft as well as my own, and had chosen that commanded by Richard Brook, gentle-born and a man of many skills. Proud of his physical strength, which he no doubt regarded as a direct endowment by God, Mr. Powell carried a roll weighing nearer eighty pounds than the sixty I had specified as the maximum, and included his big Bible and a box of soap cakes weighing about ten pounds, some of which no doubt to give fellow wanderers not so provident as to cleanliness next to godliness. Winifred, tall and strong, despite her delicate and dreamy beauty, made nothing of a roll that appeared to weigh at least forty pounds. Also in her left hand she carried a deerskin bag, its top lashed with many thongs with intricate knots, and the tension of its neck made me think it weighed at least three pounds, and perhaps more.

Her sire had strode past me in bitter silence, but she stopped and spoke.

"Martyn, I am glad you were chosen captain."

"You have always wished me well. But did you obey the order not to bring gold or coin?"

"You should know I would not. Do you remember the chunk of pure copper that was in the temple of the Wingineos? You mentioned it to Richard and he to me. He said it could be smelted with tin dishes to make bronze arrowheads, but when I saw it I thought it might be a meteorite and asked him to give it to me. He did so—and since it impressed Indians enough that they kept it with their kewas, I thought it might be useful on our journey. It was no trouble to bring."

I did not recall seeing it in the temple but in a hut, plainly a slip of memory. If it was deemed a meteorite, it might indeed be useful— my own reading about the Black Stone of Mecca and a remark by Doctor Jones had taught me as much. Still I marveled over this young girl whose depths I would never know. She had been lost to me, and won by Richard, and as she walked on I switched my thoughts to the venture ahead of us, and wondered how much of it, if any, the world might ever know. Quite possibly nothing; so easily it might come to pass that the fate of Raleigh's second colony would remain forever a mystery. Death would come to our last survival in some yet unknown and undreamed refuge; the years would pass; the darkness would not be penetrated; it would become deeper the more that scholars searched. It was of no great matter, the vanishing of one hundred and ten English people into the forest primeval; still in every generation for a century or more a few men might wonder. A few might dream dreams.

Suddenly I took thought of the big logbook in the fort, from which a few pages had been torn, perhaps to be burned or buried by Indians who thought the writing there was sorcery. But about five hundred sheets were blank. The wing feathers of wild geese furnish excellent quills; lamp black mixed with water made a legible ink. Swiftly I made my way there, got the book, put it in a canvas bag, and stowed it in our biggest boat.

And now the time had come for our departure. In the glooming the scene seemed bleak; the dimming waters under the rounding moon, the green of the forest turning to an ever darker gray. Yet there was one romantic touch. Captain Irish's piper had decided to stay with us, when the tall ship sailed; he was with us now and he had brought his pipe.

Thinking of what might await us, God knew I could not deem it excess baggage. As the men paddled the rafts out of the harbor, he played the wistful and heartbreaking "Still through the Hawthorn Blows the Cold Wind," its words well known to many of our West Country men and women, who broke into song.

The sun had set behind a band of roseate cloud. According to West Country beliefs, particularly those of our seacoast, this was a good omen:

"Red sun at night, sailor's delight;
Red sun in the morning, sailors take warning."

6

But I would have rather have no cloud in sight. The dusk was long-drawn, this of no danger to us, because of its very deceit, persuading the eyes that they could see almost as far as in broad daylight, when actually vision faded out in a few hundred yards. The light wind was holding well, its direction south by west all we could desire. The moon was high in the sky and would set well after midnight, nearly an hour later than last night. And this reflection checked with a jerk the flow of my thoughts: last night's setting of the moon had ended the tryst between Richard and Cheewink; and a minute or two later—from their couch to the place of her finding was only a stone's toss—her remembrances of Richard's embrace, his strength and his passion and perhaps his tenderness, and her own ecstasy and sense of victory, had been suddenly cut short.

Had the assassin leaped at her from ambush, or had he met her and walked with her for a few steps, explaining he had waited for her, he wanted to talk to her, he was not angry but she must make up her mind . . . Perhaps she had been uneasy but had she been deeply afraid she would have run away at sight of him, and what Indian, let alone what white man, could have kept pace with her light feet in the darkness? And suddenly she could not make up her mind, for this along with her lovely eyes was darkened by one sudden thrust of the accursed steel.

"A good, clean beginning," Doctor Jones remarked to me, watching the coast recede.

"All's well so far," I answered, careful to limit the remark, lest an evil spirit make me repent my boast.

"You know, Martyn, I can hardly believe that so much could have happened between dawn and dark."

"It is hard to believe."

"I am sorry to mention this. But all is not well, as you well know." The physician stood close at my side and spoke in the merest murmur, which the light lapping of the rippling sea against the raft drowned out of all ears but mine. As a refuge from what he had just proposed, I thought of how truly seaworthy was a well-built raft. It was unsinkable, and even unwashable except in high seas; it would rise and fall with the waves. Even our baggage would not slide off and be lost, because the builders had secured light logs along all four sides. The slits between the logs had been so well covered with nailed slats that no water whatever washed up on what we could properly call our deck. The paddlers maneuvered the oblong raft, preventing its veering to port or starboard, with complete ease. Still I wished it was provided with some sort of rudder.

Doctor Jones had spent his apprentice days as an army doctor. He was used to seeing sudden death and grievous wounds; what he had seen this morning did not prey on his mind as it did on mine. Still he was conscious of grave aspects of what had happened that I had so far mainly excluded from my thoughts.

"I do not believe it was an Indian who did it," Doctor Jones went on. "I don't see how he could have obtained Richard's knife, unless he had left it somewhere, and Weechee saw it on his belt when he parted with you last night."

Weechee was now close to me, where she belonged. She had squatted, her easiest position, and was gazing calmly ahead into the moonlit gloom.

"And if not," continued the remorseless murmur of the doctor's voice, "he was a colonist and with us now."

"Not a reassuring thought," I answered. But after all, I should be used to having a ruthless murderer in my immediate environs. The evidence had indicated my mother had been slain by someone she knew well. Thank God, that was far across the sea.

"I'll name you the most likely prospects. One—although you will not like to have me say so—is Richard himself. A very sharp-witted murderer might easily use his own knife for such a crime—especially one with an odd handle all would recognize—believing that very fact would remove him from suspicion. When a man signs his name to a murder, one's first thought is that someone forged it, and he is the victim of an iniquitous plot. Another suspect, and you'll want to drown me for saying so, is Winifred. What she said inadvertently today—then made a point of it—that the murder could be her work,

and in fact she had the most obvious motive. You believe you know
her too well to admit the merest possibility of this being true, but I
can tell you that no human being knows another human being through
and through, your best friend, your beloved, your own brother. Every
one of us has secret depths into which no one peers. She said something
today that indicated depths of the most secret and strange sort—I wish
I could remember what it was. Mark you, I am only having intel-
lectual exercise, which I have no right to impose on anyone—I no more
believe that that beautiful and idealistic young woman committed such
a crime than that I myself did it, walking in my sleep. My main
suspect, against whom a good lawyer might make a convincing case,
is Edward Powell. What is his motive? That an Indian girl had copulated with his beloved daughter's betrothed? You know his hatred
of interracial copulation—we all know his fanaticism, his unfaltering
belief that he alone, of our colony, represents the God of Vengeance.
But his guide is the Scriptures, his inspiration is the prophets, so
he cannot forget the commandment 'Thou shalt not kill.'

"I wonder what made him such a fanatic," Doctor Jones went on.
"The Welsh are a fiery people—a bit fey in the modern meaning of
the word—I too am a Welshman and should know—still there's
something in his life, perhaps terrible and strange, that was not in
most Welshmen's lives. Well, I'm going to convince myself that it
was some man of our colony, probably obscure, possibly prominent,
who himself was in love with Cheewink, who had lain with her, and
thought he owned her; and murdered her in a passion of jealousy.
From the thickets he had watched the dalliance and then the embrace of Richard and his Indian sweetheart. I can hardly doubt that
next to getting money, sexual jealousy has caused more murders than
all other causes combined. I assure you, Martyn, as a trained thinker,
that this hypothesis is the most sensible and the most likely. He had a
disordered mind—or it became violently disordered by what he saw.
And in this case, it is not likely to happen again."

I wished he had not said this last. His saying it seemed to make
it less true. I did not know why. I did not wish to find out. Again
I sought the North Star, found it with ease, and assured myself that
our course was south by west.

I had not yet lighted my torch. The moon, still bright and rounding, cast enough light that no raft had any trouble following its
forerunner at a safe distance of one hundred feet, and I could dimly
make out the shadow of the last in the line, at almost a cable's
length. We progressed to my total satisfaction for another half hour,
before I had a faint feeling of change. When I tried to detect its
source, I could only tell myself that the stars *seemed* dimmer in the

most minor degree. But instead they should brighten, as our scene spun farther from the light of the sun.

Just then I found Manteo at my elbow. He too spoke in a low murmur.

"Martyn Sachem, the wind is rising a little, and I think veering a little, and a faint mist has spread between us and the stars."

"Do you expect bad weather?" I asked, after a brief pause.

"Not at all. But I expect the wind to keep on rising to a brisk blow, and to keep on veering more and more northward."

"Enough that we might have trouble making in to Man's Bay?"

"No. The paddlers would have to work harder, if the wind rises fast as it veers more to the south, but they can make it safely. Already we are only an hour's drift from Man's Bay. But you had better light your torch."

I did so at once, by shooting sparks from my flint against a pinch of tinder at the end of the torch, and, as the latter began to smoke, blowing on it. When the oil-soaked reeds made a bright slow-eating flame, I held the torch so it fully revealed Manteo's face.

"Your voice reveals thoughts you have not put in words," I told him, and the mere forming of that sentence revealed my mastery of the Croatan language.

"Aye, I have thoughts I have not revealed. To you I say again we can easily make into Man's Bay. But what if we did not try? What if we took full advantage of this north wind? It is not likely to change without first giving sign, and we could not be more than a few miles from the mainland. I believe, but I cannot be sure, that we could paddle in even against a west wind, for it could not be tempestous so close to the land. And every mile we drift southward takes us farther from the Croatan."

"In plain words we might make Marsh End without abandoning the rafts?"

"Martyn Sachem, we might make the bay behind the end of the barrier reef that Lane Sagamore called Cape Lookout."

A great thrill coursed down my spine.

"And at no greak risk?"

"There is always risk no matter what you do. But there may be safety, too, in gaining the grounds of the Muskhogeans."

"How soon?"

"Before tomorrow's sunset."

"And I, God help me, must make the decision, and I will."

"Aye, Martyn Sagamore, you will."

Chapter XIV

THE FUGITIVES

1

The wind was rising at a rate impalpable in any brief period of observation, yet it turned my thoughts to the choice which soon I must make. As again and again I took note of the wind, always it was perceptibly higher. I knew true north by finding the Polar Star; as far as I could tell the wind blew straight from it. *And no south wind could blow it out,* I thought. *They had puffed their mightiest ere now, but Old Trusty burned serenely in his place out from the pointer stars, a never-failing pilot whether for an outward or a homeward sail.*

Nor need I rebuke myself for this kind of revery. Nearly half an hour must pass before I must decide our course, and then the decision must be made on inspiration more than studied judgment. The terms of the problem were extremely simple. The farther southward we were thrust by the wind, the wider would be our separation from Croatans and their allies, but the greater would be our danger of being swept out to sea or of being shipwrecked on the coast. The first of these perils was very real; the second could lose us our supplies, or bog us down in marshes from which our boats would have great difficulties in our rescue. On the other hand, the landing of the rafts at Man's Bay would be easy, but the chances of our capture by hostile Indians far greater.

In twenty minutes more the wind was blowing steadily and briskly between fifteen and twenty miles an hour I guessed, cool but not in the least cold, causing the oblong rafts to pitch noticeably and rhythmically, but not rock to our discomfort or our hardly notice. The paddlers kept them in line, straightforward and not wheeling and at the same approximate distance from each other, but their labors became heavier. Manteo observed all these things and then came to my side.

"Martyn Sagamore, it is time for you to order the landing at Man's Bay, if that is still your intention."

"Now?"

"Aye. The rafts can be worked westward as they drift southward, and not miss the beach. But if you wait much longer, the drift might be too great and they would run into the marsh beyond."

I drew one long breath and gave the command that so boldly shaped itself upon my lips.

"Keep our present course."

This word bull-voiced Doctor Jones shouted to Richard commanding the raft behind mine. "Aye, aye," came Richard's reply, full and ringing in the wind; and then we heard him shouting the same command to the raft behind. I could not have made the last raft captain hear me, had I shouted against the wind, but it flung into my ears his clear, and, as far as I could tell, untroubled response. Yet certainly some if not all of the captains knew I was not carrying out the plan I had proposed and the majority had approved a more audacious plan, perhaps fraught with greater danger from the sea, if less danger from Indians.

They could not help but perceive that I was taking advantage of the wind to get some place as soon as possible. Such is the temperament of man, as opposed to that of woman, to like just this. Men are bolder than women, but not nearly as brave in many respects, and especially in confronting and bearing pain. When the contest is purely physical, against the old and pagan gods, man ignores physical dangers that appall women; indeed he loves to challenge these gods; yet when a woman decides to risk something she will often risk all, and it is man at his best who painfully tries to weigh chances, compute percentages, and reckons risks when he fights his fellow men for pelf or glory. I would have no trouble with my followers as long as I kept going forward at whatever danger. But by nature they cannot endure boredom, and would quickly turn on me if ever I could not think of what to try next.

Man's Bay, with its hard beach, dropped behind us. Staunchly the wind held in the north; ever Polaris hung where I hoped and expected him to hang, above and behind me. When I asked Manteo if he thought the wind would rise still more, he shook his head, and I wondered by what process of thought, or superstition, or previous observation, he had come to that opinion. As any wind can fall to utter death, any wind can rise to heights terrible and almost unimaginable—at the whim of whom? I could only hope, in a childish way, that Manteo was right. Even now the paddlers must wield their blades faster and with greater force to keep the rafts head on. On the other hand if we affixed sea anchors, the materials of which we had in plenty, these would reduce the labor to a minimum but greatly reduce our speed.

In any case we must maintain this speed until we were opposite Marsh End, about a mile below a peninsula which Lane's colonists, for reasons unknown, called Roanoke Marshes. This point Doctor Jones had estimated to be nine and one half miles from our stockade. Here a marsh that ran from immediately below Man's Bay ended abruptly in sand and gravel. This beach was about five and one half miles south of Man's Bay beach where I had first proposed to land and burn the rafts.

Not only the added distance gained would increase our chances of complete escape from the Croatan. Below the outjutting peninsula called Roanoke Marshes our rafts and boats would be hidden from the sight of the Croatan village and of canoes not far out in the strait.

The idea came to me to have the sea anchors rigged, ready to cast out as soon as possible, although they would not be needed for at least an hour. On our raft was one of the colony's gentlemen who never in our experience had been seen to do one trick—which landsmen would call one lick—of manual work; although he had supervised repairs of the stockade. So I presented myself to him, standing in the fore end of the raft, out of the salt spray sometimes flung up by the impact of a wave on our stern.

"Mr. Richard Berry," I said courteously, "kindly get shears from the boxes, a roll of canvas, and fifty fathoms of cord, and rig eight sea anchors, the canvases to be five feet by five."

"Mr. Sutton, I have never seen a sea anchor, and would not know one if I saw it, let alone know how to make one."

"Nothing could be simpler. To the corners of each of the five-foot canvases you bend—that means to attach firmly—the end of a forty-foot line. About fifteen feet from the canvas gather up all four lines and tie them together in a big knot. The remaining twenty-five feet of the four lines should also be knotted at intervals as our main sea-anchor line."

"I suggest, sir, that you appoint this task to one of the paddlers, skilled in the work of common seamen."

"I will do so gladly, if you take his paddle. He would be happy to make the exchange, because the paddling must be strenuous for the raft to maintain way."

"Then I will consent to direct a suitable hand and see that he does not loiter in the task."

"I consider you a suitable hand for a simple task of this kind, and

I am obliged to tell you you must obey my order at once, or suffer disciplinary action."

Mr. Richard Berry almost lost his breath with astonishment. "Would *you* dare to threaten *me?*" he demanded, incredulously.

"Dare, sir, is not quite the word. I am in command; it is my duty to give orders, and see that they are obeyed. All persons above infancy must fish or cut bait."

"I have a notion I should defy you, to test the legality of your high-handed action."

"Defy me, if you like. My first response will be to throw you overboard. You are a good swimmer and will certainly be able to clamber aboard one of the rafts. True, the seas are somewhat cool, but healthy exercise with a paddle will prevent a chill."

I must guard myself, I thought. I was enjoying this brush with this lofty fool; I felt my lips drawing back with a pleasant sensation. I caught myself hoping he would resist, so I could make swift and brutal use of the peasant muscles that had mangled a prison guard in far-distant Wiltshire. And then I heard a low voice at my side.

"I do not like you, Señor Marteen, when you look like that!"

"Forgive me, Weechee. I forgot my place. Master Richard, it will be necessary for all of us to work if we are to live. I will show you how to tie the knots. I ask you to work willingly, for the benefit of all."

2

When I had explained the principle of the sea anchor—in this case a canvas fastened at its forecorners and dragged behind a wind-driven craft—he demonstrated quick hands at cutting the cloth and tying the lines. He did not complain when a tarred line smeared his hands, or at his cramped position on the deck of the raft. He finished four of the anchors, its lead line ready to make fast, in just about an hour. Then at a word from me Thomas Hewett left his post of observation to help with the chore, and four other anchors were made ready in a half hour more.

In this period the wind-blown rafts had passed Roanoke Marshes, the outline of the peninsula dimly visible in the pallid glint of the setting moon. In its lee, I had led the flotilla on a southwest course, the paddlers struggling mightily, until we coasted within a cable's length of a long, dark gray beach. Our sounds had not once given us less than a fathom of water here and I knew that we could make the shore by brisk paddling whenever we wished. So it took no strength of will on my part to decide to continue our southward flight all night long unless the brisk wind out of the south began to veer easterly. The casting of our sea anchors greatly reduced our speed, but saved the men an immense amount of labor in maintaining way; and indeed they could loaf at stroking and rest when they pleased.

I thought upon this old, fast friend of seafarers known as the sea anchor. On my first great journey and on this one, more than once the ships had heaved to, and by the aid of their drags kept from being gale-driven far off their course. Were we not in deadly danger of striking reefs? There was some risk certainly, but Lane, Sir Francis Drake, and Sir Richard Grenville had all reported that this coast was clear of reefs as far as their observations could detect. And although we had had the sense of swift travel, actually it had been slow, because we had neither hulls nor sails against which the wind could exert force. On several occasions when hunting deer or buffalo Manteo had ventured this far south in his canoe.

We were still drifting southward, but there were several peninsulas or headlands to round which the paddlers must stroke strongly. My torch was burning out and I was about to light a second, when Cuthbert White brought his long boat in easy talking distance of our raft. He suggested that I light a candle from the dying flames, screen it well, and discover if any of our company had the not uncommon gift of night sight. We could tell in a few minutes, he said. If one of us had the gift in a notable degree, he would be able to make out the dark line of the coast in dim contrast with the starlit sea. This would increase our comfort—blackness would not longer press about our craft, as when the torch had flared—and add a moiety to our safety.

The experiment proved a complete success. Some of our number reported that visual perception of the coast "came and went" but Winifred, whose large, pale-colored eyes were her most lovely feature, called that she could detect it with entire ease. All but one of us were warmed and pleased that she could be useful to us as well as so beautiful to our sight. The exception was Weechee, who sat down by herself and sulked.

In all truth our company took comfort in this lookout, in the person of one already such a lovely although somewhat mysterious addition to our number, and a sharply increased sense of safety. When the paddlers rested their blades, they stretched out and slept. In the darkness the men could relieve their needs over the log railing of our stern; and our only grown-lady passenger, Jane Mannering, did the same to the embarrassment of no one. I had not kept track of Weechee but I had no doubt of her common sense in matters such as this.

The stars appeared to burn brighter as seems to be their wont just before dawn. This phenomenon was commonly called "false dawn," but I had never been able to decide whether it was real lumination or an optical illusion. But one fact was beyond dispute. We were out of any region claimed by the Croatans and beyond the divide between them and the Muskhogeans.

Some of our number could make out the barrier reefs like a dim pencil drawn the whole width of the slowly, vaguely paling eastern sky when Winifred called that the mainland shore we were following was curving inward and westward rather sharply. Manteo told me he believed that it was the beginning of a headland that was one of the gates of a large bay, the near side of which had swampy shores. He advised me to continue our coastwise course until we raised the point, then turn again straight south and make across the bay to sheltered waters fronting a dry, firm beach, and there land the rafts and go to shore. He was almost certain, because of signs he had seen such as lesser headlands, and his estimation of our drift, that this was what his people called Wild Hog Bay, named so from Wild Hog Point on its far side.

I was inclined to believe Manteo, even though naturalists had long ago decided there were no wild hogs indigenous to this part of North America. However, the Huguenot Ribaut had had tame hogs at his ill-starred colony, and some of these might have escaped. Manteo told me also that when he was an urchin the beach we were making for had been the scene of a love feast of the Croatans and the Muskhogeans. However, the Muskhogeans proved to be corn growers more than hunters, would not make a treaty with the alien Croatans, and the two tribes had become estranged.

All of this was good news as, in the rapidly clearing light, we made for the long crescent of a sandy, pebbly beach. No one would dispute our landing; no pursuers were in sight as far as eye could reach. And then we saw certain sign that we were in Muskhogean country. Moored in a swamp creek at the western end of the beach were two boats which would amaze an uninformed explorer. They were flat-bottomed, blunt-ended crafts resembling English punts.

Manteo seemed more exercised by the fresh-water creek than by the boats. "Martyn Sagamore, tell your tribe not to drink of the stored water, but dip their utensils here," he told me with somewhat more emphasis than was commonly put on his suggestions.

I did not see much sense to this, as this was a well-watered country and surely we could refill the casks whenever we liked. Also, the swamp water would probably taste and smell of rotted vegetation. Finally, I wished I could avoid giving any orders for some hours, wherein the tired-out men could eat and drink and then sleep awhile in comfort on the sunny beach. Still there was almost always sound sense in the great chieftain's directions to me, and I complied.

"Also tell them to light no cooking fire, but eat the cold corn cakes and dried venison."

"Manteo, isn't that unduly harsh? I see no sign of changing weather. Except for that patch of filmy cloud, in fact a mere haze, far to the northward—"

"Martyn Sagamore, that is not vapor, but smoke from cooking fires, lighted by Storyteller as you bade him, to gull the Croatans."

"How could it be visible at this distance?"

"At what distance, Martyn Sagamore? The wind could not thrust against our low-lying rafts; we are pushed along by waves on the surface that of themselves move very little. How far say you, are the false cooking fires lighted by Storyteller?"

"The least they could be is forty miles."

"The most they could be is twenty of your English miles. The brisk wind has fallen to a light breeze, still the Croatan canoeists would paddle that short way with ease in four hours, and in the haste of fury, in three hours. They ate breakfast in the dark before dawn; the smoke from their cooking fires has drifted afar and disappeared; what are they doing now? Perhaps most of them are sharpening arrow points, replacing worn-out cords and fletching, and some are painting their faces and bodies, or affixing bright feathers in their war bonnets, but a few are out in their canoes, lying all but invisible against the coastal growth, as their eyes search the village scenes as the eyes of a falcon search grass for a huddling hare. Already they have marked the absence of men and women busied around the houses. Perhaps they have not guessed the truth; it would be hard to guess because they know our three little boats could not transport all our colonists to the mainland in one night, and they think of our raft—it was your contrivance that only one has been visible at a time—as a fishing platform. But we do not know that they were deceived. It is an equal chance that they have found out we had eight rafts—that would be in accordance with the stealthy ways of Indians; they have no books to read in an idle hour, so often they steal forth to spy. Of a certain they will soon know or surmise that we have water transport of some kind, because the colonists have disappeared, and only Storyteller remains where only yesterday they swarmed about. And of a certain they will soon know that the raft they had seen had disappeared, and perhaps instead of one 'marsh house,' as we called it, there were several."

At that moment Vestryman Thomas Ellis came up the swamp creek, and in ill-temper, hardly giving us a glance, dipped his bucket in its waters. These he immediately tasted.

"I am not going to drink that stinking water," he declared.

"You'll drink it, or go dry," I answered harshly, in great perturbation of mind because of Manteo's message.

"What do you mean, sir, by addressing me in that fashion?"

"I beg your pardon, Master Ellis. I am trying to save your life along with the others."

"Good God! I thought it was saved already. Is there a new threat?"

"The same threat, Manteo believes, and in any case there will be one new threat after another until we find a refuge."

"Well, what is it? What can we do? The men are dog-tired."

"Tell the people to eat what food they brought and light no fires, and all to rest an hour; then we must continue our journey."

"I voted to fight it out at the fort, where at least we had cannon, but the rank and file voted to follow you. Captain, I will give them your orders."

Thomas Ellis marched away. With aching eyes I searched Manteo's face.

"But I thought it a surety that the Croatans would not cross the contested ground."

"And they would not, to steal Muskhogean corn or even maidens. But since we spoke of that, I have reconsidered Weoanza's words. I recalled she had given her word, for me to carry to the palefaces. She is a great Weoanza, yet her word we have disregarded; she is no longer bound to wait until sundown to light the fires and send up the smokes to signal in the Croatan kinsmen."

"Twenty miles! We are only at the edge of the Muskhogean country!"

"Aye, and we must get deep into it, where the corn grows green and tall, and there are many villages and countless temple mounds before the Algonquin peoples will quit our trail."

3

Then there was nothing for me to do but return with Manteo to the beach where our fellows were hastily eating a cold breakfast, and then to stand in their midst and explain why in one hour from now we must launch all rafts and boats, and continue our southward flight.

These stout-hearted English people did not flinch from this worsening of news, and not one other voice was raised in rue of our desertion of the fort. In a few minutes over an hour, the rafts and boats were again loaded, and we were rounding Wild Hog Point, the paddlers stroking not frantically but steadily and with rhythm. Mostly young men, much of their strength had been restored by a scanty breakfast and an hour's rest. Yet I wished we had taken time to rig a sail for every raft. We had enough canvas; we could have cut poles for spars; we had tools by which we could set in the center logs strongly braced masts. What wind there was was again out of the northeast, to waft us southwest, and enough to puff the sails we had not spread, and to add two or even three miles an hour to our crawling gait.

Then we rounded a sharp, eastward-jutting, marsh-grown cape beyond which our southwestward course was visibly straight except for a lesser projection less than two miles down the coast sharply veering southwest. We rounded this also short of two hours, the boatmen idling at their oars in order to stay alongside the rafts. Patently the spirits of the people had risen with the sun; the flight in the dark of last night had been a bleak and forlorn experience; now the sun was high and burning, the water gleamed, all could see what we were doing and where we were going; and all were committed to a long flight and therefore more hopeful and resolute. Before noon we had crossed the mouth of a small bay and were rounding a point so abrupt and considerable that Lane's men had given it a name—Long Shoals Point. From hence the coast ran due west for more than two miles and then we must cross the mouth of a wide estuary of the Long Shoals River to a point that marked the southmost land that Manteo had ever visited, before he had sailed with Lane.

On this trip we searched our rucksacks for the last meal ere we landed to try to buy corn from a native village and drank some of our stored water, although the waters of the estuary were brackish rather than bitter salt, and we could have drunk of these without harm in extreme need.

Actually we did not know when we could make shore, for this whole coast was marshy. It was Doctor Jones's opinion that we were no longer following the shore of the mainland, but that of large sea islands, separated from each other by salt creeks and runs. All we knew for certain was that we were drifting ever deeper into Muskhogean country which the Croatan's more northerly allies, having no personal feud with us, might be loath to enter. Also these allies could not be summoned overnight. What if the Croatan, finding us fled from Roanoke Island, decided to follow us and make lone war against us? They could catch us in their swift canoes, but they did not outnumber us, in fact the moccasin was on the other foot, and we believed we could beat them off.

The afternoon waned; every headland and seamark in our fore drew so slowly alongside. At sundown Thomas Warner, by some magic we did not penetrate, produced a big bag of jerked venison, enough to put in every hand one stick, and every bite we chewed long, ere we washed it down with a sip of fresh water. So nourishing was this fodder that our oars and paddlers freely declared they could ply onward until moonset.

But this would be dangerous sailing. We did not know where we were in this welter of sea islands; so far we had depth in plenty but at any moment could be driven on reefs or into marsh. Our navigation consisted in keeping our directions by the polar star and entering any water passage that led south or southwest. But on no account would these beguile us into the storm-swept ocean, because of the immensely long barrier reefs of sand or mud which we saw ran as far south of Cape Hatoraske as Roanoke Island was north. We were making our journey between these reefs and the mainland or its close-lying sea islands.

The rounded moon was dipping in the west, and dawn was near, and I was wondering whether we need drop our anchors, when a strange thing came to pass. My just-lighted torch was mirrored by another, flaring equally bright, in the dim distance. It could mean the approach of a fleet of canoes manned by Croatans, but if we must fight in the dark, so must they. I knew that Manteo did not believe that this was the meaning of the signal. He knew Indians, and he gravely doubted they would announce their nearness when enough moonlight limned the waters that they could take us by surprise.

"Friend or foe?" I asked Manteo in a breathless mutter.

"I cannot say for certain, but I think it is a friend."

The light was not as far distant as it first seemed. It grew rapidly brighter; the boat that brought it was traveling fast; after ten minutes had crept by we could see its shadow in the torch's flare, and it was such a shadow as a canoe would cast. And then a bold voice rang out.

"Manteo Sagamore!"

"Hough!" the great chieftain answered.

"Tell Martyn Sagamore there was no sense in continuing a show of cooking fires, for before sunrise the Croatans knew that all the palefaces had fled. So I came swiftly by the shortest routes in my canoe."

"Storyteller, you are welcome as when, in the deep of winter, with its dark days, a tribe of your people and mine beheld your approach on your endless journey, so once more they may build a high fire, and sit in a ring, and hear of the heroes of old!"

"For the love of Manitou, Manteo," I begged, "ask him if the Croatan are close behind." This Manteo did quickly.

"No, and such allies as took the warpath have barely gained the Croatan village. What they will do tomorrow only the werowance know. Tell the palefaces that tonight they may rest well!"

"With the boats and the rafts lying at anchor?" Manteo asked.

"Nay, on good dry ground, nigh a village of the Muskhogeans. Follow my torch!"

This thrilling message I immediately translated for my fellows, waiting with straining ears. A shout went up that rang far and wide over the waters, and the water creatures felt its vibrations in their element, and it may be that they paused in their occupations, whether hunting one another, feeding on swamp vegetation, or performing fertility rites undreamed by man. Perhaps more than one little fish escaped sudden death as his pursuer's ferocity was for a second arrested by this unknown tremor in their fastnesses.

A moment later, Storyteller brought his canoe alongside our lamp. My latest curiosity about his coming to us was instantly satisfied—how he managed to handle his torch when he needed both arms to stroke? By the same token I perceived why it had held so steady. In front of him was a metal tripod supporting a three-inch cylinder half a foot long. My first guess as to its origins was wrong: the metal was not iron from Europe but bronze, and the holder was decorated by *repoussé* work, indicating a sun shooting out rays, and various mythical animals. This was almost certainly the smithery of Mexican Indians, quite possibly the ancient Aztecs, which he had stored in his canoe.

If its making was a mystery, a greater one was its ever falling into Storyteller's use. But the greatest and most esoteric mystery was Storyteller's countenance in its down-spreading rays. Had I eyes to see, thereby I could have understood his genius. I perceived noble purpose, unweakening resolve, and enormous cerebral energy. I would have seen the same in the face of Homer as he recited his epic poems in the halls of Attic kings, and because I had read those poems, with their flood of sharply visual images, I still might believe he had been blind in old age, but before then he had seen as deeply and as truly as any seer that ever lived.

It was no wonder that wandering Indian storytellers were known as the Blessed Men.

"Martyn Sagamore, will you have the flotilla follow me?" he asked most courteously, yet with the humility beheld in men who know their own greatness.

"Truly," and the thought struck me if any member of our party was so dull and base as to warn me against the act, reminding me that Storyteller was an Indian, perhaps treacherous as the rest, and might lead us into an ambush, I could not have withheld my fist from striking him in his blind eyes.

"Then we will take yon little channel to the left of the land. Now Martyn Sagamore, hold your torch aloft, and wave it in a circle like unto a sun, which is the signal to the Muskhogean to expect visitors."

4

We gained the village in half an hour's paddling. Its supper fires had been newly fed, and I was able to make a swift survey of its main features and the faces of the people courteously waiting in front of what I took for a temple mound. Their flat-bottomed, blunt-ended boats of American cypress, at least thirty of these, lay in a row at a kind of landing in a little cove: the bow of each was secured to a deep-driven stake. A bold stream had its mouth a few paces distant and several racks for drying fish indicated heavy runs of herring and shad in season, and fresh-water fish of various kinds in abundance.

The town's main street lay roughly parallel to the stream, and hence the houses were not in a straight line. These were square or oblong structures, each in its own yard, and planks had been employed niggardly in their building, a wonder to me since the moon revealed the seriated tops of heavy forest not far beyond what I took for cornfields. Broken limbs had been used in erecting the walls of the houses, willow saplings, and a great deal of thatch. Other streets ran parallel to the main street.

The village was ancient and occupied a fine site, Manteo told me in an undertone. A few enormous trees gave shade year after year instead of being cut down for planks or firewood. In fact I was to learn that the Indians conserved their heavy forest, where the survival of the most fit was the law, and there was almost no underbrush. Only when a great tree fell could seed take root in its place, and the survivors grew to enormous height and thickness of bole. Thus the forest furnished many food plants, and in its depths roamed countless herds of deer, and a few huge buffaloes made their stolid, resistless way. Manteo had already told me that the Muskhogean were rarely known to ring trees to kill them, and thus gain crude fields reachable by sunlight where corn would grow; and instead grew corn as far as possible in natural meadows.

The men I saw looked amazingly well grown and the women handsome and strong. It was their custom to put weaklings and afflicted children to a merciful death. It happened that a band of forest dwellers whose sole occupation was hunting had arrived only a few days before, and these were peculiarly impressive men, lithe and tall, who were trained to run down deer and buffalo, the chase being often of more than fifty miles between dawn and dark, and in this the two-legged runners were usually victorious, four-legged animals not being capable of such prolonged exertion. The fact caused me to think that man was superior to beasts not only in mind but also in physique.

Only in specialized activities, such as the arboreal agility of squirrels or the incredibly long hunting runs of wolves, did the lower animals surpass us.

The hunters had long, strong bows, possibly of gumwood. Some had spears with long, sharp heads. But the arrows that I saw appeared made of very straight, tough cane, these used for shooting small game. Some of the bronzed, lithe men had slings, that biblical weapon with which expert stonecasters obtained such deadly skill. They had brought in many deer, some of which had been deposited in what they called the "Miko" crib, from which guests were served. Also the crib had its grainery, so that visitors never lacked corn. Miko was the Muskhogean word meaning werowance or magician.

Storyteller received first honors from our greeters, and by far the highest honors, many of the women kneeling at his feet. The most proud sachems touched one knee to the ground before him, a form of obeisance which antiquaries believe was common in West Britain ten centuries ago. And at once he asked the Muskhogean sagamore if his palefaced friends could spend the night here.

The language was different enough that I caught only an occasional word. Manteo was in the same boat, but I saw Weechee's pretty ears prick up, and at once she confided to me that assent had been given. Storyteller's next question concerned the Croatans, and this exchange he immediately translated for my benefit, and I reported it to my fellow colonists.

"The sagamore bids us have no fear the Croatan will follow us here. In the first place, the corn harvest has been good, showing the Great Spirit and the lesser spirits have given them their favor, and the tribe has danced the Corn Dance, and many of the young men long to put on warpaint and win another such victory as their fathers won over the Hatoraskes twenty years ago, and they could want no better foes than the Croatans, with whom the Muskhogeans have had a long-drawn quarrel over lands. You are most welcome, declares the great sagamore, and after you have feasted, you may sleep in peace, and your hosts will waken you when they go to work in the fields, or the strong-thighed hunters when they return to the forest, or the children in their play."

Our supper was indeed a feast, fresh venison, spotted-tailed bass, and corn cakes being served on wooden platters, and there were large wooden bowls of squash, sweet potatoes, and unknown forest products. The night being warm caused many Muskhogeans to sleep out of doors, surrendering their beds of skins to their guests.

A brief consultation between the Storyteller, Manteo, Doctor Jones, and myself resulted in the decision to remain here two more days, in

which we would beach our boats and repack our goods for a southward march the following day, our three boats keeping pace just off
the coast transporting some of our heaviest luggage. The sagamore
here could be expected to furnish us a guide to a big village ten
miles distant amid a group of lakes which Doctor Jones thought almost directly west of Cape Lookout.

Because almost all the Indians we would encounter north of Cape
Fear River and many farther south would belong to clans of the great
Muskhogean nation, I spent those days in learning all I could of their
ways. By and large, they were farmers and hunters, although no few
smaller villages on the numerous coasts were settled by fishermen. The
farms' main crop was maize, although yams, squash, melons, and a
variety of bean were widely grown. The fields were held in common
by the villagers, although every family had its row of every kind of
crop, these too worked by all hands. The clans gave freely to one
another in case of crop failure. Marriage was a strong institution,
usually monogamous, although if a husband died, his brother must
take the widow to wife, second in status to his first wife who remained
head of the house. Women arranged all marriages, social status being
an important consideration; and the two chosen to be married to each
other had no voice in the matter. No great to-do seemed to have been
made over intimate relationships between bachelors and unmarried
girls, but adultery as the English knew it was severely punished.

Betrothal was observed by the prospective bride and groom eating
an ear of boiled corn together. "I eat corn with you," said the youth,
calling the maiden's name, and she answered "I eat corn with you,"
and called his name. Later he left the carcass of a deer at the girl's
house; if she dragged it inside and cooked it, then served some of
the meat to the giver in the presence of witnesses, the twain were
married, the bride's and the groom's fathers not even being consulted. The mother had the right to kill any infant that she did not
want, whatever her reasons, and twin babies were almost always
killed, being regarded with horror.

Children belonged to the mother's clan, not the father's. I could
not escape the conviction that among the Muskhogeans, the men
stood definitely lower than the women. Yet an adolescent boy had a
hard time qualifying as a man and a warrior: until then he had no
status worthy of the word, being ignored or kept at menial jobs. When
his voice began to change, he went into the forest where he fasted
for ten days and performed rigorous religious ceremonies. On his return—often he failed to do so, one way by which the tribe rid themselves of weaklings—he was bled copiously by the werowance or miko.
This was supposed to rid him of any evil spirit. Then he was given

the name he must bear all his life long, and this appeared to have great occult importance in his destiny.

The aged were respected, but if very old and enfeebled were killed as an act of mercy.

Certain clans seemed to be hereditary enemies, although the insult or misdeed that had made them so was usually long forgotten. War parties were frequently formed from one of these clans to raid and harry the other. The participants were usually young men, eager for the right to wear a scalp lock and thus win prestige in his own clan. This was real and sanguine war; often the prestige seeker never returned to the cooking fires of his kinsmen; sometimes the whole party was captured alive, in which case their fates were precariously tilted. Some were make blood brothers of their capturers, for despite their ancient feud no clansmen ever forgot they were branches of the same mother tribe that we knew as the Muskhogean. In this case the initiates must break all bonds with their native clan. Some became slaves of the victorious clan. But sometimes the captives were dedicated, one might say, to Death, a somewhat different religious experience than being a human sacrifice to a god. The magical principles involved were extremely complicated and not easily penetrated by western thought. The dedication was performed with fire.

Muskhogean life was ridden by superstition. A member of a war party or even a hunting party must turn back if he had a certain kind of dream or heard the call of certain species of birds. On the other hand Muskhogeans had a high sense of honor and were hospitable to strangers. They were also keen traders without being cheaters. Inland Muskhogeans had storehouses of skins and hides, copper, flint, mica, and pipestone, which they could exchange for coral, dried fish, colorful sea shells, and the hair tubes made from the central column of the conch shell, worth four deerskins, from the storehouses of coastal tribes. Muskhogean braves rarely wore plumes or anything like a war bonnet but each had a coronet of swan feathers for ceremonial occasions.

Young women usually wore their raven hair long; married women in certain clans must wear theirs tightly bound. Men wore a belt of snakeskin from which hung an apron of strong cloth I did not recognize, but which Storyteller told me was made of the shredded bark of the mulberry tree. A woman usually wore a short skirt of deerskin, sometimes of Spanish moss, and various necklaces; in winter she wore over one shoulder a mantle of mulberry-bark cloth.

Ceremonies were frequent, and their meaning often unknown to Indians outside of the nation or even the individual clan. Ceremonial dress varied a good deal, but it always included paint and the warrior's pouch on a shoulder strap containing pipe, tobacco, and a talisman—often a piece of quartz. On a war party the leader carried a charm box, reminiscent of the ark of the ancient Hebrews, even though it contained not holy symbols, but images of the Snake and the Panther, mightily important in what might be called the Muskhogean pantheon, although in fact these were not gods but creatures to be propitiated by magic ceremonies. Thunder and lightning created great awe in the Muskhogean heart; the four winds were symbolized and sometimes personalized, and their good will invoked by magical practice.

Some one animal was sacred to every clan. Many individuals regarded another animal as his peculiar friend or guardian, and this custom was common to numerous different nations. Weechee's "totem" —a word Doctor Jones had taught me—was her namesake, the common swallow.

The Muskhogean funeral ceremonies seemed most strange, but probably no more so than those of other nations. If a warrior died at home, the grave was dug under his bed, deep and wide enough to contain all of his personal possessions and the corpse in a sitting position. The tribe mourned four days with high fires day and night. If he was away at war, his bones were later exhumed and put on a platform. If a warrior died in battle and his body was recovered, it was immediately elevated, the bones to be sent home later.

Most Indian families had four houses, a winter house where cooking was done all year, the roof of which had a hole to emit smoke; an airy summer house, a storehouse for trade goods, and another for farming tools, provision, and the like. For beds and lounging they used platforms built against the wall, on which lay animal skins. They had pottery as well as wooden dishes, containers made of shells or gourds, and sometimes copper as well as stone instruments and weapons. Farmers prized the shoulder bone of a buffalo as a blade for a hoe.

They had different ceremonies for different purposes. The grasping of another's elbow by the hand was a sign of friendship. They played hard at different games and wagered their most precious possessions on the outcome.

On the whole these Muskhogeans were a superior Indian nation. Yet I would not like to have our colony join them, live their life, and ultimately be absorbed by them. Merely thinking of it caused me to wonder what we would do, where we would go, if the Spanish at St. Augustine refused to accept us. The latter outcome I thought most likely, almost certain in fact, although I would not dream of confiding these expectations to anyone but Manteo and Tom Warner; curiously enough, not even to Richard. In this case there would remain for us two choices, one to establish and maintain a colony until some Old World ship would rescue us and carry us to England. In all truth, I thought such a project beyond our powers. We would be menaced by hostile Indians; worse than that, we would have no hope, no joy in life, to keep our spirits high; hence we would surely lose our unity and die or be killed out. The other choice was to ally ourselves with some truly superior tribe of Indians, where life was good. But the trick lay in these last four words. Could Indian life ever be good enough to be worth the while of white folk of the higher civilizations?

5

The generic name of our hosts seemed to be Muskhogeans; but this term included a multitude of peoples and tribes, with varied dialects and customs. These friendly Indians' more precise name was Tuscarora, and quite likely they were separated in several branches; and Storyteller told me they occupied at least thirty villages. The name could be translated, he said, as "Gatherers of Hemp." I did not inquire as to the name of the village where we were so genially entertained, and later I regretted this omission on my part, for what in a small way was a great event occurred there.

The first sign of it was that Weechee did not partake of the midnight supper. When I asked the reason she replied sourly in one word,

"*Agruras.*"

"That is Spanish for bellyache," Thomas Warner, who was close beside me, explained.

"Weechee, why do you speak Spanish, of which I know not one hundred words, instead of Croatan, of which I am the master?" I inquired.

"Because I am sick and tired of Croatan," the maiden burst out, an angry glint in her eyes. "And if you are the master of Croatan, why have we had to run away from them, for nearly two whole days and nights?"

"I meant the language, not the people, and you know it."

"I am sick of both. I wish the Caribs had sold me to a rich and noble Spaniard, instead of to that *hijo sucio de la chingada, el señor,* from whom I ran away into the thorns. I would not have run away from a grand *señor*. I would wear silk and satins and emeralds in his *sala,* and not be bounced about on a bumpy raft, splashed with salt water, catch no wink of sleep, and then have to walk *lejísimo* with a thirty-pound roll on my back and then be burned at the stake by redskins."

"A domestic altercation, I presume," Thomas Warner remarked dryly. "I depart forthwith."

Although my Spanish vocabulary was indeed limited, I knew what *hijo sucio de la chingada* meant—dirty son of a whore. *Lejísimo* was a Spanish word that Tom frequently used, meaning a very great distance.

"Where will I sleep tonight?" Weechee demanded, hardly pausing to catch her breath. "I am sick and tired of sleeping in the same room with you. I think I will ask the great Storyteller, who is an old but great and noble man, if I can sleep in the same room with him, and when he leaves us, if I may go with him."

"Do all this at your heart's desire," I answered, which took her somewhat aback.

"Anyway it is not seemly that I sleep in the same room with a young man. Not that he will give way to passion for me—his only longing is for the preacher's daughter, and he cannot have her because handsome Richard has already got her—still I am a chief's daughter—a greater chief than you have ever seen—and I must do nought that reflects upon him. Aye, I mean it. I will be your friend, and find out things for you, but no longer your roommate. I will be thankful to you ever for saving me from *el señor,* but no longer follow you about like a dog. *Adiós!*"

She had been squatting near my easy seat on the grass. She sprang up, and stalked away to where Storyteller was sitting on a kind of stool with staghorn legs especially placed for him, and at once began a sparkling conversation. Now and then she would clap her hand to her belly and almost bend down with pain.

And then I knew what had happened. The sign has been given, along with the pain, that she was no longer a child, but by Indian counting a marriageable young woman.

6

When the feast was over, Weechee darted to the second-best house in the row, vacated by a sachem for Storyteller's use. Storyteller himself took the opportunity to give me a few words of advice.

"Your charming little friend and companion—I knew almost at first glance she is no more than that—is crossing the divide," he told me. "She has told you that she wants to quit your house, and my advice is, that you express the regret I know you feel, but make no protest. This is a delicate time in any maiden's life. I think she sees no future

for you and her together; and she is perfectly right if you intend
to take a white woman for your wife. She would not play second
flute to any woman. Master Richard would want her if his betrothal
to the preacher's lovely daughter is permanently broken; the youth
you call Thomas—whose father was slain by the Wingineo—would
take her in a trice. But perhaps she will marry the son of a great
Indian king you will meet on your travels."

"You once said, great Storyteller, that you believed you knew to
what nation she belonged. Would you care to tell me now?"

"I will tell you what I believe, although I cannot be sure. The
thought keeps coming to my mind that she is of the Calusa tribe,
which is ruled by what you would call a king, like unto Philip of the
hombres. I have never visited their nation—it dwells at too great
distance—and I cannot vision you and your followers making so
great a march. I do not know their tribal language, although it is
said that some of them speak Cusabo also, a language I do know.
She is very proud, this child. I doubt if she could be happy with a
white-man husband; on your journey some stalwart son of the sagamore is almost certain to desire her, and now she can lawfully marry,
I am almost persuaded you should let her go."

I was almost persuaded also, but certainly I would not let go for at
least a year. Then she would be well past fourteen, at which age many
English maids were wedded; and this was the usual age, so I had
been told, among all but the best-born in Spain and Italy.

But when she left me, it seemed that my very being would be
reft. In all case the void would be hard to fill, if possible at all.
I could think of only one damsel, perhaps not wholly inaccessible
to me now, who might do so.

On the next day's journey guided by the tall son of last night's
host, Weechee marched rather stately beside me, not frolicking as
usual, no doubt for a good reason. The town where we were welcomed—mainly because of Storyteller in our midst, but partly, I
thought, because of the good nature of the people—was again one
of the Tuscarora towns of the far-flung Muskhogean nation. Again
it was built on a big creek, and the only readily patent difference
in the folkways was that here there were many dogs.

These were of a squat species, resembling beagles: they accompanied their masters in their boats and on the hunt, where they were
useful in unearthing burrowing animals such as badgers and rabbits
and hares. Unquestionably Weechee meant what she said about our
parting as roommates: she was beside me at the feast, sprightly and
impudent as ever, but she slept on a mat beside Storyteller's.

We rested all the following day and night. The march had been longer than the day before, and our people were not accustomed to such, carrying heavy packs. Again the sagamore appointed us a guide to a town on the coast, where we effected a rendezvous with our seafarers. The next town was on the north bank of a river, and here we had no difficulties with language, because the people there spoke a dialect of Algonquin, not greatly different from the Croatan dialect, and I must suppose, more by their customs than appearance and dress, that they were akin to the Croatan. If so, they did not know of their kinsmen's war with us, and we were most cordially received.

Already the time seemed long since the murder of Cheewink and the beginning of our flight. This last was not its only consequence; on the night of our debate Winifred had confessed her love affair with Richard, their betrothal, and her granting of his amorous desires, which doubtless she had shared. It was a wound to my spirit deeper than I would readily confess, which I tried to expel from my thoughts, but which might ache and burn a little all my life long. She had also estranged her father by this admission. She no longer lodged with him, but with the spinsters, while he made his quarters with our goldsmith, William Brown. I felt that Mr. Powell had virtually disowned her. Plainly he did not take into consideration the English folk belief, shared by many of our gentry, that betrothal was half tantamount to marriage, ending all chaperonage, and justifying carnal liberties not openly permitted in early courtship. If a babe was born of wedded parents a few weeks before its lawful time, few aspersions were cast.

But my great surprise was that Richard did not assert his rights to Winifred, and take her to live with him. I could only surmise that she had not yet forgiven him his intimacy with Cheewink currently with one with herself. It was quite possible that the latter would never be resumed. Half hidden behind Winifred's many other qualities was regal pride.

Richard did not sulk in his tent. He was the same hale fellow as before, as keen a hunter, as able a lieutenant, and as zealous for the company's welfare. Of course I did not speak of this matter even to so old a friend, but when we were fletching some deerskins side by side, he confided in me.

"I don't blame Winifred for breaking off her affair with me," he said. "I had cut her to the quick by my current pursuit of Cheewink. Nor do I blame Mr. Powell for ordering the breach—he is a fanatic through and through, and of course abominates miscegenation along with every sexual liberty condemned in Scripture. But, you know, Martyn, in some ways I feel relieved. Winifred is the most beautiful girl I have ever seen and now ever hope to see, but I have an odd feeling I'm not up to her. I know of no man who's worthy of her in marriage, and God knows I'm not. I would be sure to disillusion her sooner or later. I'll make out with available spinsters as long as this lasts."

I thought this over, and I thought I could understand what Richard meant in regard to Winifred. I knew by sweet experience that she was sensual; but even in this she was not quite earthy, and I knew too by bitter experience that she too was fanatical in religion. Few men would want to marry a second Jeanne d'Arc, whom she sometimes summoned to my thought; or a maiden to whom the Scotch applied the word fey. But I idolized her—at last I could face the fact—and I would not have yielded her up so tamely as did Richard.

But two of Richard's remarks had sped my thoughts far from Winifred.

"Richard, you used the phrases 'and now ever hope to see,' and 'as long as this lasts.' Did that mean you really have not much hope of surviving our present adventure?"

"I did not mean that. I meant more than that—I doubt if any of us will survive. Up until now everything has gone wonderfully well, but we've barely begun the long march from Roanoke to St. Augustine, and from there God knows where if the Spanish colonists turn us away. They won't feel very kindly toward any kind of Englishman since the visit of Sir Francis Drake."

"So you've heard about that."

"Yes, I did. Most of the colonists accepted your statement that he took only a modest tribute. That is hardly the way of Sir Francis when he's dealing with the dons. But I won't speak of this to our fellow colonists."

"Letting that go—what do you think is our greastest danger?"

"We're surrounded by danger of almost all sorts. It's everywhere you look. Doctor Jones has told you, as he told me, that there are criminal tribes ranging all over these coasts—perhaps over the whole continent. They live by murder and rapine. In ourselves we are weakly defended and we're rich pickings. Now we're staying at big villages but that won't be the case always. If the Spanish win the war that I don't doubt is waging, they'll have time to teach us a lesson for poaching on the lands they claim, and, in case of victory over England, the lands they own. There's the chance of a plague by which many tribes have been wiped out. If we go hungry long enough we can die by starvation or eating some poison plant. We can drink poison water. We can be caught in a forest fire. Most likely of all, we can die out by attrition. Repeated ambush that can take a few of us at every clip. Bears and wolves when our powder's gone, raiding our camps at night. Just giving up under hardship, one man after another dropping out. That's the way that hundreds of Cortés' men died when they were fleeing from the Aztecs. There are said to be enormous swamps south of the Savana River and in the north end of Florida. We're so few among so many. I still wish we had defied the Croatan and fought it out at Roanoke Island. I think you made a fatal mistake, Martyn, but if so I won't hold it against you."

"The hell of it is, my lad, you might be right."

I had never before spoken so familiarly with Richard, son of the franklin Thomas Wade and Lady Isobel Wade. The fact startled me.

7

Winifred Powell took more notice of me now than during her affair with Richard. Almost all women, I suppose, are attracted by power; this may be a phase of their natural drive to conceive and bear strong children. When a stranger stag challenges and then defeats a stag followed by several hinds that he had protected, these will immediately follow the winner without a backward glance at their late lord. Just now I wielded a great deal of power, since the main of the colonists were presently satisfied with my leadership. I had the friendship of Manteo and could speak his language, and a sort of patronage from Storyteller. Also the exodus from Roanoke had gone well so far.

Yet I found difficulty in ascribing to Winifred ordinary feminine traits. She appeared to act and feel individually in all matters. I could not doubt that her dealings with me in Wiltshire still held great meaning for her, and still aroused her emotions and perhaps her passions. When our eyes met in a gathering of colonists she would give me her strange and wistful smile, then touch the amulet supposed to contain a strand of St. Winfrid's white hair which I had retrieved for her at sore cost and at the gain of being chosen by Sir Walter Raleigh—if at last it proved a gain and not total loss. Indeed, a flood of feeling swept me then, in the recall of our love-making on the porch of her house immediately after my foolhardy rescue of her treasure. Often I recalled my deliverance from sentence as a felon, in which I could not doubt she played a large if not indeed a heroic part. Truly, there was a strong bond between us which would live as long as we both lived. In deeper truth, I could not deny that I idolized her.

Perhaps she would not have broken with Richard—I ached to believe it—unless she had been torn between him and me.

After about our ninth march from town to town with Indian

guides and on dim Indian trails, about twenty days from Roanoke, during which we had included crossing a great estuary in our hosts' boats—we gained Cacores, a town on Trade Creek nigh the mouth of a tidal river three miles wide that joined the open sea at what our mariners called Cape Fear. It had a lovely setting, the night was warm, and the moon, about three days old, was a brilliant crescent in the west. Our hosts, originally of Iroquois stock but now hardly distinguishable from Muskhogeans in customs, dress, and appearance, were most genial. Instead of listening to Storyteller around the big assembly fire, I stood with Winifred in the outer circle of the throng. When I stretched my hand and found hers, warm and silky smooth, I led her away into the shadows. Perhaps Richard saw our departure —it was his habit, retained from boyhood, to keep track of me; and I am sure that Weechee did so, but she glanced quickly away.

Winifred and I found a little knoll beside the moonlit waters of the creek and sat down there, both of us to listen to its pleasant murmur and I to smoke my Indian-clay tobacco pipe of which I had become fond. Indeed, these were our first occupations, each lost from the other in his own thoughts; but I reckoned we both had other plans, although I was not at all sure these would coincide.

"We became separated, didn't we, Martyn?" she asked at last in her soft voice with its faint tones of sorrow.

"Yes."

"It happened because I fell in love with Richard. Falling in love is a most strange human habit. Or should I call it a capability? Perhaps the better word is a gift. The more fortunate the person, the more frequently he or she falls in love—sometimes with a potential and lifelong mate—which almost everyone craves—sometimes with a gray-haired poet, man or woman—sometimes with a lake or a rock or a little stream—sometimes with a song—sometimes with an old house with children looking out the windows, by an old, untraveled road. Rather commonly that mate-love is lifelong. But it was not that kind into which I fell with Richard. I wanted him to possess me but not keep me forever. It was his handsomeness and especially his virile beard and his hearty laughter that wakened that. But oddly enough, Martyn, I have never fallen in love with you."

"I think I sensed that."

"Maybe it isn't very odd. You are not boyish enough; you are too strong. I have kittled with you—I think that is the word the peasants use—and wanted to do more; still I was not and am not now in love with you while my eyes turn into stars. If we had stayed in England, I would likely have married Richard, a completely successful marriage. We would have had children, position, I would have been proud of him and he of me; the first passionate love would have turned into a deeper love, that of needing each other not only for bodily bliss and relief, but every hour and at every turn—in sickness and in health, as the service reads. On the contrary I could never have married you. The wall was too high. That wall has disappeared but the magic was only incense rising from the forest. I could marry you now if we both wanted to, but I don't think either of us does. It isn't that kind of feeling, I mean all of it, every kind, that makes for happy marriage; there are many feelings and one in particular. At least that is true of me. Is it true of you?"

"Of course."

"I don't see why we can't have it—not regularly but occasionally. You are not involved in that way with Weechee. We would not be hurting anybody but my father—and his feeling would not be pain but outrage. If we do it, we won't let him know it, at least at first. It would be exquisite pleasure in itself. By not being in love we could each concentrate on his own pleasure, not worry about his partner's. Now I must say something that I would not dare say to a less intuitive, a more narrow-minded man. I want to honor you as well as please you. You had the potential to rise and you realized it. To surrender to you—I won't call it that—to make love with you will express in some way what I feel about your returning my amulet, and how you were punished for it, and how you bore it. I have never expressed it before, I have done little and all that will increase my pleasure in the act. Should I say, I want to reward you? I suppose not, yet every woman knows it is true; she has it in her power to give a truly noble reward, if she has eyes to see, a mind that remains clear."

"You rewarded me, Winifred, a thousand times over when you saved me from conviction as a felon and many years in prison."

"Did you know about that? I suppose, as would most young men, you thought I had made a noble sacrifice. You could not be more mistaken. Judge Willoughby was a wonderful man. Strictly speaking, to him I lost my virginity, but if I had retained it and let you go to prison for serving my great need, I would have lost it to someone else, perhaps not nearly as worthy. That is so because I too easily fall in love. It was very hard for that judge to suppress evidence— in that he was admirable; his taking out on you his own shame for doing it by giving you so long a sentence—well, that was ignoble in the extreme. Also his well-known severity is perhaps ignoble but perhaps it is an uncontrollable passion with him, as is my father's fanaticism. But we are wandering from the subject."

"Winifred, you look at everything perfectly straight—or completely askew—and I'm not clear-headed enough to know which."

"Well?"

"What am I going to do here and now, you ask. Why, what both of us want to do."

"You are right. What both of us want to do. Whether that is right—in wanting to, I mean—is a hard question. I do not believe we should seek its answer. Everything is different here than in England. Martyn, are you torn apart with yearning? Kiss me long and deep, and let's see what happens."

What happened was that I saw her quickly bared limbs and her extended arms. I saw her face, when I held it between my hands, and it lay in the Moon's pale bath. The Moon too would gaze on no other for a while, for it mirrored her in some mystic way.

Winifred was the daughter of the Moon. Or, perhaps in the person of Lilith, or even some more ancient nature goddess, Winifred had had incestuous union with her father the Sun, whereby the Moon was born. Or, perhaps, these sublime relationships had come into being not in dim centuries gone, when the wheel of time had only begun to turn and unwind the years, and instead but lately, in a year when I myself was born and toddling. The waxing Moon had shown through an open window facing east upon the vulva of Enid, out of the Gwynedd kings of Wales. Because the Moon was herself a nature goddess, no male seed had been needed, and thereby Enid had kindled and given birth to this Moon child in my arms.

Now she lay in the close clutch of my mortal limbs. The consequence, not what I clearly saw but what I knew with certain knowledge, was transport; and because this is forbidden to earth-crawling human beings, Jove's mighty rage might waken and he would hurl his bolt. I, Martyn, had made venereal union with my goddess. I had stolen from the Olympians transcendental experience, as had earthborn Leda in her passage with the divine swan, or as had come upon a shepherd lad in the arms of a swan maiden in a downy bed beside the Baltic Sea.

Both of us wakened; we were back on earth, but Winifred asked that I leave her for a little while, so she could sleep.

I spoke the words that came to my lips, without thinking.

"No, I cannot leave you here alone. When I looked for you, I might find you lying cold, with cold and solid and real steel thrust deep in your side."

Chapter XV

THE WILDERNESS

1

Aye, such punishment might be dealt us both, not for stealing from the gods as my wildly aroused imagination had envisioned at the zenith of our bliss but for arousing a frenzy of jealousy or hate in some fellow colonist, and the thrust given by hands as mortal as my own. As we walked the short distance through open ground to the big bonfire, I thought upon that unknown slayer, still in our midst, and still I could only postulate his motive. Even this much was possible only by my believing what I wished to believe, that he was one of our bachelors who had lain with Cheewink, was enthralled by her, and had vowed and kept that most base of vows, that if he himself could not have her to himself, no one could have her. I had trouble refraining from hastening our pace.

Apparently Weechee did not glance at Winifred and me as we gained the circle of listeners to Storyteller's recital. She was crouching between Richard and a young, wonderfully handsome Cacores warrior, the former's whole mind upon her, since he did not know the language, and a good half of the latter's attention wavered to her again and again. Well, by Indian law and custom she was eligible for marriage; the like by English law and by the customs of our forefathers. She wore a bright metal headband, accenting the gloss of her raven hair, a deerskin knee-length skirt, red sandals, and a swanfeather cloak given her as tribute by the Cacores Sagamore. Among the Muskhogean tribes, only the werowance and the Blessed Men wore such cloaks. I could only assume that the local chieftain recognized her as a Calusa far from home, and because of her headband, a daughter of a king. The garment left one pale-brown shoulder bare and glossy in the moonlight. The esoteric beauty I had just experienced could not blind me to the perfection of its structure.

After a pleasant night, we spent the next day at this cordial town, gorging on lobsters, crabs, shrimps, and scallops, and the tasty tentacles of octopi. Some arrowheads were sharpened, bow cords oiled, muskets cleaned and greased, clothes mended, and pack rolls rearranged; still I felt the day largely wasted, since I was in great haste to gain a warmer realm before the break of winter. On the following day we made a long march, first northwestwardly to skirt a tidal river which the sagamore told us was named "Lisbeth"; and again we felt a haunting by Sir Walter Raleigh and his adoration of the Queen. Thereafter we made straight west to the upper muck of Mudflat River, to find nearby another town whose people called themselves Shakori, but who were plainly Muskhogeans. Here we could not rendezvous with our rowboats, because Mudflat Inlet was unnavigable except with poled flat-bottomed punts. But in these the townsmen cheerfully put us and our goods on the west bank of a long tidal creek emptying into the mudflats, saving us God knew how long a trip to encircle its headwaters.

On the morrow we made again straight west, to the neck of a bay that I thought was called Shifting Bar Inlet on the *Lion's* charts. On this march we had no Indian guide—the Sagamore of Shakori had explained that there was "bad blood" between his people and those of the neighboring village—but we could follow a well-blazed trail. This region was sparsely inhabited: the only town from which we could expect help in crossing tributaries was named Sioua, its people a mixed tribe little known to early Spanish explorers. However, we hoped that our rowboats could enter the inlet and keep off its shoals to rendezvous with us.

We were greeted with more than the usual courtesy and cordiality. The sagamore told Storyteller that except for his age and infirmity he would himself had gone forth in search of a buffalo, to provide a welcome feast; however, his young warriors had lately netted what he called black ducks, plainly a non-migratory species, and we would not go hungry. Their leader was a deeply tanned man of about thirty, his head plucked bald except for a black scalp lock, and who was called Bear Hunter. In fact he had lately entered a thicket after a wounded bear and had been chased by the animal into a thicket of needle thorns. This incident was related by one of his followers amid gusty laughter. Certainly he wore evidence of its truth, the skin of his face showing several livid scratches. Oddly enough I did not notice any scratches on his hands. Also I observed that his eyes were large and gray, not beady and black like most Indian eyes. Still, we had seen one or two blue-eyed Indians.

Their houses were not as good as in other towns we had visited, and their weapons weaker and not as well kept. Amid the "black ducks" served us were a dozen brace of a fresh-water gallinule which we called coots, not at all like the English coot, but tolerably good eating, and which I suspected was the main fare of the Siouan. When the warriors gathered about the cooking fire, they wore ceremonial dress, hardly different from that of the Muskhogeans, and in addition wore pendants of snake fangs on their chests suspended by well-cured snakeskins around their necks.

The sagamore was too old and short of breath to deliver an oration of welcome, so his son-in-law Bear Hunter would be his delegate. He explained he would first speak in the Old Tongue, as an honor to their forefathers and such others of us who might understand it. Then he would speak to the Storyteller in the New Tongue, who in turn would repeat his expressions of welcome.

Even Storyteller could make nothing of the so-called Old Tongue. But Bear Hunter's voice indicated that he was exhorting his followers to the most strict obedience to his commands. Once he pointed northward, evidently speaking of whence we had come, and the stern faces of his hearers took on an animated expression. I did not like our hosts as well as usual, and I could not tell why. Still I passed a signal arranged between all our male colonists and me, which caused them one at a time, and without attracting attention, to make sure that the hilts of their sheath knives were in easy reach of their right hands.

The New Tongue was certainly a dialect of the Muskhogean language, and perfectly understandable to Storyteller. Evidently it was in replete if not fulsome praise of us, because Storyteller often bowed his head in modest acknowledgment. And then John Hynde, my fellow jailbird, did an unseemly thing. He rose from his place and came, bent, and murmured in my ear.

"That man's a renegade Englishman. Those scratches are where he shaved off his beard with clam shells when they saw us coming. I think they intend to garrote us with those snakeskins."

John Hynde had done his part well in the deliverance of this heart-stopping warning. The gestures and the movements of his head all indicated he was telling me a pleasant thing, or making a suggestion of how we might reward the Siouan for their hospitality.

I nodded my head with feigned enthusiasm, while asking what seemed a careless question.

"What evidence have you got?"

"In his first speech to his men he said what sounded like Croakumshire. I first thought it was a coincidence, then I decided he had said Croakumshire. The word used to be a joke about Northumberland, the way of talking there, but it became London thieves' cant for kill-

ing someone. Send him to Croakumshire, and that meant the garrote, knife, or pistol. Cap'n, you better act fast."

I made a mockery of laughter and waved John Hynde to his seat.
But what in God's name would I do now?

Bear Hunter had begun an eloquent address directly to Storyteller.
Meanwhile he made a motion with his finger, indicating a large circle,
and other motions imitative of beating a drum. Now I signaled great
and immediate danger, then spoke to my wise friend in an undertone.

"What is he saying? There's a plot to kill us. Be careful."

"I'll let you know, pretending to make my remarks to him." And
this was as quick thinking as I had ever seen.

"Bear Hunter!" Storyteller cried, on his feet and in a resounding
voice. "I will tell the palefaces of the honor you mean to pay us, employing the language we have in common." This he pronounced in
the Croatan tongue, which in all probability Bear Hunter did not
know. If he did, Storyteller could be trusted not to reveal our suspi-
cions.

"Men of the ships, the Siouan wish to pay us great honor. It is a
ceremony that their forefathers paid to Ribaut, to De Soto whom
Bear Hunter calls Seeker of the Magic Fountain, and other great
white sagamores who visited the village. The drums will be brought
forth, and then warriors, numbering four score, will dance in a ring,
first in front of us, and then behind us, and then pay us the final honor
of hanging their sacred snakeskins around our necks. It is a like honor
to that the Wingineos paid George Howe before my coming, giving
him a full quiver of their finest arrows. How may we reply to this
great favor; why, it will leave us breathless! Martyn Sachem, speak
to your followers. We must not shame ourselves before our generous
hosts."

Most of the men had caught my signal of immediate and deadly
danger; a few had repeated the seemingly innocent gesture for those
who missed seeing it. They seemed calm, some affected smiles, but
all were listening with extreme alertness.

"When warriors dance behind us they intend to loop their snakeskins about our necks, truly a great honor, so they say," I said in English. "It is the same as the Wingineo paid George Howe. Give them
your silver breast pins such as Cheewink's lover gave her beside the
sea. Do so all at once, as the dancer behind you removes from his
neck the garment of honor. I hope that the great Bear Hunter will
choose me as the first to be honored, as is my right. Do as I do."

By intense concentration and self-control I was able to say this in
what seemed a pleased and gratified tone. I did not believe that Bear

Hunter had read my riddles because of half-forgetting his native language through its little use. Only Edward Powell left our circle to lean against a tree.

But in ghastly fear of making a horrible mistake, I asked Storyteller to question the speaker further, speaking the tribal language and taking utmost care. His answers might strengthen the evidence of intended massacre, or cast doubt upon his guilt.

"Bear Hunter Sachem, the palefaces wish to know the meaning of the honor, and why it is given them. When you have spoken, I will speak to their leader."

"Know then, Great One, that the large black snake with gold stripes like a chain on his back is our tribal totem," Bear Killer explained to Storyteller, pausing while the latter translated the former's reply. "The black snake kills many of the poison snakes with rattles in their tails, they are his favorite food, and so at the ends of our skins of honor, we wear the rattler's fangs. It means we are the black snakes, and our prey is the poison viper. And for the time that you wear them you become our brothers, and may have our wives and daughters for the night, and when we part tomorrow, our thoughts and well-wishes will go with you, and yours will stay with us."

This was good enough Indian thinking, and totemism at its best. Perhaps it was almost too good, for usually it is confused and mingled with other cults, and I doubted if this was of native origin and instead the invention of a murderous English renegade. No Indians I had met had wanted to put their totems in alien hands, even for one night. And I could sense a growing excitement and impatience in the faces and involuntary movements of the warriors.

Still I was in doubt whether to commit the rash and bloody act that I proposed—until a whim of fate relieved that doubt. One of the young squaws was wearing a silver crucifix on a leather thong, which holy emblem no Spanish priest would have ever given or sold to a heathen.

"Storyteller, tell Bear Hunter that we covet the honor, also we will relish tonight the lending of their wives and daughters, and we bid the warriors bring forth the drums and begin the sacred dance." I heard myself say it in half disbelief. We were committed to shedding blood in ghastly measure.

Three drums were brought forth, before which old men squatted. Again resounded the *boom*, boom-boom, *boom*, boom-boom that we had heard at the long-ago feast of the Croatan, evidently a favorite rhythm with the mainland Indians. The warriors formed a circle within our circle and began their dance, prancing and stamping, wildly gesticulating, and shouting, and the squaws began to howl and hiss, whereupon I could not doubt that they were parties to the plot. Bear

Hunter led the file of more than sixty warriors, and because he was an Englishmen, not an Indian, he could not control his countenance as stolidly as the rest. There was hate in his drawn lips and gleaming eyes, and I thought a frenzy of blood lust. All our men had followed my example in getting to their feet. They were waiting in an extremity of suspense, yet they seemed calm.

Blessedly they did not have to wait long. After twice dancing their inner round, Bear Hunter led the way through our circle, choosing his exit on the right side of Storyteller, then turning right, so that these Indians, right-handed as was every one I had seen, would have his right arm nearest to a white man's back. One complete round behind us would bring Bear Hunter up to my rear, for I stood at Storyteller's left. And that would be the crucial and fatal time, a matter of seconds in which to act, by which actions we lived or died.

I turned my head to follow the file of frenzied dancers. Pausing now and then as various warriors jumped up and down, many of them hissed like snakes in fury. The nightmare *boom,* boom-boom, *boom,* boom-boom quickened a little as the file neared the end of its round. Bear Hunter came up behind me. There he stopped, whereby no warrior danced behind Storyteller. As Bear Hunter pranced in frenzy, I turned just enough to watch him out of the side of my eyes. He began to remove his snakeskin neck band. He lifted it over his head. He raised his arms to loop it over my head, and I saw the tension of his grasp on each side of the snake-fang pendant. My hand leaped like a striking snake to the hilt of my hunting knife. With a hideous and inhuman yell, I plunged its blade with all my strength into his naked breast.

My followers were only a trice behind me. As I had bade them, they did as I did. All but one of them struck home; he, Thomas Ellis, who had waited almost too long, and the loop was about his neck, and only the swift, strong hands of the youth Thomas Smart, whose own attacker lay dead at his feet, prevented the quick crossing of the ends about Ellis' neck and the hard jerk that would break his larynx. Almost in every case the conspirators tumbled on their backs, with such simultaneity that the effect was grotesque, a formal feature of a death dance; and only gushing blood destroyed the illusion.

This last would have been a horrid sight, if I had seen it sanely. As it was, I loved it with the love of a beast of prey as he tears out the great vein of his quarry's neck, a love that lived in the darkest cellar of my soul. All of the sixty or more dancers were dead or mortally wounded, but there were more than sixty warriors in the tribe, to the number of a score who had not taken part in the dance, and I did not try to stop my followers as they fell upon them with their bloodied knives. They fought back bravely but without hope, and only three of my men received flesh wounds before the last of the Siouan warriors reeled backward and pitched like a falling tree.

The aged drummers continued their wild beat as though in implacable defiance of death. It drowned out the moanings and death rattlings of mortally wounded Indians; and this, along with the scarlet pools and gushings every way one looked, was like a madman's nightmare coming true. The squaws shrieked as they fled into the forest, some of them clutching babies; and so did terrified children. But I did not call to them that we would spare them, I was in too great haste to search the houses, to find visible and palpable evidence of similar slaughters by a tribe that lived by murder.

It was easy to find in plenty. The deerskin bags of the warriors were heavy with plunder stripped from innocent dead whom these Siouans had ambushed and had dealt as they had plotted to deal with us. There were silver and brass and occasionally gold amulets, copper earrings of the style of far-distant tribes, coral and shell necklaces and headbands taken from butchered women, knives of alien pattern, beaded garments such as I had never seen, egret plumes, swan-feather robes, fishing gear of Spanish make, golden crosses and crucifix, pearls, a golden snuffbox that might be Aztec, and indeed every kind of precious possession their victims had obtained by toil or trade. This was a type of criminal tribe rarely if ever seen by explorers: they did not rove through the forests to fall on unsuspecting villages. Instead they waited in peaceful guise in murderous ambush.

Our worst find was a great heap of human bones, revealed by the drying in a drouth of a pothole or marsh. We could not bring ourselves to examine them closely; we could only roughly number them as representing at least two hundred skeletons. This represented their kill in the last three or four years; for those dumped here before then would have rotted away.

Our colonists were strangely quiet; the scene itself had an uncanny hush. The men wiped their knives and restored these to their sheaths and then looked at me, their eyes asking a question.

"We will not spend the night here," I directed. "There is a good trail leading to the creek and we will go *up* the creek a short distance and make our beds on the ground. It is a warm night, without likelihood of rain. We will rise before the sun and make for the town of Waccama, on Little River Inlet. There we will surely meet the boats unless they are lost, for if they could meet us at this hellish village, they would have come before now."

On second thought, I wondered if "hellish" were the right adjective. Certainly so, by English thinking. The sick notion came to me that the idea would have been incomprehensible to the old men of this village, survivors of the slaughter. Storyteller had told me that the Siouans were a large and widespread people, probably of Sioux origins. The most were hunters and farmers; some were fisher folk. But the warriors of this town called Sioua neither hunted nor farmed nor fished with industry; their occupation was murder. Quite possibly their minds worked like those of the Thuggee in India, whom visitors to India had described. No doubt when they could not kill safely by ambush or surprise, they fought bravely if the resisting force was not too large. It was entirely probable if not certain that they regarded themselves as the elite among all the Siouan tribes: they took the biggest game.

We could be sure that their miko or werowance highly approved their ways; and these wizards were backed by their kewas. I would have gladly burned their temple if I could have summoned up any more energy for violence; but the act would have been useless now and therefore folly. The warriors' wives, mothers, sisters, and children took wholesale killing for granted; they were used to it; it was their way of life. No doubt all but babbling toddlers knew of tonight's plan when scouts had reported a large party of palefaces making toward their village. The elder children had watched from doorways for the climactic scene, when the warriors would have looped their garrotes around our necks and violently pulled the ends. Also they would have watched with shining eyes and much laughter as our possessions were stripped from our corpses; but would yawn when these were being dragged away to dump in their garbage pond. Later tonight the braves and their wives and sweethearts would have made passionate love; the warriors worked up by wild excitement and glorious triumph; their women carried away by their lovers' virility, indeed magnificence in their sight, and by the fabulous richness of the spoil. I could imagine their wriggling in ecstasy, their wildly thrusting thighs, their breathless embraces, their love-lighted eyes. The dimmest feeling of remorse was unthinkable. And this was the way that the human mind and soul could be debauched by circumstance and habit.

But my imagination, its activities permitting me so many glimpses of beauty and nobility, was likewise accursed. It went on churning.

Such debauchery would never end as long as the race endured, by any reclaiming that I could vision. Instead I saw a vision of the near future, in which Richard's dark prophecy came true. Only by the wildest fluke of chance had Bear Hunter let slip English thieves' cant into the address he had made to his followers and John Hynde had happened to identify it. How easily we might encounter an Indian tribe that rightfully hated all white men for their cruel abuse; a tribe vastly outnumbering us and wiping us out with feelings of pride and glory. And if we escaped the knives and the arrows, there remained those perils Richard had enumerated—plagues, swamps, starvation, death by attrition.

Perhaps we would have done better to have died at our camp, fighting to the last man against the united tribes of the Algonquins. What will we have gained, worth having, at the end of the road? Still accursed areas of my imagination could not concede such a lame conclusion. We would fight on.

2

A single instance of aftermath of our bloody work at the assassin's town of Sioua was either of most slight or no importance. Still I will record it, as an example of the effect of our deed on one Siouan wife. I had posted a guard over our camp on the creek above the village, eight men to stand four watches of two hours each, on the wild supposition that the runaway squaws or even the old men who had been spared might steal upon us with the knives of the slain to take a moiety of revenge. One of the guards, Thomas Smart, wakened me soon after I had fallen to sleep in the black and silent nadir of the night, to tell me that a young squaw had approached him and by pronouncing my name Martyn, which she had heard some of my followers call me, and by sign language, caused him to understand that she wanted speech with me, under a water oak within the watchman's lines.

"Is she a Siouan?"

"She lived in the Siouan town. I remembered seeing her there."

"Is she armed?"

"I don't see how she could be. She's wearing nothing but a short skirt of shredded bark and I saw her good in the watch fire. There were no suspicious bulges anywhere."

"She gave you no hint of what she wanted?"

"She spoke to me in what I recognized as Croatan, but I haven't picked up the language. By the way, she's a remarkably beautiful young squaw."

I had no wish to look upon a beautiful young squaw of the degenerate Siouan, still her tidings might be of importance to our party and might go a little way toward solving the mystery of their departure from normal Indian behavior. Also I was curious about her speaking Croatan, wondering if she could have any connection with our former neighbors across Croatan Sound.

I approached the tree and perceived her shape in a far-darting gleam of a watch fire. The line of fires that the watchmen kept burning was beyond the tree, and there was no way for anyone to steal upon me or the sleepers, since in other directions there was impenetrable marsh. I noted that the remnant of the moon was just topping the eastward forest.

She stepped out from the tree's shade to let me see her plain. With the moon's and my night-sight's aid I could see that she was young, lithe, and had a vivid beauty, not common or yet extremely rare among Indian women. She spoke to me at once.

"Great sagamore, my name is Memeo," she told me in Croatan. This was also the name of a New World woodpecker. "I was the woman of Bear Hunter, whom you slew."

"Then you came here from afar."

"From Pompuik. My tribe was conquered by the Tuscaroras, and our maidens sold into slavery. Bear Hunter was among the conquerors, and he bought me—I had seen twelve suns—and I was his woman for three moons before I knew that he was a paleface. I have been his woman for three suns."

"And now?"

"He hated his own brethren and killed as many as he could and because this was against nature, I did not like to have him touch me, and I cheated him in a way the old women know and had no baby by him. It was seen that you have no woman and slept alone. I am used to the ways of a bad white man who hated his brothers and I can quickly become used to the ways of good white men who love their brothers. I am skilled at all tasks suitable for women. I have never had a baby and I have remained like to virgin—if you doubt me, give me your hand."

Smiling, I shook my head.

"Will you not try me? The grass is soft, and there is deep shade under the tree, and the night is warm, and my bosom is on fire, as is my whole body."

"Why should you desire me, Memeo? You have not seen me before today's sunset."

"Sagamore, I saw the flash of your knife and the flash of your eyes when you slew Bear Hunter. I have waited until now in a great burning. And I know if you tried me once, you would pine for no other woman. I know all the little tricks of muscle that men love. Also, you would take me with you on the great march, whence I do not know. There I would be of help to you and your followers, because I went with Bear Hunter when he led twice ten of his warriors against a little village on a river called Cumbahee."

"Are you in danger here, Memeo?"

"Oh, great danger! Only two moons ago Bear Hunter and his warriors made war against the village of Minsal—the name means small shells—on a branch of these very waters. Some of the warriors escaped the snakeskin loops, and now they will seek revenge by killing all our old men, perhaps our women and children, and surely they will kill me, the woman of Bear Hunter. Take me with you, great sagamore! Why, you will halt the marches before sundown in your haste to bed with me. Besides"—and she lowered her voice a little—"I know where Bear Hunter had hidden gold."

"I cannot take you with me, widow of Bear Hunter. I cannot touch a woman he has touched. There is no room for you among our marchers."

"You cannot?" she asked, incredulity in her tone.

"I will not. Speak no more."

"Bah! You are not a man, but a reed! Bear Hunter hated his brethren, but he was a man truly, and I lied when I told you I did not love his mighty arms and thighs and his pitiless heart! I am the daughter of a werowance, and I know many magic spells. These will be cast against you, and you will be eaten by dogs! I spit in your face."

She did so literally, and as I wiped away the spittle, she darted away. I went back to my bed and almost instantly fell asleep.

On the following day we gained a peninsula between the eastward and westward branches of what Ribaut had named Little River. From this point we spied our boats two cables' length down the main creek and beckoned them to join us. After a happy reunion, we refilled their water casks and food bags, and John Hynde told them the story of our near-slaughter the preceding night almost as a jest, but this was because its horror was still upon him, and he wished to conceal the fact or his mind dodged it. Yet this sensitive man had been born in the slums of London; he had been daubed by their grime; he knew the cant of thieves and murderers; he had himself thieved and had been sent to prison; and was now one of my staunchest men.

His hearers had little to say. They themselves had had close calls; they were used to sudden and deadly threats to their lives. Danger was becoming their element.

Having arrived three days before and explored Little River and its main branches, they told us that in three trips they could ferry us across the western branch of the river, whereupon we could march behind four miles of marsh and come out on a firm beach, where they would be waiting for us. They had found it by exploration of the coast for about ten miles, and from a high sand dune they could see no inlet several miles farther. It would be most pleasant if the parties could keep in sight of each other as long as possible. They would be able to

net large hauls of scalefish and shellfish, which would spare our pantry.
Also when we encountered tidal rivers they could ferry us across.

Storyteller had traveled this route several years before. He recalled
a stretch of beach that we could follow for about twenty miles before
we would encounter a maze of sea islands. Well, we could swing
around those islands, and find the beach again. That would be easier
than a cross-country journey whereby we must cross without aid of
boats two great rivers which Storyteller knew by their Indian name
Peedee. As to our welcome at the coastal villages, our wise guide was
not certain. The legend still lived of how Vásquez de Ayllón had kid-
naped seventy Cusabo Indians who were never seen again; that had
occurred a half century before, on a coast far southward, but the
storytellers and the mikos had long memories. Our bringing no tall
ships would allay the people's fears.

So we crossed a channel less than two hundred fathoms wide, and
were poled across a marsh of equal width, the reeds of which all but
touched the surface in a tide swollen by a southeast wind. On the
shoreward side both parties camped for the night, sleeping under and
over oiled cloths because of light rain. In the morning the boatmen returned to Little River, making for its mouth, and told us they would
see us when we had marched behind the four miles of coastal marsh.
The beach we found was indeed firm, a fine sand beach on which I
dreamed of white folk reveling in centuries to come.

The remainder of the day was the most pleasant we had spent
since our flight began. The mid-September sun was genial: porpoises
sported and gave fishes fits a cable's length from the sands, and not
much further we could see our fellows in their three craft. About sundown we found a small village of Indians on the shores of a lake half a
mile long, two hundred yards wide, and a furlong back from the
beach. So small a village had never before been honored by the visit
of a storyteller, one the Blessed Men, and the people had never
before seen palefaces.

These villagers, numbering about a hundred men, women, and
children, were patently but by no means miserably poor. Their name
was Waccamba, the same as a noble river. They had no metals of
any sort; the points of their weak arrows lacked flint tips and had
been merely hardened and sharpened in the fire. Their spears were
canes likewise sharpened; their fishhooks were sea shell, merely a
narrow cutout shaft with a point running up from its end at a forty-
five degree angle. They had no nets, only clumsy-looking weirs, although their boats were patiently fashioned of cypress, and flat-
bottomed for traversing marshes. The feast they spread for us was of
cakes made of a coarse flour obtained by grinding the small acorns

of water oaks, clams that were presumably the mainstay of their lives, dried or fresh fish, crabs, lobsters, giant shrimps, and scallops. The crabs and perhaps fish had been caught mainly in pits that they dug in the sands above low-tide line, and from which, when the tide had risen and again receded, they retrieved their catch.

For flesh they had a variety of seafowl, some of them blue-billed ducks and a few English mallards, and fresh-water gallinules from their reed-rimmed lake, and curlews and sandpipers of various size. But the most had a fishy flavor and were probably merganser ducks, scooters, and such like. They served us no venison, for which omission their headman apologized to Storyteller, although he proudly told him that from the palm and scrub forest back from the beach some of their hunters occasionally brought home a deer.

Their houses were brush huts, and these they emptied for our use. We would not have accepted this generous offer because of the rank smell of the abodes if a rain storm, patiently waiting until Storyteller completed a heroic narrative, had not begun its chilling fall. The Indians cheerfully retired to some sheds, open on three sides, screened only on the side facing the sea, but well roofed with palm fronds, containing racks for drying fish, yet protecting these from the wet. All of our women along with babes and toddlers would sleep in the chief's house, the largest in the row, while we men found room to lie down in the smaller houses. The boatmen had their own protection against the rain. These were canvas tarpaulins which they fastened to the gunwales of their boats by an ingenious arrangement of wire hooks over nails. Lying under the thwarts all hands made out somehow.

After clasping our elbows with their right hands, grinning, and bowing, the villagers bade us good-bye, then watched us out of sight. Our boatmen ferried us across a narrow inlet terminating in a patch of canes, and in the afternoon we followed a peculiarly beautiful beach and camped out amid some dunes at the northern end of a cluster of sea islands separated by creeks and marsh. This was the end of our beach march here. From hence we must take a circuitous route to rendezvous with the boats on the estuary of the rivers Peedee. This march and the crossing took two days from the spare number ere the break of winter.

3

Storyteller warned us that our progress southward would be painfully slow from henceforth almost to St. Augustine. The coastal lands lay only a few feet above sea level, and contained vast marshes sur-

rounding the bays and estuaries of mighty rivers. To avoid the marshes
we must march far inland, and hence the boats must advance far up
the rivers in order to ferry us across. In the case of the first two
floods, the northern Santee and the southern Santee, the crossing
would be at least fifteen miles from the sea. A blessing that might
turn out a curse, perhaps the ultimate one of death, was a large
Indian population in this region, occupying towns beyond count. These
were prosperous folk, planting corn in the savannas between the
waters, hunting deer and bear and small game in the dense woods,
and taking great harvests of fish from the innumerable rivers, creeks,
and lakes. Among the Indian tribes were the Winyaw, whose lands
we had gained, the Seewee to our southward, the warlike Yemasee,
and the mighty Cusabo, farther south. Beyond these were the
Apalachicola, the name meaning "People of the Other Side," which
might refer to their living across a tremendous river, the largest
that Spanish explorers had observed south of Chesapeake Bay. They
belonged to the Muskhogean nation, and comprised its largest division. They were friends of the Spanish, which did not augur well for
them being our friends.

Before we set out, Storyteller, Cuthbert White in command of the
boats, Doctor Jones, Thomas Warner, Richard, Manteo, and I con-
ferred together. I had removed about half a dozen blank sheets from
the logbook I had taken from the fort at Roanoke, and we made
ink from lantern black mixed with water, and Doctor Jones had a
quill pen. Our plan was to pool our knowledge of the vast country
we must traverse to gain the great river of the Apalachicola, a distance
that Doctor Jones, who had poured over every Spanish, French, and
Indian map he could get hand on, estimated at no less than three
hundred miles by crow flight, St. Augustine lying about seventy-five
miles farther on. Manteo was second to myself and Richard in use-
lessness to the conference. He had already reached the southern end
of his known world. Our two mainstays were Storyteller and Doctor
Jones, in that order of importance. Still we proposed to make three
copies, and an extra in case one were lost, one of these for me, one
for Cuthbert White, and one for Doctor Jones. We spent the whole
morning at the task, charting the marchers' course generally westward
below the Santee swamps, across country to what was known as Buffalo Ford, not far below the junction of the Wateree and the Con-
garee, these rivers being branches of the Upper Santee. We could not
be ferried lower down across either of the Santee's two estuaries because of the impenetrable marshes that lay between.

From Buffalo Ford we must march sharply southeast to the great
bend of the Edisto, the site of an Indian town called Chehaw, where

if all went well we would meet the boats, these entering the river a little north of a sound Ribaut had named St. Helena. Again marching southeast, with Indian guides honoring not us bearded palefaces, but our Blessed Man, we would again try to effect a rendezvous at the head of a sound about thirty miles below St. Helena, at the Indian town of Xoxi. The river known to Ribaut as Fleuve Grande in the region of Port Royal, entered here, and we were hospitably received at a town called Talapo. From hence there was an Indian trail to Sonepah, and the river was famed for its broad savannas along its lower waters.

Storyteller furnished us the names of fully twenty towns on or near our course. To traverse it required sixty-five days, each of which had varied events and yet gave the impression of sameness. In all truth they were somewhat alike in hardship, uncertainty, and lesser or greater perils, and they had such a dreamlike quality that I feared I was going mad. When we had no guide, we frequently lost our way, and had to backtrack a weary way to obtain orientation. Where Indians admitted us into their towns, they usually provided us with shelter, but at numerous towns they would admit only Storyteller, and it was by his persuasions that they furnished us a meal, sometimes two, and, on rainy nights, helped us erect pavilions. In some towns the folk spoke Muskhogean, at others Hitchiti, and at others mixtures of both languages or dialects of one or the other. Very rarely was Storyteller stumped. At not a single town did his hero-tales fail to attract an enthralled circle of listeners.

In the swampier regions progress would have been impossible without cutting our way by machetes or following deer trails. In marvelous contrast was the primeval forest, which exemplified the law of the survival of the fittest, only trees especially adapted to the climate and terrain being able to find root and thrive, eliminating almost all thickets, creepers, and scrub trees. Only by the death of one giant could another giant drive down its roots in search of water and nourishment and thrust its top to the skies. But a low herbage, adapting itself to deep shade, furnished fare for deer and other game, and our flanking parties of archers and in hungry times our musketeers almost always could provide meat for the evening meal.

These forests were hushed, constantly they reminded our marchers of cathedrals erected on a divine scale; even on windy days the little flame of a new-lit fire need not be guarded, and we knew of the rushing air only by a swishing sound of waving treetops far over our heads. Through these we marched almost in silence along deer paths or occasional Indian footpaths. Here, if we lacked a guide, Manteo was the leader of our files, because he was the best able to maintain

his directions, not I thought by any psychic faculty but by occasional
glimpses of the sun and by the growth of moss on certain sides of
the tree trunks.

No day was without hardships, whether only labor before dawn or
after dark, or cold streams that we must wade, bogs, or, among the
very worst, a region of "down timber"—the trees felled by some tor-
nado of extreme violence, and forming an all but impenetrable mesh.
In such regions the men swore as they squirmed over or under fallen
trunks and treetops. Oddly enough Winifred very frequently wept,
and this was a marvel, for she was not nearly as given to weeping
as our other women. On the other hand, among the standing giants
she seemed exalted, her eyes not overly brilliant, but soft and beautiful and often wide with awe. Among our most cheerful marchers, and
certainly the most nimble, was Weechee.

Our ranks suffered attrition, and the wonder was, that this was
not greater and more rapid. Only three lost their lives, one of them
the urchin son of Ambrose Viccars, struck in the calf of the leg by a
hugh rattlesnake. Doctor Jones had immediately applied a tourniquet,
and shallowly cut the swelling, pressing it to squeeze out the venom,
but the boy lived only two hours. Another variety of rattlesnake, whose
markings were in diamond-shape, stung Thomas Topan in the neck
when he had tripped over a rotten log, and he died in under three
minutes. And in under three days his widow Audry took up with
Richard Berry, gentleman.

We had dug him the usual shallow grave, and as usual, Edward
Powell had pronounced a prayer for his soul. As usual, he had made
the formal request that a wooden cross be raised, with the victim's
name and the year burned on it with a red-hot ramrod, but we could
spare neither the time nor nails to erect such a monument.

Nor was there much time for love-making, which is the first stage
of Nature's process of replacement of those who die. The belief was
common in the colony that Winifred and I were lovers, but there
was no fact on which to base that belief, still I could not deem it
precisely untrue. We met rather frequently, behind the glare of the
cooking fires, but scarcely touched each other. She offered an explanation for her restraint which I accepted as true but not as the
whole truth.

"That other interpassage was so beautiful," she said. "I think we
were both enchanted in a very real sense—the moon, the forest, our
awful loneliness, the dangers to our very lives we had lived from
minute to minute, from hour to hour, from day to day. I feel—I almost
know—what we experienced that night can never be recaptured. We
met on some distant and magic threshold where we had met once ago;

who can say it was not in a previous existence? Now I want us to know each other as people. I want to find out if we can ever be married, provided we survive and find a haven where something like ordinary life can go on; or whether there are insuperable barriers between us. I do not mean our stations in England; these are wiped out forever. But reared as I was, by a fanatical father and a mother who could never forget she was a daughter of the Gwynedds in a day when kings and queens were regarded and considered themselves gods and goddesses, I can't conform. I have almost nothing in common with the squires' daughter or even the daughters of noblemen, let alone the best of the girls we have with us. And you, Martyn, have such a superb gift of leadership that it may be genius. You are truly a ruthless man in getting your way—or should I say in carrying out your plans for the colony? Can I use the word deadly? I think it is the right word. I heard how you beat the prison guard. You would have indeed thrown Richard Berry overboard that night, if he hadn't yielded. I do not believe we could make a successful marriage—still I want to find out."

But while I told her a good deal of my past life, my childhood experiences and dreams, what I thought and felt, she was really the greater talker, mainly of her own life and long-ago life in Wales. She told me that King Arthur, about whom such a vast cloak of myth had formed, was certainly a Welshman from the Taff River. She never doubted that he really lived and was the great commander who had won seven victories over the Saxons and stopped them in their tracks in southeastern England, and arrested their conquest of all Britain for seventy-five years. He was first called Ambrosius— which became Ambrose. After his first victory over Vortigern, King of Wales, he was given the name of Artay, a deity in the pagan religion of Cambria identified with Hermes, the Roman Mercury. He was the nephew of Merdin, the last of the great Druids, who in myth became Merlin the Magician.

She told me of other early deities of ancient Wales—using the word Cambria, which was the Roman name of that land set apart by mountains and possibly by its people from the main of Britain. It was never really conquered by the Romans, although certain of its regions were occupied. Even now its nobility and many of the folk still wanted to be Welsh, not English. Many were its tales of both bloodshed and beauty, and these she recounted to me in her sweet low voice that lent them power. Always the Cambrians were warring with the men of Eire who came across the Irish Sea in their coracles, and ravished, burned, and slaughtered. Many Cambrian heroes emerged, many were sent to Dalor, god of death. The folk were given to great jubilations or to deep sorrows, and their chief deity, after Lud himself, was Dagda, god of the corn.

Once she asked me a strange thing.

"Martyn, we think of time as ever moving forward. Can it never retreat?"

"I do not know what you mean."

"Why couldn't it? We know nothing about time. Certainly our party is retreating into time—would not you say so? We are fighting the wilderness for survival as did our ancestors. The people we meet, with whom we foregather and make friends whenever we can, are a Stone Age people. Slowly we are adopting their way of life, possibly their way of thinking. My father is a fanatic in his fundamentalist religion, yet in some ways he is the most civilized man in our party, in that he most fiercely resists our becoming renegades from European civilization."

So different was my mind from that of Mr. Powell's, that I deemed him the least civilized man in our party. However, an incident at a town called Coosaw, lying southward of the Salkehatchie River, and peopled by Yemasee Indians, lent strength to her argument. They were known to Storyteller as a peculiarly warlike tribe and we feared our reception there, but actually it was one of the most hospitable since our dealings with Bear Hunter. The people vacated about twenty houses for our use, the smallest of which I shared with Storyteller, Weechee spending the night with Ananias and Eleanore Dare. Amid a circle of eager listeners, he began telling a long tale I had heard before. Somewhat tired, I strolled off to my night's lodging.

Winifred followed me there. She was not amorous, as I first thought and no doubt hoped; she was only lonesome and wanted to talk. Truly she had almost nothing in common with our other spinsters and very little, I concluded, with any of our company; and I did not fully understand what impelled her to confide in me. Seated on one of the shelves that served the house owners as bed and lounge, she told me that she had taken a vow of chastity to keep until we arrived at some sort of destination, where she would choose a husband from quite a number of ever-ready wooers. She had sworn by Queen Boudicca of what was now Norfolk, who toward the end of the first century had led a rebellion against the Roman conquerors of whom thousands were killed. But it had failed at last and the Queen took poison. Most certainly she had not been a saint, since she led an army of pagans, but was forever a heroine among the Welsh.

Winifred and I fell to discussing chastity, held in such reverence by many peoples of widely varying degrees of civilization, and almost disregarded by other peoples. Losing it except to a lawful husband was certainly not a deadly sin, instead a venial sin by folk-thinking of our times, a far worse offense when committed by a girl of name than by a peasant girl, but always a danger to such formidable institutions as wedlock, legitimate descent, and inheritance of property, because it could so easily bring about the borning of bastards. In the glimmer of an Indian lamp—a bowl of oil with a rag wick—we had talked nearly an hour when the curtain over the door was drawn aside. Then there entered, very quietly, Edward Powell.

"May I come in?" Mr. Powell asked in complete calm. "I have waited patiently for Winifred and you to complete your orgy."

When I started to protest, Winifred shot me a warning glance. Although I could not begin to guess why, she was plainly willing for her father to think she and I had done what he supposed.

"I saw you both slip away from the gathering," he went on. "Of course I knew your intentions. I thought I would not deprive you of your iniquitous pleasure; in fact I could not do so if I tried, and could only postpone it. I recalled that Winifred was no longer a virgin; she had committed the same sin, then with the excuse of betrothal, with Richard. I do not believe there were any others; I cannot call her wanton because she has had only one lover at a time. So what I have come to say will require only a moment, if you will give me leave."

"Yes, sir, of course."

"I cannot blame you overmuch, Martyn. I myself have known illicit yearnings. When the Lord said that he who looks wantonly upon a woman is as guilty as he who commits fornication with her, He pointed His finger at me. All my prayers have never absolved me from that sin. But I am of stronger stuff than you, Martyn; you yielded to those yearnings while I did not. In my later life I have been able to suppress them utterly; the Devil knows it is useless to try to tempt me; I laugh and spit at him. This is not of what I wished to speak when I came here. It is of the future."

I glanced at Winifred. She had seated herself on the shelf-bed, I stood in respect to Mr. Powell. I had the sense of her feeling stronger than her father. I was not sure but that she had felt so for some years. I wondered why. I greatly wished that I knew why.

"Yes, sir," I answered Edward Powell with due courtesy.

"I do not wish you two to be married. In fact, I would refuse to perform the sacrament, and there is no other in our company who has the right. I refuse because it would no longer be a sacrament, but an empty gesture, by which I will not waken the rage or incur the contempt of the Lord God. It no longer matters to me if you both continue to sin. The Lord will deal with the matter in His own way, and this without fail. Hear me, both of you—I say without fail. Your living together, what would be called in England a common-law marriage, would not lessen the sin—there is no such thing as a common-law marriage; the relationship would still be an abomination before the Lord. But such a relationship, I mean living together, would have a devastating effect on your followers. They would think I had condoned your wickedness, and I would much rather have them laugh at me, behind my back, for what they might think is my ignorance of wickedness done in stealth. If you do it, so can they. The other unwedded maidens would take up with the man of their choice; all the rest would get Indian girls, and commit the sin for which God punished His Children, that of mingling their blood with the heathen."

"I doubt, sir, if we Englishmen could be called His chosen people."

"That, I grant; but He has divided one people from another, one race from another, by unmistakable marks. Having white skins, we are the sons of Japheth, not of Ham who was black. The writing is plain to read. May I ask, sir, that you and Winifred continue to do your wickedness in stealth? That you do not try to lend to it the merest shadow of respectability? It is so little to ask." And this last moved me to pity.

"Sir, I think you should put the question first to Winifred."

"She heard what I said. Winifred, will you grant your lawful father this favor?"

"Certainly, if that is the way you want it," Winifred replied in a soft, compassionate voice.

"Will you give me your solemn promise, to hold as long as we are on this terrible march? When we reach civilization, when we are under canon or civil law, perhaps you can be reborn; although your sins are as scarlet, He can make them as snow; and in that case I will myself perform a wedding ceremony for you and the man of your choice."

"I will give you my solemn promise, to hold until we are settled in St. Augustine!"

"Great God! A Roman Catholic settlement! Once I cried out in deepmost woe, 'Eli, Eli, why hast thou forsaken me!' Now I have no doubt He is testing me as He tested Job. Still, the Spaniards are Christians, not dark-skinned savages. Even my respected friend, Doctor John Jones, is a member of that faith. What I truly wish is that we had not listened to Martyn, and if I could not have persuaded the Croatans to forgive the deadly sin committed by one of our number, to have died on our knees in the fort. Aye, I wish we had all died then, because we would have gone before the Bar of Judgment with fewer sins upon our souls than we have now. And hark ye both: I am not a misanthrope; I have obeyed the ordinance to love my fellow men and to serve them the best that I can. And I am not so blind as to fail to see one good that can come out of the wickedness between you and your illicit lover."

He fell silent, and after long pause I must ask, "Would you care to tell me what it is? I grant your sincerity, and your zeal to do what you feel is right—"

"What I *know* is right!"

"Very well. What I am trying to say is, I wish to understand you fully as possible."

"I mean, in a sense, I will sacrifice my own daughter for the good of the hundred souls who are in our company, of which you are the leader, and let her walk the dark road that leads to Hell. As long as you have access to the beautiful body of my daughter Winifred, you will not turn to the body of an Indian girl. Yes, I mean Weechee. Only Winifred is saving you from that abominable sin. And your committing it would cause almost all other of our unattached men to commit a like sin. God smote down many who had worshiped the Golden Calf, but not all. He will smite down many of our sinners, but I am doing what I can that He may not smite down all."

"As long as I desire Winifred and she me, and we yield to that desire, I will not make love to Weechee."

"So be it. Now I will take my leave. Winifred, will you come with me, or do you wish to stay longer with your lover?"

"I'll come with you. In a little while I'll go to my quarters with the spinsters. And soon I too will pray to the True God."

"At my knees? If not there, before what shrine?" Fixing his sad eyes on me, he went on, "Our leader has not seen fit to erect a shrine in the wilderness."

"Sir, I pray your forgiveness. There was so little time. Ours is a savage battle between life and death."

"All the more need for a shrine. Still, you have done the best you could, that your eyes could see, that the Devil let you see."

"I will find a shrine," Winifred broke in, her eyes softly glimmering, her voice melodious, her beauty breath-taking. "Whenever we walk in that great, hushed forest, I feel I am in church."

Chapter XVI

OKE FENOKEE

1

Greatly to my satisfaction, Weechee had not yet chosen a husband, perhaps because no attractive young bachelor in our company had set out to woo her earnestly and with ardor. I felt almost certain that Richard could have won her, if he tried: the explanation of why he did not try seemed partly that he was in love with adventure, especially deer hunting, at which he was the most successful of any of our nimrods. Partly his reluctance might be a consequence of his blighted love affair with Winifred, which he did not try to renew but which still haunted him. Possibly he felt he would be poaching not on my preserves but on my reserve.

While these undercurrents flowed, Death did not stay his hand. Two men died, smothered in muck, when they tried to take a short cut across a marsh, and we stood about a few minutes, saying almost nothing, and then marched on. One man climbed a tree to club a porcupine and fell out and broke his neck.

In our thinking that the Indian term "People of the Other Side" referred to the dwellers of the south bank of the great river we had gained, known to the Spanish as *El Rio de los Sabanas*, Doctor Jones, Manteo, and we others deciding our routes had been mistaken. Possibly it meant inhabitants of the region of the Ogeechee River, farther south, or the Olatama, called the Altamata by some tribes, about sixty miles southward by crow flight.

These concerns were for the future. Just now our party was confronted by a crisis, nonetheless serious because it posed no immediate danger and caused no talk; in fact it remained unknown except to our leaders. The town we had just reached was called Guale, a term applied to other towns and regions, and was actually a name of or applied to an Indian nation. This nation was certainly related to the Muskhogean or Muskhogogee, the speech and customs of both being closely akin, and very alike in appearance. Doctor Jones thought that Guale was the name for what Ribaut had called the Muskhogean nation.

The crisis was simply that we wished to winter in this large town, and the sagamore had not yet given his permission.

It was Thomas Warner's clear observation and thought that put us into position for bargaining. He had observed that the Guale had extremely powerful bows, the average weight, meaning the force necessary to bend them into a deep crescent, being around sixty pounds. But their arrows with flint heads were large and heavy enough for light spears. "I think it would be impossible," he told us, "that they can launch such arrows with tolerable accuracy at more than forty yards."

"Why don't the fools know it and use lighter heads?" I asked.

"I can give one reason, applicable all over the world to all peoples —reluctance to change old ways. What was good enough for their grandsires is good enough for them; and this of course omits all change of conditions since their grandsires' times. Perhaps Manteo can give a practical reason. Ask him, Martyn."

When I had done so, Manteo gave a rather eloquent reply.

"The wooded swamps above and below here, so a hunter told me, throng with deer. These are the hunting grounds of the deer slayers among the Guale, and may extend a mile or more on either bank, and the same is true for a five-day journey of a hunting party westward and inland. The swamps produce shrubbery and grasses that the deer crop, but never is there a blessing upon the greatest or the least of creatures without its curse. The curse upon the deer would appall my heart, that of Manteo, not merely the hearts of the timid hinds and, though they seek to hide the truth with the proud bearing, the hearts of the horned stags. All of us know the *cuguara;* five times the weight of a greatest wild cat; we have seen his tawny coat as he skulks the thickets; and the dartings of our torches on his eyes have shown like great emeralds as he prowls about our camps. It is these that the Guale fear, not without cause! Because of them their arrow shafts are bowed down with heavy heads, for they think that only such can plunge their way into the vitals of *cuguara,* and put out the iniquitous and almost unextinguishable fire of his life ere he charges with great snarlings and tears down the hunter."

Manteo fell silent. The rest of us fell into thought. My own brain wheeled wildly. Then I spoke.

"Manteo, what if you challenged the chief to tournament, fifty of our archers against fifty of his best, to shoot into hempen mats which are countless in the town, hung upon stakes not at forty but at one hundred paces? Would he accept?"

"Aye, Martyn Sagamore! It would shame him not to do so, and all men on earth love tournaments as they love interbinding their limbs with their beloveds'."

"I think if we would beat them not in a close match, but out and far, and make them seem as bunglers, the chieftain would take thought of how many deer we could kill for the tribe in the hungry days of winter, and invite us to stay in the houses vacated by the Altamata Guales who grow sickly in cold weather and have gone southward to their old town, Tulufina, where the winter sun is warmer."

"I think so too," Doctor Jones broke in, his face beaming at the prospect.

"Manteo, it will do no harm to try," I told him, "and perhaps the tournament can furnish Storyteller with a scene to describe in one of his noble tales."

With Storyteller himself acting as interpreter when one was needed, Manteo indeed challenged the Sagamore of the Guales, known by a name almost unpronounceable in English, meaning "He on whom the sun shines on dark days," and which our irreverent English immediately reduced to Sun Target. He did so in a lofty manner, to which the Guale gave a lofty but affirmative reply. The news of the coming match immediately excited the whole town. It was held on a small savanna of about five acres about ten minutes' walk from the main street. Twenty targets were set up at one hundred paces, at which a hundred archers would discharge three arrows each. These hempen mats were ideal for the purpose, for the arrows would penetrate and stick without doing the least harm to the arrowheads.

What I thought would happen, did happen. The long bows that Tom Warner had fashioned were distinguishable only by an expert from those used by English yeomen at the battle of Crécy. I believed them to be without peer except for the short, more deeply curved bows of bone and ivory employed by those great archers, the Scythians. Our fifty archers had become skilled by practice, hunting, and most of all by determination and concentration wakened by the desperation of our need. They beat the Guales' picked men as Alexander's steed, Bucephalus, beat the great chargers from the hippodromes of Darius, Emperor of Persia. Our arrows were immediately distinguishable from Guale arrows; when the contest was over, our shamed opponents did not even accompany the judges as they made the count of hits at these easy targets. There were English arrows to the count of nearly eleven twenties against six twenties of heavy-headed Indian arrows sticking in the mats.

Storyteller acted as our ambassador to the humiliated and sullen Sagamore of the Guales. First presenting a gift of one of our four remaining burning glasses and demonstrating it could start a fire at noon in the winter sun, he said that it would be useless for the palefaces to attempt a boat race in open water, let alone high marsh, in the full-moon tide against incomparable Guale boatmen in their flat-bottomed craft, because we would be shamed by our poor showing. Storyteller must have given a hint of the deer we could furnish the whole town in the deep of winter when fish were scarce and the waterfowl, obtainable in season by slings hurling ounce-weight stones, had all flown southward. The outcome was that the sagamore did indeed invite Storyteller, the Sagamore Manteo, and the palefaces to remain with his people until the now brief days were of equal length with the nights.

We did so, and fared well. Six days a week, our fifty archers made from five- to ten-mile marches from the town at the head of the estuaries to the nearest deer grounds, and so numerous were the deer that rarely any pair of hunters returned without the carcass of a deer slung on a shoulder pole. Twenty or more deer provided every family one meal of red meat every day.

It happened that more than twenty of the Guale warriors who wintered in the more genial sun of the Altamata went there unaccompanied by their wives or daughters. In the first place, young women are less mindful of cold weather than are young men, proved by the fact they are comfortable in lighter dress. I had noticed that Indian women swam or waded in waters more chill than white men relished. In fact Doctor Jones had told me what I deemed an anatomical fact: that women had a thin layer of fat under the skin which Nature had not seen fit to give to men. Also some of their women did not like the long tramp of sixty or more miles. Adultery was a sin severely punished in the Muskhogean nation; but the definition of the term among Indians was somewhat loose; the offense was in major or minor degrees. Certainly the lending of wives to honored guests making long visits was a somewhat common practice in certain tribes. As a matter of fact, the explanation of which I did not attempt to seek, what Reverend Powell called miscegenation became for the first time somewhat common between our bachelors and fine-looking Indian women.

It was no shock to the older heads among our males, who realized human needs as well as the necessity of regulation of their gratifying. Doctor Jones was among this number. He pointed out that no civilization of which he had ever read had not provided for the latter by custom or institution. Even his church, while never condoning copulation except by married couples, had countenanced concubinage as practiced between Spanish colonists in the West Indies and healthy Indian girls who had been solemnly baptized in the Christian faith. Another great factor in Doctor Jones's complacency was these more northerly tribes did not suffer from a social disease common but not severe in its effects among Mexican Indian women, but devastating when contracted by white men.

At the opposite end of the pole was Edward Powell. He did not rave or rant; but he was deeply grieved as well as outraged, and demanded that I put a stop to the race mingling by imposing the most severe penalties for its occurrence. This I was not in position to do by spiritual or temporal force, or so inclined. Yes, some children of mixed blood would be the consequence. But the child goes with its mother, by law and custom; in everything but tint of skin they would grow up into Guales as good as their half-brothers or sisters. Other objectors to the behavior of our wayward bachelors were our spinsters and married women. The latter did not desire pursuit by these men; without exception they were faithful wives; but on principle they fitted the ancient phrase, dogs in the manger. No men with present wives that I knew of joined these forays as far as I knew. I did not join them because of a temporary troth I felt with Winifred and of a far more mysterious and illogical thing, my relationship with Weechee. Richard did not, partly because avid hunting exhausted his energies and inclinations and forces within his being kept secret from all.

The winter was damp and chill, but no more severe than Wiltshire winters. Since our present latitude as revealed by the astrolabe was about twenty degrees south of Wiltshire, this was hard to understand. We fed well enough; we kept our persons reasonably clean; we repaired our gear; because of constant hunting our band of fifty became truly expert archers. March brought temperate weather, so I did not await the spring equinox for all the party under me, marchers and boatsmen alike, to resume our southward journey.

On a warm and sunlit morning, when the boatmen had taken their seats on the thwarts, and our marchers had formed their lines ready to throw their packs upon their backs, the Guale bade us farewell in a fashion not even Doctor Jones had ever known to have occurred between seeming-stolid Indians and palefaces. The squaws assembled, and one of their virgins, a beautiful maiden, took her stand in front of them, her breasts bared. She sang the stanzas of a song we thought extempore, of deep and poetical meaning, and all the women joined in the chorus. It was in the minor key, with beautiful and touching phrases, and a song of woe.

When the song ended, I nodded to Weechee. Instantly she removed her deerskin shirt, and began to sing in the language of the Calusa. She had a pure sweet voice, clear and strong, and she sang a song she had remembered between sleep and wake, without knowing the meaning of the words. When she paused, all of we palefaces joined in a chorus which was at least in the spirit of the stanzas, and not in great disharmony with the melody. It was a peasant song that we sang at harvest home, and these were its simple words:

"Goodbye, dear fields, in summer so green,
In the sun's bright shine, and the rippling wind,
Hark to the song of our Harvest Queen,
And do not believe we are dumb and blind.
We know whence comes our power to do,
To toil and to dance and to sing and to love,
Aye, all of these wonders derive from you
And through you we are blessed by our God above."

Weechee retired from her position and put on her shirt. Our boatmen began to stroke their heavily laden crafts. Our marchers slung their packs for the short walk to the Guales' landing, to which the braves were running in order to man their flat-bottomed punts. Each of these with a single rower took three of our party for the mile-wide crossing of the estuary. Our sea division took down the estuary toward the sea; when our marchers had landed and the elbows of our left arms had been pressed by friendly hands they followed a well-beaten path that led to Chatufo, a Guale town at the confluence between the Ogeechee and Canochee rivers. This region we would gain before sunset tomorrow and here we would meet our boatmen to ferry us to the southern shore.

Whether at last we gained a refuge or if we were foiled, whether we lived or whether we died, we were living a great adventure.

2

Ogeechee River was a small river, as North American rivers flow. Still we spent three days in its crossing because of the swamps that flanked it on both sides, densely thick with avid growth, with many creeks deep enough to drown us, mudbanks, and treacherous ponds, and infested with rattlesnakes, the largest having diamond-shaped markings on their backs, and with a spade-headed viper, mainly a fish and frog killer, not quite as large but mud-colored and dangerous. Because of the white membranes in his mouth that we saw when he opened his fanged jaw, the men called him cottonmouth. The men poled the boats when they could; and when they could not our whole band portaged them through thickets, over rotting logs and amid stumps. We reached high, dry forest at last, the boats returning to the main channel and from thence to the sea. Daubed with mud from head to foot, Winifred knelt to her Deity—somehow I felt He was not the same as Him we worshiped—and wept.

In a clear stream we marchers bathed, the men and women not as careful as once they were to shield our nakedness. Our soap cakes were long since exhausted; now we used a mixture of fine wood-ashes with deer-fat, what we called Indian soap but which Wiltshire peasants and even yeomen knew well how to make. Thereafter we marched behind a welter of rivers and marshes entering great sounds on either side of St. Catherine's Island, to a point on the Olatama, also known as the Altamata, to a great loop just above the juncture of the north branches and the south branches at the estuary. This was the appointed rendezvous with our boats, which we had reached in six days' march, but our marchers who had penetrated the swamps to the riverbank watched and waited four days more in growing despair, until they finally spied the two larger boats making bravely toward them. The smallest boat had sprung an irreparable leak, but its crew of two and most of its cargo had been saved.

Again we crossed the swamp to the northern bank of the river, were ferried across, and forced our way through the swamp beyond its southern bank. Again we washed our clothes and bathed our bodies in the first clear stream we found. Winifred entered the water from behind a thicket, yet while she did not once expose her body except as a fading glimmer, every one knew that she swam naked. Other spinsters followed her example, with not such care as she had taken. It did not matter to me—modesty had become a luxury we could hardly afford—and the men paid little mind; still our descent from the customs of civilization must be checked at some point. Oddly enough, Weechee, who had gone stark naked as a child slave on Saona Island, wore a loin cloth, which I suspected was the same Thomas Warner had furnished her so far away in distance and event, but not much more than a year by the implacable count of time.

The moon waxed and waned, once, twice, thrice. Long since, the great flocks of northward flying waterfowl looked down at our stumbling, to them almost stationary file; and now we saw only wood ducks of gorgeous feather. From the Altamata we had crossed two nameless rivers, far less than she, yet flanked with swamps where grew white cypress and water oaks, the latter draped with moss. Our boatmen, by making a long loop, ferried us across both rivers and told us that they emptied in a bay we had passed on our northward sail to Roanoke, which they remembered by a headland our captains called Pelican Point, thronged with these very birds.

This spring and summer we had lost four men, one of them Thomas Ellis, who had stopped on the Indian trail, clutched his breast, turned black in the face, and died. And on the very next march Jane Mannering was struck in the breast by the shaft of an ambushed Indian, of whom we caught no glimpse. When she died in the middle of the night, only whimpering a little, it struck me that King Death had begun to spurn us commoners, and to choose gentry and near-gentry for his attendants in his dark halls.

Deer were numerous; Indians extremely rare. The latter did not breed fast enough and were killed off too soon. We camped out far more frequently than before, but with no great discomfort; actually we were learning, as soldiers do, to provide for ourselves well; and the heavy rains from which we could only partly shield ourselves with our oiled cloths, chilled us ere we were again warmed by the ardent sun. Another change in our circumstance was that we encountered fewer deciduous forests and more pine forests. The species had longer needles than on any pine trees I had seen. They furnished us with a great quantity of rosin, and because they were magnificently tall and thick of bole, there was no heavy underbrush; hence our walking was better than before.

Often and more often we made our marches without Indian guides. An equal worry was that Storyteller had been this far south only twice in his years of wandering; except for his amazing memory we could not have found the few towns and Indian trails. I began to fear we would not reach St. Augustine before we must halt for winter. It would not be severe, but all-day exposure to blowing and chill rains might undermine the health of my sturdy followers. Also, the Spaniards were more likely to accept us at the break of winter, because my fifty archers could contribute so generously to their food supply.

The Indian name for this whole region, Storyteller told us, was Gama; and he had no notion what the word meant. To the south were regions called Timucua and to the southeast again Guale. I could no longer untangle the complex of Indian tribes; and for such as follow us, or ever read this chronicle, there were Yui, Yamiscarron, Timucua, Talassee, Oconee, and Saturiwa. The boundaries of their hunting ground was most vague. Actually I believed that all were members or a kin of the great Muskhogean nation.

As we approached the crossing of two great Indian trails, one running generally north and south and the other east and west, I had an evil dream just before waking in the September dawn. In this dream, black clouds had spread swiftly across the sky, eclipsing the sun, and then a torrent of rain poured down upon me. I was almost blinded by it but could feel its spreading flood creeping toward my knees. I waked depressed, and then tried to rationalize the dream, and looked backward over our course to see if we had made some disastrous mistake. After crossing the greater of the two rivers, we wished to make for a river called Santa Maria by the Spanish on which we were to rendezvous with our boats. Storyteller thought it only one day's march; but a friendly faced Timucuan Indian whose right hand was cut off at the wrist, and who was gathering black walnuts, told us it was about twice this far. Also it went westward rather than southward as Storyteller had assumed. Hence we must follow the south bank of this river which he called Satilla, and the greater of the two Indian trails led in this direction.

We marched fully twenty miles in two days. Since we had hurried because of threatening clouds, and had met with no time-consuming obstacles, I considered it possible that we had marched twenty-five or even thirty miles. Various lesser trails had branched off both northward and southward, and early in the morning, under a densely clouded sky, the main trail dwindled to what was little more than a footpath. I expected the heavy downpour of my dream, but it did not come, and instead the path wriggled from right to left and back again. About noon it made a rather sharp turn, but I could not tell the direction. On such occasions on dark days it was Thomas Warner's practice to put the point of his knife against his thumb nail, where it almost always cast a perceptible shadow. Today we could not detect it, nor could the sharp, young eyes of Weechee. Manteo's usual guide, the growth of moss on the tree trunks, likewise failed us. So we put blind faith in a brook which the trail followed, and which we deemed must lead us to Rio Santa Maria.

Our blind march might have been fifteen miles. All were tired and discouraged, with hauntings of fright, and we camped in expectation of heavy rain. It did not fall in the morning and I determined to take the first well-worn trail we should encounter, that would certainly lead to some village. We had hardly started when I located the sun in breaking clouds which revealed the frightening fact that we had been traveling north. Only a little farther on our trail it turned sharply west, enlarged by an entering trail from the north.

We came to a native village, but we durst not enter it, for at least a hundred braves began shouting in fury, drawing their bows. I presume they took us for Spaniards, the tale of whose kidnapings and other cruelties to the Indians had sped far. Our shouting "No *españols*" and "No *hombres*" did not the least good. But the brook had grown larger now, flowing generally west, and we were certain a big river was not far off.

Actually it was twenty weary miles. We gained its banks in a forced march, and camped on its banks. This we dared not doubt was the headwaters of the Santa Maria, the only considerable river of which we had heard in this part of the country.

On its south bank ran a good Indian trail through thickets; this we followed until it ended at a ford, but rainfall had swollen it to the degree that we dared not attempt a crossing. We could only follow it, as if in a trance of fatigue and fear, in blind faith that it was the Santa Maria. But it led us to no village and instead into swampy ground.

What could we do but go on? Follow a brook to a stream, a stream to a river, a river to some settlement—this is the oldest of advice to persons and parties who have lost their way. Perhaps the swampy ground would soon again turn firm. Instead it began to quake beneath our feet.

Thus my dream came true. We had entered a dim swamp, the dimensions of which we did not know, but these it must certainly have, and somehow, some way we must find its end.

Often as we plunged onward, up to our knees in mud, I thought upon turning back the weary way to where we had received advice from the one-handed Indian. But could we find the place in the immense unpeopled forest and the maze of Indian and deer trails? We began to encounter runs, to cross which we must wade hip-deep. There were few heavy brush thickets, indeed the cypress were tall, their knees huge in girth, and draped with darkling moss, but there were many vines, to cut through which we used our hunting knives. We saw half a dozen immense alligators on a sand bar in the river. All of us broke off sticks because of numerous snakes—especially those we called cottonmouth and another species with a pink belly, the color running up under its lower jaw—and whether these were poisonous we knew not. There were palmetto palms, around which the ground was dry, but huge rattlesnakes with diamond-shaped markings far more numerous. Wild flowers, many of them highly colored and beautiful, were species we had never seen. There were large snow-white lilies that somehow made me think of Winifred. I would pluck her a bouquet, I thought—and then wondered if I were mad.

If not, I would soon be so; and so would all my followers. The swamp was utterly and deathly silent except for the occasional hiss of a snake, the harsh outcry of a bird, or the rush and splash of an alligator entering some pond or sun. The trees mourned in low-hanging moss.

We were doomed now, I thought. This was the end of the trail upon which we had embarked so bravely, at my provocation. Instead of Indian arrows, we would smother in muck. God knew I wished that I had confessed to a murder I did not commit, whereby my fellow colonists would still be relatively safe on Roanoke Island, instead of my having led them to death in this woodland hell. Nor was doom as far distant as I had first believed. William Berde, that stout yeoman, disappeared from sight, so suddenly that he had no time to utter an outcry, and the only trace of his vanishing was wet, bubbling sand. We were marching abreast rather than in file, testing for firmer ground, and one after another of my companions found death instead. Anthony Cage was bitten on the thigh by an immense snake coiled on top of a rotted root. Once he had been High Sheriff of Huntington and he was a brave man, for he killed the snake with his club, beheld its diamond-shaped markings, and then quietly lay down as if going to bed. It must be that the two-inch fang had pierced an artery and injected venom there, for he waved at us feebly, panted heavily for no more than a moment, then cast his soul.

John Prat, urchin son of Roger Prat, began to cry out from a run he had tried to wade, and his sire leaped to help him, only to be clutched by muck and sucked under, and I reckoned they had died in each other's arms or hand in hand. At a big run all of us joined hands, but in crossing we waded in muck, and the chain became broken, and when we gained the farther bank, three of our number had disappeared, John Ernest, Thomas Smith, and Agnes Wood, who had hoped to join her husband, John Wood, one of the fifteen or eighteen men left by Sir Richard Grenville, and at last had done so. Five minutes later James Lacy, shrinking back from a *cuguara* boldly stalking toward us, stepped into quicksand and died screaming.

We had already waded across a shallow lake. Now there spread before a large lake, with reed-grown banks, and its ends we could not see because of the dense woods. And then I saw something that caused a weak glow of hope to rise in my soul. In the deep shade of a cypress tree on the farther bank was what looked like a boat, with a shape in one end that might be an occupant. But I could hardly believe the latter was an Indian, it looked so small.

"It is a little Indian boy," rose a voice beside me. Weechee's sharp eyes had told her so. "He's fishing."

We began to shout. It was a wonder, almost a miracle, he did not take fright at our frenzied band, hasten to the bank, and disappear. Instead he raised his anchor and picked up his paddle and began to stroke in our direction. The prayer rose in my heart that Storyteller could speak to him. After what seemed an interminable wait, that prayer came true.

3

At about fifty yards from us, the boy checked his stroke and called. Indeed he asked a question, of which I caught one word which was *hombre*, the Indian's common name for a Spaniard.

Storyteller shook his head and in some tongue I had never heard him speak answered that we were not *hombres*, but Englishmen.

Storyteller's very appearance reassured the lad. Fearlessly he stroked to the bank, pulled his boat into the reeds, and walked to meet us. At once he and Storyteller fell into conversation. The lad was pointing due south.

In a moment Storyteller turned to me, his face beaming, and revealed what he had learned.

"He asked me how we had gotten here. He seemed incredulous when I told him we had followed down a river. Then I asked him if it was Rio Santa Maria, and he answered no, it was Rio Suwannee. But the headwaters of the Santa Maria are only one day's march, and he knows a path through thickets and around the deeper runs and the beds of quicksand. But first he will lead us to his father's hut. His father is a *cimarrón*. That means an outcast from his tribe."

All of our band except Storyteller, Manteo, Weechee, and I watched with pale, strained faces as the lad, turning sharply, hastened to his boat. Then all of us laughed wildly as we perceived his errand. He had gone to get his day's catch—a string of catfish.

When he left his roughly made shallow-draft boat, he did not lock it or even tie it to a stake. Plainly there was no one to meddle with it in this vast swamp, and no hard wind among the close-ranked trees to set it adrift. He told Storyteller that his name was Tomay. It recalled to my mind the name of Towaye, the Croatan Indian who had deserted our colony soon after our arrival at Roanoke. Storyteller could not tell me what the name meant; all that I knew was, I would never forget it.

With his fish string in one hand and a pole for testing the firmness of ground, he began to lead us along the shores of the lake, then took off on a deer path in a generally eastward direction. The path had many curves and loops to avoid heavy muck and quicksand, and his young eyes were ever alert for a mottled hide in the grass or fallen leaves. However, we passed within twenty yards of a veritable herd of huge crocodiles, twenty at least, lying close together on the sandy bank of a woodland pool. In less than ten minutes he had fetched us to a hut, with a roof of palm fronds, walls of fallen tree-branches, and wattled with clay or mud. It had a door, but no windows or chimney, so perhaps there was a hole in the roof for emitting smoke from some sort of fireplace used on days of heavy rain.

Tomay's sire, a fine-looking Indian of about thirty-five, emerged from the hut to meet us, and dropped on his knees before Storyteller. When the latter bade him rise, he gestured toward us and asked one question.

"*Españols?*"

"English."

"I have no name," the Indian went on in what I guessed was the Cusabo language, a guess that Storyteller verified when he translated the utterance. "I have no woman, no tribe, no friend, no miko, no kewas, not even a son from my loins although I have Tomay, whom I stole from the Oconee when he was an infant. I am a *cimarrón;* meaning one cast forth from his people. I may not leave Oke Fenokee, but it gives Tomay and me a living, and now and then we may trade healing herbs and snake fangs and skins with Timucuans on the lower Rio Santa Maria for things useful to us. Will you and your people eat the food gathered and cooked by such a one?"

"Aye, and in joy."

"I have stored cakes of the corns of water oak, wild honey, dried fish and venison in abundance, sweet tubers that are good baked in the fire, the eggs of waterfowl pickled in brine, some raccoon, opossum, and wild cat meat likewise salted and sun-dried but belike too rank for your taste, and the aged juice of swamp apples and berries and grapes to wash down what you put in your mouths and do not spit out. When you address me, pray you address me as Siminole, for as I told you, my name is lost to me forever, and hence I have no spirit to go to the Sun when I die."

"Siminole, we will rest a short time, scrape off some of the muck and mud, and then eat and sleep."

We would never know, Storyteller told me, what offense this man had committed whereby he was so banished and bereft. Of this he was forbidden to speak. But when the two had talked a little more, Storyteller told me that Oke Fenokee meant "Quaking Ground." The outcast said that on the morrow he would lead us to the Trader's Trail on the Santa Maria, which followed the river to the sea. He was careful not to touch any of us with his hands or body, and he managed without giving offense to avoid our touch.

After our abundant supper, the two talked again, and when Storyteller had given a minute description of the one-handed Indian who had misdirected us, Siminole had identified him as a Guale whose hand had been hacked off by the Spanish for some unknown offense. The "outside" people knew him by the Guale name for the fiddler crab, which scuttle in great numbers in tidal runs at low tide, and which have one long claw and one short.

"Fiddler Crab's heart is black with hate for all palefaces," Siminole said simply.

Our party gained Rio Santa Maria in two easy and safe marches. Once there, all bathed and washed mud-daubed clothes. We were now off the quaking ground and only one sharp fear remained in my bosom and brain—that our boatmen had given us up for lost and were seeking us on some distant coast. Out of the three remaining burning glasses, I gave Tomay one and showed him how to use it. I had two left, one for myself and one to give away in some extremity of fortune.

Siminole would accept no gift of any kind, and made but one entreaty—that Storyteller cut a cane, and strike him thrice as hard as he could across his naked back. Knowing his people well, our brown-skinned, latter-day minnesinger did so. Then we saw what was almost a smile on Siminole's face. The foster father and his foster son tramped homeward without a backward glance.

To our inexpressible joy, we found our boatmen the following day. They had drawn up the two boats and pitched camp on the riverbank and had sworn to stay there a full moon if need be; and if by then we did not appear, Cuthbert White, himself a Roman Catholic, would entreat shelter for himself and his companions from Franciscan monks who had a priory at San Pedro, near St. Augustine; and by their help, return to Europe. They had had mishaps and minor adventures, but none had been such fools as to wander into a vast and deadly swamp.

Had we turned directly south from the southernmost loop of the Satilla River we would have gained the north bank of the Santa Maria in two days' march. Had we not been misdirected because of one man's hate we would have saved the lives of eight of our companions and not been lost in the wilderness fifteen or more days—I had lost exact count—and marched well over a hundred unnecessary miles. I had proven a faulty leader and gave thought to resigning my post. This I discussed with Richard, Doctor Jones, Ananias Dare, Thomas Hewett, Thomas Warner, and Cuthbert White. Without a single exception, all urged me to remain in command, reminding me that the most brilliant military commander had never fought a major battle without loss of life. I did not make the proposal to Edward Powell, because I knew already how he would answer: that I do so immediately and appoint him in my place. But the main reason I retained my position was that I had not lost confidence in my leadership, that I knew of none in our party who was better fitted, and that I loved power.

There was a beach path to a point on the Tolomato River across
from St. Augustine, and an inland path west of that river and the
far-flung marshes of other rivers. The choice was an easy one, on
account not only of the villages of peaceful fishing tribes on the coastal
strip, but of it being shorter, better walking, and requiring no more
and perhaps less crossing of waterways by boats. Again we could keep
abreast and in touch with our boatmen. So we marchers set off southward down the beach of Guale Island, discovered and named by
the French, and where a few Spanish and French settlers now lived
at peace. It was just below the Santa Maria entrance and from its
southmost point, to be gained in two easy marches or in one if at all
pressed. We must be ferried across Bird Island Sound to the northern
beach hardly a league long, march the three miles, be ferried again
across a narrow inlet, march along a beach for less than half a mile,
then be ferried across a broad inlet of Rio San Mateo. Then we could
be landed on the north end of one of the longest unbroken beaches
our seafarers knew, running approximately forty miles south by east
to St. Augustine Inlet.

We had now changed our identity, although not our nationality
which we could not hide. It came about through Doctor Jones's abrupt
suggestion immediately after being landed on Guale Island.

"Hark to me, Martyn," he said. "If we are to keep peace with any
Spanish we should meet with, and especially with the dwellers of
St. Augustine, we had better forget we were once of Raleigh's colo-
nies."

"Because all Spaniards love not Raleigh?" I asked, after a brief
start.

"His name is anathema to all Spaniards and all Indians under
Spanish sway. In all truth, they abhor him. Along with Sir Francis
Drake and Sir Richard Grenville he stands as the arch-type of English
privateer, buccaneer, and pirate most hated by King Philip. All Spanish
and their Indians know that Drake and Grenville were involved with
all of Raleigh's ventures. To have the least chance of being admitted
to St. Augustine—England and Spain are almost certainly at war—we
have to claim to be a misguided and foolhardy group of private English citizens who decided to settle in the New World, found our own
money, hired a ship, and landed at—well, say near Cape Hatoraske.
The very mention of Roanoke—Raleigh putting Lane there threw Philip
into fits of rage—would damn us."

"Would not the St. Augustine officials know that White's colony had
disappeared and put two and two together?" I asked.

"I would say that would be highly unlikely. They might not even
know of its establishment or that Lane fled to England. You have

personal knowledge of the vast distances of the New World—truly we
all have cause to—but there is virtually no communication between
nation and nation—almost none between tribe and tribe. There are
no roads, only dim paths. There are no letters, only signal fires on
very rare occasions and once in a blue moon an Indian storyteller
wandering from village to village. For the love of God, do not let
anyone let the Spanish know we are Raleigh's people. Do you agree?"
And I had never heard Doctor Jones speak more earnestly.

"I certainly do agree. The plan and its reasons will be announced
to all after supper tonight. We will deal with the Governor of St.
Augustine through an ambassador, and he should speak Spanish
fluently, and that means Thomas Warner. We will hold our people
back from their barricades. But even so, if England and Spain are at
war as we both believe, I can hardly credit the citizens of a town
ravished and probably burned by Sir Francis Drake three years ago
accepting Englishmen of whatever skin. I would far more likely expect
their cannonading."

"I am well aware you harbored that doubt, almost a conviction,
from the first. So did I. But you were on firm ground when you saw
we must flee Roanoke or be massacred, and you had to hold out
some sort of hope for the fly-by-nights. Any man essaying to lead the
people must lie plausibly when necessary."

"Sir, I thank you for that understanding. It is a deep consolation
to me for my great mistake that cost eight lives."

"Forget that if you can, Martyn. And as for almost certain refusal
at St. Augustine, I think you have an alternate plan, harbored from the
first. If it is what I think, I will approve of it."

"Yes, I have an alternate plan. In the language of a card game called
Hazard, I have an ace in the hole. If it wins, we would find safety
and a living until the war is won or lost. To quote an old saw—while
there's life, there's hope."

4

We made the march to the southern tip of the Island in one day.
Here we met the boats and spent the night on the beach; then were
ferried across Bird Island Sound before noon the next day. In the
afternoon we marched three miles, were ferried across an inlet hardly
a cable's length in width, marched along three furlongs of coast, and
then were ferried across the mouth of the San Mateo to a Satawuran
town named Moloa. In the three long marches that followed, Fate
and the weather could not do enough for us in the way of Indian
villages and cloudless skies. These Indians were Satawura, fishermen

and clam diggers and waterfowl hunters with bows and arrows. In spring they ate hen-size eggs that giant turtles laid in the sand. In one of these villages we found an anchorite, the first paleface we had seen since our bloody meeting with Bear Hunter. The recluse gazed upon us mildly but did not answer the questions Tom Warner put to him in Spanish. Perhaps he was vowed to silence.

Then, in four trips, our boats landed us below the marsh fronting St. Augustine. There were still fire-blackened ruins, reminders of Drake's raid three years before, but a new town was being built, its *presidio* already raised. As we were assembling, outside an earthen embankment, I spoke briefly with Weechee. Knowing the business was grave, she fixed her slightly slanted eyes on mine.

The month was October; more than a year had passed since she had come to flower; and she was no longer the little girl I had found in a thicket on Saona Island off Santo Domingo. Well past fourteen, she stood five and a half feet in her sandals; she had the high-breasted slender form seen in the elite tribes, hunters and warriors; and her countenance was of a different cast from any Indian maiden I had observed. It was obviously Indian, under her raven-black hair; and her cheekbones were wide, her eyes long, narrow, and brilliant, and forehead and nose on the same slant. Also it was patently aristocratic, with narrow nose, finely molded bones, and rounded lips. These I had not kissed for some days. I had known I could not do so in a brotherly fashion; and the vow I had made to Governor White on the night of her finding, now antedated, still put me in restraint. But for that matter, I had not kissed Winifred either; she did not by sign or word invite me to do so.

"Weechee, we are going to ask admittance to the town, to remain here through the winter and perhaps longer, until a ship of some neutral nation will take us home."

"I will not go across the sea," she answered. "I will find an Indian who with his wife will take me to my father's tribe, and there he can be sure of generous reward."

This remark was a fortunate one, for me; it led straight to what I had wished to say without quite knowing how to begin.

"Weechee, I do not think we will gain admittance here. The people are Spanish and have reasons to hate us English. In that case, could we not all go to your father's tribe? Would he refuse us permission to dwell there, I know not how long, and fish and hunt and raise corn?"

"I do not know that my father still lives. I have not seen his face for six suns. But if he does, would he refuse friendship with the chieftain who saved me from *el señor?*"

"Not if he is a great chieftain."

"He is the greatest in all this land. This is shown by his name, which only lately I have remembered. He is head chieftain of the Calusa nation, which in width is five twenties of what you call miles, meaning a distance we can walk briskly in ten and five tiltings of what Doctor Jones calls his minute glass. My father's kingdom is in length ten twenty miles. And the name by which he is called by underchiefs is Tzin Cacique."

Even if Weechee's estimation of her father's nation was wildly ex-aggerated, I could not doubt the breath-taking significance of this title. Certainly it had been borrowed from the Aztec nation, and Doctor Jones had used it repeatedly on his dissertations on Cortés' con-quest of Mexico as written by Spanish priests and translated into Latin. It meant no less than head chieftain or noble chieftain.

"Weechee, do you wish to go there?"

"It is my heart's wish, but I think it is a very long way."

"You are sure it is part of the great land that the Spanish call Florida?"

"Yes, I am sure. A great Spanish *cacique*, in splendid dress, who came to my father's house when I was eight years old, called it so."

"Do you want me to come there also?"

"Yes, if Winifred is not then your woman."

"Well, I will soon know whether I can come, or must stay here."

A Spanish officer from the *presidio*, escorted by a small guard, was making toward the embankment outside of which waited Thomas Warner and our colonists, all of whose faces revealed deep strain. The two men spoke for perhaps ten minutes; then the officer turned sharply on his heel and returned to the *presidio*, no doubt to report to a superior. As soon as he had told our people that the Spanish answer would be forthcoming soon, Thomas Warner reported to me.

"I told the don what you said to tell him, no more or less. But he told me quite a lot of news. Spain and England are indeed at war. The last visit of a Spanish ship to St. Augustine was in August. King Philip had assembled what the officer called the Armada, the greatest fleet of warships in history, so he said, with the intention of invading and conquering England. It sailed from Lisbon on May 18—one hun-dred and thirty vessels, mainly galleons, and seventeen thousand sol-diers. The officer believes that the invasion and conquests are by now established fact."

My heart sank but I spoke boldly, for Weechee's ears as well as Thomas Warner's.

"If Drake and Sir John Hawkins are in command of the English fleet, I doubt it."

"There is some more news that bodes ill for our welcome here. The Governor of St. Augustine, a grand *señor,* is not in residence now, but is on a warship gone north with no other purpose than to destroy Sir Walter's colony, which he thinks is on Chesapeake Bay."

"Well, any way you count it, it's a good thing we got out of Roanoke when we had the chance."

"I'll return to my place at the gate. The Spanish officer told me that the answer would be given us in a few minutes and will be from the alcalde and the captain of the garrison."

The officer had been quite right; there had been no prolonged conference; he reappeared, walking briskly. To Thomas Warner he spoke no more than two sentences, then turned his back and walked away. Only shaking his head to the question in the imploring eyes of our comrades, Thomas came straight to me.

"The answer is short and to the point. We will be admitted only as prisoners of war, which of course means slavery. And if we will not surrender we must take ourselves off at once, or they will fire on us with all the guns of the *presidio.*"

I went up and faced our little throng. It had once numbered one hundred and twelve; now there were about ninety. They already knew they had been refused—the shake of Thomas Warner's head had told them so—yet they stood staunchly and I knew, God help me, that the hope I saw in their faces was born of confidence in me.

"Form your lines and sling your packs," I told them, "and we'll march to the landing place of our boats. Then we'll be ferried across as fast as we can to what the Spanish call Isla de Conch, which is across Rio San Juan from the beach we left this morning."

Only one voice was raised in reply—that of Edward Powell.

"'Vengeance is mine, sayeth the Lord.' And I am his proven prophet."

Two crossings had been made of the mile-wide estuary, in the crowded boats, and I was waiting with about twenty-five of my fellows for the third and last, when a visitor approached our hushed cluster. He wore the cowl and gray cloak of the Monastic Order of Saint Francis, whom we called Gray Friars, and he carried under his arm a roll of paper about five feet long. This he presented to me in complete silence.

Before I could speak he turned his head and spoke one phrase to our whole company: *"Vaya con Dios."* (God go with you.)

When he had gone I unrolled the scroll and gave it one quick glance. It was a hand-drawn map of the great land the Spanish called Florida, showing some rivers and bays and lakes, but the larger part of it was marked *Tierra Desconocida.* I had heard Thomas Warner use this expression many times and need not be told that it meant "land unknown."

"Storyteller, please ask the Timucuan if he knows the name of the good priest, who regards us as heretics and yet has shown us mercy?" I proposed.

The Timucua, in the region of St. Augustine, were one of the most unique, I could truthfully say outlandish, of all North American tribes. They were obsessed with the adornment of tattoo; not only their faces and arms but every inch of skin on their bodies was covered by tattoo in various colors and highly elaborate designs and symbols. They wore a minimum of clothes—in their own encampments they probably went naked—but seen at a distance a Timucua warrior appeared fully dressed. The greatly decorated fellow to whom Storyteller spoke made pompous answer.

"That is the great werowance of the palefaces, who has come hence from his mission at San Pedro, Father Balthasar Lopez."

From other Indians, some of them far away, I had heard mention of this Franciscan friar, one of six or so in all Florida, whose mission was a league distant from St. Augustine. I could not doubt that he had heard of our approach to the town, and perhaps from a distance he had seen our paltry line and knew well how we would be received at the barricade. Yet he had gone out of his way to help us pursue our journey. I thought that his action should be stern reproof of his fellow Catholics who persecuted Protestants, and Catholic haters and beheaders among so-called reformists. Yet the day was still far off, although inevitable, when some great Pope would unite the strengths of all Christian faiths against the enemies of the Son of Man and of mankind itself.

The two boats were now returning. Our remainder got aboard with their rolls, and the rowers stroked strongly against the making tide. We landed on Conch Island near a fishing village, and since the sun was low, we pitched camp here for the night. After our supper of toasted fish and maize cakes bought from the Indians with colored cloth, I had some of our number gather driftwood for a high fire. It was somewhat scarce on this beach, because of its use by Indians; still we found enough. The wood had absorbed so much salt that it burned with beautiful red, green, and orange flame.

Standing in the center of the ring of travelers, I repeated the message that Thomas Warner had brought from the alcalde and the captain of the Spanish garrison. But, I continued, I knew of a certain haven both from the Spanish and from hostile Indians, and there we could dwell, hunting and fishing and raising corn, until we were rescued. This might not occur for several years if the Spanish won the war, but its outcome would not affect our safety. Perhaps the greatest of all nations on the North American coast—Storyteller had informed me that the Calusa was certainly one of the very greatest—would be our protectors. He himself had never visited it, but he had heard it described as a good land, of very rich soil and an abundance of game; Weechee had been born there, the daughter of its head chieftain, and she had assured me of our welcome there.

At these last tidings the faces of the people brightened. They had long realized that she was the daughter of a great sagamore; at first they had often spoken of the help she might be to the company, and now their words would be proven true.

"How far is it?" Edward Powell asked civilly, almost his only utterance since his outburst at the command and the threat we had received at St. Augustine.

"Sir, I do not know, and anyway I do not believe it matters very much. It is certainly our best chance, and maybe our only chance, to survive."

"Shouldn't our whole body—or at least the leaders—hold a conference before we decide?" Richard Spencer asked.

"I decline to hold a conference. But if you like you can vote whether or not you still want me as your leader. If you wish to elect some other, I will obey his orders."

"I offer myself for the position," Edward Powell said quickly. "It was what God intended from the first."

"Sir, we others are not so sure of God's intentions as you are," Doctor Jones said quietly after a short pause. "I move that Martyn Sutton remain our leader. If you are with me, raise your right hands."

Every right hand but three shot up swiftly and decisively. After a few seconds Richard Spencer raised his hand. The two that did not raise were Edward Powell's and the Storyteller's, and the latter did not know the point at issue, and anyway he took no part in the paleface discussions. Whereupon almost all the people clapped their hands.

"Any Injun country that's good enough for ye is good enough for me," declared my fellow jailbird, John Hynde, in a ringing tone.

"Yes, we will go on with high hope," Doctor Jones said quietly. "We have fought a good fight so far, under our young leader, and we will continue to fight whenever we are called upon to do so. It may be we will never see British shores again. If not, and the most of us live to considerable age, not meagerly but well, and have proved our British hardihood, indeed our heritage, and have adventures and a fair share of human life's rewards, I think we should never rue our departure from England and our fate. Martyn, there are too small casks of Italian brandy in the larger boat that have never been broached. Also we have a copper kettle, not yet traded, which can be filled and refilled. Let us pass that bowl, and all of us take one or two swallows of the cordial drink. And we will drink to our brother-hood, our fellowship in adventure, in joy and in sorrow, in good times and bad, and in victory and defeat. And that brotherhood is itself a victory for our lonesome human souls."

Not to my amazement, but to my own immeasurable joy, a great shout went up. The Indians came out of their houses and gazed at us in the great silence of surprise.

Chapter XVII

LAND OF WIDE WATERS

1

The moons waxed and waned. The seasons changed. Our luck alternately rose and fell. When on the march our pace was faster than before, because every member of our land party was a trained marcher, rid of all unnecessary fat, and with practiced, almost tireless muscles. He knew how to traverse deep sands with a minimum of effort, to feel his way with short poles across bogs, to recognize shallow waters from deep before he was in them, to make his way through thorn thickets when he must, but otherwise circumvent them. At various times we fed heartily, at other times our fare was meager, sometimes we half-starved.

When Doctor Jones's astrolabe told us we were about thirty miles north of the twenty-eighth degree of latitude—Roanoke Island was about the thirty-sixth degree, and hence about five hundred miles by crow flight from our starting point, but eight hundred or even more because of our wanderings—we received what our most pious could well believe a direct dispensation from Providence.

On a day of heavy inshore wind we saw what was plainly a ship on fire, a mile or more down the coast, and perhaps a mile from the sands. The vessel blazed fiercely because of the wind, and suddenly there was a great, towering burst of flame amid wildly flying debris, followed a few seconds later by the deafening roar of an explosion. We could not doubt that flame had reached the vessel's powder magazine, and unless some of her hands had already fled her in her boats, not a human soul was saved.

We scanned the seas in vain in search of boats, but the sharpest eyes in our company made out what they had first thought was a school of porpoises near a sandspit extending from near the apex of a cape about a mile wide at its base. Then I was more inclined to believe the strongly swimming herd of eight or ten large creatures were some unknown species of sea monster. Not until they gained shallow water and then waded out on the sandspit, did I perceive they were horses.

In that instant of recognition also I perceived their great value to us, if we could catch them. Circumstances were almost incredibly favorable to our doing so. Beyond doubt they had come from the deck of the burning ship where they had been haltered; as the flames had neared them and they had begun to plunge, some merciful sailor had cut their halter ropes and driven them overside. Horses are good swimmers; the brisk wind was landward; but they were tired enough to stand awhile in the sunlight about halfway the length of the spit.

I bade all our men lay down their rolled packs and advance on the double-quick to the foot of the spit. Here we formed our line, about two yards apart, and began a slow advance toward the little herd. They saw us but took no alarm; they were used to the smell and sight of men; but as the spit narrowed and we closed ranks they began to give us uneasy glances and move outward on the spit. We continued our slow advance. Our intent was to come quietly up on the beasts, grasp their halter ropes which were from three to six feet in length, and hang on for dear life, even if some of us were dragged through the sands.

One mare allowed her rope to be grasped without trying to burst through our line. The others, in sudden panic, made the attempt; and getting in one another's way, and some of us being knocked down, we could not prevent the escape of two. But we had caught six, more precious to us than their weight in gold, and these quickly became docile.

From hence forward they would bear no graceful *caballeros*, but heavy packs. When the time would come to forsake our boats to go inland at about, I thought, twenty miles north of the twenty-seventh degree of latitude, they would be invaluable not only as burden bearers but for swimming us across, we clutching their tails, rivers too deep to wade.

I had chosen this course by detailed examination of our Spanish map, and by close questioning of Weechee. My most exciting discovery on the former was the words *Calusa Rey*, which I need not show to Thomas Warner to recognize as "King of the Calusa." A point indicated what was almost certainly his capital, which lay toward the southern end, near the western side, of the land called Florida. It lay to the southwest of an immense lake, the largest body of assumably fresh water that we had seen in all our travels, named *Lago Grande Calusa*.

My questioning of Weechee had been a long process, resulting in my gathering a little more information almost every day. The Indians that we saw in small temporary fishing villages on the coastal strip, she did not recognize as Calusa and thought they were a mixed breed, but occasionally she pricked up her ears at some word they uttered. But she could understand their lingo no more than did Story-teller. In our trying to circumvent what we thought was a beach lagoon but which proved to be an arm of the vast lagoons separating the coastal strip from the mainland and which we must cross in boats, we had come across a town indubitably Calusan. I identified the tribesmen instantly by their countenances, darker than Weechee's but like hers in general feature, and I would have surmised their identity by their obvious superiority over any Indians we had seen. The Spaniards had written that their only equals in the New World of their explorations were the Aztecs and the warlike and untamable Caribs, and presumably of the same basic stock. In fact the Calusa might well be Caribs, arriving here in their long dugout canoes not many centuries before.

In the same instant that I recognized these townsmen as Calusa, some of their number so recognized Weechee. They stared at her briefly, then glanced away, and I could hardly doubt that they sur-mised that she was of noble Calusan birth, by not only her aristo-cratic countenance but her metal headband. What was she doing with a pack of palefaces, they asked themselves? But they tried to give no sign of their curiosity; they stood aloof from her and from us. They were a tall, copper-colored people, with immense natural dignity that changed into hauteur when they exchanged glances with us white folk. The women's breasts were high and fine, their waists narrow, their limbs long; and they had long smooth muscles. Their scanty garments were plaited strips of palm leaf or interwoven Spanish moss; the warriors had coon tails fixed to their belts behind. The sides of their palm or cypress-wood houses were open to the air except for deep eves; some were of two or even three stories. The heads of the tools that I saw were either of conch shell, turtle shell, or bone. Their bows were heavy; their quivers indicated long arrows; but I could not see whether the points of these were metal or flint.

One very pretty maiden, clad only in a palm-leaf skirt, wore cop-per earplugs. I saw Weechee touch her own ears. Her eyes were in-drawn and brilliant, as she gave ear to the quiet talk of the Calusa.

"Walk among them Weechee," I told her. "If you understand any-thing they say, try to answer. Try to tell them you are the daughter of Tzin Cacique, on your way home."

She came up to them with grave demeanor, as was proper to a

princess of her nation. She did not permit intense strain that I knew
she felt appear in her face as she tried to answer their questions. To
an old headman who addressed her as *señorita,* and who evidently
had had dealings with the Spanish, she spoke very slowly; pointing
to herself.

"*Hija* . . . Tzin . . . Cacique . . . Calusa." She had used the Spanish
word for daughter, by which she was often addressed by Thomas
Warner.

The effect on the old underchief was startling. His stolidity was
instantly lost; he stared at Weechee as though he could not believe
his eyes, then at us. I motioned for Thomas Warner to go forward.
He did so, and spoke in distinct and simple Spanish. With painful
slowness, the aged Indian attempted to answer. He pointed to his
own ears, plainly referring to the absence of golden plugs in Weechee's ears.

I heard Thomas Warner's reply and caught the word Carib, and
then *prisionero.* The Indian nodded with his mouth agape; and I
surmised that he had heard of Weechee's abduction by the Caribs,
but still could not credit her presence here, so far from the Caribbean
islands, among palefaces of dress and appearance such as he had
never seen. Then Storyteller joined the group. He too could not speak
Calusan, but he spoke Cusabo, and soon he found an interpreter.
To a gathering throng he told in a voice charged with feeling of
Weechee's sale to *el señor* and her rescue by Martyn Sagamore. At
the story's close many of the Calusa women stretched out their hands
to Weechee, palm upward, their heads bowed, and the braves touched
one knee to the ground. The thought came to me to ask them to send
runners to the capital of Tzin Cacique Calusa, to tell them of our
going thence, but I did not yet know our route on which his followers
could meet us. We were only on the fringe of Calusa country and
would touch at many nearer towns. From these we could dispatch
our tidings so his anxious wait would not be unduly long.

We observed a good deal of gold in throat and arm ornaments
worn by both men and women. Many of the women and girls
had necklaces of what William Brown thought were fresh-water pearls
and beautiful jewelry of conch shell combined with gold or with
pearls. They fastened up their raven-black hair with pins of bone or
turtle shell. Some of the knife blades we saw were the cutting-teeth
of various sea creatures, such as giant sharks or barracudas. But we
were most startled by the sight of several *machetes* with steel blades,
unquestionably Spanish. Their gold must have been obtained from
the looting of Spanish ships, wrecked on some dangerous coast where
kinsmen dwelt; we could explain their use of steel, and in some

instances of cloth of European weave, by trade with more southerly
Calusa who had crossed the Yukatan Straits in long Carib-like dugout
canoes to trade with Cubans. Certainly there were no Spanish forts
or towns of any consequence in this part of Florida, or we would have
heard of them. Their temple mound—Doctor Jones ventured it might
be of funereal use as well as a house for kewas—was by far the largest
we had seen.

"Martyn, have Storyteller ask the Cusabo Indian if these people
have gold that they will trade for colored cloth or mirrors, or clasp
knives," the doctor proposed. "We still have some in the saddlebags,
and we need the pure malleable metal without delay."

Instantly I knew our need—to adorn Weechee.

When we departed the town three days later, we had half a pound
of nuggets. Also its citizens filled our food baskets with every kind
of edible in their pantries, including a flour called sof-kee. It was the
product, Storyteller learned, of a thick root made from a foot-high
plant with yellow and orange cones. Also we were given fresh and
dried venison and fish, palm cabbage, red beans we had not seen
before, and reed bags of nuts. To drink, they gave us earthen jugs
of the juice of wild grapes; to smoke at our leisure, a wooden chest of
tobacco leaves. A little girl stole up and presented Weechee with a
huge bouquet of flaming-red poinsettias. A guide would escort us to
a village fifteen miles southward.

Storyteller reported to me his interview with the Cusabo-speaking
Indian. The latter had never been to the far-off capital of Tzin Cacique,
but by report he believed it to be on the northern rim of a vast
swamp of cypress trees, to the north of a district of immense,
uninhabitable grass plains, impenetrable thickets, countless shallow
lakes, and forest. It was a journey of one or two days from the wide
windy waters now known as *Golfo de Mexico*, much farther inland
than Carib slave catchers had ever been known to raid.

Encountering Weechee at a bubbling spring at dusk after our next
day's march, I told her of Storyteller's report. It was not at Tzin
Cacique's capital that she had been captured and her mother and
brother killed by the raiding Caribs, she said—catch the *diablos* coming anywhere nigh it—but on a pleasant beach where dwelt her mother's sister, the wife of the Sagamore of the Calusahachee, a tribe paying
tribute to her father, the king. Also she repeated at least a hundred
words of the Calusa language that she had heard our hosts of yesterday
pronounce, and which she had instantly recalled from long ago. If and
when she found her tribe, in short of a month she would be as fluent
as ever in its speech.

Then she grew pensive, started to speak, hesitated, then blurted out, "Something has come between us, Martyn, since you found me in the briar patch."

"I know of nothing."

"I do, and I will speak her name. It is Winifred."

"For a full month I have seen Winifred only in the company of others."

"But you dream of her at night. I do not blame you; she is so beautiful. And her skin is white as a swamp lily, and mine as brown as a sandpiper."

And it had a like reddish tinge, also, I was thinking. And then I looked upon Weechee herself, tall beside me, high of head, beautiful of throat and shoulders, her eyes still picking up the dying light in the way of jewels. Memories of some passages between us stirred my pulse.

"How old are you, Weechee?" I asked.

"Ten and four, and I have been a woman for more than a year. What do you care for that? The last time you kissed me was when the moon was young and in the west, and that was a good-night kiss, no more than a brushing of my lips. Well, that was all I wanted. Save your real kisses for Winifred, but be careful she does not bite you with her sharp teeth."

"What do you mean by that last?"

"Nothing that you want to hear."

Fourteen, she had said, and a year had passed since her first flowering. The oath I had taken to make no amatory addresses to her was no longer in force.

"Let us have our good-night kiss now, Weechee, though it may be more than a mere brushing of our lips."

"No matter what it is, it will mean nothing."

"I intend that it will mean a great deal to me."

Both of us were naked above the waist, our custom now in hot weather, and drawing her close I felt the firmness behind the silky skin of her well-grown breasts. Her lips remained still at my first kiss, then she drew a sharp breath, and they grew warmer and more rounded. Then we were both involved in the first kiss of ardor we had shared, the first that invited and perhaps imaged love, that exquisite caress peculiar to human beings, ancient, and mysterious in its connotations and effects. Weechee trembled in my arms. Her heartbeat quickened against mine. Her parted lips implored a deeper kiss. Wildly aroused, I would not have known the outcome if she had not burst out of my embrace and flung away.

"It still meant nothing," she told me, in rising anger.

"It seemed to, Weechee."

"Have you ever seen a forest fire—in a stand of young pines, when a hard wind is blowing, and after a long deep drouth? I did, when I was a slave to *el señor*. One tree after another bursts into sudden flame. Instantly it is bathed in flame. The fighters are helpless, they can only run. The place of safety they make for turns into the place the priest in a black gown told the people they would go when they died if they had been bad. Trees down wind, many paces from the fiercest flame, catch fire before the red tongues touch them. Thus it was with me, when you held me so close and kissed me. A little fire that ever burns within my body, and is not my fault, becomes a great fire. It does not mean I want to be your woman and join our naked bodies. When I come to my father's house I will become Richard's woman. He wants me more than you do, and needs me more. I can make him happy. He has never been truly happy."

"Weechee, I don't know what you mean."

"I mean since he was a little boy. And it's all on account of you."

"Please talk sense, or not at all."

"Sense. You are blind not to see it. You told me that in his old home he was rich, the son of a sagamore and a caciquess. Why should he come to this wilderness, sweat like a slave, risk his life, go cold and hungry? Because you come, you who lived in a little house, whose father labored in the fields, and you wanted to be a sagamore yourself. Always he asks where you are, what you are doing, even when he is alone with me and I let him kiss me a little, and hug me. Is it not true that wherever you go he is sure to come? You have some awful hold on him that I do not understand. I think you have had a werowance cast a spell on him."

"Weechee, it is true that we both like to compete against each other —at hunting for instance. But it is a friendly rivalry. He liked to beat me—"

"But he never does beat you. You always win."

"That is not true. I win one round, we call it, and then he wins one. He is a great sportsman."

"And you are a great fool! Well, he will win once against you—he will win me, if that counts for anything. If you really wanted me, and he won me, it would count the whole world to him. Sometimes he takes from his pouch a little seed he picked up from the ground, looks at it so sadly, and then puts it back. He found it on the day that you found me in the thorn thicket. He wanted Winifred when you did, but she let you make love to her, and now you don't want her very much, and he doesn't either."

"We are not talking about Winifred. Richard picked up that little nut or acorn after he had made a bad miss at a deer; and so it was my turn to take the next trophy—any game we saw—and it turned out to be you. Are you sorry he missed, for if he hadn't, he, not I, would have had you."

"I'll not say I'm sorry. That would be a lie. I have been happy with you—when I was a little girl I was in love with you—if you don't think a little girl can fall in love you are a bigger fool than I said. And if I'm still in love with you—a little—I'm going to be his woman after I get home. And then he will get well from his trouble that I do not understand. The curse that was laid on him will be gone forever."

She darted away to join the people about the cooking fire. I stared after her, dumfounded, yet with an eerie feeling I could not put by. My common sense told me that what she had told me could not possibly be true. Or else it had a grain of truth that I too could not understand.

2

Our party was now making toward an Indian trail shown on my Spanish map, running east and west, the eastern terminal of which was about a hundred miles southward of Cape Horse. I judged it an important footpath, used by many Indians and perhaps a few Spanish missionaries, for it ran clear across Florida, almost touching the northern end of Lago Grande Calusa. At this point there was an Indian town, with the harsh yet rhythmic name of Okeechobee.

We had gained the mainland about twelve miles south of Cape Horse only by swimming the rested horses on a long line fixed to their halters and bent on our largest boat a full two miles across Rio de Indio. One man poked at the lead horse with a pole to keep him from trying to swim over or get in the boat. There we came to a firm beach on which we marched thirty-five miles, encountering only two rivers, both of them minor, which we forded at Indian crossings a few miles above their mouths. This journey we had made in exactly a fortnight when we came on a sharp turn westward of the Indian trail, north of an inlet running eastward and then southward. It received the waters of another minor river, which we crossed in our boats, again swimming the horses. On its farther bank we must leave our boats, which pained us but could not help, since we could not portage them to the next large river that our map revealed, westward more than twenty miles.

The great part of this march was along a very slightly elevated ridge with cypress swamps both to our north and to our south. We encountered two villages at the edges of these swamps, their dwellers unmistakably Calusa, but living quite a different life than the Calusa in the coastal town. They too ate sof-kee but the main source of their living was the swamps, these by no means as dense and dark and dangerous as the Great Swamp that was the source of Rios Santa Maria and Suwannee. Their trees were draped but not shrouded in moss. Sunlight found its way down, and amid its ponds and runs many deer fed, and the portals of the houses were often decorated by the massive horns of buffalo. Woman's work was making sof-kee, gathering other food plants such as palm cabbages in the woods, swamps and pine forests, cooking, plaiting palm leaves, and curing deer, buffalo, bear, and *cuguara* skins, and the furry pelts of otters, wild cats, raccoons, and a swimming mammal, resembling a muskrat, which Doctor Jones did not believe was a rodent but a carnivore. The hunters killed and skinned a great many large snakes, the skins of which were a valuable article in trade; but the first trade they made was often the hunter's life.

Because of snakebite and other fatal hunting accidents I noticed a marked plurality of women over men. Girls must often wait until they were sixteen or seventeen to find husbands, and hence polygamy was an accepted and common practice. This fact distressed Edward Powell infinitely more than it did me, and considerably more than any of our fellow travelers, even a few of our married or unmarried women among whom the martial shoe was on the other foot. Indeed except for polygamy the villages could hardly have survived, let alone increased their numbers.

We had never before seen such indefatigable, bold, cunning, and skillful hunters as these Calusa swamp rangers. They had flat-bottomed boats for certain uses, but also very light and buoyant rafts made of canes. Richard drew one of their bows and guessed its weight at fifty pounds. Their long arrows were handsomely painted, fletched with gaudy feathers, and usually tipped with beautifully worked flint, but we saw some with shark-tooth points. These arrows were highly prized; long searched for if lost. I took it that they lost very few, for the simple reason they were almost always found in the bodies of their quarry. We marchers had encountered archers to equal our very best.

Also we were nearing, very slowly, the capital city of Tzin Cacique, called *Calusa Rey* by Spaniards. His given name was Antonio,[*] and he was a younger son of the great Carlos, he who had wed the sister of Governor Menéndez de Avilés. We could not have advanced at all

---

[*] Historians record the name of only one son born to the marriage of Carlos and the sister of the Spanish Governor Menéndez. This son was named Felipe. But it is conjectural that these had a younger son of the likely name Antonio, since his mother was Dona Antonia.

except for paths cut by the Calusa through stretches of indescribably dense forests of vine-hung trees whose kind I knew not, and we would have barely crawled except for their rude bridges of tree trunks crossing runs and bogs. Soon we must send runners announcing the approach of Tzin Cacique's lost daughter, in strange company. Now we must begin preparations for her arrival.

William Brown had completed a pair of golden earplugs of our easily worked gold. Each was a decorated disk of gold fixed to golden stem about half an inch long and nearly a quarter of an inch thick, near the end of which he had bored a hole for a pin to hold the plug in place. It was now Doctor Jones's unwelcome duty to reopen the holes in the lobes of Weechee's ears, and keep these open until the slight wounds healed. Did we have a small set of essential surgical instruments? What did I think he was, a faith healer? Of course he had such a set in his pack roll. In fact I had seen it before, when he had tried to save the life of Jane Mannering, shot in the breast by an Indian in ambush.

While Weechee sat on a stump, Doctor Jones thrust the end of a scalpel into the now-closed apertures. She did not make a sound, although tears kept flooding her eyes as he worked to spread apart the flesh, and ever she brushed them angrily away. With a needle he inserted thongs, and these she must work back and forth at frequent intervals. This operation was performed near the big town of Okeechobee on a minor river emptying into Lago Grande Calusa, once called by the Spanish *Gran Laguna de Mayaimi*. By the time we reached what was a mere pond in comparison, actually about nine miles long lying off the southeast corner of its expanse, the minor wounds had healed. With William Brown beaming at his side, Doctor Jones inserted the golden pegs fixed to the golden disks, and inserted the pins. With other ornamentation our gold had provided, Weechee was fairly well adorned to meet her sire.

By now we had seen *pa-hay-okee,* which was brown saw grass mainly covered with foot-deep water stretching for countless miles, dotted here and there with mile-wide patches of forest or rocky hummocks. Its assembly of fresh-water birds was probably unequaled anywhere in the world. Amid its waterweeds and weed thickets were white ibis, noble wood ibis, blue herons that looked man-tall, little blue herons in implausible flocks, white herons whose lovely flight and numbers suggested Heaven's hordes of angels. There were flamingo like flying flame, egrets of beautiful plume, swimming fowls of scores of species, and in awesome contrast, far-flung flocks of grisly vultures that nested on the wooded islands. But on its shores there were trees we had known in England, and New World trees of friendly aspect, and in these sang mockingbirds; and jays, grackles, and small crows uttered their harsh cries. Nor were flowers forgotten in this wilderness of water and wild growth, and riots they were of blue, yellow, and red blossom.

And now we had sent runners, to announce Weechee's approach, and now she was almost miraculously relearning her native language at every village where we rested one day or more. To hear and recognize one word caused her to recall scores of associated words. Thus her returning to her native tongue was far swifter than had been Thomas Warner's. He had been a slave in Santo Domingo for seventeen years; Weechee a slave to *el señor* only three years and my companion about two years.

Doctor Jones, William Hewett, Richard, and I discussed the wave of optimism, born of an increasing sense of security, sweeping our company. Except for almost unimaginable disaster, we would gain the Calusa capital in ten days despite the great swamps we must wade or circumvent, and the many rivers and runs that we must cross. Our living, breathing Passport would assure us the help of the Indians we met, not only in transport but in supplies. Happily not many of our company conceived of an only too possible happening at the capital itself—Tzin Cacique's refusal to let us establish an English colony in his domains.

Our march of the past thirty days had not been particularly arduous, but our advance was exceedingly slow. Except for Indian pathways which were originally game trails, these following the highest ground and leading to the best fords and most shallow marshes, we would have been immobilized. In all truth this whole, immense area encircling the fresh-water sea called Lago Grande Calusa was a kingdom unlike any other in the world of which I had heard or read, unexplored, unconquerable by a Spanish Army, and forbidden territory to all except those whom its dwellers welcomed and helped to come here. From each village a Calusa guide had led us to the next village along our course. It was a strangely and wildly beautiful domain, but impenetrable to strangers. Despite what weapons they might have and the abundance of game, they simply could not have made their way into its fastnesses.

Great stretches of it were watery grass plains, agleam in the torrid sunlight. But there were also vast reed beds, and pathless forests. The worst part was the mangrove thickets, minatory in their aspect; the best were the cypress woods, with their rich grass, which in times of torrential rains became all but illimitable shallow lakes. Its single greatest blessing was the scarcity of mosquitos. The only explanation for this phenomenon we could hit upon was a fearful competition for existence in the marshes and saw grass glades; rare was the wriggler that escaped being eaten by small fish, and lucky the insect that escaped the swarms of swallows and nighthawks and bats.

The news of our approach had spread far and wide. We were met on the trail by the headmen of every village and town; where we would lie for the night was decided by chiefs and guides and provision was made for our lodging. With us palefaces, the warriors did not fraternize. They saw to our wants but themselves remained aloof, their faces inscrutable, sometimes I thought cold. On the contrary Storyteller was most honorably received; Manteo had his due as a great sagamore from afar; the reception of Weechee, invariably the house-guest of the headman and his wife at every town and village, was ceremonial, never familiar. She had long ago been relieved of her pack roll. Other than official welcomers, it seemed to me that only children, presenting bouquets of multicolored flowers, ever came close to her.

At various towns she had received gifts such as fresh-water pearls set in gold rings and once a glimmering necklace of these jewels, with a pendant of conch shell and pale jade. Jadite in many forms was a frequent gift, this stone in high esteem among the Aztecs. With her gold armbands set with emeralds, she was at last properly arrayed as a Calusa princess, daughter of the Tzin Cacique, the latter an Aztec title. Obviously the Calusa, probably of Carib origin, and living a life unique in the New World as far as I knew, had borrowed many ceremonies and perhaps customs from the Aztecs. And although Storyteller was deeply revered, his knowledge of the Calusa language was scant in the extreme, and our only avenue of communication with our hosts or perhaps our tolerators was Weechee herself. In the past month she had fully recalled the speech of her early childhood.

My heart was sad, because I could not help but believe that with all the changes Weechee had escaped from me forever.

3

We made our last march to the capital city of the Calusa; but if Doctor Jones expected even a shadow of the glories that Cortez had found at the end of that long causeway of Montezuma, he had built in vain. True, an honor guard of eight spearmen met Weechee at the entrance of an embankment, actually a closable dike against high water. There were hardly more than a thousand families living on roughly parallel streets and cross streets, each in its own lot, having one, two, and three-storied houses with deep eaves and open sides, their frames of palm or cypress, and with thatched roofs. The main structure on every lot was decorated in some measure with strings of garlands of gorgeous blossom in honor of Weechee's return. But the people stood in their doorways or close to the houses, silent but with jubilant faces; and only little children brought bouquets to her, so many that they must be carried by her guardsmen.

These were tall men, wearing one feather in their hair, necklaces of quartz, armbands of copper, and in the case of their captain, gold. Their only garb was a belt holding a sheath knife with a flap before and coon tails behind, and a short cape decorated with the red feathers of the flamingo.

The royal residence could not be called a palace. Amid a cluster of smaller buildings it occupied a square on the highest ground of an elevated plain of turf-grown coraline rock on which the city was built. It was larger than an English cottage but not the abode of an English squire; it too was of palm and cypress wood, and painted red with geometric designs in black and white. Our column was halted some hundred paces from the door; out of the house came a very tall pale-colored Indian, possibly six and a half feet, and certainly no more than forty years old, wearing egret plumes in a golden headband, and a robe of what was called feather-cloth, first seen and probably made in Mexico, the feathers being those of the flamingo, the swan, and the great blue heron. His bearing was haughty in the extreme; and I thought that his handsome face would have been radiant if he had given rein to his emotions. Two paces behind him and preceding her attendants, walked a stately woman in feather-cloth jacket and skirt, her black hair confined by a golden headband and conch-shell pins. Her jewelry was a necklace of large pearls and gold earplugs and bracelets set with emeralds and jade. Her complexion was notably darker than the king's, and she was some years younger and of royal beauty.

Weechee dropped on her knees before Tzin Cacique. Immediately he raised her up, bent and received her kiss upon his lips. She then knelt to Tzin Caciquess, who raised her up and embraced her. The three then retired into residence, but the captain of the royal guard came toward us walking ahead of a fine-looking Indian whom I immediately recognized as of a different tribe from the Calusa.

"Mayaimi," Storyteller murmured in my ear. "I think I can talk to him."

The newcomer bowed low to Storyteller, and then spoke in what I thought was the Mayaimi language. When he paused, Storyteller immediately translated his words into Croatan, which I, raising my voice, repeated in English. My followers listened with anxious faces.

"My name is Outlander," the Mayaimi began. "I came hence from the Calusahachee, where I had taken a Calusa woman when Tzin Cacique's capital, Tampa, stood nigh its mouth. My tribe is a subject tribe of the Calusa. And here Tzin Cacique looked upon me with favor, and I became his mouth in speaking unto the Mayaimi."

"Hough!" Storyteller pronounced.

"Now I speak the message of Tzin Cacique, for you to bear with tongues to the ears of the palefaces. He welcomes your visit here, and bids you all be seated at your comfort, and his own servants will bring trays of bread and meat and fruit for your refreshment. Thereafter he will himself appear before you, and speak to you winged words."

The last phrase made me think of Homer. It was no wonder that the same thoughts and images would appear in the poetry of the Ancient Greeks as in the orations of the Calusa. In a sense both lived in their Heroic Age.

When we had eaten, the interpreter returned to the royal residence. In the meanwhile he had answered some of Storyteller's questions, as to the distance to the sea and to Key Sombrero named by the Spanish. When he emerged, it was in the train of Tzin Cacique, now being carried in a panoplied litter, no doubt a copy of an Aztec litter, by six bearers. Some of his headmen marched behind.

The litter was set down in our fore. Immediately the interpreter stepped close to the king and with bent head, listened to his utterance. This he immediately translated for Storyteller's understanding, who in turn repeated it to me in Croatan. This I recited to my fellows.

"So speaks Tzin Cacique. He bids you ask what reward he can bestow upon you, worthy of his gratitude for our rescue of his daughter, snatched from his bosom six suns ago by the Caribs and sold by them into slavery."

The Mayaimi paused while the king spoke again, after which I transmitted his words to my comrades.

"And Tzin Cacique asks what reward he may bestow upon you for your long march hither to restore his daughter to his arms . . . He bids you not be bashful in speaking forth your desires, and these not be niggard, because of his four children by his queen, Weechee is the only survivor. His eldest son was slain by the Caribs when she was taken prisoner. Two younger sons died in honor, one in knife against claw in battle with a wounded bear, and the other when he had challenged, in the way of the Calusa warriors, a shark of great size and manifold teeth . . . Although he slew the monster with his spear, he himself died by the bleeding of many wounds."

My hearers stood silent for a long moment. Then Eleanore Dare, wife of Ananias, with her yet unweaned baby in her arms, spoke in a wistful voice, more to her husband than to me.

"I suppose he would have no way to transport us to England."

"Not now, certainly, and probably never," answered Ananias Dare. "Martyn, I suggest you make the proposal that was discussed—that he permit us to found a colony in his domains and have his men help us build houses and lay our fields, and give or lend us corn until we can harvest our crop."

Actually the Calusa had very little corn, so in translation I changed the word to sof-kee, the source of Calusan bread. When the request reached Tzin Cacique, he looked at us with a quiet wonder which seemed to me touched with pity. Then he made solemn answer, which at last I could give my comrades.

"Tzin Cacique can permit no people other than his own people to dwell in his domain," Storyteller had said. "Outlander and his woman have become his own people, obeying his law, employing his speech, living the life and following the customs of the Calusa. Still he will not have us driven forth until, after two tests of our worth, he will make an offering of honor to us, out of his thanks to us for delivering his daughter Weechee, her maidenhead unbroken, to his arms."

Torn between heartbreak and hope, my comrades listened to the murmur of talk between the king and his interpreter. The former pointed to something of medium distance in the royal square. I could see nothing but the rotten stump of what probably had been a noble poplar tree, now long fallen. Then it seemed to me he indicated the longbow that I carried unslung on my shoulder. Again Storyteller spoke to me in Croatan.

"Tzin Cacique has named the two tests that we must pass before he will make a proposal in counter to ours," I told my comrades. "I do not know what or where our failure or our success in this test may lead, but plainly it is of utmost moment to Tzin Cacique and if Richard and I cannot win against two of his warriors, at least we will come close. Richard, he bids us take turns shooting at the rotten stump upwind more than one hundred paces. The target appears easy, but the range is medium long, and the wind will make the shot difficult. We are each to launch ten arrows, so will two of his best archers. Will you compete, old friend?"

"I wouldn't miss it," Richard answered with a slow grin.

Then while Tzin Cacique was giving orders to one of his attendants, Edward Powell hastened to my side.

"Martyn, this is heathenry," he burst out. "I cannot yet guess what proposal this heathen king is about to make—perhaps the establishment of our colony in the domain of a tribe other than his own, under a chief not as imperious as he—still civilized people should not be judged by the prowess of two of their leaders with bow and arrows. Let me speak to him. Let me tell him how, if he lets us remain here, his people will receive benefits immeasurable, their heathen gods cast down, their wicked practices changed to godly practices, under my hand. If I had been here, when his sons were killed, I would have saved—"

"Mr. Powell, I must ask you be still. This is a critical moment in our lives. The king is already looking at you—"

"Bid Storyteller translate—"

"Be still. That is the command of your leader. For the present, keep out of it."

"God forgive you! Will you promise me that I will have an audience with Tzin Cacique?"

"I cannot promise. I will speak later to Doctor Jones and other leaders."

Happily the king was occupied giving instructions to two archers who had come on the run from a nearby building, which I took for a mess house or barracks of the king's guard. Richard and I were fastening the loops of our cords in the notches of our half-drawn bows. I was wondering if I should have called Thomas Warner instead of Richard, or appointed him to my place. Another moment with Edward Powell would have so unnerved me that I would have had to do so. The truth was that in this ancient sport and prowess, Thomas was fully the peer of either of us. However, his special talent lay in fine shooting at very long ranges on still days.

The two guardsmen had already removed their feathered cloaks and were slinging their bows. Each of us four contestants was told to loose ten arrows. In twenty minutes we had done so, shooting rapidly, while Tzin Cacique watched first in boyish delight and then with a suggestion of incredulity in his handsome, well-mastered countenance. Richard and I had shot no better than the two Calusa, but fully as well. More of my teammate's and my arrows hit nearer the center of the stump than did our opponents', but one of mine, caught in a gust of wind, had missed the target clean.

The second test astonished me beyond expression, a natural reaction to say the least, but it also waked an eerie feeling as though I were dreaming. I did not doubt that Richard experienced a like sensation, and his memory was moved as was mine. The game I was asked to play with a third warrior called up was in essence quarterstaff. Instead of two poles, the contestants must use long stout canes. My opponent's staff had a small, very sharp, arrowhead set in its tip; mine had what

I guessed was a shark tooth. Obviously points were won not by one player striking the other, but by pricking his skin.

The intelligent Mayaimi explained to Storyteller, and he to me, that this would be a mock-fight in representation of a spearman's aquatic battle with a shark, which was the single greatest test of a Calusa warrior's prowess and indeed his manhood, with the possible exception of fighting a manta ray, a sea monster of frightful size and aspect. At certain seasons, when runs of cobias brought many big sharks into shallow waters, parties of warriors visited the coast about thirty miles distant; and rather commonly not all of their number returned. The spearing of huge crocodiles in their own lakes and swamps was almost as dangerous, because these reptiles turned with utmost ferocity upon pursuing swimmers.

For this game I must bare my body above the waist. I had had no choice but to undertake it myself in my part as the leader of the palefaces: this was the wish and hence the command of Tzin Cacique. But he had Storyteller tell me not to be ashamed if I did not bleed my opponent even once in a game of five points, because even if such contests were known in my own tribe, I had probably had no practice in my long journey hither. Actually my skill with a quarter-staff had by no means died in my body; the very journey of which the king spoke had quickened my muscles and limbered my bones and I could not be in better physical condition. In the match that took fully half an hour I received three pricks that brought blood, and gave my opponent two. I truly believed that the king could hardly believe his eyes.

One watcher, Winifred, seemed in a spell. I remembered that she had been a spectator of my long-ago match with Richard that was somehow, although I could not trace the intervening steps, the beginning of a long series of adventures. I wondered if today's duel was the end of a richly adventurous road, or a new beginning.

"And now I will tell the palefaces how they may remain in my domains—the only way," Tzin Cacique declared, sitting upright in an open palanquin, and with regal voice and mien. "It is for themselves to become Calusa. I cannot and will not rule a divided people. Their tribe differs in minor ways from mine, in speech, in color of skin, in religion, no doubt in countless customs." Then, in direct address: "Still we will accept you as brethren, first because you befriended my daughter greatly beloved, and second, because you have shown stout hearts in your long march here from the hunting grounds of the Croatan, of whom I have heard, and thirdly, most important of all, I think my people would be strengthened, and not weakened, by your addition."

This message I could hardly bring myself to interpret to my follow-

ers, despite a glow I could not deny in my heart. Only Doctor Jones
spoke, he after a long pause. For once, Edward Powell was stricken
speechless and could only stare aghast.

"Does he mean intermarriage?" Doctor Jones had asked. "Of course
he does! Still, find out all you can."

Oddly enough, the king's next remark fully answered the doctor's
question.

"Because of our way of life many of our best and bravest young men
die before they have seen twenty suns. By word of the Great Spirit
of the Waters and the God of the Dead with whom our mikos hold
speech, it is permitted that my warriors take second and third wives,
although it is not a good custom among people who trace descent
through bowl and pestle." Obviously the latter term was the equivalent
of "distaff" in English speech. "Thus I will expect every wifeless male
except the miko in your party to accept for his wife the woman appointed to him, by myself and my councilors. But these will be not
ill-favored girls, shrews, or wantons, and will be skilled at womanly
tasks. You will learn our speech. You will join in our great hunts and
our great fishing. In case of war—but what people would dare challenge us, lest it be the Caribs coming to our coast in their dugouts, in
such numbers as come the wild geese from the north in the cool
moons—you would fight to the death beside us. Together we will
dance the sof-kee dance, the buffalo dance, the snake dance, the swan
dance, the dance of the darting fishes. With us you will perform ceremonies before the kewas; the children you bear will have Calusan
names; your own names will be forgotten. Alike forgotten will be your
brethren and your women in your native land. When you die your
bones will lie in the ground or in our burial mounds. Your maidens
may marry palefaces if they choose, but in this generation only; their
daughters must marry Calusa braves and your sons Calusa maidens,
so you emigrants will become indistinguishable from us Folk of the
Wide Waters.

"But you need not make your decision now. You will wish to confer
together, but I must know your answer on the night of the full moon.
If you decline our invitation, you must begin your journey the following day, and guides will be provided you to the borders of my
kingdom, in any direction that you choose, and also we will furnish
you bread and meat that far, in payment of my debt to you when
you provided meat and bread and loving care to the Caciquess
Weechee. Now you may retire to a shelter against rain that has been
erected twenty-twenty paces from my abode."

Tzin Cacique spoke to his bearers, who at once raised his palaquin
and bore him toward his house. The Mayaimi gestured courteously

and we fell in behind him. In silence and in a daze we followed him
to an immense pavilion, a hundred feet long and half of that wide,
with corner posts and ridge poles and pillars of cypress poles supporting a low-eaved roof of palm leaves as a shelter against rain.
There we found our pack rolls and other possessions, and a generous
supply of sof-kee cakes and fried venison, fish and toasting sticks of
green wood, fruit, and most strange, many festoons of flowers.

4

The Indian mind can hardly credit the fact that palefaces prefer
to sit rather than squat. Still a few rude benches had been provided,
toward one end of the pavilion, and near the opposite end a Calusa
carpenter had built what he no doubt prided himself was a genuine
paleface chair, having four legs, a plank seat, and an upright plank
back. This was obviously intended for our chief, when councils were
being held. But with dignity and as by divine right, Edward Powell
took his seat there, thus facing the company. When our eighty and
a few more assembled, he spoke in quite a matter-of-fact, calm voice,
as of a matter already settled.

"Of course the idea the king proposes is not only wicked. It is
fantastic—impossible—unthinkable."

After brief thought, Doctor Jones replied.

"Sir, I will speak of its moral aspects only as far as to remind you
that these apply only to morals as we define them, which are English,
Hebrew, and in general and broadly speaking, those of Western civilization. Even in the West, morals differ among different nations and
classes. But Tzin Cacique's invitation is not in the least fantastic in
his able mind, or in my mind. I know of nothing that makes it impossible, let alone unthinkable. Indeed it must be thought upon with
great earnestness by us all."

"God above! To trade our Christianity, our civilization, what we owe
to God and to our native lands, and our heritage, for a savage, iniquitous life not as teachers but as fellows with a tribe of heathen Indians.
Mr. Thomas Hewett, will you comment on this?"

"Yes, sir, I will, by Mr. Sutton's permission. I remind you, Reverend
Powell, that he is the proper person, as our elected captain, to lead
this discussion, not yourself."

"You know what he'll say!"

"Sir, as a lawyer, I try to avoid premature opinions. I wish to hear
what he will say."

"Mr. Hewett, you would be favoring the company if you express
yourself freely," I told him.

"Instead, I will ask a question," Mr. Hewett replied. "What, sir—and I ask this question of all—is our alternative from accepting the king's invitation?"

"I would rather die!" Edward Powell cried, losing his uncustomary calm.

"I am sure I wouldn't," observed Doctor Jones, lighting his tobacco pipe with flint, steel, and a pinch of tinder.

Ananias Dare, a diffident man, not really fitted for leadership, coughed nervously and spoke.

"I cannot propose an alternative," he said. "I can merely remind you that if we accept the invitation of Tzin Cacique, it means not only our obliteration as English people, but our disappearance from history. Our fate will never be known. No explorers will come here in our lifetimes, and for perhaps a century after our deaths; this particular area of Florida is no man's land except for Indians almost without contact with other Indians. Large areas in the moors of Devonshire have remained inaccessible to men, in fact unexplored, unsurveyed, to this day, despite the shire being inhabited by Englishmen for a thousand years. The paths into this vast wilderness, this labyrinth of marsh are known only to the Calusa and allied tribes. When at last palefaces—before God, I am turning into an Indian ahead of time —I say when white adventurers finally come here, and anthropologists make a study of the people, almost all trace of a white infusion in their blood will have been lost, and if there is such a thing as throwbacks, or avatism, skins paler than most will be ascribed to albinism or to any one of several factors other than the truth. English customs, speech, and religion will have disappeared. We are less than ninety in all. Within a circle of twenty miles radius from where we stand, there are at least nine thousand Calusa Indians. What of it?—so our more adventurous may ask. I ask it, because my wife has a babe just learning to toddle, the first white child born in Virginia. But pray do not take this into your considerations. I would rather she become the matriarch of a line of half-breeds, quarter-breeds, and descendants with an ever receding fraction of white blood, than die in the wilderness, by starvation, or exhaustion, or by the bite of a poisonous snake."

"Sir, I have pity on your weakness," Edward Powell said with deep feeling.

"What is weakness?" Doctor Jones demanded, abruptly taking his pipe from his mouth. "What is strength? It is a strong thing, a noble thing, for a man or woman to die for a great cause, but what great cause would be served by the death in the forest of Ananias Dare, his good wife, and his infant child?"

"The cause of God," Edward Powell answered quietly.

"I do not see how it would benefit the cause of God. God gave us birth, not with the intention of our dying in our youth or our full manhood, but of our living, if we can, to three score and ten or by reason of strength, four score. If we stay here, we must do lip service to a heathen religion. In our hearts we can still pray to Whom we believe is the Christian God. But we cannot do so, if we leave this haven, wild and heathen though it may be. I think our hearts will be stilled by death. I believe in heroism, the risk or even the surrender of our lives for the benefit of others; I am no hero, still there are many causes, including human health, for which I would risk death or die. Here I can practice my profession and perhaps save several lives in the course of the years; my skeleton rotting away in the illimitable forest could not do so. Racial purity? No race has ever been pure-blooded. Well, I have said this much; I will say the rest. I am now over forty years old, and a widower. I propose that we accept the invitation of Tzin Cacique on the terms he offers. If we do so, besides practicing my profession as well as I can, I will live an adventurous life. As for my own intentions, I will take a second wife, and take my word for it, she will be comely, a good helpmeet, and bear me sturdy children. I have nothing more to say."

"God help you," cried out Edward Powell.

"I thank you, sir." And Doctor Jones puffed hard on his pipe, to revive its glow.

A long silence ensued. It was broken at last by a girlish voice, soft and melodious.

"May I speak?" asked Winifred Powell. And she stood pale-colored and lovely, illuminated by a shaft of sunlight that had found its eager way to her through a rift in the palm-leaf roof.

"Ask Martyn, not me," replied her sire. "He is in command."

"Certainly you may," I said.

"I see no point in taking a vote now. Its outcome—the vast majority would vote to remain here under Tzin Cacique's protection. Forgive me, Papa, but I would vote with that majority, unless conditions change between now and the full moon, the period allotted us in which to decide. Alive, we may serve the True God, in secret when necessarily; dead in the wilderness, our souls, sped to Heaven and everlasting bliss, can serve Him as He commands. But a miracle might come to pass before the moon rounds. If England has won her war with Philip, Sir Walter Raleigh could have sent a ship, and when he found us gone from Roanoke, his search parties might finally find us. I agree with Doctor Jones that the chance would be very slight. But I would want us to regard our stay with the Calusa as temporary— we need not say so, but do so in our hearts. A more likely outcome than rescue by English people would be our migration to another tribe, a tribe of corn growers instead of hunters, for instance the Muskhogeans who live more like white people. The young men will love these swampy fastnesses because of the adventurous life, but I think it would be better for us and our children to live in some other part of the New World, our houses in uplands instead of moors, perhaps under ancient oaks such as we have seen. In any case, let us wait for the beautiful full moon before we vote. Tzin Cacique will prize us all the more and think we have given consideration to alternatives if we keep him waiting."

This last sentence in Winifred's address most impressed her hearers. A good many nodded their heads; no objection was raised to her proposal. As for me, I considered the matter settled; no search party would find its way to the Calusa capital before the full moon, or for many moons thereafter, for many suns, and in all probability not within our life times, or when any face of our descendants remained truly pale.

But many issues remained unsettled. And this fact was in the back of my head when for my own pleasure and refreshment, I went to seek the Princess Weechee.

5

She was not hard to find. In fact, she was strolling in plain sight in the royal square. When she saw me, she came on the run, unprincesslike conduct, I thought; but wholly characteristic. It caused me to recall a saying among real Oriental Indians, not Red Indians, once quoted by Doctor Jones in discussing a book written by a retired factor from Portuguese India: "Where there are no eyes, there is no caste." The same was true in considerable measure in England.

"Wah!" she burst out, an exclamation I had heard before. "No doubt the palefaces have been searching their hearts and wagging their tongues! Did you decide to stay with the Calusa or be eaten by bears and wolves in the wilderness?"

"The decision will be made formally in the time allotted us," I answered. "But I can tell you now, there is not one chance in twenty-twenty-twenties that we will go."

"I am glad. I have come to love many of the palefaces, and like almost all. We have been through so much together; we have made such a long—what was the word you used?"

"Odyssey, I guess. Maybe I called it a Marco Polo journey."

"I think it was as far as from here to the moon."

"You are wrong there, Weechee."

"Here you will have the life that you love. My father, Tzin Cacique, will make you a sagamore under him. You can hunt and fish, fight *cuguara,* bears, and if you are a good enough swimmer, spear huge alligators or even sharks. Unless you marry one of the paleface maidens—and I know you won't want any of them except Winifred, and she is going to choose Richard, or you would have done so before now—my father will assign you the most beautiful of the unmarried Calusa girls."

"Is there any danger of him assigning you to me?"

"He might if I asked him to, and I courted you passionately. You see, we trace descent through our mothers, not our sires, the bowl-and-pestle side we call it, although we are not like the Muskhogeans, where marriages are arranged by the mothers. But I cannot court you passionately, even if I wanted to: my position is too high. All I can do is find out if I want you, and then tell my mother, Tzin Caciquess, what I decide. But if I should decide that I do—and that is very unlikely—still you could refuse me. That would be against Calusa custom, but I could tell them that you are an outlander, also my rescuer, and they would make an exception in your case. Then I would marry my cousin—he has speared three big shark and at least a dozen big alligators. He is the warrior that beat you at the mock fight with a shark this morning."

Meanwhile she was walking ahead of me, talking over her shoulder. We were following a hardly perceptible path that led up a very beautiful stream, and it might be that she had a particular destination. Weechee had her own ways of finding out what she wanted to know. She was not, I recalled, particularly modest in the western meaning of the word. And now she was the Caciquess Weechee of the royal line of the Calusa.

We came to a long reach of quiet water surrounded by heavily branched cypress trees. It was reminiscent of the pool where I had bathed her mud-plastered and thorn-scratched body on the day of her rescue from *el señor.* She tested the sunlit water with her finger, and pronounced it quite warm. This was no wonder, because the day was hot and the almost tropic sun had been shining on it most of the afternoon.

"Why not go swimming?" she asked. "This is the private swimming and bathing place of the royal family. Neither of my parents will come here today and I have no living brothers. No one else comes here."

"I think that would be delightful."

She stepped behind a bush growing on the bank, laid down the little leather bag she almost always carried on a strap over her shoulder, and then she became a pale blur. A moment later her naked body was a pale blur in the clear water. I slipped off my own scant clothes and joined her. For a few minutes we dived and splashed and raced, in the way of swimmers. Because she belonged to an aquatic race, her swimming surpassed mine in every respect. Then she stopped and spoke in a not quite steady tone.

"I need a bath," she said. "I have not had a good, warm bath since the new moon. Will you reach in my leathern bag and get the little flask of soap? It is almost like that we made on the march, fine wood-ashes mixed with deer fat, but it has musk in it, and it smells good."

I got the flask of baked clay, uncorked it, and poured a little of its contents into my hand.

"Stand in water up to your waist," I directed.

"I would rather lie down in the shallows as I did before."

This she did, a lovely sight, and to my great joy I need not today feel guilty at my feelings toward her, and repress them with the full strength of my will. I must impose a limit on my actions even if she did not—the fate of the colony might depend on that—but at least I could take exquisite pleasure in my office. So I lingered over soaping her beautifully molded shoulders and then her young breast. She did not speak but gave one long sigh; its full meaning I did not know. Only the Greeks knew the full beauty of a maiden's breast, I thought —trying to maintain some sort of order in my mind—they alone as far as I knew had sculptured it in its perfection. But every natural male knew its attraction, innate in his being since the race began.

While she sat up, I soaped her back, and when she lay down again, her tapered and beautiful thighs. Then she tried to speak in a casual tone, but the attempt was a failure.

"Are you not going to—bathe—me—all—over?"

"Without fail," I answered.

When I had completed the exquisite rite, she spoke again.

"You can examine me—as you did before—to see if I have been wanton with Richard or with anyone, which was my right, since the promise you made Sagamore White has not bound you for many months—still you are my rescuer and a sagamore; and whoever you wed, it is a fit thing that she be a maiden."

"Weechee, I cannot, for that would be more than a young man's flesh can bear without giving way."

She mumbled something in the Calusa tongue, no doubt an insult, and started to get up. But I put my arms about her beautiful breast, and her mouth could not forbear from meeting mine. It was the deep, long kiss of love.

Chapter XVIII

SHE OF THE DARK VEIL

1

On my return to the pavilion I found Doctor Jones and Edward Powell starting out to look for me. The swift thought crossed my mind that they were an odd pair, one so learned and broad-minded and humanitarian, the other so fanatical in religion that he had lost contact with reality. But this thought came to me only to steady me and prepare me to meet a crisis. I knew by the expressions on their faces that a situation of profound gravity had come to their attention.

"We must have Manteo's help with this," Doctor Jones told me, while Edward Powell stood stricken and white. "Will you bring him here?"

"Mr. Powell can summon him, while you tell me what has happened," I answered. "Sir, he is fletching arrows by the footbridge across the stream. Beckon with your finger, point to me, and say, 'Sagamore.' He will come at once."

Edward Powell hurried away on his errand, welcoming any action to relieve even momentarily the intense strain on his mind.

"Martyn, I can tell you the events leading up to a terrifying discovery," Doctor Jones said, the inner strength of the man evidenced by his quiet tones. "You can see from here a gap in the trees. As we were standing about in the sunlight, a wild bull buffalo crossed there. He had his muzzle close to the ground, I think he was following scent, possibly of a buffalo herd. At once Richard declared his intention of following him and shooting him with bow and arrow. He said something about it adding prestige to our company in the eyes of Tzin Cacique, but I think he was moved by love of the chase of the biggest game he had ever hunted. Winifred immediately announced she would go with him and since she is a good marcher, almost tireless, he made no objection. In fact I think he was delighted at the opportunity to take a great trophy in her presence."

The North American buffalo was indeed a trophy worthy of any huntsman, however skilled. They were quite rare in this part of Florida as far as I could tell, by no means numerous in any forest we had visited; but Storyteller had told me they were common east of the mountain range flanking the seaboard for a great distance northward, and southward to at least as far as the headwaters of Rio de Savana. On the prairies westward of the Father of Waters, other wandering storytellers had told him, the animals ranged in vast herds.

Doctor Jones had arrested his narrative briefly to brace himself, I thought—and now resumed it.

"Richard and Winifred set off—but Manteo and Mr. Powell are in sight. Tell Manteo to follow the spore of the bull, which should be easy in the soft ground, and we can probably catch up with them fairly soon, as Richard certainly can't track as swiftly as Manteo. Also ask Mr. Powell to walk with him or closely behind him. I think he'll understand I want to talk with you privately. He has already heard the little I know—I had to come to him first—God knows I don't want him to have to hear it again. I'll tell you when we're on the march."

This was almost immediately. The tracks of the buffalo bull were perfectly visible but some of them were blurred and I did not know why until Manteo told me.

"There are two buffaloes," he said. "The bull is following the scent of a cow buffalo. She is probably in heat."

We set off, Doctor Jones and I walking about a hundred feet behind Manteo and Mr. Powell. At once he began a recital to which I could hardly bear to listen, involved with terrible events that had occurred across the sea.

"Today there was an occasion to move Winifred's pack roll and other possessions, because they were directly under the smoke hole in the roof, and clouds were gathering in the west, the usual source of a thunderstorm," he began. "The Mayaimi Indian suggested we do so and he moved Winifred's pack. I picked up that leather bag she always carries. When I once asked about it, really making conversation with a pretty girl, she told me it contained a chunk of pure copper she had taken from the temple of the Wingineo—she thought it would be useful to William Brown for making armbands for Indians or for smelting with tin dishes to make bronze. That sounded rather fishy, but I accepted it, although now and then the bag has bothered me, especially since she kept it, and did not throw it away, when we were lost in that hellish swamp."

"She told me about the same story."

"Well, Martyn, it does not contain a chunk of copper. When I was moving it, I saw where a seam had begun to burst out for about six inches. I could not resist taking a look. It contained two pieces of metal, one of which I had seen before. It was a bronze hook, shaped a little like a horseshoe, with a hole in one end. It had been found in a stand of giant oak trees in your part of Wiltshire—it was several inches underground—and given to the Reverend Stephen Burberry of Ames-bury, who was something of an antiquary and collected things like that. I knew him fairly well. We had tastes in common. He told me that it was an authentic mistletoe hook, the end of a long pole being fixed in the hole. Its like was used in Druidic rites, before and during the Roman occupation of Britain, and a century or so in Wales after the occupation. After the murder of an innocent, dim-witted wood-man, who had been chopping down the oaks at his master's orders, the lumber to be used in shipbuilding, I happened to be writing Reverend Burberry, and, on a chance, asked if the crime had occurred in the same stand of timber where the mistletoe hook was found. He replied that it had indeed, and strangely enough, the hook had disappeared from his cabinet."

"Doctor, that story is scaring the stuffing out of me," I told him.

"Worse is yet to come. I wrote again, asking who under heaven would steal the hook, without monetary value, except possibly another antiquary who like most hard hobby riders is not always in his right mind. He wrote back that no antiquary had visited him in many months, and the last people to whom he had shown the relic was a Welsh preacher, living in your part of Wiltshire, and his beautiful daughter. He added, in a jocular vein, he could hardly accuse either of these, and in fact the preacher had called the hook a heathen abomination."

"You said that worse was yet to come. I wish you'd tell me, and get it over with."

"I don't know that worse is yet to come. The hook I saw with my own eyes; the other metal object in the bag only reminded me of something you told me, one night when we two were sitting late by the cooking fire. You said that when you were growing up your father, digging to unearth a badger, came on a sealed, watertight box made of copper. He thought it might contain treasure, but it contained some things which seemed to have no relation with one another. Tell me again, if you remember, what they were."

"I remember too damned well. There was a human skull, some broken glass, a couple of inches of some sort of oil, and a hatchet head that proved to be tin."

"I thought about these and I did find a connection," Doctor Jones went on. "The broken glass could have once been a bowl, containing the head of a great Druid preserved in oil. These too played a part in Druidic rites. Legend has it that when Ambrosius—some believe he became Arthur in Welsh myth—fought Hengist the Saxon, a glass bowl containing the head of the last great Druid was carried before the victorious army. After the bowl was broken—perhaps in the burying or by an earthquake or even the impact of a falling tree—the flesh would decompose and leave the skull. Well, a hatchet with a tin head was also used in Druidic ritual. The box, then, had been buried by Druids, maybe the priests, maybe the worshipers, for one of several reasons. One, to keep the holy objects out of the hands of the Romans, who chopped down the sacred groves. Or maybe out of the hands of the early Christian priests, who had a hard time suppressing Druidism in the West. Then my cursed memory would not let me alone. Was there, or was there not, the head of a tin hatchet involved in the so-called Wiltshire murders?"

"You are making it as easy for me as you can. It was I who told you that after my mother was killed, my father said that the only thing he missed about the home acre was that tin hatchet, to which he had fitted a haft, but which wouldn't hold an edge, and which he couldn't possibly connect with Mama's death."

"You told me too there was some kind of design engraved or worked on the lock of the metal box. Did you say a stylized tree?"

"Yes, I did."

"Wasn't there the same kind of design on the gold clasp of the pearl necklace Winifred wanted so bad?"

"Yes, there was."

"That could not have been a Druidic sign. There was tree worship in America—almost everywhere in fact—but it was not associated with Druidism as in ancient Britain."

"I wish you would go ahead and tell me the rest that you know about the hatchet. You know something."

"Yes, I do. I wish to high heaven that I didn't. Well, I'll tell you if it chokes me. The other metal object in Winifred's bag was a tin hatchet head with a blunted edge."

We tramped awhile in silence, then I asked, "Is that all?"

"About all, thank God, of which I have any personal knowledge. Winifred has made several utterances about trees—once, 'Forgive me, ancient trees'—something of the kind. That could mean nothing and probably does. She keeps speaking of the True God instead of a just God. Is it possible there is still a Druidic cult in Wales? A great many ancient cults keep on reappearing after they are supposed to have died out. Especially this happens in times of religious conflict, as has afflicted England ever since Luther—especially since Henry VIII."

"The cult of Modo?"

"That was a murder cult, arising after the Romans departed Britain. It had nothing to do with Druidism, and has never reappeared in England as far as anyone knows. Just now there's a good deal of talk among English peasants of witches and witch masters and goblins and so on. But tell me this, Martyn. Is it conceivable that beautiful young girl could become involved with a revival of Druidism in Wales?"

"Perfectly possible—if her mother did. If there were still a Welsh throne, Enid Powell could have been the most likely claimant. She was of direct descent from Owen Glendower and the Gwynedd kings. She might naturally cling to the old Welsh religion, more fanatically because England had conquered Wales. But she was murdered too—I too have got to speak plain—and Winifred didn't do it. She worshiped her mother and was away from home at the time. But Doctor Jones, you don't know about little Owen. He was Winifred's brother, about two years old. Apparently he walked into a stream against which he had been warned. That was natural enough —but Reverend Burberry and I found something when we walked down the stream, and which he never showed the sheriff but took home. It was a curved piece of wood, cut from a very large tree trunk, its ends slightly raised. It had some iron bands."

"That is a description of an ancient British shield."

"Did it have any connection with Druidism?"

"Not directly. But an ancient test for bastardy in Britain and Wales involves babies and shields, too. The babe was placed in the hollow of the shield and put in a stream. If it floated the babe was legitimate, otherwise not."

We were getting deeper and deeper into a great forest, dank but unflooded, grown to ancient and immense cypress trees. Their incurved knees began to have an eerie aspect. A huge rattlesnake hissed at us and then in slow writhings moved from our path. A beautiful angel took off from beside a woodland pool in soaring, divine flight, but it was only a snow-white heron. I steadied my sick and reeling brain.

"Let's sum it up," I said in harsh tones. "A traveler was murdered on the road we lived on—but Winifred had barely learned to walk. My mother could have been killed by a fanatical follower of an ancient religious faith for the sake of a sacred hatchet. A woodman could have been killed as a warning against anyone cutting down what was once a sacred and sacrificial grove of the Druids. Someone left a crudely drawn picture of human sacrifice on Mr. Powell's bed—after he had incited a crowd of young people into pushing over some of the still upright pillars of Stonehenge. A baby was drowned near where Reverend and I found an ancient British shield which could have been washed out of the ground by a flood. Winifred kept and cherished a hatchet head and a hook used in Druid worship. But Enid Powell was hanged while Winifred was a day's travel distant. Doesn't her innocence of that murder remove her from suspicion of any other?"

"Maybe it does," Doctor Jones replied, speaking very slowly. "I believe it does. But on this continent, across the ocean from Wiltshire, a Croatan girl named Cheewink was wantonly killed because of a love affair with Richard. That brings all the rest straight home."

2

The great adventure that had begun in violence would end in violence. This was no mere figment of my disordered fancy; it was intuition, which is an inward seeing based not on superstition but on the secret workings of the mind as it examines fact. Had someone in our party aroused the Furies from their foul nests? Must we expiate ancient evil in battle and bloodshed? I feared this coming meeting with Richard and Winifred. Weechee had surmised a bond, the origins of which I knew not, between him and me. I was fated to play a leading part in the terrible climax. I smelled a storm of illimitable fury.

Mighty trees, I would pray to you for protection if it were any use! Even now, the storm is beginning to break, the warning only faintly ominous as yet, a natural and innocent sound, like that a barn-yard cow might make when, as our peasants put it, she is "bulling." The reply was the explosive snort of a bull, then a prolonged bellow. This was how Fate moved, one certain step after another, to her dreadful destination—giving little sign, and all of this reassuring explanation. I called to Manteo in a low voice.

"Bid Doctor Jones and Mr. Powell wait here, because they are unarmed."

"Aye, that is wisdom," he replied. "Martyn Sagamore, I know not what awaits us beyond yon thickets, but I fear it in my inmost heart."

It was right, it was in the poetry that Fate must ever write, that Storyteller and Manteo should be with me in the tragedy that soon must strike. They were not participants; the actors were Richard,

Winifred, and me; but they were my boon companions. We three had made possible our journey to this terrifying goal.

Beyond the thickets, that looked like common thickets, was the rendezvous long predestined, toward which we had been implacably marched. Behind them waited Fate in her dark draperies and how did we know that she was not greater than all the gods? Now we were peering through them, but we did not see her in any form that the mind could recognize.

We saw the bull in his godly rut. He was himself a god, as all young, clear-eyed people not yet scourged from the breast of nature, have ever perceived; or else gods took his bull-form. He was the inspiration and the ominous, stolid or raging, central figure of a thousand cults, because he was identified with the act of perpetuation of all creatures. Nigh him the cow buffalo made coy and jerky movements, not yet showing readiness to accept his primordial embrace despite her burning.

Carefully I searched the shadows and the areas dusky with thickets in search of Richard and Winifred. I found them soon, invisible to the near-sighted monsters, standing hand in hand. And now the bull rushed bellowing upon his beloved, he reared up, his forelegs on and flanking her back, his back arched up. He began making his puissant thrusts, fast and faster, with remorseless wrath and resistless power. It was a demonstration of the implacable fecundity of nature, and the envious cocks in the grass and shrubbery must watch, and so must serpents, remembering the mere lascivious intertwining of their matings, and so must little man and woman watch, enthralled.

The act replete, the bull's loins emptied and tormenting him no more, the cow shook herself, aware that her womb yearned no more. She snatched a bite of grass. But Richard, who had nocked an arrow, and was drawing his bow in deadly intent, suddenly let it fall. Instead he turned on Winifred, and my first frenzied thought was that he meant to kill her, but he only clasped her in rough arms and threw her to the ground. Instantly he snatched up her skirt, spread wide her thighs, unbelted his own garment, and then in savage haste he satisfied the sudden lust the scene had wakened in them both. Then he stood upright, fastening his belt, and snatched up his bow and fallen arrow and looked for the two buffalo, now out of sight in the dusky forest. In the sweep of his gaze he saw me.

He saw me, and he knew I had seen him. And for reasons beyond ken, this broke the last threat of a weakening cord of restraint, and set free an ancient, aching, but sternly mastered passion. Looking at me, he snatched an arrow from his quiver and nocked it on his cord.

Not until he started to draw his bow did I cry out, "Don't shoot at me, Richard! I am your friend!"

"My friend! I hate you to black hell. Shoot for your life, Martyn! This is a duel to the death! I can endure no more." And even as he yelled, he was bending the bow with great force, and I sprang behind the nearest tree.

But this was a young cypress, slender of trunk, in the beauty of youth, but not yet heavy of bole as were her elders. It was no adequate shield from the arrows of that terrible archer, Richard, so I shouted again.

"Think what you are doing! Have you lost your mind? I am Martyn —you are Richard. We have been friends since early boyhood."

"Friends!" he mocked, meanwhile shifting from side to side to get a better view of me, his bow more than half drawn. "Brothers, you mean! And always you have beaten me, I the lawful son, but can you beat me now? Look to yourself, Martyn! This is our last contest, and he who wins last, wins all."

He launched his arrow. Only a quick shift to one side spared me from a disabling wound; even so the arrow grazed my naked arm and brought blood. Winifred shrieked and fled. Before he could nock again, I sped to a nearby tree, hardly more protection than the first.

"Draw your bow, you fool!" Richard bellowed. "Do you think I'll spare you if I get one clean shot? You are always the gentleman. I am the rude peasant that takes every chance he can get."

Once more his arrow hummed, piercing my cap, for he had held a little high. And now wild fury stopped the pangs of my broken heart, and my lips drew back even as I raised and drew my bow. And before he could get his aim, I sped an arrow that cut his breeches leg, and I saw a stain of blood on his bared thigh.

"Two hits out of three! Damn you, do you remember? And the next hit will win the bout!"

We both shot again, but we could not properly aim as we sought to guard ourselves behind the slender trunks, and both shafts flew wide. On a like impulse we both sped toward trees with massive boles, but beheld each other full in the open, and on a like compulsion, irresistible to any hunter of the heart of Richard and me, we both stopped. Aye, we were willing that the duel be decided by swiftness of getting off a well-aimed shot, not by agility or cunning.

We both nocked an arrow, we both drew with great swiftness as well as power, we both aimed; and the range was point-blank, no more than forty yards. Neither of us could miss if we loosed cleanly the same instant, and that would be a gleeful conclusion to King Death, and Fate would deem it one of her most poetic passages in all her dealings with human prey. But I loosed half a second sooner than did Richard, and instantly flung to one side. He loosed an equal time before my arrow plunged into his breast, but I no longer stood where he aimed, and I heard its hornet-hum in my ear and did not feel in my body its merciless point. When I looked again Richard had dropped his bow, and now he threw wide his arms and toppled on his back.

I ran to him, and he gazed into my eyes in a long glance that both asked and answered a question, but what the question was, I would never know.

"Richard, why did you force me to do this?" I asked, my eyes streaming tears. "If you had told me that your father lay with my mother and I sprang from his loins, I would not have held it against you. I would not have hated even him, since it would have been by my mother's consent—"

"Oh, you fool!" he interrupted me, in a voice still strong. "You hopeless fool. Thomas Sutton was not the cuckold; my father Thomas Wade was the cuckold; your father the servant, mine the master. If the reverse were true, I would have never given it a thought; landlords are forever tupping their tenants' wives. But my father, of no high birth, was wedded to Lady Wade."

"I don't believe it. It could not have been managed in secret—"

"The more fool you. Don't underrate the conspiracies of two determined women who like and understand each other when a crisis rises! It was a simple matter of both Thomas Wade's wife and Thomas Sutton's wife going on an extended visit to kinsfolk at the same time, and one passing her newborn brat into the arms of the other." And Richard heaved a troubled, painful sigh.

At that instant Manteo and Doctor Jones ran up, and stood staring in hopeless silence. Neither Richard nor I gave them more than a glance, so intense was our concentration upon each other; of such vast importance was this last intimacy. Mr. Powell followed, at a firm and steady pace, and stopped a short distance away, yet in hearing of our voices.

"Richard, how did you discover—"

"For the love of God, don't ask me inconsequential questions! Don't you know it hurts to talk? Your cursed arrow did not pierce my lungs, but cut some big vein or little artery, and I'm bleeding like a pig in my chest-cavity. Well, you didn't beat me as a peasant against half a nobleman; but as one half-nobleman against another. Martyn, we've got to wind this up fast. My heart's beginning to beat against a barrier. What more have you got to say? Say it quickly."

"Did Winifred kill my mother?"

"No, Enid did, because your mother refused to give her the blunted hatchet."

"Did Enid kill the woodman?"

"Yes. To teach folk a lesson not to cut down ancient oak trees."

"Did Winifred drown little Owen?"

"No, that was an accident. Winifred, who knew you were the son of Lady Wade, got it in her silly head that Thomas Wade knew it also and was laying up with Enid in reprisal against our mother. She gave the baby the old Druid test for bastardy, seeing if he would float in an old Welsh shield that Enid had. The damned shield sunk under his weight."

"What made Enid such a fanatical Druid?"

"The word is Druidess. She was the descendant of Owen Glendower and the Gwynedd kings, but Druidism was a dying cult, almost dead in fact, and that makes its few remaining members all the more fanatical. What god can live, what religion can remain true, without worshipers? Happily, the Druid church was a stand of mighty oak trees, and these progenerate, and thus last longer than man-made churches of board or brick or stone."

"Do not utter such words, Richard," Edward Powell said in what was almost his customary resonant voice, "when about to meet your Maker."

"He's more forgiving than you think, Reverend Powell," Richard answered. "Maybe he'll forgive Lady Wade for lying with a peasant and bearing him a son." With agonizing effort, Richard turned his head and again addressed me. "And it was Enid, with Winifred's help, who left that bloody-sacrifice picture of Mr. Powell on his bed. I guess that gave him the first clue."

"Clue to what? Enid was herself murdered."

"You thick-headed ass! How did you ever become leader of the colony, the position I so terribly craved to win over you at last? Enid was not murdered. She was duly hanged for committing heathen-religious murder by her husband, who counts himself the deputy of God."

"I *am* His deputy," Edward Powell said quickly.

"Then there's only one more question. Try to answer it, Richard, for our souls' sake. Who killed Cheewink?"

"The answer won't be much relief for your cursed soul. It was Winifred, of course, her first murder. She had inherited her mother's amenability to its commission, but not the same zest. I had my knife, I was with Winifred, she went off, and I had lost my knife. She did it out of plain jealousy and fury. She counts herself a princess higher than any Tudor, and she loved yours truly, now on his way out."

Saying so seemed to make it so. After a few deep gasps, Richard turned on his side, the last touch of color faded from his pale face, his troubled breaths became farther and farther apart, and so he died.

3

The troubles of our colony, before we could descend to happy savagery, were not yet over. We were still sons and daughters of law-ridden England, and Winifred must be tried for murder.

The trial would be held in the open space assigned to our use, if the weather was fair; otherwise under our pavilion. By tacit consent of our former colonists, I appointed Ananias Dare as judge and William Hewett as Winifred's defender, and William Brown as prosecutor for the distant Crown fading into dimness. Since she had readily confessed to the crime, Mr. Brown had no duties except to assist Mr. Hewett in appointing a jury. In performing this task the two men chose jurors not because of their feelings for or against Winifred. Instead they took twelve of the most honorable and level-headed men in our number.

Richard's body was buried almost at the spot where he had fallen, dressed in his best raiment, with his weapons beside him, and wearing a seal ring bearing the coat of arms of his mother's family. Edward Powell spoke briefly and with restraint, mainly of Richard's fidelity to the company in the long march, and pronounced a brief prayer for the rest of his soul in God.

Because of a drizzling rain, the trial was held in our pavilion. Ananias Dare was given our only chair. Mr. Hewett and Winifred shared a bench, William Brown and the only witness who would be called, Doctor John Jones, occupied another. The jurors and spectators were to stand, the former having been given a blank sheet of paper torn from the log I had brought from Roanoke Island, a quill pen, and a wooden cup containing a little ink made from lantern black and water. Their duty was to find the defendant guilty of murder in the first degree or innocent because of unsound mind at the moment of the crime. In the case of the first she was to be immediately dispatched; of the second she would be set free.

Mr. Brown was the first to address the jury. The point of his speech was that murder was a high crime not only against the victim but against society, always it had been held so, that the murder had been one of passion, and its forgiveness would cause other crimes of passion in our new abode. Mr. Hewett delivered a longer address, to try to show that Winifred had an insane mother, Enid, a father whose religious passion was at least uncommonly intense, and that Winifred's own fanaticism in an ancient, pagan, primitive religion was in itself proof of an unsound mind. This fanaticism she had proved by her attachment to two so-called objects of the Druid ritual, the tin head of a hatchet and a mistletoe hook. To obtain the former her mother had committed murder. To get hand on the latter Winifred herself had committed theft. Then he put one question to the prisoner.

"Winifred, you wear a silver locket on a golden chain about your neck. A locket usually contains a most dear possession. The jury has a right to know what is in it, thus better to peer into your emotional life. It may or may not throw light on whether you are of sound mind. Will you permit me to open it?"

"I do not want you to lay impious hands upon it," Winifred replied in a firm voice, on her feet and erect and proud. "But I will tell you what is in it. I lied when I told Martyn Sutton it was a lock of white hair from the head of St. Winfrid, whom I called my patron saint. If I showed you the white hairs the locket contains you would readily believe me. But Winfrid is not my patron saint. I hate his memory; he too persecuted the Druids and ordered the cutting-down of almost the last of the Sacred Groves. My locket contains white hairs from the forelock of the last great Druid, his name Merdin in Wales; known in foolish myth as Merlin the Magician."

"You may resume your seat."

"No, I will not. I will speak the whole truth. I adored my mother, accepted her fervid faith almost with her milk, certainly as soon as I began to understand human speech. She killed a traveler on the road to obtain this locket that he had stolen from the secret shrine that the few remaining Druids had in Wales. He intended to sell it to a curiosity shop; but one of our own, who rode a swift horse, told my mother that he was certainly the thief, and to obtain it at all costs. She gave it to me when I was six years old, explaining how she had recovered it. Also she told me how she had been forced to kill an innocent peasant woman to obtain the sacred hatchet head of tin, and thereby my love for her, indeed my adoration, waxed greater. Later, as a warning to the owner, she killed a woodman who was cutting down trees in the very last of the Sacred Groves remaining in Wiltshire. He was a dim-witted fool, not himself to blame, but an example had to be made. I helped prepare the crude drawing of human-sacrifice to put on my father's bed. You may ask, since he was such a bitter and implacable enemy of my mother's and my God— his name is Lud, and the city of London was once Ludtown—why we did not conspire to put him to death. We could not bring ourselves to do so. He was kind to me, and he loved my beauty if not me myself. My mother loved his embraces."

It was no wonder that Winifred was aware of her own beauty; otherwise she would have been blind. The skies had darkened in the last few minutes; one could imagine that what daylight remained had difficulty shooting in the right direction to find its way under our eaves; and Winifred's face and form somehow gathered it up. Before our march her complexion had been markedly fair—the Lily Maid of Astolat was probably Welsh—and although it had tanned in the beaming sunlight of the beaches, since we had traversed the forests of Florida it had once more paled. Her eyes were ever luminous and now so in a fascinating degree, perhaps because of emotional excitement. She appeared utterly without fear. Her posture was that of someone chosen for most lofty office—a queen or prophetess.

"My mother was a woman of passion," she went on. "I suspected that in her later life she had taken advantage of the prerogatives of the ancient queens of Wales—as did Goneril, daughter of King Lear in ancient legend—and perhaps she accepted the embraces of Thomas Wade, a neighbor of common birth but of riches and power, and a virile and impressive man. I suspected that my little brother Owen was his bastard. So I subjected him to an ancient test practiced in ancient Wales, which doubtless the Druids countenanced. In all truth I knew that the antique shield in which I placed him would sink with its weight of bronze except for a miracle. But before now, in countless instances, the water witches bore up a babe of lawful birth, or Belisame the Just did so, or Tor, God of Thunders and hence of rains by which streams flow. I thought that even Lud, my lord the Sun, would prevent his drowning. It came to pass that my brother did drown. My dam made him welcome beyond the Sea Mists, and did not blame me; for part of our holy lore had been lost, and doubtless I had failed to observe a ceremony performed with the holy mistletoe before I put Owen to the test. Hence, your honor, appointed to be my judge, at this point I had committed no heinous crime."

"I have heard what you said, Mistress Winifred, but will make no comment," answered Ananias Dare.

At this moment there came a brilliant flash of lightning, that caused an afterimage on the eyes, and not far distant, since the crash of thunder ensued almost immediately. Winifred cast her eyes upward as in mute worship.

"Now I come to my dealings with Cheewink, the Croatan Indian girl, and to her I did evil," Winifred said in her soft voice. "A savage, Cheewink did not know the offense she had committed against me, Winifred, out of the Gwynedd kings, by seduction of my lover. Even if he were the instigator, for he was a lusty man, with ungovernable passions, still I was incensed, and I prayed to Dagda, god of the corn, he who loves troth between two lovers, and received his sign that Cheewink should pay the penalty. That evening I had sat with Richard in the moonlight, and he kissed me and embraced me only lightly, and made an excuse of weariness from hunting for not joining his body with mine in the embrace of love. Well I knew he had a rendezvous with Cheewink. The knife in his belt was in reach of my hand. I took it, intending to return it before he observed its loss; then I lay in wait near the meeting place of him and Cheewink. I walked at her side and she perished without pain. Still I could not retrieve the knife, so deeply it was thrust and perhaps caught between the bones, but that did not matter, for certainly Richard would not be accused of her slaying, since the knife had a carven handle which all our party had seen and knew, and he being a man of wit, indeed of high intelligence, this alone declared his innocence. So her death is on my soul. To this, no more, I plead guilty. Nor do I ask the indulgence or the mercy of this court. If my life must pay for hers, I will make no protest. For as is promised to worshipers of Lud, my lord the Sun, my soul will pass beyond the Sea Mists to another realm. Nor will my body be abused if I am hanged to the bough of a noble tree. That bough will send down shoots of greenery, and these and creepers will enfold my bones, until they become part of the tree itself. Now I will stand down."

She did so, and if Ananias Dare or any other of our company had tried to speak, he could not have made himself heard. Amid flashes of lightning, almost blinding in their brilliance, there were long and repeated peals of thunder—no wonder at this time of year in this well-nigh tropical region. Still the effect was as though they had waited for Winifred to finish her address, that this was its emphasis, and that the nature gods had either applauded or condemned her. Then a heavy silence fell, that I thought a prelude to a downpour. A few big drops, each distinctly heard, fell on our palm-leaf roof. All we hearers were in a wrought-up state. The voice of Ananias Dare, raised at last, and certainly carrying forward the drama nearer its dread conclusion, came almost as a relief.

"This court desires the expert opinion of Doctor John Jones. Doctor Jones, always our trusty adviser, in your opinion was Winifred Powell in her right mind when she lay in wait for the Indian girl, Cheewink, and stabbed her to death?"

"Sir, I cannot answer that question. She may have been the victim of temporary insanity caused by jealousy. This plea is often made in English courts in cases of this kind, and only rarely if ever has it been regarded by his lordship, the Queen's judge. But if you ask me if Winifred was insane previous to that night, or is now insane, I must give my opinion that she was not, and is not. The term 'illusions of grandeur,' is sometimes heard when the question of insanity is raised. There are enough facts backing Winifred's statement regarding her royal birth, that such pride, loftiness if you will, that her statement disclosed is quite natural and perfectly sane, if certain members of the Tudor and the Stuart dynasties were considered sane. Except for Henry VII, and in a lesser extent, Queen Elizabeth, both of these dynasties embrace the doctrine of the Divine Right of Kings. It is true that Winifred is a fanatical member of an antique cult, now almost extinct in England proper, although it still has no few devotees in Wales. That should not be taken into consideration by this court except as regards her willful risk of the life of her infant brother, which resulted in his death. Her father is a fundamentalist of the extreme sort—a fanatical Puritan. If we hanged all the devotees of antique or unorthodox religion living in the British Isles, spiritualists, Pythagoreans, practicers of magic, faith healers, Rosicrucians, numerologists, Zoroastrians, sun worshipers, Isis worshipers, fetishists, necromancers, demonists—there is an almost endless list—we would be perpetrators of a massacre dwarfing St. Bartholomew's. I feel that under these circumstances the jury should consider only the slaying of Cheewink, a perfectly human act, alas all too common. The only excuse I can make for Winifred is that loving her murderous mother, and a fanatic in her mother's paganism, she had come to think that the taking of a human life did not matter very much. It is an attitude commonly taken by habitual murderers."

Doctor Jones sat down. Ananias Dare thanked him courteously, then began to instruct the jurors. He was a plain man of few words.

"Gentlemen of the jury, this is not an English court. England is far away and perhaps lost to us forever. But we have no other guide than British courts. In those courts, not the judge perhaps, but certainly the Queen's prosecutor, would point out the consequences of the killing of Cheewink by Winifred Powell. Our colony was forced to leave Roanoke Island. In our long and arduous march, more than twenty people died who otherwise might have lived. You may now consult together, and give your verdict."

Edward Powell rose to his feet. "Your honor, I have a request to make, impelled by duty," he said in a shaking voice. "If my daughter is found guilty and is sentenced to death, I ask to be her executer."

"That is a most strange request, Mr. Powell," Ananias Dare replied.

"Only so in eyes that will not see. I will choose the manner of her death, and administer it with my own hand. If the duty were left to any others they would be guilty of breaking the Commandment 'Thou shalt not kill.' But I am the deputy of God; His only deputy in this lost congregation. I am like unto Jephthah the Gileadite, who slew his own daughter out of his love of God."

"If she is found guilty, and you intend to carry out the sentence of death that I would then impose as mercifully as possible, I will grant your request."

"Sir, I will do my duty."

"I will not refuse you, Reverend Powell," Ananias Dare declared after brief reflection, and in evident relief. And I suppose it was natural enough that every spectator of the trial, including the jury, also looked relieved.

No rain was falling and the jury filed out of the pavilion. I was in a state of mind to be grateful for any boon, even one so slight as our being saved the sight of the huddled jurymen, while we others crowded out of hearing of their consultation. More likely they would have gone out in any weather, rather than be watched as they did their dreadful work.

They were absent only a few minutes. They took their former places and their hastily elected foreman, the yeoman Mark Bennett, took a step forward.

"Mr. Foreman, has the jury reached a verdict?" Ananias Dare asked in a voice held steady by great strength of will.

"Aye, your honor, that we have," Mark Bennett answered in his country accents.

"I will bid the prisoner rise and face the jurymen."

Winifred did so, and stood tall and proud. Mark Bennett returned her gaze.

"Mistress Winifred Powell, us jurymen find ye guilty of wanton murder, wherefore ye must die."

The bad dream I had dreamed before, on several occasions, always under different circumstances, with varying characters, began to weave again. But it was, and never had been, a dream. It had been only my mind's reluctance to accept facts that I knew were real.

"I thank the judge, the jury, and all the people for a fair trial," Winifred replied in soft and lovely tones.

Then Edward Powell bustled out. There was no fit word other than bustle. We heard him at work, opening one of our boxes. No one gazed in that direction, but too well we knew it was a box containing hempen rope protected from the rain by a tarpaulin. Then we heard a scraping sound. Presently he reappeared, his eyes feverishly bright, picked up the bench on which Winifred and Thomas Hewett had sat, and lugged it out. In hardly half a minute he reappeared, stood in the door, and addressed us in the tone of voice he had employed in addressing congregations, and in that which he had addressed Ananias Dare when he had asked to be chosen our leader.

"Winifred, you will come with me. I request all others to come also, to be spectators of the vengeance of the Lord upon evildoers. There is no rain to wet you. That is by the Lord's provision. This evildoer is my daughter Winifred, but that does not blind me to my duty, or weaken my will in the least jot. As ye sow, so shall ye reap. That is the dictum from on high." And the dream I dreamt intensified into nightmare.

"Stop talking, Papa, and get it over with," Winifred said gently. Stately we saw her walk from under the pavilion and follow her father into a grove of cypress trees growing nearby. From one of its limbs hung a hempen rope, with a noose at its end. Directly under it was the bench.

"Stand on the bench, Winifred," Edward Powell directed her.

She mounted it in graceful movements, then faced our little throng, all deathly pale and wide-eyed. Edward Powell also stood upon the bench until he had affixed the noose around Winifred's slender neck. And at that instant Weechee slipped two things into my hand. I knew by their feel what they were—my own bow and a deer arrow with a needle-sharp point.

"Be quick," Weechee murmured.

No one stood in my way as I nocked the arrow and began to draw the bow. I do not believe that any of our number watched me; they only watched Edward Powell, meanwhile fervidly praying that I could launch my arrow, and it would dart swiftly and in a true course, before he would draw aside the bench. "The Lord have mercy on your soul," we heard him say, as I took certain aim. Then as he bent toward the bench, I loosed my shaft.

Then my nightmare ended, and I returned to the good earth and to my fellows, as the arrow rose in a graceful arc, then darted down to its certain mark. It struck Winifred in her soft and beautiful throat that I had kissed, then plunged deep. Although the noose tightened as she toppled, she did not feel even the rough hemp against her tender skin. Had her soul already fled beyond the Sea Mists? That was as good a destination as any, I supposed, for any soul in flight.

4

Antonio, Tzin Cacique, had given our party until the moon rounded to make our decision whether to unite with his tribe. He had so spoken on the fourth day of the new moon. More than a week remained before that rounding, and the day after Winifred's trial and its awesome conclusion, he suggested to me through his Mayaimi interpreter and Storyteller that I undergo a test put to young men of high enough station to aspire to chiefdom. It was to disappear with one companion in the forest, both of us wearing nought but moccasins and breechclouts, and with no equipment but our fire-making gear and our bows and arrows, subsist for one week without help from anyone, and return in good health and strength. I accepted immediately, and asked Thomas Warner to go with me.

We decided to make for the coast, where we could be sure of sea food in case of a migration, by no means uncommon, of deer from their usual haunts. I would have liked to have gone to the ruins of Old Tampa, Carlos' capital before the royal seat had been moved inland, and which was near the mouth of the Calusahachee River; but the distance was long and the trails marshy, so we made for the region of Cape Romano, the scene of so many wreckings of Spanish treasure ships and hence a principal source of Calusan gold.

The trail pointed out to us, kept open with machetes, led us through one of the heaviest jungles we had ever penetrated. It was a dark mass of tough custard-apple trees, gigantic leather ferns, vines that appeared knotted by the Devil to arrest progress, and willow and elderberry trees. Its only grace was numerous mockingbirds with their sweet song and the roseate flash of flying red-winged blackbirds; but its dominant voice was harsh and vaunting, being that of the ribald and raucous outcries of blue jays, Florida crows, and grackles. We emerged from it at last on a coast thick with palmettos with needle-pointed leaves.

We had no difficulty finding food and drink and both Thomas Warner and I knew how to throw up palm-leaf shelters against tropical rainstorms. In fact, our easy subsistence made me suspect that Tzin Cacique wanted me to be absent from the colony's councils in the next few days, perhaps fearing I might prevent the desperate flight and consequent death of our more faint-hearted that he would accept, but did not desire, in his tribe. I experienced a narrow escape from a coiled diamond-back rattlesnake, every inch of seven feet long, in our deer path. I had not made out her form in the mottled, fallen leaves, but Thomas behind me had done so. Speaking quietly, he bade me halt, not jump sideways or back, and quickly nocked an arrow which transfixed the brute's neck. In a niggardly count of seconds I would have been in her easy-striking range, about three feet—the extremely large rattlesnakes being almost always females. She could have injected enough venom in my foot or leg to drop me almost in my tracks.

On our fifth day at our hastily erected bivouac, which we expected to vacate on the morrow's dawn to begin our thirty-mile march to the capital, Thomas Warner and I received by strange means almost certain evidence that England had won her war with Spain. But the same occurrence posed to me a moral problem of greater difficulty than any with which I had ever been forced to cope. Might I be spared its like again! And years must pass before I would have any clear inkling whether my decision was in part right, or wickedly wrong.

Coming out of a palmetto thicket, Thomas Warner and I had climbed a sand dune grown to weeds and vines to scan the coast ahead, always our wont. When we peeped over its crest, what we saw, of all things under heaven that we could least expect, and which awed us to the core of our beings, was a large, fat-bellied trading ship riding at anchor about three miles from the beach.

We would have known her for English, even if she had not proudly flown the English flag. For a moment we remarked on the almost surety of England's war with Philip having ended with his abject defeat—possibly the destruction or certainly the repulsion from English shores of his great Armada—or an English trader, lightly armed, would not venture so boldly into what once were forbidden waters. These remarks delayed our facing our awesome dilemma of such personal import to both of us.

A ship's boat had just been put overside and was making for shore, probably to refill water casks. This would be a chore requiring at least three hours; more likely the vessel would linger here all afternoon and well into the evening, so the boat could again take advantage of the flood tide, to ease her over the sand bars. Thomas Warner and I had abundant time to meet the boat and inform them that more than eighty English castaways, the remnant of an English colony at Roanoke, were at a Calusa city hardly more than thirty miles distant, a great many of them, all of the women and some of the men yearning to go home.

He and I crept down the sand dune, through the palmetto grove, and seated ourselves on a fallen tree trunk. His expression was so solemn that I nearly laughed aloud; I felt that my own face was flabby from indecision. Still there were two sides to the question, each with many facets. We sat in silence, pondering with all our might, before he spoke.

"Mr. Martyn"—so he always addressed me when grave matters were afoot—"what do you think is your bounden duty?"

"The duty, whatever it is, is on both our shoulders and our souls."

"No, sir, that is not true. Where you go, I go, if you'll permit me. What you do, I do, by that same permission. I told you that long ago. I was a slave for seventeen years. My kinspeople have disappeared or scattered. I have no life save what I have with you. You, sir, must make up your mind. I can only remind you of facts on which to base it."

"Well, then, I do not know what my bounden duty is in this case. Until now it was to try to preserve the colony by leading the people to some sort of refuge. If we let the ship go her way, my bounden duty will be to help the people in adjusting their lives to Calusan life, so that they may be as happy as possible. If we declare their presence nearby to the ship's crew, my responsibility has ceased; her captain will command them until they reach England; then they will scatter to their homes and resume their old lives."

"Sir, I must correct you again. They can never resume their old lives. Experience such as we have undergone has changed them forever—their lives in England will be different from before we set sail."

"In general, I agree with you. They were snatched from modern times into the Stone Age; there are difficult adjustments to be made before they can again feel at home in modern times. I'll tell you something that Weechee told me lately. I do not know if it is germane to the subject. Long ago, about half a century I believe, a party of fifty white men, deserters from a Spanish vessel, made their way to the then capital of the Calusa, which was called Tampa, near the mouth of the Calusahachee River. After about six months their officers found them, and invited them to return to duty, promising them that no charges would be made against them, and they would receive no punishment. The men refused to leave their Calusa wives. I think that is why the Calusa headmen and others have paler skins than most Calusa we saw on our march."

"No, I cannot see that it is relevant to our problem. What would happen, Mr. Martyn, if the question was put to vote by our people?"

"They would vote—the majority I mean—to stay here. But I do not think it would ever be put to a vote. The women will not let it. I do not know how they would go about to stop it; still I think they would manage it somehow. If the men insisted on voting, the women would still win. They would wail about the children raised in barbarism; they would start walking toward the frontier; they would use all the weapons in their arsenal, and these are mighty powerful where weak man's nature is concerned. We men have a great chance to escape from civilization—female dominance to put it bluntly—the only chance we'll ever get—but it looks as if we're going to miss it, my good friend Thomas."

"Would they be as happy through the years to come if they went home?"

"That is an unanswerable question. Doctor Jones could return to his

studies and his practice of medicine; Thomas Hewett could plead before justices and jurors; little Virginia Dare would grow up and marry
a white man, not an Indian. Would their lives be longer there? I presume so, probably so in the case of our men, the vast majority of our
party."

"But is the length of any one's life the most important thing?"

"That, I doubt. Happiness, if decently obtained, not at the expense
of others, seems to me more important; a very great many elders, perhaps the most, have outlived their positive happiness. Some find happiness in the success of their children. Some find heartbreak in their
desertion by their children, or their children's calamities."

"Then, I think you should confine the question to where our people
would be happiest, as long as they live, in England or living with Indians in the New World. Not where they could do the most good for
other people. It would be impossible to decide, I believe, whether we
could do more or less good for the Calusa than we could do for
our neighbors if we returned to England. I make bold to suggest a
strong chieftain could stop human sacrifice of slaves and prisoners,
which the Calusa make every year to what I might call the God of
Death. Storyteller has heard about it—he didn't want to tell you yet,
for reasons I can guess—but he told me. He has picked up enough
English words—and I enough Croatan words—that along with us making signs I understood him."

"Did Storyteller believe there was any danger of them sacrificing
us?"

"None whatever, if we united with the tribe."

"We might stop it. If I get to be sub-chief, and master the language
well, I think I could invent some directions from the God of Death
himself, that he wants the practice stopped. I am a pretty able liar,
when the need arises."

"You want to stay here, don't you, Mr. Martyn?"

"Yes. I'm in love with Weechee. I'm in love with adventure. I want
new sights—new experiences. I suppose I'm in love with power. I don't
want to be a peasant any longer—and I would be one, in England,
despite what honors I earned there—the gentry would never stop saying, 'I remember when.' I don't want to marry one of our peasant
girls, the only suitable marriage I could make. I want to marry a
Calusa princess. I want to hunt buffalo and deer and wild turkeys
and geese and ducks; I want to fish in rivers and lakes in which few
hooks have ever been lowered; I even want to fight alligators with a
spear, maybe sharks too, maybe even the deadly dangerous sea cows
called manta rays. I want to have a part in magic rites—forgive me,
O Lord, but they are more exciting to a man like me than attending

Church; I want thrills up my backbone. I want to do the sof-kee dance and the dance that brings deer into arrow range, and the dance that starts the run of cobias into the river. I doubt if most men like civilized life. Except for their women they would choose to hunt, fish, and fight dangerous beasts with short-range weapons—ever risking their lives instead of living safely but tamely. Our large majority are males. They're an adventurous lot, or we wouldn't have got this far. But our women want security, I suppose; and as usual they would carry the day. I want to be underchief of the Calusa nation—perhaps someday Tzin Cacique. They are not strictly Stone Age Indians. They have made off with enough loot from sunken Spanish ships, or taken it in tribute from the coastal tribes, to have useful things as well as pretty things, and they get along fine."

"Well, sir, I'll make a suggestion," Thomas Warner said, his voice trembling a little, when I paused my declaration because of spent wind.

"All right. What is it?"

"Although a peasant, you always longed for power. You told me so; your father told you so. Now you've got it. Why don't you exercise it? No one but you and I need ever know this ship stopped here; I think it was a chance in a thousand. Why don't you keep your mouth shut about it? Why not make the decision yourself? Isn't that the prerogative, possibly even the right, of men of power? Until now the rich people and the highborn people and a few very smart people have made the decisions; unless they were too harsh the crowd obeyed them like sheep. Now a former peasant has an opportunity to make a great decision. Why don't you do it?"

"By God, I will. We'll return to the settlement and be Calusa and be damned."

"Good for you, Mr. Martyn Sutton."

So we shook hands, and with no more mention of the ship, returned to our bivouac. There we prepared for tomorrow's march for—home!

And shortly thereafter, when the moon had waxed to the full and begun to wane, I would go forth into the forest and with my resilient bow and deadly arrow I would slay a deer. This I would dress and then carry the meat to the house of Tzin Cacique, and leave it at the door for Weechee. And she would bake or fry some of it over an open fire, and invite me to share it with her before witnesses. And thus she would become my woman in the eyes and by the law of the Calusa. And we would dwell together, and she would bear me babes with pale-brown skins and brilliant black eyes and we would be Cacique and Caciquess when we had grown old. And we would hear no more and care no more about the doings and the wars of my once-brethren and their troubled times across the seas. Instead we would hark back to ages gone.

I would dwell with beauty and adventure and the comradeship of my fellows. What more could a man ask?

EPILOGUE

I, Martyn Sutton, native of Wiltshire, England, now known as Sachem Cacique in the capital of the Calusa Indian nation in the great land of Florida, so-named by the Spanish in the times of Fernando de Soto, write this document with a good quill and lampblack ink, as an explanation of my writing the above chronicle of the history of the second colony planted by Sir Walter Raleigh on Roanoke Island off the coast of Virginia.

It so happened that I had paper in abundance—over four hundred blank sheets in a large logbook which the first Roanoke Colony had left in the fort. My hand-writing, taught me by Mistress Clara Barton (God rest her soul) long ago in my native shire, is small and neat; hence I have been able to recount the fortunes of the colony, and preceding events which effected these fortunes. All this I have put down in the five years since the colony, forced to fly Roanoke on the threat of massacre by Indians who had made a just charge against us, united with the Calusa Indians at their capital city named Carlos in honor of the greatest of Calusa chieftains, who treated with the Spanish Governor Menéndez in the year 1566, and whose sister became the beloved wife of the great chieftain. This city at the time of this writing lies south and west of the main body of great fresh-water sea, called by the Spanish *Gran Laguna de Mayaimi,* and which we knew as Lago Grande Calusa.

As for my own fortunes, in these five years I have fairly won the title above mentioned, second in honor in the Calusa nation only to that of my father-in-law, known as Tzin Cacique. His daughter, my wife Weechee, had borne me three children, two boys and one girl, who give us both great joy, and who are the pride of their royal grandsire.

Why did I undertake the labor of writing the chronicle? In the first place it was not only a labor but a joy, to recount the great experiences, the tragedies and the triumphs of the colonists, and a moving experience for me to tell of previous events which proved such a factor in our fortunes. But my main impulse was the slowly growing realization that unless I did write this chronicle, providing a chance for it to reach and be read by people who live long after our times, historians would never know the fate of the colony of English people mysteriously vanishing from their settlement at Roanoke, and it would remain forever unknown. It so happens that our present haven is in a region so inaccessible to travelers and explorers, that I doubt if any will come here in the remaining years of this century or in the next century. By then our people will have mingled their blood with the blood of the Calusa. Our descendents will be Calusa of somewhat paler color than is common, our English names and language will be lost. Our coming hence will be woven into tales told by wandering Indian storytellers, so adorned with myth that no part of them will be recorded by historians. Indeed any report of our presence here will be explained away by fact, known to the Spanish, of deserters from Spanish ships settling many years ago in the Calusa capital of Tampa, near the mouth of the Calusahachee, and long since deserted and fallen into ruin.

As for my fellow colonists who joined the Calusa nation, so far they have fared well according to my present standards of good or ill, which of course are greatly influenced by my present environment and the standards of my fellow tribesmen of darker skin. Our archers have proven equal to native Calusa archers; paleface hunters are as skilled and as successful as those native to the tribe; like our Calusa brethren we have become an aquatic people, proven by our trophies won in battles with great crocodiles, sharks, and manta rays. Our hitherto unattached males are happy with their beautiful and fruitful wives of darker skin. In courage and hardihood and in other qualities held in honor in the Calusa nation, we newcomers have not been put to shame, and indeed are reckoned by our brethren as full peers.

Even in such difficult skills as tracking game we have won their respect. Most of us have learned how to make beautiful or useful objects out of conch shell and other materials available to us, and he who was once William Brown, an English jeweler and goldsmith, can equal if not surpass any native Calusa in making superb ornaments out of copper, and gold and silver, obtained from Spanish ships wrecked on our dangerous coasts.

Acting on his declared intentions, Doctor Jones indeed wedded a "comely" Indian girl assigned to him by Tzin Cacique, indeed one of the beauties of the Calusa nation; and she was also, as he had specified, a good worker. However, his medical practice was not in the least what he had expected. A good English physician of his time, he found himself outclassed by Calusa physicians, who had adopted the medical practices of the Aztecs who in turn had learned much from the Incas. These Calusa doctors knew five hundred healing herbs, he told me ruefully, to his fifty. Moreover, they were definitely better surgeons than the Europeans of his times. Yet he came to high honor among them, and hence throughout the nation, when he recognized a disease causing chills, fever, and prostration as the same as was widespread in southern Europe and which could be arrested and often permanently cured by the taking of a white, inordinately bitter powder obtained from the bark of the quina tree in Peru. This powder Doctor Jones readily obtained through the regular channels of trade between the coastal Calusa and the Aztecs. In the speech of the Calusa people he became known as "the hot-skin doctor."

The one member of our party that I thought surely would meet disaster was the once fanatical preacher, Edward Powell. He became something of an anchorite, living at the outskirts of the town, and spent most of his hours in meditation. Thereby the curiosity that native Calusa people felt about him changed into superstitious wonder and then to awe. Hence he is regarded as a great werowance and his needs are generously met and he sits at the left of Storyteller at the left of Tzin Cacique; I sitting at the right, at great tribal assemblies. Also he has done more, by an occasional rare utterance, to stop the abhorrent practice of human sacrifice at the Feast of Death than all the rest of us put together. Once, indeed, he boldly cut the thongs confining the captive Indian intended for sacrifice, and even Tzin Cacique, let alone a lesser Calusa, did not raise a hand to rebuke or punish him.

What can I do with the chronicle, now that I have completed its writing? In all truth I do not want it known to the world in my lifetime or that of Weechee's and my children or even grandchildren, lest some well-intentioned people would try to rescue us or them from savagery. At last I have hit upon a possible solution of my difficulty.

Not far from the town of Carlos there is a deep pit in the ground and the coralline formation beneath. Doctor Jones has no doubt that it was caused by a meteor, falling there with incalculable speed and force. It is no doubt still buried in the rock, and it seems to me, perhaps in centuries to come, it will be recovered by curious geologists. It may indeed attract gold seekers who might regard the pit as a likely place to look for treasure buried by Spaniards or by Indians who had looted Spanish ships. I am almost certain that in time to come people from across the seas will dig there, certainly so if by then they have invented a device that would reveal metal underground, as the divining rod used in England reveals water.

Also there has come into my possession from a looted ship a box of pure copper, no doubt once used as a treasure chest, and being of soft metal, its cover can easily be made watertight by simple pounding of its edges to fuse with the box itself. In this I will deposit my writing, and by digging out the coralline rock at the base of the pit, easily conceal it from any casual glance into the pit, or superficial examination thereof.

This action I will now perform. Thereby I will break the last cord that binds me to my native land, sever my one remaining link with the past. No one has addressed me as Martyn Sutton for more than two years; instead they have called me by the name given me by the Calusa, which translated into English means Bear Hand, which I regard as a compliment, since the paw of a bear is not only wonderfully strong but, in meeting his own needs, adroit. This is my familiar name in the tribe; in all ceremony I am addressed as Sachem Cacique.

But Weechee calls me what dwellers of my native land would term a pet name. It is not quite amenable to English translation. The nearest I can come to it is "My Beloved."

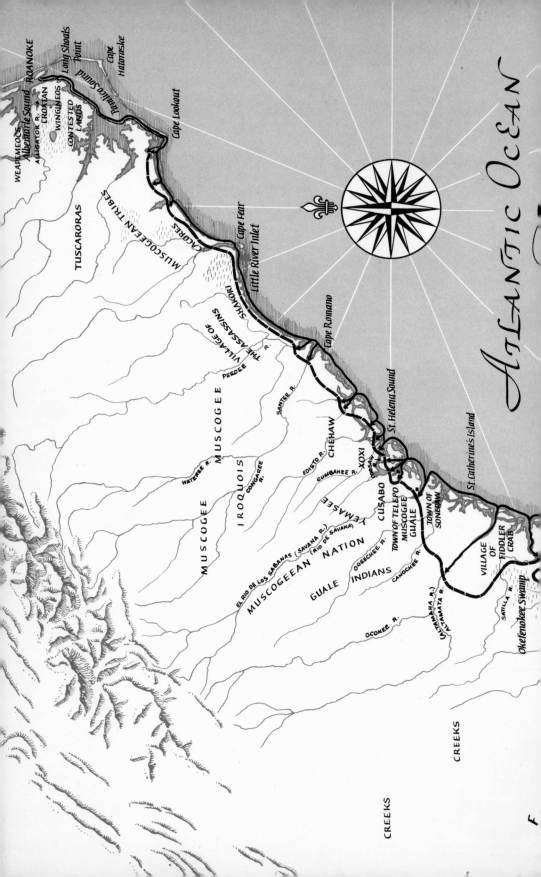